The Lost Princes of Ambria

Royal fathers in search of brides!

Come to the breathtaking land of Ambria and
get swept up in Raye Morgan's captivating
world of feel-good fantasy as you fall in
love with royal daddies who juggle duty,
fatherhood—*and finding their perfect wives!*

Secret Prince, Instant Daddy!
Single Father, Surprise Prince!
Crown Prince, Pregnant Bride!
The Reluctant Princess
Pregnant with the Prince's Child
Taming the Lost Prince

All Available Now

Dear Reader,

This is the last book of a series of six about the Lost Princes of Ambria—a lovely, fog-shrouded, fictitious island nation off the coast of Western Europe. All the princes have been found and brought back home again. Their family, which was shattered and torn apart when their parents were killed by the Granvilli rebellion almost thirty years ago, is reconnected and healed about as well as it can be. Goodness and mercy are back in the land.

Too bad all our problems can't be solved so easily—but then, we're not royal, are we?

Last year we saw the Westminster Abbey wedding of Prince William and beautiful Kate Middleton, and all the excitement and celebration that surrounded it. This wonderful couple brought back star power to the British monarchy—a sense of special magic that reminds us why fairy tales so often feature princes and princesses. Larger than life, the focus of dreams. No wonder we love it all.

Prince Max and the woman he loves, who is secretly raising his child, need a bit of that magic to find their happy ending. They have to struggle through misunderstandings, a kidnapping and a heavy shared sadness that almost destroys their love. I hope you enjoy being a witness to the way they manage to capture their dream.

Thank you for reading my story.

Regards,

Raye Morgan

RAYE MORGAN

Taming the Lost Prince

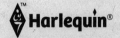

TORONTO NEW YORK LONDON
AMSTERDAM PARIS SYDNEY HAMBURG
STOCKHOLM ATHENS TOKYO MILAN MADRID
PRAGUE WARSAW BUDAPEST AUCKLAND

ISBN-13: 978-0-373-17806-3

TAMING THE LOST PRINCE

First North American Publication 2012

Copyright © 2012 by Harlequin Books S.A.

The publisher acknowledges the copyright holder
of the individual works as follows:

TAMING THE LOST PRINCE
Copyright © 2012 by Helen Conrad

KEEPING HER BABY'S SECRET
Copyright © 2009 by Helen Conrad

PLEASE RECYCLE
THIS PRODUCT IS RECYCLABLE

Recycling programs
for this product may
not exist in your area.

Raye Morgan has been a nursery school teacher, a travel agent, a clerk and a business editor, but her best job ever has been writing romances—and fostering romance in her own family at the same time. Current score: two boys married, two more to go. Raye has published more than seventy romance novels, and claims to have many more waiting in the wings. She lives in Southern California, with her husband and whichever son happens to be staying at home at the moment.

Books by Raye Morgan

PREGNANT WITH THE PRINCE'S CHILD*
THE RELUCTANT PRINCESS*
CROWN PRINCE, PREGNANT BRIDE!*
SINGLE FATHER, SURPRISE PRINCE!*
SECRET PRINCE, INSTANT DADDY!*
BEAUTY AND THE RECLUSIVE PRINCE
THE ITALIAN'S FORGOTTEN BABY

The Lost Princes of Ambria

Other titles by this author available in ebook format.

This book is dedicated to Nick and Jenn, and most of all to CB, the new prince in our family.

TAMING THE LOST PRINCE

Raye Morgan

CHAPTER ONE

PRINCE MAX leaned out over the edge of the wrought-iron rail on the balcony. A light rain was falling but he hardly noticed. He was at least the equivalent of five floors up. The castle garden below looked farther away than that. A strange, shivering impulse inside made him wonder what would happen if he jumped.

Too late now. A few weeks ago he could have jumped. He could have ended his worthless life with a flourish. No one would have cared.

But now he had a new life—new responsibilities. People were beginning to expect things of him. What the hell made them think he could possibly deliver?

Actually, this might be a better time to jump. Maybe he would find out he could fly. It looked so simple. All he had to do was spread his wings. He knew what it felt like to fly. He'd been flying ancient crates from past wars for years now. Flying planes was the one thing he knew he was good at. But taking that leap on his own would be different.

No, he wasn't going to jump. He wasn't going to

mock his fate by trying to fly without a plane. Self-destruction wasn't really his style. But he did have a peacock feather he'd picked up in the castle gardens. He held it out.

"Fly and be free," he muttered to it. And then he let it go. It began its long, meandering flight toward the ground and he leaned out even farther, watching it go. It flashed back colors, blue and green and gold. As it neared the ground, it started to spin crazily. He laughed. "Go, baby," he murmured to it. "Do your thing."

The feather hit the ground and his laughter faded away. Now it was caught, just like he was. A short flight to nowhere.

"Hey," a candy-coated feminine voice said to him. "Don't lean out so far. You'll fall."

He closed his eyes for a moment. Was he ready for this? Did he need it?

"You okay, mister?" she said.

He turned slowly, wondering if she realized who he was. Probably not. He was dressed for hiking, not for the ball. But he thought he'd seen her before, passed her in the halls. He recognized the look. And he knew the drill. Either he gave her a simple friendly nod and went on his way, or he smiled at her suggestively and things went on from there. His choice. He could tell she was ready. Eager even. A part of him groaned.

But he couldn't give in to that. What the hell? He was young. Life was there to be lived. And who knew how much longer he'd be free to follow where his urges led him?

"I'm fine," he said, and he smiled.

"You're wet," she countered flirtatiously.

He shook his head like a sheepdog. Water flew everywhere. She gave a little shriek and then she laughed.

"You'd better come on to my place and get dry," she offered.

"Your place?" he repeated questioningly.

"Sure. My room is on this floor. I'm only a few doors away. You need to dry off. You wouldn't want to catch a cold, would you?"

His gaze made an exploratory journey down the length of her, from her spiked, fire-engine-red hair, down to her full lips, lingering on her hourglass figure. His look was insolent. He knew it. And he also knew she was the type of woman who liked that sort of thing.

"Sure, why not?" he said. Anything was better than joining the other royals at this ridiculous ball the queen had cooked up. A few hours with this willing playmate might be just the thing to help him get rid of this feeling of doom that was hanging over him. "You're like an angel of mercy, aren't you? Always on the lookout for someone in trouble."

Her smile had a wicked sparkle to it. "Not really," she said. "I'm kind of picky about who I help."

He raised an eyebrow. "And I made the grade?"

Her eyes widened appreciatively. "Oh, yeah. You'll do."

He pretended to bow. "I'm honored."

She giggled and led the way.

Queen Pellea swept into the royal office and glared at Kayla Mandrake. "So where is he?" she demanded.

Kayla jumped up from her desk, shaking her head. That sinking feeling she'd been fighting since she'd found out who the new prince actually was had come back with a vengeance. "I haven't seen him at all," she said. "I thought he was supposed to be here…."

Pellea grabbed the back of a chair, her knuckles white. "Of course he was. He was given complete instructions. And he blew them off, as usual. Everyone is waiting in the ballroom."

"Shall I make an announcement over the speaker system?"

Pellea looked pained. "Oh, Kayla, you've been in Paris all this time and you don't know how things have been. This guy is driving me crazy."

Kayla held back a grin. That was Max. He drove everyone crazy.

"He'll settle down," she told the queen without really believing it herself. "Once he understands the way we do things."

"The more he understands, the more he flouts the rules. You're going to have to go out and track him down."

Pellea made a sound of angry impatience and tossed her head in frustration. She was wearing a spectacular gown—deep blue silk threaded with gold, strapless, form-fitting, with a skirt cut to move sinuously as she danced…or walked. Kayla felt frumpy in her simple skirt and sweater.

"And I hope you're prepared to kill him when you find him," Pellea said dramatically.

"Your Majesty," Kayla began, beginning to give in to a touch of anxiety. She was trying to think of a new excuse for him on the fly—but something that wouldn't get her fired. The queen did have her emotional moments.

"Don't." Pellea held up a hand like a crossing guard. "I don't want to hear any tales of woe. I don't want to hear explanations and confessions. All I want is Prince Maximillian here where I can punish him." She shivered with what looked like anticipation. "Or his head on a platter. That would do." Her dark eyes flashed. "Do you understand?"

Kayla nodded. Despite everything, she was working hard to suppress a grin. She didn't dare let it show. Pellea was so angry.

The trouble was, she knew very well that the Max she had known was sure to make Pellea even angrier as time went by. There was nothing she could do to avoid it.

"Yes, Your Majesty. I'll do my best."

"Just find him!"

Queen Pellea swept out like the storm she could sometimes resemble. Kayla took a deep breath and steadied herself. What now? How was she supposed to find a rebel prince who obviously didn't want to be found?

It was always this way with Max. Rules were

made for other people, not for him. He was easily
the most infuriating—and the most charming—man
she'd ever known. Just the thought that she would
see him again any moment gave her a thrill that was
electric. But it also gave her a dull, pounding headache. How was she going to work this? Heaven only
knew.

She started by making a few phone calls. There
were guards everywhere and security officers working the monitors at special locations. If he was in the
castle, someone must have seen him. And some had.
She got a lead here and there, and finally, an actual
sighting from a hall guard who'd seen him disappear into the apartment of a local girl who was well-
known for partying.

"Of course," Kayla muttered acidly. "I should have
known."

She started off toward the place like a rocket, but
deep in her heart, she dreaded the whole confron-
tation ahead of her. What was she going to do once
she got to the door? Barge in on a seduction? She
shuddered as she punched in the floor designation
on the elevator panel.

"Darn you, Max," she whispered. "Do you always
have to make life so hard?"

She thought about the last time she'd seen him,
almost two years ago, his thick, bronzed hair disheveled, his eyes bleary with pain. Emotional pain.
They'd both been in agony that night, both mourning
over the same tragedy. The next thing she'd known,
he was gone.

The elevator doors slid open silently and she stepped off, heart beating, head aching. It was only a few steps to the doorway. She stood in front of it, wishing she were anywhere else. Her phone buzzed and she pulled it open. It was Pellea, of course.

"Yes?"

"Have you found him yet?"

She sighed. "I've got his location. I'm about to go in and see...."

"Watch him," Pellea warned. "If there's a balcony, he'll jump."

Kayla gasped. "You don't think he's suicidal, do you?"

"Oh, heavens no. He defies death for the fun of it. I swear he's got to be an adrenaline freak."

Kayla considered that seriously. "You know..." she began.

But Pellea wasn't waiting to hear other views.

"Last week, we had a gathering of the new princes at the ski chalet, a meeting for them to get to know each other better. We'd barely begun cocktails when Max and the chalet manager's two beautiful daughters took off on snowmobiles, racing off into the mountains as though it were nothing more than a free snow day. And they didn't come back."

"Oh."

"No excuses the next day, of course. He thinks his smile covers all bases."

"I see," she said for lack of anything cogent to add. She felt a little lost with the queen battering her with complaints like this. A part of her wanted to defend him, but how did you defend behavior like this?

"Last night it was dinner with the Italian ambassador. We're about to sign an important treaty with them. He didn't show. And what was the excuse? He'd stopped in at a pub and got involved in judging a karaoke contest and lost track of time."

"Oh, Max," Kayla said in soft despair.

"So I say, watch the balcony. He'll tie a rope to the edge and pretend he's Tarzan. Don't let him get away."

"I won't." She only wished her determination was as stout as it sounded.

Pellea sighed. Maybe her tone hadn't been convincing. "Give me your exact location. I sent a couple of security officers up to help you. I'll key in directions for them."

That startled her. "Help me do what?" she asked after giving the queen her location.

"Make sure he doesn't escape. We'll tie him up and drag him in if we have to."

"We will?" She knew Max and she was pretty sure that wasn't going to be done easily. This whole thing was beginning to resemble a nightmare. She stared at the door to the target apartment. Max was supposedly in there. They'd told her he'd gone in with a woman. Did the phrase *love nest* come to mind? This wasn't the way she'd imagined their reunion might pan out.

"Now I want you to be forceful," Pellea encouraged. "You must take him by surprise."

Kayla gasped in horror as a picture of what that might mean spun through her head. "You mean… burst in on him without warning?"

"If you have to. Whatever you do, you've got to stop him from disappearing again. Call me when it's over."

"Yes, Your Majesty. Of course." She hung up just as two security guards stepped off the elevator and marched over to join her.

"Sgt. Marander, ma'am, at your service," the one who seemed to be in charge announced. "Here's the master key. We're here to back you up. We'll be right behind you."

She chewed on her lower lip. "Can I knock first?" she asked, rather forlorn.

His stare was steely cold. "I'm afraid not. Her Majesty specifically recommended a surprise attack. She's afraid he'll…"

"Escape by jumping off the balcony. Yes, she told me as much."

He glanced at her and frowned. He probably heard the reluctance in her voice and didn't approve. "Sorry, miss. Instructions from the queen are not to be taken lightly."

She took a deep breath. "All right," she said, straightening her shoulders and heading for the door. "Here I go."

She closed her eyes and turned the key in the door, letting it swing open. "Max?" she asked breathlessly, not daring to look. "Are you in there?"

There was an ominous moment of startled silence

and then a deep voice cried, "Kayla! What are you doing here?"

She forced herself to squint through one slightly opened eye. And there he was, standing before her, completely clothed. Very civilized. Not scary at all. She gasped in relief.

"Oh, Max," she said, half laughing. And as he threw his arms around her, she sighed and went limp in his embrace. "I can't believe it's really you."

He hugged her, kissed each cheek, dropped a quick one on her lips and, finally, leaned back to take a look.

"Hey, gorgeous, it's been almost two years, hasn't it?"

She nodded, her head swimming. He was still the most beautiful man she'd ever seen, still hard and handsome, still looking like a playful rascal and a bit of a rogue. His thick rust-colored hair seemed to have a constant breeze blowing through it, his mischievous blue eyes were framed by eyelashes so thick it was almost criminal, and his mouth looked so deliciously sensual, it ought to be censored. That was Max, just as she remembered him. Lord, how she'd missed him!

"So what are you doing here?" he asked, looking completely bemused.

"I came to...to sort of arrest you. In a way." She made a face. What a farce.

"Arrest me?" At last he focused on the security guards behind her. He frowned. "What did I do now?"

"Oh, Max," she sighed. "Why can't you be good?"

"Kayla, my sweet," he said, grinning at her, "you know that's not in my nature."

But he was genuinely happy to see her. Taking her in was like a good shot of whiskey. One look and he was transported two years back in time, back to those sidewalk cafés with the red umbrellas along the Mediterranean coast, back to the balmy breezes and sunlight filtering through the palms, back to hearing suggestive songs played by small combos while they'd sat sipping chichis, the local drink that tasted a bit like a Mai Tai and packed a punch like an angry kangaroo. The things they'd done, the things that had happened, the choices made, the regrets— it all still churned inside him. He couldn't let it go.

But he also couldn't regret knowing Kayla. She'd always been a joy. It was fantastic seeing her again.

"This is Kayla," he said casually to the redhead who was standing behind him, looking terrified. It appeared she wasn't used to having castle security barge in through her locked door. "Her husband was my best buddy in the old days when we flew sorties out of Trialta together."

"Oh," the redhead said weakly. Her teeth seemed to be chattering. "Nice to meet you, I'm sure."

"Yes," Kayla responded and tried to smile at the girl.

Max saw the confusion in her eyes and realized she was still digesting the situation she'd burst in on. It was pretty obvious she thought she'd found him having a "moment" here. That was hardly the case, though the redhead seemed to have thought it might turn into one, too.

But he hadn't been able to conjure up any interest. He'd been polite. He'd chatted. He'd accepted one small drink and the redhead had worked hard at creating a seductive scene. But he'd found himself looking out at the stars in the inky sky and listening to the strains of the orchestra from below in the ballroom, and all desire for that sort of satisfaction had melted away.

But before he found a way to explain all that, the two guards stepped forward and began to slip metal restraints on his wrists.

He looked down, startled. "What the hell is this?"

"Sir," Sgt. Marander said in an unfortunately pompous tone, "consider yourself in the custody of castle security."

Max blinked. He couldn't accept this. Handcuffs? They had to be kidding. He quickly saw two or three ways out of the situation. He could easily handle the guards and…

But then he looked up and met Kayla's worried gaze. Her pretty face, her dark, clouded eyes and her long, silky blond hair all created in flesh a picture that had haunted him for two years. Adrenaline still sizzled inside him for a few seconds, then began to drain away.

He wasn't going to run from Kayla. Now that he'd found her again, he didn't want to lose her until they'd had a chance to talk. If he could mine her memories and join them with his, maybe he could slay some of the demons that kept him awake at night. Maybe.

"Please, Max," she was saying, reaching out and putting a hand on his arm. "It's really important to Queen Pellea that you make an appearance at the ball."

He smiled down into her anxious gaze. "There is nothing I'm looking forward to more," he lied smoothly. "Now that you're here, I'll have someone to dance with."

She jerked back, pulling her hand away. "Oh, no. Not me. You're supposed to be meeting eligible ladies of rank. That's not me."

He stared at her. "Kayla, what's the deal? Do you work for the royal family, or what?"

She nodded. "Yes. I've known the queen since we were kids together and my sister's husband is in the guard. Pellea offered me a job and I jumped at it." She shrugged, palms up. "I love it here."

He frowned, not sure what to make of that. When they'd been in Trialta, he'd assumed she was as much of a vagabond as he was. Now to know she had royal ties…

But what was he thinking? He was the one who was supposed to be a prince.

Still, he didn't like being corralled this way. He could tolerate going to the ball if they let him come on his own terms. This way was just too much. Kayla or no Kayla, he was back to wanting to get the hell out of here. But his hesitation had meant he was locked up.

"Hey, I'll come with you willingly," he noted. "But could we get rid of these handcuffs?"

She hesitated, looking down at them. Then she gazed up into his eyes.

He smiled. She sighed.

"Sure," she said, wondering if she were risking everything but hardly caring. She looked at the security agents. "Let him go."

The sergeant glared at her. "But, Miss…"

"I'll take the responsibility," she said. "If he bolts, I'll tell the queen it was my fault."

The man shrugged and used the key, but he didn't look happy about it.

Max smiled and flexed his wrists and looked toward the balcony in the redhead's room. He could make it in two bounds and be jumping for freedom in seconds. Everything in him was ready to go. Why the hell should he stick around when he knew he was going to hate the results?

CHAPTER TWO

KAYLA could read Max's mind. She knew him too well. She saw the glance as a way out and she moved in smoothly, taking his hand in hers, lacing their fingers together. If he was going to run for it, he was going to have to drag her with him.

"You're all mine now," she told him archly. "I'm calling the shots."

"Is that right?" he said, looking skeptical, but amused. "I thought I was the one who was supposed to be royal all of a sudden." He raised one quizzical eyebrow. "You've heard, haven't you? Now they've got me pegged as one of the lost princes. Can you believe it?"

She shook her head, smiling at him. "I'm finding it hard. When I realized it was you…" She shrugged and closed her eyes as she relived those moments, and when she spoke again, her voice was shaky. "Max, I thought you were dead."

He looked at her for a moment, then managed a crooked smile. "Which time?" he asked softly.

Her phone buzzed. She knew it was the queen. Pressing her lips together, she shook her head.

"We'll have to talk later." She reached for her phone but she didn't let go of his hand. She'd learned a lesson or two over the years, and one of them was to look both ways before stepping off the curb.

"Yes, Your Majesty. We're on our way."

Ten minutes later they were in Pellea's public parlor while she flitted about and generally let Max know he was on thin ice with her. Kayla watched, but hardly listened. She knew the queen was crazy about him and was just trying to convince him to behave.

At the same time, she herself was a bit impatient with all this. She felt as though every nerve ending was vibrating right now. There were so many things to take care of, so much to consider. Max was back and she had to figure out how to fit him into her life again. She had a thousand questions for him. There was so much she wanted to know, so much they'd missed. So much they needed to discuss.

For instance, had he come close to marrying anyone in the last two years? Was there someone out there? She was hoping there was, but the signs weren't good. If he had someone serious in his life, she could move on without any lingering doubts. Couldn't she?

The funny thing was, she couldn't imagine him married. He didn't have a married way about him. His beautiful eyes had a look that said he was always searching for something and not very satisfied with what he'd found. You had a sense that there was something missing in his life, but he wasn't sure what it was and he knew he hadn't seen it yet. Just seeing that in him scared her.

But the queen seemed to have no forbearance left for all that. She knew what she wanted from Max and she wanted it now.

"The first thing we're going to do is get you into some decent clothes," she said, rummaging through her closet.

"What? You don't like my style?" He said it in a tone that might have seemed insolent if he hadn't paired his words with a look of pure innocence that caught Pellea by surprise, making her laugh.

"Now I see what the problem is," she told him, shaking her head. "You just don't know any better. You need to learn a thing or two about being a prince, don't you?"

"If you insist." His mouth twisted but he bent forward in a sweeping bow. "Anything for you, my beautiful queen."

Despite everything, Pellea colored slightly, then glanced Kayla's way. "You've got to admit, the boy's a charmer," she said out of the side of her mouth. "I think he's a diamond in the rough, too. We'll see what we can make of him." She smirked. "Heat and pressure. That's how you get perfect diamonds. Are you game?"

He didn't answer but she'd already turned away and was hunting through a closet again, muttering about sizes and ruffled shirts.

He looked at Kayla and shrugged, as though to say, "They've got me this time," and she smiled at him, her heart full of affection for all he'd meant to her in the past. She wasn't sure what the future would bring. But things were never dull when Max was around.

Her smile faded as she remembered that there was something more lasting than memories between them, something more precious than life itself. And that was when she decided it was time for her to go.

"Your Majesty, if you don't need of me here…"

Pellea poked her head back out of the closet. "Go ahead, Kayla," she said. "I know you've got work to do. I won't keep you."

"Thank you," Kayla said, then she turned and gave Max a stern look. "You will be good, won't you?"

"At what?" he teased with a lopsided smile.

She glared at him. "The guard is outside so don't think you can get away with anything," she murmured to him out of Pellea's hearing.

He gave her a "Who? Me?" look. She shook her head and started for the door. "Have a lovely time at the ball," she said over her shoulder. "I'm sure you'll be the star."

And she was out the door before he had a chance to say or do anything else.

She hurried back to the office, hoping to get some work done that she'd neglected while she was off chasing princes. It had been a hectic week. Pellea had sent her to represent the DeAngelis royal family at a financial conference in Paris. She'd hated leaving for a whole week, but the fact that the queen had that much faith in her had been wonderful. She'd worked herself to the bone trying to live up to expectations and she was exhausted.

And while she was gone, the search for the last of the lost princes of Ambria had struck gold. First Mykal Marten, whom she'd met before she left for the continent, had been confirmed as the fourth prince. And then the news had come that the fifth and last prince had been discovered. When she saw the name—Max Arragen—in a newspaper account, she hadn't thought much of it, but then she saw a picture. It was blurry and taken from a distance, but the jaunty set of the shoulders had made her think of Max—her Max. She'd gasped and begun to wonder.

It wasn't until she'd returned home to Ambria a day ago that she'd seen a good picture and realized that Prince Max really was the man she'd known in Trialta as Max Arragen two years before. And that sent her into a virtual tailspin.

She'd only known him for about six months, but the time they'd spent together had been crazy and intense. He was her husband's best friend, and they'd both been working as contract pilots, flying reconnaissance missions against the tyrannical regime of the North African nation of Trialta on the Mediterranean. They'd lived like young people involved in war often do, working hard during the day, partying at night like there was no tomorrow. They were fighting for the rebels and thought they were invincible.

She couldn't believe he was back in her life again—at least in a peripheral way. He always managed to inject excitement and surprise into everything, like no one else she'd ever known. She remembered times in Trialta where it had seemed she and Eddie were in the lead vehicle in a continuous car chase—and Max was at the wheel.

And then came the day when Eddie didn't return from a mission. The wreckage of his plane was found, and all the parties stopped. Kayla had clung to Max at the time and they'd mourned together, hardly believing that the Eddie they both loved so much could be gone forever. No one else could have understood how deep their grief was.

But that was then. Things had changed, for both of them. Surely he'd had some life-changing experiences since she last knew him. And she'd had a beautiful, wonderful child.

What would it be like to be friends with Max now? She was a little bit afraid to find out. She wasn't the wide-eyed innocent she'd been two years before. She had some secrets of her own. And how would she keep them from him, now that he was going to be living right here in the castle?

She buried her worries in work, staying an hour longer than normal. And then, once she'd put away her papers and shut off her computer, she gave in to temptation and made her way down to the ballroom instead of going straight to her room.

She took a back entrance and climbed the stairs to a seldom-used interior balcony that overlooked the entire floor area. The orchestra was playing a waltz and the couples swept across the floor, around and around, the women like flowers in their beautiful dresses, the men resplendent in gold-edged uniforms of white or blue or crimson. Despite everything, it took her breath away and made her heart beat faster. A scene like this would make anyone want to be noble, especially if they'd been raised on fairy tales.

She watched for a few minutes longer, caught up in the magic. How wonderful to be royal and to live as though you were the star of it all. Just being here in the castle made her feel as though she were blessed. But it also made her feel a new and more intense responsibility to her country and her people. She wondered if Max would start to feel a little of that soon.

She could pick out most of the princes. So handsome, every one of them—so tall and strong. They looked like men who were confident in themselves and ready to take on the world. She could hardly believe Max was about to take his place alongside of them.

There was Prince Mykal, sitting on the sidelines, still recovering from a horrendous motorcycle accident from a few months before. Prince David, one of her favorites, was dancing with beautiful Ayme, who had recently become his bride. Prince Joe, still looking like a California surfer with his sun-streaked hair, was laughing with Kelly, his own new bride. And newly crowned King Monte had Pellea in his arms and was leading her around the floor with such obvious passion, you'd think the honeymoon was starting that night. That made her laugh softly to herself.

She searched the crowd. Where was Max? Her gaze lingered a moment on Princess Kim. She was glad to see her looking happy after all that she'd been through on the enemy side of the island with the Granvilli partisans. It was good to have her safe and sound, back in the castle where she belonged. But where was Max?

At first worried, she began to get angry. If he had slipped away again…!

And then she saw him.

Max was standing with a group of men she didn't recognize. As she watched, the men moved away and a beautiful dark-haired woman was brought up to be presented to him. Kayla felt a tug on her heartstrings, but she tried desperately to suppress it. She couldn't be jealous. There was no sense behind it. She had to keep it down. Max was not hers and never had been. Never would be, especially now that he was a prince. There was no justification for any jealousy. She couldn't let it happen.

She watched as they danced. He moved so well, as if he were floating on air. He was talking to his partner and she was blossoming in his arms. He could have been born for this—and of course, he really was!

The dance was over. She could breathe again. And now, she really had to go. But she watched for just one minute more, and suddenly his head was tilted up. He was looking right at her. And as she watched, he lifted a glass of champagne and smiled at her, giving her a toast. Her breath caught in her throat and she gasped. He gave her a nod, and then a lascivious wink. Her face felt hot as she pulled back, away from where anyone could see her. She was laughing, though. That wink was guaranteed to keep her warm that night. Trust Max!

But as she turned and left the balcony, her amusement evaporated. She couldn't do this. She couldn't be watching Max from afar and reacting every time he noticed her. Nothing good could come of this. Much better that she should stay as far away from him as she could get. If he really wasn't attached, it would be his duty to find a bride as soon as possible. Watching him fall in love would be tough to take. And if he ever found out…

No, keeping in touch with Max was much too dangerous. She had to find a way to avoid it.

She hadn't eaten since breakfast and she was starving. Glancing at her watch, she knew it was too late to pick up Teddy before he went to sleep. Her heart ached as she thought about that. She missed him. Her baby was only a little over a year old and she missed him when she had late days like this. Sighing, she knew she had to speak to Pellea about it. She really didn't want to be away from her child this long. At the same time, she was so lucky to have this job…

She stopped in at the all-night café and got a salad to eat once she got home.

Then she headed for her sister Caroline's room, just two doors down from hers.

"Hi," she called softly, opening the door with her own key. "How are they?"

"Sleeping like lambs," Caroline said, rising from the couch where she'd been reading and coming to give her sister a hug.

Just two years apart, they looked enough alike that there was always someone who asked if they were twins. Caroline wore her blond hair short, pixie-style, and had a more sleepy, languid look about her, but otherwise, they were practically replicas and had always been especially close.

They stood together looking down at where the two little boys, one dark-haired like his father, the other as blond as his mother, lay side by side, sound asleep.

Caroline's husband, Rik, was a rising star in the Ambrian royal guard. Right now he was on a mission on the Granvilli side of the island and would be gone for a few days. Luckily, whether Rik was home or not, Caroline loved having Teddy in to play with her own boy.

"Why don't you leave him here for the night?" she suggested. "He's used to sleeping here after the last week when you were in Paris. And it was so hard to put them down tonight, I hate to wake them up and have to start all over again."

"Are you sure?" Kayla felt guilty, but she was so tired, it sounded like a good thing to do.

"Absolutely. You're only two doors down. I can get you over here fast if I need you. Just come on over first thing in the morning and it will all be good."

She stayed for half an hour, sharing her salad with her sister while they talked, watching her baby while he slept.

And then she was back in the corridor, on her way home and looking down toward the public area, wondering how the ball was going. It was interesting to live this way, with everything happening so close at hand. The castle lifestyle was growing on her. She had been new to it a year before when she'd come to work here, but she was used to it now and it seemed a comfortable way of life. She compared it to living on a huge cruise ship.

She opened her own door and went in, yawning and kicking off her shoes as she did. A tap on a switch turned on a soft light in the kitchen, which did enough to light the path to her bedroom. She made her way slowly through the apartment, casting off clothes as she went, first her jacket, then her skirt, then her sweater.

She was thinking about crashing straight onto her bed and closing her eyes and not opening them again until morning. Heavenly peace. No dreams, please. Just wonderful sleep. Her eyes began to droop in anticipation.

But it was not to be. Two steps short of her destination, just as she was reaching back to unhook her bra, a dark hulk rose from her overstuffed chair in the corner.

"You know," the hulk said ruefully, "I'd love to let you go on with this, but I have a feeling you'd hate me in the morning. Just a hunch."

She screamed, grabbing her sweater back again and pressing it to her chest. At the same time, Max jumped forward and took her by the shoulders.

"No, don't scream," he said urgently. "I get into so much trouble when women scream."

She glared up at him, quickly pushing him away, startled and exasperated all at once. She could smell alcohol on his breath, but that was hardly surprising. Still, she was wary enough to be careful.

Handsome men, liquor and a moonlit night—the recipe for disaster.

"Then don't jump out at them from dark corners, maybe," she suggested sharply.

He shrugged as though anxious to make up for scaring her. "Okay, okay. It's a deal."

"Oh, Max." She glared at him as she tried to keep covered in all the most delicate areas. "Why did you let me get this far before you said anything?"

His eyebrows rose. "Are you kidding me?"

"Oh!" She shook her head, but she was calming down. "Look that way," she insisted, pointing to the wall. "And don't turn around until I tell you to."

He turned obediently and she began to search her drawer for fresh clothes to wear. "What are you doing here?" she demanded at the same time.

"I wanted to see you. We need some time to talk. Old times and all that."

She pulled on a comfortable top.

"Maybe call first next time," she suggested grumpily as she dug for something to pull over her legs. "How did you get in here anyway?"

He chuckled. "Princes pretty much rule around this castle. You tell people you're a prince and they want to do things for you. The housekeeper couldn't wait to do me a favor."

"That's a problem." She sighed. "Okay, you can turn around."

He turned and looked at her and he was knocked out. Here he'd just come from a royal ball filled with beautiful women who'd all spent half the day in the beauty shop and were dressed to kill and no one he'd seen there turned him on the way Kayla did wearing a simple sweatshirt and black leggings, with her hair looking like a tornado had just come through.

"I think I love you," he said, taking in all her rumpled glory and smiling. "I know I've missed you like crazy. It's so good to see you again."

She gazed into his warm blue eyes and melted. She knew he was kidding, that this was his way of joking about emotions instead of dealing with them. But she also knew he was recognizing the ties between them and ready to embrace them, just like it used to be.

Still, she had to wonder if he remembered that last night as clearly as she did. He had done nothing to indicate it. As far as she was concerned, she hoped he had a touch of amnesia. That night had been a crazy rush of pain and grief and anguish and they hadn't handled it very well. Best to forget it. If they could.

She gave herself a moment to really look at him. Pellea had found him a striking uniform to wear to the ball, but he'd taken off the jacket and pulled open the shirt, displaying some gorgeous skin and manly chest hair. Now he looked less than formal. She shook her head at the sight, but despite everything, she enjoyed seeing him. She always did.

"How did you get away from Pellea?"

He shrugged. "It wasn't easy. The woman was watching me like a hawk."

She sighed and sank into a chair, gesturing for him to sit on the couch across from her. "She'll probably be calling me any minute to organize a search party."

He moved her discarded jacket and dropped down onto the arm of the couch, then leaned toward her. "You won't give me up, will you?" he said with a puppy-dog look.

"Are you kidding?" she told him crossly. "Of course I will. I'm not risking my job so that you can play hooky."

He laughed. "Good point." Then he frowned. "What is your job exactly?"

"I'm the queen's personal assistant. I do whatever she needs to get done but doesn't have time to do herself."

It was a good job and she was proud of it. As a

single mother without anyone to count on but herself, she was lucky to have it. If she ever lost it, for any reason, she would be in real trouble. There weren't many good jobs for women in Ambria right now and the queen was a wonderful woman to work for. With a two-year-old of her own, Pellea understood the problems Kayla had to face and was ready to give her a lot of leeway.

"Ah," Max said, "impressive. Quite another level from the job you had in Trialta."

She smiled, thinking of it. "Selling T-shirts to tourists from a kiosk on the beach. Yes, I didn't get much chance to show my skills and talents at that one."

But it hadn't mattered then. Her days were spent waiting for Eddie to come back from a flight, and her nights were filled with wine, music and friends. For a few months, life had been carefree and exciting. But you had to pay for everything, one way or another, and she'd been paying the price ever since.

Max was staring at her as though he could see what she was thinking. "And yet, here you are, barely two years later, assistant to the queen."

She gave him a look. "I do have a university education, you know."

He appeared surprised. "No, I didn't know. When did you get that?"

She smiled. "Long before I first met you."

"No kidding." He frowned, thinking that over. "That's more than I've got. And they think they want me to be a prince."

Her smile wavered a bit. It was true. From what she knew of his background, he might have a bit of trouble. He'd never been shy about it. While sipping drinks in the sidewalk cafés of Trialta, he'd regaled them with tales of his childhood living on the streets, always making it sound hilarious rather than tragic. But she'd often thought the raw tattered ghost of deprivation lingered in the shadows of his eyes.

He'd had a rough childhood. Any breaks he ever got he'd worked hard to achieve. That was very different from what most royals experienced. The newspaper accounts had filled in some of the parts of his background she hadn't known before, but she didn't know how accurate they were.

"From what I've read in the newspapers and magazines, they seem to think that you were spirited off on the night of the rebellion," she said to him musingly. "When the Granvilli family attacked and burned the castle—when your parents, the king and queen were killed, and all the DeAngelis royal children went into hiding."

She shuddered just thinking of it. Those poor kids!

"Do you know how you escaped? Do you have any idea who it was who saved you by carrying you off that night?"

His shrug was careless, as if he didn't know and didn't really care. "Whoever they were, they didn't take very good care of me. By the time I was seven or eight, I was fending for myself on the streets. Before that, there were various strangers—at one point I think I was staying with a pickpocket who tried to teach me his tricks. But as far as I know, nobody was around for long at anytime. There's no one I can claim."

It broke her heart to think of a child being abandoned like that. She knew from his stories during their Trialta days that he'd been taken in by a fisherman for a while, but the man was cruel and he eventually ran away. It wasn't until his late teens when he was given a corner to sleep in and a job cleaning the chapel that he met a wonderful older man—a pastor—and his kindly wife, who made it their business to see that he was clothed and had a safe place to stay.

The pastor had a hobby of flying ancient aircraft—planes from twentieth century wars. Pretty soon he was teaching Max the ropes, introducing him to aviation, and after that life was much brighter. Max joined the Ambrian Air Force as soon as he was old enough. And that was pretty much all she knew.

"And no one ever guessed you were one of the lost princes," she murmured, looking at him wonderingly.

He laughed shortly. "Did you guess?"

She spread her hands out. "No."

"Neither did I. That shows you how long the odds were."

"Yes." She sighed. "How horrible for you to be treated like that as such a young child. I'm glad the Granvillis are paying the price for their treason now."

He stirred restlessly. "That's life. Sometimes you win, sometimes you lose."

"And sometimes they pull the chair out from under you, just when you think they've given you a throne to sit on."

He grinned at her appreciatively. "A cautionary tale, Kayla? Reminding me not to count on anything?"

She nodded. She couldn't help it. She'd always been a cautious one. Her only times of going crazy had involved marrying a flyer and then letting grief make her lose all control when he died. "Count no chicks before they hatch."

He cocked his head to the side. "Wisdom as well as beauty."

"Nice of you to notice." She rose, feeling a little too nervous to sit for long. "Would you like a drink? Iced tea? A cup of coffee?"

"A beer?" he suggested, following her to the little kitchenette.

"I think I have one." And she did, ice cold and ready to drink. She pulled it out of the refrigerator and popped the top for him.

He took a long sip, sighed with satisfaction and leaned against the counter, looking at her. "So what have you been doing all this time?" he asked her. "You didn't come straight here from Trialta did you?"

"No. I've been here for less than a year."

"And what were you doing before that?"

She hesitated. Her heart was thumping in her chest. It was time to come clean. She had to tell him. He would find out soon enough anyway. And if he thought she were trying to keep it from him, he might think…

She shivered.

"I…uh…I had a baby." She forced herself to look him in the eye and not waver. "A little boy. I call him Teddy."

"Teddy?" He blinked at her.

"Yes. He's at my sister's right now, down the hall. Maybe you can meet him tomorrow."

And she stared into his eyes, searching for doubt, searching for memories, searching for anything that would tell her he'd guessed the truth.

CHAPTER THREE

MAX's reaction came a beat too late. Kayla knew he'd had a quick second to think before he let his natural instincts take over. What was he thinking in that flash of time? What was he feeling? His crystal-blue eyes didn't show a thing. But that tiny hesitation did.

"Teddy," he said, sounding pretty normal. "You named him after Eddie, huh? Great."

He licked his upper lip quickly, then smiled and reached out to give her a one-armed hug. "Kayla, I'm so glad you have a piece of Eddie to hold on to. That is very cool."

He was looking right into her eyes now, seeming completely sincere. "I can hardly wait to meet him."

Glancing down, she realized, to her horror, that her fingers were trembling. Quickly, she shoved them under the hem of her sweatshirt.

"How about you?" she said, a little breathless. "I guess you're not married."

"Married!" His laugh was short and humorless. "You know me better than that."

"If Pellea has her way, you soon will be."

His deep, painful groan made her smile.

"Did you meet anyone interesting at the ball?"

"That wasn't all the ball was about, was it?" His groan was louder this time. "Oh, lord, do you think she's going to have more of them?"

"Of course. You have to marry someone. The others are all paired up already. Pellea wants to get you settled as well."

His sigh was heartfelt as he leaned wearily across the little counter. "Why don't you marry me? Then we can forget all about this nonsense and just be happy."

She looked away. The very suggestion sent something skittering through her like sparks from fireworks and she took a quick, gasping little breath, trying to suppress the feeling.

Marrying Max—what a concept. Luckily, that would never happen, not even for the sake of convenience. There was no way Max could ever take care of her and her baby. It wouldn't work. She'd been out in the world with him and she probably knew him better than she knew any other man, other than her husband. Max was born to be a bachelor.

Even Eddie had said so. "Max will never get married," he'd told her when she tried to have a go at a little matchmaking at one point. "He's like those animals that die in captivity. They can't be tamed. They can't even be gentled. Leave Max alone. He'll just break their hearts. And yours, too."

Eddie was right, as usual. Max was not a man to hang your heart on. She shook her head and got up the nerve to meet his gaze again. "Sorry, Max. You're going to have to walk that lonesome valley on your own."

His mouth twisted with a bit of pretended chagrin, but he wasn't really thinking about what she'd said. His gaze was skimming over her face, searching in her eyes, looking for something in the set of her lips. She wasn't sure what he expected to see, but it was disturbing, and she turned away, heading back to the living room.

She could feel him watching her, as though his gaze were burning a brand into her back. She forced herself not to look, and finally he came after her and sank onto the couch.

"Come and sit down by me," he said.

His voice was low and there was a new element in it…something different, something mysterious. She felt wary and her pulse stuttered and then began to move a bit faster. There was a sense of being a bit off-kilter. Somehow, the room seemed warmer. A new tension quivered in the air. Every time her eyes met his, the tension seemed thicker, more insistent, like a drumbeat beginning to make itself heard across a rain-forest jungle.

She took a deep breath and held it for a moment, trying to calm herself. They were just friends, but she worried that he might be edging toward something more. She couldn't let that happen. Not again.

"Come on," he coaxed. He wasn't smiling but his gaze was warm. Almost smoldering.

She shook her head and dropped back into the chair. "No. I think I'll stay here."

"What's the matter?" he asked her.

She licked her dry lips. "I think we need to keep a demilitarized zone between us," she said, trying to sound casual and friendly at the same time.

His eyebrows shot up. "What are you talking about?"

She took a deep breath. How to begin?

"I'm serious, Max. I don't think we ought to be close. You're moving into a whole different sphere of life. I don't belong there. Let's not start anything that will have to be…" She shrugged, not sure she wanted to put it into words.

His bright gaze clouded and he appeared bewildered by what she'd said. "But you seem a part of this castle stuff and I'm just a beginner," he pointed out. "What are you talking about with this 'different sphere' business?"

She wondered for just a moment if he were really that naive about the class structure in their society. Ambria had always been a remote, self-absorbed little kingdom. Islands tended to breed peculiarities in animals and people if they were cut off from the mainstream for too long. Now that the monarchy had taken back control, after a twenty-five-year exile, and some of the old customs and rituals were being revived.

Royalty was royalty. It was special. That was all part of establishing authority and building back the old foundations. They were meant to be set apart from the common Ambrian. That was just the way it had to be.

"I'm an employee," she told him cheerfully. "You're a prince. Never the twain shall meet."

He made a face as though he thought that was complete tripe, but he would accept her judgment for the moment.

"We can still be friends, can't we? We can still talk."

"Sure."

He frowned. "I'm counting on you for that, you know."

That was just the problem. "Max…"

He took in a deep breath. "Here's the deal, Kayla. I don't know what I'm doing here." His gaze was hard now, insistent, and yet at the same time, completely vulnerable. "I don't know if I can stand too much of this prince stuff. It's not me."

"Oh." A flash close to pain went through her. He thought he couldn't do this. And yet, how could she be surprised? This was exactly what she would have expected if anyone had asked her. But that didn't mean she could let him go down this road without a struggle. He had to see how important it was.

"I'm willing to give it a go. For now. But I'm not feeling too confident. Most of my life has been lived on the other side of the divide. I don't know if I can adapt."

"Of course you can." She wished she could find the words she needed to get through to him. "Max, you were meant to be a prince from the beginning.

Don't you see? The part where you lived on the streets was the mistake."

"I'm not so sure about that." He winced, then went on softly, his eyes looking dark and luminous, his voice barely hiding the years of uncertainty he'd lived through.

"Sometimes I think I never got a family because I didn't deserve one. I was a misfit. A pretty bad misfit. And maybe I didn't ever get that kind of family love because…" He looked up and met her gaze. "Because I'm just unlovable."

She gasped. He wasn't joking. His expression was serious, questioning. Now she had to stop herself from going to him, from sliding down beside him and pushing away his pain with her arms. And at the same time, everything in her wanted to do it.

"Max! How can you say that? Women adore you!"

He stared at her for a moment, then gave a half laugh, half grunt. "That's not love, Kayla. That's something else."

Her head went back in surprise. Who would have believed Max would be the one to see the difference so clearly? But still, he seemed to be utterly blind to his own strengths. He was always so carefree and debonair. She'd never known he had this insecurity at his core. She had to make him see how wrong it was.

"Oh, come on. What did we used to call you? Mr. Casanova. A new girl on your arm every night."

His sigh was full of regrets. "You see, that's just

it." He took a long drink from his beer and stared into space. "Lots of new girls. No true love."

It was hard to believe that a man this appealing, this attractive, thought he couldn't find his soul mate. She looked at him, so handsome, so adorable. Her fingers ached to run through that thick auburn hair. It took all her will to stay where she was.

"Haven't you ever been in love?" she asked him.

"Not really." He squinted at her, thinking it over. "I don't think so. Not like you and Eddie." His smile was crooked. "I used to watch you two together and I think I hated you almost as much as I loved you."

"Oh, Max…"

"You know what I mean. It was pure jealousy. You two were so good together, so…so devoted." His voice broke on the word and she had to close her eyes and bite her lip to keep from going to him.

Devoted. Yes, that was exactly the way it had been. When she'd found Eddie, she couldn't believe her luck. They'd met in an elevator in their apartment building in Paris. As they traveled up the floors, people got off, but the two of them remained, until they were alone and looking at each other tentatively across the empty car. Their eyes met. Love at first sight. And when they finally got to her floor, he admitted his had been four stops before. How could she not invite him in for a cup of coffee? Two months later, they were married.

When he'd died, she had thought life was over. She moved in a dark, menacing fog, blindly searching for some way out of the pain, not really believing it was possible. For days, she was obsessed, thinking of ways to join him. And then she realized she had someone else to think about.

"Do you remember...?" Max's voice choked.

She stiffened. Here it came. She had to keep a cool front. Still, she had to tell the truth, at least as far as it was safe.

"I remember too much," she said softly.

"Me, too." He finished off his beer and looked at her. "I think about Eddie every day."

She nodded, closing her eyes. "Me, too."

She wasn't going to cry. She had to hold it back. For a moment, she let herself recall the way it had been being married to Eddie. Sunshine every day. Champagne for breakfast. Walks on the beach and dancing barefoot to a reggae tune. Driving with the top down. Love in the afternoon. Eddie was the best. The very best.

But she couldn't let herself think about him too much. That was a temptation that could sap her life away.

"Remember that day we went sailing in the bay," he said, "and your straw hat flew off and Eddie and I jumped into the water and raced for it?"

She nodded, trying to smile. "We had a picnic on that little island and we ate all those cherries."

"And then spent an hour rolling in the sand, moaning, with the worst stomachaches imaginable."

She managed a half grin. "I thought we were going to die."

He laughed. "I wanted to die."

His words seemed to echo in the room. Eddie was the one who had died, not long after that sunny day.

She closed her eyes again. They had to stop this. No good could come of it. They were laying treacherous emotional land mines all around. If they didn't stop, something was going to explode.

She wanted to stop. She tried. But somehow she couldn't keep the words from coming.

"I remember when you and Eddie would fly off into those big thunder clouds," she said softly, staring into the past, "like two falcons challenging the sky. It was so scary, but so magnificent. It made me shiver every time. I could hardly breathe. You were angels flying into the danger zone. And every time you came back victorious, another strike for the good guys, another strike for justice in the world." She turned to look at him, emotion almost choking her. "I was so proud of you both."

He didn't answer. Instead, he shook his head and looked away, and she knew his voice was probably too rough to use right now.

She should stop. She should push this all away into the past. But she couldn't. It was as though she had to get this out in the open in order to let it go. She tried not to say anything more, but the words came anyway.

"Everyone was proud of you. You were heroes. The best. The brightest stars."

She swallowed hard, then reached out across the coffee table and took his hand.

"And then, on that dark, rainy day in November,

you took off together, as usual, but you...you came back alone."

She blinked, wondering why there were no tears in her eyes. She usually had tears by now when she went over this in her own head. Why wasn't she crying?

"I stood there and watched your plane fly in, and I knew in my heart what it meant. But I didn't want to accept it. I kept thinking, no, he'll be coming. He's just had engine trouble or took a wrong turn or..." Her voice choked and she took a deep, shuddering breath. "I kept staring into the horizon, looking for that black spot to appear against the sky."

Her words seemed to echo against the walls as they both sat quietly, waiting for the pain to fade.

"Eddie was the best guy I ever knew," he said at last, his voice rough as a rocky beach. "It should have been me."

"No..." She held his hand as tightly as she could, with both her own.

"He was true and honest and brave. Not like me."

"No," she said fiercely. "Don't ever say that."

His face was twisted with pain. "Kayla, Kayla, it should have been me."

She was next to him on the couch now, and she wasn't sure how she got there. But she had to be with him, as close as she could get. She had to remind him of his own worth, his own value. She couldn't let him feel this way.

She took his beautiful face between her hands and stared right into his eyes. "Eddie was a wonderful

man. But so are you. You're just as good and precious and worthy."

He looked at her and winced, as though the light
was too bright in that direction.

"I would trade it all to have him back again," he
muttered.

She shook her head. "I don't think you can make
bargains like that. I don't think you can trade yourself. What happens, happens. We have to use it to
make ourselves into better people."

"Yeah." He tried to twist away from her, then gave
it up. "But it shouldn't have been Eddie. Not Eddie."

Her fingers dug into his hair and he looked down
into her eyes. He was going to kiss her. She knew it
and she knew she should stop him. She tried. But as
his arms slowly wrapped around her and he pulled
her body close, she could only sigh and raise her
mouth to find his.

The moment was electric. They'd come together
as though it were inevitable, as though they were
pulled by a force they weren't strong enough to fight.
Everything in Kayla cried out with need for Max. In
this primal moment, he was hers and she was ready
to surrender again. Just like before. She clung to him,
clung and arched into his embrace, waiting for the
touch of his tongue.

His face came closer. She could feel his warm
breath on her lips. Closing her eyes, she sighed and
offered her face to him.

And that was when the door to the apartment flew

open and Pellea came storming into the room like a Valkyrie.

The two of them stared at her, mouths hanging open in shock, still tangled in each others arms. She glared back, her hands on her hips as the door slammed shut behind her.

"What the heck is going on here?" she demanded.

Max frowned, not letting Kayla go. "Doesn't anyone ever knock in this place?" he quizzed right back at her.

"You're a fine one to talk," Kayla said, sotto voce.

Pellea's nostrils flared. "I knocked. Nobody answered. I guess you were too busy with this…this…" Her hand waved around in the air but she couldn't find a word that would suit. Still, her annoyance was clear.

Kayla began to pry herself loose from Max's octopus embrace and rose quickly in order to show respect for Pellea's position, hoping Max would notice and follow her lead.

"Oh, Pellea, don't get upset," she said, half laughing at the crazy situation. "We're old friends. Max was Eddie's best friend. They flew together in the Mediterranean."

Pellea's mouth made a round circle for a moment. She looked from one to the other of them. "Wow," she said. "I had no idea."

Kayla looked back at Max. He was grumpy and she couldn't really blame him. But she was glad Pellea had interrupted them. If anyone needed an intervention, it was the two of them. She gave him a look and he slowly rose beside her.

"I didn't realize he was the man I'd known until yesterday, when I first saw his picture in your office," Kayla explained.

Pellea frowned suspiciously. "You didn't say anything."

"I…I needed some time to get used to it. You see, earlier I had thought he'd been killed in Somalia months ago and…"

"Wait." Pellea held up her hand. "Your husband was killed flying for the Trialta National Forces, wasn't he?"

"Yes. He and Max flew together there."

Pellea looked skeptical. "And you never had any idea he might be royal?"

Kayla shook her head. "Never. I would have laughed at anyone who suggested it."

"Hey," Max complained in a low voice.

"Oh, never mind." Pellea looked at Max, then at Kayla, and shook her head and her look turned thoughtful. "That just makes it all more interesting, doesn't it?"

Kayla had to fight hard to resist rolling her eyes. "If you say so," she muttered, wondering what the queen had up her sleeve now.

She was carrying a portfolio, obviously something she'd brought in to show off for some reason. But her attention had been diverted. She glared at the recalcitrant prince.

"I feel like I'm going to have to put a homing device on you," she warned him.

He frowned, looking rebellious. He glanced at Kayla, then looked straight at the queen. "Is this prince job a twenty-four-hour commitment?" he asked suspiciously.

"Of course," Pellea said sharply.

"Of course not," Kayla said at the same time.

She certainly didn't want to contradict the queen, but she thought they'd better widen the discussion a bit before Max said something he would regret. The look on his face already set the stage for handing in his resignation as a royal. She didn't think the queen should portray it with quite such a heavy hand. Talk about scaring the quarry away! A little finesse was in order.

"The other princes don't have homing devices," she explained sensibly.

Pellea frowned at her. "The other princes don't need them."

Kayla shrugged reluctantly. "Good point."

And don't you forget it, Pellea seemed to say with her flashing eyes, though not a word passed her lips. She turned to Max and her face softened.

"Did you enjoy the ball?" she asked him hopefully.

He hesitated. Kayla bit her lip and prayed. For once in his life, was he going to be good? She knew there was a struggle going on inside him.

"Yes, Your Majesty, I did," he admitted at last. "You put on an amazing show. I was impressed."

Pellea looked pleased. "There, you see? If you would just relax and see what we're all about, you'll learn to love us in no time at all." She was smiling now, looking at both Kayla and Max with affection. "You'll see," she added, and then her smile faded and she took a deep, deep breath.

"But there's something else," she said, sliding the portfolio out from under her arm. "Take a look at this."

Sweeping aside the things on the coffee table, she pulled a poster out and spread it out on the flat surface.

"All right," she said dramatically, looking at Max. "Now explain this, mister!"

Max and Kayla stepped closer and looked down at the poster. Bright red with startling black writing, it displayed a large picture of Max and the announcement Max Arragen, Wanted, Dead or Alive!!!

CHAPTER FOUR

THE silence in the room was electric. All three seemed frozen in place. Finally, Kayla looked up at Max and asked simply, "What does it mean?"

He didn't meet her gaze. "I have no idea," he said softly, still staring at the poster. His mind was working like a buzz saw, cutting through all options and leaving shards of rejected possibilities behind. What could he possibly have done...?

Pellea crossed her arms over her chest and glared at him. "Okay, if nothing comes quickly to mind, let's go over the facts. As you can see, this was issued by the small nation of Mercuria. Have you ever been there?"

He raised his head and looked at the queen. This was a can of worms he would rather not have to deal with, but it seemed he would have no choice.

"Yes. I've been there."

"When? What were you doing there?"

Kayla was glaring at him now, as well. Interesting that they both seemed to assume he must be guilty of something. But then, he probably deserved that.

If he didn't want people to suspect shenanigans, he should have lived a different sort of life. Was it too late to change? Probably. He frowned.

"I spent a few months there last year. I did some work for the government. Actually, I helped them set up their air force."

Pellea's eyebrows rose at that. "And then what happened?"

He thought about it for a moment. Funny how things that seemed so mundane at the time became so impossible to explain to anyone. This looked a little more serious than he'd expected. But try as he might, he couldn't remember having done anything illegal while he was there. He hadn't robbed anyone. He hadn't run off with the royal jewels. He hadn't stolen any plans. The only thing he could think of that might apply had been a broken relationship with a rather beautiful… Well, he wasn't going to tell these ladies about that. They wouldn't be happy to hear it. And anyway that had been over a year ago.

He faced them squarely and tried to look candid. "I have to think it over and see if I can figure out what they are actually talking about."

"You can't tell us now?" Kayla asked.

He looked at her and shook his head. "No. I'm sorry. You're going to have to wait until I get a bit clearer on just exactly what they're objecting to."

Kayla and Pellea were both staring at him with wide-eyed wonder. Both sets of eyes contained the same horrified expression. It was pretty clear that they both thought that anything that couldn't be explained right here, right now, in simple language, had to be pretty darn bad. He looked at them both and shrugged, hating to feel defensive this way. Why should he have to explain himself?

But he was trapped. Sooner or later, they would probably know everything about his life—even things he didn't know. Still, why make it easy for them?

"I haven't led a perfect life. I've done things I'm not proud of. Things I wouldn't want to tell you about."

Pellea nodded as though she'd thought as much, but Kayla appeared surprised and troubled. He regretted that. But he still wasn't going to tell her everything he'd ever done wrong in his life. He wasn't going to tell anyone.

"I'm sorry," he said simply. "But I'm going to find out what they are accusing me of before I start spilling my guts and go admitting to every crime known to have happened in the last ten years. You understand?"

He looked at them. They looked back, and it was clear they didn't understand. It was obvious neither one of them had ever done anything to be ashamed of in their lives. Or not much, anyway. They stared at him with huge eyes and didn't say a thing. He groaned.

Suddenly, he was a little angry. "You know what? I didn't ask for this gig. I don't know much yet about what it means to be a prince. And I'm starting to feel like it's going to crowd me a bit. I live my life pretty free and easy." He shook his head, looking from one to the other of them. "I don't know, maybe that sort of living is incompatible with royal structure. What do you think?"

They just stared and he began to feel uncomfortable. In his experience, women talked over everything. They never quit. What was with the silent treatment? Did they really think he'd done something so awful it couldn't be talked about at all?

He was about to ask about that when Pellea made a move toward him. As he watched, she walked up and grabbed him by the front of his shirt, pulling his face down inches from hers.

"Promise me you won't run away," she said fiercely.

That was a tough one. "Um…for how long?"

There was a pause while she seemed to digest his attitude and realize he was close to an edge she didn't want to reach. She closed her eyes for a second, then opened them again. "Promise me you will give this a month."

A month. Could he take a month of this constant royal oversight?

He shook his head. "How can I do that?" he said, his tone almost sarcastic. "I may have to go serve time in East Slobovia here." He gestured toward the poster, then pulled back and used his most disarming smile. "How about a week?"

She winced and made a concession to reality. "Two weeks."

He glanced at Kayla. She looked like she was

holding her breath. He drew in a long breath himself and nodded as he looked back at the queen.

"Okay. I can give you that."

She let go and gave him a pat where she'd been grabbing his shirt. "Come to me tomorrow and be ready to tell me everything," she said as she headed for the door.

"I'll tell you what I feel you need to know," he countered as she opened it.

She whirled and glared at him. "Listen, Max. I hope you understand that you must take this seriously. So far, I've been able to keep this nonsense out of the king's notice. But if things get more dicey, I'm going to have to go to him with it."

Kayla bit her lip, wanting to stop Pellea. Didn't she see how he resented being talked to like this? Didn't she notice the sarcastic twist to the corner of his mouth, the veiled anger in his deep blue eyes?

She was actually surprised he hadn't said anything. He was used to talking back and walking out. It wasn't going to be easy for him to learn to hold his tongue and take honest criticism. Was he going to be able to handle it?

"Tomorrow," Pellea said. "And you will tell me all."

"Or at least as much of it as I know myself."

She threw back an exasperated look, but this time she didn't stop. In a few seconds, the door was closing and he and Kayla were alone again.

She turned to him, her eyes huge and dark in the lamplight.

"Max, what did you do?"

He took a deep breath and faced her. This was almost funny. Maybe someday they would look back and laugh. But not today.

"You know what? I don't have a clue." He saw the skepticism in her eyes and he looked away, swearing softly. "I've done a lot of things, Kayla. Nothing ever seemed bad enough to deserve jail time. Or death." He turned back and looked at her. "But you never know. People take things more seriously than you think at the time."

She shook her head slowly, almost in wonder. "Mercuria. It's a simple little country. You never even think of it. It's smaller than Ambria. What can they be so upset about?"

He shrugged, a little annoyed that no one seemed to have any faith in him. But he knew that wasn't fair. He'd given no one any reason to trust him. When you lived on the edge of a knife blade, like he had, you had to know that people were going to back away in horror now and then. It came with the territory.

"I'd have to see more than a picture on a Wanted poster to know that for sure."

He gave her a long, slow look, then shrugged again and headed for the door.

"I'd like to see a full description of my crime," he said, managing to sound lighthearted and carefree again. Free and easy. That was the way he wanted to live. "You've got to see what you're charged with before you can mount any sort of defense. Basic legal advice."

He turned and gave her a wink, then made it out the door and into the castle hallways.

Kayla watched the door swing shut and she drew air deep into her lungs. Secrets. He had secrets.

Well, funny thing. So did she.

The following morning when she got to work, Kayla found the queen involved in a dispute between a kitchen prep assistant and the royal chef. She was claiming the older man had promised to advance her and now he seemed to be spending all his time giving extra training to the pretty new pastry chef.

"Who knew my fabulously exciting days as queen would be filled with this sort of relationship management?" she complained to Kayla. "I might as well be working for the local department store." She sighed. "But I do feel sorry for her. He has been leading her on."

"Call the chef in for a nice chat, tell him that his grilled rosemary scallops are to-die-for and mention that reports of favoritism will be noted on his permanent record," Kayla advised. "And just to be safe, make sure he knows canoodling in the broom closet will be frowned upon."

Pellea shook her head. "You see it all so clearly, my dear. I know exactly why I hired you."

Kayla gave her a quizzical smile. "No regrets?"

Pellea pursed her lips and slid down into the chair opposite from where Kayla sat at her desk. "Okay. Let's get into it." She fixed her with a steady look. "Do I have anything to worry about?"

Kayla managed to look completely innocent. "In what way?"

Pellea gave her a look. "I think you know what I'm talking about. I have plans for Max, so it would be best if we put all our cards on the table, don't you agree?" She thought of something and her eyes narrowed. "By the way, where was your baby last night? I didn't see any evidence that he was with you."

Kayla's heart began to beat a bit harder. "He was nearby. He was staying down the hall with my sister."

"Oh." Pellea still looked skeptical.

Kayla leaned forward earnestly, determined not to let Pellea go down the road she obviously had been moving toward.

"No, it's not like that. Teddy often stays with Caroline when I work late. She watches him during the day, and her little one is the same age. He was already asleep…"

She stopped, realizing she was giving too much information. That was always the perfect way to sound absolutely guilty as charged. Taking a deep breath, she added simply, "I had no idea that Max was going to drop by."

Pellea blinked rapidly. "Just how close were you and Max in the old days?"

"We were good friends. Very good friends." She sighed and looked directly into the queen's eyes. "What you saw when you came in was a result of us both remembering Eddie and comforting each other over losing him that way."

Pellea held her gaze steady and slightly shook her head. "It looked like more than that to me."

Her heart rate made another lurch. "Pellea, I adored my husband," she said forcefully. "He was my life." She shook her head, hair flying about her shoulders. "Max loved him, too. Everybody did. He was a wonderful man." Reaching out, she took Pellea's hands in hers. "Please understand. Max and I were never…"

She stopped short, turning red. She couldn't really say that, could she? To her horror, she realized it was a lie. And she couldn't lie to Pellea of all people. She stared, wide-eyed, not sure how to get out of this trap she'd wandered into.

But Pellea didn't seem to notice. She nodded, searching her eyes with a sense of sympathy and compassion that didn't leave any more room for suspicion. "Okay. Oh, Kayla, I understand, and I'm sorry if it seemed I was implying anything more." She smiled with a sweetness that had once been her trademark, but wasn't often seen of late. "I won't do it again."

"Thanks." She smiled back, feeling a sense of relief that her friend and employer cared enough to make that pledge. And yet, in the pit of her stomach there lurked an aching tangle of guilt.

As of now, it seemed she was the only one who remembered what had happened that last night in Trialta. She had to keep it that way. But how could she do that when temptation was always lurking?

Somehow, she had to work at distancing herself

from Max. She had to be unavailable when he was around. It shouldn't be too hard. He was going to be very busy getting to know the rest of the royals and learning what his duties and responsibilities would be here in the castle. She would try to stay just as busy somewhere else. She might even ask for another assignment on the continent, one where she could take Teddy with her.

Yes, that was a good idea. She would leave the castle for a while. She would do something. She had to fix this. And she would.

"Did he tell you why Mercuria wants him to come back and stand trial?" Pellea asked.

"No. He didn't seem to know why."

"Hmmph." Pellea didn't sound convinced. "It's a real problem, you know. We owe that country a lot. They helped us during the war. Without their help, we might not have succeeded. And now that we've got a sort of truce going, they are the ones who act as go-between, our line of communication to the Granvillis. They're strong allies. I can't turn my back on a solid request like this. I can't ignore our friends. They won't be there for us next time if I do."

The worry in her voice sent Kayla's nerves quivering. They couldn't possibly be considering giving him up to the Mercurian royals—could they? Impossible.

"Send out the diplomats," she suggested, only half joking.

"Oh, definitely. Droves of them." She smiled, but it faded quickly. "I've got to admit, it worries me quite a bit. I'm going to have to make a call to them soon. I've got to tell them something. Max is going to have to level with me. And regardless, we'll have to find some way to either meet their demands or placate them."

"Meet their demands?" Kayla repeated, her dread growing.

Pellea gave her a reassuring pat. "Placating is probably safer," she noted. Then she made a face. "If we sent him back to them, lord only knows what he might do."

Kayla was beginning to rebel. After all, he wasn't all that bad. A bit nonconformist, of course, but all in all, he was definitely a good guy, at least in her experience with him.

But Pellea was still thinking of examples. She shook her head. "Last night at the ball, when he was presented to the old duchess, my Great-Aunt Judis, I was afraid he was going to say something like, 'Hey, Toots, could you get me a refill on this drink while you're up?'"

Kayla's eyes widened. "He didn't!"

"No, he didn't." She raised a significant eyebrow. "But there's something about him that keeps making me scared he will."

Despite her regard for him as a man, Kayla knew exactly what she meant. She frowned, trying to key in to the heart of the matter.

"He just doesn't have the proper instincts."

"Exactly."

She looked up hopefully. "He'll learn."

Pellea sighed. "Of course he will. But can we wait around for that to develop on its own? I think not." She drew in a deep breath. "So I'm getting him a superior teacher."

"Really?" Kayla's heart fell but she fought against it. This was just what had to happen. He had to learn his place in the scheme of things and she had to keep her distance from the entire process. It was all for the best and she knew it. "Who is that?"

Pellea stared at her, lips pursed as though she were annoyed with her somehow.

"A wonderful woman. She's perfect for this assignment. Her only flaw is that she is rather slow on the uptake at times." She gave a sound of exasperation. "It's someone he already respects and has a great affection for."

"Really?" She was still frowning. She hadn't realized he knew that many women here. But what was she thinking? He always knew women, wherever he happened to be. "Do I know her?"

Pellea threw up her hands. "It's you, silly. And you have exactly one week to perform a magical transformation."

Max arrived at Pellea's office in a somewhat surly mood. He'd spent the morning thinking about what he was going to say to her and nothing very good had come to mind. He decided to go for the basics—to tell her why he'd been in Mercuria and how his work there went. Then maybe she could weave some sort of conspiracy out of it all.

"Good morning, Your Majesty," he said cheerfully as she rose to greet him. He kissed both cheeks and smiled at her.

"You just missed Kayla," she told him. "I sent her on an errand." She gave him a sharp look. "But that will give us a chance to talk openly, won't it?"

He frowned, not sure he appreciated her implications that there might be things he could tell her that he wouldn't tell Kayla. Still, he followed her lead and sat across from her at her desk.

"I take it you have something to tell me?" she said, looking almost eager.

He shrugged and took a deep breath. "I've made some inquiries. I've got a few ideas."

"Good. Tell me what they are, because I don't have a clue."

He chewed on his lower lip, then admitted evasively, "I don't really have anything definitive."

She looked disappointed. "You don't know why the Mercurians are angry with you?"

He laughed shortly. "Angry, sure. Ready to lock me away in a dungeon…not so much."

Pellea's eyes were cooler now. "Why don't we start at the beginning?" she suggested. "Maybe there's something you're just not noticing. Why don't you tell me everything? All about your time in Mercuria."

He felt his jaw tighten, but he knew he really couldn't blame her. So he tried to do it her way.

"Okay. It all started when an old flight instructor of mine recommended me to the Mercurian Army as someone who might be able to help them get an air force organized and trained. I flew over, met the king and talked to the military people in charge. It seemed like a decent little country, trying to emerge onto the global stage, but without a lot of money and mainly ancient aircraft at their disposal. The jets were going to have to come later. Anyway, I thought I could help them. Why not? So I signed on."

"How long were you there?" '

"Not quite a year."

She nodded, thinking about what he'd told her and frowning. "Were you successful?"

"I thought so. We got a good skeleton of a program started."

She nodded again. "Did you know they were helping us with our war effort?"

"Of course. That was one reason the project appealed to me. I'm Ambrian, too."

"Why did you leave?"

That was a harder question. There were too many threads making up that answer to get into right now.

"Actually, around that time some old flying friends of mine showed up and talked me into coming over to join the fight for the restoration of the monarchy here in Ambria. It sounded like fun. Aerial combat and all that. And I was growing tired of all the bureaucracy I had to deal with in Mercuria. I wanted to get back into real flying again. So I joined up." He looked at her expectantly, his story over.

She sighed, shaking her head. "Which tells me a lot," she muttered, "and nothing."

"Exactly."

She studied his face for a moment. "Were they angry that you left when you did? Did they feel you hadn't completed your commitment?"

He shook his head. "There might have been a little of that, but no one actually complained. They knew I was ready to go."

He leaned forward. She deserved a better answer, but he just didn't know what he could tell her that was going to give her the information she needed.

"Pellea, I did a lot of things that someone might look back on and decide were…out of bounds, perhaps. We were flyers. We raised hell. That's what we do."

Slowly, she shook her head. "I'm pretty sure this is more than raising hell," she said. "You don't say 'dead or alive' about a little carousing."

"Okay, maybe…maybe an old girlfriend decided to take some sort of revenge. Maybe an innkeeper decided to blame me for a fight that might have torn up his bar and is suing for damages. Maybe someone who felt slighted by me in some way wants a pound of flesh. I just don't know. And I'm not sure what you want me to do about it." He shrugged. "Do you want me to issue an apology?"

"What? No. Of course not. Not until we know just what this is about."

He bit his tongue, wishing he could lose the defensive attitude. He knew he hadn't been living an exemplary life. He regretted it. Talking with Pellea, he wasn't proud of it. But it was lousy being asked to explain it. Life was complicated enough without this stupid wanted poster arriving from Mercuria.

He sat back. "Leave it to me. I think I can handle this. It might take a little time, but I'll get in touch with people I knew when I was there. I'll let you know for sure when I think I've really got it pinned down."

She nodded slowly. "Do that," she said. "But make it soon."

Kayla knew Max was going in to see Pellea first thing and she hoped they would be able to settle matters. It might be better if she could be there to help things along, but she had some business on the other side of the castle and knew she would probably miss him. So she left Max a message to meet her in the hall of portraits, and to her surprise, he was right on time.

The fact that there *was* a hall of portraits was a miracle. During the original rebellion, when the Granvillis had burned most of the castle and killed the king and queen—the parents of the current crop of princes, as well as of King Monte, Pellea's husband—they had destroyed everything they could get their hands on that might remind anyone of the deposed monarchy. A lot of paintings burned that night, but many of the most important ones were spirited out by various servants who hid them with relatives for the twenty-five years of the Granvilli regime.

After the restoration of the DeAngelis monarchy, when the castle archivist began to collect them and bring them home, there was a wave of emotion in the populace that touched them all. It was so very important to have these beautiful pictures to tell the story of what their history had been.

Kayla found Max gazing up at a huge stately portrait of his great grandfather. The fine-looking royal was wearing an ermine-lined cape and looking quite imperial and majestic.

"Quite a handsome bunch, your ancestors," she noted, sliding in beside him and looking up as well. She felt proud for him, proud for Ambria. She only hoped he understood what it meant to be a part of this.

"They certainly seem well-turned out," he agreed. "But then, you've always got artistic flattery on your side when you're royalty." He gave her a mock jab in the ribs with his elbow. "The artist makes them beautiful or he doesn't get paid, I would think."

"Maybe." She gave him a sideways look. "But from the evidence presented by your brothers, I'd chock it all up to good genes."

He shrugged and she frowned, not sure he was sufficiently impressed.

"After all, the blood of these very people flows in your veins," she pointed out.

He grunted. "Let's hope none of them were bleeders or vampires," he said lightly. "Don't those two things tend to run in this kind of family?"

For some reason him saying that made her absolutely furious. Did he really not understand how important his own family was? Or was he just trying to drive her crazy?

"There is no such thing as vampires," she said through clenched teeth.

"Maybe not," he said, his blue eyes sparkling with amusement. "But I'm going to start being more careful with the morning shave. You never know."

"No one in the DeAngelis family has ever shown any signs of hemophilia," she protested, trying hard not to let him see how annoyed she was. "Just forget it."

He gave her a look that infuriated her even further, then shrugged again and turned away as though it hardly affected him anyway. She took a deep breath and forced herself to calm down. She knew she was being overly sensitive, and that he was playing on her emotions like a skilled musician. She had to hold it back. She couldn't give him the satisfaction of showing her feelings like this.

Slowly, she followed as he examined one portrait after another. She'd been here often in the last few months and she didn't have to look at the labels to know who each one was. She was ready to answer any of his questions, but he didn't say another word and she wondered what he was thinking.

No matter what, he had to be fascinated by the imposing DeAngelis family. Who could help it? And to think that he'd suddenly found out he was one of them.

They'd walked the length of the hall and then they both went out onto the terrace that overlooked the royal fields. Leaning against the massive stone guardrail, he smiled at her and her annoyance with his attitude began to melt away. She really couldn't resist that smile.

"Did you talk to Pellea?" she asked.

"Oh, yeah. We had a little chat."

"And?"

He eyed her questioningly. "What? You think I'm going to tell you everything I told her?"

She pulled back quickly. "No. Of course not."

He laughed and reached out to push her hair behind her ear and then pull her closer again. "But you know I would. If there was anything to tell."

"You didn't come up with anything?" Her skin tingled where his fingers had touched and she frowned, trying to ignore it.

He hesitated. "Not anything sure. Or substantive." He shrugged and changed the subject. "I can't get over you being here like this," he said. "What are the odds that we would both end up in the Ambrian castle? That was certainly a stroke of luck."

"Yes, wasn't it?"

She looked at his beautiful eyes and the hard, tanned planes of his handsome face and she knew he belonged with the men and women in those huge, gorgeously painted portraits in the hall. Someday his image would hang there with them. That was his destiny. Surely he knew that. Didn't he?

"So how did Pellea find you, anyway?" he was asking her. "You said your sister had something to do with it?"

"I told you we'd known each other before. When my sister and her husband moved here, Caroline went to Pellea and told her about me and my situation and let her know I was looking for a job. It just so happened that she was looking for an assistant. So everything fell into place."

"Good timing. Life can happen that way sometimes."

She nodded ruefully. "Not often."

"No." A shadow flickered through his gaze. "Not often."

They stood silently for a moment, each thinking private thoughts. Kayla was remembering Eddie and she was pretty sure he was, too. But she didn't want to get started on that again. They had work to do.

"I guess you're wondering why I asked you to meet me here," she said at last.

He grinned at her using such a well-known cliché. "The question had crossed my mind a time or two," he admitted. "And then I decided you just wanted me to learn to connect with my roots."

"A simple goal, I would think."

He grimaced. "So okay, I looked each ancient ancestor in the eye and took his measure. And the women, too. And I was impressed." But he seemed a little impatient. "What else do you want from me?"

She drew a deep breath in slowly, wondering how to put this. She had no idea how he was going to take it. For all she knew, he might storm off and never speak to her again. Finally, she just blurted it out.

"Okay, Max. Here's the deal." She steeled herself. "Pellea wants me to teach you how to act like a prince."

CHAPTER FIVE

Max stared at her and for a moment, Kayla thought he hadn't understood. But a faint smile quirked at the corners of his mouth and he repeated slowly, "Pellea wants you to teach me how to act like a prince?"

She nodded, waiting.

He gave her a look as though this was about as kooky as he'd thought things could get. "Really?" he said with a twist to his smile. "Who taught you?"

That was a good question and keyed right in to her deepest fears about this assignment. But she wasn't going to let him know that. She hadn't asked for this. In fact, she wished it hadn't occurred to Pellea at all. But it had, and here they were, stuck with a project to do.

"I'm very observant," she said cheekily. "Don't worry. I won't steer you wrong."

He grinned, watching her with a slightly lascivious expression. "I'm not worried at all. I have every intention of becoming teacher's pet in a major way."

She pretended to frown. "Don't count on that,

mister. I'm a tough grader. You're going to have to earn your graduation papers."

"It's a deal." He pretended to look at his watch. "You've got two weeks to make me into royalty. Better get moving."

She wasn't crazy about the way he set it up like an adversarial position, but she'd known from the start that she would have to work fast. He didn't have to remind her. His attention span wouldn't last long. And he proved it by jumping to a new topic in seconds.

A man had walked by holding a baby, and they both looked up as the baby made a cooing sound. She met Max's wide eyes and they both smiled.

"Hey, when do I get to meet little…Teddy, did you say his name was?" he asked.

She felt a surge of unpleasant adrenaline.

"Yes, uh…Teddy."

He looked at her curiously. "Is he here at the castle with you?"

"He stays with my sister during the day. I'll… uh…make sure you get to meet him soon."

"Good." He frowned and she knew he was wondering why she was so hesitant. "I'll bet he looks just like Eddie."

Color filled her cheeks. She tried to force it back but it just kept coming. Had he noticed? Did he see how uncomfortable she was with this?

"He's a little young to look like anyone right now," she said breathlessly.

But he didn't seem to notice her reaction. He was

looking into the past, his brows pulled together, and thinking of how it had once been. "Thank God you had his baby," he said softly, reaching out to touch her cheek. "Thank God there's a piece of him left in the world."

Her mind was racing. She had to think of something. Hopefully, he would forget about Teddy once he was thoroughly invested in taking on the royal mantle. That had to be her goal: to convince him that becoming a prince was something he wanted to do, that it would engage his mind and spirit like nothing else he'd ever done. Once he opened himself to it fully, he would be so busy, so connected with what was going on here in the castle, that he would forget about her and her son. They would just fade into a pleasant memory for him, and then her life could go on as it had before he ever got here.

But he was still frowning at her, searching her eyes. She pulled away from his hand and turned to look at the distant sea. They were miles away, but she thought she could hear the waves pounding on the rocks.

"Listen, what about this Mercuria situation? I know you don't know exactly what their beef is, but you must have some idea of what set them off." She turned back to look at him. "Any clue at all as to what their problem was?"

He stared at her for a moment, then gave a bitter laugh. "You mean why they want to lock me away in their particularly nasty tower and torture me with bad food? No. I'm still not sure what that is all about."

She frowned. "Come on, Max. You must have a secret opinion. Or two."

"Oh, yeah. I've got some thoughts on the matter." He frowned and shifted his weight from one foot to the other, as though suddenly uncomfortable with those very thoughts. "But you wouldn't like them."

That gave her a momentary pang, but she was game. "Try me."

He made a face. "I'd rather not."

She looked into his eyes. He was serious.

"Max, this isn't a game. We have to find out the truth. This has to be dealt with."

He nodded slowly. "Of course."

She waited. He stood very still and watched her. She sighed with quick exasperation and tugged on his sleeve. "Max! Tell me! Delve down into your deepest intuitions and tell me what you think it just might be."

He grimaced, then looked back at her and shrugged. "Okay. If you really want me to do this, here you go. This is just a guess, but…" He took a deep breath, then looked out at the distant mountains. "I think they want me to marry their princess."

She stared at him in shock. He glanced at her and sighed.

"And here you thought this was the only royal gig I had lined up," he said grimly. "But no. I've got my choice. Lucky me."

Kayla swallowed hard. She hadn't expected some-

thing like this. Staring at Max, she tried to get her
mind around these new developments. Everything
inside her was aching for a denial. He couldn't…
could he? He hadn't…had he?

"Is there…uh…a reason they would be demanding this? I mean, their charges were pretty hard-line,
even if they weren't explicit."

His blue gaze skimmed her features. "You mean,
did I compromise the girl's reputation in some way?"
he said with a trace of sarcasm and a touch of resentment. "No, Kayla. I did not."

"Oh." Relief flooded her, leaving her breathless.
And then she realized she still didn't know any of
the details. "Then…?"

"The Princess Nadine is fifteen years old," he
told her, looking almost angry. "She decided to get
a teenage crush on me. I didn't do a thing to encourage it. Believe me, I do have certain scruples. But
girls that age…" He shrugged and looked toward the
heavens for help.

It was ridiculous. Maddening. And ultimately, he
had a feeling it would be quite embarrassing. There
had to be a way to handle this without everyone
knowing what the Mercurians really wanted.

Princess Nadine was a lovely girl, but she was
much too young to be handed off to an old guy like
him. He'd only seen her a few times and he'd managed to keep those visits short. He couldn't go back
there. There was no telling what would be demanded
of him. The family running the country was a few

bricks short of a load at times. One might even say, crazy as loons.

"It's not a good situation."

"Oh."

"She decided she wanted me. And her daddy, the King of Mercuria, gives her whatever she wants."

"Oh, dear."

"Yes. 'Oh, dear'." He finally looked her in the eye. "So how am I supposed to explain this to Pellea? Especially when I don't even know if it's true?"

She thought for a moment. It was a problem. The queen was not going to be happy, and this put her in an awkward position in regard to an international relations situation that would just tangle things into knots. She could see why he hesitated to tell her about it.

But he would have to.

"You haven't said anything to her about this?"

"No."

She nodded. "Explain it to her just like you did to me."

He looked skeptical. "I don't think she'll buy it."

"If it's the truth, what else can you do?"

He gave her a baleful look and shook his head. "Run away?" he suggested, only half joking.

"Never," she said firmly.

He looked weary. "You know, this is just a guess. I don't have any evidence. I'm not sure this is the exact thing pulling their chain. For all I know…"

"You've got to tell her. Right now."

"Right now? But…"

She dug for her mobile and held up a hand to stop him. "I'll see if she's in," she said, punching in Pellea's office number. "She's not there," she said after a moment. "But her message says she'll be right back."

Leaning on the stone guard wall, he was watching her from under dark, lowered lashes. "You're bound and determined to make sure I do the right thing, aren't you? And by that, I mean the 'royal' right thing." His eyes narrowed further. "You remind me of a prison warden I once knew."

She looked up at him, doggedly set in her goals. "I'm going to make you into a prince," she said coolly. "And you're going to like it."

He didn't smile. His blue eyes looked as cold and hard as sapphire stones. "Or else I'll bow out," he said softly.

Holding his gaze, she shook her head slowly. "Over my dead body," she promised, enunciating each word carefully. "You're sticking this out, mister."

He stared a moment longer, and then his lip began to curl. "Damn," he said huskily. "Do you know how sexy you look when you're giving me orders?"

"Oh!" She turned and started away, furious with him again. Was he ever going to take anything seriously?

"Hey." He caught up with her and grabbed her upper arm, pulling her around to face him. "I'm sorry. I'm sure you thought that was condescending, didn't you? I didn't mean it that way. I was just being honest."

She glared at him. "Be honest with Pellea. She's the one who counts. And believe me, she's ready to give you every chance in the world. But you have to level with her. Come on." She linked her arm with his and gazed up at him, intense and a bit anxious. "Let's go on over to the office. She ought to be back any minute. And you can tell her yourself. She'll listen."

He gave her a skeptical look. "She'll try to see my side of things?"

"Oh, absolutely. She's really very understanding."

"I really don't understand any of this and what's more, I won't have it!"

Kayla recoiled. She'd never seen Pellea so angry. She glanced apologetically at Max, but he was scowling at the queen. Oh, brother, did she ever regret forcing this little conversation.

They had come back to the office and found Pellea just arriving, a sheaf of papers in her hand. Obviously, she'd had news. She'd greeted them both the way someone thoroughly annoyed might, and as things were going, that did seem to be exactly what she was.

Pellea took a deep breath, closed her eyes and tried to calm herself. "All right. I'm going to try not to shout. That sort of thing is never becoming in a queen." She gestured at them, slipping into her desk chair. "Sit down. We'll do this the right way." But her eyes flashed at Max. "Now tell me again, what exactly have you heard from Mercuria?"

Every muscle he owned seemed to be locked in stone. "As I said before, not much."

There was a hard line to his mouth that Kayla didn't like. She knew he resented being talked to the way Pellea had done, but she could also see that he was holding back. She only prayed that he was in control of his emotions. And that Pellea was, too. Sinking into a chair, she tugged on his sleeve to get him to sit down, too.

"I do have some calls in to some people and a friend is trying to look into this further, but…" He shrugged. "So far, not much."

"You're right," Pellea said evenly. "That's not much." She waved an official-looking document at him. "I'll tell you what I have. We've just received it. It's from their foreign minister." Her eyes blazed.

Max's head went back defensively and his eyes were hooded. "What does he have to say?"

She rattled the paper. "He says we have five days to the deadline and at that point, they expect us to hand you over."

A muscle pulsed at his jawline. "And if you don't hand me over?"

She glared at him. "They're going to invade."

Kayla gasped. "What? Oh, Pellea, that can't be."

The queen looked at Kayla, at a loss and showing it. "That's what they say, right here." She held up the embossed announcement, complete with signatures and an official stamp. "Read it and weep."

"They won't invade," Max scoffed. "They don't have the man power." But he perused the document carefully, reading every line.

Pellea seemed to be counting to ten. Finally, she said a bit breathlessly, "Maybe they won't actually invade. Maybe this is all bluster. But that doesn't fix everything. We still owe this country a lot. We need to pay them back, in kind if not in cash. What are we going to do to satisfy them? What are we going to do about their demand to have you extradited?"

His gaze was steady and firm. "We're going to tell them to pound sand, I hope."

"No." She shook her head emphatically.

His face registered a tiny flash of shock, then one eyebrow rose quizzically. "You want me to go and stand trial?" he asked incredulously.

"Of course not. But we don't get around it by yelling at them." She threw her hands up. "We consult. We sympathize. We question. We find ways to talk them out of their anger. We don't give them exactly what they want, but we make them think we did."

Max frowned, not sure he bought her song and dance. "But we still don't know exactly what they want from me."

"No. We don't, do we?" Pellea tapped the toe of her shoe against the tiled floor and stared at him steadily. "The only one here who could possibly know is you. So what do you think it is? If you were to venture a guess."

Max stared back. Kayla waited breathlessly, expecting him to find a way to tell the queen about the princess, just the way he'd told her. She waited. And waited.

But Max didn't say a word about that. Instead, his handsome face seemed to have cleansed itself of all emotion, all thought, and he said evenly, "I think you already have a theory. Don't you? Why don't you tell me what it is?"

"A theory? No." She pulled another large sheet of paper off her desk and brandished it. "But the foreign minister of Mercuria seems to have one. Here's what he says." She held it up and began to read, just skimming to the pertinent words and phrases.

"According to the foreign minister, while you were in their lovely country, enjoying their delightful hospitality..." She took a deep breath before going on, setting up a nicely dramatic pause. "You stole a horse, hijacked an airplane and made off with an important ancient historical national artifact." She lowered the paper and looked him in the eye. "And you say...?"

He was shaking his head, half laughing, but without amusement. "That's insane. I never took any artifact."

Kayla groaned and Pellea's eyes widened. "But the horse and the airplane...?"

He grimaced. This was all so stupid. "Listen, I can explain."

Pellea looked at Kayla. Kayla looked at Pellea. They both groaned.

"No, really," he said, feeling unfairly outnumbered. "There was no money in the treasury. They gave me the plane in lieu of payment for services rendered. I can prove it."

Pellea's eyes flashed. "Good. You'll have to. Do you have papers?"

He hesitated and then he shrugged. "I'll have to take a look. I must have something somewhere."

She nodded as though she'd known that all along. "And the horse?"

He drew in a long breath. "That's a longer story."

"Of course." She was glaring again. "And the artifact?"

His eyes blazed at that one. "Now there, I have no idea what they're talking about."

Pellea's eyes narrowed. "Oh, but I think you do."

"Do you?" His back was really up now. "Then why don't you tell me?"

She searched his eyes for a moment, then shrugged. "We're going to put together a letter of explanation," she said, completely dismissing the subject of the artifact for now, "and send an ambassador right away."

"For this?" he said dismissively.

She turned and looked at him. "Don't you understand how important this is? We have to soothe ruffled feathers as quickly as we can." Her eyes flashed and her hands smoothed down the bright red dress she was wearing, the outfit that was making her look like a Spanish dancer. "Unless you'd like to go back and explain it to them yourself?"

He winced. "I don't think that would be a good idea."

"Just so," she said, as though that proved some point she'd been making all along.

Watching all this, Kayla was at a loss. She knew Max was being cagey. Why hadn't he brought up the princess? Why did he treat Pellea like someone he had to keep things from? She wished he would lay it all out for her. If they didn't handle this properly, war could be the result.

Either that, or extradition. She shuddered.

"Pellea, does Monte…does the king know about this?" she asked her.

"No." Her face crumpled and for a second, Kayla was afraid she would cry. But she regained her composure quickly, taking Kayla's hand in hers and squeezing it as though grateful she had her support and understanding. "No, he's got his own international relations problems right now. I don't want to bother him with this. I have to begin taking care of these things on my own and not go running to him with everything."

Kayla nodded sympathetically. Working with Pellea, she had seen for herself what a precarious tightrope she walked trying to become effective without becoming either obsessive or too dependent. She and Monte had been like the perfect couple from the beginning, in more ways than one. Their royal marriage was a partnership and Pellea worked at it night and day.

Max rose, looking moody. "Your Majesty, let me just say this. The list you received from the foreign minister sounds like a bunch of excuses to me. I don't know what's really behind all this." He stopped and swallowed hard. It really wasn't easy for him to delve into his life and try to find explanations for this. But he would try.

"Why not wait until I find out something from my contacts in the country. Just hold on until then. Maybe we'll have something we can work with."

Pellea nodded, looking distracted. "Of course. You'll let me know, won't you?" She waved them off. "Until then, I'll be counting on Kayla to manage things. So go, both of you. Get some lunch. I'll talk to you later."

Kayla looked back as they closed the door. A jagged little piece of her heart tore at the look in Pellea's face. She bit her lip and turned away.

They walked away from the office. Kayla eyed at Max sideways and wondered how to broach the subject that was begging to be discussed. She kept expecting all this to be cleared up, and instead, she was just getting more confused.

"You want to explain all that to me?" she said at last, when he didn't volunteer anything.

He looked down at her and raised an eyebrow. "You mean, why I didn't tell her about Princess Nadine?"

She nodded. "You could start with that."

He shrugged and kept walking. "There was nothing about it in the complaint. So maybe I'm wrong. Maybe that's not what this is all about."

She stopped him and searched his eyes in wonder. "You don't believe that."

He glanced back at her, frowning. "Who cares what I believe, Kayla. What does it matter?"

"Of course what you believe matters. How are we going to get to the bottom of all this if we just throw out theories without exploring them?"

She saw the torture in his eyes and melted. "Listen." She grabbed his arm and pressed close so she could talk to him softly. "Whatever they think you did, whatever it turns out to be, we'll handle it. Nothing is going to drive you away. We won't let it." His gaze locked in hers. "I won't let it," she whispered, her love for him in her eyes.

He reached up and his hand cupped her chin, fingers trailing across her cheek. He didn't say a word, but something in his eyes said volumes. *I need you, Kayla,* they seemed to be saying. *Don't ever leave me. I don't want to live without you. Never again.*

She saw it as clearly as though he had said the words aloud. But she also saw what followed—a regret, a denial. She'd seen his true feelings, but at the same time, she saw why he couldn't act on them. It was all there. As Pellea had said, read them and weep.

He dropped his hand and looked away and she put distance between them and cleared her throat.

"Tell me about the horse," she said coolly.

Something flashed in his eyes and he turned away, then steeled himself and turned back and said, "Let's get some food first. Where's the closest place to get some food around here?"

She led him there and they entered the fast-food

His eyes were troubled as he remembered how it had been for these people. "The whole family had one goal—keep those horses. But while I was living there, they had to get rid of two of them. They just couldn't keep up with expenses. They were about to lose their house and they couldn't...." He shook his head as though the words just wouldn't come for a moment.

"I would have tried to help them, but the Mercurian government wasn't paying me at the time. So I didn't have much in the way of resources." He looked down at his hands. They were clenched into fists. Slowly, he made them relax.

"But we managed to get together enough money to keep the most important one, a beautiful horse named Belle. He belonged to the Minderts' eight-year-old daughter, Mindy. She rode her every day. It was magical to watch the way she and that huge horse had a rapport between them. It would have been a crime to separate them."

Kayla murmured something and reached for his hand again. His fingers curled around hers, but he didn't seem to know it. He was wrapped up in his story.

"The public affairs minister and I had a falling out. Bottom line, he hated me. He tried to undercut me a couple of ways that just didn't work out. And then, all of a sudden, he took Mindy's horse away." His voice deepened roughly. "He had some trumped-up national security reason. They were supposedly confiscating all horses in the sector."

He turned to look into her eyes. "It was a bunch of bull. I went to him to try to get it rescinded. He called the guard, tried to have me arrested." He shrugged. "I got away." He gazed at the wall again and took a deep breath. "I found out where they were keeping Belle and I stole her back. I took her and I rode her right across the border."

He looked back at Kayla as though to see how she was taking that. She looked right back. So far, she wished he hadn't done it, but she didn't see how it was going to be a capital offense. These things could be explained…couldn't they? Maybe Pellea could authorize a payment?

But Max was still telling his story.

"I managed to have the Minderts meet me. They were about to lose their land anyway. It was time for them to go. I got them out of the country and on their way to Switzerland. They have family there." He took a deep breath and looked at her. "And Mindy has her horse back."

"Oh. I'm glad. But…" It did seem a large price to pay for a horse. She admired him for his instincts to help, but… "Max, you could go to prison for this." Not only that, but he could also be giving up his place in the royal family.

"Yes," he said simply. "I might." He stared hard into her eyes, his own silver with passion. "But, Kayla, I don't really care. There was something more important than that involved. And I would do it again. I would do it tomorrow."

CHAPTER SIX

MAX's hand tightened on Kayla's. "You see, there's more to this story. Mindy is a sweet and adorable girl. You would love her. But more than that, Mindy…" His voice choked a bit and he cleared his throat. "Mindy is blind, you see. Belle was her life companion, her only joy. You understand?" He searched her eyes, looking very serious.

She drew her breath in sharply, and then she nodded slowly. She did understand. She had to admit, Mindy's blindness made all the difference. The fact that he had thrown away everything he had in order to help the child…she was touched by what he'd done. "Yes. I think so. I do understand."

He nodded, as though satisfied with her answer and by what he could see in her eyes. "Good. It had to be done."

She stared at him. Yes, it had to be done. And he'd done it. He was a man who went ahead and did things. He didn't wait to see how the wind might blow. He made things happen. Suddenly, her heart

filled with affection for him. So he stole a horse—
so what!

"And you...?" she asked.

He shook his head. "I never went back. It was time
for me to go anyway."

She took a deep breath and sighed as though she'd
just been through something important. "Wow. You
were a hero."

"No." He shook his head and appeared pained. "It
was my fault the horse was taken in the first place. I
should have been more obsequious to the minister. I
don't ever seem to be able to learn that lesson."

"And I don't suppose you were much of a hero to
the Mercurian regime, were you?"

He gave a short laugh. "Hardly."

"So by the time you left, they already had a pretty
deep grudge against you."

"So it seems."

Their tea was getting cold and the first round of
sandwiches had arrived. Luckily, they were delicious
and Kayla began to relax. It was wonderful what a
little bit of tea and some yummy finger food could
do. She was feeling so much better about everything.

He had reasons for taking the plane and reasons
for stealing the horse. Surely he also had an explanation for the historical artifact. Whatever that was.
But she wouldn't bug him about that right now. All
in good time.

She definitely wouldn't let herself get caught up
in so much worry about it any longer. She had work

to do. She was supposed to mold him into a prince in a week. It was time to get going on that little job.

"We've got to get back to the essential things we've been tasked with," she told him between bites of a watercress delectable. She gave him a significant look. "Prince lessons."

He rolled his eyes but didn't balk. "I'm game," he said with resignation. "What do I do next? Cut my hair in a pageboy?"

"Nothing so old-fashioned as that," she assured him. "But I think we ought to make a list." She pulled a notebook out of her huge purse. She'd brought it along just for this sort of thing.

"A list?" His look was wary.

"A list of all the things the modern nobleman must be."

He gave her a crooked grin so endearing, she felt something move in her chest. He'd grinned at her with just that look before. She had a quick flashback to a day on the beach down on the Mediterranean, a day so bright and beautiful, it made her think her world had been enchanted. Max and Eddie were competing to see who could build the best sand castle. And she was just sitting to the side, watching them and laughing at their silly macho banter. The sea was turquoise blue, the sand was sparkling, the sun was liquid gold.

A perfect day. A perfect time. A bittersweet sense of nostalgia swept through her and she had to hold back tears. Nothing would ever be so special again.

She pulled herself back into the now and Max was still making fun of her list.

"I'll see your modern nobleman list," he teased her. "And then we'll raise the stakes and make a list of everything the non-noble should know before attempting to play the royal game. That one I might be able to shoot for."

She shook her head. "Don't worry. This doesn't mean you have to absorb everything all at once. It's more of a wish list." She wrote on the top of the page, The Attributes of the Perfect Prince.

"Perfect?" He groaned. "Might as well toss it right now."

"Will you stop it?" she said, raising her pen to her cheek as she thought things over. "I know. We'll start with physical appearance."

He seemed surprised. "You don't think I've got the looks for the job?"

She flashed him a satirical glance. "As far as the basics, you'll do. But there's more to it. There's a certain way that a prince carries himself."

He grinned. "Arrogance and disdain? I think I can handle that."

She pretended to glare at him. "No. Confidence and competence mixed with a certain sense of approachability. Leadership and the common touch, all wrapped up in one handsome package." She wrinkled her nose. "Do you understand what I mean?"

He looked back and then sighed. "I think I get it."

"Good." She nodded. "Work on that, please."

"Oh, sure. No problem."

"And then there is your manner of dress."

He looked down at his casual shirt and Levi's and eyed her questioningly.

Her look back was scathing and she shook her head. "I'll get together some pictures to show you what you can do on that."

"Spend money," he said cynically.

"Yes. But carefully. I'll teach you the tricks."

"No kidding?" His smile was nothing if not provocative. "I didn't know you had a few of those up your sleeve."

She grinned back and tapped him with her pen. "Be ready for anything."

"Oh, I will."

"But right now," she said, shifting gears and getting serious again, "I want to see how you walk."

He blinked at her. "What?"

"Your walk. Is it royal enough? Does it need more backbone? Insouciance? Perhaps a bit more savoir faire?"

"Listen, I'll do anything you want, but I'm not going French."

She laughed. "You only wish you could be French. The French know how to walk."

"I've never been put down for my walk before."

"Let's see it, then."

He blinked at her. She couldn't mean what she seemed to mean. Could she? "What?"

She gestured for him to stand. "Do it."

His eyes were clouded. "Do what?"

She leaned toward him, holding back a laugh at

his hesitancy. "Walk across the room. Let's see what you've got."

"Here? Now?" He looked around the room, his face worried.

"Yes, here and now." She bit back a grin and decided it was time to take pity on him. "Oh, don't worry. Something simple. Just a quick turn and back again."

She almost laughed out loud at the look he gave her. It was obvious the whole concept was a huge embarrassment to him. Funny. Had he never been conscious of how he came across before?

"Just get up and walk over to the counter and pick up a tray of sweets and bring them back here. No one will know you're on display."

He took a deep breath, his look as close to a glare as she'd ever received from him. "All right," he said grudgingly. "But be kind."

Rising, he threw her an exasperated glance and started across the room. His walk was slow, strong and controlled and she knew right away there was nothing she could suggest to improve it. The set of his shoulders, the tilt of his head, the length of his stride—his manner of carrying himself might not be particularly royal, but it was about as good as it could get.

And then she noticed something odd. It was like a force field moving through the room. Every single woman, even those who couldn't have possibly seen him get up from where they were sitting, was turning her head in his direction. What was he—magnetized? She watched, eyes wide and hand over her mouth, as he picked up the tray and started back. They were all staring.

And it wasn't that he was so handsome. There were other handsome men in the room. There was more to it than that. There was a sense about him—a little bit of danger, a little bit of bravado and a lot of something else. She bit her lip, trying to analyze just what it was. Those gorgeous eyes seemed to say he knew things other people didn't—secret things about life and love. And whatever those secret things were, they seemed to draw the attention of every female imagination in the place.

"Wow," she breathed as he sat down again.

He lifted a dark eyebrow sardonically. "I was that good, was I?"

She rolled her eyes. "No," she told him briskly, not willing to let him know the power he had, just in case he wasn't sure of it yet. "I was just thinking what a lot of work we have ahead of us."

He winced and looked rebellious. "I can save everybody the trouble and forget the whole thing," he offered, only half joking. "If even the way I walk isn't good enough…"

"Isn't good enough," she echoed weakly, shaking her head. It was no use. He might as well know the truth. "Someone should call out the paramedics," she whispered to him wryly, leaning close so as not to be overheard. "Half the women in here are about to swoon right off their chairs after watching you walk across the room."

He eyed her skeptically, a cloudy, slightly bewildered expression in his eyes. Then he spoke with such honesty, she was taken aback. "Kayla, come on. Don't mess with my self-confidence like that. I'm feeling shaky enough about this whole royal thing. I don't need you, of all people, to be mocking me."

She recoiled in surprise. She hadn't meant to do that. She hadn't thought anything could ruffle his famously appealing feathers. Evidently, he wasn't quite as cocky as he seemed. To think that he had never noticed the effect he had on women was a revelation.

"I'm sorry," she said quickly. "I'm just as new at this as you are. I was trying to stick to a light tone and I guess I went a little too far." Reaching across the table, she took his hand in hers and leaned forward, looking into his eyes earnestly. "Max, you've got a great walk. Manly and noble and full of confidence. At least, that's the way it comes across and that is what counts. You were born to be a prince, no matter how you want to fight it. It's in your blood."

He squeezed her hand and didn't answer, but his eyes were smiling.

"But we aren't finished," she added quickly. "There are a lot of superficial things you need to learn. We still have a long way to go."

He nodded, agreeing with her. "'And miles to go before we sleep,'" he said softly.

She gasped and smiled. "A literary quote. Very good. Knowing good poetry is a real plus in a prince."

"Eddie taught me that one." His eyes clouded. "Too bad it wasn't Eddie who got the chance to be a prince. He would have done a bang-up job of it, wouldn't he?"

As she watched him, something caught in her heart. "Max, Eddie was great. I miss him constantly. It just kills me that he had to die. But…" And here was the hard part. It was true, but hard to say. "Max, he was no better a person than you are."

Max winced as though she'd slapped him. "Don't say that. Of course he was."

"No." She shook her head. "He wasn't perfect. He was a man, just like you are. He had his good days and his bad ones." She tried to smile. "He could be darn grumpy when the weather didn't suit him. You remember."

A slow grin erased Max's frown. "I remember."

Their gazes met and held. Max began to lean closer, his eyes filling with smoky memories.

"Kayla," he began huskily.

But he never got any further. A shriek filled the room, a sound like a fire engine coming through, and they both jumped back, startled.

"Oh, no," Kayla said as she leaped to her feet and whirled. And just in time. A child who could barely toddle was racing toward her as fast as his chubby little legs could take him.

"Teddy!"

He threw himself at her, practically flying through the air, and she caught him and pulled him up into her arms, half laughing, half scolding. "Teddy, what are you doing here?"

"I am so sorry," Caroline said, rushing in behind him with her own little boy in her arms. "We saw you through the glass. And once he knew his mom was in here, there was no stopping him. He climbed right out of the stroller!"

Holding Teddy in her arms was like being close to heaven and Kayla always reveled in it. But there was another emotion lurking. Guilt. Leaving her baby with someone else was something she had to do, but the guilt never completely left her, no matter how busy and involved she was at work. She held him tightly and whispered soothing words against his adorable head, and he whimpered and pressed in close. And the guilt welled up inside her.

She looked up, realizing there were other issues that had to be dealt with. Her sister was smiling at Max, but she hadn't told her anything about him and she obviously had no idea who he was.

"Caroline, this is an old friend from back in my Trialta days. Max Arragen. He...he and Eddie were really close. They flew together...."

"Nice to meet you." Caroline frowned as she held out her hand for his. "Wait. Max Arragen? Aren't you...?"

He gave her one of his devastating self-deprecating smiles. "The new prince. Yes."

Caroline's eyes lit up. "Congratulations," she said, glancing at Kayla. "I had no idea. Wow. You must be really excited with all this hoopla."

"Oh, yeah. Something like that anyway."

"I feel like I should do a little curtsy or something."

"No. Please." He seemed genuinely embarrassed and she laughed.

Kayla watched them and she had to smile. Her sister resembled her quite a bit, but her blond hair was cut short and perky. Caroline was the friendly, outgoing sort, while Kayla had always felt she was the shy one, the quietly competent one whose work no one really noticed. And yet, here she was, having lunch with a prince, working for the queen... Maybe it was time to reassess her self-image.

"Ma-ma," Teddy said, tugging on her collar and adding something indecipherable that probably meant, *Let's get out of here and have some 'mommy and me' time together.*

The words weren't there but Kayla heard the message loud and clear. She looked up at Max, waiting for him to finish chatting with her sister and notice the baby.

"We were on our way to the playground," Caroline was saying. "If you two have any lunch hour left, why don't you come along?"

Kayla looked at Max. He was staring at Teddy. Her heart began to race. What was he seeing? What did those sharp eyes catch? What were the vibes that were getting through to his instinctive reactions?

It was hard to tell. He was smiling, but something in that smile was beginning to stiffen up. Had he noticed? Had he taken a quick assessment of whom

Teddy might look like? It was an exercise that was completely familiar to her. She'd done it periodically ever since her baby was born. She was blond with dark eyes. Eddie had been the same. But Max had dark bronzed hair and shockingly blue eyes. And so did Teddy.

It didn't mean anything. Of course it didn't. There were all sorts of combinations possible with the logic of genetics. She knew that. He knew that. But still…

"This is Teddy," she told him, wishing her voice wasn't shaking. "Teddy, this is Max. Say 'hi.'" She made him wave, but his little baby face was rebellious.

Max hesitated. He didn't seem to have much experience socializing with babies and in the end, he smiled awkwardly and said, "Hi, Teddy."

Teddy turned and hid his face against her neck. Kayla searched Max's eyes, trying to guess what he might be thinking. She didn't see any clues. But she also didn't see the sort of appreciation for her beautiful child that she might have expected.

"I think he's tired," she said, knowing it sounded like an excuse.

"Oh, sure," Caroline chimed in helpfully. "He didn't have a nap this morning and he usually goes down for a half hour or so."

Teddy still had morning naps? Had she really been out of his daily routine for so long that she didn't know it any longer? She felt a sudden sense of remorse. She should be with her baby today. He needed her. She needed him. He was clinging to her and she was getting the message.

As she pulled him closer, he turned to look at Max. Teddy's expression didn't change, but his lower lip thrust out and his little hands dug deeper into the fabric of her blouse. *This is my mom*, his face said. *She belongs to me.*

"Cute kid," Max said shortly, but there was no warmth in his eyes as he turned away.

Kayla made her decision. "I think we're going to have to put off doing more work on our prince project," she told him. "I really feel I need to go to the playground with them. I've been neglecting Teddy so much lately. Do you…do you want to come along?"

She waited as he mulled it over, hoping he would say no.

"I've got a few things I've got to take care of," he said at last, his gaze touching hers, then veering off again. "I'll catch you later."

"Okay." Relief flooded her. This was just too nerve-wracking to keep up much longer.

She didn't look at Max again. Her attention was all for her baby. Caroline gave her a questioning look and she knew that her sister wanted to get filled in on a few details and get a fix on her feelings, but she wasn't up to discussing Max and all that he meant to her. Too much had happened too soon and she needed to reevaluate.

But right now it was Teddy's time. She turned her face away and began a baby-talk discussion with her son. Her sister would have to wait.

* * *

Max wandered down into the main castle courtyard and out along the man-made miniwilderness where he could lose himself among the trees. A small babbling brook ran cheerfully past a large flat rock, and that was where he settled, out of sight of the walkways.

Normally, he wasn't much for introspection. He thought of himself as a man of action. He didn't tend to second-guess himself, to try to analyze why he did the things he went through or why the results had been good or bad. Navel gazing was just not his style.

But today he felt like a little self-analysis was in order. He'd just spent an hour in a meeting with two of his brothers—Prince Mykal, who had been identified as one of the royals only a few weeks before Max had, and Prince David, who had caught sight of him in the hallway and invited him to join them in a discussion of renovations to a still-destroyed area of the castle.

Much of the original and ancient castle had been burned on the night thirty years before when the Granvilli family had mounted a successful rebellion and taken over Ambria, killing the king and queen and establishing their vicious dictatorial regime. That night, each of the royal children had been spirited away by various servants or friends or members of the administration and hidden from the Granvillis. It had taken twenty-five years for the princes and princess to begin to find each other again. Their fight to win back their country had been successful and now there was only a remnant of the Granvilli faction that held a remote part of the island to deal with.

David was the second oldest prince and considered second only to King Monte in importance. Tall and dark, he had a serious air about him.

"Max, I'm glad to see you," he said when he met his brother in the hall. "I've been neglecting you, I know. There are so many issues coming up right now. I really want to get you more involved in management matters. We all have to share the burden of managing the castle, and eventually, the nation at large." He gave him a firm pat on the back. "I'm meeting Mykal in the blue meeting room right now. Why don't you join us?"

Max was glad to do just that. He was still new enough at the castle to be a little starstruck by his brothers and he wasn't sure he would ever get over being impressed by them. He'd been told a little of David's background. He'd been raised by a family in the Netherlands, and since he was six when he was taken, he remembered where he'd come from. But he also knew it had to be kept secret, and it wasn't until he was in his twenties that he and Monte found each other and began to plot their return to power. As the two oldest, they were regularly considered the head and heart of the family.

Mykal was almost as new to this as Max was, and it showed. Still recovering from a terrible motorcycle accident, he had trouble sitting for long, and by the time an hour had passed it was obvious the meeting had to be adjourned for the day.

But Max sat with them at the long, shiny table and made small talk about how he was settling in. Then the real work of the meeting had begun, and he was very quickly over his head. The talk was all architectural plans and cost estimates and zoning regulations, things he had never dealt with before. He listened carefully and filed information away to learn more about later. But he was definitely out of his element, and what's more, though he liked and admired them, he didn't feel any special connection. They were brothers, but it didn't feel the way he had expected that sort of relationship to feel. When they all rose, shook hands and parted ways, his head was swimming.

That feeling was still with him now. He was glad to have carved out an hour to be on his own. There was a lot to think about. He was feeling a bit shaky about what he ought to be doing and generally undecided about his own future. Bottom line—what the hell was he doing here living in a castle?

The whole prince thing just didn't feel right. He'd never asked for it. He'd been happily flying reconnaissance missions over the Granvilli territory when he'd been called in to the commander's office and asked to take a battery of tests. He still didn't know who had nominated him for testing or why.

If only he'd refused and walked away right at that point, none of this would be happening. He'd be off flying in someone else's war.

Still, what was stopping him from doing exactly what he pleased right now? He could go. He could find someone else to fly for. He would keep his promise to the queen, but once that was over, he wasn't so sure he was going to stick around. After all, what was really keeping him here?

Right now, he would have to say it was mostly Kayla. He hadn't expected to find her here, but now that they had reconnected, he knew he didn't want to lose her again.

Kayla was important to him. She always would be. He remembered those days in Trialta as the best days of his life. He and Eddie had hit it off like brothers, born to be together, and Kayla had been a huge part of that bond.

Funny. When he'd heard she had a child, he'd assumed her baby would be an extension of that. That he would love the kid as a small form of Eddie. But the reality hadn't fit in with the vision. There was something about that baby...

He was definitely a beautiful baby boy. But looking at him, something hadn't felt right. Something about the kid bothered him, made him want to look away quickly, and he didn't want to feel that way about Kayla's baby. Very strange. Maybe he ought to stay away from the kid until he was a little older.

A twig snapped and he turned his head, sure someone was coming into his little clearing. He didn't want company. He stared into the brush, ready to scowl a nonwelcome. But no one appeared. He stared harder, his gaze darting from one gap in the greenery to another, looking for movement. Nothing. Funny…he was sure he'd heard someone.

And it had happened before. He remembered getting the same feeling when he was wandering through the halls, earlier. A feeling that he wasn't alone.

Suddenly he had a prickly feeling on the back of his neck, and he stood, turning slowly, hands balled into fists. Yes, damn it, someone was watching him. Maybe he couldn't see it, but he sure as hell could feel it.

CHAPTER SEVEN

KAYLA looked up, startled, as Max came into the office. There was a thunderstorm brewing in that handsome face.

"Max," she said, but he walked right past her desk and confronted Pellea.

"I want to know why you've got somebody following me," he said curtly. "Don't you trust me? Has it really come to this?"

Pellea looked up and gaped at him, bewildered and showing it. "What are you talking about?"

"Look, I've made you a promise. I may be unreliable in superficial ways, but when I make a promise, I keep it. There was no call for you to send spies to watch over me. I don't like it."

She was shaking her head, looking at him as though he'd lost his mind. "I don't have anyone following you," she protested earnestly. "Really, Max. I swear."

His anger seemed to pulse in the small room. He took a deep breath, trying to calm himself. He knew he was over-the-top and taking it out on Pellea wasn't going to fix anything. This wasn't really her fault. He'd been angry when he thought it was, but her outrage told him differently, and he began to cool down. If he were honest with himself, he knew his own doubts and insecurities were more to blame for this outburst than anything the queen could have done. He needed to get a grip.

"I was just down in the courtyard, in among the trees, and someone was there watching me. I know it."

She shrugged. "There may have been someone watching you, but I didn't tell them to. Believe me, Max. I wouldn't do that." She made a face. "Not yet, anyway."

He looked at the ground and shook his head. For someone trying to learn to act like a prince, he was doing a lousy job of it. He looked up with a rueful smile and made a slight bow toward her.

"Your Majesty, please forgive me. This was rude and uncalled for. I had no right to attack you like this and I'm sorry."

Pellea's smile lit up the room. It seemed she knew earnest regret when she saw it. "Of course I forgive you. This is not supposed to be a fight. We're both on the same side." She rose from her desk chair and came out to throw her arms around him and then kiss him on both cheeks.

"Listen to me," he told her. "I will make you a pledge right now. I won't do anything behind your back. If anything happens, I'll tell you. If I decide I have to leave, I'll tell you. No secrets."

She nodded. "Good." One last pat on his cheek and she turned. "And in the spirit of openness, sit down. I'll give you the rundown on our latest outreach to Mercuria."

He sank into a chair across from her, but glanced back at Kayla. She gave him a wink and a tiny approving smile. Ridiculously, he suddenly felt much better.

"All right, here's the news. We've sent our ambassador to Mercuria."

Max nodded. "And what message does he take with him?"

Pellea shuffled papers on her desk and brought up the pertinent ones. "In answer to their charges, we respond thusly—it is our understanding that the airplane was given to Prince Maximillian, formerly known as Max Arragen, in payment for his help in establishing the Mercurian Air Force and therefore not an item that can be reclaimed."

She looked up for his approval, and he nodded.

"As for the horse, we made it clear that we feel there was a misunderstanding and a wrong done to the horse's owner, who now has regained possession of the horse. If they like, we are prepared to pay damages for the loss of it to the Mercurian government." She nodded toward Kayla. "I've had that whole episode explained to me. Kayla repeated what you told her this morning."

He glanced back at Kayla again and nodded. "Sounds reasonable."

"As for the historical artifact, I let them know that

we have no idea what this might be or how it might have come into your possession. We shall await clarification. Barring that, we are unwilling to count that as a serious charge against you."

"Wow. I'd say that pretty much covers all the bases."

Pellea nodded. "Now we wait to see how they take it. We should have their response tomorrow." She gave him a significant look. "And then, we'll see."

He heard the warning in her voice. She was seriously worried about this.

"You've said the Mercurians were a big help in the fight to regain Ambria for the DeAngelis royal family," he said musingly. "What made them come in on your side?"

Pellea shrugged. "As you know, Mercuria is a tiny stretch of land along the coast, not even as large or as important to this area as Ambria, whose main source of wealth comes from tourists, mainly in gambling. Some wags have called it nothing more than a casino with a nice beach. But they have been traditional allies of ours, and the fact that they have a monarchy, just as we do, cemented our ties more recently."

He nodded. "And they are the closest country to you, aren't they?"

"Yes. Just an hour by boat will bring you right to the foot of the Mercurian castle. You could almost consider them a neighbor."

"Do you know King Juomo personally?"

"No, I don't. I guess the families had personal ties back in the dark ages, but as far as I know, none of us have come face-to-face with any of them. As I understand it, they are rather reclusive."

He nodded. "Yes. Very reclusive. And very strange."

"So I've heard." She made a face. "That doesn't bode well. It's hard to judge how they will take this. What do you think?"

He shook his head. "I have no idea. King Juomo liked me, until he didn't like me anymore. And I'm not sure what made the change."

"Oh, well." Pellea waved a hand dismissively. "We shall see. And I need to get back to work." She smiled at him. "Cheer up. We'll get through this."

He smiled back. "Of course." Taking a deep breath, he rose, took his leave of the queen and pivoted to Kayla.

"Do you have time to go get a cup of coffee with me?" he asked, looking at her without any clear emotion.

She glanced at Pellea, who nodded her permission, and smiled. "Sure," she said, reaching to pull her tiny clutch purse out of her larger bag. "I won't be long," she promised the queen.

She almost had to run to keep up with Max's stride once they were out in the walkway. His walk was strong and aggressive, with a hint of residual anger still hovering over his mood.

"Will you tell me why you're so upset?" she asked.

He gave her a sideways glance and didn't respond as they came out onto the public corridor and up to the coffee bistro. It was packed with people and the lines were long.

"There's a vending machine a little farther out this way. We can get coffee and go out on the balcony."

They got their coffee in paper cups from the machine and made their way outside. The balcony was small, but there was a table flanked by two chairs, and they went to it after a quick look over the railing. The blue skies were gone and a cool wind blustered in and out of the crevices and still neither of them had said a word.

Max stared down into his coffee. She watched him. Finally he looked up and met her gaze.

"You know what?" he said. "I want to go."

Her heart jumped. His eyes looked hard and unhappy.

"Where?" she said.

He shrugged. "Away. Anywhere. Something new. Something different." His blue eyes held hers. "This isn't the life for me."

"Max…" She reached for his hand and held it tightly.

"I don't feel like I belong here. I don't think the way these people do. My instincts don't work here. I really feel I need to go."

"Max…"

His wide eyes stared right into her soul. "Will you go with me?"

She stared at him. How could he ask such a thing? Didn't he realize she had a life here? A son? She couldn't go anywhere she felt like. She had commitments.

He could read her refusal in her eyes. The child.

Of course. What was he thinking? She had the child. He pulled his hand away and looked out at the grey skies.

A cold wind blew in and Kayla shivered.

"Here, take this," he said, slipping out of the denim jacket and handing it to her. "Unless you still scorn it?" he tried to tease, his smile unconvincingly stiff.

"I never scorned it," she protested, shrugging into it and huddling gratefully in the warmth his body had left inside. "I love jeans jackets."

"Just not on princes."

She pulled the jacket in close and looked at him. "Not true. Max, I know you want to wear the clothes you feel comfortable in. And you should be able to. But you have to know what's expected of you in certain situations. That's all. We're not trying to change the fundamental you."

He grunted, and she leaned closer. "Tomorrow we'll go clothes shopping and I'll show you what I mean."

He stared at her and finally a smile began to tug at the corners of his mouth. "I guess that means you don't think much of my plan to leave," he said, eyes smiling sadly.

"I think it stinks. You promised Pellea two weeks. You'll manage to stick it out that long. I know you. You won't run."

He wasn't so sure she knew him as well as she thought she did. Running was what he'd done all his life—running from his problems, running from expectations, running from commitment. He knew it was time for him to grow up and stop running, but he wasn't sure how to do that.

"You won't run," she repeated confidently, and he merely smiled and let her think she had him pegged.

"At least you won't really need new clothes tonight," she mentioned. "Pellea has a dinner planned for all you princes, but it's beer and pizza and football on the television."

His smile evaporated in an instant. This was the first he'd heard about it. He scowled, but she wasn't cowed.

"You need to interact with your brothers more," she said. "Once you get to know them better, you'll feel more welcome here."

"Maybe." He didn't look convinced, but the sun came out from behind a cloud at that very moment, and it was as though liquid gold was streaming down all around them.

She laughed and went to the railing, enjoying the warmth of the sun, and he followed. The countryside around the castle looked magical. It was late afternoon and the shadows were long and colors intensified.

"Do you ever go walking down by the stream?" he asked her, pointing it out below.

"No, I've never been there."

He grabbed her hand. "Let's go," he said spontaneously. "You'll love it."

They took the elevator down and walked quickly through the corridors and onto the back patio, hoping to catch as much sunshine as they could before the cloud cover took over again. He took her hand and led her through the trees to his favorite rock. She scanned the area, enchanted with the rustling leaves and babbling brook. Then she got a thoughtful look.

"Is this where you were when you thought you were being watched?" she said accusingly.

"Yes, it is." He looked excessively innocent. "Why do you ask?"

"You just wanted me to come down here to see if I could help you catch the culprits, didn't you?" She pretended to take a swipe at him.

He laughed. "No," he said, fending off her mock attack and grabbing her wrists. "Though come to think of it, two sets of eyes are better than one."

He pulled her close until their faces were within inches of each other. She smiled into his eyes. He smiled back and something electric happened. He was going to kiss her. She could feel it. Her breath caught in her throat and she pulled back quickly, heart pounding.

"I don't see anybody," she said breathlessly. "I don't hear anybody. I think you're getting paranoid."

"No. Someone was there." He pulled her back against him. "But I don't care anymore."

He saw alarm in her eyes—denial, dismissal and a lot of worry, but like he'd said, he didn't care anymore. His mouth took hers as though he had a right to it, as though he'd gone through all the reasons why she wasn't his for the kissing and decided to throw them out the window. He wanted her. He'd always wanted her. And now that he had her in his arms, he needed to feel her heat, taste her warm sweetness, touch her beautiful body.

His hands slid under the jacket, under her sweater, up her slender back and she arched her softness against his hard chest. His kiss was hungry and hot and she answered it back the same way. The wind swirled around them. Leaves blew around their feet. The water from the brook sang a happy song, and time seemed to stand still.

It was meant to be a short kiss, just something quick and loaded with commitment and affection, but he never wanted it to stop. If it had been up to him, it never would have. But she knew it couldn't last.

"Max."

He was kissing the curve of her neck, tasting her skin, devouring her sweetness.

"Max!"

Pulling back, he looked at her groggily. She was laughing.

"Max, stop!"

He shook his head, then groaned and let her go. Running his fingers through his hair, he tried to get his balance back.

"Sorry," he muttered. "You just feel so good. I want to hold you forever."

She looked into his eyes, smiling, loving him, but not sure what to say. They couldn't do this. He couldn't kiss her this way. There was something intoxicating between the two of them. Once they started, they didn't seem to know how to stop. Reaching out, she cupped his rough cheek in her hand and smiled sadly.

And then, without a word, she stepped away carefully and sank down to sit on the rock. He followed and sat beside her.

"Eddie would have loved this place," he said softly, and then winced, wishing he'd kept his mouth shut.

She didn't look at him. She didn't say a word, but he knew she what she was thinking.

They were silent for a few minutes, watching the water, and then Max started talking about his brothers again, haltingly at first. And then he just kept going, talking as though they had never stopped.

"You know, there's a big difference between me and the other princes," he said at one point. "They all grew up in families. They might not have been the right families, but at least they had that. I think I'm the only one who sort of got thrown out with the trash."

His words might have been bitter, but she was glad to notice that his tone was more bemused.

"Actually," she told him, "Prince Cassius—the one we all call Joe—had a pretty rough time of it as well."

"Prince Joe? The surfer prince?" He had to grin. He'd met Joe.

She nodded, smiling. "That's him. Whoever was supposed to hide him that night didn't show up and the kitchen maid ended up taking him with her when she ran, hiding him under her shawl on the boat. She didn't know what to do with him, so she took him back home to England, whereupon she promptly died and left him to be raised by members of her family who had no clue who he was."

"How did he end up in California?"

"The family emigrated and then the parents got divorced and they all pretty much split up. I guess it wasn't much of a warm-and-toasty family after all. Sort of dysfunctional. The way I heard it, he took off pretty young and then he joined the military."

Max nodded. "Okay. Joe and I might just have a little bit in common. Maybe I'll have a chance to talk to him tonight." He made a comical face. "Pizza and beer," he repeated, shaking his head. "I guess she really does want to make me feel at home. That's practically my daily diet as it is."

"She's doing her best." She looked at him whimsically. "I don't think you realize how much better this is going to make things for you," she said simply.

He groaned and the anger flared in him again. That was the last thing he wanted to hear.

"Don't tell me how wonderful this is for me and how it's going to change my life. I don't want my life changed. I like things the way they've been. I don't want to be a prince."

She was frowning at him now. "You don't want to be a prince because you don't want to have to conform to rules and standards. You don't think anyone else should have a say in how you should act, do you?"

He blinked, not used to tough talk from her. "So? What's wrong with that?"

Her eyes flashed. "Grow up, Max. It's time for you to stop playing at life and start living it."

Maybe I don't want to.

He didn't say it. The words popped out onto the tip of his tongue, but he wisely held them back, and as he thought them over, he realized how childish they were. What the hell. She was right. It was time for him to grow up. Grabbing her hand, he pressed his lips to the center of her palm, then looked up at her, smiling.

"How did I do without you all this time?" he said huskily. "Eddie once said to me that if anything ever happened to you, he wouldn't want to go on alone. And I can see why."

His words sent a shock through her. She closed her eyes and thought about them for a moment. Then she looked at him, trying not to be resentful. "And you're wondering how I've managed to go on so normally without him?"

"No," he said, looking shocked at the thought. "That isn't what I meant to say at all."

"Then why did you say it?"

He shook his head, trying to remember what had been in his mind at the time. "I just wanted to remind you to remember how much Eddie loved you."

She pulled her arms in close. "I don't need reminding. I remember very well. I remember it all the time." She still felt resentful as she looked at him. "I didn't get to where I am without a lot of pain, you know."

He nodded, searching her face, staring into her eyes. "I know that, Kayla. There was enough pain to go around." He winced and looked away. "I felt it, too. After Eddie died, I went a little crazy for a while."

"Didn't we all?"

"No, I mean it." He looked back at her. "I took stupid chances, did stupid things. In some ways, it almost felt as though I couldn't live life normally anymore. If a guy as super as Eddie could get killed like that, what right did I have to be happy?" He frowned, remembering. "I began to make careless mistakes. At one point, I did something stupid and I had to ditch my plane. I bailed out in time, but it was a while before they found me." He shook his head. "That woke me up."

"That was when I saw the report on the news. I…I really thought you were gone, too."

He nodded. "It was hard to accept a world where the best people got snuffed out like candles. No real reason. Just here one moment, gone the next. To see a good guy like Eddie get killed so easily and a waster like I am get lucky every time—it didn't seem right. I was having a hard time with that."

"Max, Eddie's gone. I don't think you've completely faced it yet."

"Have you?"

"Yes. I've tried very hard. There's a part of me

that will always love him and miss him horribly. But most of life has to go on without him. I either go on or I throw myself off the balcony."

His eyes darkened with horror. "You wouldn't do that."

"No. I couldn't do that. I have Teddy."

He looked startled, as though he'd forgotten.

"Teddy is my whole life now," she told him carefully, wishing she saw a smile or a look of affection or something friendly toward her son. How could this man not feel something? "Do you understand that?"

"Yeah, I think I do."

She thought about the fact that he'd never really lived in a family. Maybe he didn't understand what it meant to have a child, how it consumed your soul. It was true that as far as she could see, he didn't react well to Teddy and she didn't know why. But maybe this was a part of it.

Or maybe it was something else, something about Teddy's background that threw him off. And if that was what it was, she knew she didn't want to face that at all.

"I've got to get back."

He nodded. "I'll walk with you."

They started off and once again, they both fell silent, as if they had talked about things that needed some mulling over before they mentioned them to each other again. At the door to her office, Kayla smiled at him.

"Could I come by and see you tonight?" he asked. "After the pizza party?"

Her smile disappeared. "No," she said slowly, thinking it over on the run. "I think it would be better if we kept our relationship on a completely professional level. Forget that we're friends."

He looked as though he thought she was nuts. "Forget that we're friends?" He shook his head, his anger beginning to hint at a return engagement. "No. That's carrying things too far. I'll be circumspect during prince lessons, but once they're over, you're fair game."

"Fair game?" she repeated, puzzled.

"You got it. You can run but you can't hide."

"What are you talking about?"

"This." Taking her face in his hands, he bent down and kissed her softly. His lips were warm and his solid male earthy scent made her head spin. His kiss was sweet and sincere and somehow much more effective than the wild one out by the little river. It brought tears to her eyes and left her gasping, aching for more.

"And that's just a sample of things to come," he told her, giving her a triumphant grin and turning to go.

Speechless, she watched him go, her cheeks burning. It wasn't until he was out of sight that she remembered she still had his jacket.

She was fixing Teddy a nice peanut butter sandwich for dinner, because that was all he would eat besides eggs and bananas. He was dancing around the apartment, bobbing his head and pretending to play a little plastic guitar, when the phone rang.

"Hey, it's me."

Amazing how his voice could send sparkles through her bloodstream. She remembered the kisses and the sparkles intensified.

"Max. What is it?"

He paused, listening. "What's that noise in the background?"

"Oh, it's just Teddy. He's so funny. I wish you could see him. He's sort of singing and dancing and banging things. But you may ignore at will. Go on."

"He makes a lot of noise for such a small kid."

"You don't know the half of it," she said, laughing. "He's only just begun."

"Hmm."

Once again Kayla got the impression that he didn't like her baby much, and she frowned.

"Well, I just called to tell you my place has been totally ransacked."

"What? How did someone get by the guard?"

There was an extensive network of security in the castle, but it was especially concentrated in the royal wing.

"That's a good question."

"Did they take anything?"

"I don't think so."

"What were they after?"

He paused, then said, "I think it's all related. The

people watching me, the people going through my things. What do you think?"

"It would seem logical I guess. But you have no idea who they are, right?"

"Right. Still, I think it's related to this. Now if I could figure out what they're looking for…"

"How about an historical artifact from Mercuria?" she suggested, eyes widening as she thought of it.

"I was thinking the same thing." He paused. "Anyway, I just wanted to tell you to be careful. I've told the guards to watch your apartment more vigilantly than usual. So if you notice a lot of cops hanging around, you'll know why."

"Okay. Thanks." She frowned. "Do you think it's people from Mercuria?"

"I'm sure of it. No one else has a grudge against me at the moment. At least, no one that I know of."

"Are you still going to the pizza party?"

"Sure."

"Good. What are you wearing?"

"Kayla! I'm not a girl. Who cares what I wear?"

"No, I mean…I forgot to give you back your denim jacket. I left it in the closet at the office. Remind me later to give it back to you."

"I have another one."

"Oh. Hey, I guess you really do like them, don't you?"

He ignored that and when he spoke again, his voice was lower, almost husky, with a feeling she didn't want to name.

"Hey. I miss you."

Her heart gave a lurch. "No, you don't. You just saw me an hour ago."

"I know. But I still miss you."

"Max, don't. You can't…"

"I know. But I still miss you. Can't help it. See you tomorrow. Good night, Kayla."

"Good night, Max." She closed her eyes to stop the tears that were suddenly threatening. "Happy pizza."

They met for breakfast at nine. She flushed when she saw him waiting for her in the little crepe café. She couldn't help it. All that crazy kissing had made her jumpy for hours.

But he didn't seem to remember it. He had a lot to tell her about his pizza party with his brothers the night before. He'd obviously had a pretty good time, though he wasn't ready to call it that.

"It was okay," he said slowly as he savored the hot cup of coffee the waitress had served him. "I still don't feel really comfortable with them, but they are a great group. I like them all."

And then he went on to tell her in minute detail everything everyone had said. She smiled, listening to him, slowly picking at her blueberry crepe. Could it be that he was beginning to feel a little better about being here?

He had an omelet and a brioche, but he looked tired. And then he yawned.

She frowned. "Didn't you get enough sleep last night?"

He hesitated, looking a bit chagrined. "Actually, no. On my way back from the pizza party I met an old flying buddy I hadn't seen for a while. We went and had a few drinks and…"

She bit back the words that came to mind, but he read her thoughts in her eyes.

"I know, I know. I'm supposed to be learning to be royal, not carousing with old friends." He glowered at her. "The royal life is looking about as appealing as a term in prison."

"It's not that bad," she said, smiling at his funny face. "Royals go out with friends all the time. In fact, some even get in a lot of trouble all the time. Just read the tabloids. But…"

"Kayla, I know what you're worrying about. We're back to the need for me to grow up. I know. I'm working on it."

"I know." She made a face. "I don't mean to be your constant scold. That's not much fun for either of us. And you deserve to have fun." She gave him a silly grin that just oozed affection. How could she help it? She adored him and adored the way he told her what he was thinking all the time. There was very little about Max that was inscrutable.

And then she sobered. "Just don't forget how serious these times are. The war may be officially over, but there is more work to do. This truce with the Granvillis is going to lead to us taking over their area soon and who knows how that will go?"

He looked at her carefully. "You're sure of that, are you?"

"Of the Granvillis surrendering? Everyone says it's about to happen."

He raised his eyebrows. "Funny thing. This old flying buddy I met last night? He has some ties to the Granvillis and he thinks they are getting ready for a new surge."

Her heart sank. "Oh, no."

"He seems to think they're getting some international help they didn't have before."

She shook her head, knowing how terrible it would be if the war heated up again. "You'd better tell Monte," she said anxiously.

He looked away and shrugged. "I might," he said slowly. "I've got to think it over first."

"What?" The very thought that he might hesitate to tell his brother and king something that might be vital to national security floored her.

He glanced back, looking defensive. "It was a private conversation. Just talking with a friend. I can't back any of it up. I'm not sure if he was on the level or just trying to recruit me."

"Recruit you!"

He nodded. "They need flyers." He looked at her, hard. "That's what I do, Kayla. I'm a flyer. It's what I love. I told him I'd think about it."

"But…" She bit her tongue and turned away, horrified. Didn't he see that doing something like that would be tantamount to treason? She had to find a way to make him understand that he was now a part of the heart and soul of the Ambrian people, and of this royal family. Their destiny was his destiny. All the rest would flow from that.

Turning back, she looked at him, so handsome, so rebellious. She thought of Eddie. He'd been the kind of man who always did the right thing without effort. He was never tortured by doubts the way Max was. But he'd loved the vulnerability in Max as much as she did, and Eddie's own certainty was part of what drew Max to him, as she knew well. Two men, so different, yet both such quality guys. Max just didn't know the extent of his virtue yet. But he would work it out. She had faith in him.

"Max, you're representing the DeAngelis royal family now," she said quietly. "And the nation of Ambria. That has to be your highest priority."

He gave her a skeptical look and the corner of his mouth jerked down. She sighed, thinking about what she would say to him if only she could.

Max, you didn't really grow up here. You have love of country in your blood, but not in your experience. You need both in order to understand what the others take for granted. You will. But you need to be introduced first. How am I going to make sure that happens?

She ached to say those things, but she knew he wasn't ready to hear that right now. He was still feeling resentful.

"No matter what, I won't be a spy," he said, turning to look into her eyes. His jawline hardened. "I won't rat on my flying buddies."

She was so tempted to launch into a lecture on

duty and patriotism and how those things had to come first, but she stopped herself. She was acting enough like a schoolmarm to turn Max from a best friend into an enemy. She had to learn a few things herself—things about when to hold 'em and when to fold 'em. So she bit her tongue and smiled brightly instead. After all, they were still trying to convince him that he should stay.

She knew one thing. Everyone who came in contact with him wanted him to hang around. But he was so bored with the whole thought of being a prince. She was afraid one of the other offers that kept pouring in would tempt him and he'd be gone.

CHAPTER EIGHT

HALF an hour later, Kayla and Max were taking the elevator down to the main floor, where the gymnasium was located. The gym had a marquee, like an old-fashioned movie theater, and today it was advertising a basketball game that night. But as they walked in, half of the pictures posted in the display boxes had to do with minor sports and most of those were fencing.

"Have you ever studied fencing?" Kayla asked him as they entered the cavernous room. All the princes had been trained and Max would have to learn as well.

"Never." He pretended to wield an imaginary foil. "We didn't do much of that in the crowd I ran with."

"Well, take a good look," she said with a sweep of her hand. "Because you're going to have to learn."

"This lame stuff?" He looked down over the edge of the railing and suddenly hoped his voice hadn't carried that far. Down below were numerous men in white clothing, holding very slender swords.

"Why don't you put on a suit and go in and give it

a try? It might just open your eyes." She snickered. "Or kill you."

He gave her a baleful look, but before he could make a rejoinder, someone hailed him from the floor.

"Hey, Max. Come on down here and give me some competition." The fencer pulled up his mask and slashed the air with his foil.

Max laughed, realizing it was his brother Joe. "I don't know one end of a sword from another. I'd probably end up stabbing myself," he called down.

"I was just like you a few months ago," Joe said. "Hey, I spent most of my growing up years on a surfboard in California. What did I know about these ancient ritualistic sports?" He grinned. "But I learned. And it's a lot of fun, actually. Gives you a good workout, too. We'll have to get you set up with lessons."

"Cool," Max said back. "If a surfer boy can learn, I guess a seat-of-the-pants flyer can."

"Absolutely."

"Though I don't know if I can fit it in," Max added, teasing Kayla, though he was still talking to Joe. "I'm real busy learning how to be a prince, you know."

"You have somebody teaching you?" Joe cried. "Hey, how do I get in on that gig?"

"I'll tell Pellea you're interested," Kayla told him with a laugh.

"Do that." He saluted them both. "See you later," he added as he pulled his mask back down and took the ready position.

"He doesn't need any lessons," Max said in admiration. "Look at him."

She did, then she turned back, eyes sparkling. "Max, you ought to look at yourself. You look just as good as he does. It's only a matter of time until you have the confidence to carry it off without a waver."

"Sure," he muttered out of the corner of his mouth. "Whatever you say, teacher lady. I'm here to learn."

Next stop was at the tailor. Mr. Nanvone's father had been the royal tailor thirty years before, and now his son had taken over. Max was less enthusiastic about this visit.

"Why don't we just wait awhile and see if we're really going to need formal wear and all that stuff?" he suggested as they reached the shop. Mannequins in tuxedos lined the show windows. "After all…"

Just then a smartly dressed man emerged from the shop doorway. It took a double take for Max to realize it was another of his brothers.

"Max," Mykal said jovially. "Come to get your fancy formal wear ordered?"

Max made a face. "Unfortunately, it does seem to be the goal here."

Mykal laughed. "We all have to do it. You want to play, you've got to wear the gear."

Max looked him over and blurted out, "What made you decide?"

Mykal looked wary. "Decide what?"

Max shrugged. "Whether you wanted to play or not."

They stared at each other for a long moment and then a grin broke through Mykal's reserve. "So you're still at that stage, are you? Wondering if it's all worth it." He patted him on the shoulder. "Been there, done that. And as you see, I'm still here."

He gave Kayla a wide smile, winked, then turned back to Max.

"Listen, come see me one of these days. We'll talk." And he was off.

Max watched him go, still favoring one side of his body over the other. Max sighed and then turned and followed Kayla into the tailor shop.

"I guess that motorcycle accident really did a number on him, didn't it?" Max murmured to her.

"Yes. He almost died. He had shrapnel in his back, very close to his spine, and they didn't want to operate because of that. But Mykal decided he would take any chance to be whole again, so he insisted on surgery."

Max nodded. "Brave guy." He squared his shoulders. "If he can do this, so can I. Where's the man with the measuring tape?"

Kayla laughed as Mr. Nanvone instantly appeared from behind the curtain barrier into the back room, a measuring tape in his hand.

His session didn't last very long, but by the time the measuring and other necessary particulars were finished, he seemed exhausted.

"The questions were the worst," he told her as they left the shop. "'Which do you prefer,'" he mimicked, copying the tailor's accent, "'ostrich- or pearl-gray, teal or military green, oxford or gold-ore brown.' Too many decisions!"

"Hold it," Kayla said, reaching for her phone. "There's a message from Pellea." She read it quickly. "She wants us to come in right away. They've had a response from Mercuria."

Her gaze met his and he reached out and took her by the hand.

"Let's go."

But as they walked toward the elevator, Max's mood grew more somber.

"I've got a bad feeling about this."

Kayla looked up at him, curious. "What do you expect to go wrong? Things like this usually go on forever. We send our ambassador, they send theirs, they talk, they negotiate, they go back to their respective corners and it all starts again. You hardly ever see anything actually resolved."

He considered her description as they got onto the elevator and punched in the right floor. "I'd feel better if I knew what that historical artifact they think I took was. I mean, one person's historical artifact could be another person's used piece of trash. I wish I had some idea of what we're looking for."

Pellea's face wasn't giving away any clues as they walked into the office.

"Thank you for getting here so quickly," she began. "I feel like things are escalating and I don't want them to spin out of control."

"Of course not," Kayla agreed. "What have you heard?"

The queen waited while they took chairs, then continued. "I think I explained to you how the charges were addressed by our ambassador. He handed our letter to King Juomo personally. Here is the king's response."

She held up a large, embossed and very official-looking document.

"'The plane and the horse are nothing to us. We are willing to let them go. The artifact is everything. We must have it back. There is only one way we will accept its return. Max Arragen must himself bring it back to Helgium Castle and offer it by hand to the Princess Nadine. No other method will suffice.'"

Pellea looked up and cocked her head in Max's direction. "Princess Nadine?" she said questioningly. "A new element has been added. Care to elaborate?"

Max sighed and looked guilty. "I should have told you about Princess Nadine."

Pellea's eyes flashed. "Yes, you should have."

Quickly he told her the same thing he had told Kayla, explaining how crazy this was, at least in his opinion. "She's just a teenaged girl with a teenaged crush. Nothing more."

"A teenaged girl with the power to start a war." Pellea glared at him. "And possibly have you executed."

Executed. That was an ugly and very serious word. Everyone in the room seemed to reverberate to the vibes coming off just the sound of it for a moment.

Pellea was the first to break out of the spell. "All

right, here's the rest. 'You have only three days left to comply with our demands. We are preparing for an invasion.'" She looked out at the others. "An invasion. The man is crazy, but then, those who invade other countries often are."

There was a long silence, and then Max looked up.

"Why don't I go? They can't hold this whole country responsible for me if I'm not here and haven't officially been made a part of the royal court. Just call me the black sheep, the one you can't control, the one you can do nothing about. They can't expect you to pay for my crimes."

"Impossible. You are a prince of Ambria. We can't let you go."

He looked down again, then up. "You know, I didn't do anything," he said softly to Pellea.

She half smiled. "Max, if I thought you had done anything at all with a fifteen-year-old girl, we wouldn't even be talking here anymore."

He looked relieved. "Of course not."

Kayla moved restlessly. "I think you should tell the queen about what happened to your rooms last night."

Pellea turned a questioning face Max's way. "Yes?"

"When I got in late last evening, I found my apartment ransacked. I think it was probably Mercurians after that darn artifact, whatever it may be."

"Interesting." She frowned. "Why weren't you better guarded?"

He shrugged. "I've talked to the captain of the guard. I think conditions will improve."

"Good." She frowned again as he told her the situation and what had been done to his things.

"You're sure nothing was taken?"

"As far as I can tell."

"And you think it was the Mercurians?"

He nodded. "I'm sure of it."

"Well, I guess we all had better be on our guard," Pellea warned. "Those darn Mercurians."

"Mercurians!"

That was the first thing Kayla thought when she opened the door to her own apartment later that afternoon. Everything looked normal at first, but she could tell. She had the distinct feeling that things were different. Strangers had been in her place. Nothing seemed to be missing. But there was a sense of invasion. Her personal space had been violated. She was sure of it.

She called Max right away.

"They tried hard to put everything back just the way it was," she said. "But I can tell. These creepy people have been all through my things. Ugh!"

"Did you call the security guards?"

"No." She felt a bit abashed. "I called you."

"I'll call them. And I'll be there in a few minutes."

"Oh, I don't want to bother you, Max. I know you have things to do."

"I'm coming over and I'm bringing my toothbrush and jammies."

"What? You can't stay here."

"Try and stop me."

She had to laugh after she hung up. He did have a way about him. But amusement fled when the security people arrived and claimed they couldn't find any evidence of a break in.

"How can you be sure your things were moved? Suppose you moved them yourself and forgot you did it?"

She had a feeling they were snickering at her behind her back, but they got serious when Max arrived. He wasn't pleased that they hadn't been watching her apartment more carefully, as he'd requested. They promised to be more vigilant.

"You see, you don't have to stay," she told him once they'd gone. "I'll be okay."

"Yes, you'll be fine. Because I will be here with you."

"Really?" She gave him an exasperated look. "And how long do you plan to stay here?"

"Until the Mercurians stop looking for the artifact."

She made a face at him. "That could take a long, long time."

"Look, this is just for tonight. We'll deal with the rest of our lives later. Okay?"

He had a few errands to run but he was back an hour later. He'd been looking forward to his night with Kayla with mixed feelings. It would be a delight to be with her, even if the mood was platonic, but he knew that Teddy probably came with the package.

When he arrived at the door and glanced around the room, sure enough, there was the kid, sitting in a little plastic chair and playing with a stuffed dinosaur.

He wanted to like Teddy. The child was beautiful with huge blue eyes and a head of dark bronze curls. He looked adorable. But the kid hated him. He really seemed to have something against him. But that wasn't fair. He was only a baby. Babies didn't hate. Did they? They wanted what they wanted the minute they wanted it. Teddy wanted his mama and didn't want to share her with some strange man. Who could blame him?

Sure. He grinned to himself. That was all it was. He had to stop letting his imagination run away with him.

He'd thought about this ahead of time. He knew what he had to do. He went right up to the child. "Hi, Teddy," he said in a friendly manner. "What's that you've got there? A tyrannosaurus?"

The blue eyes glanced up at him and shot back down to stare at his toy.

There you go, he thought. *The kid hates me.*

He was at a loss. He'd never had any experience with children this age and he had no idea how to deal with them. He looked up at Kayla for help.

She stepped forward and he thought she seemed a little nervous. "Teddy, can you say 'hi' to Prince Max?"

Obviously not. Teddy's lower lip came out and he stared very hard at his dinosaur.

"All right, we'll work on that later," she said with

forced cheer. "But you're going to have to learn to be polite to visitors."

"Leave him alone," Max murmured to the side. "Let him get used to me." As if he knew the secrets to popularity with the Rugrat crowd.

She produced a batch of oven-fried chicken that was as good as anything the colonel made, along with crispy biscuits and a nice green salad. Even Teddy took a few bites. She'd also made some rubbery green gelatin squares that were so tough, they could play catch with them. Once he saw those, Teddy suddenly had an appetite. He came over to watch, hanging on his mother's leg and leaning his head on her knee, and when Max tossed a square into the air and caught it with his mouth, Teddy couldn't help it—he just had to laugh.

When it was time for bed, Teddy went down fairly easily.

"Help me tuck him in," Kayla urged.

"Why?"

She gave him a look and he reluctantly followed her into the bedroom. When Teddy saw Max, he hid his face in the covers.

"You see," Max whispered to her. "He doesn't want me to be here when you tuck him in."

"He's a child," she muttered back. "You're a grown-up. You're the one in charge of the situation. Don't let him con you."

So he helped tuck Teddy in. But the kid still seemed to hate him. He wasn't sure why that should be—or why he cared. He'd known other kids who didn't seem to adore him and it had never bothered him before. Maybe it was the fact that he'd expected to have instant rapport with Eddie's boy. That hadn't happened.

He came out into the kitchen and helped her with the dishes, taking a towel and drying them as she put them up on the counter, sparkling clean. They talked about old times and laughed about old stories. And Kayla realized that Max was really her only link to Eddie, physical or emotional. The memories were all in his head, like they were in her heart. Was that what drew her to him so strongly? Was that what made her feel something very close to love whenever she looked into his eyes?

No. It was more than that. Much more. If only she could pin down exactly what it was.

She got him a beer and she made herself a cup of hot tea and they sat on the couch and talked softly.

She stretched and smiled at him. "You know what? In this very moment, in spite of everything, I'm very happy."

"Why?"

"Because you're here. And because you seem to be at peace in a way. Not quite as tense and restless as you usually are."

She was right. It was good being with her this way. She made him happy, too. He looked at her pretty face, her soft brown eyes, her beautiful lips and he felt an ache where his heart should be.

"You need to be kissed," he murmured, looking at her mouth a bit hungrily.

She shook her head and began to appear wary. "No, I don't."

"Yes, you do." Reaching out, he touched her chin, then curled his hand around her jawline. "Or maybe I should say, I need to kiss you. That might be more honest."

Searching into his deep, mysterious eyes, she laughed softly. His hand felt so warm on her skin and his breath was even warmer on her face. She needed to pull away, let him know she couldn't let him keep the promise that was smoldering in his eyes. But somehow, that just wasn't happening.

"You don't need to kiss me," she said. "Kisses are for lovers. We're not going to do that."

A slight frown creased his brow. "You don't get it. I do need to kiss you. And you need to kiss me. Just me and you. And nothing about Eddie."

She closed her eyes for a moment, and then she looked into his again with a tiny, sad smile.

"I don't want you to do anything that you'll regret," she told him, half joking.

He frowned. "What is it that you regret?"

She shook her head, letting her sleek blond hair brush against his hand. "I don't regret anything. There was a time when I did. But I got over that quickly enough." Turning her face, she caught the palm of his hand against her lips and put a kiss there. "One look into my baby's eyes, and regrets faded away," she added softly.

He stared at her and a look of pain flashed in his eyes. "Kayla…"

"Hush." She put a finger to his lips. "Just kiss me." And he did.

His mouth was hot and hard on hers and she moaned low in her throat, a deep, primal sound of pleasure. She'd been so lonely for so long, to feel his arms around her, to feel the joy of his true affection, seemed to bring her out of a long sleep and into the sunlight. Their tongues met, caressed, tangled, then seemed to meld together into one smoldering focus of heat and her whole body was ready to burst into flames.

"Oh!" she cried, pulling away and staring at him. "Oh, my gosh, Max. We can't even kiss without setting the world on fire. What the heck?"

He lay back against the pillows on the couch and started to laugh. She batted at him, then started to laugh as well, falling on him and holding him close as they both enjoyed the moment.

"Just let me hold you," he murmured, face buried in her hair. "I just want to feel you against me."

She nodded. "Me, too." And then she sighed. It took a while for her body to calm down. She knew in her heart that they would make love again and it would be soon. But not now. For now, this was enough. In fact, it was a certain brand of heaven.

A sound from Teddy's room made her get up to check on him. She looked down at her sleeping child and her heart was so full, for a moment, she couldn't breathe. She came out with a new determination. It was time.

"Max, we have to talk about it."

He looked up, startled at her tone. "Talk about what?"

"That night. That night after Eddie died."

His heart began to pound in his chest. "No. We don't have anything to talk about." His words were defensive and so was his tone. He was scared to talk about it. Anyone could see that.

She gestured for him to follow her. "Come here. I want you to look at this baby."

"No. Kayla…"

Reaching out, she grabbed his arm. "Come here. Look at him. You have to."

He came reluctantly, sure that this would do no good and make no difference. What was the point?

He looked down. Teddy really was a beautiful child. Something was fluttering in his chest.

"Look at him," she was saying softly, almost whispering. "His face is so sweet when he's asleep. Those big round cheeks." She turned to look at him. "If his eyes were open, you would see how blue they are."

"Kayla." He winced.

"He's an adorable, sweet little boy. And you're not letting him into your heart."

He closed his eyes, searching for an inner strength he wasn't sure he was going to find.

"Is he mine?" His voice was tortured, vibrating with pain.

"You know the answer."

He closed his eyes again and turned away, pushing

his way back out to the living room. She followed, wondering if he'd felt what she wanted him to feel.

"How could we have done that, Kayla?" he was muttering angrily. "How could we have betrayed Eddie like that?"

"At the time we did it, it seemed like a sacrament. A tribute. An homage to his life. It was only later, in the sober light of day, that it seemed like a betrayal."

He nodded. "I remember it well."

Suddenly she turned on him. She threw a pillow at him and then cried fiercely, "Max, don't you dare regret it! Don't you dare!"

"Kayla…"

"That night, after we found out there was no hope of finding Eddie alive, we were in shock. The pain was so great—do you remember? We turned to each other to stem it. We told ourselves we were celebrating his life, but we were really trying to pay back the fates for what they'd done to us…to Eddie."

He nodded but he didn't say a word.

"All we could do was cry and hold on to each other. And somehow, we ended up doing something we never meant to do. But it happened." She pulled on his arm. "Don't deny it! It happened."

He turned his head away.

"A miracle came out of that, despite everything. My sweet baby. Our sweet baby. Don't you dare deny that."

Max took a deep breath and turned back to look her full in her tearstained face.

"No. I won't deny it. But I do regret it."

He took her in his arms and she cried and cried.

It was a few hours later. Max was asleep on the couch. He raised his head, wondering what he'd heard, and then he realized it was Kayla. She was singing softly to her baby. He listened, staying very still. There was something in that voice, something in the love she had for her child, that gave him chills. It touched him like nothing else and tears came to his eyes, stinging.

He'd never thought it would happen. He was the perennial bachelor. He was famous for it. No woman had ever been able to make her way through that tough shield of reality and reach his heart. Only Kayla had. And yet, he couldn't get around it. To love her was a betrayal of Eddie.

CHAPTER NINE

"LISTEN," Max said as he left in the morning. "I won't be able to stay with you tonight. Can you make arrangements to stay with Caroline?"

"Maybe." Kayla knew she sounded defensive, but that was how she felt. She knew he was upset, that things said and done from the night before had thrown him off again, and she resented it. "We'll see."

He hesitated, as though he wanted to argue with her, but then thought better of it. "Okay," he said. "I'll call you later."

And he was gone. She stared at the door as it closed, a lump in her throat. He was regretting again. She was losing him.

She fixed breakfast for Teddy and took him to her sister's, then hurried on to the office. Pellea was on a tear, racing from one project to another, barking out orders and ideas, and Kayla didn't have time to find out what had been decided as a response to the Mercurians. And then, suddenly, Max was back and he didn't have the scowl he'd had that morning.

"Look at this," he said, his blue eyes sparkling with new energy. "Research has come up with a picture of the artifact."

He had a thick book with beautiful photographic illustrations, and there was a huge picture of the item in question. They gathered around and stared at it and for a few minutes, no one said a word.

"Wow," Pellea said at last. "No wonder they want it back."

The historical artifact was a beautiful medallion on a thick gold chain. The background was encrusted with rubies and emeralds and the centerpiece was a huge, elongated, multifaceted diamond. It took a moment or two to realize that the gems formed a picture of a green field and a tree with rubies as apples. The diamond in the center seemed to represent a huge waterfall. On the next page, the image of the backside showed a date almost four centuries old and the name Mercuria.

"Wow," Kayla breathed, echoing the queen. "I've never seen anything so gorgeous."

"And probably worth more than ten small countries thrown together," Pellea said. "Max, did you ever have it in your possession?"

"Are you kidding? Do you think I could have forgotten something like this? Or mislaid it? I've never seen this before. And I damn well know I never held it in my hand."

They looked at each other.

"How about this?" Max asked after a moment of silence. "Do we have some sort of video communication system set up with King Juomo? If so, I could tell him face-to-face that I didn't take this and don't have it, without actually going there."

Pellea nodded. "We've got the capability. Heck, I could do it from my notebook. But as I understand it, it will take some time to set up the official, royal version that they can use, too," she said. "I'll try to have the technicians on it right away." Then she frowned. "In the meantime, you be careful. People have been known to do some ugly things to get their hands on a piece of jewelry like that."

"Don't worry. I've got my eyes open." He gave a simple bow to the queen and a faint smile to Kayla, and then he was out the door.

Kayla was glad to know he was now certain he had not taken the artifact, but she was not so happy with his new dismissive attitude. She was mulling over how to respond to it when Pellea walked up and leaned on her desk with both hands.

"What are we going to do about Max?" she said in a quiet voice, meant to stay clear of any eavesdroppers.

Kayla was startled. "Why? What's wrong?"

"Nothing new. Just the usual. I'm still worried about his lack of commitment to becoming a prince. His heart isn't in it. Not yet."

She only hesitated a moment before taking the plunge. "I'm afraid you're right. At least, in part. I think he's coming around, but it's going to take some time."

Pellea sighed. "The others seemed to be able to

make the adjustment to royal status quickly and easily. I don't know if he's just too rigid in his ways or what. I'm really afraid that he might not be able to do it." She shook her head, looking worried. "There's something wild and free in him. Something that resists rules and borders. I'm not sure he'll be able to stay."

Kayla knew the queen was emotionally invested in Max's success, still, she was surprised to see she had tears in her eyes. Kayla reached for her hand and held it with genuine affection.

"Oh, Pellea, don't give up on him."

"Oh, I can't. We need him. The family won't be whole without him. Like a family portrait with one face cut out. Can you imagine? Impossible! It will kill Monte if he doesn't stay. Now that the war is basically won, now that Leonardo Granvilli is dead, he has such plans for this country."

"I'm sure he'll stay," she said, wishing she could sound more convincing. But that was hard when she wasn't sure what she was saying was true. "He just needs seasoning."

Pellea dried her eyes and gave Kayla a watery smile. "I still have hope. I do have one ace in the hole, you know. You see, I have one piece of bait, one promise, one prize that just might keep him here."

Kayla looked innocent. "What is that?"

Pellea laughed. "You!"

"Me? Oh, no, no, no, no."

"Yes, you, my dear. It's obvious the two of you are in love. Or hadn't you noticed?"

Luckily, a visitor arrived in time to save Kayla from having to answer that. She went back to work, typing as fast as she could, her cheeks hot and rosy. What Pellea was suggesting was insane. She knew Max well enough to know he wasn't husband material. He wasn't even father material. He was a wild man. And after last night, she was afraid there was no hope of anything taming him.

Kayla sent a message asking Max to come for dinner, and to her surprise, he showed up, despite the fact that he hadn't contacted her all day. It was funny how lonely that had made her. In just a few days she'd become used to hearing from him constantly and she missed it when it wasn't there. She served meat loaf and mashed potatoes and he had two helpings. Though he started out seeming a bit distant, he soon warmed up as he told her about talking to the king of Mercuria on the video phone connection.

"We weren't exactly buddies when I was working on organizing the air force last year," he said. "But we did work together often and we got along well. Unfortunately, he doesn't seem to remember all that."

"What did he say?"

"He insists I have the artifact. He says he has proof."

"Proof? What sort of proof?"

Max hesitated. Then he made a wry, apologetic face and told her the truth. "He says that Princess Nadine gave it to me personally when she knew I was leaving. She supposedly gave it to me so that it would bring me back to her." He looked at a loss. "Believe me, I barely ever spoke to the girl. And she never gave me anything. I was hardly ever that close to her."

Kayla nodded, thinking hard. She had no doubt at all that Max was telling the truth. But how could the princess have thought she was giving it to him when she wasn't at all? And where was it now?

Teddy was playing about their feet as they finished their dinner. He had a large, open plastic bus and a small plastic horse and he was very intent on making the horse drive the bus. It seemed to make perfect sense to him that a horse would be driving. But at one point the horse fell out and the bus ran right over him.

Teddy gasped. Max reacted without thinking, reaching down to save the horse. "Poor little horsey," he said, pretending to make the animal neigh back at him. "The horsey wants to go back in the bus," he told Teddy, as though he'd understood the neigh. "Here." He put him back in the driver's seat.

Teddy stared up at him, eyes wide. Then, suddenly, he grinned right up at Max. It was a bright grin, a complete grin, full of joy, no holds barred. Max's heart almost stopped. He'd never known. No one had ever told him what a baby's smile could do. It knocked him out and then some. He felt something explode in his chest and realized it was his heart starting up again.

Teddy had already forgotten the moment and gone

back to playing with the bus. Max turned and looked at Kayla. She smiled at him.

"Wonderful, isn't it?" she murmured.

She understood. He didn't have to say anything and she understood. He glanced back at Teddy, at his own sweet baby. A baby who didn't hate him after all. He could hardly breathe, he was so happy.

They talked softly for a while longer, and the euphoria faded. He still didn't feel right about how Teddy had come to be. It had been wrong and he feared he would have to pay for that wrong, somehow.

"Are you okay?" Kayla asked.

He looked at her. She was so beautiful with the lamplight making a halo behind her beautiful hair. He wanted her—wanted her in his life and in his bed and in his dreams. Wanted her with an ache that throbbed inside and almost made him crazy. But he wasn't ready to tell her so. He had so many things to think about and he was having trouble keeping it all straight.

He might leave. Just go. He'd done it before. In fact, it was the way he normally operated. Stay in one place as long as it pleased him, then, when things got tough, just go. He might do it again. He didn't want it to happen. He was trying, really trying to change his ways, to find meaning in life and stick to it. But he knew himself well enough to know it might not work that way. He might just go.

He got up to leave. He had to go out on his own and figure out what was in his head and in his heart.

"Thanks for the great dinner," he told her. "Promise me you'll stay with Caroline tonight."

"I will. As soon as you're gone, we'll go over there." She searched his eyes. "Will I see you tomorrow?"

He avoided meeting her gaze. "I don't know. I've got a lot to think about. I may go off on my own for a while." He shrugged. "And I have to decide what to do about Mercuria. I can't let them attack this country." He shook his head, looking bemused. "What a concept, huh? Like a comic opera. But they are just crazy enough, they might do it."

Kayla went up to say goodbye, then went on tiptoes and kissed him on the lips, surprising him. "I love you," she told him.

Everything in him cried out for him to take her in his arms and give her what she deserved, but he held back. He held her shoulders and felt her lovely rounded flesh, so warm, so inviting. But he held back. She didn't mean that she was in love with him. She loved him. She had always loved him, just as he'd loved Eddie. They had all loved each other. But that didn't mean they were in love. Was he in love with her? That was just one more question he had to deal with.

He had to figure this out.

"Goodbye. I'll call you."

She nodded and watched him go, then turned to her son.

"No crying," she told herself sternly. "We have things we have to do."

She packed Teddy's bag and then went into the closet to get some things of her own to take along to Caroline's. She'd finally brought the denim jacket back from the office and then she'd forgotten to give it to him again. Even worse, it had slipped off the hanger and lay on the floor. She picked it up and pressed it to her face, reveling in the scent that reminded her of Max. Then she put it back on the hanger, noting that it was an awfully heavy jacket. And she finished packing and grabbed her son and headed out to her sister's apartment.

The next day was unusually busy and different from their normal routine. In the morning, there was a meeting Pellea had set up that she wanted all the princes—and Princess Kim—to attend.

"I'd like all of the new princes to meet with the prime minister," she told Kayla that morning, "and begin to get an idea of what they need to study about our history and foreign policy matters. They need to begin developing what their duties will be. That, of course, will depend a lot on each one's individual skills and talents and how they can be used to best serve this country."

Pellea's face was quite serious, as though she'd given this a lot of thought. "Some of them still don't realize that they can't keep up the sort of lifestyle they are used to if they want to be serious about this royalty business."

"Yes, I agree with you," Kayla said softly, wondering if she mainly had Max in mind.

Pellea went on, completely filled with her own sense of purpose. "When you take on this way of living, you are taking on a responsibility for the lives, happiness and well-being of your people. And that means everybody in this castle, everybody on the royal side of the island, and even those rebels still siding with the Granvillis. Because eventually we'll win them over, too, and the kingdom will be united again."

Kayla nodded. "Have you told them all where and when?" she asked, wondering if she ought to give Max a call to remind him.

"Yes. Ten o'clock in the blue meeting room. And then, of course, we have the picnic luncheon for the French foreign minister and his family, out on the south lawn. Practically everyone in the castle will be coming to that one. Free food does tend to gather a crowd."

The phone began to ring and the queen was soon engrossed in one conversation after another. Meanwhile, Kayla tried to get hold of Max. She called, she sent messages, she even emailed him, but there was no response. As time went by, she began to be concerned, wondering what could have happened to him. She knew he'd planned to go off on his own for a while to think things over, but surely he was checking his messages.

Unless...

Unless he'd left the island. Unless he'd decided just to go. Her heart raced and she got a sick feeling in the pit of her stomach.

"All right, I'm off to the prime minister's meeting with the princes. I'm sure you'll be able to handle things while I'm gone. I'll go straight to the picnic from there. And don't you forget to come to that. Afterward, we'll work on the response to Mercuria."

Kayla nodded, wondering how long it would be before she got a panicked call from the meeting telling her to find Max. When the hour went by without that call, she began to relax. Surely Pellea would have called her if he hadn't shown up. Maybe everything was okay. Maybe she was letting her imagination run away with her.

And maybe she would go to the picnic luncheon after all. Max might even be there. She put away her work and hurried over to the other side of the castle, glad she'd worn dark slacks and a crisp white shirt rather than her usual skirt and sweater. She was dressed for a picnic.

She came out on an upper level and looked down. From where she was standing, she could see the royal platform. And there were Pellea and King Monte and all the princes. All the princes except one. No Max.

Her heart fell. Where could he be? She bit her lip and tried to calm down. There was no point running around like a headless chicken. She had to be logical. The first place to look would be at his rooms.

Going back quickly through the halls, she made her way there in ten minutes. The usual guard was gone and when she knocked, no one answered.

Strike one. Where could she try next? Okay, he'd said he was going off on his own to think. He'd shown her his favorite place to do that, the flat rock by the stream. There was a balcony that looked right down over that area. That would provide the quickest access. She raced toward it.

There was an eerie feeling in this side of the castle today. The usually bustling halls were empty. Everyone was at the picnic. Kayla tried to calm herself down, but she was feeling a bit spooked.

Finally, out of breath, she reached the balcony, and with it, a sense of instant calm. She leaned out over the balcony railing, breathing in the fresh air and reveling in the feeling of freedom. White clouds scudded across a china blue sky. It was a beautiful day and a beautiful setting. Looking down, she didn't see Max, but she did see a glorious view of the countryside, and she knew Max was down there somewhere. Surely he would begin to feel better about everything after a few hours walking about the grounds. She knew she would. She leaned out a bit farther and searched the hills and valleys for a sign of him.

All in all, she was glad she had brought her baby here to the castle. She had a good job and a nice place to live. No complaints. The only element lacking was a daddy for her baby. Other than that, things were coming up roses.

Finally, a movement caught her eye, but it came from right below where she was standing. Two men were struggling with a large push cart. From her vantage point, she could see a large white van parked in a stretch of trees toward the main road. It looked like they were headed that way. But why not bring the van down to the castle and load their cargo in a convenient place? Only one reason she could think of. They were doing something illegal.

And that was certainly the feeling you got from watching them. Their movements were a little too quick, and a lot too furtive. Funny. What could they be transporting that they knew they shouldn't be? Equipment they'd stolen? Machinery they'd found in a storeroom? The entire contents of someone's living room?

That reminded her of the way her place had been manhandled and Max's ransacked. She looked at the men more carefully. Was there anything about them that could be said to seem Mercurian? Not really. They looked like normal workmen. But still…

A siren sounded, making her jump. Sirens were not unusual. There seemed to be a fire drill every week, mostly because of the legacy of the castle burning during the Granvilli rebellion. But this was no drill, not in the middle of a state picnic luncheon. She frowned and looked down at the workmen. The siren seemed to have panicked them. They were running now, pushing at each other and shouting. The pushcart hit a rock and nearly overturned. The canvas cover came off and their cargo was revealed. There was a man lying inside, scrunched into a curled-up position. The man was either dead or unconscious, and he looked very much like Max.

She gasped. The cover was quickly restored, but she knew what she'd seen. Could this be the Mercurians? They looked so guilty. Had they grabbed Max? She wasn't at all sure that was who she'd seen, but still, just the possibility threw her for a loop.

Her heart was pounding like a drum in her own ears. Her hands were shaking so hard, she could barely use her mobile to call security. It rang and rang.

"Come on!" she muttered, nearly crazy.

And finally someone answered.

"Quick," she cried. "This is Kayla Mandrake. I've just seen two men kidnapping someone. I think it might be Prince Max."

"No, can't be," he said. "The princes are all at the picnic. I just saw them there."

"Did you see Max?"

He hesitated. "He's the new one, right? I don't think I've ever seen him, so…"

"Please, please, come quickly. They're going to get away!"

"Lady, listen, do you hear that siren? We're short-handed right now. We've got that darn picnic and now everyone else is out responding to the fire in the library area. There's no one here but me and I can't leave the phone. Listen, call back in about ten minutes. I'll see what I can do then."

"What?"

She couldn't believe it, but she didn't have time to argue. She tried Pellea's number, and then Caroline. Something was wrong; she couldn't get anyone. There was no one to help her. She looked down.

They still hadn't reached the van. Maybe she could catch them herself.

Oh, sure. Catch them and do what? Yell at them a lot? Besides, she would never catch them before they got to the van. And then, who knew where they would go?

But wait. She did know where they would go. What had Max said? She remembered his words— "Mercuria is an hour away," or something like that. An hour away from where? The docks.

The docks! And that wasn't very far. In fact, she knew a shortcut. Caroline and her husband had twin motor scooters that they had used on weekend getaways before their boy was born. She still had a key to Caroline's scooter on her key ring. She could take that scooter and make it across the dunes to the docks before the van got past the traffic signals. There would be officials at the docks. Someone would be there to help her.

She raced down the hall to the stairway. She didn't have time for the elevators. The whole time she ran, she kept looking for someone who might help her, but the halls were empty. She would have to do this herself.

She made her way to the parking garage and found Caroline's scooter. Miraculously, the engine popped on with no trouble, and she was off, dashing for the dunes.

There was a small part of her brain that kept poking her, saying, *What if it is just a body? What if... what if...*

And she pushed it back, saying, *No! They may have said dead or alive, but everything they've done proves they want him alive. So don't even think that!*

She veered off the main road onto a dirt track that cut out about a mile of driving to the docks. The little scooter was racing along and she was feeling very scared, but strangely exhilarated at the same time. She saw the craggy outcropping of the rocky point ahead. That meant the docks were only a few minutes away.

As she came around a curve, the main road was spread out below and she saw the white van. It was turning around. She jammed on her brakes and pulled to a stop.

A man was running from it and another lay on the side of the road. A shot rang out, and then another. Her heart in her throat, she started down the incline, racing to get to the place where the trees stood near the road and she could get a view of the van as it passed without being seen herself.

If her guess were right, that should be Max driving. It looked to her as though he'd overpowered his kidnappers and taken off with their van, but she couldn't be sure. Ditching the scooter behind a small hill, she ran for the edge of the road and made it close enough to see, gasping for breath, just as the van came around the corner.

It was! She could see Max driving. It looked like he had a bloody head wound, but he was driving and as far as she could see, he was alone.

He'd done it! What a guy! Jumping for joy, she

yelled and waved her arms, but she was still too far into the trees and he didn't see her.

She had a small, empty feeling when he drove on past and left her there, but she knew it wouldn't be long before she caught up with him again. She turned to run back to her scooter, and that was when she felt the dart go into her neck. She reached to pull it out, but her hands never made it there. In seconds, she was out like a light.

Max had been back at the castle for over an hour and had told everyone his story of being kidnapped by Mercurians. Even King Monte had come by to hear it personally. The whole thing seemed crazy, but everyone wanted to hear it.

Max had spent most of the morning out on his flat rock by the little river, thinking his life over and trying to make some important decisions. He knew Pellea wanted him at the prime minister's meeting, and he had come back to the castle for that, but just as he was coming in through the big double doors, someone had shot a tranquilizer dart into his neck and he had collapsed. He'd woken an hour or so later to find himself locked in a storeroom. This time they put him out with a rag soaked in chloroform, and he woke up in the back of the white van on his way to the docks. His hands were tied, but not very well, and he had no trouble working them free. Then he'd bided his time, not letting the two men know he was awake and that his hands were free. Finally he got his chance and he overpowered one of them. The driver pulled over to help his friend and Max threw the first man out and dealt with the second. Then it was a simple matter of grabbing the keys and taking the same transportation back again, minus the kidnappers this time.

"Though one of them did shoot at the van as I drove off," he told his attentive audience. "Luckily, he wasn't much of a shot."

Security at the docks had been alerted but they hadn't found the men.

"I'm calling out the army on this," Monte said with a scowl. "I want someone charged and put behind bars. We have to nip this sort of thing off right away. We can't have criminals running around kidnapping people."

By now, Max had asked where Kayla was a number of times and no one seemed to know. And then a call came in from the dockyard police saying they had found Caroline's abandoned scooter near the road to the docks, and Pellea and Max began to piece together different bits of evidence and get a vague idea of where she might be. Their conclusions were grim.

Once Pellea questioned the security guard who had been on duty that afternoon and found out someone had called in saying Max had been kidnapped, the picture became clearer.

"Kayla obviously saw the kidnappers taking you off and when she couldn't get security to help, she grabbed Caroline's scooter and went after you herself."

Max stared at Pellea, stunned.

"They have her," he said in a low, gravelly voice. "The bastards have her." He turned to look for his keys. "I've got to go."

CHAPTER TEN

"Hold it."

Monte held a hand up and stopped Max cold.

"You're not going anywhere."

Max's face darkened rebelliously. Right now he wasn't in the mood to take orders from royals, no matter who they were. But before he had a chance to say anything, Monte continued and explained his position.

"I'm not trying to pull rank on you, Max. But we have to stop and think things through before we act. We need to be sure we are doing the smart thing to get the results that we want and not just more bloodshed. You swimming the channel in a burst of adrenaline, showing up on shore with a knife between your teeth, is just going to get you killed. We can't succeed without a plan."

"What sort of plan?"

"I say we go in at midnight."

"Who's 'we'?"

"All of us royals. The warriors of the DeAngelis regime. We've got a very fast, very slinky boat that can enter areas without making a sound. I'm thinking four of us will take it."

"Four?" Mykal asked the question.

Monte nodded. "Sorry, old man, but I don't think we ought to risk you on this mission. You're not healed yet. We'll use you as a coordinator back home."

Mykal nodded reluctantly.

"Okay, so we've got Joe with his special forces training. And you, Max—you've been in combat. David is the best strategic thinker I know of. And I'm a pretty good leader." He shrugged. "What else do we need?"

"A plan," Max answered, still restless and not sure this was going to work. He liked to work alone. That was what he was used to. And every minute they delayed was a minute more Kayla had to endure whatever they were putting her through.

"A plan would be good," Monte admitted. "That's why we're going to take a few hours to think about it. We'll meet at eleven and go over our thoughts and put something together.

Max stared at him, trying not to let his resentment show. He knew what Monte was saying was smart, but he wanted to go now. He clenched his jaw and kept his opinion to himself. Monte knew what he was doing and he was exhibiting good leadership. He had to let this play out. Still, he ached to go right into their castle and save Kayla. If someone was hurting her, they were going to pay.

"I'm preparing a message for King Juomo and his

ministers," Pellea said. "I'm telling the king that this nonsense has to end and that he'll personally pay for anything that happens to Kayla." She took a deep breath and looked around at them all. "You know it is possible that this is just a fringy, rogue element who has masterminded this," she said.

"You think so?" Max challenged her. "You don't think the king sending a poster saying I was wanted dead or alive was a little rogue, a little fringy?"

"Of course it was."

"Yes. The whole Mercurian royal family has been cuckoo for years."

"Which means you can't base your estimates of what they might do on normal reactions. Be ready for anything."

Max couldn't face going back to his room alone and thinking any more. He wanted to take action. It killed him to wait. He had to do something to take his mind off it. So he stopped by Caroline's apartment and asked to see Teddy.

Caroline was worried. He could see it in her face, and when he decided to take Teddy to Kayla's and fix him some dinner himself, she readily agreed, but caught him before he left.

"Are you going to save my sister?" she asked earnestly. "Can you guarantee me that she's going to be okay?"

He took her hand in his and gazed deep into her eyes. "I guarantee she'll be okay," he said gruffly. "Or I'll die trying to make that happen."

She stared back for a moment, then nodded, satisfied. "Okay," she said. "I'll hold you to that."

"Come on, Teddy," he said, looking at his little boy. "You want to go with me?"

Teddy gave him a steady gaze but didn't look enthused.

"Go with Prince Max, honey," Carolyn said. "I'll bet he could fix you a nice scrambled egg for your dinner." She said as an aside, "He really likes scrambled eggs," and Max nodded, smiling as the little boy got up and came to him.

"I'll bring him back in an hour or so."

He bent down and picked him up and they said goodbye, but Teddy was stiff in his arms until he saw that they were going to his own apartment. Max realized he probably thought he was going to see his mother, so he began talking to him as they entered the room, keeping him occupied as long as possible, and it seemed to work out all right.

They sat on the floor and Max began putting together a set of fat train tracks meant for toddlers, while Teddy pushed the train engine and tried to make train noises. The tracks were going everywhere, and since the door was open to the coat closet, soon they were going there, too.

Max looked at the little boy he was playing with and he couldn't help but smile. This child was his son. And then Teddy looked at him and gave him that beautiful smile again, and he felt it—the connection. Finally. This really was his son. He could feel it now.

He got up to go fix Teddy some scrambled eggs. He couldn't eat anything himself, he was too tied up in knots, but he fed his boy. And then he paced the floor and thought of Kayla.

Suddenly he noticed a flash of light and he turned, puzzled. A sort of reflection was on the wall. He turned again, trying to figure out where it was coming from, and realized Teddy had pushed his toys into the closet and was pretending it was a cave. But something he was playing with had made that fantastic reflection, all dancing, shimmering lights.

He went into the closet and the first thing he noticed was his own denim jacket, lying on the floor. Realizing it must have fallen, he picked it up and put it on a hanger, then looked down at Teddy. The boy had a thick gold chain around his neck and he was playing with the pendant hanging from it. Max frowned and took a closer look, and then his blood began to pound in his veins and his heart did a flip in his chest.

"What the...?"

It was the artifact. He was staring down at a million-dollar diamond and his son was playing with it.

He turned away, struggling for breath. The historical artifact that threatened to ruin his life, the jewel-encrusted icon worth millions, was in the hands of a toddler. He turned back.

"Teddy, Teddy, where did you get that?"

Teddy didn't seem to know, but Max looked at his own denim jacket and realized what must have happened.

"It was in my jacket all this time," he muttered in hazy wonder. "And it took Teddy to find it."

And Teddy didn't want to give it up.

"Sorry, kid," he told him. "I've got to take this from you. I can't let it out of my possession again. Lives may depend on it."

Looking at it, he was sure this was what the king of Mercuria wanted. He didn't want Kayla. He didn't even want Max. This was basically the crown jewels of the nation and he wanted his treasure back.

How had it ended up in his jacket pocket? Maybe someone ought to ask Princess Nadine that question. He grabbed his denim jacket and put it on, then slipped the artifact back into the hidden, inside pocket, making sure it was secure.

"Thanks, Teddy," he said, picking the boy up and giving him a big kiss. "You're the hero tonight."

He got together the baby's things and he felt as though he were walking on air.

"Okay, Teddy," he muttered. "You're going to have to go back and stay with Caroline, because I'm going to get your mama back."

He knew he was supposed to wait for his brothers to go with him, but that was three hours away. He had to go now. Kayla was all alone and scared and he couldn't wait any longer.

Max had lived in Mercuria for almost a year and he knew all the little inlets along the coast and he could find them, even in the dark. He pulled his boat into a cove and tied it fast to a stand of pilings, then went ashore. It was a short walk to the castle. Mercuria was an old-fashioned country. The new, modern methods of security and border entry hadn't been introduced as yet. Very few people came to visit, because, after all, who cared about Mercuria? They had sat tight in their little isolated peninsula for decades and most people didn't even know they existed.

Max knew certain passwords, certain door codes, and before long, he was in the central living area of the castle, smiling at his old friend Sven, doorkeeper to the royal family.

"Hey, Sven," he said.

"Max!" Sven, a big, burly Swede, stepped out to clap him on the back. "Hey, good to see you, old buddy. It's been a while. So you're back?"

"Ah...yes, I'm back."

"And you're going into the royal center?"

"If you're going to let me, yes, I am."

"You don't have a pass, I suppose."

"Do I ever?"

Sven laughed. "No, can't say that I've ever known you to arrive with the proper pass." He shook his head with pure affection. "Come on in. Shall I announce you to anyone?"

"No, thanks. I'm going to go in and see who's available. Hopefully, I'll find the king isn't busy and has time to talk to me."

"Oh, sure. I think someone said he's in the greenhouse right now."

"Okay. I'll just hang around until he gets back."

"Sure."

He'd given a lot of thought to where they might be holding Kayla. There was a guest room on the first floor, off the library. If they were being extra special nice, they might have put her there. He slipped around the kitchen where he overheard two kitchen maids gossiping, and headed straight for the library, then the guest room. Empty.

That left the women's jail on the second floor. He took the stairs, hoping he wouldn't pass anyone on the way, and came to the fortified area that had been built especially to hold female prisoners. He'd known a housemaid who'd been accused of stealing and had been kept there for weeks. He'd felt sorry for her, visited her often and finally won her release when the real culprit was identified. He knew the way in and the way out and he could pick the main lock at will. A few clicks and he was in.

Two cells faced each other, divided by a corridor between them. In one cell, just as he'd expected, there was Kayla, sitting on a bare cot and looking unhappy but otherwise unscathed. But what he hadn't expected was to find Princess Nadine sitting in the other cell, face muddy with the effects of a lot of heavy crying. She looked up when Max entered, and her face brightened considerably.

"Max," she said, jumping up and going to the bars. "You came for me! Finally!"

But his attention was all on Kayla.

"Max!" She reached out her hand and he took it in his, pulling as close to her as he could.

"Are you all right?" Kayla asked anxiously. "How's your head?"

He'd forgotten all about his head wound. He touched it gingerly. "It's okay. How about you?" His gaze ran over every inch of her, searching for any signs of wounds. She looked a little mussed and had a bruise on one cheek, which made him swear softly. Her hair could use a combing. But she was the most beautiful thing he'd ever seen. "Did they hurt you?"

"No. Well, they did stick me with a tranquilizer dart."

He grinned at her. "Me, too."

She grinned back. "But other than that, they've been okay."

"Max!" Princess Nadine called, sounding like the spoiled child she was. "Come see about me."

He looked over his shoulder. "Why is she in here?" he asked.

Kayla shook her head. "I'm not sure. I think her father put her in here as a sort of trap for you when you returned to get her."

"Get her?"

"They seem to think you two have a love affair going on."

"In her imagination, maybe."

"Or maybe her father is just mad at her."

"I'm not mad at all, young lady," said a deep, sonorous voice.

Max turned quickly. King Juomo was coming down the center aisle. Dressed in eighteenth-century royal garb of brocade and velvet, he looked splendid and ridiculous all at the same time.

"My daughter is incarcerated for a very specific purpose." He smiled and made a slight inclination of his head toward Max. "I'm glad you made it. We've been waiting for you. Now we can get on with things."

"Your Majesty, with all due respect, I would like you to release Kayla right away. You have no right to hold her here. She has nothing to do with any of this."

He batted that pesky demand away. "I hear you're a prince now, my friend. What a lucky occurrence that is. Now my daughter will be doubly royal, won't she?" He put his head to one side, thinking hard. "Not to mention the unbreakable ties our two nations shall have with each other. Won't that be lovely?"

"Your Majesty," Max said bluntly, "I'm not going to marry your daughter."

"Oh, but I think you are. You see, I won't release your little friend here unless you do. It's quite simple, really." He smiled. "I've had the men in to fire up the old torture room in the dungeon. Quite a few nice old-fashioned machines in there. Can tear a body to ribbons, you know. I don't think your little friend will like it much. We will strive for historical accuracy, but still, her screams are going to be hard to take."

"Wait a minute." Max stared at the man as though

he could hardly believe he was sane. "You're threatening to torture Kayla if I don't marry Princess Nadine? Are you crazy?"

"Not at all. I've been tested. I'm quite sane." He threw a dour look Kayla's way. "And not mad, either."

"I meant angry," she told him quickly. "Which is what I'm beginning to get. This is so absurd. I don't believe for a minute that you plan to torture me. You know very well international law forbids it."

He frowned. "Since when?"

"You don't keep up much with international affairs, do you? It's been that way for years. You can't get away with it. They'll string you up."

His laugh was jovial. "They'll have to catch me first."

"Really? And exactly where will you run to?"

He looked at Max. "I quite like your friend. She has a lot of spirit. Maybe I'll marry her myself." He giggled. "We'll have a double wedding."

"Daddy!" Nadine was sobbing.

"Hush, child. You wanted him and I told you I'd get him. Now he's here for you. Show a little gratitude."

"Tell you what," Max said sensibly, "I don't think anyone is marrying anyone at this point. But I do have a bargain for you. I might be able to produce your historical artifact."

"You'd certainly better produce the artifact. If you don't, you're all going to lose your heads."

"Oh, for heaven's sake," Kayla muttered just loud enough for Max to hear. "Now he thinks he's the Red Queen."

"If I can produce it," Max went on doggedly, "I'm sure you'll be gracious enough to let us both go free."

The king's eyes widened. "You and Nadine?"

"No. Me and Kayla."

He was frowning. "How does that help my little daughter? She loves you so."

"Daddy!" Nadine called.

"Hush. I'm negotiating here."

"But Daddy, I don't want him anymore. I hate him."

The king turned and glared at his daughter. "What?"

"I hate him. He didn't come back the way he was supposed to. I waited and waited."

"Well, he's back now. I went to a lot of trouble to get him for you."

"I know." She pouted. "I used to think he was really cute. But not anymore."

Max and Kayla exchanged significant glances.

"I don't understand," the plump man blustered. "I thought you couldn't live without him."

"Yeah, well…" She made a face. "He's not as cute as the new stable boy. Daddy? Please? I want the new stable boy."

Kayla grinned. By now she'd pretty much decided this whole thing was a thinly disguised farce. She couldn't believe anyone this silly could run a country.

"Maybe *I* ought to take a look at the new stable boy," she said brightly. "Who knows? Maybe I'll like him better, too."

Max turned to glare at her. He wasn't quite as ready as she was to assume this was an annoying but basically harmless situation. The king was off his rocker and pretty ridiculous, but that sort of person could go from farce to tragedy in a heartbeat.

But before he could say anything, there was a commotion in the hallway. There were shouts. A gun was fired, then another. And deadly silence.

They all stood very still, each holding his breath, listening for clues as to what this meant. Suddenly, the door to the cell room burst open and Monte appeared, with the guard Max knew as Sven in front of him with revolver pressed into his back.

"Your Majesty," Monte said to King Juomo, "so nice to meet you at last. We've come to take our people back, if you don't mind. The keys, please."

King Juomo seemed dumbfounded and very scared. Hands trembling, he produced the keys. David came in behind Monte and took the keys from him, opening the cell where Kayla had been sequestered and giving her a friendly smile.

"I always love it when they send in the cavalry," she noted approvingly.

"I don't know," Max said sardonically as he looked around at his brothers, "I thought I was doing okay on my own."

"It never hurts to get backup," Joe told him. "And anyway, thanks for trying to cut us out of the action."

"How did you know?" he asked, quietly admitting to himself that he'd never been happier to see a gang like this show up on his side.

"Caroline called Kimmee. Kimmee called Pellea."

"And we figured the rest out on our own," Monte said.

Max shook his head and grinned at his brothers. Reaching into the pocket of his jacket, he grabbed the artifact and drew it out. "Here you go," he told King Juomo, handing it to him.

The king looked at his daughter. "So you were telling me the truth?" he cried.

She nodded sulkily. "I put it in his pocket for safekeeping. I wanted it to be with him always, wherever he went. I knew it would bring him back to me, one way or another." She sniffed. "And now I don't want him."

"You see what folly it was to do that?" the king roared at her. "You see what trouble you caused?"

Her face crumpled but the princes were ready to leave her to her father's care and they began to head for the exit.

"It's been grand," Kayla said, saluting the king as she passed him. "Sort of like a visit to Freedonia without the Marx Brothers."

He looked rattled but it was evident he was starting to get color back in his face, and they hurried, not wanting to get bogged down in another discussion with him. Joe covered their departure, making sure the guards they'd disarmed on the way in weren't getting any ideas. And then they were on the boats and heading for home.

"There's something exhilarating about a good rescue operation," Monte said. "No casualties. Just some good clean fun."

"Fun." Max looked at Kayla, feeling drained.

She grinned at him. "All's well that ends well," she said.

Max groaned. "Another one of the quotes I'm supposed to learn, huh?"

She nodded and moved closer, putting her head against his shoulder and enjoying the cool, clean spray from the ocean. She loved Max. And she was in love with him, too. It was a good day that taught you a life lesson that big. She meant to savor it.

In the morning, Max went to Kayla's to have breakfast with her and her baby. He sat eating a delicious breakfast pastry that Kayla had picked up at the bakery and drinking black coffee and listening to Kayla talk to Teddy and feeling as though he'd won the lottery. This was great. This made him a happy man.

Suddenly he realized something. It broke over him like a shooting star, spreading sparkling gobs of fire all around. Being a flyer was important, but not everything. Being a prince was going to be his life's work. But the one thing he really cared about above all others, the one thing he wanted to do with his life, was to protect Kayla, to protect her and cherish her and make her happy. And loving Teddy was a part of that.

He sat back and marveled at how simple it all was once he'd let himself break free of all the old hurts and fears. He'd spent much too much time tied up in knots of doubt. No more doubts. No more regrets. He loved Kayla. Therefore, he would live his life to honor her. And that was all there was.

Could he do that? Could he be a father? Why the hell not?

He looked across the table at the woman he loved. "Will you marry me, Kayla?"

She pursed her lips and pretended to be thinking it over. "I don't know. I'll have to think about it. There's a lot to consider." She searched his face and shook her head sadly. "If only you were as cute as the stable boy."

He groaned. "I'm going to trade you to King Juomo. You'll be happy there. He really knows how to treat a lady."

She grinned happily. "Okay, I'll marry you. Let's do it quick."

"Before we change our minds?"

"Never." She held her glass of orange juice up as a toast to him. "I'll love you forever, Max. Forever and everywhere and always."

"Me, too."

Teddy made a noise. It sounded very much like words.

Max frowned. "Did he just say, 'me, too'?"

Kayla nodded. "It sure sounded like it."

"You know what that means?"

"Tell me."

"We're a family now."

Rising from her chair, she went to slip onto his lap and put her arms around him.

"Sealed with a kiss."

* * * * *

KEEPING HER BABY'S SECRET
Raye Morgan

CHAPTER ONE

DIANA COLLINS woke with a start and lay very still, her heart beating hard in her chest. She stared into the dark room. She'd heard something. She was sure of it.

It was midsummer and her windows were all open. That was nice for ventilation, but not so wise for safety, even out here in the country. Silently she railed at herself. She'd known she should do something about getting bars on the windows or...

But wait. There it was again. The intruder wasn't stumbling around in her little turn-of-the-century cottage. He was still outside. He was...singing.

Slowly she lifted her head. She knew that song. She knew that voice.

"Cam," she whispered, and now a different brand of adrenaline was shooting through her veins. She smiled.

"Cam, you idiot!"

Slipping out of bed, she went to the window and looked down toward the lake. She could just make out a dark figure lounging on the pier. The moonlight glinted on a bottle he was holding as he leaned back to let out a wobbly high note.

"Oh, Cam," she said despairingly, but she was laughing. It must have been ten years since she'd last seen him. Joy flashed through her as she dashed around the room, searching for a robe to throw over her light nightgown—and to conceal, at least for the moment, her rounded belly.

Everything was going to be…well, not okay, but better. Cam was back.

Cameron Garfield Wellington Van Kirk the third was feeling no pain. There was no denying it—he'd been indulging. And since he almost never had more than a single glass of wine at dinner these days, he'd been affected more quickly and more thoroughly than he'd expected. He wondered, fleetingly, why he seemed to be bobbing in a warm, mellow glow. It was unusual, but rather nice.

"Maybe a little too nice," he muttered to himself in a Sam Spade accent, trying to look fierce and world-weary at the same time. It didn't really work. But did that matter when there was no one here to witness it anyway?

Never mind. He was going to sing again. Just one more swig from this nice bottle and he was going to sing that song about Diana.

"'I'm so young, and you're…'" he began tunefully, then stopped, frowning. "Wait a minute. I'm older than she is. This song doesn't make any sense."

An owl called from across the water, then swooped by, its wings hissing in the air.

He turned and there she was, coming down toward the pier, dressed in lacy white and looking like something ethereal, magic—from another world. He squinted, trying to see her better. He wasn't used to thinking of her as part angel, part enchantress. The Diana he'd known was a girl who had both feet firmly placed in a particularly earthy sort of reality. At least, that was the way he remembered it.

"Diana?" he whispered loudly. After all, he didn't want to wake anybody up. "Is that you?"

She came closer and he watched, fascinated, then blinked hard and shook his head. It was his old friend Diana all right but it looked like she was floating. Were her feet even touching the ground? Her cloud of blond hair shimmered around her and the gown billowed in a gust of wind and he felt a catch in his breathing. She was so beautiful. How was it that he'd managed to stay away this long?

"Cam?" she said, her voice as clear as the lake water. "Is that really you?"

He stared at her without answering. "If this is heaven," he mumbled as he watched her, enchanted and weaving dangerously right next to the water, "it's more than I deserve."

"It's Apache Lake, silly," she said as she came onto the pier and headed right for him. "Heaven is still to come."

"For you, maybe," he muttered, shaking his head as he looked her over.

She might look magical but she was all woman now—no longer the barefoot girl with the ragged cut-offs and the skimpy cropped top and a belly-button ring—and like as not a set of bruises administered by her bully of a father. That was the Diana he'd left behind.

This new Diana was going to take some getting used to. He made no move to give her a hug or a kiss in greeting. Maybe that was because he wanted to with a sudden intensity that set up warning flares. And maybe it was because he'd had too much to drink and didn't trust himself to keep it simple.

"Some of us are still holding our options open," he added irrelevantly.

Her answering laugh was no more relevant, but it didn't matter. She was laughing from the pure joy of seeing him again. She looked up at him, still searching his face as though needing to find bits and pieces of the Cam she remembered. She noted how he was still fighting back the tendency to curl in his almost-black hair. And there were his startlingly blue eyes, crinkling with a hint of laughter. That was still the same. But there was a wary reserve that hadn't been there before. He was harder now, tougher looking. The sweetness of the boy had been sloughed away and in its place there was a cool, manly sort of strength.

For just a moment, her confidence faltered. He was large and impressive in a way she didn't recognize. Maybe he'd changed more than she was going to like. Maybe he'd become someone else, a stranger.

Oh, she hoped not, but her heart was in her throat.

"Hey," he said.

"Hey yourself," she said back softly, her dark eyes luminous in the gloom as she searched for clues in the set of his shoulders, the lines of his face. "What are you doing here?"

He frowned, trying to remember. Everything seemed to have fuzzy edges right now. He'd been on his way home—if you could call the house where his parents and grandfather lived his home. Yeah, that was it. He'd been on his way home, and then, he'd taken a detour....

Suddenly the answer was clear. He'd thought he was just stopping by to say hello to an old friend, putting off the homecoming he had waiting for him at the Van Kirk family mansion on the hill not too far from here. But now he knew there was a flaw in his thinking. There had been another motivation all along. He just hadn't realized it. He'd come to find the person he'd missed most all these years. And here she was, not quite the same, but good enough.

He looked down at her, needing nothing more than the Diana she was today. He soaked her in as though he'd been lost in the desert and dying of thirst. She promised to be something better and more satisfying than mere alcohol could ever be.

They said you can't go home again, and maybe that was true. Things could never be the way they'd been before he left. But that was okay. The way Diana had turned out, things might just be better.

"What am I doing here?" he repeated softly, still struggling with blurry thinking. "Looking for you."

"For me?" She laughed dismissively, looking over his shoulder at the moon. "I think you're looking for someone who isn't here anymore."

"You'll do," he said simply.

They stared into each other's eyes for a long moment, their memories and emotions awakening and connecting in a way their words could never quite explain.

"I thought you weren't ever coming back," she said at last, and her voice had a catch in it that made her wince. Tears of raw feeling were very near the surface and she couldn't let them show. But to see him here, standing on her pier, just as he had in those bygone days, sent her heart soaring.

She looked at him, looked at his open shirt and wide belt, his attractively tight jeans and slim hips, the way his short sleeves revealed nicely swelling biceps and she shook her head. He was so like the young man she'd known, and yet so different. The dark hair was shorter and cut more neatly, though it was mussed a bit now and a spray of it still fell over his eyes, just like always. The face was harder, creases where dimples used to be. But the gorgeous eyes were just as brilliantly blue, sparkling like starfire in the moonlight.

For so long, she'd been afraid his last declaration to her would come true. Even after all these years, the memory of those final words had the capacity to sting deep down in her heart.

"I'm out of here, and I'm never coming back."

She'd thought her world had melted down that day. And now here he was, back after all.

"Naw," he said carelessly. "I never meant it. Not really."

She nodded. She accepted that. She'd waited for a long time for him to show up again. She'd been so sure he would, despite what he'd said. But after years, when it didn't happen, she'd finally started to lose faith.

She remembered when he'd left. She'd been an angry and confused eighteen-year-old, trapped in a broken home, grasping for a reason to thrive. For so long, he'd been her anchor to all that was good in life. And then he'd left and she'd felt adrift in a world without signs or shelter. She'd been so very all alone.

"What I can't understand is why you're still here," he said.

She lifted her chin. "Where did you think I'd be?"

He shrugged. "I don't know. San Francisco maybe. Becoming sophisticated." He half grinned. "Gettin' swanky."

"Swanky?" She laughed. "That'll be the day."

As if on cue, he began to softly sing the Buddy Holly song of the same name, still staring soulfully into her eyes.

"You're drunk," she accused him, shaking her head as though despairing of him.

He stopped short and grimaced. "No. Impossible." He stared hard, actually trying to convince her. "You can ask anyone. I don't drink."

"Cam!" She looked pointedly at the bottle in his hand.

He looked at it, too, then quickly looked away. "Hey, anyone," he called out a bit groggily across the lake, forgetting all about keeping it quiet. "Tell her. She needs to hear it from a neutral source."

She bit her lip, trying not to laugh at the picture he made. "There's no one out there," she told him simply.

"Sure there is." He turned his heavy-lidded gaze on her. "Look closely, now. Can't you see them?"

Turning to lean on the railing, she looked out across the lake to the stand of pines and cottonwoods shivering in the breeze. It was so good to be here in the night with Cam, almost as though a missing part of her was back in place, where it should be.

"See who?"

"Us." He moved closer and spoke very near her ear. "Cam and Di. The boy and girl we used to be. The ghosts are out there."

She could feel his warm breath on her skin. It made her pulse beat just a little faster and she was enjoying it, for now.

It had been so long.

She'd tried asking about him over the years, first in the village, then at the Van Kirk mansion when she'd been there in connection to her job, and the response she had was minimal. She'd told herself that it looked like he was gone for good, that he'd had some sort of rift with his family that couldn't be repaired—that he was never coming back. She'd tried to convince herself to forget about him. But his influence on her was embedded in her soul. She couldn't shake him loose, no matter what.

And at the same time, she'd always known that she could never really have him. But that was a tragic fact of life, something she'd accepted as a given.

She turned and looked at him. "I don't see anything," she told him, determined to be the realist to his crazy dreamer. "There's nobody out there."

"Sure there is." He frowned as though it was a puzzle that needed solving. "Maybe you should have some of this," he said, brandishing the bottle and looked at her hopefully. "Your vision might get better."

She shook her head, rolling her eyes as she did so. He looked at the bottle, drained it, then frowned, silently reproaching himself. She had a right to hate drinking. She'd certainly suffered enough from the stuff.

"Okay. I'll get rid of it." Easy enough for him to say. The bottle was empty now.

"Wait!" She stopped him from sending it sailing out into the water, snatching it from his hand. "Don't litter in my lake. I'll put it in the trash can."

He blinked at her but didn't protest, leaning back on the railing with his elbows and watching her with the trace of a smile on his handsome face. She tossed the bottle and turned back to him. Her heart lurched at the picture he made in the moonlight, part the man he was now, part the memory of the boy. There had been a time when she would have done anything for him. And now? Hopefully she knew better now.

Looking out across the water again, she pretended to squint and peer into the moonlight. "Wait a minute," she said, looking hard. "I think I see them now. Two crazy kids stomping around in the mud."

"That's them," he said approvingly, then looked down at her. "Or more accurately, that's us."

Us. Yes, they had spent time together on that side of the lake. How could she forget? Some of the best moments of her life had been spent there.

Cam was always fighting with his grandfather in those days. After a particularly bad argument, she would often find him down at the far side of Apache Lake, fishing for rainbow trout. She would sit and watch and he would tell her stories about the valley's history or his sister's latest exploit or… sometimes, what he wanted to do with his life. His dreams involved big things far away from gold country. Whenever he talked about them, she felt a sense of sad emptiness inside. She knew she would never be a part of that world.

He always used catch and release, and she would watch regretfully as he threw the shiny, silvery fish back in and they watched it swim away. He didn't realize that she could have used it for dinner. More often than not, the refrigerator at her house was bare and her father was off somewhere burning through the money that should have gone to food, pouring it down his throat in the form of bargain wine. But she never said a word to Cam. She was too embarrassed to let him know her dinner would be a cheap candy bar that night.

Such things were not a problem any longer. She had a nice little business that kept her comfortable, if not exactly rolling in wealth. These days she was more likely to try to cut down on calories than to need to scrounge for protein.

Times had changed. She'd traded a rough childhood for an adulthood that was a lot nicer. She'd been a damaged person then. She was okay now.

Her hands tightened on the railing and she bit down on her lower lip to keep it from trembling. Who was she trying to kid? A woman who was content with her life didn't take the steps to change things that she had recently done.

He hadn't noticed yet. She resisted the urge to pull her robe more carefully over her slightly rounded belly. He was going to have to know the truth some time and it might as well be now.

Well, maybe not now. But very soon.

"Remember the night before I left?" he was saying, his voice low and slightly hoarse. "Remember…?"

He let his voice trail off and she closed her eyes. She remembered all right. She would never forget. It was the one and only time he'd ever kissed her. It wasn't much of a kiss—not at all the kind of kiss she'd yearned for. His lips had barely touched hers. But she still considered it the best kiss she'd ever had.

She felt him touching her hair and she sighed. If she turned to look at him, would he kiss her again? She tried it, moving slowly, opening her eyes to look up into his face. For just a moment, she thought he might do it. But then a look of regret came into his eyes and he turned from her, moving restlessly.

Her heart sank, but she scolded herself at the same time. What was she thinking? A romance with Cam was not in the cards—never had been.

"So where have you been all this time?" she probed to get her mind on other things.

He shrugged. "Pretty much everywhere. Served a few years in the Navy. Worked on an oilrig in the Gulf. Spent some time as a bodyguard in Thailand. The usual stuff."

She nodded. This was definitely not the sort of thing his mother would have bragged about. If he'd been at law school on law review, spent time working as an aide to the governor, or made a pile of money on Wall Street, she would have made sure the local paper covered it in minute detail. Cam had always had a tendency to turn away from the upper class path to respect and follow his own route to…what? That had often been a bone of contention between him and his family.

But who was she to complain? It was exactly that inclination that had led him to be her protector for those early years. Their friendship had started when she was in middle school. Her father was the town drunk and that meant she was the object of vile names and other indignities that adolescent boys seemed compelled to visit upon those weaker than themselves. Cam was a couple of years older. He saw immediately what was going on in her life and he stepped in to make it stop.

That first time had been like magic. She'd gone for a swim at the park pool. None of her friends had shown up and suddenly, she'd been surrounded by a group of boys who had begun to taunt her, circling and snapping at her like a pack of wolves. She knew she could hold her own against one boy, or even two or three, but there were too many this time and she panicked. She tried to run, which only egged them on, and just when she thought she was going to be taken down like a frightened deer, Cam appeared on the scene.

He was only a few years older than the boys, but his sense of strength and authority gave him the upper hand and they scattered as soon as he challenged them. He picked her up, dusted her off and took her for ice cream. And that began a friendship that lasted all through her school years. He was her protector, the force behind the calm, the one who made everything okay.

Even when he'd gone away to university, he'd checked on her whenever he came home. He treated her like a big brother. The only problem was, she'd never been able to completely think of him that way.

No, from the start, she'd had a major crush on him. It hadn't been easy to hide. And the effects had lingered long after he'd skipped town and left her behind. In fact, she knew very well it was her feelings for him that had ruined every relationship she'd attempted ever since.

"So you've pretty much been bumming around the world for ten years?" she asked, frowning as she looked at him again. Whatever he'd been doing, it actually looked to be profitable. Now that she noticed, his clothing was rumpled, but top-of-the-line. And that watch he wore looked like it could be traded in for a down payment on a small house.

"Not really," he told her. "The first five years, maybe. But then I sort of fell into a pretty lucrative situation." He shrugged. "I started my own business in San Diego and I've done pretty well."

"Good for you."

He shrugged again. "I've been lucky."

She knew it was more than that. He was quick, smart, competent. Whatever that business was, he was evidently successful at it.

"And all that time, you never thought a simple phone call might have been in order?" she asked lightly. "A letter, maybe? Just some sign that you were still alive and well?"

She bit her lip again. Was she whining? Better to drop it.

He shook his head. "I figured a clean break was the best way," he said softly.

She winced. That was exactly what he'd said that night, after he'd kissed her. But she wasn't going to complain anymore. It wasn't like he owed her anything. When you came right down to it, he'd done more for her than anyone else ever had. What more could she ask for?

That was a dangerous question and she shied away from it quickly.

"So what brought you back?" she asked. "Are you back for good?" The words were out of her mouth before she could stop them and she made a face, knowing she had sounded altogether too hopeful.

He looked at her, then at the moon. "Hard to tell at this point," he muttered. Turning, he looked back toward the little house she lived in. She'd done something to it. Even in the dark, it didn't look so much like a shack anymore.

"Your old man still around?" he asked.

"He died a few years ago," she told him. "Complications from pneumonia."

Complications from being a rotten drunk was what she could have said, he thought bitterly. She was better off without him. But that being said, you didn't get to choose your relatives and he *was* her father.

"Sorry," he muttered, looking away.

"Thanks," she said shortly. "For all the grief he gave me, he did manage to hang onto this little piece of property, so it's mine now. All five acres of it."

He nodded, then smiled, happy to think of her having something like this for her own. Whenever he'd thought of her over the years, he'd pictured her here, at the lake. It was so much a part of her.

"I had a funeral for him," she went on. "At the little chapel on Main. I thought it would just be me and him." She shook her head, remembering. "Do you know, most of the town came? I couldn't believe it." She grinned. "I even had a cousin I'd never met before show up, Ben Lanker. He's an attorney in Sacramento and he wanted to go over the will for me, to see if all was okay." She laughed shortly. "I think he was hoping to find a flaw, to see if there was some way he could get his hands on this property. But I'd had everything nailed down clear and legal when I was dating a lawyer in San Francisco, so he was out of luck."

He laughed along with her, pleased to know she was taking care of herself these days. Looking at her, he couldn't imagine her being a victim in any way.

"So tell me, Cam," she said. "The truth this time. I'm still waiting to hear the answer to my question. What brings you back to your ancestral home?"

He sighed. "It's a fairly easy answer. I'm just embarrassed to tell you."

That made her laugh again. "Oh, now I *have* to hear it. Come on. The raw, unvarnished truth. Give it up." She smiled at him. "What did you come home for?"

Giving her a sheepish look, he grimaced.

"Okay. You asked for it."

She waited expectantly. He took a deep breath, as though this was really tough to admit.

"I came home to get married."

CHAPTER TWO

THE smile froze on Diana's face. She blinked a few times, but she didn't say anything. Still, it felt as though Cam had shot an arrow through her heart.

It shouldn't have. She had no right to feel that way. But rights didn't wait on feelings. She stared at him, numb.

"Married!" she finally managed to say in a voice that was almost normal. "You?"

He coughed discreetly. "Well, that's not actually technically true."

She blinked. "Cam!"

One dark eyebrow rose provocatively. "Take it as a metaphor."

"A metaphor!"

He was driving her crazy. She shook her head. It was too early in the morning for mind games.

"Will you tell me what is really going on?"

He sighed. "Let's just say my mother has plans. She thinks it's time I settled down."

"Really." Diana took a deep breath. So…was he getting married or wasn't he? She was completely confused and beginning to get annoyed. "Who's the lucky girl?"

He looked at her blearily. "What girl?"

She wanted to throw something at him and it took all her strength not to snap back through clenched teeth. "The girl your mother wants you to marry."

"Oh." He frowned as though he didn't see how this mattered. "There's no specific girl. More like a category of women." He shrugged and raked fingers through his tousled hair, adding to his slightly bewildered look. "She has a whole roster picked out. She's ready to toss them at me, one at a time, and I'm supposed to catch one of them in the end."

Diana took a deep breath. This had been the most maddening conversation she'd had in a long time. The strongest impulse she had right now was to push him into the lake. How dare he come back here this way, raising old emotions, raising old hopeless dreams, and then slapping her back down with vague news of pending nuptials? Was this a joke? Or was he just trying to torture her?

But she knew that wasn't really it. He didn't have a clue how she had always felt about him, did he? Well, despite the position it put her in, that was probably a good thing.

Holding all that in as best she could, she looked out at the moonlight on the lake. Funny. Cam had come home and within minutes she had reverted back to being the little raggedy urchin who saw him as her white knight. For years she'd clung to his protection, dreaming that one day, when she was older, he would notice that she wasn't a little girl anymore, that she'd grown into a woman.

She sighed softly. It had always been a stupid goal, and still was. He was from a different world and only visited hers when it suited him. He wasn't available, in other words. And even if he were, what she'd done to her own situation alone would rule out any hopes she might have. She should know better by now. A little toughness of her own was in order. No more shabby girl with her nose pressed to the windowpane.

She tilted her head to the side, a bemused look on her face as she worked on developing a bit of inner strength.

"Let me get this straight," she challenged. "You came back because your mother wanted you to?"

He blinked at her groggily. "Sort of," he admitted.

She shook her head, eyes flashing. "Who are you and what have you done with the real Cam Van Kirk?" she demanded.

"You don't buy it, huh?" He looked at her, trying to be earnest but too groggy to manage it well. The swath of dark hair that had fallen down over his eyes wasn't helping. He was looking more vulnerable than she'd ever imagined he could look.

"Actually," he murmured, "neither do I."

"What does that mean?"

"Come on, Di, you know how it is. You grow up. You begin to realize what is really important in life. And you do things you never thought you would."

Sure, she knew how it was. But she couldn't quite

believe it. Not Cam. Not the young rebel she'd idol-
ized for so many years.

"What happened to you, Cam?" she asked softly,
searching his face.

He moved toward her, his hand reaching in to slide
along her chin and cup her cheek. She pulled back,
looking surprised at his touch and pushing his hand
away.

And as she did so, she forgot to hold her robe
closed and it fell open. Her rounded belly was obvious.

"Whoa," he said, jerking back and staring at it,
then looking up at her face. He shook his head as
though trying to clear it so that he could deal with
this new development. "What happened to *you?*"

"It's not that big a mystery," she said quickly, pulling the robe back. "It happens a lot, in case you
hadn't noticed."

He stared at her for a moment, his brow furled,
and moved a bit further away, purposefully keeping
his eyes averted from her midsection.

"Did you go and get married or something?" he
muttered uncomfortably.

She looked away and he frowned. The downside
of that possibility was suddenly clear to him. He
didn't want her to be married. Given a choice, he
would rather she wasn't pregnant, either. But that
was clearly settled and he could have no influence on
it. But the married part—no, if she were married he
was going to have to leave pretty quickly and probably not come back.

Why hadn't he considered this possibility? Somehow it had seemed natural to find her here, just where he'd left her. But of course things had changed. It had been ten years, after all.

"No, Cam," she said calmly. She pulled the robe in closer and looked out at the lake. "I'm not married."

Was he supposed to feel relief at that? Probably not. It was pretty selfish of him. But he couldn't help it. Still, it left a few problems behind. There had to be a man involved in this situation. Cam blinked hard and tried to act sober.

"Who's the daddy? Anyone I know?"

She shook her head. "It doesn't matter."

He shrugged. "Your call. So I guess you're doing this on your own, huh? Are you ready for that?"

She gave him a quick, fleeting smile. "I'm fine, Cam. I can handle this."

Something stirred inside him. Was it admiration? Or regret? He was a bit too groggy to tell. But the Diana he'd left behind had seemed to need him in so many ways. This one, not so much. That was probably a good thing. Wasn't it? If only he could think clearly, he might even be able to tell.

"Well, you know, if you need any help…" he began.

She turned on him, ready to be defensively self-reliant, and that was when she saw what looked like blood. It was trickling down out of his dark hair, making a rivulet in front of his ear. She gasped, then looked more closely, detecting a lot more that had started to dry against the collar of his shirt.

"Cam! What's this?" She touched it and showed him.

"Oh, just a little blood." He pulled out a handkerchief and dabbed at it.

"Blood!"

He gave her a melancholy smile. "I had a little accident. Just a little one."

She stared. "With your car?"

He nodded. "The car wouldn't go where I tried to get it to go. I kept pulling on the wheel and saying, 'Come on, car, we've got to get to the Van Kirk mansion,' and the stupid car kept saying, 'You know you'd rather go see Diana.'" He looked at her with mock earnestness. "So we crashed." He waved toward the woods. "We smashed right into a tree."

"Cam!"

"Just a little one. But I hit my head pretty hard. Didn't you hear it?"

She stared at him, shaking her head. "Oh, Cam."

"It wasn't very far away." He frowned. "I'm surprised you didn't hear it."

"I was asleep."

"Oh." He sighed and stretched out his arms, yawning. "Sleep, huh? I used to do that."

She noticed the dark circles under his eyes. For all his handsome features, he did look tired. "Maybe you shouldn't drink when you drive," she pointed out sharply.

"I didn't." He shook his head. "The drinking came later."

"Oh."

He shrugged. "Just a bottle I found in the trunk after the crash. I brought it along to tide me over while I waited on your pier for the sun to come up." He looked forlorn. "I was planning to invite myself for breakfast."

How did he manage to look so darn lovable in this ridiculous state?

"It's still a little early for breakfast." She sighed, then reached out and took his hand. "Come on."

"Okay," he said, and started off with her. "Where are we going?"

"Where else would the prodigal son go? I'm going to take you home."

The drive up to the Van Kirk mansion was steep and winding. Diana had made it often over the last few years in her little business van. Alice Van Kirk, Cam's mother, had been one of the first people to hire her fledgling floral styling company to provide fresh arrangements for the house once a week back when she'd originally started it.

The sky had begun to lighten, but true dawn lurked at least a half hour away. Still, there was enough light to let her see the turrets and spirals of the Van Kirk mansion ahead, reaching up over the tops of the eucalyptus trees, shrouded in the wisps of morning fog. As a child, she'd thought of the house as an enchanted castle where royalty lived high above the mundane lives of the valley people, and it looked very much like that now.

"Are they expecting you today?" she asked.

When she didn't get an answer, she glanced at Cam in the passenger's seat. He was drifting off to sleep.

"Hey!" She poked at him with her elbow. "I don't think you should let yourself sleep until you see a doctor. You might have a concussion or something."

"Hmm?" he responded, looking at her through mere slits where alert eyes should be.

"Cam, don't fall asleep," she ordered.

"Okay," he said, and his eyes immediately closed all the way.

"Oh!" she said, exasperated and poking him with her elbow again. "Here we are. Which door do you want?" She grimaced. "I don't suppose you have a key, though, do you?"

He didn't answer and his body looked as relaxed as a rag doll. With a sigh, she pulled into the back entrance, using the route she was used to. The servants' entrance she supposed they probably called it. The tradesmen's gate? Whatever, it was just off the kitchen and gave handy access to the parts of the house where she brought flower arrangements once a week. She rarely ran into any of the Van Kirks when she came. She usually dealt with Rosa Munez, the housekeeper. Rosa was a conscientious employee, but she doubted the woman would be up this early.

"How am I going to get you in there?" she asked, shaking her head as she gazed at the dark house.

Turning, she reached out and pushed his dark hair back off his forehead. His face was so handsome, his features so classically perfect. For just a moment, she ached, longing to find a place in his arms. But she couldn't do that. She had to be tough.

"Cam," she said firmly, shaking his shoulder. "Come on, wake up."

"Okay," he murmured, but his eyes didn't open.

This made things a bit awkward.

Slipping out of the car, she went to the door and looked at the brass handle, loath to try it. She knew it would be locked, and she assumed there was a security system on the house. Everyone was obviously still asleep. What the heck was she going to do?

Stepping back, she looked up at the windows, wondering if she could climb up and get in that way, then picturing the embarrassment as she hung from a drainpipe, nightgown billowing in the breeze, while alarm bells went off all through the house. Not a good bet.

Turning, she went back to the car and slid into the driver's seat.

"Cam, I don't know what we're going to do," she said.

He was sound asleep and didn't even bother to twitch. She sighed with resignation. She was going to have to wake up the whole house, wasn't she? Now she regretted having come without changing into day clothes. But she hadn't been sure she could keep Cam in one place if she left him to go change, and she'd thought she would just drop him at his doorway and make a run for home. She should have known nothing was ever that easy.

"Okay. If I've got to do it, I might as well get it over with," she said, leaving the car again and going back to the door. Her finger was hovering half an inch from the doorbell and she was bracing for the sound explosion she was about to unleash on the unsuspecting occupants, when the door suddenly opened and she found herself face-to-face with Cam's sister, Janey.

"Diana? What in the world are you doing here?" she demanded.

"Janey!" Diana was immediately aware of how odd she must look standing on the Van Kirk doorstep in her filmy nightgown and fluffy white robe. The shabby slippers didn't help, either.

Janey, on the other hand, looked trendy and stylish in high end jogging togs. A tall, pretty woman about a year younger than Diana, she was evidently up for an early morning run and determined to look chic about it. Diana couldn't help but have a quick catty thought wondering which of the local squirrels and chipmunks she might be trying to impress. But she pushed that aside and felt nothing but relief to have a member of the family appear at the door.

She and Cam's sister had known each other forever but had never been friends. Janey had been aware of the close ties between Diana and her brother, and she'd made it very clear in very public ways that she didn't approve. But that was years ago. When they saw each other now, they weren't exactly warm, but they were perfectly civil.

"Janey," Diana said, sighing with relief. "I've got Cam in the car. He was in an accident."

"What?"

"Not too bad," she reassured her quickly. "He seems to be basically okay, but I think a doctor ought to look him over. And…well…" She winced. "He's been drinking so…"

"You're kidding." Janey followed her to the car and then they were both fussing over her brother.

"Cam, you blockhead, wake up," Janey ordered, shaking his shoulder. "We haven't seen you in years and this is the way you arrive?"

He opened one eye. "Janey? I thought I recognized your dulcet tones."

She shook her head. "Come on. I'll help you up to your room. I'm sure Mother will want to call Dr. Timmer."

"I don't need Dr. Timmer," he grumbled, though he did begin to leverage himself out of the car. "If Diana can take care of herself, I can take care of myself." He tried to pound his own chest and missed. "We're a pair of independents, Diana and I."

Janey gave him her arm and a quizzical look. "I have no idea what you're talking about," she said crisply. "Come on. We'll let your friend get back to her…whatever."

"Diana is my best friend," he murmured, sounding almost melancholy. "My favorite person in this valley. Always has been."

Janey chose that moment to notice Diana's baby bulge. Stopping short, she gasped. "Cam! Oh, no!"

Despite his condition, he immediately recognized the way her mind was trending and he groaned. "Listen, Janey, I just got into town at about 2:00 a.m. Not even I could get a lady with child that fast."

"Humph," she harrumphed, throwing Diana a look that took in everything about her pregnancy and the fact that she was running around the countryside in her nightgown, delivering a rather inebriated Cam to his old homestead. It was obvious all this looked pretty darn fishy to her.

Diana almost laughed aloud. If Janey only knew the irony involved here. "Can you handle him without me?" she asked the other woman. "I'd like to get home and try to get some sleep. I do have an appointment back here with your mother at eleven."

"Go, go," Janey said, waving a hand dismissively and turning away.

But Cam didn't turn with her. He stayed where he was, looking back at Diana. "I was just getting used to having you around again, Di," he said. "A little later, when I've had some sleep…"

"You'll be busy getting caught up on all the family news," Janey said quickly. "And learning to give up living like a drifter."

"Like a drifter?" Cam looked up as though that reminded him of something and Diana laughed.

"Watch out, or he'll break out into song on you," she warned his sister as she turned for her car. As she walked away, she heard the Cam's voice warbling, "'Here I go again…'" She grinned.

Cam was back. What did this mean? Right now, it meant she was full of sadness and happiness at the same time.

"The thrill of victory and the agony of defeat," she murmured nonsensically as she began the drive down the hill. A moment later, tears were streaming down her face and she had no idea why.

But Cam was back. Good or bad, things were going to change. She could feel it in the air.

CHAPTER THREE

CAM woke to a pounding headache and a bunch of bad memories. It didn't help to open his bleary eyes and find the view the same as it had been when he was in high school. That made him want to close the world out and go back to sleep again. Maybe he would wake up in a better place.

No such luck. He opened his eyes again a few minutes later and nothing had changed. He was still a wimp for having let himself be talked into coming back here. Still an unfit driver for having crashed his car just because of a freak tire blowout. Still an idiot for having had too much to drink and letting it show.

And still bummed at finding Diana more appealing than ever and at the same time, totally unavailable. Life wasn't exactly glowing with happy discovery for him right now.

Then there had been the humiliating way he'd returned to the green green grass of home. His mother had tried to pretend he was fine and gave him the usual hugs and kisses a mother would bestow upon a returning miscreant. But, his father barely acknowledged his return. And Janey was plotting ways to undermine him and making no bones about it. He groaned. The outlook wasn't bright.

There was one more gauntlet to brave—the most important one right now—his grandfather. There was no point in putting it off any longer.

He made the water in his shower as cold and stinging as he could stand. He needed to wash away the previous day and start over. Maybe if he could just start fresh...

But he already knew it was going to take all his will to be able to stay and do what he'd promised he would do—save the family business, and in so doing, hopefully, save the family.

Funny that it would be up to him. When he'd left ten years before, his grandfather had just disowned him and his father had refused to take his side. His mother was upset about his choice of friends, and his sister was angling to take over his position in the family. To some extent, a somewhat typical twenty-one-year-old experience. But it had all been a culmination of years of unhappiness and bad relations, and something had snapped inside him. He'd had enough. He was going and he was never coming back.

Leaving Diana behind had been the only hard part. At eighteen, she'd still been gawky, a coltlike girl whose antics made him laugh with quick affection. She thought she needed him, though he knew very well she was strong enough to handle things on her own. She was fun and interesting and she was also the only person who seemed to understand what he was talking about most of the time.

But that was then. Things were different now. Diana had proven she could make it on her own, no problem. She'd done just fine without him. And she now belonged to somebody else. She could deny it, but the facts were right there, front and center. She was pregnant. That meant there was a man in her life. Even if he was out of the picture for the moment, he was there. How could it be any other way?

And all that was just as well, actually. Without that complication, he knew he could have easily fallen in love with her. He'd known that from the moment he saw her coming down to the lake, looking like an angel. He responded to her in a way he never did with other women, a combination of past experiences and current attraction. Yes, he could fall hard. And falling in love was something he was determined never to do again.

For just a moment he thought about Gina, the woman he'd lived with for two years and had almost married. But thoughts of Gina only brought pain, so he shrugged them away.

He needed to focus on the purpose of his return. He needed to get ready to face his grandfather.

Diana parked in the same spot she'd used earlier that morning. This time there was a buzz of activity all around the compound. Workmen were putting new doors on the multiple garages and a painter was freshening up the long white fence that edged the driveway. Across the patio, two men were digging postholes for what looked to be a new barbecue center. With all this action, she could see she wasn't going to need to contemplate a break-in this time. Sighing with satisfaction, she slid out of the car and made her way to the back entrance.

She'd traded in her nightgown for a sleek pantsuit she'd picked up in Carmel a few months before. Luckily she could still fit into it. She'd chosen it out of her closet specifically to rival anything Janey might be wearing. It had a high collar and a loose jacket that hid her belly and she knew she looked pretty good in it—always a confidence booster.

The back door was propped open and she went on into the huge kitchen, where Rosa, elbow deep in flour, waved at her from across the room.

"Mrs. Van Kirk is out in the rose garden," she called. "She asked that you meet her out there to go over some new plans."

"Fine." She waved back at the cheery woman and headed into the house. She'd been here often enough lately to know her way around. This place that had seemed so special to her as a child, and then so scary when she was friends with Cam but never invited in, was now a part of her workspace.

Walking down the long hall, gleaming with Brazilian cherry hardwood, she glanced into the library, and then the parlor, to check on the large arrangements she'd brought just a few days before. Both looked pretty good. Ever since she'd stressed to Rosa that the stems could use a trim and fresh water every few days, her masterpieces were holding up better than they had before.

The Van Kirk mansion was beautiful in a way few houses could be. The quality of the original materials and workmanship shone through. The rich past and full history just added luster. It made her happy and proud just to be here, walking its beautiful halls.

As she rounded the stairwell to head into the dining room and out the French doors, Cam surprised her by arriving down the stairs and stopping right in front of her.

"Good morning, Miss Collins," he said smoothly. "You're back."

She cocked her head to the side and looked him over, fighting hard to suppress her reaction as her heart began a frantic dance in her chest. Here he was. It was really true. She hadn't dreamed what had happened the night before. Cam was back in her life, just when she'd thought it could never be.

He looked so good. Morning sunlight was even more flattering to his handsome face than starlight had been. Dressed in khakis and a blue polo shirt that matched his eyes, he looked hard and muscular as an athlete but gentle as a lover at the same time.

The perfect man—hadn't that always been the problem? She'd never found anyone better. It made her half-angry, half-thrilled, and practically hopeless. Now that he was back, what was going to happen to her peace of mind?

One casual meeting and she was already straying into thoughts she'd vowed to stay away from. A simple look into that silver-blue gaze and her breath was harder to find and she was thinking moonlight and satin sheets and violins on the terrace. Given half a chance, she would be sliding into his arms, raising her lips for kisses....

No! She couldn't let that happen.

Very quickly, so quickly she hoped he didn't even notice, she pulled herself up short and forced a refocus. Cam was a friend and that was all he could ever be.

So think friend, she ordered herself. Lover thoughts are not allowed.

"Yes," she agreed, putting steel in her spine. "I'm... I'm back."

His gaze swept over her. "You're looking particularly lovely today," he noted, a slight smile softening the corners of his wide mouth.

The corners of her own mouth quirked. "As opposed to what I looked like yesterday, after midnight?" she said, half teasing.

His grin was crooked. "Oh, no. After midnight you looked even better. Only..."

"Did you see a doctor last night?" she broke in quickly, eager to forestall any flirting he might have in mind. They had to keep their relationship on a certain level and she was bound and determined she would be the watchdog of that if he wouldn't be.

"I guess so." He shrugged. "I was pretty much out of it."

"Yes, you were."

Looking chagrined, he put his hand over his heart

and gazed earnestly into her eyes. "I don't drink, you know. Not really. Hardly ever."

If she wasn't careful, he was going to make her laugh, and that was almost as dangerous as making her swoon.

"So you said."

"And it's true. If I'd found a box of crackers in the trunk of the car instead of a bottle of booze, I'd have been all crumbs last night, instead of the sauced serenader I devolved into."

She choked and his eyes sparkled with amusement at his own joke.

"But I do want to apologize. I was rude last night. I took over your lake and ruined your sleep and generally made myself into a damned nuisance."

He meant it. He was really apologizing. She met his gaze in solemn candor. "You did."

"And I'm sorry." His blue eyes were filled with tragic regret.

She laughed softly, shaking her head. She'd missed him, missed his candor, missed his teasing and missed what often actually seemed to be his sincere sensitivity to what she was feeling. But she had to admit, that sensitivity could sometimes slosh over into a subtle mockery and she was afraid he might be working his way in that general direction right now.

Still, they were friends, weren't they? She was allowed to act like a friend, at least.

"I'm not," she said firmly. "I'm not a bit sorry."

She smiled up into his face. "Despite everything, it is good to have you back in the neighborhood."

"'Despite everything,' you say." He looked skeptical. "Seriously?"

Her smile deepened. "Of course."

The warmth between them began to sizzle and she knew it was time to pull back. But it felt like resisting quicksand to do it. If only she could allow herself this small island of pleasure. Soon enough she would leave and hopefully wall off any further contact with Cam, except the most casual and occasional kind. Would it really ruin everything to let herself enjoy him, just for this warm spring morning?

Yes. He was looking at her mouth and it sent shivers all through her. She couldn't risk even a tiny moment or two of weakness. Determined, she pulled away.

"I drove by to look at your car this morning," she said over her shoulder as she started to walk toward the French doors that opened onto the gardens.

"How's it doing?" he asked, walking with her.

She glanced at him sideways. "You didn't tell me you'd had a tire blowout."

"Didn't I?"

"No." She stopped in the doorway, turning to face him again. "It's too bad. I sort of liked your story about fighting the wheel in order to get to my place."

He snapped his fingers. "That was exactly what I was doing when the blowout occurred."

She grinned. "Right."

Mrs. Van Kirk, wearing a wide-brimmed sun hat and carrying a basket filled with cut flowers, was out among her prized rosebushes and as she turned, she spotted the two of them and began to wave. "Yoo-hoo! My dear, I'm over here."

Diana lifted her hand to wave back and said out of the corner of her mouth, "Who's she talking to, you or me?"

He stood beside her in the doorway, looking out. "I'd say it's a toss-up."

She glanced at him. "She's your mother."

His eyes narrowed suspiciously as he looked out at where she stood, waving at them. "Sometimes I wonder," he muttered.

Diana didn't wonder. In fact, she didn't have a doubt. Cam looked so much like his mother, it was cute—or frightening, depending on how you looked at it.

"Well, I'm going to go to her," Diana said, turning to leave.

He hung back. "I'm not coming with you. I've got a command audience with my grandfather."

"Oh, no." Stopping, she looked back at him. "Is this the first you've seen him since you came back?"

He nodded, a faraway look in his eyes. "This should be interesting."

To say the least. Diana winced, remembering all those old, painful arguments with the old man when he was younger. She could see by the look on his face that he wasn't as optimistic about the coming meeting as he might pretend.

"I'm surprised you're not taking in a bodyguard," she said lightly, only half joking. "I remember those sessions you used to have with him." Her eyes widened as she recalled some especially wild fights they'd had and she shuddered. "He put you through the wringer."

Cam nodded and he didn't smile. "That he did." His gaze skimmed over her face. "You want to come with me?"

She reared back. "Not on your life. When I was suggesting a bodyguard, I was thinking more along the lines of one of those burly fellows digging posts for the new barbecue center out back."

He laughed. "I think I can handle my grandfather," he said. "I'm older now. Wiser." He cocked an eyebrow. "More agile."

Diana shook her head, suppressing a grin. "And besides," she reminded him. "From what I hear, he's often bedridden. I guess that would give you an advantage."

He laughed again. "Exactly."

Word was that his grandfather was in rapidly failing health. With Cam's father spending most of his time at spa resorts that specialized in "rest cures" and his sister reportedly caught up in playing musical husbands, that left Cam to support his mother and help make some decisions. She was beginning to realize that those circumstances were probably part of the reason he'd agreed to come back home.

"I'll come out and join you if I survive."

"Okay." She winced as she started out through the

rosebushes. She shouldn't be encouraging any of this "joining" or chatting or anything else with Cam. Her goal coming in had been to have the meeting with Mrs. Van Kirk and then get out of here as quickly as possible. It was becoming more and more clear that staying away from Cam had to be her first priority.

The older woman came toward her, smiling.

"Oh, my dear, I'm so glad to see you. Thank you so much for coming by. Come sit with me in the garden and Rosa will bring us some nice tea."

Diana smiled back and followed her to the little gazebo at the far side of the flower garden. Her relationship with Cam's mother had undergone a complete transformation in the last few years. When she was a teenager, she knew very well the woman had considered her a guttersnipe who would contaminate her son if she didn't keep a constant vigil. The one time Cam had tried to bring her into the house, Mrs. Van Kirk had practically barred the door with her own plump body.

Years later, after Cam was long gone and Diana had started her flower business, the woman had hired her periodically, acting rather suspicious at first, but warming to her little by little as the quality of her work became apparent. By now, her affection for the girl she used to scorn was amazingly obvious to everyone—and sometimes resented by Janey.

But Diana was comfortable meeting with her, and she settled into a chair across from her in the gazebo, thinking once again how similar some of her features were to Cam's. She'd been a beautiful woman and was still very attractive in a plush sort of way. Her hair was auburn where Cam's was almost black, and her look was soft rather than hard, but she had the same blue eyes and sweet smile he did.

"I want to tell you how much I appreciate you bringing my son home last night after that terrible accident," Mrs. Van Kirk began. "He was certainly out of sorts for a while, but Dr. Timmer assures us there will be no lasting injuries. He was so fortunate it happened so close to your place." Her gaze sharpened and she frowned. "How exactly did you know the accident had happened?"

"Just lucky I guess," Diana said breezily. This was not the time to go into reasons why Cam felt at home enough on her property to use it as a refuge. "I was glad to be able to help."

"Yes," she said, gazing at Diana as though seeing her with new eyes. "Well, anyway, we'll have tea." She signaled toward the kitchen, where Rosa had appeared at the door. The housekeeper waved that she understood, and Mrs. Van Kirk turned back to the subject at hand.

"Now, I want you to take a look at my new roses." She pointed out a pair of new English heirlooms. "What do you think of them?"

"Oh, they're lovely. That soft violet color is just brilliant."

She looked pleased. "Yes, I've hired a new rose expert to come in twice a week and advise me. I want to make sure I'm getting the right nutrients to my little babies. He's very expensive but I'm so pleased with his work." She looked up. "Perhaps you know him. Andre Degregor?"

Diana nodded. "Yes, he's quite good." And an internationally recognized rose expert. "Expensive" was probably putting it mildly.

"You seem to be doing a lot of work on the estate," she noted, giving the older woman an opening to get the conversation back on track.

"Yes." She settled down in her seat and gave Diana a significant smile. "And that's why I wanted to see you. I'm going to begin a major project. And I want you to take a primary role in the preparations."

"A project?" she echoed brightly. What type of project would involve a flower stylist? She was beginning to feel a faint thread of trepidation about this. "What sort of project?"

"It's something I've been thinking about for a long time." Her eyes were shining with excitement. "I'm planning a whole series of various social gatherings—teas, dinner parties, barbecues, card parties—all culminating in a major ball at the end of next month."

"Oh my," Diana said faintly.

"On top of that, we'll be hosting quite a few guests between functions. I've hired a wonderful caterer from San Francisco—for the whole month!" She laughed with delight at the thought. "And I want to hire you for the decorating. If all goes as planned, this will be quite an undertaking."

"It certainly sounds like it."

"Now, I'm going to want you to put some extra

effort into your weekly arrangements and prepare to work up an entire decorating plan for the various parties."

"Really." Diana's smile felt stiff and artificial as she began to mull over the implications. She had a very bad feeling about this. Ordinarily she would be welcoming the new business, but something told her she wasn't going to like this once she got the full picture.

Rosa arrived with a tray containing a sterling silver teapot and two lovely, egg-shell thin porcelain cups with saucers, along with a plate of crisp, slender cookies. Out of the corner of her eye, Diana could see Janey making her way into the garden and she offered up a fervent prayer that the young woman would find her way out again before stopping in to see them. She had enough to deal with here without Janey's caustic comments.

"You have such a good eye for decorating, Diana. I'm really going to be counting on you to help make this very special."

"What is the theme going to be?" she asked as Rosa poured the tea.

"Well, what could be more obvious?" She waved a hand dramatically and leaned forward. "I'm planning to introduce Cam back into the society he should have been a part of all these years," she said emphatically. "That's the theme."

"The theme," Janey said, flouncing into the gazebo and flopping down into a wicker chair, "is that Mother wants to marry Cam off to the most important socialite she can find for him, and preferably the one with the most money. He's raw meat for the voracious upper crust marriage market."

Her words stung, but Diana kept smiling. After all, she'd known this was coming, hadn't she? Cam had said as much, though he'd tried to take it back. He'd come back home to get married.

"Janey!" Mrs. Van Kirk said sharply.

Her daughter shrugged. "It's true, Mother, and you know it. We need the money."

The woman's sense of decorum was being challenged by her daughter's gloomy vision of reality and she didn't like it at all.

"Janey, I will thank you to keep your acid tongue to yourself. We have no financial problems. We've always been able to live just the way we've wanted to live. We're going to be just fine."

"Dream on, Mom." Janey looked at Diana and shrugged. "She won't look out and see the tsunami coming. But you might as well know it's on its way."

The older woman pretended not to hear. "Now, I want you to think this over, Diana. I'm hoping you'll be free." She sighed happily. "Such a lot of activity! It will be just like the old days."

"What old days are those, Mother?" Janey asked, the tiniest hint of sarcasm edging her tone.

"Oh, I don't know." Her mother frowned at her. "Things were more hectic when you children were younger. We had parties. Remember all those picnics we had when you were sixteen? It's been a long time since we've had an actual event here. It's exciting, don't you think?"

Diana was torn. On the one hand, she liked Cam's mother, despite her eccentricities—or maybe because of them. On the other hand, she didn't want to be involved in roping Cam into a marriage—any marriage, good or not. The very thought was darn depressing. It would be awful to see him make a bad marriage just for his mother's sake, but it would be almost worse to see him falling in love with some beautiful young debutante.

Either way, Diana would be the loser.

But that was crazy and she knew it. Cam would marry someone. He had to. It was only natural. She only wished he would do it far away where she didn't have to know about it.

"Poor Cam is going to be sold off to the highest bidder," Janey said. "I wish him better luck in marriage than I've had. But then, I tend to marry penniless jerks, so there you go."

"Janey, please," Mrs. Van Kirk said icily. She'd had enough. "I'd like to talk to Diana alone. We need to plan."

For a moment, Diana thought Janey was going to refuse to leave, but she finally rolled her eyes and rose with a look of disdain on her face. Diana watched her go and for once, she wished she could go along.

How was she going to tell Cam's mother that she couldn't do this? She hated to disappoint her, especially when she was so excited about her project.

But the situation was downright impossible. She was going to have to find the right words…somehow.

And in the meantime, she was going to have to find a way to keep Cam at a distance.

CHAPTER FOUR

FILLED with comforting tea and discomforting misgivings, Diana skirted the house as she made her way back toward her car, hoping to avoid seeing Cam.

No such luck. He came around a corner of the house and met her under the vine-covered pergola.

"Hey," he said, looking surprised.

"Hay is for horses," she said back tersely, giving him barely a glance and trying to pass him.

"Channeling our school days, are we?" He managed to fill the passageway, giving her no room to flee. "I guess the meeting didn't go so well."

She looked up at him and sighed. "Oh, it went fine. I'm just a little jumpy today." She made a show of looking at her watch. "I've really got to go. I'm late."

He didn't buy it. Folding his arms across his chest, he cocked his head to the side and regarded her narrowly. "Late for what?"

She hesitated, not ready to make something up on the fly. "None of your business," she said instead. "I just need to go."

He stepped forward, suddenly looking concerned, glancing down at her slightly protruding belly. "Are you okay? Do you need help?"

He was being too darn nice. Her eyes stung. If he kept this up, she might end up crying, and that would be a disaster. Shaking her head, she sighed again and decided she might as well tell him the truth. Lifting her chin resolutely, she forced herself to meet his gaze.

"I'm going to be perfectly honest, Cam. I...I need to keep my distance from you. With all these plans and all that's going on, I can't spend time with you. It just won't work."

He looked completely baffled. "What are you talking about?"

She took a deep breath and plunged in. "Your mother just spent an hour telling me all about the plans to find you a wife. She wants me to help." She took a deep breath, praying her voice wouldn't break. "I don't think I can be involved in that."

"Diana, it's not a problem." His laugh was short and humorless. "She can look all she wants. I'm not getting married."

She blinked up at him, not sure why he would say such a thing. "But you said last night..."

He gave her his famously crooked grin. "I think I said a lot of crazy things last night. Don't hold me to any of them."

"Cam..."

"I'll tell you one thing." He grimaced and raked his fingers through his dark hair, making it stand on end in a way she found eminently endearing. "I'm never going to drink alcohol again."

"Good. You'll live longer and be healthier." She shook her head. She wasn't really worried about that. "Why did you say you'd come back to get married if you don't mean to do it? Maybe the alcohol brought out your true feelings."

He groaned. "What are you now, a psychologist in your spare time? Forget it. This is a 'don't try this at home' situation." He shook his head, looking at her earnestly. "Diana, my mother has been trying to get me to come home and get married for years. I've resisted. I'm still resisting. But she's still trying. That's all there is to it."

She frowned suspiciously. "Okay, you're saying you didn't come home to get married?"

"Of course not."

She waved a hand in the air. "But then why is your mother planning all this?"

"She's always planning things. That's how she lives her life." He shrugged. "Let her go on planning. It'll keep her busy and out of the way."

She frowned, not sure she could accept that. "I don't know."

Reaching out, he took hold of her shoulders, fingers curling around her upper arms, and stared down into her face. "Okay, Diana, here's the honest truth. My mother can make all kinds of plans, for all kinds of parties. She can even plan a wedding if she wants to. But I'm not marrying anybody." His added emphatically, "Anybody. Ever."

Anybody...ever...

The words echoed in her head but it was hard to think straight with his warm hands holding her and his hard body so close. A breeze tumbled through the yard and a cloud of pink bougainvillea blossoms showered down around them. She looked up into his starry blue eyes and had to resist getting lost there.

"What happened to you, Cam?" She heard the words as though from far away and it took a moment to realize the voice was her own.

He hesitated, staring down into her eyes as though he didn't want to let her go. The warning signs were there. She had to pull away. And yet, it seemed almost impossible. When her body wouldn't react, she had only her voice to reach for as a defensive weapon.

"Cam, what is it? What do you have against marriage?"

Her words seemed to startle him and his head went back. He stared at her for a few seconds, then grimaced.

"Once bitten, twice shy," he muttered, releasing her and making a half turn away from where she stood, shoving his hands down into his pockets.

Watching him, shock shot through her system and she barely avoided gasping. What was he saying? Did he really mean what it seemed he meant?

"You've been married?" she said, coming down to earth with a thump.

"No," he responded, looking back at her, his eyes hard. "But I did come close. Not a pretty story, and

I'm not about to tell it. Just understand I've been in-oculated. I've stared into the abyss and I've learned from that. I won't need another warning."

She didn't know why she was so disturbed by what he was saying. He was a normal man, after all. No, strike that, he was an abnormally attractive man, but with a normal man's needs and desires. Of course he'd had women in his life these last ten years. Naturally he'd been in love. What could be more ordinary? Just because *she* was a nut case and couldn't forget Cam for long enough to have a rela-tionship with another man didn't have any bearing on his experiences. Some amateur psychologist she was; she couldn't even fix her own life, much less dabble in his.

"Well, if that's true, you'd better tell your mother," she said, grasping at the remnants of their conversa-tion to steady herself on. "It's not fair to let her give parties and invite people."

"I said we should let her make plans. I never said she could put on any parties."

She shook her head. "That doesn't make a lot of sense."

"Don't you think I know that?"

He looked so troubled, she wanted to reach out and comfort him. If only she had the right to do it. But then she remembered—even if she had that right, she would have had to stop herself. She couldn't risk doing anything that might draw them closer. She had to think of her child.

"I've got to go," she said, turning and starting toward where her car was parked.

"I'll walk you out to your car," he said, coming along with her.

She walked quickly, hoping to stay at least an arm's length from him. She just had to get away.

"Diana's Floral Creations," he said aloud, reading the sign painted in pretty calligraphy on the side of her tiny little van. "Interesting name."

She threw him a look over her shoulder. "It's pretty generic, I know. I'm creative with flowers, not with words."

"No, I meant it. I like it. It suits you."

She hesitated, wanting to get into her car and go, but at the same time, not wanting to leave him.

"What made you go into this flower business stuff?" he asked her, actually seeming interested.

She smiled. This was a subject she loved. She was on firmer footing here. "I've always been good with plants. And I needed something to do on my own. I took horticulture classes in college so I had some background in it. Then I worked in a flower shop part-time for a couple of years."

He nodded, his gaze skimming over her and his admiration for her obvious. That gave her the impetuous to go on, tell him more.

"It's really a wonderful line of work. Flowers are so special, and used for such special occasions. We use them to celebrate a birthday, or a baby being born or two people getting married—or even the life of someone who has died. They add something to the most emotional times of our lives. And that interests and excites me."

"And also just to decorate a room," he reminded her, since that was what she was doing here at his house.

"Yes," she agreed. "But usually flowers are used to represent an emotion. They're symbols of feelings people have a hard time expressing in words." She stopped, coloring a bit, not used to being so effusive about her line of work. For some reason, she'd felt the need to tell him, explain. Well, now she had. She turned to her car, ready to make her escape.

But he stopped her once again.

"I'm glad you have something you love so much," he told her. "The business I've been running is a bit more prosaic." He hesitated, then grimaced.

"Okay, Di," he said, looking down at her. "I might as well get this off my chest. Here it is. The real reason I came home, the reason behind everything I'm going to be doing for the foreseeable future."

She waited, heart beating, wondering if she really wanted to hear this. She knew instinctively that whatever it was he was about to reveal would have the effect of tying her more closely to this family—this crazy outlandish bunch of people who had once scorned her and her family. And now he was going to tell her something that would make her care about them. It didn't seem altogether fair. But then, life wasn't often fair, was it?

He turned from her, flexed his shoulders and then turned back.

"There won't be any parties. There can't be any parties. The fact is, there's no money."

Diana heard what he said, but she couldn't quite digest it. Janey had said things that had let her know money was probably a consideration, even a concern, but to say there wasn't any... That just seemed crazy. These were the Van Kirks. They had always been the richest family in town.

"What? What are you saying?"

"I've just been talking to Grandfather, finding out how bad it is. He already outlined the situation to me over the phone a few weeks ago. That's why I came home. And now I know the rest of the story." He took a deep breath and a pained expression flashed across his face. "My family is on the verge of losing everything."

Her head came up. Despite the things his sister had said, she would never have dreamed it could come to this. "You mean bankruptcy?"

He nodded. "I came home for one reason, Di. I came home to try to save my parents from losing their home."

"Oh, Cam, no."

He went on, detailing where the problems lay and how long they had festered, but Diana was thinking about his mother and remembering how she'd seemed oblivious to the dangers as Janey had taunted her with them. She'd thought Cam's sister was exaggerating, but it seemed she was wrong.

She knew without having him explain it that the issue went back years and years. Many of those old fights Cam had with his grandfather centered around the old man's fear that Cam would end up being a drone like his father was. She'd been vaguely aware at the time that Cam's dad had tried running the family affairs and had failed miserably, mostly through his own weaknesses. The grandfather had been trying to groom Cam to be a better manager. Even though Cam hadn't stayed here to take his father's place, it seemed he'd found his way in the world and made something of himself. And now it was Cam whom the grandfather had turned to in hopes of getting the family out of this mess. She wondered if he really had the experience. She knew he had the family background for it. And with his grandfather as his mentor, surely there would be hope that he could use his younger energy to turn things around.

No wonder Cam had been called back. Someone had to rescue the family, she supposed. Why he'd decided to let them pull him back, after all he'd said when he left, was another question, one she couldn't answer.

But there was no doubt the situation was dire. Bankruptcy sounded so radical. And the Van Kirks not living in the Van Kirk mansion? Unthinkable.

Still, this couldn't be her problem. She couldn't let it be. The more Cam talked, the more she wanted to go to him, to throw herself into his arms, to tell him she would help in any way she could. But she couldn't do that. She had to get out of this situation. Her baby had to be the main focus of her life, the reason for living. She couldn't get distracted by old longings. She had to get out of here and leave temptation behind. And that meant leaving Cam behind.

"I'm sorry all this is happening," she told him, trying to be firm. "But I really can't be involved. Do you understand?" She gazed up at him earnestly.

He nodded slowly. "Sure. Of course. You have your baby to think of. You need a calm environment. Don't worry about Mother. I'll explain things to her."

A few minutes later, she was in her car and heading for home again, only this time she wasn't crying. Her face was set with determination. She was going to be strong if it killed her.

Diana was up a tree—quite literally—a black oak to be exact. It wasn't something she usually did and that was probably why she seemed to be so bad at it. It was a typical well-meaning rescue mission gone awry.

She been jolted awake early that morning by small, piercing cries from outside. When she'd wrapped herself in a blanket and stepped out to find what tiny creature was in distress, she'd been led, step by step, to the big old black oak. Looking up, she saw the cutest little black kitten staring down at her with huge golden eyes.

"Oh, no, you don't," she'd grumbled at the time, turning back toward the house. "I know very well you'll have an easier time getting down from there than I would in going up. You can do it. You just have to try." She glanced over her shoulder at the little one as she returned to the house. "And then I hope you'll go back wherever you came from."

That had been hours earlier. In the meantime she'd made herself breakfast, taken the time to do a bit of bookkeeping for her business and returned some phone calls, including one from her attorney cousin Ben Lanker in Sacramento. It seemed their uncle Luke, the last survivor from the older generation, had died a week before and left a piece of property in the mountains to the two of them, jointly, as the only remaining descendants in their family. She'd received something in the mail that she hadn't understood, but Ben explained what was going on and suggested they get together and talk it over.

She was tempted to put him off. She already had the only piece of land she'd ever wanted and from what Ben said, the inheritance from Uncle Luke might turn out to be more trouble than it was worth.

But then she remembered that she'd been suspicious of her cousin in the past and she decided maybe she'd better look into the facts.

"One shouldn't look an inheritance in the mouth, I suppose," she muttered to herself.

It could just be that Ben was trying to pull a fast one. He had that slippery lawyer way about him. So she told him she would get back to him soon and find a time when they could get together and go over the situation to see what would be best.

In the meantime, the little cries had grown more pitiful with time, wearing away at her like water torture. When storm clouds began to threaten, she finally decided she had to bite the bullet and climb up or she wouldn't be able to live with herself when the worst happened. She kept picturing the exhausted kitten losing all strength and falling to its death through the gnarled branches.

"I'm coming," she said reassuringly as she hoisted herself up with a foothold on the first major branch, regretting that she didn't have any ladders tall enough to do this job. "Just hold on."

It had been a while, but she'd climbed this very tree often when she was young. The only problem was, she wasn't all that young anymore. Muscles and instincts she'd had at that age—not to mention the fearlessness—seemed to be gone. And the tree was a lot bigger. And she was pregnant. To her surprise, that threw her balance off in ways she hadn't expected. But she kept climbing, reaching for the kitten. And every time her fingers almost touched it, the silly little bugger backed away and climbed higher.

"This is not going to work," she said aloud, staring up at the infuriating cat. "I'm not going any farther. You're going to have to come to me."

Fat chance. The golden eyes just got bigger and the cries just got more pathetic.

"Oh, never mind," Diana said, turning away and giving up. And then she looked down.

Somehow, she'd come further than she'd thought. The ground looked very far away. And as she clung to a space between a branch and the trunk, she began to realize she was going to have a heck of a time getting down.

And the kitten was still crying.

"You little brat," Diana muttered to herself. "Look what you've done. You've got me up a tree. How am I going to get down?"

"Meow," the kitten chirped.

And the rain began.

"I can't believe this," she moaned as drops began to spatter all around her. "Why is everything going wrong at once?"

And that was when she heard Cam's car arrive.

"Oh, no!"

She hadn't seen him for the last two days. She'd almost begun to think he might have taken her last words to heart and might just let her be alone, not try to pull her into his life again. But here he was, so she supposed that had been a bad guess.

She sat very still and watched as he turned off the engine and slipped out of the car. He looked around at the trees and the lake, but his gaze didn't rise high enough to notice her and she kept quiet while he went to the front door and knocked. The rain was still light, but it was beginning to make rivulets down her neck.

"Diana?" he called. "You home?"

Now it was time to make a decision. What was she going to do—let him know she was stuck in a tree? Or just sit here and let him drive away again and try to figure out how she was going to get down on her own in a rainstorm?

It was a rather big decision. She felt like a fool sitting here. And yet, she was liable to break her neck if she tried to get down by herself. It was pretty obvious what her decision was going to have to be, but she put it off as long as possible. She couldn't even imagine the humiliation she was going to feel when she began to call out to him, pitiful as the little animal scrabbling around on the branch above her.

Luckily she didn't have to do that. He heard the kitten screeching and finally looked up into the tree on his own. She looked down. He looked up. He fought hard to hold back a big old grin that threatened to take over his handsome face. She tried hard not to stick her tongue out at him. They both failed.

He came over and stood right under where she was. "Good view of the valley from up there?" he asked.

"The best," she answered, her nose in the air. "I come up here all the time."

"Do you?" He bit back a short laugh. "I see you have your faithful feline companion with you. What's the kitty's name?"

"Once you name them, you own them," she warned. For some unknown reason, she was unable to keep the annoyance from her tone. "Do you need a kitten? I'm putting this one up for adoption." She tried to move a bit without losing her footing. "The only catch is, you have to climb up here and get her."

"Well, I don't need a cat," he admitted. "At least not today. But I will help you down."

"I don't need any help," she said quickly, then bit her lower lip. What was she saying?

"You can get down by yourself?" He just couldn't hold the grin back and that was infuriating.

"Of course."

He shrugged. "Okay then. I'll just leave you to your own devices." He turned as though to head for his car.

"Cam! Come back here." She shivered. She was really getting wet. "Of course I need help getting down. Why do you think I'm sitting here like a lump of coal?"

He tried to control the chuckle that was fighting its way out. "A little humility is a wonderful thing," he noted.

She glared at him, but followed his instructions and a moment later, she took the last leap of faith and ended up in his arms. He held her for a moment, her feet just off the ground, and looked down into her wet face.

"Why is it that every time I see you I want to smile?" he asked.

She tried to glare at him. "You're probably laughing at me."

"No." He shook his head, and his eyes darkened as he looked at her lips. "That's not it."

She drew her breath in and pulled away, regaining her footing and turning toward her little house. "Let's get out of this rain," she said, and as if on cue, it began to pour. They'd barely made the porch when she remembered something.

"Oh, wait! We forgot the kitten!"

"No problem," he said, pointing just behind her.

She whirled. There it was, looking like a drowned rat and staring up at her with those big golden eyes. Despite everything, she laughed. "You little faker! I knew you could get down if you tried."

"I guess you could call this a mission accomplished," Cam said as he opened the door and they all rushed into the warmth of the little house.

"I'll get towels," she said, reaching into her tiny bathroom. "We'd better dry off kitty first. She's liable to catch pneumonia, poor little thing."

Her gaze flickered over Cam as she spoke and she couldn't help but notice the rain had plastered his shirt nicely against the spectacular muscles of his wonderful chest. Why that should give her a sinking feeling in the pit of her stomach she couldn't imagine, and she looked away quickly.

"Here," she said, handing him a towel. "You take this one."

She caught the kitten as it tried to make a dash for the underside of her couch, toweled it down and then let it go. It quickly scampered into the next room.

"I ought to put her out so she can find her way home," she said, shaking her head. "But how can I put her out in the rain?"

"I think you just got yourself a cat," Cam noted, slinging the towel around his neck after rubbing his thick hair with it. "Here. You need a little drying off yourself."

She opened her mouth to protest, but he was already applying a fluffy fresh towel to her wild hair.

"I can do it," she said, reaching for the towel.

"Hold still," he ordered, not letting it go.

She gave in, lifting her face and closing her eyes as he carefully dabbed at the raindrops on her nose. He smiled, remembering the time he'd had to clean her up in similar fashion after a messy exploding bubble gum incident. She'd had more freckles then, but otherwise she looked very much the same.

Then she opened her eyes and the memory of Diana as a young girl faded. She was anything but a young girl now. She was a warm-blooded angel just as he'd seen her the other night. As he gazed down into her dark eyes, he had the sense that his larger vision was picking up details so sharp, so clear, that he could see everything about her—the tiny curls at her hairline, the long, full sweep of her eyelashes, the translucent shimmer of her skin, the clear outline of her beautiful lips. She was a woman—a beautiful, desirable woman, a woman he had known most of his life and loved just as long—loved as a friend, but the affection was very strong just the same.

And yet this was different. This was something more. A jolt of arousal went through him and he drew back quickly, as though he'd touched a live wire. But he didn't turn away. He stood where he was, watching her as she reached for the fluffy towel and began to rub her hair with it.

He knew he'd had indications of this sort of response to her ever since he'd come back, but this time it was so strong, he couldn't pretend to himself that it was anything but exactly what it was. That presented a bit of a problem, a bit of a conflict. He considered her his best friend, but the way he was feeling today was light years beyond friendship. Did he have a right to feel this way? Or was this a big mistake?

She dropped the towel onto the couch and looked at him, a challenge in her dark eyes, as though she had a sense of what he was feeling and wanted to warn him off. He felt clumsy and that wasn't like him. He just wasn't sure…

"Why did you come here today?" she asked him.

He raised one eyebrow, startled at her question. "I wanted to see how you're doing."

"I'm doing fine." She said it crisply, as though that ought to take care of the matter, and he might as well be going.

But that only put his back up and meant he was going to be staying all the longer.

"Actually I haven't been around for the last few days," he went on, "I was down in L.A. talking to some money people, bankers I've got contacts with, trying to work out some sort of deal to stay afloat, at least for now."

The challenge faded from her gaze and a look of concern began to take its place. That reassured him. The Diana he knew was still in there somewhere.

"Any luck?" she asked.

"Marginal luck." He hesitated, then went on. "I did talk to a real estate broker about selling the house."

"Oh." Her hands went to her mouth and her eyes took on a look of tragedy. "That would flat out kill your mother."

"I know."

"You didn't…?"

"Not yet. I'm hoping to avoid it."

She sighed and nodded. "Have you told her there won't be any parties yet?"

He grimaced uncomfortably and didn't meet her gaze for a moment. "Not totally."

"Cam!"

"It's making her so happy to plan." He looked back at her ruefully. "I hate to burst the bubble on her dream."

"But she's hiring people like Andre Degregor and the caterer from San Francisco. You've got to stop her."

He knew that. He had to do something very soon. But right now all he could think about was how this new electricity he felt between the two of them was working out. Not well, he took it, from the look on her face. She was wary and guarded and wanted him to leave. He rubbed the back of his neck and frowned thoughtfully, about to ask her why. But the kitten was back, looking for attention.

"Oh, kitty, what am I going to do with you?" she said, smiling down at it. "I don't need a kitten. I'm having a baby."

His immediate sense was that she'd said that as a reminder to him, and he took it to heart. He knew she was having a baby. That very fact made the way his feelings toward her were evolving all the more problematic.

"What you do need," he said to her, "living out here on your own, is a dog. Whatever happened to Max?"

"Max?" She smiled, thinking of the golden retriever she'd grown up with. "Max died years ago. He was really a great dog, wasn't he?"

Cam nodded, remembering. There was a time when Max had been part of the whole picture, always bounding out to meet him when he came to fish or to see Diana. Realizing he was gone left an empty spot. Nothing lasted forever. Everything changed.

Moving restlessly, he turned and looked around the room.

"You know, I've never been in here before."

She looked surprised, then nodded. "No one was allowed in here while Jed was alive."

His mouth twisted as he remembered. "Your father was something of a barnyard dog around this place, wasn't he?"

"That he was."

He turned back to look at her. She hadn't invited him to sit down. She hadn't offered a drink or something to eat. She wanted him to go, didn't she? He frowned. Funny, but he didn't want to leave. Everything in him rebelled at the thought.

"I came close once," he pointed out. "I came over here full of righteous anger and tried to come in to talk to him."

She looked up, curious. "What about?"

"You. I came to tell him to stop using you for a punching bag."

She flushed and shook her head. "I'm sure he agreed immediately, once you explained to him how naughty it was to beat up on your teenage daughter," she said dryly.

"He pulled out his shotgun." Cam grinned, remembering. "I took off like a scalded cat." He glanced down at the kitten, now wrapped around Diana's ankles.

"No offense intended, kitty," he said glibly before raising his gaze to meet Diana's. Their gazes caught and held for a beat too long, and then she pulled away and turned to pick up the kitten and carry it into the kitchen where she put down a tiny dish of milk from the refrigerator.

He watched, thinking about that time he'd come looking for Jed. He'd called the older man out and told him if he hit her again, he'd take her away from here. She'd told him again and again not to do it, that it would only make things worse for her. But when he found her with bruises on her upper arms and a swollen knot below her blackened eye that day, he'd raged with anger. He'd had enough.

"You do it one more time and I'll take her with me," he'd yelled at Jed. "You won't see her again."

"Where do you think you're going to take her?" Jed had jeered back at him. "Won't nobody take her in."

"I'll take her to my house. We'll take care of her."
Jed had laughed in his face. "You can't take her

to your house. Your mother would die before she'd let a little white trash girl like my daughter in on her nice clean floor. Your mother has higher standards, son. You're living in a dream world."

And that was when he'd come out with the shotgun.

Cam had gone home. He told his mother his idea. Funny thing. He'd been so sure his mother would prove Jed wrong. But the man had turned out to have a keener understanding of how things really worked than he did. His mother had been horrified at the idea. She wanted no part of his crazy scheme. Her reaction had been part of what had motivated him to leave home.

Strange how that had changed. Now Diana was one of his mother's favorite people.

She came back out of the little kitchen and looked at him questioningly, as though not really sure why he was still here. But Cam was still lost in the past, mulling over what had happened with her father in the old days.

"When exactly did your dad die?" he asked her.

She told him and he nodded. "Your dad had a grudge against the world and he set about trying to drink himself to death just to spite us all."

She looked troubled and he added, "I suppose your mother dying pretty much threw him for a loop at some point, didn't it?"

Her gaze rose to meet his again. "My mother didn't die. She left when I was six years old."

That sent a shock through him. "I thought she died."

She nodded. Turning from him, she began to collect the towels. "That was what he wanted everyone to think. But the truth was, she couldn't take it anymore and she headed out. Leaving me behind."

Cam felt a wave of sympathy. He could hear the barely concealed heartbreak in her voice. He started to reach for her, but the moment he made a move, he could see her back stiffen, so he dropped his hand back to his side.

"Have you ever heard from her?"

"No." Her chin rose. "And I don't want to."

"I would think you would want to reconnect, especially now with the baby coming."

She whirled, glaring at him. "You know what? My pregnancy is not up for discussion in any way."

"Oh. Okay."

He frowned. His first impulse was to let her set the rules. After all, she was the one who was pregnant. Pregnant women needed extra care, extra tolerance, extra understanding, from what he'd heard. But the more he thought about it, the more he realized he was bending over backward a bit too much. This was getting a little perverse, wasn't it? He turned back and faced her.

"You mean I'm supposed to ignore your baby and pretend it doesn't exist? Is that what you're asking?"

Her face was set as she went on folding the towels and she didn't answer.

Being purposefully defiant, he asked, "So how far along are you, anyway?"

"Cam!" She glared at him, pressing the stack of towels to her chest. "I will not discuss this with you."

He shook his head. "Sorry, Di, that's not going to fly any longer. I need to know what's going on with you and I need to know now."

CHAPTER FIVE

"Diana, tell me about your baby."

She stared up at him, holding his gaze with her own for a long moment, then she turned and began to march from the room.

He caught up with her, took her by the shoulders and turned her back.

"Come on, Di," he said, carefully being as gentle as he could be, especially in his tone. "You can't run away from it. Tell me."

"Why?" She looked up but her eyes looked more lost than angry. "There's nothing to tell."

He shook his head and his hands caressed her shoulders. "You can't do this. You can't keep it all wrapped up inside you."

She looked almost tearful. "You don't know what you're talking about."

"That's just it. I'm trying. But you've got to let me in."

She shook her head, her hair flying wildly around her face.

"Come on, Diana. We're friends. Remember? We need to stand together."

She looked up, still shaking her head, but slowly. "Cam…"

"It's me, Cam. You can count on me. But you've got to trust me first."

She sighed and he smiled, coaxing her.

"What are you going to name your baby, Di? Have you picked anything out yet? Tell me. Please?"

She swallowed hard and looked away. When you came right down to it, there was no one else in the world she trusted like she trusted Cam. That was just a fact of life and she couldn't deny it.

"I'm going to call her Mia," she said softly. "My mother's name was Mia."

At any other time, Cam would have been horrified to feel his own eyes stinging, but for once, he didn't care. "Oh, Di," he said with all the affection he had at his disposal. "Oh, sweetheart." And he pulled her close against him. "That's a beautiful name."

Her arms came up, and for just a moment, she clung to him. He pressed a kiss into her hair and held her close. And then she pulled away, all stiff again, and took a step back.

"When is Mia due?" he asked, hoping to keep the connection from breaking again.

But she shook her head and looked as though she regretted what she'd already told him.

"What are your plans? How are you doing physically? Diana, what can I do to help you?"

She took another step away from him. "I'm fine," she said shortly. "Just leave it at that, Cam. I'm doing fine."

He shook his head. "Don't lock me out, Diana."

She stared at him for a long moment, then sighed and said, "Don't you see? I have to lock you out. If I don't..."

"What?" He shook his head. He didn't see at all. "What will happen if you don't?"

She swallowed hard, as though this was very difficult, but she held her shoulders high and went on quickly.

"Here's the deal, Cam. You were my savior when I was a kid. You defended me from the bullies. You made life seem worthwhile. I was going through a pretty rough time where it looked like the world was against me. And then you came."

She closed her eyes for a moment, remembering that day. "And suddenly I had a champion. It made a huge difference in my life and I thank you for it to this day. But..."

He sighed. "Oh, yes, I thought I could sense a 'but' coming."

"In some ways you ruined me."

He stared at her, shocked. "Ruined you?"

"This is how. My expectations in what a man should be, in what I wanted in a man to share my life, became unrealistic. You raised the bar so darn high, I couldn't find a man who could clear it."

He looked at her in complete bewilderment and was close to laughing, but he knew that would be the kiss of death.

"That's nuts."

"No, it's true. I'm serious." She shrugged and

sighed. "I don't know if it was the real you or my enhanced imaginary you."

He groaned. "You make me sound like an action figure."

"But that image was hard for any man to overcome." She bit her lip and then went on. "I tried. For years, I tried. But I couldn't get you out of my mind." She hesitated, wanting to leave it at that. Going any further would be getting a bit risky. But she knew there was a bit more that she had to say.

"So I finally took some affirmative steps and moved forward. I had to. And now suddenly, here you are." She shook her head and looked at him as though pleading for his understanding. "I can't let myself slide back to being that dependent little girl I was in the past. I just can't let that happen."

"I understand that," he said, though it was only partly true. "I respect you for it."

She searched his eyes. "But do you understand that I can't be around you? You distort my reality."

He hesitated, wishing he knew how best to deal with this. Bottom line, he didn't want to take himself completely out of her life. He just couldn't imagine that happening. And he still didn't really believe in all this on a certain level. "That can be fixed."

"No, it can't." She took a step back away from him, as though she'd begun to realize he didn't really understand at all. "I have a baby to think about now. She has to be my focus. Cam, I just can't be around you. I can't live my life hoping to see you smile, hoping to have a minute with you, watching as you go on with what you do. Don't you see that?"

She meant it. He could see it in her face. He rubbed his neck and frowned at her. "This is crazy."

"It only seems crazy to you because you haven't thought about it like I have. Believe me, I've lived it for years. I think I have a better grasp of what I have going on inside, in my heart and soul, than you do. I know what I'm talking about." She looked so earnest. "Please, Cam. Don't come here anymore."

Now that was just too much. "What are you talking about?"

"I need you to leave me alone."

He shook his head, still avoiding the implications of her insistence. "So you're telling me…"

"I'm telling you I need space. This is a hard time for me right now and I need space away from you while I learn what I can do, and what I need."

He felt very much at sea. On one hand, he could understand that she might have had some problems. She was raised to have problems. How could she have avoided it? But he didn't see why she was taking it all so seriously. The problems all seemed repairable to him. If he wasn't around, if they were never together, how could these things be fixed? No, her insistence that he stay away didn't seem reasonable.

There was only one explanation he could think of, one factor that might make her so adamant about keeping him out of her life, and she wasn't bringing it up at all. Turning slowly, he asked the pertinent question.

"Is the baby's father liable to show up anytime soon?" he asked.

Something changed in her face. Turning on a dime, she strode to the door and threw it open.

"Go," she said.

And there was just enough anger brewing in him by that time to do exactly what she said without another word.

It was two days later before Diana saw Cam again.

Thursday was her regular day to change the flower arrangements at the Van Kirk mansion. She usually went in the afternoon, but once she found out that Mrs. Van Kirk was going to a garden club lecture at 10:00 a.m., she slipped in early in hopes of missing her. The last thing she wanted was to have the woman try to pin her down on when she would be available to begin work on the "project."

From what Cam had told her, she assumed the project was as good as dead. Though she felt sorry for Cam's mother, that did get her off the hook as far as having to come up with an excuse as to why she couldn't participate. It just wasn't clear when Cam would finally tell his mother the truth. She was going to have to have some sort of conversation about it sooner or later, but hopefully things would be settled down before that came about.

She parked in her usual spot and saw none of the usual family cars. Good. That meant she had the house to herself—except for Rosa, of course. And then there was the grandfather.

She'd never had a conversation with the old man, though she'd seen him out in the gazebo a time or two when she'd come to change the flowers. Funny, for a man who had been such an influence on the valley, and had made such an impression on Cam's life, he was almost invisible these days. As far as she knew, he spent most of his time in his room in a far wing of the house. Even though she would be working in the house for the next hour or so, she didn't expect to run into him.

She replaced the sagging gladiolas in the library with a fresh assortment of spring flowers and moved on into the dining room where she began weeding out lackluster roses and replacing them with a huge glass bowl holding a mix of yellow tulips and deep purple Dutch irises. At the last minute, she pulled out a few extras and a couple of bud vases and headed for the stairs. She always liked to put a small arrangement in Mrs. Van Kirk's sitting room, and while she was at it, she might as well surprise Cam with a small vase, too. Just because she didn't want to meet him face-to-face didn't mean she wasn't thinking about him.

Thinking about him—hah! She was obsessing on him and she knew it had to stop. But ignoring him when she was handing out flowers wasn't going to fix that problem.

She dropped off one vase in Mrs. Van Kirk's room, then went down the hall to where she thought Cam's room must be. The door was slightly ajar and she knocked softly, then pushed it open enough to confirm her assumption. There was a large bed and a bedside table and cabinets against one wall. Banners and sports items from ten years before filled the other wall. Nobody had made the bed yet and the covers were thrown back casually.

"Naughty Cam," she murmured to herself. What was he waiting for, maid service? He should make his own bed.

She set the small vase with one yellow tulip and one blue iris on the stand beside the bed, then stood back to admire it. Her gaze strayed to the bed itself, and she noted the impression on the pillow where his head had been, then groaned at the way it warmed her just to think of him asleep. She really was a sucker for romance—as long as Cam was the man in the fantasy.

A noise from the hallway turned her head and in that same moment, the door to the attached bathroom opened and Cam came out wearing nothing but a very skimpy towel.

She froze, mouth open, disbelief paralyzing her. In the split second it took to recognize him, he erased the distance between them with one long step, grabbed her and put a hand over her mouth. She gasped as he pulled her tight against him and nudged the door closed with his foot.

"Shh," he whispered against her ear. "Someone's in the hall."

She only struggled for a second or two before she realized that he was just trying to keep her from speaking out loud and making it obvious to whomever was out there that she was in here with a nearly naked Cam. She nodded and then she sagged into his arms and he slipped his hand from her mouth and just held her. The voices went past the room slowly. She thought she recognized Janey's voice, but not the woman with her.

But it hardly mattered. By the time the voices faded, she was lost in a dream. She was in Cam's arms. Hadn't she always imagined it would feel this way? She looked up into Cam's face. His eyes were brimming with laughter, but as she met his gaze, the humor evaporated quickly, as though he could see what she was feeling, and his arms tightened around her.

She had to pull away, she had to stop this, but for some reason, she couldn't. Every muscle she possessed was in rebellion. She felt like she was trying to move in honey—she couldn't do it. Her body, her mind, her soul, all wanted to stay right there and be held by Cam.

His eyes darkened and a sense of something new seemed to throb between them. And then he was bending closer and she gasped just before his mouth covered hers. At that point, she gave up trying. Her own lips parted and her body seemed to melt into his. She accepted him as though she'd been waiting for this all her life.

And she had.

Cam hadn't exactly planned to do this. In fact, he'd been pretty rough on himself, swearing he wouldn't do this or anything like it in rather strong terms. All those things she'd said had been rattling around in his head for the last two days. The more he thought about it the more they didn't make any sense to him—and his own reaction to them made even less sense. He'd always known she had a bit of a crush on him, but he hadn't taken it seriously. That had been long ago—kid's stuff. Things had changed. He'd changed. That was just the point.

So had she changed, too? Were his instincts right? Had her crush turned into something stronger? And if so, what was stopping her from following her instincts and responding to these new currents between them?

The baby's father, of course. What else could it be? On a certain level, he had to respect that. The bond between a woman and the father of her baby was sacred, even if there were problems between them. He had to stay back, out of the way, and let her deal with the things she needed to deal with.

On the other hand, where the hell was the guy? What kind of a jerk was he? How could he leave Di alone to handle all these life changes on her own? She needed support. She needed her friends around her, if nothing else. As a good friend, how could he ignore that?

But she'd asked him to stay away. Reluctantly he would do the honorable thing and keep his distance, leave her alone.

But, dammit, how could he do that if she showed up in his bedroom like this? *Game over, Diana!*

He had her in his arms and he wanted her there. He had her fresh, sweet scent in his head and the excitement of her touch on his skin and the feel of her soft, rounded body against him and he wanted to drown himself in her body. There was no going back now.

Diana was finally beginning to gather the strength to resist where this was going. It was so hard to push away the man she'd wanted close for most of her life but she knew she had to do it. She couldn't believe, after all she'd been through, after all the serious thinking she'd done on the subject and all the serious preparations she'd made to resist her feelings toward him, here she was, lost in his kiss and loving it. How could this be?

Maybe her response to the temptation that was Cam was so strong because it had been so long since a man had held her and kissed her…but no, it wasn't a man's touch she craved. It was Cam's touch. Only Cam.

She finally mustered the force to pull away from him, leaning back, still in his arms.

"Oh, Cam," she said in despair, her gaze taking in his beautiful face and loving it.

"Hush," he whispered, leaning forward to drop a kiss on her neck. "Unless you want Janey bursting in here to demand an explanation."

She sighed, shaking her head. "Admit it. This isn't working."

He kissed her collarbone. "What isn't working?"

Reaching up, she pushed hard to make him release her. "Our plan to stay away from each other."

He looked amused. "Hey, don't try to pin that plan on me. I never liked it much anyway."

Her sigh was a heartfelt sign of regret. "I thought once I told you face-to-face…"

"That didn't work, did it? Want to try something else?"

"What?"

"This." He leaned closer again and began to nibble on her ear.

She pushed him away. "No! Cam, we have to try harder."

"Hold on." He shook his head, looking down at her in disbelief. "Di, you need to decide what you really want. You order me out of your life, then show up in my bedroom. Either you've developed a split personality, or you're conflicted in some way."

"I was just delivering flowers," she said plaintively, knowing it wasn't going to fly as a serious defense.

"Ah, the old delivering flowers ploy."

"Cam, I didn't mean to start anything like this."

"Didn't you?"

"I thought you were gone."

"You were wrong."

"Obviously." She managed to get a little more space between them, her gaze lingering on his wide shoulders and the beautiful planes of his naked chest. Just looking at him made her stomach do a flip and made her knees begin to tremble. She had to get away from him quickly or she was going to be lost. She closed her eyes and pressed her lips together, then opened them again with more determination. "Now how am I going to get out of here without running into your sister?"

"I heard her go back downstairs a minute ago. You should be in the clear."

She stared at him. She hadn't heard anyone go by again. She'd been deep into kissing him, too deep to be able to process anything else. But he hadn't been, had he? That was something to keep in mind.

Turning away from him, she gathered her supplies, her hands shaking and fingers trembling, and headed for the door. He pulled it open for her and smiled.

"Give me a minute and I'll get dressed and…"

"No." She shook her head. "I'm going, Cam. This doesn't change anything."

His eyes darkened. "The hell it doesn't," he muttered.

She shook her head again, looking out into the hall to make sure it was clear. "Goodbye," she said. Avoiding his gaze, she hurried away.

She made a quick trip through the first floor rooms, giving her arrangements a last-minute check, then turned to leave and almost ran into Janey.

"Hello." Cam's sister was dressed in a black leotard with a bright pink sweatshirt worn over it. Her hair was up in foil, being colorized. Diana quickly made the assessment that the voice she'd heard in the hallway was her hairdresser. She knew the woman came to the house on a weekly basis.

"I saw your car," Janey said. "I was wondering where you were."

"I was putting flowers in a number of rooms," Diana said, trying hard to sound innocent and casual. "And I'm running late."

Janey's green eyes flickered. "Well, how's that baby coming?" she asked.

Something in her tone put Diana on alert. "Just fine, thank you," she said, looking at Janey hard before starting for the kitchen.

To her surprise, Janey stepped forward and blocked the doorway, looking at her speculatively. "You know, there are people who have practically come out and asked me if Cam is the father."

Diana's heart lurched but she stood her ground. "How interesting. Too bad you don't know the answer, isn't it?" She felt a twinge of regret. Why didn't she just tell the woman Cam wasn't the father and put the question to bed? But hadn't Cam already tried to do that? Janey wouldn't believe her no matter what she said.

"Mother is still planning her parties," Janey said coolly, her eyes flashing. "You do understand what these parties are about, don't you?"

"I think I have a vague idea."

Janey nodded. "We need Cam to marry a rich girl. That's pretty much our only hope of getting out of our current financial difficulties."

Diana held her anger in check, but it wasn't easy. "Good luck to you," she said, and stepped forward in a way that signaled she wanted to go through the doorway.

Janey didn't move out of the way, but her eyes

narrowed. "So tell me, how does that fit in with your plans, exactly?"

She glanced down at Diana's rounded belly, making it very clear what she was talking about. She was worried that Diana was going to try to snag Cam for herself. Diana's anger was truly simmering now. How dare she! Well, she could just go on wondering. No matter what she was told, she wasn't going to believe it.

"I don't have any plans, Janey," she said, meeting the other woman's gaze with her own clear vision.

Janey arched an eyebrow. "Don't you?"

"No." She arched an eyebrow in return. "In fact, the parties are going to have to go on without me. I'm going out of town for a while. So you're going to have to find someone else to try to bully." With one firm hand, she gently pushed a surprised Janey out of the doorway and made it past her. "So long."

She walked quickly through the kitchen and out to her car, swearing softly to herself as she went. That woman!

It wasn't until she was in the driver's seat and starting the engine that she remembered what she'd said to her and she half laughed.

So she was going out of town. Funny, she hadn't realized she had a trip in her future until she'd told Janey. But now that it was out in the open, she was glad she'd thought of it. It was probably her only hope to stay away from Cam. And with a little distance and a bit of perspective, she might even think of a way to fall out of love with him.

CHAPTER SIX

DIANA was back in town.

She'd been gone a little over a week. She'd left her occasional assistant, Penny, in charge of supplying arrangements to her weekly clients, and she'd spent a few days in San Francisco with her old roommates.

She'd made a run up to Sacramento as well, hoping to catch her cousin, Ben, but he was gone on business, so she missed him. They had since connected by phone and he was coming to Gold Dust today so they could meet. He had some things to show her.

She was very curious as to what he was up to. Having her uncle leave them a piece of property together was interesting but she wasn't sure if that wasn't going to be more trouble than it was worth. Hopefully Ben would clear some of this up when he arrived.

They were meeting at Dorry's Café on Main and she was on her way there now. She lucked into a good parking place in front of the library under a big old magnolia tree. It was a short walk to the café, but she needed the exercise.

She had a lot of things on her mind, but mostly, she was thinking about Cam. Had absence made the heart grow fonder? Not really. She couldn't get much fonder. But there definitely had been no "out of sight, out of mind" involved, either. Thinking about Cam sometimes seemed to be her main state of being. She was getting better and better at it. And it had to stop.

But there was something else on her mind as well—or should she say someone else? She could feel Mia move, just a flutter, like a butterfly caught in a magic net, but that tiny bit of movement made all the difference. Mia was real to her now like she hadn't been before. Mia was her baby, her child, the center of her future and that meant that Mia was all the world to her.

She was definitely showing, and proud of it. But that made for a different atmosphere as she walked down the streets of the little Sierra town she'd lived in all her life and interacted with the people. Strangely she felt almost as though someone had painted a big red A on her chest when she wasn't paying attention. Suddenly everyone was noticing that she was carrying a child, and most of the looks she was getting were not sympathetic.

Still, what she saw wasn't really old-fashioned small town disapproval. What she had to face every day was even more annoying—blatant curiosity. Everyone wanted to know who the father was. They all knew very well that she hadn't dated anyone for over a year. She had taken a few trips to San Francisco, but other than that, she was busy working with her flowers and hanging out at her lake, with nary a male in sight.

Of course, things were different now. Cam was back.

And it seemed Janey wasn't the only one with suspicions. It was amazing how many ways people could contort a simple conversation into hinting around at the question—*was the baby Cam's?*

Everyone knew that Cam had been her champion once upon a time. Now she was pregnant—and he was back. Was there a connection? It was difficult to find a way to come right out and tell them there was nothing to the rumors when they never actually put the darn thing into words she could refute. They just said something here and left a little hint there and gave her looks that spoke volumes.

She was working on a way to deal with the problem without getting too rude, but as time passed and more and more people got bolder and bolder with their probing, she was beginning to think rude might be the only way to go.

But she smiled and nodded to passersby as she made her way to Dorry's. Maybe this was just the price you had to pay for living in a small town. And bottom line—she loved it here.

Cam saw her going into Dorry's and he stopped on the street to have a two-minute argument with himself. He knew she didn't want to see him or talk to him, but the fact was, he wanted very much to see her and they had plenty of things to discuss. She'd been gone for a week and he'd missed her. That morning in his bedroom had proven one thing—she wanted him. The fact that he wanted her was a given. But no matter how she protested, she'd let the cat out of the bag, so to speak. Left to its own devices, her body would take him in a New York minute. It was just her heart and mind he had to convince.

Just thinking about that morning made him throb and he knew it was going to be very hard to stay away from her. He wanted to talk to her. Hell, he wanted to be with her. Should he leave her alone, give her a few more days of peace? Or should he get on with this?

They were friends, first and foremost. He valued her like he had valued few others in his life. And from the moment he'd seen her the other night, a new element had been added. Of course she knew that. He hadn't been very subtle about it. She attracted him in every way possible.

But he wasn't a nut case. He knew she was out of bounds right now and he respected her need to stay away from him most of the time. He didn't agree with it and he didn't like it, but he had every intention of keeping his distance—for the moment. Until he convinced her it was pointless.

But did running into her here in town count? Not at all, he decided at last. After all, this was casual and public and totally nonthreatening. So he might as well go on in and say hello.

Great. That was settled. He strode confidently toward the café and went in, waving to plump, friendly Dorry with her head of gray curls and nodding to

Jim, the tall, skinny mechanic who had worked on fixing his car and was now up to his elbows in a big, juicy cheeseburger. But all the time, he was searching for a familiar looking blonde.

And there she was.

"Hey, good-lookin'," he said, sliding into the booth across from her and smiling.

She looked up and winced. It was like looking into the sun. The light from the big bay window shone all around him, giving him a halo effect. That, along with his dazzling smile, sent her reeling for a split second or two. He was too gorgeous to be real. Maybe she'd just invented him in her head.

Everything about him looked smooth and clean, from the tanned skin showed off by his open shirt, to his beautiful, long-fingered hands. For a moment, she thought she'd lost the ability to breathe. Whenever she saw him unprepared, he made her react this way. No other man had ever affected her like this. Why oh why? It just wasn't fair.

"Go away," she said hopefully, but there was no strength of will behind her words.

"No," he said calmly. "You've admitted that we are friends. Old friends. Dear friends. And friends get together now and then and shoot the breeze. That's what we're doing here."

She raised her gaze to the ceiling and said plaintively, "It would be better if you would go away."

"We're adults, Di," he said pleasantly as he reached across and took a bread stick from the basket the waitress had put on the table. "We can sit in a café and talk."

She looked worried. "Can we?"

He grinned and waved the bread stick at her. "You bet."

Diana shivered and shook her head, trying to ground herself and get back to reality. "Some other time, maybe," she said, and as she said it she seemed to pick up confidence. "I don't have time today. I'm meeting someone."

"Oh?" He tensed and his sense of humor seemed to evaporate without a trace. Suddenly he was very guarded.

"You'll have to leave before he gets here."

So the person she was waiting for was male, was he? Cam stared across the table at her. She looked nervous. Her usual calm was not evident and her hands were fluttering as they pushed her hair back behind her ear, then reached for her glass of water, then dropped back into her lap. Was he making her nervous? Or was it the pending arrival of her visitor?

He went very still and stared at the wall. His first guess was that this was the father of her baby whom she was meeting in this public place. Had to be. In which case he wasn't leaving until he got a good look at him.

He turned his gaze back and met hers squarely. "Diana, I'm going to be up-front about this. My instincts are to throw you over my shoulder and run off to a cave for the duration."

Diana had unfortunately just taken a drink of water and she nearly spewed it across the room. "What are you talking about?" she sputtered hoarsely, still choking on the water as she leaned across the table in hopes no one else would hear this.

"I'm serious." He leaned forward, too, speaking as softly as he could, but with definite emphasis, and gazing at her intently. "I want to take care of you. I want to protect you. I want to make sure you and your baby are okay." He grabbed her hand and held it. "Everything in me is aching to do that. And I have to know." He grimaced. "Are you going to marry this guy?"

She blinked at him. "What guy?" she asked in bewilderment.

"The father of your baby. Mia's father."

"Mia's… Oh, Cam." She almost laughed, but not quite, and her fingers curled around his and then her eyes were suddenly shimmering with unshed tears. "You're crazy."

His hand tightened on hers. "That doesn't answer my question."

"Who says I have to give you an answer?" She smiled through her tears. "But I will. No, I'm not going to marry anyone. I'm like you. No wedding in my future."

He set his jaw with resolution and looked deep into her eyes. "Okay," he said. "Then I'm warning you, I'm going to do what I have to do."

"As long as you leave me with my feet on the ground," she teased him. "And no caves, okay?"

He shrugged. "Like I said, I'll do what I have to."

The waitress arriving with the salad she'd ordered saved Diana from having to respond to that. She drew back and sat up straight and looked across the table at Cam. She couldn't help but love him for his concern for her and her baby. Still, that didn't change anything.

But this was no place to have that argument. As soon as the waitress was gone again, she picked up a fork and began to pick at her food, and meanwhile, she changed the subject.

"Your mother was on my answering machine twice in the last few days. I'm going to have to call her back eventually. What am I going to say to her?"

His wide mouth twisted. "A warm hello would be nice, I suppose."

She studied his face. "Have you told her yet? Does she understand that you aren't going to be doing the parties?"

Leaning back, he sighed and looked troubled. "I have told her as firmly as I can muster. What she understands and doesn't understand is another matter."

"Meaning?"

"Meaning she is so deep in denial…" He straightened and rubbed his neck. "Well, I did try to have it out with her yesterday. I'm afraid there was a little yelling."

She put down her fork and stared at him. "You didn't yell at your mother!"

He grimaced. "Just a little bit." He definitely

looked sheepish. "She drives me crazy. She just won't face reality."

"Didn't you show her some documentation? Facts and figures? Spreadsheets and accounting forms?"

He nodded. "Even an eviction notice."

"What?"

"For one of our warehouses in Sacramento."

"Oh." She sagged with relief. The picture of Mrs. Van Kirk being carted out of her home by the sheriff with an eviction notice was a nightmare scenario she didn't want to see played out in the flesh.

"But I showed it to her to try to convince her of how serious this is. Well, she got a little hysterical and ran out to go to her precious rose garden and fell right down the garden steps."

Diana's hands went to her face in horror. "No! How is she?"

Cam was looking so guilty, she couldn't help but feel sorry for him, even though she knew his mother probably deserved the pity more.

"She was pretty shaken up." He sighed with regret. "And she broke her ankle."

"What?"

He shook his head, his eyes filled with tragedy. "All my fault, of course."

"Oh, poor thing."

He gave her a halfhearted smile. "I knew you would understand."

"Not you! Your mother." But she knew he was only trying to lighten the mood with a joke, and his quick grin confirmed that.

"Don't worry. It's a hairline fracture sort of thing. The orthopedist said she'll be better in about a month and good as new by Christmas."

Diana groaned. "She's got a hard row to hoe," she said. "It's hard sitting still when you're used to being busy all the time."

"True." He looked at her speculatively. "So now we're reversing a lot of plans," he went on more seriously. "We're firing a lot of the workmen she hired and we're letting the caterer from San Francisco go. And the rose expert. And the barbecue center will have to wait for flusher times."

Diana sighed, shaking her head. "I suppose you'll be laying off the floral stylist as well, won't you?"

"Is that what you call yourself?"

She nodded.

He grinned without much humor. "Yup, she's a goner."

Diana sighed again. "Your mother's been my best account."

He gave her his finest cynical sneer. "Such are the ripples in a stagnating pond."

She laughed. "Now that's just downright silly," she told him. "The Van Kirks are not stagnating. I thought you were going to see to that."

He nodded, his eyes brimming with laughter. That was one thing he loved about her, she seemed to get his silly jokes and actually to enjoy them. Not many people could say that.

"I'm doing what I can. I still can't say we've saved the house. But I'm working at it."

"I'm sure you are." She gave him a quelling look. "Now if you would just buckle down and marry some rich gal, all would be forgiven."

"Right."

"But if you're not going to have the parties…"

He frowned uncomfortably. "Well, about the parties…"

"Yes?" she said, one eyebrow arched in surprise.

He made a face. "We're sort of compromising."

"What does that mean?"

"She was so devastated, I had to give her something. So there will just be one party. A simple party. No fancy chefs, no rose experts."

"I see."

"Mother, Janey and Rosa are going to have to do most of the work themselves." He hesitated, narrowed his eyes and gazed at her as though evaluating her mood. "But since she's flat on her back right now, we need a coordinator to take charge."

Diana's head rose. Why hadn't she seen this coming from farther away? She knew she was staring at him like a deer in the headlights. She was thinking as fast as she could to find excuses for saying no to him. She had to say no. A yes would be emotional suicide.

She could just imagine what it would be like, watching beautiful young, rich ladies from the foremost families in the foothills, dressed in skimpy summer frocks, vying for Cam's attention while she was dressed like a French maid, passing the crudités. No, thank you!

"Janey could do it," she suggested quickly.

"Sure she could," he said out of the corner of his mouth. "If we want a disaster to rival the Titanic. She'll undermine it all she can." He gave her a significant look. "There's only one person Mother would trust to handle this."

She stared back at him. "You can't be thinking what I'm thinking you're thinking."

He shrugged and looked hopeful. "Why not?"

Slowly she began to shake her head. "You couldn't pay me enough. And anyway, didn't you say you were broke?"

He nodded. "That's why I'm hoping you'll do it for free."

She laughed aloud at his raw audacity. "There is no way I'm going to do this at all. Save your breath, Mr. Van Kirk. I refuse to have anything to do with the whole thing."

This could have gone on and on if it hadn't been for the arrival of Diana's visitor. He stopped by their booth, a tall man, handsome in a gaunt way, just starting to gray at the temples, and dressed in an expensive suit. Cam hated him on sight.

"Hello, Diana," he said, smiling coolly.

"Oh." Diana had to readjust quickly. "Hi, Ben. Uh, this is my friend Cam." She threw out a pointed glance. "He was just leaving."

Cam didn't budge. He made a show of looking at his watch. "Actually I think I've got a little more time."

"Cam!"

"And I've got a sudden yen for a piece of Dorry's

apple pie. It's been ten years, but I can still remember that delicate crust she used to make."

She glared at him, and so did Ben, but Cam smiled sunnily and went on as though he hadn't noticed the bad vibes, chattering about pie and apples and good old home cookin'.

"Cam," Diana said firmly at last. "Ben and I have something personal to discuss. You've got to go."

He gazed at her intently. "Are you sure?" he said softly, searching her eyes. He wanted to make certain she really meant it, that she didn't want him to stay and act as a buffer for her.

She gave him a look that should have warned him that she was losing patience. "I'm sure. Please go."

He rose reluctantly and flashed her friend a sharp look, just to let him know he was going to be keeping an eye on him.

"Okay," he said. "I'll be over there in the corner, eating apple pie. In case you need me."

She closed her eyes and waited for him to go. Ben looked bored. Cam went.

But he didn't go far and he kept up his survey of what was going on from a pretty good vantagepoint. They were talking earnestly, leaning so that their heads were close together over the table. It tore him up to watch them. If this was really the guy...

Their meeting didn't last very long. Ben pulled out a portfolio of papers that he showed her, but he packed most of them away again and was obviously preparing to leave. Cam felt a sense of relief. There had been nothing warm between them, none of the sort of gestures people who had an emotional bond might display. If there had ever been anything between them, he would say it was pretty much dead now. In fact, Diana looked almost hostile as Ben rose to leave. And as soon as he was out of sight, she looked up and nodded to Cam, as though to beckon to him. He was already up and moving and he went to her immediately, sliding in where the other man had been sitting.

"I need your help," she said without preamble. She had one piece of paper that he'd left behind sitting on the table in front of her. "Because I don't know how to do this."

"Do what?" he asked. "Sue the guy? Charge him with abandonment? Get some money out of him for child care?"

She was shaking her head, wearing a puzzled frown. "What are you talking about?"

He blinked. "That wasn't the father of your baby?"

She threw her head back. "Oh, Cam, for heaven's sake! Ben is my cousin. I told you about him."

"You did?" Her cousin. It figured. The body language had been all wrong for lovers, or even current enemies who were past lovers. He should have known. Feeling a little foolish, but even more relieved, he took a deep breath and calmed down. "Oh. Maybe you did."

"Never mind that," she said, staring down at the paper. "Here's the deal. Ben's a lawyer. He always seems to be looking for a weak spot to exploit." She looked up, wrinkling her nose. "You know what I mean? Our uncle Luke, my father's older brother, died last week. I met him a few times years ago and he came to my father's funeral. But to my shock, he had a little piece of land in the mountains and he left it to Ben and me."

"The two of you together?" That could be a seemingly lucky break but with a sword of Damocles hanging over it.

"Yes. I assume he thought we would sell it and share the revenue or one would buy the other out. Whatever."

"Okay. What's the problem?"

She frowned, chewing her lip. "Ben wants to buy me out. But…" She made a face, thought for a moment, then leaned closer, speaking softly. "I know this is going to sound really horrible, but I don't trust him. Everything he says seems logical enough and it sounds good and all. But, well, he tried to find a way to get a piece of my lake property when my dad died. He wasn't all that open about it, but I could tell he was snooping around here for a purpose. And now I just can't help but wonder…"

"Better safe than sorry," he agreed. "Where's the land?"

"That's just it. He seems a little vague about that. He does say it's out in the sticks, far from any amenities and there seem to be some encumbrances on it that are going to make things difficult. I did get something in the mail myself, something from my uncle's lawyer, but I couldn't make heads nor tails of it and when I tried to call him, the number didn't

seem to work. Ben gave me this paper with the par-
cel number and coordinates, but as far as a map on
how to get there, he was very unhelpful."

"Has he been out to take a look at it?"

"He says he has. He says it's pretty barren.
Flatland with not even a lot of vegetation. No views.
Nothing."

Cam nodded, thinking that over. "So you're a bit
skeptical."

She made a face. "I hate to say it, but yes. Color
me skeptical."

"And you would like to go take a look for yourself." He nodded again, assessing things. "I think
that's good. You need to know a little more about
where it is and what condition it's in before you make
any drastic moves."

"I think so," she said. "For all I know, it's a garden paradise or a great site to build a house on." She
squinted at him hopefully. "I just thought you might
know what state or county agencies to go to and
things like that. Or maybe you have connections in
the Forest Service?"

"I know some people who might be able to help."
He looked over the paper for another moment. "Can
I take this with me?"

"Of course."

"Good." He folded it and put it in his pocket, then
gave her a sardonic look. "I'm going to have to pull
some strings, you know. I might have to call in some
favors. Use my family's influence." His smile was
suddenly wicked. "And after I've done all that, going

out of my way, putting my reputation on the line, going all out to do something for you..." His shrug was teasingly significant. "Well, I'm sure you're going to be more open to doing a favor for me in return."

It was obvious he was still trying to get her to manage the party for his mother—the last thing on earth she wanted to do.

"Cam!"

His wide mouth turned down at the corners for just a moment. "Just think about it. That's all I ask." He patted the paper in his pocket. "I'll get back to you on this." His smile returned to being warm and natural. "You'll trust me?"

"Of course I'll trust you." She smiled back at him. It just wasn't possible not to. "Now go away," she said.

Actually he was late for a meeting at the mayor's office, so for once he obeyed her. But first, he leaned forward, caught her hand in his and brought it to his lips, kissing her palm.

"See you later," he promised, giving her a melting look.

She shook her head, half-laughing at him as he slid out and left the café. But as she looked around the room at the glances she was getting, her face got very hot. It was obvious a lot of people had witnessed that hand kissing thing and could hardly wait to get on their cell phones to tell their friends what they'd seen.

Small towns!

CHAPTER SEVEN

IT ONLY took Cam two days to get all the information Diana needed to make a trek up to see the land. She was thrilled when he called her with the news. So now she'd fed the kitten and watered her flower garden and dressed herself in hiking clothes and was ready to go. This was totally an adventure and she was looking forward to it. She just had to wait for Cam to show up with the map of the location of where she was going.

She knew she was not acting according to plan. She'd sworn she was going to stay away from Cam—far, far away. She wasn't going to risk falling back into the patterns that had ruled her life for so long. She was a grown woman with a child on the way and she couldn't afford to act like a lovesick teenager.

She knew asking for his help put her in a weaker position in refusing to help his mother, and yet, she'd done it anyway. Somehow Cam kept weaving his way through the threads of her days, finding a reason here, an excuse there, and before she knew it, she was almost back in the fold, tangled in his life, loving him again, unable to imagine a future without him.

It had to stop. Right after he gave her the map. She had the grace to laugh out loud as she had that thought. What a ridiculous fool she was!

She heard his car and hurried out to meet him, hoping to get the map and send him on his way. He got out of the car and leaned against it, watching her come toward him with a look of pleasure on his face. She couldn't help but smile.

"Oh, Cam, don't do that."

"Don't do what? Enjoy you?"

She gave him a look. "Do you have the map?"

"Yes, I do."

She looked at him. Both hands were empty.

"Where is it?"

"In the car."

"Oh." She tried to look around him. "May I have it?"

"No."

She stared at him. "What do you mean?"

His eyes sparkled in the sun. "I'm the keeper of the map. I'll handle all navigational duties."

She put her hands on her hips and gave him a mock glare. "That'll be a little hard to do, since you'll be here and I'll be the one approaching the site," she said crisply.

"Au contraire," he countered smugly. "Since we're going in my car…"

"No way!"

"And I have the picnic prepared by Rosa this very

morning and packed away in an awesome picnic basket, with accoutrements for two."

She drew in a quick breath. "I never said you could come with me."

He gave her the patented lopsided grin that so often had young ladies swooning in the aisles. "That's right, you never did. But I'm coming anyway."

Fighting this was probably a losing battle and not worth the effort as it stood, but still, she frowned, trying to think of a way out. "Can I just see the map?"

"Sure. But I'll hold it."

She groaned at his lack of trust, but that was forgotten as he spread out the map and showed her where her property lay.

"Ohmigosh, that's really far from any main roads. I thought it would be closer to Lake Tahoe."

"It's uncharted territory. Just be glad it's not winter. Think about the Donner party."

She shuddered. "No, thanks." She frowned at him, trying to be fierce. "Now if you'll just give me the map."

He smiled and dropped a sudden, unexpected kiss on her forehead. "I go with the map. Take it or leave it."

She shook her head, but a slight smile was teasing her lips and her heart was beating just a little faster. "What a bully you are."

"Guilty as charged. Let's go."

They went.

It was a lovely drive through the foothills and then into the taller mountains. They passed through small idyllic towns on the way, and little enclaves of farm or ranch houses. Cows, horses and alpacas seemed to be grazing everywhere on the still-green grasses. They talked and laughed and pointed out the sights, and all in all, had a very good time. The final segment was a fifteen-mile ride on a dirt road and that was another story. For almost half an hour, they were bouncing so hard, conversation was impossible.

And then they arrived. Cam brought the car to a stop in a cloud of dust and they both sat there, staring out at the open area. For a moment or two, neither said a word.

Finally Diana asked pitifully, "Are you sure this is it?"

"Afraid so," he said.

She turned to gaze at him, a look of irony in her eyes. "I don't think there could be an uglier patch of land in all the Sierras, do you?"

"It's definitely an ugly little spud," he said out of the side of his mouth, shaking his head. "I don't think anyone is going to want to build here. There are no trees, no view, no nothing."

"No paved road," she pointed out, wincing as she looked back at all the rocks and gullies they were going to have to go back through. "Looks like the best thing to do would be to take Ben up on his offer and let him buy me out."

"Maybe." Cam frowned, leaning forward on the steering wheel. "Though I can't help wondering why he wants it—or whom he's going to sell it to. I can't see one redeeming element here."

She let out a sigh. "Darn. I was hoping for a bit of good luck for a change."

"Ya gotta make your own luck, sweetheart," Cam said in his best Sam Spade imitation. "That's the way the game is played."

She made a face at him and admitted, "I don't even see a place to have a picnic here. And we passed a nice park about thirty minutes ago. Shall we go back?"

The ride back wasn't any better than the ride out had been, but they found their way to the nice park and sighed with relief when they got there. The park had tables with built-in benches and they set up their feast on a nice one under an oak, in full view of the small river that ran through the area. Rosa's lunch was delicious. They ate and talked softly in the noon day sunshine. A group of children played tag a short distance away. Mothers with strollers passed, cooing to their babies.

Diana took a bite of her chicken salad sandwich as she watched the passing parade. "Funny how, once you're pregnant, you suddenly notice all the babies that pop up everywhere."

He gave her a covert look. She'd brought up her pregnancy on her own. Did this mean that the moratorium on mentioning it was lifted? Just in case, he made sure to tread softly.

"You're going to make a great mom," he noted.

She flashed him a look and for a moment, he

thought he was going to get his head handed to him. But then her face softened and she almost smiled.

"What makes you say that?" she asked.

"I get a clear vibe from you that seems encouraging," he said. "You seem to be settling into this new role you're about to play in the world."

Now a smile was definitely tugging at the corners of her mouth. "It's funny, but it has taken me a while to fully realize what I've done, what I'm about to do. Mia seems very real to me now. I can hardly wait to hold her in my arms. I only hope I'll be a good mother to her."

"I have no doubts. I remember how you took care of your father."

"Do you?" She looked at him in surprise, then with growing appreciation. "I don't think most people remember that, or even noticed at the time." She shook her head. She'd spent too much of her young life taking care of him and getting little thanks for it. But she'd done it out of duty and a feeling of compassion for the man. And though she'd gone off to the big city as soon as she could, to leave all that behind her, she'd come back when her father needed her and no one else would have taken care of him as he lay dying. So she did it.

Funny. She'd left Gold Dust because of her father and then she'd returned for the same reason.

"He needed someone to take care of him. It was a cinch he couldn't take care of himself."

He waved a carrot stick at her. "You were taking care of him when you were too young to be taking care of anything more than whether your socks matched."

She smiled. Trust Cam to have paid attention and to have realized how difficult it was for her when she was young. How could you not fall for a guy like that?

She was quiet for a moment, then said softly, "I loved him, you know."

He looked at her and saw the clouds in her eyes. He wanted to take her in his arms, but he held off, knowing how she felt about the situation.

"Of course you did. He was your father." He shifted in his seat. "Did you ever know your mother at all?"

"Not much." She shook her head. "She took off before I was six years old and never looked back."

"That's a shame."

She tilted her head back and smoothed her hair off her face. "I'm not so sure. If she was worth knowing, she'd have made a point of letting me know her." Her laugh was short and spiked with irony. "At least my father stuck around."

They packed away the remnants of their lunch, put things into the car, and walked down to watch the river roll by. There were just enough boulders and flat rocks in the river's path to make for a pretty spectacular water show. They followed the river for a bit, then sat on a large rock and listened to the rushing sound.

"You need something like this at your place," he told her. "Your lake could use some shaking up."

"I've got a nice stream," she protested. "That's more my sort of excitement. Something manageable and contained."

He laughed, leaning back beside her and tossing a flat pebble into the river. "That's all you want out of life, is it? Something manageable?"

"What's wrong with that?"

"Not a thing." He tossed another pebble. "But back about the time I left, I thought you had plans to go to the city and become a model." He shifted so that she could lean back against his shoulder instead of the hard rock. "What happened to that?"

She hesitated, then gave in to temptation and let her body snuggle in against his. "Kid dreams," she said airily.

He turned his head, savoring the feel of her against him. A sudden breeze tossed her hair against his face and he breathed in her spicy scent. "You would've been good," he said, closing his eyes as he took in the sense of her.

"No."

"Why not?" Opening his eyes again, he was almost indignant. "You've got the bones for it. You could be a model." Reaching out, he touched her hair, then turned his hand, gathering up the strands like reins on a wonderful pony. "You...Diana, you're beautiful."

He said it as though it were the revelation of the ages. She smiled wryly, appreciating his passion but knowing it was just a bit biased.

"I'm not cut out for that sort of life," she said simply.

"Chicken."

She shook her head. "No. It's not that."

He went very still for a moment, thinking over her situation. "Maybe you should have gone for it anyway," he said softly.

She moved impatiently, turning to look at him. "You don't understand. I know more about it than you think I do. I lived in San Francisco for a couple of years after college. I did all those things you do when you live in San Francisco. I went to parties in bay-view penthouses, danced in sleazy discos, dated young account executives and overworked law students. Climbed halfway to the stars in little cable cars. Lived on a houseboat in Sausalito for a few months. Worked at a boring job. Had my car broken into. Had my apartment robbed. Had a lot of fun but finally I'd had enough and I wanted to come home. To me cities are kind of those 'great to visit but don't make me live there' sorts of places."

He smiled, enjoying how caught up in her subject she'd become. Reaching up, he touched her cheek. "You're just a small town girl at heart."

"I guess so. I love it in Gold Dust." She threw her head back, thinking of it. "I love to wake up in the morning and see the breeze ruffling the surface of the lake. I love the wind high up in the pines and the fresh smell after a rainstorm. I love that feeling of calm as the sun sinks behind the mountaintops and changes the atmosphere into a magic twilight."

"I understand," he said. "That's part of what pulled at me to come back." He hesitated only a few beats. "That…and you."

The moment he said it, he knew it was true. Through all the turmoil, all the hell he'd gone through with Gina, Diana had always been in the back of his mind, a calm, rational presence, an angel of mercy whose care could heal his soul. He'd always pushed the memories away, thinking they were a crutch he'd held on to in order to comfort himself, like a favorite fantasy. But now he knew it was much more. What he felt for Diana might be fairly hopeless, but it was real and true and strong inside him. It was more real than any other part of his life had ever been. His gaze slid over her, searching the shadowed areas along her neckline, her collarbone, the upper swell of her breasts.

She turned toward him slowly, as though in a dream. She knew he was going to kiss her. She heard it in his voice. Her heart was thumping so loud, she wasn't sure if she could breathe. He was going to kiss her and once again, just for this moment, she was going to kiss him back.

She didn't wait, but leaned toward him, her lips already parted, and his arms came around her and she clung to him, moving in a cloud of sensual happiness. Was this real? Was that really Cam's body that felt so warm and wonderful against hers?

It was over too soon. She sighed as he pulled back, then smiled up at him.

"How can I miss you if you won't go away?" she murmured, half-laughing.

"What is that supposed to mean?" he asked, touching her cheek with his forefinger.

"It means you're always there," she said, straightening and moving away from him. "You're either in my life or in my dreams. I can't get rid of you." She said it lightly, as though teasing, but she meant every word.

He watched her through narrowed eyes, wondering why she appealed to him more than any other woman he'd ever known. Holding her felt natural, kissing her had been magic. He wanted her in his bed, in his life. But what did that signify? Right now, it was just confusing.

It was later, as they winged their way home, that he brought up the topic she'd been dreading all along.

"You haven't been over to the house for a while."

"No. I was gone and then…" She let her voice taper off because she knew there was no good excuse for her sending Penny to take care of the arrangements at the Van Kirk mansion one more time, even though she herself was back in town.

"My mother is asking that you come see her," he said, glancing at her sideways.

"Oh, no," Diana said, her eyes full of dread. "She's going to beg me to take over the party plans, isn't she?"

He nodded. "Yes."

She wrinkled her nose. "Tell her I've got the flu."

This time his look was on the scathing side. "I

make it a practice never to lie to women," he said, and she wasn't sure if he was joking or not.

She smiled sadly just the same. "Only to men, huh?"

He suppressed a quick grin. "Of course. A man can handle a lie. Likely as not, he'll appreciate a well-told one. Might even appropriate it for his own use in the future, and thank you for it, besides."

"Unlike a woman," she countered teasingly.

"Women only appreciate lies about themselves, and then only if they're complimentary."

She stared at him, struck by how serious he sounded all of a sudden. "What made you so cynical about the human race?" she asked him.

For just a moment he was tempted to tell her about Gina, the only other woman he'd been close to loving over the last ten years, about how she'd nearly pulled him into an ugly trap, teaching him a lesson about feminine lying he would never forget. But at the last moment, he decided it was a story best kept to himself and he passed over it. It was all very well to use episodes from the past as lessons in guarding one's trust like a stingy uncle, but to inflict those stories on others was probably too much.

"Life does take its toll," he said lightly instead.

"Are you done?" she asked.

He glanced at her in surprise. "Done doing what?"

"Done running around the world looking for affirmation."

He gave a cough of laughter. "Is that what I've

been doing? And here I thought I was looking for adventure all this time."

She shrugged, loving the way his hair curled around his ear, loving the line of his profile, loving him in every way she possibly could. She'd missed him so. She would miss him again when he left. And she was sure his leaving was inevitable. She didn't know when, but she knew he would go. And this time, she refused to let her heart break over it.

"Tell me why you went in the first place? The real reason."

"You mean, beyond the fight with my grandfather? It's pretty simple. The age-old story." He maneuvered through a traffic circle in the little city they were passing through. "I had to go to see if I could make it on my own without the Van Kirk name boosting me along. I didn't want to end up like my father. And I didn't much want to end up like my grandfather, either. I wanted to be me."

She nodded. That was pretty much what she'd expected. "And now?"

He grinned. "Now I'm thinking my grandfather isn't such a bad model after all."

"Interesting." She thought about that for a moment, then went on. "Has anyone ever told you that a lot of people thought you left because of Lulu?" she informed him, watching for his reaction.

He looked blank. "Lulu?"

"Lulu. Lulu Borden. You remember her." She hid her smile.

"Oh, sure. Tall, curvy girl. Lots of red hair. Nice smile. Kind of flirty."

"That's Lulu."

He shrugged. "What does Lulu have to do with me?"

"Well…" She gave him an arch look. "She started showing right about the time you disappeared. A lot of people figured you were the one who got her that way. And that was why you took off."

"What?" He gaped at her in horror until she reminded him to keep his eyes on the road. "If a lot of people thought that a lot of people were wrong."

She nodded happily. "I was pretty sure of that, but it's good to hear you confirm it."

He frowned, still bothered by the charge against him. "What did Lulu have to say about it?"

"She married Tommy Hunsucker, so she's not sayin' much."

"Geesh." He shook his head with a look of infinite sadness. "Maligned in my own hometown."

"Sure," she said cheerfully. "Where better to have your reputation besmirched?"

"And now they think I'm a daddy again, don't they?" he said cynically, looking at her growing tummy. "At least the town has a lot of faith in my potency."

She grinned. "Legends speak louder than facts sometimes," she admitted.

"Speaking of legends…" He hesitated, then went on bravely. "Tell me why you aren't going to marry the father of your baby."

All the humor drained from her face and she seemed to freeze. "That is not up for discussion."

He turned to look at her. "Di…"

"No. I'm not going to tell you anything." She shook her head emphatically and her tone was more than firm. "This is my baby. The father has nothing to do with it."

He winced. "That's not true."

"It is true," she insisted fiercely. "That's it." She held her hand up. "End of discussion."

He didn't press it any further, but he thought about it all the rest of the way home.

It was late afternoon before they turned onto the Gold Dust Road and came in sight of her little house by the lake.

"Getting back to the point," he said as he pulled up before her gate. "Will you go to see my mother?"

"Wow, that was a subject I thought we'd left in the dust way back there somewhere. Or at least we should have."

She thought for a moment before answering. She wanted to give him the benefit of the doubt, an even chance, a fair hearing, and all those other tired clichés that meant he probably had a point to make and she ought to let him make it.

He moved impatiently. He obviously thought she'd taken enough time to come up with a fair decision and he was beginning to think she was dragging her feet.

"Listen, Di. I owe my mother something. I owe her quite a bit, in fact. I wasted a lot of time trying to figure out what life was about and what my place was in the general scheme of things. By the time I'd sorted it all out, I was back where I'd started. But by then, I realized family was more important than anything else. And I needed to make up for some things with mine. So that's why I came back. Unfortunately they're in more trouble than I can easily deal with. But this, at least, I can do for her. I can let her have her party. And she needs help to do it."

Diana listened to him and agreed with just about everything he said. He was a good son after all. And she knew she could help. She sighed.

"All right, Cam. I'll go to see your mother." She shook her head. "But I can't go tomorrow. I've got a doctor's appointment in the morning and I won't be back in time."

"Here in town?"

"No." She looked at him speculatively, then amplified a bit. "I decided from the first that I'd better go to a clinic down in Sacramento. I found a good doctor there. And I didn't want everyone in town knowing all about my pregnancy."

He nodded. "Probably a wise move," he said.

"So I'll plan to come by and see her Friday," she went on. "I'll talk to her." She winced. "But I'm afraid I'm only going to disappoint her."

He grunted and she couldn't tell if he was agreeing with her or dissenting.

"I still don't feel comfortable being a part of the great wife search," she told him, "especially if you plan to thwart your mother on it. If you really mean it, that you won't marry anyone, I hope you're planning to tell her the truth from the beginning."

"She knows how I feel."

"Does she?" Somehow, doubts lingered. "Cam, let's be honest. Your mother is looking for a bride for you, like it or not. It's not exactly fun for me to be a part of that."

"Why is that?" He gazed challengingly into her eyes. "Tell me what bothers you about that?"

Her lower lip came out. "You know very well what it is," she said in a low, grating voice. "It's not really fair of you to make me say it. You know exactly what it is and you know there's no cure for it."

With that, she grabbed her map and slipped out of the car, heading for her little lonely house.

Cam sat for a long time, not moving, not reaching for the ignition, just staring at the moon. And then, finally, he headed home.

CHAPTER EIGHT

DIANA dreamed about Cam, about his kiss and how lovely it was to be in his arms. And then she woke up and there he was on her doorstep.

"Doughnuts," he said, holding out a sack of them like a peace offering. "For your breakfast."

"Thank you," she said, taking the bag and closing the door right in front of him.

"Hey," he protested, and she opened the door again, pretending to scowl at him.

"Too early," she said. "You're not even supposed to see me like this."

"I'll close my eyes," he lied. "I came early because I didn't want to be too late to take you to the doctor."

She stared at him, and slowly, she opened the door wider for him to come in. Turning, she looked up at him. "I don't need anyone to take me to the doctor," she said stiffly.

"I'm not trying to horn in on your private business," he assured her. "In fact, if you want me to, I'll wait in the car. But I think you ought to have someone with you, just in case. And since the baby's father isn't around to help you, you can count on me. I'll be around in case something happens, or whatever."

You can count on me—the words echoed in her head. She knew he meant it, but she also knew he couldn't promise anything of the sort. "Cam, I really don't need help."

He stared down into her wide eyes. "Yes, you do," he said firmly. "Di, I know you can do this on your own. You're very brave and you've tried your whole life to do everything on your own. I know you don't actually, physically, need any help. You're strong. You've done it all on your own forever."

Reaching out, his hands slid into her hair, holding her face up toward him. "But everyone needs somebody. No one can chart his own course forever. I'm here now. I can help you. I can give you some support and be around in case you need a shoulder to lean on. You don't have to be alone."

To her horror, her eyes were filling with tears. She fought them back. The tears were a sign of weakness, and she couldn't afford to show that side to anyone. But as she fought for control, he was kissing her lips, moving slowly, touching gently, giving comfort and affection and a sense of protection that left her defenses crumbling on the floor. She swayed toward him like a reed in the wind. He was so wonderful. How could she resist him? A part of her wanted to do whatever he said, anytime, anywhere. And that was exactly the part she had to fight against.

He pulled back to look at her, his gaze moving slowly over her face, a slight smile on his own.

"Please, Diana," he said softly. "Let me be there for you. I'm not asking for anything else. Just let me be there."

She was really crying now. Deep sobs were coming up from all her past pain, all her loneliness, and she was helpless in his arms. He pulled her up against his chest and stroked her hair. When she could finally speak again, she pulled back and looked at him. How was she going to make him understand?

"Cam, don't you see? I can't start to depend on you. If I do that…"

"I'm not asking for a long-term commitment and I'm not offering one," he insisted, holding her loosely, looking down into her wet, sleepy face and loving it. "But I am here now. I can help you. You could use a friend. I want to be that friend. That's all."

She closed her eyes. Didn't he understand how dangerous this was for her? Didn't he see how much she loved him? She had to send him away. It was the only chance she had for strength and sanity.

She felt him move to the side and heard paper rustling and she slowly opened her eyes and then her mouth to tell him to go, but before she got a word out, he popped a piece of doughnut inside it.

"Let's eat," he said cheerfully, and his comical look made her laugh through her tears. She chewed on the delicious confection and laughed at his antics and somehow her resolutions got forgotten for the time being.

But she knew this wasn't the end of the matter. She might let her guard down for now, but very soon, she would have to erect it again. She knew that from experience. So she would let him come with her to her doctor's appointment and she would be with him for another day. And she would love doing it. But it couldn't last and she couldn't let herself be lulled into thinking that.

"If I were one to sing old Elvis songs," Diana muttered to herself the next afternoon. "I'd be singing that 'caught in a trap' song right now."

She was going to help Cam's mother. She'd always known, deep down, that she would end up doing it. The mystery was why she'd tried to fight it for so long. A lot of needless Sturm und Drang, she supposed. She was a pushover in the end.

"You're completely spineless, aren't you?" she accused herself in the hallway mirror. "Shame on you!"

Mrs. Van Kirk had looked so pathetic lying back on her chaise longue overlooking her rose garden, and she'd been so complimentary about Diana's talents on all scores—and when you came right down to it, Diana liked her a lot. She felt sorry for her, wanted to help her have her silly parties, wanted to make her happy. So in the end, she agreed to take over all the planning for the event. She was to be totally in charge of it all.

So now she was enlisted to help find Cam a bride—what fun.

There was still the problem of how she would be paid. She'd assumed Cam was serious when he'd teased her about doing it for free, but he assured her she would be paid for her work—someday.

"How's this?" he said. "You'll have the first option on our future earnings."

"What earnings?" She knew he was working hard on setting things to rights, and she supposed there was income from the Van Kirk ranch to throw into the mix, plus some of his funds borrowed from his own business. But it all seemed like slim pickings so far.

He gave her a grand shrug. "We may just go in the black someday."

She rolled her eyes. "Great. I'll be looking forward to it."

"Seriously, Di," he said, catching hold of her shoulders to keep her from running off. "I'm going to make sure you get compensated. Just as soon as I've saved this house and have a little spare cash to take care of things like that."

She looked up at him and barely kept herself from swooning. He looked so handsome, his blue eyes clear and earnest, rimmed with dark lashes that made them look huge, his dark hair falling over his forehead in a particularly enticing way. She could feel his affection for her shining through it all. He was hers—in a way—for the next few days, at any rate. Then, if his mother's plans came to fruition, he would be some other woman's. And Diana would be left with nothing but memories.

"Forget it," she said, shaking her head, pushing away her dour thoughts. "I'm doing this for your mother. And that's it."

Of course, it turned out to be even more work than she'd thought it would be. There was so much to do. The event itself was to be called a Midsummer Garden Party to welcome Cam back to the foothills and from what they'd heard, it was already stirring interest all over the valley and environs far and wide.

"Everyone from the Five Families will be attending," Mrs. Van Kirk told her matter-of-factly.

Diana knew who the Five Families were and it made her cringe a little. The Van Kirks were one of those five, though they might be clinging to that distinction by their fingernails at the moment, hanging by the thread of their past reputation. They were all descendants of five Kentucky miners who'd come here together in the nineteenth century as forty-niners, discovered gold in these hills, settled the land and established the town of Gold Dust. They were the aristocracy of the area now, the movers and shakers of local affairs all through the valley, the main landowners and definitely the richest people around.

It was only natural that Cam's mother wanted him to marry one of the young women from that group. Why not? Not only did they have the money, they had the background to rule the area. And Cam was a natural leader as far as that went. So here she was, working hard to help him take his rightful place—

at the top of the social ladder and right beside some simpering debutante.

Well, maybe she wouldn't be simpering. In all fairness, the women from the Five Families spent a lot of time doing charity activities and working on cleaning up the environment. But still, they were eligible to marry Cam and she wasn't. So a little resentment didn't seem so out of line, did it?

But she had to shove that aside and concentrate on the work at hand. Establishing a theme came first. They needed something that would allow them to make cheap, easy party dishes instead of the gourmet selections that had been the choice when the fancy chef was being engaged.

She gathered Cam and Janey together and the four of them brainstormed and what they finally came up with was a Hawaiian theme.

"Hawaiian?" Janey wailed. "That's so retro."

"Exactly the point," Diana said. "That way we don't have to spend money on fancy decor items. We can use flowers from both your gardens and my fields. We'll string leis as party favors and have flowers to clip in the hair of ladies who want that. We'll have rose petals floating in the pool."

"But the food," Janey moaned.

"Don't worry, it'll be fine—very colorful and much cheaper. Things like bowls of cut up fruit will serve two purposes—decorating as well as eating. And as for the more substantial items, I have a friend, Mahi Liama, who runs a Polynesian restaurant in Sacramento. I'm sure he'd do a lot of the food for us. Maybe some pit roasted pork and chicken long-rice and poi. The rest will be mostly finger food that we're going to be fixing ahead and freezing and popping in the ovens at the last minute."

Janey groaned. "What a drag. I like it when we hire the work out a lot better."

Diana gave her a pasted on smile. "It'll be great. Just you wait and see."

The invitations came next. They couldn't afford to have any printed up, so Diana scavenged up some lovely notepaper she found in the bottom drawer of a beautiful carved desk in the den and put Mrs. Van Kirk to work doing them by hand. That was something she could do sitting down and it turned out she had gorgeous penmanship.

"The trick is to make it look like we are taking advantage of your handwriting skills and creating something unique without letting on that it's an economy measure," she told the older woman.

"Shall I add a little Hawaiian looking flower, like this?" Mrs. Van Kirk suggested, proving to have drawing talent as well.

"Perfect," Diana said, pleased as punch. "These will be so special, people will save them as keepsakes."

Buoyed by all the praise, Mrs. Van Kirk got busy and had a dozen done by noon on the first day.

Diana conferred with Cam about the seating arrangements. It turned out that he had rummaged in the storage sheds and found at least twenty round tables and a huge group of wooden folding chairs to go with them, supplies obviously used for parties years ago. They needed cleaning up and some repair, and probably a coat of spray paint, but it seemed doable and he was already on the job.

There was a large patio suitable for dancing. With a few potted plants arranged along the outer perimeter and a few trellises and arbors set up, it could look stunning. Diana was beginning to take heart. It looked like things were falling into place pretty easily. The whole family was involved, including a few cousins who stopped by occasionally, and despite the whining from some quarters, she generally thought that a good thing.

She was especially glad to find a way to get Janey to help out. Once she remembered that Cam's sister had been quite a musician in her younger days, she knew exactly how she could use her talents.

"Here's what you do," she told her. "I've called the high school. They have a small jazz combo, a pianist and a couple of different choral groups. I think one's a cappella. Hopefully they can do some low-key Hawaiian tunes. Their music director says they need the experience in playing in front of audiences, so I think we could get them really cheap and they could trade off, one group playing during the opening cocktails, another during the meal, another for the dancing, etc. You go talk to them and see what you can arrange. You'll be in charge of picking out the music. It's all yours."

"You know what?" Janey said, actually interested for once. "Adam, the man I've been dating, has a teenage son who does that Djaying thing at dance clubs to make a little extra money. Maybe he would help out."

"That would be great." She made a face as she had a thought. "Just make sure you have right of approval on everything he's going to play first. We don't want any of the raunchy stuff some of the kids like these days."

"Indeed," Janey said, drawing herself up. "Wouldn't fit the Van Kirk image."

Diana grinned at her. "You got it."

And for the first time in memory, Janey smiled back.

They had been working on party plans for three days when Diana got a present she wasn't expecting—and wasn't too sure she wanted. She was out in the garden cutting back a rosebush in order to encourage a few blooms that looked about to break out, when she noticed a strange sound coming from the toolshed. It sounded as though an animal had been locked in by mistake.

Rising with a sigh, she went to the door and opened it. Inside she found a small caramel-colored ball of fluffy fur. The puppy looked up at her and wriggled happily.

"Well, who are you, you little cutie?" she said.

Kneeling down beside him, she pulled out the tag tied around his neck. "Hi," the tag said. "I'm Billy and I belong to Diana and Mia Collins, only they don't know it yet."

"What?"

She rose, staring down at the dog as Cam came into the shed.

"What do you think?" he asked, a smile in his voice if not on his face.

She whirled to meet him.

"*You* did this," she said accusingly.

He put a hand over his heart. "Guilty as charged." He wiggled his eyebrows at her. "A friend of mine had a whole litter of these cute little guys. I picked out the best one for you."

She frowned, feeling frazzled. "Cam, I can't take care of a puppy."

"Sure you can. I'll help you."

She sputtered, outraged that he would take it upon himself to do this to her. He looked at her earnestly.

"Di, calm down," he said. "You know very well you need a dog. This little fellow is going to grow up to be a good watchdog. He'll be there to protect you and the baby when…well, when I can't."

She understood the theory behind the gift. She just wasn't sure she appreciated the motives.

"Cam," she said stubbornly, "if I decided I needed a dog, I could get one for myself. And right now, I don't need a dog."

He didn't budge an inch, either. "You need the protection. Living alone like you do, out there in the sticks, it's too dangerous." He gave her a trace of his lopsided grin. "You never know what sort of madman might show up drunk on your pier in the middle of the night."

She turned away. So that was it. The dog was supposed to take his place. Was he just trying to ease his guilt over the fact that he was not going to be there for her when she needed him in the very near future? She could never have him, but she could have his dog. How thoughtful of him. She was tempted to turn on her heel and leave him here with his bogus little animal.

But she looked down and saw a pair of huge brown eyes staring up at her, a little tail wagging hopefully, a tongue lolling, and she fell in puppy love.

"What am I going to do with you?" she asked the pup.

Billy barked. It was a cute bark. An endearing bark. And it cemented the future for Billy. He was going home with her. There was no doubt about that. Still, there were problems and concerns attached to this gift.

She frowned, biting her lip and thinking over the logistics of the situation. "But I'm over here all day. I can't just leave him alone at the lake, not at this age."

"I agree," Cam said. "That's why I rigged up a dog run alongside the shed. You can have him here with you in the daytime. He'll go home with you at night."

Cam had thought of everything. She looked at him, loving him and resenting him at the same time. Slowly she shook her head. "I don't know what my little black kitten is going to think of this," she said.

"They're both young. They should be able to adjust to each other quickly."

She looked up at Cam. A few weeks before she hadn't had anything. Now she had a baby and she had a kitten and she had a dog. The only thing she still lacked was a man of her own. But you couldn't have everything, could you?

She shook her head, looking at him, loving him. He shrugged, his arms wide, all innocence. And she laughed softly, then walked over and gave him a hug.

"Thank you," she whispered, eyes shining.

He dropped a kiss on her lips, a soft kiss, barely a gesture of affection, and turned to leave before she could say any more.

It was at the beginning of her second week of work on the party that Diana came face-to-face with Cam's grandfather for the first time. She'd been working hard on all aspects of the preparations and she'd gone into the house to get out of the sun and found herself in the cool library with its tall ceilings and glass-fronted bookcases. It felt so good, she lowered herself into a huge leather chair and leaned back, closing her eyes.

At times like this she was getting used to communing silently with baby Mia, giving her words of encouragement, teaching her about what life was going to be like once she emerged from her protected cave and came into the real world. She knew the baby couldn't really hear her thoughts, but she also knew that something was communicated through an emotional connection that was getting stronger every day. Hopefully it was the love.

The minutes stretched and she fell asleep, her hands on her rounded belly. The next thing she knew, there was an elderly man standing over her, peering down as if to figure out who she was and just exactly why she was sleeping in his chair.

"Oh!" she cried, and she jumped up as smoothly as she could with the extra weight she was carrying. "I'm sorry, I…"

"Sit down, sit down." He waved his cane at her sternly. "Just sit down there and let me look at you, girl."

She glanced toward the exit, wishing she could take it, but reluctantly, she sank back down into the chair and tried to smile. She knew right away who this was, and if she hadn't known, she would have guessed. She could see hints lurking behind the age-ravaged face of a man who had once looked a lot like Cam, blue eyes and all.

"So you're Jed Collins's daughter, are you?" he growled. "You sure do look like your mom. She was one of the prettiest gals in the valley in those days."

"Th…thank you," she said, still unsettled by this chance encounter. "I think."

He nodded. "She ran off when you were a little one, didn't she? Ever find out what happened to her?"

Diana bristled a bit at the sense that he seemed to think he had a right to delve into her family matters at will. But she reminded herself that he probably thought of himself as a sort of elder statesman of the community, and she held back her resentment, shaking her head. "No, sir. Never did."

"You ought to get Cam to look for her. He could find her. That boy can do just about anything."

"I don't want to find her."

He stared at her for a moment and then gave a short shout of laughter.

"You're as tough as she was, aren't you? Good. Your dad was weak and he couldn't hold on to her. But who'd have thought she was tough enough to go off and leave her baby girl behind like she did? I'm telling you, nobody expected that one."

His casual assumptions outraged her. Who did he think he was to make these judgments on her family members? And yet, he was bringing up issues no one ever dared talk about in front of her. So in a way, it was sort of refreshing to get things out in the open. She'd never really had a chance to give her thoughts on the situation before, with everyone tiptoeing around it. Now was her chance, and she took it.

"You call that being tough?" she challenged, trying to ignore the lump that was rising in her throat. "For a woman to leave her six-year-old daughter behind in the care of a man who had no ability to handle it?" Her eyes flashed with anger, and that was reassuring. She would rather have anger than tears. "I call it being selfish and cruel."

He reared back and considered what she had to say as though he wasn't used to people disagreeing with his proclamations.

"Well, you would I suppose. But you don't know why she did it, do you? You're judging results, not motives."

She drew in a sharp breath. "You're darn right I'm judging results. I'm living the results."

He chuckled. "You've got fire in you, I'll say that," he said gruffly. "I know that grandson of mine has always had a special place in his heart for you." He frowned, looking at her. "But we all have to make sacrifices."

"Do we?"

"Damn right we do." He waved his cane at her again. "He promised me years ago he would marry one of the gals from the Five Families. I had everything set up and ready to go when he lit out on me. Left that poor little girl in the lurch."

He stamped his cane on the ground and suddenly he looked exhausted, leaning on it.

"Now he's going to have to make up for it." He shook his shaggy head. "He's a good boy. I knew he'd come through in the end. Not like his worthless father."

Diana stared at him. This was all news to her. "Cam was set to marry someone when he left ten years ago?" she asked softly, heart sinking. That would explain a lot. And make things murkier in other ways.

"Darn right he was. Little Missy Sinclair. Now he'll finally get the job done."

Cam appeared in the doorway before the old man could go on with his ramblings.

"Here you are," he said to his grandfather. "I didn't know you'd come all the way downstairs." He threw Diana a glance as he came up and took the old man's arm. "Come on. I'll help you back to your room."

"I'm okay, I'm okay," the older man grumbled. "I've just been talking to the Collins girl here. Pretty little thing, isn't she? Just like her mama."

"That she is," Cam agreed with a grin her way. "And the more you get to know her, the more you're going to like her."

"Well, I don't know about that," he muttered as his grandson led him away. "We'll see, I suppose."

Diana sat where she was as they disappeared down the hallway. She would wait. She knew Cam would come back down to talk to her. And she had some things she wanted to talk about—like secret engagements and leaving people in the lurch.

She looked up as he walked back into the room.

"Sorry about that," he told her with a quick smile. "He usually doesn't come downstairs these days. I hope he didn't say anything…well, anything to upset you." His gaze was bright as he looked at her and she had the distinct impression he was afraid exactly that had happened. And in a way, he was right.

"He did say something that surprised me," she told him, wishing her tone didn't sound quite so bitter, but not knowing how to soften it right now. "I didn't know you were supposed to marry someone just before you ran off to join the circus ten years ago."

He sat down on the arm of her large leather chair

and shook his head as he looked down at her. If her use of that phrase for his leaving didn't show him that she still harbored a grievance from those days, her tone would have given him a clue.

"Di, come on. I didn't run off to join the circus."

"Well, you might as well have." She bit her lip, realizing she was revealing a reservoir of long pent-up anger against him for doing what he'd done and leaving her behind. Just like her mother had. Funny, but she'd never connected those two events until today, when Cam's grandfather had forced the issue.

"There were a lot of reasons behind my leaving at the time," he told her, taking her hand up and holding it in his.

This was all old news as far as he was concerned. He'd thought she understood all this. Of course, he had to admit, he'd never told her about the arranged marriage that never happened—mostly because he'd always known he wouldn't go through with it. And so had the so-called "bride." It had never been a major issue in his thinking—except to avoid it.

"Mostly I needed to get out from under the suffocating influence of my grandfather. And part of what he was trying to force on me was a marriage to a girl I had no interest in marrying. But that was just part of it."

She nodded, digesting that. "Who was she?"

He hesitated, thinking. "Tell you the truth, I forget her name."

"Missy Sinclair?"

He looked at her penetratingly. "If you knew it, why did you ask?"

She shrugged. The turmoil inside her was making her nauseous. "Did you ask her to marry you at the time?"

"No." He began to play with her fingers as he talked. "It wasn't like that. Me marrying Missy was cooked up between my grandfather and Missy's grandfather about the time she was born. I had nothing to do with it and never actually agreed to it. Never."

Diana took in a deep breath, trying to stabilize her emotions. "Where is she now? Is she still waiting?"

"Are you kidding?" He laughed and went on, mockingly. "Selfish girl. She couldn't wait ten years. She went ahead and married some guy she actually loved. Strange, huh?"

She finally looked up and searched his blue eyes. "You didn't love her? Not even a little bit?"

He pressed her fingers to his lips and kissed them, holding her gaze with his own the whole time. "No, Diana, I didn't love her and she didn't love me. It was our grandfathers who loved the idea of us getting married. We both rebelled against it. The whole thing was dead on arrival from the beginning. The only one who even remembers the agreement is my grandfather. Forget about it. It meant nothing then and means nothing now."

She closed her eyes. She really had no right questioning him about this. What did she think she was doing? He had a right to get engaged to anyone he wanted. She had no hold on him, even though the things he did could hurt her more deeply than anything anyone else alive could do.

If only she had followed through on her original intention to stay away from Cam. Now it was too late. She was heading for heartbreak on a crazy train and there was no way to get off without crashing.

CHAPTER NINE

BABY MIA was moving all the time now. Diana was bursting with joy at the feeling. The tiny butterfly wing flapping sensations had grown into full-fledged kicks. She would feel Mia begin to move and she would bite her lip and her eyes would sparkle and she would think, "There you go, little girl! Stretch those little legs. You'll be running in no time."

It was hard feeling like she couldn't tell the people around her what was happening. One afternoon, she couldn't contain it any longer. Mia was kicking so hard, it was making her laugh. She sidled up to Cam, who was overseeing some workers who were building a trellis and whispered to him.

"Give me your hand."

He looked at her, surprised. He'd just come back from a meeting with some bankers, so he was in a business suit and sunglasses and looking particularly suave and sensational. But he did what she asked, and she placed his hand right on the pertinent part of her tummy.

He stood very still for a moment, then turned to her with wonder in his eyes.

"Oh my God. Is that…?"

"Yes." Her smile was all encompassing. "Isn't it funny?"

He stared at her, his blue eyes luminous. "It's like a miracle."

She nodded, filled with joy. He took her hand and pulled her behind the gazebo where they could have a bit of privacy.

"How amazing to feel a new life inside you," he said, flattening his hand on her stomach again with more hope than success. "Di, it's wonderful."

"I can't tell you how transporting it is," she agreed. "It's really true. I'm like a different person."

His smile grew and took in all of her. "No," he said, cupping her cheek with the palm of his hand. "You're the same person. You just have new parts of you blossoming."

She nodded happily. Impulsively she reached up and kissed him, then turned quickly and retreated, back to work. But his reaction had warmed her to the core. She loved her baby and having him appreciate that, even a little bit, was super. Just knowing she had her baby with her was enough to flood her with happiness. All the worries and cares of the day fell away as she concentrated on the baby she was bringing to the world.

She had some qualms about raising Mia alone, without a father figure to balance her life. She'd gone through a lot of soul searching before she'd taken the plunge into single motherhood. Was it fair to the child? Would she be able to handle it? She knew she was taking a risk and that it would be very hard, but she also knew she would do what was best for her baby, no matter what. And once she'd taken the step, she hadn't looked back for one minute.

She'd begun to buy baby clothes and to plan what she was going to do with the second bedroom in her house, the one she was converting into a nursery.

"I'll paint it for you," Cam had offered. "You shouldn't be breathing in those paint fumes while you're carrying Mia."

She'd taken him up on that offer and they had spent a wonderful Saturday trading off work and playing with Billy and the kitten. While Cam painted the room pink, Diana made chocolate chip cookies and worked on a pet bed she was constructing for the puppy.

Afterward, they took fishing poles out to the far side of the lake and caught a few trout, just like they had in the old days, catch and release. Diana made a salad for their evening meal and afterward, Cam found her old guitar and sat on the couch, playing some old forgotten standards and singing along while she watched.

A perfect day—the sort of day she would want for her baby to grow up with, surrounded by happiness and love. If only she could find a way to have more of them.

She walked him out to his car as he was leaving. The crickets were chirping and the frogs were croaking. He kissed her lightly. She knew she shouldn't allow it, but it was so comforting, so sweet. She leaned against him and he held her loosely.

"What would your father say if he could see you now?" he wondered.

She thought for a moment. "If he could see me now, he'd be out here with a shotgun, warning you to go home," she said with a laugh.

"You're probably right," he said. "Maybe it's just as well he's gone."

"I do actually miss him sometimes," she said pensively. "And I know I'm going to wish he could see Mia once she's born."

"Better he's not here to make her life miserable, too," Cam said cynically.

She sighed, knowing he was right but wishing he wasn't. If only she could have had a normal father. But then, what was normal anyway?

"He apologized to me toward the end, you know," she told him.

"Did he?"

She nodded. "He told me a lot of things I hadn't known before, things that explained a lot, things about his own insecurities and how he regretted having treated my mother badly. It's taken me some time to assimilate that information and assign the bits and pieces their proper importance in my life. Just having him do that, filling in some gaps, put things into a whole new perspective for me."

"No matter what his excuses, it can't justify what he did to you," Cam said darkly. Anger burned in him when he remembered how those bruises had covered her arms at times.

"No, I know that. I want to forgive him, but it's hard. It's only been very recently that I've even been able to start trying to understand him...and my mother...and what they did."

He held her more closely. "You deserved better parents."

She sighed. "I'm trying to get beyond blaming them. In a way, they only did what they were capable of doing."

He didn't believe that, but he kept his dissent to himself. If she needed to forgive them to make her life easier, so be it. He had no problem with that. He only knew that *he* didn't forgive what they'd done to her and there was a part of him that would be working to make it up to her for the rest of his life.

Billy began to yip for attention back in the house. They laughed.

"I guess I'd better get going," he said.

He looked at her from under lowered lids, looked at her mouth, then let his gaze slide down to where her breasts pushed up against the opening of her shirt. His blood began to quicken, and then his pure male reaction began to stir, and he knew it was time to go.

She nodded, but she didn't turn away.

He wanted to kiss her. He wanted to do more than that and he knew it was folly to stay any longer. Steeling himself, he let her go and turned for the car. Reaching out, he opened the door, but before he dropped inside, he looked back. And that was his fatal error.

One look at her standing there, her hair blowing around her face, her lips barely parted, her eyes full of something smoky, and he was a goner. In two quick steps he erased the space between them, and before she could protest, he was kissing her, hard and hot.

She didn't push at him the way he thought she would. Instead her arms wrapped around his neck and she pressed her body to his. He kissed her again and this time the kiss deepened.

She drank him in as though he held the secret of life, and for her, in many ways, he did. His mouth moved on hers, his tongue seeking heat and depth, and she accepted him, at first gladly, then hungrily, and finally with nothing but pure sensual greed.

This was what he'd been waiting for, aching for, dying for. All the doubts about who she might really want in her life dried up and blew away. He had her in his arms and that was where she belonged. He was going to stake a claim now, and if any other man wanted to challenge it, he'd better bring weapons.

Diana gasped, writhing in his embrace and wondering where this passion had come from. It had her in its grip, lighting a fire inside that she'd never known before. Every part of her felt like butter, melting to his touch. She knew this was crazy, this was playing with fire, but she couldn't stop it now. She wanted more and she wanted it with a fever that consumed her.

Billy barked again, and just like that, the magic evaporated, leaving them both breathing hard and shocked at what they had just been through.

"Oh my," Diana said, her eyes wide with wonder as she stared at him.

"Wow," he agreed, holding her face with two hands, looking down into her eyes as though he'd found something precious there.

"You…you'd better go," she said, stepping back away from him and shaking her head as though that would ward off temptation.

He nodded. "Okay," he said reluctantly, his voice husky with the remnants of desire still smoldering. He didn't dare touch her again, but he blew her a kiss, and then he was in his car and gone.

Diana watched him until his taillights disappeared around the far bend. Then she bit her lip and wondered why she seemed to be into torturing herself.

"The more greedy you get," she told herself, "the more you're going to miss him when he's gone."

But she had to admit, right now, she didn't really care. Right now she had gathered another memory to live with. And she would surely hold it dear.

The work was going well and the party was only a couple of days away. Janey had thrown herself into picking the musicians and the music, auditioning all sorts of groups as well as the high school kids. Every spare moment was filled with food preparation, mostly of the finger food variety—lumpia, teriyaki chicken wings, pineapple meatballs, tempura shrimp, wontons and everything else they could think of. Rosa set out the ingredients and Diana and Janey began to cut and mix. Rosa manned the ovens. Janey cleaned the trays. And once each batch was cooked, it was filed away in one of the massive freezers the estate maintained.

Meanwhile Mrs. Van Kirk was busy going through the RSVP returns and setting up place cards for the tables.

"The Five Families are coming en masse," she announced to everyone, happily running through her cards. "The eligible young woman count is at eleven and rising fast. Once they find out Cameron is up for matrimonial grabs, they sign up without delay. He's quite popular among them, you know."

Diana didn't have to be told. She already knew and she was sick at heart about it. She knew this was the last gasp as far as her relationship with Cam went. His family wanted him to marry a rich lady and that was what he was going to have to do. He might not know it yet, but she did.

He felt guilty for leaving his family in the lurch ten years before. He was ready and ripe for the picking as far as expiating that guilt and doing what would make his family happy and solvent went. He was going to have to marry someone. He just hadn't faced it in a calm and rational way.

Her mind was made up. She was going to endure this party to the best she could and then she was going to head home and stay away from the Van Kirks for the rest of her life. Every one of them. She would have Penny come and do the weekly flower arrangements and she herself would have no further contact with these people. That was the only way to preserve her happiness and her sanity. It wasn't going to be easy, but she would keep her allegiance to her baby uppermost in her mind and she would fight through the pain. It had to be.

Cam sat in his car staring at the Van Kirk mansion. He'd been in Sacramento doing some research and he had some news for Diana, who was inside, working on party preparations. He wasn't sure how she was going to take it. He wasn't sure how he took it himself.

His grandfather had mentioned the fact that Di's mother left her at a young age and that no one knew exactly why she might have done such a thing. Was she running off with another man? Had she reached the end of her rope dealing with her drunk of a husband? But if that was the case, why did she leave her child behind? In this day and age, the answers to such questions were a lot easier to find than they had been in the old days before computers and public access to so much government information.

At first Cam had resisted looking into the matter. After all, if Di wanted to know these things, she could have instituted a search herself, years ago. To go ahead on his own was to intrude where he had no right to. And yet, once his grandfather had brought it up, the mystery had nagged at him until he'd had to find out for himself.

His dilemma now was whether or not to tell Diana that he'd done it. And whether or not to tell her what he'd found as a result. What made him think that she actually wanted to know?

But it had to be done. Swearing softly, he got out of the car and started into the house, ready to go looking for Diana. The time of reckoning was at hand.

"Hi," she said, looking harried. "Listen, I need to talk to you. Ben has been calling me."

He reacted quickly to that, turning his head to stare at her. "What for?"

"He wants me to commit to selling out my portion of the inherited land." She appealed to him, a worried look in her large dark eyes. "What do you think? Should I do it?"

He hesitated. He hadn't been able to find out anything that would make him counsel that she turn Ben down, but something about this whole deal didn't seem right to him.

"Maybe you ought to wait," he said.

Diana seemed impatient. "Wait for what? We saw the land. It's not worth much. And I could use the money." She patted her rounded tummy. "I've got a baby coming, you know."

"I know." He smiled at her obvious joy every time she thought of or mentioned her baby. "I've tried to find out if there is any reason he would be so hot to have it, but so far, I haven't found a whisper of anything that would lead in that direction."

He'd come looking for her to tell her what he'd

found about her mother, but as he gazed at her now, he thought twice and decided to hold off. She had too many things on her mind as it was. This business about her mother would just add to her worries and she didn't need that. He thought for a moment, then shrugged.

"Oh, what the hell. Go ahead and sell to him. Why not?"

"Okay. I'll give him a call and tell him to write up his proposal. He said he would send me a check once it was signed." She looked up at him, eyebrows raised in question. "Maybe you could use the money to help with…?"

"Forget it," he said, but he grinned at her. "The amount we need is way beyond what you'll be getting. But thanks for the thought. I appreciate it."

She nodded. "Okay then." She noted a worried look in his eyes and she frowned. "Cam, how's the search for funding going? Have you had any luck yet?"

He shook his head briefly and gave her a fleeting smile. "No. With the economy the way it is, no one wants to take a chance."

She hated to see defeat in his face. "What about your business in San Diego? Have you thought about…" She almost gulped before she dared say the word. "Selling it?"

"Don't you think I've tried that?" He ran a hand through his hair, regretting that his response had been a bit harsh. "Of course I've thought about it.

I've even put it on the auction block. So far there have been no takers."

"Oh." She was beginning to realize that this was really not looking good. It just might be that the Van Kirks were going to lose their family home and all the land they'd held for over a hundred years.

Funny how that sent a shiver of dread through her. What did she care, after all? These were people who had scorned her and her family all her life, until very recently. While she and her father had scrimped and clawed their way to a bare bones existence, the Van Kirks had lived a wealthy life of ease and comfort.

Or so it had seemed from afar. Once she got to know them better, she realized they had their own problems, their own demons to deal with. With wealth, your priorities changed, but the obstacles were very much the same. Life was no bed of roses no matter what side of the fence you lived on.

"You mean that darned old Freddy Mercury knew what he was talking about?" Cam said when she tried to explain to him how her thinking was running.

"Only if the Van Kirks end up as champions," she retorted, giving him a snooty look. "No time for losers, after all."

He put his forefinger under her chin and lifted it, looking down into her face. "We're going to come out of this okay, Diana," he said firmly. "I promise. Somehow, someway, I'm going to save the family farm."

She couldn't help but believe him. He had always been her champion, after all.

* * *

It was two days later that Cam came to her in a hurry just as she arrived at the estate. She'd barely risen from her car when he came rushing up.

"Diana, I need your help," he said without preamble. "Please. Find Janey and get her to take my mother downtown."

"What for?" The request was a little surprising, as Mrs. Van Kirk hadn't set foot off the grounds since her accident.

"Find some excuse. We've got to get her out of here. We've got appraisers and bank people coming to take a look at the house. It'll kill her if she sees that. She'll put two and two together and get…zero."

"Why are they coming?" Diana asked, not too good at putting two and two together herself.

"Why do you think? They want to take measurements and do evaluations." He gave her a dark look as he turned away. "Let's just say the vultures are circling."

That was an ominous thing to say and she shuddered every time she thought of it. But she did find Janey and prompted her to convince her mother to go into town for a bit of window-shopping. The real thing was off the budget for the foreseeable future. She watched as they drove off in Janey's little sports car, Mrs. Van Kirk complaining about the tight fit all the way. Just as they disappeared down the driveway, a limousine drove up and disgorged a group of businessmen who reminded her of a scrum of ravenous sharks.

Cam went out to meet them and began to take

them on a tour of the grounds, talking very fast all the while. She wondered just what line of fantasy he was trying to spin. Whatever it was, they seemed to be listening attentively.

It wasn't until he brought them into the house that she began to realize something was wrong. She heard shouting and as she ran toward the front of the house where the noise was coming from, she began to realize it was Cam's grandfather who was causing a ruckus.

Old-fashioned cuss words were flying as she burst into the library where Cam was trying to quiet the older man. The bankers and appraisers were shell-shocked, gathering against the far wall of the room like a school of frightened fish.

"Get out of my house," Cam's grandfather was yelling. "I won't have you bloodsuckers here. I'd rather die than give in to you thieves. Where's my shotgun?"

"Get them out of here," Cam told her as she skidded to a stop before him, pointing to the group of visitors. "I'm going to lock him in here."

She shooed the men away, then turned back. "I'll stay here with him," she heard herself say, then gaped in horror at her own suggestion. The last thing in the world she wanted to do was stay here with this raving madman, but at the same time, she couldn't see locking him in here all alone. He was too old and too honored a member of this family to be treated like that.

"Really?" Cam looked at the end of his rope. "Great. Thanks, Di. I'll make it up to you, somehow."

He took off after the others, locking the door behind him, and Diana turned to look at the grandfather.

He'd finally stopped yelling and he sagged down onto the couch, his face turning an ashen shade of gray. She quickly got a glass of water from the cooler in the corner and handed it to him. He took a long drink and seemed to revive somewhat. He turned to look at her and frowned.

"They want to take my house away," he told her shakily. "I can't let them do that."

"Cam is going to try to fix it," she said, wishing she had more faith in the fact that a fix was possible. "I think these men are just here to gather some data."

He didn't answer and for a moment, she thought he'd forgotten she was there. Then he turned, gazing at her from under bushy eyebrows.

"Let me tell you a story, girl. A story about family and friendship and history."

She glanced toward the door. Surely Cam would be coming back to rescue her soon. "Well, if it's only a short one."

"Sit down."

He did have a way with words—a strong and scary way. She sat down.

"I'm sure you know all about the Five Families, how our ancestors all worked together to establish a decent community for our loved ones here. Those bonds were still strong back when I was young. Through the years, they've frayed a bit. But two of us remained true friends, me and Jasper Sinclair. Some called our friendship historic. We were the only remaining descendants in our generation of a group of close friends who had struck out together for the California gold fields in the mid-nineteenth century, men who found their fortunes, and founded a pair of towns rimming the Gold Dust Valley."

He shook his head, his foggy gaze obviously turned backward on ancient scenes.

"Me and Jasper, we were raised to feel it our duty to maintain area pride in that culture and history. The other families sort of dissolved for one reason or another. Oh, they're still around, but their kids don't really have the pride the way they should. The Van Kirks and the Sinclairs, though, we've still got that Gold Rush story running in the blood in our veins."

Diana nodded. She knew a lot of this already, and she knew that it was a Sinclair girl that Cam had been expected to marry ten years ago.

"Jasper's gone now, but he had a passel of granddaughters. I always said, if Cam can't decide on one of those pretty girls, he just ain't the man I think he is. You see, I promised Jasper I would see to it that we kept the old ways alive. Traditions matter. That's what keeps a culture intact, keeps the home fires burning, so to speak."

Diana took a deep breath and made a stab at giving her own opinion on the subject. "You know, in this day and age, it's pretty hard to force that sort of arranged marriage on young people. It just doesn't fit with the way we live now."

He fixed her with a gimlet eye. "Some of those arranged marriages turn out better than the ones people fall into by themselves," he said gruffly. "Look at your own parents. They married for love. That didn't turn out so well, did it?"

Diana had just about had it with his casual interest in giving out his view of her family affairs.

"Mr. Van Kirk," she began stiffly.

But he didn't wait to hear what she had to say.

"Did you know that your dad and my son, Cam's father, were good friends back before the two of you were born? Drinking buddies, in fact."

That stopped her in her tracks. "No," she said softly. "No, I didn't know that."

He nodded solemnly. "I used to blame him. Your dad, I mean. But now I realize they were both weak, both with addictive problems. Funny, isn't it?"

"Tragic is more like it," she said, but the words were under her breath and he didn't hear them.

He glared at her. "Anyway, I just hope you understand that Cam has got to marry one of them girls. There's no other way. It's either that, or we are over as a family." He shrugged as though dismissing her. "Sorry, but that's the way it is."

Cam returned before he could go on and she rose gratefully, leaving him to take his grandfather back up to his room. She felt numb. She knew what the old man had been trying to say to her. He needn't have bothered. She knew Cam would never marry her. As far as he was concerned, she was pregnant with another man's child. Besides, he didn't want to marry anyone. Didn't the old man know that?

But if all that was true, why was she crying again?

Cam sat in the darkened library staring out at the moon and wondering how things had gotten so crazy. He held a crystal glass filled with golden liquid of a certain potent variety and imbibed from time to time. But mostly, he was lost in thought.

It was the night before the party. Everyone had worked long into the evening, and would be back first thing in the morning to finish preparations before the guests began to arrive. Cam felt tired down to his bones, but he knew it was more emotional than physical.

Tomorrow the grounds would be filled with partygoers. A lot of beautiful young women from eligible families would be showing off their pretty summer dresses. Most of them were just coming to have fun, to see friends, to be at a party. But he knew there were certain expectations, mostly from his own family, that he would choose one of them to court. Preferably one of the richest ones, preferably from one of the Five Families. Hopes were high that he would do something matrimonial to save his own family from being kicked out of their ancestral home.

That wasn't going to happen. Much as he wanted to do something to save his family from ruin, he couldn't marry someone he didn't love. And he couldn't stop loving someone he couldn't marry.

He groaned, stretching back in the leather chair and closing his eyes. He should never have let his mother have her way with this party. He should never have let any of them get their hopes up this way.

Janey had actually brought the subject up earlier that day.

"Look," she'd said, waving a paring knife his way as she took a break from fashioning vegetable decorations. "It's only obvious you're crazy for Diana. You don't want to marry any of those women who are coming. I'm not sure you even want to be here with us."

She waved the knife so dramatically, he'd actually stepped back to be sure he was out of range.

"Why don't you just grab Diana and go? Take off for parts unknown. Leave us behind. We'll sink or swim without you."

He shook his head. "I can't do that."

"Why not?"

"Because it turns out, though I tried for ten years to forget it, blood is thicker than water. I'm a part of this family and I do care what happens to it."

Janey looked at him as though he were demented. "You can't just go off and be happy with the girl you love?"

"No."

Janey looked at him for a long moment, then said, "More fool you," but her eyes were moist and she turned and gave him the first hug he'd had from her since they were children.

A part of what complicated things, of course, was that, even if he wanted to go off with Diana, he wasn't sure she would want to go off with him. He knew she had a lot of affection for him, knew that she'd missed him and resented that he had gone off and left her behind suddenly the way he had—and for so darn long.

But why wouldn't she tell him who Mia's father was? He didn't know anything about the man who had fathered her baby. There was only one reason he could think of for that. She must still love him, still hope to get him to return and take up his duties as her child's father. What else could it be? And if that was still her dream, how could he get in the way?

He wished he understood women better. Somehow their thought processes were such a mystery. Just when he thought he'd figured one of them out, he found she was off in outer space somewhere, running on completely different assumptions than he was.

Gina for instance, the woman he'd lived with for a substantial length of time two years before. He'd thought they had the perfect adult relationship— companionship and sex without strings. She was the one who had suggested it and he'd been glad to accept her conditions. Then, suddenly, she wanted to get married. That was a shocker. He very quickly realized he didn't love her and didn't want to spend his life with her. When he explained that to her, she left in a huff.

A few months later, she was back, claiming to be pregnant with his child. He'd felt trapped, threatened, but he wanted to do the right thing. They planned a wedding, but he was in torture the whole time, resenting her, resenting the coming child, and hating himself for feeling that way.

Out of the blue, she died in a car accident. He was even more miserable, sad for her and the baby, tortured with the way he'd acted. He wished he'd been kinder to her.

Then, when the medical reports came in, he found out that the baby wasn't his after all. The confusion that left him in lasted for months. He couldn't even think about dating again. He didn't trust any woman he met. He'd actually begun to wonder if he would ever feel comfortable with a woman again.

Then he'd come home and there was Diana. It didn't take long to realize he was probably in love with her and always had been. The fact that it was crazy and doomed didn't bother him. He was used to life not turning out the way he'd hoped it would.

A sound in the doorway made him open his eyes and sit up straighter. There was Diana, walking slowly into the room and finally spotting him as her eyes adjusted to the gloom.

"I thought you'd gone home," he said.

"I did, but I forgot to put some of the leis we strung together in cool storage. I didn't want to leave them out overnight."

He nodded. "Will you join me in a drink?" he offered.

"No, thanks." But she came close and perched on the arm of the overstuffed leather chair where he was sitting. "I've got to get on home. I just stopped in for a minute."

"I was just sitting here thinking about you. About us."

She sighed. "Cam, there is no 'us.'"

"I've noticed that, Diana. Tell me why that is."

She looked down at him, startled by his tone. "There's a party happening tomorrow that is supposed to result in you choosing a rich bride to save the family," she said crisply. "That pretty much takes care of any 'us' there might have been."

He shook his head and took a sip of his drink. "I'm not buying it, Di. There's a wall between us and I'm just beginning to realize you put it there."

"That's crazy. I didn't invent this commitment you have to your family. It's enshrined in your Van Kirk legacy. It's like a shield carved into your front door. You gotta do what you gotta do."

"No, I don't."

"Yes, you do. You know very well it's what called you back here. You are part of something you can't shake free of. Duty, responsibility, whatever you want to call it. It's part of you and you're going to do what they expect."

He stared at her in the darkness. Was she right? Was he really going to do this thing they wanted of him?

He loved his grandfather with a fierce devotion,

but he'd always resented him and his manipulating ways with almost as much passion. The senior Van Kirk had constantly tried to guide his life, but in the past, he'd resisted, sometimes violently. That was what the whole mad dash to shake off the dust of this gold country town in the hills had been all about. So he'd gone off to get out from under his family's rules and make his fortune. And here he was, coming back into his family's sphere and acting like that had all been a huge mistake. Was he really ready to follow his grandfather's wishes this time?

No. The whole idea was insane.

"Diana, I've told you a thousand times, I'm not marrying anyone."

"Really?" She clutched at the hem of her blouse and twisted it nervously. "Well, I think you ought to revisit that statement."

He frowned up at her. "What are you talking about?"

"You made a promise a long time ago, from what your grandfather tells me. And now that your family needs you to put yourself on the line, I think you ought to fulfill that promise." She knew she was beginning to sound a little shrill, but she couldn't help it. Her emotions were very near the surface and she was having a hard time holding them back.

"You need to have a nice little Five Families baby with one of those super rich girls and save the house, save the legacy, save it all. It's your destiny. It's what you were raised to do."

He stared at her, aghast. "You've really drunk the Kool-Aid, haven't you?"

"I've listened to your grandfather, if that's what you mean. And I've realized you're going to hate yourself if you don't do what you've been raised to think is your duty. You can't fight it."

He swore softly, shaking his head, disbelief shuddering through him.

"Just like I was raised to be pretty much the opposite," she went on, her voice sure but a bit shaky. "That's what my father always used to tell me. 'You're just a white trash girl. Don't get no fancy ideas, running around with a Van Kirk boy. That bunch will never accept you.' That's what he used to say. I didn't believe him then, but now I see the wisdom in accepting the truth."

"Truth." He said the word scornfully. "That's not truth. That's someone's fantasy dressed up as faux reality. You've fallen down the rabbit hole, Di. Stop listening to the Mad Hatter."

She almost laughed. "Your grandfather?"

He nodded. "Despite everything, I love that old man." He shrugged. "And you're right, up to a point. I made certain promises. I've got certain responsibilities."

Reaching up, he caught hold of her and flipped her down into his lap, catching her by surprise and eliciting a shriek as she landed in his arms. "But one thing I won't do is marry a woman I don't love," he said. "And you can take that to the bank."

"Cam…" She tried to pull away but he was having none of it.

His body was hard, strong, inescapable and she knew right away she couldn't stop him. But she didn't really want to and when his mouth came down on hers, it felt so hot, she gasped. His ardor shocked her, but in a good way, and very quickly her own passion rose to meet it. The pressure of his mouth on hers was pure intoxication. She sank into the kiss like a swimmer in a warm, inviting whirlpool, and very soon she was spinning round and round, trying to get her head above water often enough to catch her breath, but strongly tempted to stay below where his smooth strength made her giddy with desire.

He'd wanted to do this for so long, his need was an urgent throb that pushed him to kiss her harder, deeper, and to take every part of her in his hands. He plunged beneath her clothes, craving the feel of her soft flesh, sliding his hands down the length of her, sailing on the sensation like an eagle on a burst of wind. In this moment, she was his and he had to take her or die trying.

The top buttons of her blouse were open and his hot mouth was on her breast, finding the nipple, his lips tugging, his tongue stroking, teasing senses cued to resonate to his will. She was writhing in his arms, begging for more with tiny whimpers, touching him as eagerly as he was touching her.

"More," was the only word that penetrated her heat. "More, please, more!"

All thoughts of duty and responsibility were forgotten. Thought itself was banished. Feeling was king, and she felt an arousal so intense it scared her. She was his for the taking, his forever. Right and wrong had nothing to do with it. He was all she'd ever wanted. The rest was up to him.

And he pulled back.

She stared up at him, panting, almost begging to have him back against her, and he looked down at her dispassionately, all discipline and control.

"You see, Diana?" he said. "There *is* an 'us,' whether you want there to be or not. You can't deny it. And I can't marry anyone else when I want you more than I've ever wanted any other woman."

He set her back on the wide arm of the chair and rose while she pulled her clothes together.

"I'll see you in the morning," he said, and walked away.

Diana sat where she was, shaken to the core and still trembling like a leaf. She was putty in his hands. He could do anything he wanted with her and her body would respond in kind. She was helpless. Helplessly in love.

CHAPTER TEN

PARTY time!

The scene was being set for a wonderful party. Cam had recruited some old high school friends to come help him and they had strung lights everywhere throughout the yard. They had reactivated a man-made watercourse that had been built years before to run all through the gardens, and now water babbled happily, recreating the look of a mountain stream. Cam had even found a way to put lights just beneath the surface at random intervals, so the whole thing sparkled as though it was under perpetual sunlight.

Guests began to arrive at midafternoon. The sense of excitement was contagious and the air was filled with the scent of flowers and the sound of music. Diana knew very few of the people who arrived. Some were cousins of Cam's who had come by to help a time or two in the past few days. But most of the Five Families children went to private schools, so she hadn't had much occasion to cross paths with many of them, and some of the ones she did know didn't seem to recognize her.

One lucky result of the theme was that no one had even suggested she wear a French maid's costume while mixing with the guests as she had feared at the first. The Hawaiian decor meant that she could wear a beautiful long island dress and put flowers in her hair and look just as good as most of the visitors did.

"I can pretend, can't I?" she muttered to herself as she wove her way in and out of the crowd. Still, she was the one holding the tray with the wineglasses, though, wasn't she? That pretty much gave the game away.

"Oh my dear, you look wonderful!" Mrs. Van Kirk approved, nodding as she looked her over. "I love the garland of flowers you've put in your hair. You look like a fairy princess."

Mr. Van Kirk, Cam's father, was home on a rare visit, looking half soused, but pleasant. He nodded agreement with his wife but didn't say much, except, "Hey, I knew your dad. He was one of my best friends. God, I really miss those days."

And she didn't linger to hear his stories.

Everyone praised the wonderful stream and the lights and the music and once the cocktail hour began to blend into dinnertime, the food was center stage. Diana was so busy making sure there was enough and the access was ample that she hardly had time to notice anything else, but she did see Cam once in a while, and every time her wandering gaze found him, he was surrounded by women.

"I'm sure he's having the time of his life," Janey said, and for once she sounded amused rather than resentful. She had her latest date, Adam, with her. A rather short man, he seemed to follow her dutifully everywhere she went, looking thoroughly smitten, and she seemed to enjoy it.

While she was filling the punch bowl with a fresh supply of green sherbet punch doused with rum and meant to take the place of daiquiris, Janey came up and elbowed her.

"Look at there, by the waterfall. Those three are the prime candidates."

She lifted her head to look at the three beautiful young women. "What do you mean?" she asked, though she was very much afraid she already knew.

"We need Cam to pick one of them to marry. They are the richest ones."

"And the most beautiful, too," she said, feeling just a bit wistful.

"Well, the one on the right, Julie Ransom, is only semibeautiful," Janey opined. "But she's got a wonderful personality."

"Oh, great. Better and better."

"What do you care? He's got to pick one of them."

"I know."

"Tina Justice, the redhead, is said to be a bit on the easy side, but nice. And Grace Sinclair, the one in the middle, is the younger sister of Missy, the one Cam was supposed to marry years ago. She's considered just about the most beautiful woman in the valley. Wouldn't you agree?"

"Oh, yes," she said, heart sinking as she looked at the woman who was wearing a turquoise sari and standing out in the crowd. "She's got that luminous quality."

"Yes. And I think Cam likes her pretty well. So let's work on getting the two of them together. Agreed?" Janey gave her an assessing look, as though wondering how she was going to react to that, but Diana didn't give her the satisfaction of letting on.

"You get busy on that," she said lightly. "I've got some crudités to crunch."

In some ways it was nice that Janey now considered her a coconspirator rather than an enemy, but this sort of scheming put her in a very awkward position. She didn't need it. She was going to keep her distance from actual matchmaking no matter what.

Just a few more hours, she told herself, and then you'll be free. You'll never have to look at this family again. But whether you can forget them—ah, there's the rub.

It was only a short time later that she found herself listening to the three prime candidates as they chatted about Cam, ignoring her completely. She was in the kitchen, taking cheese sticks out of the oven, when they came in to wash a spill out of the red-headed girl's dress at the sink.

"They say his mother is pushing hard to get him to pick a bride tonight," she was saying.

"Tonight?" Grace repeated, looking out the window to see if she could spot him.

"Yes! Have you danced with him yet?"

"Twice." Grace sighed, throwing her head back. "He is super dreamy. I just wanted to melt in his arms. If I can get him again, I'm going to find a way to maneuver him out into the trees so we can have a little make-out time. There's nothing like stirring up the old libido and then doing the old tease for arousing a man's interest in getting engaged. And if his mother is pushing…"

"I haven't had a go at him yet," Julie said with a pout. "You all just back off until I've had my turn."

The redhead frowned thoughtfully. "You know, they also say he's got a pregnant girlfriend in the valley."

Grace nodded. "Could you put up with that?"

Julie tossed her head. "I think I could hold my own against a little piece of valley fluff."

They all laughed and began to adjust their makeup at the kitchen mirror.

Diana looked at them with distaste. She wasn't sure if they'd seen her or not. Somehow she thought it wouldn't have mattered anyway. Thinking her a servant, they would likely have looked right through her. Nice girls.

She gathered some fruit on a platter, preparing to go out with it, but just for fun, she stopped by where they were primping.

"Would any of you ladies like some grapes?" she

offered, pointing them out. "They're very sweet. Not a sour one in the bunch."

All three pairs of eyes stared at her, startled.

"No, thanks," one murmured, but it was obvious they didn't know what to make of her. She smiled and carried the tray out into the party area. But her heart was thumping and her adrenaline was up. Nice girls indeed!

The dancing seemed to go on forever. Diana managed to avoid Cam, although she saw him looking for her a time or two. She was not going to dance with him. After tonight, she was going to be a stranger. No sense in prolonging the agony.

Finally the night was drawing to a close. Adam's DJ son had taken over center stage and was announcing themes for dances. It was a cute gimmick and was keeping a lot of people on the dance floor who probably would have been on their way home by now if not for the encouragement from the DJ.

Diana was tired. She wanted to go home and put her feet up.

"The last dance," the DJ was saying on the loudspeaker. "And this one is special. Our host, Cameron Van Kirk, will pick out his chosen partner and then we will all drink a toast to the couple. Mr. Van Kirk. Will you please choose your partner?"

It was like a car crash, she couldn't look away. Which one of the beautiful young women who had come here to look him over and to be looked over would he pick? She peered out between two onlookers and there was Cam. He was searching the scene, scanning the entire assembly, and then he stepped down and began to walk into the crowd.

Suddenly she knew what he was doing. There was no doubt in her mind. He was looking for her.

Her heart began to bang against her chest like a big bass drum and she couldn't breathe. How did she know this? What made her so sure? She wasn't certain about that, but she did know as sure as she knew her own name that he was headed her way.

She turned, looking around frantically. Where could she hide? He couldn't possibly do this— could he? It would be an insult to all those beautiful, wealthy women for him to pick the pregnant party planner as his special partner. She squeezed her way between a line of people and hurried toward the side exit. And ran right into Cam.

"There you are," he said, taking her hands before she could stop him. "Come with me. I can't do this alone."

"Can't do what alone?" she said robotically, still looking for a chance to escape. But with all eyes on her, she really couldn't push his hands away and she found herself walking with him to the middle of the dance floor.

"Please welcome Mr. Cameron Van Kirk," the DJ said, "and Miss Diana Collins. Give them a hand, ladies and gentlemen."

The music began and Cam's arms came around her. She closed her eyes and swayed to the music, a hollow feeling in the pit of her stomach.

"You can't be surprised," he said very near her ear. "You know you're my choice. You always have been."

She pulled back so she could look into his face. "I know you think you made a great joke out of this, but…"

"Joke? Are you kidding?" He held her closer. "Diana, face it. I love you."

She closed her eyes again and willed this to be over. She knew he thought he loved her. And maybe he really did. But it was impossible. He couldn't do this.

The music ended and the applause was polite and the toast was pleasant. But people were somewhat puzzled. You could see it in their faces, hear it in their voices. This wasn't one of the girls he was supposed to pick.

Still, people gathered around for congratulations. And while Cam was involved in that, Diane slipped away. She headed for her car. She knew she was being a rat and leaving all the cleanup to others, but she couldn't help it. She had to get away. If she hadn't been here to confuse things, Cam would have been free to choose one of the rich girls. The only remedy she could think of was to clear the field and give him space to do what he needed to do. She had to get out of here.

She raced home, packed a bag in three minutes and called her assistant, Penny, and asked her to come house-sit, kitten-sit and dog-sit. That was a lot of sitting, but Penny was up for it. In no time at all she was on her way to San Francisco. It was going to be a long night.

Cam didn't know she was gone until the next morning when he got an e-mail from her. It was short and scary.

Cam, please go on with your life without me. I'm going to be gone for a week or two so that you can get used to it. When I come back, I don't want to see you. Please. Don't bother to reply, I won't be reading my e-mail. A clean break is the best way. Di.

He went straight to her house just in case and found Penny there.

"She said she had to go to San Francisco," Penny said when he demanded to know where Diana had gone. "I'm not sure where. She'll probably call me tonight to see how the animals are. Do you want me to give her a message?"

He shook his head. "I can't wait until tonight. You really can't give me any better clue than that?"

"Well… She did say something about staying where she stayed when she got pregnant with Mia. I think she wanted to revisit the base of her decision or something. She was muttering and I couldn't really catch her meaning."

His heart turned to stone in his chest. She was going to see Mia's father. He was sure of it. He should leave her alone. Maybe she could work something out with him. That would be best for Diana, best for Mia. Wouldn't it?

Everything in him rebelled at that thought. No! That was crazy. The man was obviously not right for either one of them—and anyway, he wasn't going to give up the woman that he loved without a fight. He was going to find her if he had to go door to door through the whole city.

But first he had to have a last meeting with his grandfather.

He took the stairs two at a time and raced down to the old man's wing of the house, entering his room with a preemptory knock.

"May I talk to you for a moment?"

The old man raised his shaggy head. "I was expecting you," he said simply.

Cam went in and began to pace.

"Grandfather, I've come to tell you that I've failed. I thought I had a line on some financing that might work out, but today I've been told that is no longer an option." He stopped and looked at his aged relative. "Everything I've tried to set up has fallen through. I've come to the end of my bag of tricks. I don't know where to go from here." Taking a deep breath, he said the fatal words he'd hoped he would never have to say. "I'm afraid we're going to lose the house."

His grandfather frowned. "What about one of the Five Family girls? I saw some that looked interested last night. Don't tell me you're going to turn them down again."

Cam took a deep breath and let it out. "I think you know I can't do what you want, Grandfather. I can't do that to any of those girls. I can't do that to myself."

"Or to the Collins girl," his grandfather said angrily. "Isn't that the real problem?"

He hesitated, swore and turned on his heel toward the door.

"Hold it," the old man called. "Stop right there."

He turned back, eyes narrowed. "Grandfather..."

"You shut up," the older man cried, pointing at him. "I've got something to say."

Cam stood still, his jaw rigid, and his grandfather calmed himself down.

"Now, I know I've been a stickler for staying with the Five Families. Me and the old men of those families—we've always wanted to keep the old times alive by keeping our community together and close-knit. We figured it would be good to get the younger ones to marry in the group and keep us strong. Crazy, probably." Shaking his head, he shrugged. "Time moves on. You can't force these things on people. I know, I've tried to do it often enough."

Cam stood still, scowling.

"What I'm trying to say," the old man went on, "is that I understand. You love the Collins girl, don't you? Even if she's having someone else's baby. Even if it means we'll lose the house. You don't care. You just want her."

"I know that's how it looks to you," Cam said. "And I'm sorry. I've done everything I can to save the house, including putting my own business up for sale. But I can't do what can't be done."

"I know. I know." He sighed heavily. "Oh, hell, go marry your girl. Start over. We'll be okay. We'll get a little place in the hills and live simply. We've gone through hard times before. We can do it again."

Cam felt as though a weight had been lifted from his shoulders. "Grandfather…"

"Just go get her." He waved his gnarled hand. "Go."

Cam stepped forward, kissed the old man on the cheek and turned for the door. He was going to do what he had to do anyway, but having his grandfather's blessing made it so much easier.

Hopping into his car, he turned toward the city by the bay. Just as he was leaving, Penny called on his cell.

"I'm only telling you this because I know she's crazy about you," she told him. "She just called and gave me the number where she's staying. It's a landline. Maybe you can use it to find the address."

Of course he could. And he would.

His research led him to an unassuming row house at the top of a hill. Wearing snug jeans and a big leather jacket, he rang the bell, not knowing whether he would find her with a friend or with the man who'd fathered her baby. When a nice looking young woman answered the door, he was relieved, and it didn't take much fast talking to get past her and into the sitting room where Diana was curled up on the couch, her eyes red-rimmed, her hair a mass of yellow curls around her face.

"I'll leave you two alone," Di's friend said, but he hardly noticed. All he could see was Diana and the wary, tortured look in her dark eyes.

"I love you," he told her, loud and clear. "Di, I want to marry you."

She shook her head. "You can't," she said, her voice trembling. Tears were threatening. From the looks of it, she'd been doing a lot of that already.

He stared at her for a long moment, then looked around the room. "So where is he?" he asked shortly.

She blinked. "Where is who?"

"Mia's father." He looked at her. "Isn't that who you came to find? I want to meet this jerk."

She shook her head. "Why do you call him a jerk?" she asked. "What do you have against him?"

"He went off and left you, didn't he? He's never there when you need him the most."

She closed her eyes and swayed. "Oh, Cam."

He stood right in front of her.

"Diana, there are some things we need to get settled. The most important is whether Mia's father is going to be a part of your life or not. Is he going to be involved in raising her? I don't think you've told me the full truth about the situation yet." He shook his head, his frustration plain in his face. "I want to know who he is. I want to know where he lives. I want to know…if you love him. I want to know what place he is going to have in your life in the future. This is very important."

She raised her face to him. "Why?"

"Because I love you. Don't you get that? And, dammit all, I love Mia, even though she hasn't been born yet. I want to take care of you. I want to be with you. But I have to know…"

She began to laugh. He frowned, because her laughter didn't sound right. Was she getting hysterical? But no. Sobering, she rose from the couch.

"Come here," she said, leading him to a table at the end of the room. "I'll show you Mia's father."

She took out a loose-leaf binder and opened it to a page that displayed a filled-in form. He stepped closer. At the top of the page was the heading, a simple three digit number. Down the page he saw a list of attributes, including height, weight, hair color, personality traits, talents. As he read down the list, his frown grew deeper. It could have been someone listing items about him. Every detail was just like his.

"What is this?" he asked her.

"That is Mia's father," she said, holding her chin high with effort.

He shook his head. "It sounds like me."

She tried to smile. "You got it."

His bewilderment grew. "No, I don't get it."

She took a deep breath. "Cam, Mia's father was a donor at an assisted reproduction clinic. I don't know him. I never met him. I only picked him out of a book of donors."

"What? That's crazy."

"Yes." She put a hand to her chest. "This is how crazy I am. I went to three different clinics and pored over charts of donors trying to find someone almost exactly like you. I couldn't have you so I tried to come as close as possible to recreating what we might have had together."

He could hardly believe what he was hearing. It sounded like a science fiction story to him. He shook his head as though to clear it. "Diana, I can't believe this."

Tears glittered in her eyes. "Do you hate me? I knew it was nuts. I felt like a criminal doing it. And…I sort of feel as though I was doing it to close that door, stop the yearning. I knew if I was going to do this, it would put a barrier between us that couldn't be overcome. But it didn't seem to matter, because there was less and less hope of ever seeing you again anyway." She took a deep breath and shook her head. "But I just had to go on with my life and stop waiting for you."

"So you got pregnant." He frowned, trying to assimilate this information. "Artificial insemination?"

"Yes."

"And then I came back."

She nodded. "How could I know you were ever going to come back? Cam, it had been ten years. Your family acted like you were dead. I had no way of knowing."

"Oh, Diana." Reaching out, he enfolded her in his arms and began to laugh. "So you're telling me you're actually carrying my baby. Or a reasonable facsimile thereof. There is no other man involved. Just an anonymous donor."

"That's it."

He laughed again, then kissed her and looked down into her pretty face. "Let's get married."

"Wait, Cam…"

"I mean it, Di. We've already got our baby. All we need is a wedding ring."

"But what about your family?"

Quickly he told her about his conversation with his grandfather. "He basically gave me permission to marry you. Not that I was waiting on that. But it does make it less stressful."

She searched his eyes. "Are you sure?"

"I'm sure." He dropped another kiss on her lips. "Say 'yes'."

She smiled up at him. "Yes."

He whooped and danced her around the room. "I love you so much," he told her. "Last night when I made you dance with me, you looked so beautiful, I could hardly stand it."

"It was a nice party. Even if it didn't get you a wealthy bride."

"C'est la vie," he said, and reached down to pick up some papers that had fallen out of his jacket pocket when he'd danced her around the room.

"What are those?" she asked, her sharp eyes catching sight of her own name on one of them.

He hesitated, then nodded for her to sit down at the table. "I got this information a few days ago but

I was holding off on telling you," he said. "You see, I did some research on what happened to your mother."

She went very still. "What?"

"And here's what I found." He spread some papers out in front of her and took another out of an envelope. "She died in a cancer clinic in Sacramento. The date makes it right around the time you were six years old."

Diana stared at the papers. "So what does that mean?"

"It's my guess, from all the records I could find and what I could piece together, that your mother got a diagnosis of stomach cancer and she went away to a cancer clinic where she could concentrate on fighting the disease."

"So she didn't run off with another man? She didn't just decide she hated us and couldn't stay with us anymore?" Suddenly Diana eyes were filled with tears again. "Oh, Cam, I don't know what to think. How do you know this? Why didn't my father ever tell me?"

"My guess is that she thought she would get well and come back and be taking care of you again. She thought she had a chance, but luck wasn't with her. She left because she couldn't take care of you and deal with your father while she was going through that."

Diana's brows knit together. "Do you think my father knew?"

"Who knows what he knew or didn't know. From what I hear, he was in pretty bad shape with the drinking around that time. She might have told him and he might have been too out of it to know what she was talking about."

"Or he might have been that way *because* of what she told him."

"True. I don't suppose we'll ever know the truth." He frowned. "So she had no living family, no one to leave you with?"

"Except my grandmother on my father's side. She was still alive. I spent a lot of time at her house in those days. But she died when I was ten."

"And she never said anything to you about your mother's absence?"

She shook her head. "Not that I remember. I was only six years old, you know. Maybe she told me something that I didn't understand at the time. Maybe she just avoided the issue. People of her generation tend to do that."

"True."

Diana drew in a shuddering breath. "It's going to take some time to understand this," she said. "To really take it all in. It's a relief to know she didn't just run off, but it's so sad at the same time, and I feel like it's sort of unreal right now. Like it's about somebody else."

He was frowning, looking at an envelope in the pile of papers he'd given her. "Wait a minute," he said. "What's this?"

He pulled it out. "Oh, I didn't know this had come. I requested some information from a friend about that land you inherited. The envelope must have been stuck in with this other stuff. I didn't see this before."

He slit it open and began to read. Without looking up, he grabbed her arm. "Diana, you didn't sign that contract with your cousin yet, did you?"

"Yes, I did," she said. "I just mailed it today."

He looked up, his eyes wide. "You've got to get it back. Where did you mail it?" He jumped up from his seat. "Quick! Where is it?"

"I put it outside for the mailman this morning. I doubt it will still be there." She had to call after Cam because he was already running to the front of the house. "What's the matter?"

The mailman was at the next house when Cam snatched the envelope from the box attached to the front of the house where she'd put it. He sucked in a deep breath and leaned against the building. "Wow," he said. "Just wow."

Turning slowly, he made his way back into the house where Diana was waiting.

"What's going on?" she said.

He waved the envelope at her. "My friend in Sacramento came through with some inside info. That piece of land? A major hotel chain is planning a huge resort there. That land will be worth twenty times what your cousin offered you for it. Whatever you do, hold on to that land."

"Wow." Diana said it, too. "Does this mean…I'm rich?"

"Pretty much."

A huge smile began to break over her face. "Then

I guess you ended up with a rich girl after all, didn't you?"

He grinned and kissed her. "See? That was my plan from the first," he said. "I just had to wait until you were rich enough to help me save the farm."

"Will this do it? Seriously?"

He shrugged. "Hard to tell. But just having it means there are lenders who will give us extensions they wouldn't give us before. It'll certainly help."

"Good." Her bubbling laughter was infectious. "This is too much. I feel like I'm in the middle of an overload situation. Turn off the bubble machine."

"This is just the beginning," he told her, sweeping her up into his arms again. "You ain't seen nothing yet."

And he gave her a hard, deep kiss to seal the deal.

EPILOGUE

MORNING crept in on little dog feet but it was a cold black nose that woke Diana from her sleep. Then two doggy feet hit the mattress beside her head and she sighed. Those feet weren't really so little anymore.

"You monster," she said affectionately, and Billy panted happily, knowing love when he saw it. "Billy's here," she told Cam.

He turned and groaned, then rose from the bed.

"Come on, you mangy mutt," he grumbled. "I'll let you out."

She watched him walk naked from the room, his beautiful body shining in the morning light, wondering how she had managed to be so lucky. All her dreams had come true. Did she really deserve this happiness? He was back in a moment and this time he closed the door with a decisive snap, then turned and reached for her before he'd even hit the bed. Making love was sweet and slow in the morning, warm affection building to hot urgency, then fading to the most intense love imaginable as the sensations melted away.

"That one's going to be our next baby," he said, letting his fingertips trail over her generous breasts.

"You think?"

"I know. I could tell."

"How?

"Magic."

Mia's happy morning voice penetrated the closed door. She was singing to herself.

"She's awake."

"She's awake."

"You stay right here," he said. "I'll get her and bring her in bed with us."

She went up on one elbow as he rose from the bed. "Are you going to tell her?"

"Tell her what?"

She smiled lazily. "That she has a brother coming down the pike?"

He gave her his lopsided grin. "How do you know it's a boy?"

"I can feel it."

He frowned skeptically. "How?"

She smiled as though the world was paradise and she its ruler. "Magic."

He laughed and went to get their child. He agreed. Life was good. And Diana was magic.

* * * * *

MISTRESS IN TRAINING

Edwina Columbia

Dorian Press

Mistress in Training by Edwina Columbia

© 2006 Edwina Columbia
Published by Dorian Press

For information on Dorian Press books, call 615/256-7642.

ISBN 1-933725-22-2

Design by Armour&Armour
armour-armour.com

First Edition 2006
1 2 3 4 5 6 7 8 9 10

DEDICATION

For my parents—Anthony and Bernice Smulczenski—who never discouraged me from trying, picked me up and dusted me off when I fell short of the mark, but most of all instilled in me the courage to never give up and the wisdom to realize there are no such things as failures, only life experiences. I love you both. Thank you for always being there when I needed you.

ACKNOWLEDGMENT

A heartfelt thank you to three beautiful women in my life:
June Lund-Shiplett, for guiding my feet down the right path.
Linda Lael Miller, for affording me the opportunity to put my foot in the door.
Kathleen Fuller, whose door to the magic kingdom of unconditional support is always open to me.
Also, a world of appreciation to the editorial staff for all their hard work on this book.

NOTE

Although I have tried to remain as true to the facts of the Regency Era as possible (with the knowledgeable help of my friend, fellow Regency lover and writer Barb Satow), this book is strictly a piece of fiction meant to do nothing more than entertain. I apologize in advance for any errors, which are solely the responsibility of the author.

"**H**E IS QUITE SMITTEN with you, you know."

Julia Freemont lowered her fluttering fan and boldly glanced back at the group of admiring young gentry slowly being swallowed into the crush at the Buckingham soiree. "Which one?"

"Most assuredly not any of *those*." Her best friend Isabella St. Clair rolled her eyes. "And your flippancy would be best saved for one of the gaggle of shallow ninnyhammers that usually shadow your every step. You know very well of whom I speak."

Yes, she most certainly did. But she did not want to think of *him*. Or the indecent thoughts he evoked. So easily recalled, given the scandalously delicious dream she'd stretched languidly awake to, only that very morn. In need of more relief than her delicate silk fan provided, she set her sights on the yawning balcony doors. Quickening her pace, she left her companion no choice but to do the same.

One foot over the threshold, Julia skidded to a stop and spun so fast that, had she not dropped her fan and grasped Isabella's shoulders, they would've ended up a shocking tangle of limbs on the floor.

"What—oh. . . ." Isabella gasped softly, espying the two men leaning casually against the stone balustrade not fifteen feet away.

"Forgive me," Julia said in a rush. "Had I realized how close you were, I would not have turned so suddenly. It only now occurred to me I might benefit more from refreshment than fresh air and—"

"You do not truly expect me to swallow that plumper, do you?" Isabella looked meaningfully toward the balcony. "One might expect cowardice from me, but never you."

Had Julia not been pricked by the hint of truth in the softly spoken accusation, she would have immediately addressed the erroneous estimation of her friend's own character. "It has nothing to do with cowardice."

"Then why does the mere sight of Mr. Barringer have you running in the opposite direction? And do not even think to convince me you feel the least repulsed by the man. Admit it. You are undeniably attracted to him."

"I most certainly am not."

"Careful or your nose will grow as long as that wooden puppet's from the story your mother used to tell us as children."

"And it would appear your head is made of the same hard substance." The words spilled out on a stream of irritation and growing frustration. "That aside, what would be the point in encouraging him? Mr. Barringer is—"

"Well-mannered. Wealthy. And ever so handsome."

"You are forgetting one very important detail. It matters not how disgustingly rich or handsome he is. Or that his grandfather is a Duke. I could never marry a *bastard*."

"Oh, my." Isabella's eyes grew to the size of gold sovereigns, alerting Julia to an unexpected presence behind her.

Chest constricting, stomach somewhere between her knees and toes, Julia turned to see the object of her disparaging comment straightening from a bend, her forgotten fan in hand. The presence of his cousin Robert, Isabella's fiancé, only added to her embarrassment. "Mr. Barringer, I. . . ."

Through a haze of mortification, she watched him gather her gloved hand within his, press her fan into her palm, and with firm pressure wrap her numb fingers around it.

"Things of worth should never be treated so cavalierly, Miss Freemont." He took his hand away. "For one day you may come to regret their loss."

The low, evenly spoken comment, delivered along with her fan, was meant for the sake of anyone close enough to hear.

The look of loud condemnation in his frosted blue eyes was meant for her alone.

Before Julia could form the basest of apologizes, he was gone.

And where before she sought a respite from the stifling heat, now she longed for nothing more than her thickest woolen shawl.

1

"THIS HAD BETTER BE damnably important, Henry," Brandon Barringer responded to his butler's interruption without looking up from the ship's lading bill he was tallying.

"I did inform the lady you were not to be disturbed, sir. However, she is most insistent upon seeing you," Henry stated dutifully, easing farther into the room.

"A lady, hmmm? I suppose this lady has a name," he inquired distractedly, more concerned with the numbers adding up in his head than the answer to his question.

"Certainly, sir. Miss Freemont."

"Bloody hell!" Brandon transferred his frown from the half-written sum and the bold, black slash that trailed off the neatly columned page to his butler's unruffled features.

"Shall I show her in?"

"No." With a dismissive wave of his hand he returned his attention to the papers on his desk. "Inform the chit I'm not in."

"Yes, sir."

"Why not inform the *chit* yourself, Mr. Barringer?" asked a soft-spoken feminine voice that snapped Brandon's head up. He saw his butler step hastily aside and an elegant, black-haired woman swish past him to enter what had, up until now, been a bachelor's private sanctuary.

"Shall I have tea served, sir?" Henry asked cordially after a slight clearing of his throat.

Setting the quill into its gold holder with exacting precision, Brandon consulted the open pocket watch on his desk and leaned back in his chair. His gaze, fastened on the sonnet-inspiring, though somewhat strained, features of the woman standing stiffly inside the door, he said, "I doubt Miss Freemont will be staying long enough for tea, Henry. You may leave us."

"Very good, sir."

"And close the door, please," he added pointedly when Henry was about to leave it open.

Julia's gaze followed the butler. His slight hesitation and the surprising glimmer of mild disappointment directed at his employer did not go unnoticed or unappreciated. But in the end, the request was carried out with quiet dignity.

. Inspired by the servant's gracious deportment, she swallowed both her pride and the automatic recrimination that leapt to her tongue at the impropriety. After all, she had barged into his home practically unannounced and, God help her, there was nothing proper about the reason she'd come.

"At the very least, a *gentleman* would stand in the presence of a lady, Mr. Barringer."

"A *lady* would not enter the residence of a bachelor without proper chaperone, Miss Freemont."

Julia stiffened her spine against his insolent scrutiny and the undeniable truth of his words. "Am I to be denied the courtesy of being seated as well?" she inquired, locking her knees against an overwhelming urge to wilt. Unsure whether the weakness stemmed from the wicked display of uncommonly muscular chest and hint of dark brown curls revealed through the slack opening of his white linen shirt . . . or from the reason she'd sought him out.

"By all means. Be seated." With a half-hearted flick of his wrist, he indicated her choice of two high-backed chairs facing him.

Julia forced herself to step forward, nearly reversing the movement when he finally rose and, with blatant disregard for the deep-brown jacket draped over the back of his chair, matched her step for step until they stood a mere two feet apart.

The small distance between them didn't eliminate the need for her to tilt her head back to meet his inhospitable gaze. And for several heart-sinking beats, standing in the shadow of his intimidation, she wondered if the task she was set upon was that of a fool.

Shaken by the thought, she swayed.

He reached out. Clasped her shoulders.

The unexpected warmth of his hands jolted her into taking a hasty step back.

His arms immediately fell away, as did the momentary softening in his eyes. "You needn't fear, Miss Freemont," he said, easing back to perch on the corner of his desk. "I imagine I have as little desire of touching you as you have of my doing so. I merely meant to steady you as you seemed on the verge of swooning."

Oh, Lord, he must think her the biggest of twits. And to make matters worse, he now thought she abhorred his touch—a misconception she would need to rectify immediately if her mission was to succeed.

"You are mistaken, Mr. Barringer." Moving in front of the chair, she readily sank into it. "I do not find your touch abhorrent in the least. I find it . . ." As he quirked his brow in interest, she searched frantically for a suitable word.

". . . acceptable," she finished lamely, nearly groaning under the weight of her uncharacteristic social inadequacy.

Her floundering composure in desperate need of a respite from his unappeased regard, Julia took great care in removing her muff and discarding it on the oval, cherry table nestled between the chairs.

From beneath veiled lashes, she watched as he adjusted his balance for better comfort. Position, proximity, and the hugging fit of his fawn-colored riding breeches afforded her a detailed view of his thickly muscled thighs as they tensed and shifted. Clearly, a confident man who relished physical pursuits, he was not small in any respect—size, stature, or presence. The observation both frightened and enthralled her, bringing with it the most peculiar unfurling sensation deep in her stomach.

"Are you going to tell me why you are here, Miss Freemont? Or are you waiting for me to broach the subject?"

Her throat constricting on a half-formed breath, her gaze swung to his. Did he know?

No sooner did the question form, than a rational blanket of impossibility settled down to silence it. How could he possibly know the true purpose of this visit when she'd only convinced herself of its necessity that very morning? An agonizingly belabored decision, settled upon after weeks of alternately restless and sleepless nights.

"I assume it is your father's gaming debt that has brought you here."

She exhaled a relieved breath. "Yes, I—"

"You needn't have bothered, Miss Freemont. You will be glad to know that even I am not *bastard* enough to hold you accountable for what he owed me."

Brashly reminded of her regrettable remark, Julia swallowed a lump of mortification.

"As far as I'm concerned," the inflexibility in his voice grabbed her attention, "the sacrifice your father made more than paid his debt."

Grief fisted her heart. How tactfully he alluded to it—her father's suicide.

"Now that your fears have been laid to rest, I think it best you leave."

Her fears laid to rest? Had her plight not been so desperate, she would have laughed at the monumental inaccuracy of his statement.

"I shall ring for Henry to escort you out."

"No! Wait!" The shrill, desperate plea burst from her lips, sounding overly loud in the densely book-lined space.

Eyeing her with surprised speculation, he aborted his effort to rise.

"Please," she said more softly. "Please, wait. You . . . you do not understand." She pushed the words beyond the increasing knot of panic in her throat.

"What is it I do not understand?"

"There . . . there are others." She forced herself to maintain eye contact, her courage stumbling beneath his dark, piercing intensity.

"By others, I assume you mean debts."

She nodded.

"I am not your solicitor, Miss Freemont. I would suggest you speak of these matters with him."

"I already have."

The long, exaggerated breath he drew was far from encouraging.

"It seems you were not the only one to whom my father owed money, Mr. Barringer. I have only recently been made aware that he'd been gambling in excess for the past seven years," her voice dropped to a near whisper, "since my mother's death."

Through the parting of her cloak, she unobtrusively fingered the emerald silk along her thigh, hoping to channel some of her agitation and perhaps draw strength from her choices. Including the gown she'd chosen to wear. The exact

shade of her eyes. Purchased months earlier on an extravagant, audacious whim. Never worn before today, because of its indecent neckline.

"Exactly what are you saying? Your father gambled away most of his fortune?"

Julia lifted her chin. "No, Mr. Barringer, not *most* of it. *All* of it."

His eyes narrowed to speculative shards as he eased off the desk and stood, then began pacing. "So you've come to me." Each word and stride made ominous by its strict measure. "Expecting what? Expecting me to help you?"

"I thought—"

"Thought what? That I would be foolish enough to hand you a small fortune?"

"No. I—"

"Or. . . ."

He jerked to a stop, his head whipping around so fast, Julia sucked in a startled breath.

"Or is it marriage you seek? Has your desperation suddenly made the taint of my birth more palatable to you? You want to be my wife?" he sneered, leaving no doubt of his feelings on the matter.

"No!" His aggravation fueling her own, she jumped to her feet. "That is not what I want." She clenched her hands. Forced herself not to turn. Not to run from the room. Refused to fall prey to her emotions—as her father had.

His nostrils flared. "If not that, why are you here? What is it you want from me?"

"To become your mistress!" Julia blurted.

His head reared back. "Mistress," he repeated, drawing out the word as if it were foreign to him.

For several long, excruciating seconds silence reigned, leaving Julia to wonder if she'd struck him mute.

Then he burst out laughing.

Slapped by indignation, Julia snatched up her muff and headed for the door.

Stunned to think she was serious, Brandon broke off his laughter and took off after her.

"Wait a damn minute," he said, overtaking her in six determined strides and physically blocking her escape route.

Her attempt to elbow past him was effectively squelched as he firmly pinned her arms to her sides. Sufficiently subdued, he searched her face for signs of subterfuge.

Found none.

"You're serious," he stated, careful to keep the surprise from his voice.

"Remove yourself from my path," she said stiffly.

"If I do, what then? Will you go to another with your offer?"

Her lush, full lips compressed into a mulish line, drawing Brandon's attention. Had he not had enough presence of mind to shake off the distraction, he surely would have missed the wisp of panic that skittered across her unblemished features.

"Answer me." Using his grip on her arms, he gave her a not-so-gentle shake.

"Whatever I choose to do will be none of your concern. I insist you step aside and release me."

Like hell he would. "I will be more than happy to, Miss Freemont, *after* I've had ample time to consider your intriguing proposition."

"What?" Delicately arched brows dipped over eyes swirling with confusion.

A man who'd grown his fortune on opportunity, Brandon took immediate advantage of her perplexity by taking firm hold of her elbow and guiding her back to her chair where

he loomed over her for a short time. Not only to assure she
stayed put, but to allow his mind to absorb her outrageous
offer. Taken totally off guard, she'd left him reeling. Not liking
the feeling one damn bit, he felt obliged to retaliate in kind.

"The first thing you must learn, *if* I agree to make you
my mistress, is to use my Christian name." Somewhat molli-
fied by the shocked expression his words produced, he
reached down and extricated the muff from her lax fingers
and flipped it onto his desk.

Still dazed by the rapid turn of events, Julia voiced no
objection to its extraction, or his frankly assessing gaze.

"I'm curious as to what has brought you to this impasse,
Julia. Have you not considered marriage to one of the
many young bucks who so faithfully sniffed at your skirts
throughout the Season? Or have they retreated like the
mongrels they are at the first hint you'd lost your fortune?"

"I believe you already know the answer to that," she
said, unwilling to rise to the bait. She hadn't deluded herself
into thinking he'd hear her proposition, open his arms, and
allow her to snuggle safely into them. Had even prepared for
a healthy dose of animosity. What she hadn't prepared for
was the unexpected pain. Not from his words, but from the
absence of the adoration his eyes once held.

"What about being a governess?"

She crinkled her nose. "Look at me, Mr. Barr . . . Brandon."
And as she'd practiced in front of the mirror, until it looked
as casual as breathing, she inhaled deeply and spread her
arms out to her sides. As hoped, his gaze fell to the generous
amount of cleavage revealed by the gaping opening in her
cape. "What mother would take me into her household to
tend her children?"

Instead of answering, his lingering gaze seared a burning
path across her chest.

Determined to appear the accomplished coquette, Julia kept her arms extended. Until they grew too heavy and heat crawled up her neck.

Giving in to defeat, she lowered her arms.

A bit too hastily, if judged by the satisfied amusement touching the corner of Brandon's lips.

"I take your point. Few women would hire a youthful, pretty governess. Unless her husband were dead and all the other men in the house eunuchs. But why a mistress? And why me?"

Regaining confidence from what she felt a soundly thought-out decision, she squared her shoulders and said, "I have no family to speak of and after the debts are paid, there will be little or no money left. Also, as you have so *delicately* pointed out, my lack of fortune and the circumstance of my father's demise have made me quite undesirable in the marriage market."

Brandon could see by the set of her jaw the admission had cost her, and for a fleeting moment thought to enlighten her to the reality that her face, body, and impeccable bloodline *were* her fortune, at least to anyone whose own sterling social standing could withstand the stigma of her father's suicide. But having her in this humbling position was a revenge his bruised pride was unable to forfeit. It was also a way to have the woman he had lusted after for so long as a willing participant in his bed.

"As to the other," she went on, "I would be frank and tell you that you have enough prestige and money to keep me in the style to which I was born. I could not endure being placed in a position of serving the very people I have stood equal to for my entire life. I have neither the skill nor desire to become a scullery maid."

Brandon was hard-pressed not to smile as he pictured

her on hands and knees, scrubbing the floor. Naked. Except for a pristine white mob cap and apron. Her firm, pale little derriere in the air, beckoning him to mount her.

As expected, his manhood stirred, necessitating a shift in position—as well as a shift in thought. Surprisingly, it was the vein of her next words that provided it.

"I had heard you'd recently released your current mistress and . . ." for the first time since starting her recitation, her gaze shied from his ". . . your expertise and prowess between the sheets is not unknown, even in the most genteel circles."

"Do tell. I must seek out and thank whoever, or should I say how many ever, deemed me worthy of such an illustrious distinction," he stated drolly, greatly entertained by both the subject and her daring in divulging it.

"I wish to learn from the best," she continued doggedly, making it plain she intended to ignore his tongue-in-cheek statement. "So when you tire of me and move on as men do," her chin elevated slightly, "I will have no problem attaining another benefactor."

Still riding the slow swell of his good humor, the last of her statement didn't immediately sink it. When it did, unexpected jealousy slammed him like a hundred-foot wave.

"Stand up," he ordered gruffly, experiencing no guilt from the wariness filling her eyes.

"Why?" But even as she asked, she rose hesitantly to her feet.

"A mistress is an expensive venture, my dear. Only a fool would purchase something sight unseen," he said over his shoulder as he moved to the door, locked it and came back to settle against the desk. Crossing both arms and ankles, he didn't have long to wait before understanding gleamed in her eyes.

"You cannot mean—"

"Oh, but I do. Take off your clothes."

Her wide-eyed gaze darted to the locked door and back.

"A mistress obeys in all things," he said in a low, intentionally detached voice. "The only wishes, *desires* that matter are her benefactor's. You are there for one reason . . . pleasure. If he is pleased, you will be rewarded. If not, punished. Or perhaps discarded."

When she gave not the slightest indication of disrobing, he continued. "That is what it means to be a mistress, Julia."

Several more seconds went by. Still she did not move. Sighing deeply, Brandon shook his head. "If you cannot even comply with my first request, you are wasting my time."

Again he waited, knowing he appeared the unfeeling bastard, telling himself it had nothing to do with jealousy, that he was doing her a favor. Best she learn from the outset what harsh realities lay down the path she'd chosen. Not that he would treat her harshly. Never that. Merely make her realize the only love she would ever receive from him was of the physical kind. He would not give her false hope by coddling her as he'd once thought to do. His resolve was tested sooner than expected when her rose-petal pink tongue darted out to swipe nervously across her lips in the most innocent of invitations, and he found himself quelling an urge to enfold her protectively within his embrace. A struggle nearly lost, until she lifted her chin to reveal eyes shining with determination.

"Very well. If that is your wish," she said and with one tug of the cloak's drawstring sent the lightweight fabric avalanching down over the soft curves of her body to form an ebony puddle on the floor.

Hell-bent on savoring every moment of his long awaited desires, Brandon took his time moving his gaze up the enticing line of her graceful body. His hungry imagination supplied an image of long, shapely legs, pliable thighs,

before he raised his gaze to linger over the gentle roundness of her hips . . . tiny waist, moving upward to a breath-hitching display of creamy flesh. Satiny, abundant mounds. Captured in a frame of delicate lace. An enticing display, whetting his appetite for more. "Continue."

Her head swiveled to the right. "But it is still day."

Brandon followed her gaze to the window and the small stream of light wheeling its way through sumptuous red velvet.

"Look at me, Julia." When she did, it was through a spray of feathery lashes. Brandon steeled himself against the innocent demureness of the pose. "A man's desire does not differentiate between day and night. Neither will your sensibilities. Your body will harbor no secrets from me."

Her acknowledgement came slowly . . . a barely perceptible nod. "I will need help with the buttons of my gown and with . . . with my stays." The request faded to a whisper.

It was hard not to admire her. She was such a fascinating, refreshing blend of innocence, fortitude, and earthy sensuality. A delightful, unexpected find in an untried miss. A purity of which he had no doubt. As the woman he'd sought to wed, he'd researched her extensively. Her most valuable qualities—an irreproachable reputation and notable lineage. Qualities he could ill-afford not to demand of his future bride, if he were to dilute the blight of his own inauspicious beginnings and ease the way for future generations. He'd lived on the fringes of Society far too long not to know its members valued only two things—money and bloodline. And now that he had ample enough of one, he was determined to buy the other.

The only bride-quality he'd hoped for himself was that of true affection. Had thought he'd found all three traits in Julia. Unfortunately, she'd already lost one, was about to lose

the other, and had crushed the third carelessly beneath the short, but lethal, heel of her dainty satin slipper the night of the Buckingham soiree. So, what did that leave?

He indulged in a slow, head-to-toe inspection of her lush form to which his swelling rod quickly supplied the answer.

Ah, yes, lust. The one thing few men found with a wife, demanded in a mistress. With all things considered, didn't Julia owe him that small recompense for all she'd taken away? And the fact the proposal came from her sweet lips, freeing him of any gentlemanly guilt, added much to the desirability of the arrangement.

It was in that instant he made his decision. A decision he wouldn't apprise her of until he was good and ready. It was to a man's advantage to keep a woman guessing. Unsure of herself, she was less likely to try her hand at control. And control of either him or his emotions was something he would never place into Julia's small, insensitive hand again.

Feeling a true lightening in his mood for the first time that evening, Brandon stepped forward. "Turn and I will help you."

Perched on a life-altering threshold, Julia willed strength to her shaky limbs. Turning, she filled her lungs with a bracing breath, only to expel it in a quiet rush at the first light touch of his fingers at the nape of her neck. Determined to concentrate on something other than the intimacy of the task he was performing with the ease of long practice, she closed her eyes. Pushed aside the prickling of moral agony that plagued her. Drew strength from the self-truth that she was not cut from a martyr's cloth and that there were worse fates than being well-fed, pampered, and nestled deep into a soft, clean bed by the weight of handsome man.

Absorbed in her thoughts, she did not notice when he moved to the next task. Not until a warm splash of breath

caressing her upper back brought on a rippling shiver and her loosened clothes took a dangerous slip.

Gasping, she slapped a palm to her chest. A natural, desperate measure that only delayed the inevitable.

What now? She curled her fingers tighter, half-expecting him to rip her clothes away. Absurdly hoping he would and save her the fateful decision.

Uncertain what to do, she waited for him to make the first move.

But the only things to stir were the wisps of hair that had escaped her chignon, set into tickling motion by his short, soft, shallow breaths.

And then, nothing. Its hollowness so profound, it took a moment for her to realize he'd stepped away.

"Continue, Julia."

There it was again. That aloofness in his voice that was beginning to annoy her.

Julia peeked over her shoulder to find him leaning against the desk once again, arms folded, ankles crossed. With one significant difference. Where before his breeches had lain smoothly across his loins, there was now a rather long, thick bulge present. Armed with the knowledge she'd caused the condition, her courage rekindled.

She may never have lain with a man, but she was well aware of how their bodies worked. Courtesy of a frolicsome, plump parlor maid and a zealously accommodating young stableboy who were so vigorously diligent in their enthusiastic demonstrations, Julia was drawn to watch from behind the slats of the neighboring stall on more than one occasion.

With the shrewd smile of the parlor maid fresh in her mind, Julia pivoted slowly and released her grip. Gown and stays swished to the floor.

The instant flare of interest in Brandon's eyes gave her the courage to reach for the next piece of clothing. Her chemise.

Once loosened, she took a brisk breath. Allowed the delicate fabric to slip down her arms. Cool air colliding with warm flesh tautened her nipples.

The surge of heat that crawled up her chest and settled in her cheeks kept pace with the slow, appreciative smile that spread across Brandon's face.

"You have beautiful breasts," he said, with the look of a starving man presented with a king's feast.

Determined to finish before her courage failed under his intense scrutiny, Julia closed her eyes and reached for the tie of her pantalets. Set free, they slid down her legs in a silky caress.

She wondered what kind of picture she presented, standing in nothing but stockings, garters, and slippers. Was he pleased by what he saw? Or greatly disappointed? Why wasn't he saying anything? Why—

He moved. She could feel it. The air in front of her warmed, letting her know he was near. She imagined his gaze roaming over her in agonizingly slow increments. Inspecting. Considering. His deep, long breaths sending warm streams down her chest to fan across her breasts and brush teasingly over her nipples. Nipples that grew embarrassingly hard.

In a state of heightened senses, she knew the exact moment he started circling her. Knew, too, when he stepped away.

"You can open your eyes."

The dry amusement in his deep voice brought them open with a snap to find him seated behind his desk, looking much as he had when she'd first arrived—contemplative and mildly annoyed.

"Get dressed."

Her heart tripped at the brusque command.

Had he subjected her to the demeaning appraisal of her body only to reject her? Was this retribution for her insulting comment all those months ago?

Moist heat swarmed in the back of her eyes. She blinked, determined he would not have the satisfaction of her humiliation.

With nothing but her dignity to shield her nakedness, she reached for her clothes.

Never more than at that moment did Brandon mourn the loss of her suitability as a wife. She was a magnificent creature. Even naked, she managed to convey the poise and regal bearing of a proud, determined queen. Cursing both her father and his own for the decisions he'd been forced to make, Brandon consoled himself with the fact that he'd at least have Julia in his bed.

Clearing his mind of all but the present, he said, "I'll have your coach brought around."

At the mention of a coach, Julia nearly groaned. Another erroneous decision to heap on the pile of the others she'd made in coming here. "I . . . I no longer have a coach," she stated softly, studiously concentrating on slipping one arm into her dress sleeve and then the other.

"How did you get here?"

"I hired a hackney."

"You didn't have him wait?"

Responding to the surprise in his voice, she looked up. "I didn't want to risk your sending me away before I could present my case."

Her chin came up with the firm declaration. Brandon nearly smiled at what was becoming an all-too-predictable action. "It seems you are a woman of many surprises, Julia. I think I shall enjoy training you."

Her brow furrowed. "You . . . you're keeping me?"

Feeling it safe to touch her now that she was partially clothed, he went to her and, ignoring her stunned look, spun her around. He prevented her attempt to turn back by keeping tight pressure on the strings of her stays as he quickly laced her up. "Who is your solicitor?" Tying off the laces, he made short work of the gown's buttons and took a step back, giving her freedom to turn.

"Mr. Farnsworth."

"How convenient. As he is also mine, it will make things much easier."

"What things?"

Brandon placed a finger beneath her chin, making it impossible to look anywhere but at him. "As your benefactor, I will deal with your father's debts."

"They are . . . considerable."

He shrugged. "The house . . . was it spared?"

"No."

"Would it pain you to never reside there again?"

"I was happy there, but am resigned not to lament over things that cannot be changed."

Brandon might have applauded her resolve, for it appeared so ironclad, but standing so close, he was able to read the hurt that shadowed her expressive eyes and see the slight tremble of her full, pouty lips. Lips he had every intention of possessing. But not yet.

Releasing her, he picked up the cape at her feet and, placing it around her shoulders, secured it with a neat bow.

"I will have my coach return you to your residence. You will have three days to pack your belongings. On the fourth day, present yourself to Madame LaFleur," he instructed, giving the name of the most famed modiste in London.

"My wardrobe is quite extensive, I assure you."

Brandon responded to her clipped words with an indulgent smile. "I have no doubt you are well versed in the latest fashion, my dear. And what you wear while in the presence of others I shall leave up to you. Unless it is something I expressly object to," he added to remind her of the control he would have over every aspect of her life. "But there are things you will wear for my pleasure alone. Things of my own choosing. Your appointment with Madame LaFleur will be for no other reason than to have her take your measurements. I will handle the rest."

Incredulous, Julia stared at him. "You cannot order clothes for me. That would be scandalous," she blurted out, only to realize how ridiculous it was in light of her new status.

"If the arrangement is distasteful, you have but to say no and leave this room. But know this—once you have chosen your path, there will be no turning back."

Julia struggled to dispel the sudden heaviness pressing upon her chest. If she left, what would she do? Where would she go? She had come to him because, bastard or no, he was one of the most powerful and wealthiest men in all of England. That he was one of the handsomest only added to his allure.

Her assessment of him brought to mind the list she'd made—the list of possible benefactors. Yet as she'd compared each to the other, it was his lips she wanted hers to be crushed beneath, his hands guiding her, spreading her. His body giving her the same pleasure the stableboy had given the parlor maid.

Looking into his all-consuming blue eyes, she took a resolute breath and asked, "If I am to present myself to Madame LaFleur on the fourth day, what shall I be doing on the fifth?"

2

STEPPING FROM HIS CARRIAGE and rushing up the stairs to avoid getting drenched, Brandon pushed through the door of his solicitor's office. He watched in amusement as two young clerks fell over themselves to attend him.

"Good day, sir," the elder of the boys said, coming to help Brandon out of his wet cloak, while the other boy relieved him of his beaver top hat.

"I believe Mr. Farnsworth is expecting me," Brandon stated. Before the youth could answer, a door behind him opened.

"Mr. Barringer, good to see you." The smile on the solicitor's face was friendly as he came up to Brandon and grasped his hand in a firm shake. "Please, come in."

Returning the man's smile, Brandon preceded him into the office. "Were you able to accomplish all I requested?" Flipping up the tails of his brown coat, he sat in a chair in front of William's desk, leaning his cane against another.

"Yes," William said, pouring a glass of his finest brandy and handing it to his client. Taking his seat, he adjusted his spectacles on the bridge of his nose. "Considering the amount of money Freemont owed you and your willingness to pay off his other debts, we were able to acquire everything with little problem. Had you not contacted me as quickly as you did, I fear the task would have been rather more difficult, as there was someone else of like mind."

"Do you know who?" Brandon asked in passing curiosity, stretching out his legs and crossing his booted ankles.

"No, although I did try to find out. It seems the interested party was as determined as you not to be identified," William said.

Brandon tipped his glass toward William before taking a sip.

Not once in their five-year association had Brandon ever regretted hiring the young solicitor. From the outset, William seemed to know what Brandon expected, and for his loyalty Brandon had allowed him to invest in Barringer Shipping. The solicitor was well on his way to being a wealthy man in his own right.

"And the Freemont country estate?" Brandon inquired. "What of that?"

"Yours as well," William informed him with a grin.

"There is something else I would ask of you," Brandon said, casually swirling the golden liquid in the glass that dangled from his fingers. "Both the London house and the country estate are to be placed in Miss Freemont's name. I also intend to set up a sizable personal account for her, which she will be free to draw upon in the event something unforeseen should befall me."

Considering the amount of money it had taken to obtain the holdings, Brandon was impressed when William didn't so much as raise a brow at the suggestion. "I want it written up in such a way that if she were to marry, the property will not pass to her husband, but will be kept in trust for her children—should there be any."

"Your generosity to others continually astounds me, Mr. Barringer. I cannot impress upon you enough how rare a person you are." When Brandon shrugged and waved off the praise, William took the hint and went on. "Might I inquire

who will oversee the running and maintenance of these properties?"

A small smile crossed Brandon's lips. "I have little doubt Miss Freemont should be quite capable of doing so ... with your guidance, of course. But, if for any reason she is unable, you will take full responsibility until such time as her children come of age and are deemed capable."

For the first time in their acquaintance, William's businesslike demeanor cracked. The look of shock on his face was so comical Brandon couldn't help but chuckle. "I was beginning to wonder if perhaps you might not be human, William."

"But ... I mean, are you sure—"

"Very sure. You have proven your loyalty and worthiness tenfold over the years. There are few people in this world I trust, William. I consider you one of them."

"I am humbled by your faith in me."

"Don't be. Were it not there, we would not be having this discussion. How soon do you think you can have the papers drawn up? I wish to leave for my estate in Lincolnshire at the earliest opportunity."

"I'll have the papers ready for your signature in two days' time."

"That will do nicely."

Finishing his drink, Brandon stood and placed the empty glass on the corner of the desk. "One last thing." When William's brown eyes were intent on his, he continued. "She is to be apprised of this *only* if it becomes necessary."

William came to his feet. "I understand."

Reaching across the paper-cluttered desk, the two men shook hands, but as Brandon turned to leave, William asked, "Mr. Barringer, might I inquire if there is a reason you feel you will not be around to administer to these affairs yourself?"

If another man had asked that question, Brandon would have taken it as intrusion into his private affairs, but he knew William well and could see the genuine concern in the solicitor's face.

"Let's just say since my grandfather's death, several things have happened I am not entirely convinced were mere mishaps."

William nodded.

Brandon picked up his cane and left the room.

Business with his solicitor concluded, there was one more stop he needed to make.

"MONSIEUR BARRINGER, HOW GOOD it is to see you." The lilting greeting of Madame LaFleur's accented voice carried throughout the quaint but stylish dress shop.

Taking the delicate hand the buxom middle-aged woman offered, Brandon brought it to his lips. Before relinquishing it, he gave it an inconspicuous flick of his tongue.

The madame's eyes narrowed slightly, but only Brandon noticed. "Please, come into my private office. We have much to discuss, *oui?*"

"*Oui,* madame, we have much to discuss," he parried and turned to the three female customers who had been watching the exchange with interest. "Good day, ladies."

"Good day, Mr. Barringer," a young miss returned with a shy smile before she was hastily whisked off to one of the fitting rooms by her mother, who gave a brief nod of acknowledgment in Brandon's direction.

Grinning, Brandon followed the modiste down a narrow hall and past several curtained rooms.

As soon as the door was closed behind them, Brandon

gave the woman a hearty swat on the rump and said, "So tell me, Maude, how's business?"

In retaliation, she swung around and gave him a good whack on his shoulder. "Don't ye be gettin' fresh with me, ye young buck. Maude ain't so old she can't plant a facer on that pretty mug of yours," she said, the French accent conspicuously missing. In spite of the threat, she reached up, twined her arms around his neck, and gave him a crushing hug.

"I take it business is good, then," he stated, releasing her.

"You'll not be findin' me complainin'," she answered, moving to sit in one of two chairs in front of a white plaster fireplace, the focal point of her quarters, quarters surprisingly understated for a woman brought up in a seaport selling her body to any sailor with enough copper coin.

Brandon would never forget the night they'd met. Having sold his commission and on his way home from India, he and his friend, James, had foolishly decided to celebrate by visiting the first drinking establishment they'd come upon. To this day, Brandon could not fathom how they'd come to awaken in an alley at the mercy of a band of cutthroats who thought nothing of gutting a bloke for no more than a sixpence. Nor could he explain, in the haze of regaining his senses, why he was so sure he'd heard one of them make reference to his grandfather's title.

Cornered and outnumbered, they were dangerously close to losing their lives when Maude had shown up with some of her sailor friends. One look at the menacing bunch and the assailants had fled for their lives.

As a reward for saving his life Brandon had convinced her, after considerable persuasion on his part, to come to London where he would help her start a new life. The combination of her talent for languages and the fact she'd once worked for a modiste before being led astray by a smooth-

talking scoundrel made it easy to decide what that life would be.

"So, what be ye plannin' for that Freemont chit ye sent me?" Maude asked in her usual forthright manner, which had so endeared her to Brandon he could not take offense.

"I wish to have a wardrobe made for her that will be designed with one thing in mind—to please a man and accommodate his needs."

When her eyebrows shot up and she sat forward, Brandon felt a boyish satisfaction at having surprised her. Considering the life she'd led, he hadn't thought it possible.

FIDGETING, JULIA ADJUSTED HER skirts for at least the tenth time. The closer they got to Brandon's country estate, the more nervous she became. This, the third day of their travel, had dawned gray and gloomy. Much like her thoughts. Had she made the right decision? Or, had she set herself on a path that was spinning out of control as quickly as her emotions?

Brandon withdrew his watch. Pleased with the progress they were making, he returned it to the pocket of his waistcoat and looked over at Julia. "If the seat is uncomfortable, my dear, feel free to make use of my lap. I would offer it willingly to cushion your sweet bottom," he said around a suggestive grin that lit his features.

It had been like this the entire trip. He had not touched her, had acquired separate rooms at each night's stop, but each gesture, each comment brought with it a suggestion of intimacy. There would be stages to her training, he'd informed her at the outset of their trip. Sensual stimulation without touching being the first.

"Still blushing, I see." Making himself more comfortable, he stretched his long, boot-clad legs out onto the seat next to her. "A rare thing in a *mistress.*"

"You can't expect me to change overnight," she groused, knowing he purposely used the word often as a reminder of her new status. But, however often he might say it, it was never within the hearing of others.

"No, I suppose not, nor would I want you to. I take great pleasure in the way the color fills your chest with a warm glow, slowly moving its way up your slender neck to settle in your rosy cheeks. A journey I anticipate one day traversing with my tongue." His smoldering gaze traveled the imagined path.

A laugh rumbled from his chest when she colored once again and turned her gaze from his.

Whatever he might have said next was lost when a shot rang out.

"Bloody bastards!" The driver's curse rent the air, and the horses shot forward.

Julia pitched headlong toward the opposite seat.

Reaching out quickly, Brandon was able to save her from landing face first against the squabs. "Get down," he ordered, shoving her to the floor.

Dazed, she obeyed.

Brandon threw back the flap. "George! George!" he yelled over the rattle of coach and harnesses and thundering of hooves.

"Here, sir."

Brandon breathed a sigh of relief.

"Took one in the arm I did," the driver yelled back. "Bleedin' like a butchered chicken, I am. Don't think I can hold 'em much longer."

"Hang on, I'm coming up."

Brandon turned to Julia, who was still huddled on the floor. "Stay there." Opening the carriage door and clinging to the frame, he stuck out one leg to find a foothold.

At a bend in the road, the coach tilted. Brandon came perilously close to being flung loose. Breathing heavily, heart pounding, he clung tenaciously to the side of the runaway vehicle. When the road straightened and the coach righted itself, Brandon loosened his white-knuckled grip and began inching his way toward the top. An instant after his leg cleared the side, they came within inches of a large tree.

With a horrific crash, the door ripped away.

The sound of Julia's terrified scream sent a chill up Brandon's spine, the likes of which he'd never before experienced.

Fighting his need to see to her welfare, he dropped into the seat beside George. Bracing his feet against the floor of the box, he added his hands to the ribbons. Together the men pulled. Even with his considerable strength added to the driver's it took several minutes before the horses eventually came to a snorting, quivering stop.

After securing the leather straps, Brandon immediately checked to see how badly his driver was injured. Although bleeding heavily, George had indeed taken the shot in the shoulder without damage to anything vital.

"You're going to be fine," Brandon said, stripping off his pristine white cravat, wadding it up, and pressing it tightly against the wound.

"Of course I will. It'll take more than a highwayman's bad aim to lay low the likes of me."

"You're a good man, George. Keep your hand on this," he instructed, taking the man's opposite hand and placing it over the cloth. "I need to check on Miss Freemont." With a light pat to the driver's uninjured shoulder, Brandon worked his way to the ground.

When he reached the opening of the coach where the door had once been, Julia was already trying to make a shaky exit. He reached up to her. She all but fell into his arms.

"I . . . I was so frightened," she said, her face pressed against his chest, clutching him desperately.

"It's over," he murmured, gripping her tighter, unsure whether it was to soothe her trembling or to ease the fear he'd felt for her safety. "I would permit you more time to recover, but we need to get George to the manor house in all haste and send for the surgeon."

"I'm fine . . . really." Reluctantly, she shoved lightly out of his arms and looked up. "You must see to George. Go."

Admiration filled Brandon. Not many women of her breeding would set a servant's needs above her own. Although she seemed composed, he could still feel the slight trembling of her body. Without thought, he leaned down and kissed her. He'd every intention of making it a quick kiss, one of reassurance rather than passion, but when her mouth slightly parted with a soft gasp, he found he was unable to deny himself a taste of her sweetness. When she went still at the first invasion of his tongue, he explored rather than probed, titillated rather than delved, causing her to grip his lapels and relax more fully against him.

A moan from George made her break away and tuck her head to Brandon's chest, a feather on her bonnet nearly claiming the sight from one of his eyes.

"Tell me what is to be done," she said, when she felt composed enough to meet his gaze.

"I'd like to place George in the coach with you. Do you think you can tend him while I drive the horses?"

"Yes, I believe so."

All the time he spoke, Brandon was removing his jacket and waistcoat. "Place this under his head." Without thought

to the cost of the exquisitely tailored garments, he bunched them up into a makeshift pillow and handed it to her. "And we'll need something to put on the wound, as I fear my cravat is likely soaked through by now." He started removing his shirt with total disregard for the inappropriateness of baring his chest to her.

Julia kept her eyes above his chin, trying to concentrate on his instructions rather than her first view of his unclothed torso.

"I'll help you up and then get George," he said, grasping her elbow, guiding her to the coach, and lifting her up into it. "We'll be home within the hour." He imparted the information as he turned to leave.

Julia dared not turn around to look at him, but even after they were well on their way to the manor house and George had fallen into a troubled sleep, she could not keep her mind from the devastating kiss they'd shared or the sight of Brandon's lightly furred chest.

A chest she unexpectedly found herself held tightly against upon reaching their destination.

3

RELUCTANT TO OPEN HER eyes, Julia stretched. Her wish, if only for a few moments longer, to stave off the reality of her circumstance.

Her arrival at Brandon's countryseat had been less than the stylish one she'd envisioned. Much to her embarrassment, she'd nodded off shortly after George had succumbed to the pain of his injury and lost consciousness.

She would've liked to tell herself she vaguely remembered being swept up into Brandon's strong arms and settled against his chilled, naked chest. That she was unaware of the orders he'd issued to the stunned servants who'd come out to greet them. That amidst a mere jumble of sounds and blurred images he'd carried her into the house and up the stairs. And, that he'd removed every stitch of her clothing and tucked her beneath a mound of warm covers, while she'd been oblivious to what he'd been doing.

Yes, she would have liked to tell herself all of that.

But the truth was she'd been jolted to her senses the instant he'd gathered her close. Although she'd at first been shocked, she had also been intrigued. His cold flesh should have robbed her body of its heat. Instead, her entire being had flamed in a way she'd never experienced before.

She should've immediately alerted him to the fact that she was awake; any well-bred woman would have. But when he'd begun to undress her, it had been too tempting to

continue the charade. For what better way to judge her reaction to his intimate touch than under the guise of sleep?

She was both appalled and fascinated that she hadn't felt the least bit of repulsion. He had stripped her, his hands brushing occasionally against her, but not once did he take advantage of her supposed state of slumber.

Oddly enough, she found herself disappointed.

Yawning, she opened her eyes and turned her face toward the light flooding its way through the opening of the lavish green velvet curtains with gold tassels.

"You have no idea how many times I've pictured you this way."

Julia squealed, her gaze swinging toward the sound of the deep voice. "What are you doing here?" she demanded, gripping the covers to her breasts.

"I believe I live here," Brandon said, uncrossing his arms and pushing away from the frame of the adjoining door he'd been leaning against.

With slow, measured strides he moved toward her, his eyes intent, as if possessing the ability to see right through the bedclothes.

"Don't be obtuse." She slid deeper beneath the covers. "You know exactly what I mean. What are you doing in this room?"

At the foot of the large four-poster with its intricately inlaid headboard he stopped. "Had I known my efforts to allow you a veil of discretion by placing you in your own room would be acknowledged by nothing but your tart tongue, I would have merely ensconced you in my bed. Although . . . a tart tongue can be infinitely enjoyable when applied under the right circumstances."

He chuckled at her confused look. "You have much to learn, my sweet, and it will be my endless delight to teach

you all there is to know in the realm of pleasure." Pinching the covers between thumb and forefinger, he gave a light tug. When she refused to release them he raised a dark brow.

Taking a deep breath, Julia loosened her grip, but to her surprise, he did not tug again, only moved around to the side of the bed.

For several moments he did nothing but look at her face and then settled on the edge of the mattress. The weight of his body took the slack from the sheet. It jerked free of her hands and revealed her breasts, while at the same time causing her to roll against him. Before she could regain either her balance or the covers, he leaned over, caging her between his arms.

"I have taken the liberty of ordering you a bath," he said in a tone so seductive and compelling Julia could not have looked away had her life depended upon it.

With a feather-light touch, he began lazily running a finger along her collarbone. "After which a tray will be brought up."

His finger moved down marginally to graze the pillowy tops of her breasts. "When you are done with your breakfast, you will meet me in the library."

The caress shifted lower to where cream flesh darkened to light brown, and, with the softest touch imaginable, he outlined each cocoa-colored areola.

Of its own volition, Julia's body arched upward.

"Where we will discuss your learning schedule," he added and bent his head.

Julia closed her eyes, emitting a soft whimper when he blew a warm, gentle stream of air across her nipple.

The mattress shifted beneath her. Julia tensed. Was it fear or anticipation? She dared not name it.

When after several long moments nothing happened, she opened her eyes.

He was gone.

FEELING LESS AT A disadvantage now that she'd bathed and dressed, Julia raised her hand and knocked on the thick, paneled study door.

"Come in." Brandon's rich, authoritative voice sounded from the other side.

Drawing a deep breath, she entered to find him staring out the window with his back to her. When he turned, she was afforded a glimpse of the well-tended rose garden.

"Close the door, please," he said, snapping shut his pocket watch and tucking it away.

Her hand still on the brass knob, she pushed the door closed, her heart skipping a beat at the sound of the latch clicking into the plate. At least he hadn't asked her to lock it. She faced him, but moved no closer.

"Please take a seat, Julia. I promise I won't bite. Not yet, at any rate," he added, letting his gaze rake her body. When her step faltered, he smiled. "No, not on the chair, over there." He nodded toward the gold brocade settee, and, while she seated herself, he walked to the sideboard. Pouring a generous amount of brandy into a beautifully etched glass snifter, he came back and held it out to her. "Here, drink this."

"No, thank you, I—"

"Take it. I have a feeling you're going to need it."

She set her jaw and gave him an intent look. What in heaven's name was wrong with her? She was acting more like a schoolroom miss than the secure, grown woman she knew herself to be. She'd been responding to his commands like a stringed puppet. "Thank you," she said, snatching the glass from his hand. With a defiant glare, she brought the cool,

smooth edge of the crystal to her lips and tossed back the amber liquid with the aplomb of an East End doxie.

Julia had a mere three seconds to savor the look of surprise on Brandon's face when a fiery cauldron of bubbling heat erupted in her stomach with a vengeance. She bit the inside of her lip to prevent the gasp trying to escape, but there was little more she could do than blink to dispel the welling of moisture that filled her eyes.

Brandon raised a brow, but refrained from commenting.

When he reached for the empty glass, Julia loosened her grip, allowing him to take it. Only when he turned to set it on a nearby table did she dare several quiet, deep swallows of air. To his credit, he allowed her a few moments before speaking.

"I have spent the past several days deliberating the best means by which to . . . shall we say . . . prepare you for your new status." Removing his black morning coat, he laid it across the back of the small couch before making himself comfortable next to her. Lounging back, he spread his arms along the top. "Since your knowledge of a man's needs is limited at best, I've decided to teach you in stages. The purpose being, when I do finally take you, you will be both familiar and comfortable with not only your body, but mine as well. Unless . . ." His gaze took in her stiff posture, slid to where her breasts were pushed up in the neckline of her dress. ". . . you prefer I continue where we left off earlier and wish me to initiate you to the whole of it today?"

The light that blazed in his eyes caused Julia to stifle a shiver. A part of her wanted to say, "*Yes, let it be done and over with*," while the other part, the part that knew she wasn't ready, screamed at her to reach for the unexpected lifeline he'd tossed. "No . . . what I mean to say is, yes, I would prefer to take things slowly."

"You're quite sure? For I assure you I am more than up

to the occasion." He glanced meaningfully at his lap, drawing her gaze there. His manhood lay long and rigid beneath the beige fabric that concealed it.

Julia felt a rush of heat fill her cheeks along with a good dose of un-ladylike curiosity.

"You blush so prettily," Brandon said, reaching out and brushing the back of his knuckles against the smooth unblemished skin of her face. "I almost regret the day it will become only a rare occurrence." With a sigh, he leaned back, hooking the ankle of one leg atop his knee.

"Unlike you, sir, I will be glad of that day, for it will mean I have learned my lessons well." Julia wasn't sure where that boldness had come from, but now that it was said, she did not regret the words. Maybe a good dose of brandy on occasion wasn't such a bad thing.

Brandon responded with a throaty chuckle—the sound a man makes when a woman unwittingly puts herself right where he wants her. "I can assure you we will practice until it is so. But for now, I think it best we get back to the reason I summoned you here, sweet Julia. To begin with, the first thing you need to do is relax. A mistress does not entertain her benefactor perched upon the edge of her seat as if she were taking tea with the Queen." He held out his hand. "Come closer."

After a brief hesitation, she placed her fingertips lightly into his palm, allowing him to draw her nearer until they were knee-to-knee, but still she sat rigid.

"It is my experience the best mistresses are skilled and comfortable in every aspect of sensuality."

"*Sound.*" He pressed a light kiss to the small delicate lobe of her ear.

"*Sight.*" Her eyelids closed briefly as he brushed each of them with his warm lips.

"*Taste*." Laying his mouth atop hers, he slid his tongue along the seam of her lips until she sighed softly, giving him the opportunity to slip in for a fleeting exploration.

"*Smell*." Nuzzling his way down her neck, he paused at the top of her cleavage to inhale the sweet scent of her gardenia perfume.

"And, *touch*." Bringing up the small hand he still held in his, he watched her eyes express wonder as he sucked gently on each fingertip. "Lean back. Relax," he coaxed.

"My stays do not allow—"

"Then you will cease wearing one."

"But—"

"Unless I grant you permission to do so."

Looking deeply into his eyes, Julia saw no compromise in their blue depths. "As you wish," she agreed quietly, wondering why she didn't feel the need to resist more strongly. On the contrary, she felt all warm and fuzzy inside. No, not warm. Hot.

Placing both feet on the floor, Brandon braced his elbow against the back of the settee and leaned her into the support of his arm as he hovered over her.

"Speech can be a powerful seduction. Not only what you say, but also how you say it. More so, by what you might insinuate. And, in private . . ." he brought his mouth to her ear, ". . . there will be no words forbidden. We will express our wishes as to where, with what, and how."

"I'm not sure I understand." Her words were breathy, hesitant.

"Given time you will." He skimmed the pad of his finger lightly across her plump lips, applying the slightest pressure. Her mouth opened slightly. He eased inside to move along the top edge of her bottom teeth.

Julia felt the strangest urge to suck his finger as he had

hers, but refrained from doing so. When he retracted his hand, she licked her lips in an attempt to erase the tingling caused by his light touch.

Brandon followed the movement. Smiled.

"Eyes—" His thumb caressed the corner of hers. "It is said they are the windows to the soul, but on a more mortal plane, I prefer to think of them as mirrors to ecstasy. In them a man wishes to see a reflection of his own needs, desires . . . lusts." Their gazes locked. "A man also derives great pleasure from merely looking. The sight of a woman's body in different stages of undress is a powerful stimulus. You will learn to become comfortable in all of them."

Her eyes widened.

"Then there is taste," he said, and, leaving her no time to comment, placed his mouth to the sensitive area below her ear. Sucked gently. Moving lower he laid a trail of tiny nips, soothing each with a caress of his tongue, working down to the tops of her soft, fragrant breasts. When he reached the edge of her gown she tensed. He felt the breath lock in her chest. He foraged on, slipping his tongue beneath the fabric to stroke across a distended nipple.

When Julia expelled a soft whimper and reached up to wrap her fingers around his forearms, Brandon raised his head.

Wonder was evident in her eyes. Also uncertainty. He decided now was not the time to tell her there were other places he would much rather be tasting. Brandon knew he needed to end this particular session. He was much too close to losing control. Clearing his throat, he leaned back, pulling her to an upright position.

"I think we shall leave smell and touch for later."

"Later?" She sounded breathy.

"Yes, later. For now, why don't you change and I'll take

you for a brief ride around the estate. I'm feeling the need for some vigorous exercise and fresh air." He stood, tugging her up with him. He glanced at the clock on the mantel. "Can you be ready within the half hour?"

She managed a slight nod.

"Good. I'll meet you in the hall." When she made no move to leave, he gave her a gentle nudge and steered her toward the door. He reached to open it. Stopped. Taking a deep breath, he turned to her. "Taste me, Julia," he commanded.

She looked up with startled eyes. "What?"

"Kiss me." He waited, making no move to touch her. "Of your own volition."

She stepped closer, lightly bracing her hand on his shoulder before rising up on tiptoes and timidly pressing her lips to his. He felt her lower herself fractionally, and then she surprised him by lifting back up and, in a bold move, slipped her tongue into his mouth.

4

BY SHEER WILL ALONE, Brandon held still, allowing her this brief experiment—an experiment that ended much too soon by his way of thinking.

She pulled away. "I should go," she said, glancing at him through lowered lashes.

"Yes, I believe that would be best," he replied, opening the door to allow her escape and closing it firmly behind her.

He smoothed the side of his hair and brought his hand around to cup the back of his neck in the hopes of relieving some tension. Failing that, he walked to the sideboard, poured himself a full glass of brandy, and dispensed of it with a single backward tilt of his head. Sighing, he refilled the glass and plopped down into a convenient chair.

Ten minutes, he told himself, shooting another glance at the clock on the mantel. Then he would go up to change.

On the other side of the door, Julia stood motionless.

Whatever had possessed her?

Her only excuse was that he'd stirred such strange feelings in her with his words and caresses she'd momentarily lost her senses. The lapse of control frightened her, but not as much as the surety it would indeed happen again. Brandon was a man well experienced in the game of pleasure, while she was a mere fledgling.

She was older than most young ladies on the marriage market, having had an unheard of number of seasons in her

twenty-three years. Since losing his wife, the one true love of his life, her father had seemed in no particular hurry to lose his daughter as well. Pampered and shielded by her only remaining parent, Julia had allowed herself to test the waters, as it were. Oh, nothing so far as to be named compromising. Merely a stolen kiss or perhaps a lingering caress just short of its intended mark.

She made a face. Except for the time a very inebriated young Lord Bothell had managed to grope her breast for a distasteful moment, for which he had received a resounding smack.

But no kiss, no touch from any of them had left her so addle-brained she'd found herself wanting to experiment further.

Until now.

Resolving to maintain better control over her rioting emotions, she forced her feet to move toward the stairs.

Forty minutes later Julia was descending the wide, winding staircase, taking great delight in the appreciative look on Brandon's face as he followed her progress. An impatient person herself, she had never thought it fashionable to keep a man waiting overlong.

"Quite fetching, my dear," he said, caressing her with his perusal as he came up several steps to meet her. "Well worth the extra ten minutes I was required to wait." Taking her hand, he turned it over, peeled back her soft tan kid glove, and applied a warm, lingering kiss to her wrist.

With predetermined forbearance, Julia allowed the familiarity, taking the opportunity to study the way his thick dark-brown hair curled over his collar. A bit long by current standards, but suited to this man. Would it feel as soft as it looked?

"Gardenia," Brandon whispered upon straightening.

"Beg pardon?" Julia returned, distracted.

"Your perfume. You dab it behind your ear. Your wrist. And . . ." His gaze slid to her chest. "Between your breasts."

Although he'd kept his voice low, Julia shot a nervous glance to where Henry was stationed by the door waiting to let them out. She'd learned that except for a few, the entire London staff was in attendance, having been sent ahead to prepare for their arrival. Relieved the older gent gave no indication of overhearing, she turned a frown toward Brandon.

With a steady tug, he prompted her to take a step down, bringing her ear level with his mouth. "It makes a man wonder where else you might place a dab of that heavenly fragrance," he whispered.

The reality that she did indeed indulge in the wicked habit of placing a drop at the base of her spine, behind each knee, and at the top of each thigh in no way made the wicked vision that popped into her head less powerful. A quick yank failed to retrieve her hand from his.

Smiling devilishly, as if wise to her thoughts, Brandon tucked her hand beneath his arm and wrapped her resistant fingers around his bulging biceps. With a look that dared her to remove it, he turned and moved aside, giving her the opportunity to step down.

Unwilling to cause a scene, Julia did so, left with the distinct impression she'd had her first lesson in smell.

Henry, fastidiously dressed in white shirt, black jacket, and breeches, bowed as they passed through the door. "Good day, Miss Freemont . . . Mr. Barringer. I do hope you have a pleasant ride."

"Thank you," Brandon said.

"Yes, thank you, Henry." Julia smiled shyly under the older man's perceptive regard. She was not sure why she felt the need to gain this man's approval. Perhaps it was because

the color of his warm brown eyes so reminded her of her father's. Kind, soulful eyes. Eyes that saw people for what they were and accepted them, faults and all.

Applying gentle pressure, Brandon drew her down the three outside steps to where a young boy stood waiting. In his possession was some of the finest horseflesh Julia had ever seen. One, a massive brown brute, easily eighteen hands high, whose mink-colored coat was so shiny it shimmered. The other, a sweet-looking white mare, its wispy mane dancing on a stir of wind. Even her father's stables had never boasted such exemplary specimens.

Julia glanced around. "I see no stepping block, sir."

"Tsk, tsk." Brandon glanced back at Henry. "A gross oversight to be sure. Remind me to reprimand you upon my return."

"Certainly, sir," Henry said with due solemnity, although Julia detected not an inkling of genuine concern.

She turned a suspicious gaze on the man standing next to her. "How shall I—"

"Like this," Brandon said, and, placing his hands tightly around her tiny waist, lifted her up and onto the mare before she could think to object.

Julia emitted a breathy gasp. Convincing herself it stemmed from the man's audacity, and not the feel of his strong warm touch, she prepared to protest. One look into his smiling face told her he was expecting her to do exactly that.

"Thank you." The courtesy was stilted as she pointedly tried to ignore the intimate rub of his thumbs against her stomach. When he finally released her, she began straightening the skirt of her periwinkle blue dress. As she felt his gloved hand sliding beneath the folds to grasp her calf, her gaze clashed with his.

She darted a glance at Henry, the boy holding the reins,

then back to Brandon. Thank God he was broad of shoulder, his body shielding his actions. She dared not breathe, let alone say anything, fearful of drawing attention to what he was doing.

His hand slid higher, caressed the back of her knee, and smoothed along her thigh. Stopped.

Julia swallowed a shriek, willing the trapped air to leave her lungs, trying hard to ignore the heat of his hand through the soft leather and the thin barrier of muslin between his flesh and hers. But most of all, trying to deny the sudden desire to have his hand move much, much higher. To appease the unaccustomed stirrings in her most feminine region.

Looking up at her, Brandon waited to see what she would do. Even with her face partially shadowed by the angle of the small, stylish jockey cap atop her head, the bright morning light clearly revealed the play of emotions across her lovely features.

Trepidation, embarrassment . . . a trace of excitement. An inexperienced miss she might well be, but she had a willingness and determination that left him throbbing. She was the perfect combination of innocence and sensuality. And he wanted nothing more than to haul her off the horse, toss her to the ground, and sink into her untouched, virginal flesh. Flesh he would soon claim.

Not now. Not here.

"Hook your leg around the horn and I will settle your other foot in the stirrup," he said, giving her thigh a light squeeze.

Reading the challenge in his eyes, Julia hesitated. If she did as requested, he would have unrestricted access to her through the split in her drawers. Her stomach curled. Her heart beat faster. With measured slowness, she did as requested.

He smiled, his face reflecting admiration.

His palm skimmed the top of her thigh, lingered, and then made an unhurried glide back down her leg. Grasping her supple kid boot at the ankle, he slid it into the stirrup.

"Are you well-seated, my dear? I am set on a vigorous ride."

His words implied more; she heard it in the smooth tone of his voice. Exactly what, she could not imagine, but was quite certain it carried some sexual implication.

"I am well ready for anything you have in mind, *Mr. Barringer.*"

"We shall see." Ignoring her formal address, he turned away to reach for her horse's reins. "Thank you, Joseph," he said, returning the boy's smile before handing the straps to her.

Julia balked at the small amount of leather he offered for her grasp. When she took it, his fingers wrapped around hers in a brief caress, and then he moved away to mount his horse.

Staring after him, Julia couldn't help but notice the high shine on his black knee-high boots or the way the buttery yellow buckskin molded the fine shape of his muscular thighs as he swung into the saddle.

Once he was settled, Henry came around to hand up a small wicker basket. After thanking him, Brandon said, "Relay my appreciation to Etienne for the picnic he prepared and tell him we shall sup lightly upon our return. If there is anything that needs my *immediate* attention, you know where to find me."

"Yes, Mr. Barringer," Henry said, stepping back.

After securing the basket behind his saddle with a strap, Brandon glanced Julia's way. "Ready, my dear?" At her nod, he turned his horse and set a leisurely gait away from the house.

Julia was thankful when Brandon did not immediately engage in conversation. It gave her time to study the

surrounding landscape—not the meticulously groomed grounds she was used to seeing at her father's properties, though well maintained. More natural to the countryside, they hinted at a controlled wildness. Much like the man riding next to her. The trappings of society might hold him at bay and a woman might think to control him, but it would be merely an illusion. He was an enigma, a challenge.

And deuce it all, she so did love a challenge.

"Are we venturing far?" she asked, turning her head to find his attention already on her.

"Dare I hope you are in a hurry to be alone with me?" He held back a smile at the flash of annoyance in her eyes.

Determined not to allow him to fluster her, she gave him a censoring look. "I was merely making polite conversation, Mr. Barringer. Must you turn everything I say into some implied intimacy?" With a small huff, she looked straight ahead.

Pulling up on his reins, Brandon reached over and grabbed the mare's bridle. Both horses came to an immediate standstill.

Julia emitted a sharp intake of breath. Her gaze flew to his.

"I will not tell you again, Julia," he said, sidling his horse so close that his thigh brushed her leg. "From this moment on, every time you address me as Mr. Barringer, I will take it to mean you wish to be reminded of exactly how *intimate* our relationship will be." His gaze slid from her wide green eyes to the rapid rise and fall of the plump tops of her breasts, and back up. "And I will give no consideration to where we are or whose company we are in. Have I made myself clear?"

Before she could answer, he released her horse's bridle, slipped his hand behind her neck, and pulled her to him.

Seated so precariously, Julia instinctively tightened her

leg around the horn of the saddle and threw out one hand. It landed high on Brandon's thigh. Thoughts of removing it vanished when his mouth connected with hers for a sweet, foraging invasion.

Brandon tried to force himself to concentrate on the kiss, the soft lips beneath his, and not the dainty warm hand so close to his crotch. Had it been a light, fleeting touch, perhaps he could have managed. But with the solid weight of her body behind it, the pressure was impossible to ignore. His manhood stirred as need flooded him. If he but shifted slightly. . . .

Something of his tension must have conveyed itself to his horse. The high-strung stallion shied, breaking the kiss and causing Julia to dig her fingers deeper.

Brandon didn't know whether to curse the animal or thank it.

Moving his hand from around her neck to her shoulder, Brandon gently pushed Julia to an upright position. He breathed a silent sigh when both her hands were once again clasped tightly around her reins. Unfortunately, the heat of her palm still lingered.

"Might I suggest we continue on to our destination," he said, with an indifference he was far from feeling. Expecting her to rebuke him for his treatment, he was surprised when her only response was to nudge her horse forward. It delighted him, the way she never responded as he expected. She was an amazingly complex creature. Taking into consideration his reaction to her, he decided it best to step up the learning schedule he'd planned.

The thought produced a twinge of annoyance. He disliked not being in control, and was not a man who enjoyed his plans disrupted. Though in this instance, there would be definite advantages.

He would instruct Julia in the pleasures of the flesh, thus creating for himself the perfect mistress. Then he would take her back to London, set her up in her own household, and get back to the business of finding himself a respectable wife.

Pleased that things were once again placed on an orderly path, he intended to enjoy the rest of the day and the delectable little puss riding next to him. Who, at the moment, was trying her best to ignore his presence. Something he would not allow for long.

"HOW LOVELY," JULIA SAID, looking out over the small lake, its entire shoreline visible from the secluded grassy area into which Brandon led her. Almost completely surrounded by trees and low-growing bushes, it seemed a world unto itself. A perfect place for quiet contemplation. Or, seduction. Julia did not delude herself into thinking Brandon had brought her here for the former.

"It pleases me that you like it." Dismounting, he came around to help her down. "I have never shared this place with anyone," he said, reaching up and wrapping his hands around her waist.

The jolt of awareness Julia felt was intense. His hands were warm and steady, as was his regard. Bracing on his shoulders, she leaned forward, expecting him to step back and lower her to the ground.

Instead, he moved in, his warm lips coming into contact with the swelling flesh of her breasts, which she'd inadvertently placed within reach.

"I—" Stifling her natural reaction to pull away, she allowed him the liberty. For as much as she wanted to rebuke

him, she wanted more to explore the sensations whirling through her.

Like a butterfly flitting from flower to flower, his firm, moist lips moved across her exposed flesh. Closing her eyes, Julia gave herself over to his touch as he continued his gentle venture. Shamelessly, she arched her head back to allow him better access. He obliged, slipping his tongue deeply into the valley between her breasts. Her nipples beaded.

Lost in anticipation, it took her a moment to realize he'd stepped back, another moment to open her eyes.

"You look disappointed, sweet. Dare I hope you are starting to crave my touch?" he asked. Lifting her from the horse, he set her on her feet.

The euphoria surrounding Julia dissipated like morning mist on the water. "I was not aware a mistress need crave her benefactor's touch. Merely tolerate it," she stated levelly, trying to break the contact of his hands by stepping back.

Brandon tightened his grip and smiled. "Are you trying to wound my male pride by saying my touch is abhorrent to you, Julia? Very dangerous ground for a woman in your position. Some men would turn out a mistress for saying such. Others would consider it a challenge." He caught her chin in his palm. "How shall I take it?"

When she said nothing, he grazed his thumb across her lips. "I believe I shall let you decide. Tell me—shall I return you to London or consider it a challenge?"

She licked her lips, but remained silent.

"You must choose. We will not leave this spot until you do. Tell me how I am to proceed."

"Challenge," she whispered.

"Beg pardon, I don't believe I heard you."

Knowing damn well he had, she subdued her temper and stated more loudly, "Challenge."

"Very well, I accept." His grin was predatory. "And I vow before this afternoon is done, you will be begging for my touch."

He turned and walked away, leaving Julia to stare after him. Moments passed before she could gather her wits enough to take up her horse's reins and lead her to the edge of the water. Barely did she notice the brush of the mare against her shoulder as the animal moved past her, planting front hooves in the soft sand, lowering its head to drink. She was only mildly aware of the gentle breeze that teased loose tendrils of hair against her cheeks, but very much aware of the man not far behind her.

Good Lord, he was annoying. Not to mention arrogant, self-assured, and so damnably handsome he had her anticipating his intentions rather than despising him for the way he treated her.

Sneaking a peek over her shoulder, she watched as he bent to his knees and began spreading the afternoon's feast onto a blanket. What he pulled from the basket seemed better-suited to formal dining than a picnic in the woods. First to appear were grapes and a bottle of wine.

Each time he reached, his dove gray riding coat pulled taut across his broad back, emphasizing the considerable width of his shoulders. Having seen him in formal attire at many social gatherings, she'd thought his size enhanced by padding. The day she'd entered his study and had caught sight of him in his shirtsleeves dispelled that notion quite neatly.

She tingled at the memory. Would he remove his shirt altogether when making love, as the stableboy had? Somehow, she knew he would.

Seeing him come to his feet, she quickly turned away.

"I'll finish taking care of the horses," Brandon said,

coming up next to her. "Make yourself comfortable on the blanket. I'll join you momentarily."

Only too happy to comply, she relinquished her mount into his keeping and walked away without saying a word.

Brandon watched her go, appreciating the sway of her hips until she demurely seated herself on the blanket and seemingly became absorbed with something in the opposite direction from where he was standing. Her facade of indifference was irksome. He would allow her the false security for the moment, but she would not be so inclined in the future. He would see to it.

5

WHEN THE ANIMALS FINISHED drinking, Brandon walked them partially into the trees and tethered them before removing his horse's saddle. Initially he had thought to leave it on, intending only to stay a short time, but Julia's lofty attitude had changed all that. Taking off his gloves, he tucked them inside the pockets of his riding coat. Removing both it and his waistcoat, Brandon hung them on a low-hanging branch. Next came his cravat, which he tied onto the mare's bridle. Henry would take its meaning and ensure their privacy.

Untying the mare, he pointed her in the direction of the path and gave her a solid whack on the backside.

Julia's head jerked up at the sound of pounding hooves. "My horse!" Hampered by her dress, she struggled to her feet. By the time she was standing, the animal was well on its way. She spun to face Brandon. More concerned with the loss of her horse than the lack of his cravat, she urged, "If you hurry, I'm sure you can catch her."

"There's no need. She'll eventually make her way home," he replied, walking toward her, opening a few buttons to reveal the upper portion of his chest.

"I. . . ." For a moment, Julia lost her train of thought. After clearing her throat, she said, "Since I cannot believe you mean for me to walk back to the house, I can only assume you intend doing so."

A bedeviling smile crossed Brandon's lips. "Come, Julia. I know you are not that naïve. I don't intend for either of us to walk. Neptune is more than capable of carrying us both."

No, she was not that naïve, but the thought of being pressed so intimately against him for the length of time it would take to return to the estate was both disconcerting and titillating. The narrow cut of her dress would not allow her to ride behind him. Which meant she'd be cradled in the strong, muscular arms he was currently exposing by rolling up his shirtsleeves. The thought of being wrapped in them sent a shiver skittering through her entire body.

By the time he stood in front of her, both arms were bare to the elbow. "Come, let us sit and enjoy the meal." He held out his hand.

Needing a distraction, she slipped her hands into his grasp, allowing him to assist her to the ground. Keeping her back perfectly straight, she shifted to her hip, bent her legs to the side, and carefully adjusted her gown so only the tips of her boots were visible.

Dropping down next to her, Brandon handed her an object wrapped in linen. "While you unwrap this, I'll open the wine," he said, picking up the bottle and withdrawing a corkscrew from the basket.

Julia became distracted by his actions. Such a simple task really . . . opening a bottle of wine. She'd seen it done before, but never by a man whose arms were bare.

His lower arms, easily twice the size of hers, were covered with a sparse matting of dark-brown hair. She became fascinated by the play of tendon and muscle beneath his skin. They shifted, tightened, and relaxed with each turn of the handle that drove the metal spirals deeper into the cork. The top of the corkscrew was lost in the palm of one large hand, the bottle encompassed by the other. Her eyes drifted

shut, imaging those same hands wrapped around each of her slender thighs as they spread her—

The pop of the cork startled her back to reality, nearly causing her to drop what she was holding. Without further delay, she began peeling back the layers of cloth, discovering it to be a large monogrammed napkin protecting a delicate, stemmed glass. She ran her finger lightly over the etched "B" on its surface that perfectly matched the one on the napkin.

Placing the goblet carefully on the blanket, she said, "If you will give me the other glass, I will unwrap it."

"There is no other."

Julia's brow furrowed. "Was there no room in the basket? Shall we take turns then?"

Brandon shook his head and smiled.

There it was again, that smug smile. How it irritated her to think he was finding amusement at her expense.

She surveyed the items on the blanket. An array of food and fruits, two bottles of wine. One plate, one set of utensils, one napkin, one goblet.

"Lovers do not take turns, they share," he stated baldly, gaining her attention.

Refusing to indulge his humor further by saying something she'd regret, she merely nodded.

He reached for the glass, his forearm lightly grazing the tops of her thighs. He made no apology, nor did she expect him to. After pouring the wine, he handed her the glass.

She accepted it, careful not to come into contact with his fingers. Watching him over the rim, she took a sip.

Brandon stretched out on his side next to her, bracing himself on his forearm. "Now, I want *you* to give *me* a drink," he said. "But first, turn the glass so I may drink from the same spot."

Shocked, yet fascinated, Julia did as asked. When she brought the wine to his lips and went to tilt it, he grasped her hand.

Holding her gaze, Brandon drew his tongue over the place her lips had touched and with a light pressure of his hand, prompted her to angle the glass so he could drink. Before releasing her, he placed a light kiss on her gloved index finger.

"Now you."

Willing her hand to remain steady, Julia rotated the glass and brought it to her lips. Still captured by his riveting blue gaze, she lightly licked the glass and drank.

"Very good." His voice was low and approving as he took the glass from her, finished the last few drops, and placed it aside. Pulling over the plate, he filled it with an assortment of food.

He levered up enough to balance on one hip. "Give me your hand."

She raised her hand . . . hesitated. "Why?"

"The flavor of leather has never appealed to me," he confessed, grasping her wrist to bring her hand the rest of the way to him.

Before she could comprehend his meaning, he began removing her glove. Not quickly, as she expected. Instead, peeling back the soft kid, placing warm, subtle kisses on every new inch of skin he exposed.

Determined to appear unaffected, Julia tried hard to ignore the spiky little tingles that raced up her arms. If the simple play of his lips on her hands could wring such sensations, what havoc would he create should he give like attention to other, more tender parts of her body? She dared not imagine.

Done with one hand, he beckoned for the other. In a

daze, Julia gave it. By the time the ordeal was over, she felt ready to swoon.

A knowing smile on his face, Brandon leaned back to a reclining position. "I think I'd like the cheese first, if you wouldn't mind serving it to me."

Julia reached for the fork.

He caught her hand.

His earlier comment regarding the taste of leather suddenly became clear. Calm on the outside, shaking within, she pinched a piece of cheese from the plate and held it to his lips. Both food and her fingers disappeared into his mouth.

Wide-eyed, Julia watched and felt his tongue slide between her fingers to capture the tidbit, his mouth sucking as he pulled back, releasing her.

It took her several moments to realize she was still holding her hand up in front of his mouth. Yanking it down, she dipped her chin. He must think her the biggest ninny to be so affected by such a simple act. After several deep breaths she brought her head up. His expression was not the least bit mocking as he held a grape in front of her lips.

"I could hardly call myself a gentleman, did I not return the favor."

Julia tentatively opened her mouth, allowing him to slip the fruit inside. The tip of his finger followed.

"Gently, love. The feel of a woman's lips along a man's flesh is a pleasure to be savored."

Unable to withstand his unwavering scrutiny, Julia lowered her lashes, sucked gently, and then drew away. At the sound of his low moan her eyes opened to discover his gaze riveted to her mouth and his eyes burning with an intensity that thrilled her.

As if awakening from a spell, Brandon broke eye contact

and reached for the wine. Unlike the previous glass, he drank the entire contents. Refilling it, he offered it to her.

When Julia dutifully turned the glass and licked it, Brandon hastily rose to his feet.

"If you'll excuse me a moment, there is something I need to attend to," he said and, giving no further explanation, strode off into the woods.

Bewildered by his actions, Julia watched him until he disappeared from sight. Hand trembling, she brought the glass to her lips and drained it.

A short distance away, assured of his privacy, Brandon braced his forearm on a tree and leaned his head against it. He closed his eyes. It took disgustingly little effort to conjure up a vivid image of Julia. Her shiny, long, black hair. Her sparkling, inquisitive, green eyes. Her moist, tender lips. The way those lips had looked when wrapped around his finger. Unable to ignore his physical needs longer, he let loose a low, ragged groan.

Reaching down, he released himself from his breeches and, taking his aching shaft in hand, applied the steady rhythm necessary to garner relief. It didn't take long. Less than a dozen strokes and his seed lay in a glistening pool at the base of the majestic tree.

Not even bothering to set himself back to rights, Brandon headed for the nearby lake. He crashed through the woods, his mind not on snapping twigs or crackling leaves, but centered on one thing: future torments he would be made to endure before making Julia irrevocably his.

Crouched down by the shoreline, idly swirling his hand in the water, Brandon stared down at the bulge of his unappeased shaft. Washed and stuffed back into his breeches, it was still hard with need.

"Damn the irresistible little minx for making me lose all

control. And damn me for allowing it," he said, shaking his head. Hoping to clear his mind, if only temporarily, he closed his eyes. Focused on the water. On the tepid liquid running through his fingers. It worked for all of two minutes, until an idea struck.

He pulled out his hand. Tested the air.

Surging to his feet, he returned to the clearing.

Julia watched him advance, his strides long and sure, his attention directly on her.

He seemed a far different man than the one she'd arrived with. His hair was tousled, brown waves caressing his broad forehead. One of his rolled sleeves had come down, billowing softly as he walked. The shirt itself was free of his breeches. He looked more a dangerous pirate than a gentleman—one bent on ravishment. She was shocked at the excitement she experienced.

"Can you swim?"

Her thoughts jerked to a stop. "No. Of course not. Who would teach me such an improper thing?"

He grinned. Squatted in front of her.

The instant she realized his intent, she scooted backward.

His hand shot out, latching onto her booted ankle. "Did you not come to me for lessons?"

"Not in this," she stated firmly, tugging against his hold. "In—"

"In seduction?" he finished for her and began pulling her.

At the sight of her dress crawling up her legs, Julia squealed. All thoughts of resistance forgotten, she made a quick grab for the hem of her dress.

When he began loosening the laces on her short boots, she made another attempt to dissuade him from his course. He retaliated by lifting her leg higher. To retain her balance,

she threw her hands back, giving him a clear view up her dress.

Knowing she could not win in a contest of strength, she gritted her teeth and refused to give him the satisfaction of struggling, even when he slid her pantalets above her knees and peeled her white stockings and garters from her legs with the detachment of a lady's maid.

"Up," he instructed, hauling her to her feet as he stood. The next things to go were her hat and jacket, carelessly added to the pile of discarded garments at her feet.

"Turn, so I may unfasten your gown."

"You cannot possibly mean for me to take off my dress. Surely when the horse returned without a rider someone set out to look for us," she said.

"If you are hoping to be rescued, I'm afraid you will be disappointed. No one will be searching for us."

The glint in his eyes and the curve of his lips immediately aroused her suspicions. Her head swung in the direction her horse had taken and then back. "You did that on purpose," she accused, planting her fists on her hips. "By what right—"

Reaching out, Brandon looped an arm around her waist and yanked her against him. "By right of ownership," he stated firmly. "An ownership you yourself gave me the day you asked to become my mistress. You are mine, Julia." In an instant, his lips were on hers. Hot—demanding—giving her no time to think. Only to feel.

And feel, she did. Right down to the toes she was curling into the blanket.

Brandon broke the contact and looked down at her. Black lashes fanned across creamy cheeks, head back, lips still puckered and seeking. The sound that escaped him was somewhere between a groan and a chuckle as he grasped her by the shoulders and turned her around.

"If you leave the dress on, it will never dry by the time we leave," he said, needing a distraction from her innocent appeal. He was determined not to let her tempt him to waver from the learning schedule he'd set. Today was a lesson in touch, and he would take it no farther.

When she was out of the dress, he spun her back.

She stood motionless. Appearing so composed Brandon might have thought her totally resigned, if not for the slight rise of her hands to cover herself before she quickly lowered them.

"Later, we will discuss the matter of your defying my wishes by wearing this," he said, hooking his finger into the top of her stays and pulling her closer.

He stared at her lips so intensely, Julia thought he intended to kiss her. She hadn't realized how much she wanted him to until he stepped back and began tugging his shirt up and over his head. She felt immensely disappointed, a feeling she had little time to dwell on when presented with the sight of his broad, naked chest. Last night, when she'd been cradled next to it, it had been cool to the touch. She wondered what it would feel like now, warmed by the after-noon sun.

She looked on with interest as he sat on the ground to divest himself of his own boots and stockings. When he stood, and made no attempt to remove his breeches, she found herself grappling with both relief and a recurrence of disappointment.

He whisked her up into his arms. With her clutching tightly around his neck, he strode for the lake.

Thigh deep in water, he released her legs. When her feet found purchase on the soft, spongy bottom, he turned her into his arms.

She gasped.

"Cold?" he asked, looking down into her upturned face.

She was certain he knew it wasn't the water that had caused the reaction. It was the hard ridge of flesh snuggled into her stomach. But she had decided somewhere between the removal of her stockings and his that she would not allow him to be amused at her expense again. She was not the silly goose he assumed her to be.

"A bit disconcerting, perhaps. But I am quite sure I will adjust," she said, still clinging to his neck.

"Of that, I've little doubt." He began walking her backward. The deeper the water, the more her grip tightened. By the time he was waist deep, her head was buried against his shoulder. "I want you to wrap your legs around me." He clasped his hands around her narrow waist and prompted her by lifting. The split in her pantalets gaped wide. The feel of her warm, hair-shrouded flesh against his stomach caused it to clench. Expecting Julia to push away at any moment, Brandon remained still, his heart thundering in his chest.

To his surprise, all she did was release a tiny sigh and relax more fully into him. When he felt more in control, he waded out chest-deep. Not wanting to release her yet, he held her against him a while longer.

"The first thing you need to learn is how to float," he stated, gripping her waist and pulling her slightly away until they were face-to-face. "Lower your legs."

Still clinging to his neck, she did as instructed. The slow glide of her legs against his was sheer torture. He straightened his arms to keep her from drifting against him. He needed to concentrate on teaching her to swim, not the weightlessness of her body and the thought of how easy it would be to release his straining shaft and plunge deep inside of her.

Shifting her to the side, he placed one arm behind her

shoulders, the other beneath her knees. "Take your arms from around my neck.

Clinging tighter, she shook her head.

"Trust me, Julia. I won't drop you. I promise," he said when she hesitated.

Brandon tried to concentrate on her face and not the water lapping at the tops of her breasts, displayed enticingly by her tight stays. Or the thought of what else would be revealed the moment he brought her body to the surface. "Close your eyes, keep your breathing steady, and lean back."

When she did, he eased her to the surface. Water sluiced from her body, leaving behind wet, clinging fabric. The thicker material of the stays protected her modesty, but from the waist down she might as well have been naked. He bit back a moan, locked his knees, and widened his stance.

"How delightful," she murmured.

With considerable effort, Brandon tore his gaze from the juncture of her legs and the dark hair peeking out from the split in her drawers.

"I feel free as a bird," she continued, eyes still shut, oblivious to the carnal picture she presented.

Brandon's gaze drifted downward.

Curious as to why he wasn't speaking, Julia opened her eyes. She should have been appalled at where he was looking and how she was displayed, but the open hunger on his face made embarrassment a fleeting thought. For the first time in her life, she witnessed raw male desire. It stirred her as nothing in her life ever had. She felt an almost frantic need for him to touch her. There. Between her legs. Where she ached.

She'd once seen the stableboy place his hand between the parlor maid's thighs, making her writhe and moan. Later that same night, alone in her bed, Julia had slid her hand beneath

her nightgown. The shock of the sensation had startled her so much she'd snatched her hand back. But the thought of a man's hands, Brandon's hands. . . . "Touch me." The words were out before she could think to stop them.

The appeal was so softly spoken Brandon believed he'd imagined it.

"Please, Brandon. Touch me."

Swallowing deeply, he turned his head. What he saw in her crystal green gaze was far removed from the wary virginal curiosity he expected. It was a woman's yearning.

"I had thought to initiate you more slowly, but since today's lesson is touch, I see no reason to deny you. Put your arms around my neck."

Once they were there, Brandon took several steps back into shallower water. Removing the arm supporting her legs, he allowed them to drift down. Her toes brushed his as they made contact with the silt bottom of the lake. Placing his hands on her waist, he used the slightest pressure to turn her to face him. "Part your legs."

He felt the slightest tightening of her fingers on the back of his neck before she complied. "Relax, sweet. The water will make this much easier."

Nodding, she took a small, stuttering breath. Followed by a deeper one.

Holding her gaze, Brandon moved his hand around to her stomach. Her muscles contracted beneath his touch. He gave her a minute to become accustomed to the feel of his hand. When she relaxed, he dipped lower. And lower. He stopped at the opening in her pantalets. His path unhindered, he lightly sifted his fingertips through her silken curls.

Using the pad of his index finger, he sought out the pleasure nub hidden within her folds.

Sucking in a sharp breath, Julia rose up on tiptoes, breaking the contact.

"I—"

"Shhh." Bending his head, Brandon touched his lips to the corner of her mouth. "Close your eyes," he whispered. When she did, he pressed his mouth fully to hers, flicked his tongue across its surface, and sucked gently at her full bottom lip.

For the moment, he focused on nothing else—nibbling and licking—until she sighed and relaxed. He worked his tongue between her unresisting lips. He worshipped her mouth with lazy exploration, as if that alone were his sole purpose and they had all day. When he felt the time right, he cupped her with his hand.

This time, she did not shy away.

6

WITH THE TIP OF his tongue, Brandon lightly traversed the surface of Julia's lips. His finger mimicked the motion, gliding across her fleshy, moist folds.

His tongue grazed the opening of her mouth. His middle finger, the opening of her womanhood.

Eyes closed tightly, Julia was awash in sensation.

His tongue entered her mouth, barely slipping inside, tentatively testing. His finger did the same, entering her to the first knuckle, gently circling.

His tongue swirled. His finger rotated.

Both tongue and finger searched deeper.

Julia clung to him, her toes curling into the soft bottom of the lake.

He retracted both tongue and finger, returning to delve more deeply with each. He repeated the motion, moving out and slipping in. Deeper each time.

Julia moaned.

Familiar with a woman's needs, Brandon knew the sound stemmed from pleasure, not pain. The water provided the natural lubricant her virginal body had yet to release.

He made the final invasion, with both tongue and finger. Surging deeply, firmly, but never too deep. Moving. Swirling. Careful not to breech her maidenhead. He would save that particular pleasure, wanting to feel it stretch against the sensitive head of his pulsing staff.

Once again, he retreated.

"Shall I stop?" he asked, sure of the answer.

"No." The hands she'd settled on his shoulders earlier gripped more tightly as her hips thrust forward to follow his retreating finger.

He stilled, barely maintaining contact, wondering how he could continue this pleasant torment without consigning himself to bedlam. His earlier self-induced release seemed to have done little to assuage his ferocious need. But he'd promised to make her beg for his touch and was determined to see it so. She would never again hide beneath the veil of martyrdom she seemed to have donned.

"Brandon, continue." The stern command was rendered less potent by the amount of desperation it held.

"Brandon?" he taunted, arching a brow. "Are we finally dispensing with *Mr. Barringer*?"

"Whatever you wish—only do not stop. I would have you finish what you started." She moved closer, seeking his caress.

Her lack of restraint pleased him. "Are you begging, sweet Julia? If so, I will accept no more demurring, or false proclamations that you are merely *tolerating* my touch." He circled her flesh with his finger.

Julia shifted to force it deeper, causing the water to swirl through her open thighs. She moaned.

"If I proceed and give you a taste of the pleasures to be found in my arms, you will turn yourself completely over to my tutelage. From this day on, you will leave behind any silly notions you were taught regarding sex and learn what it is a man truly wishes from a woman."

One flex of his wrist gave her a brief taste of more— another took it away.

"Damn you." Her nails bit into his shoulders. "Is it not

enough I relinquish my body? Would you take my pride as well?"

"I will not deal in half-measures with you. I will have it all." The determination radiating from his eyes gave validity to his statement.

Julia wanted to scream her frustration. Ashamed to think she was so wanton, she craved his touch more than her pride. A pride she'd valued highly not so many days before. But what worth was pride? She could not eat it, wear it, or use it for shelter. Only Brandon could give her all that and more.

She met his waiting gaze. "If you need to hear me beg, I shall." Her chin lifted. "Please, Brandon. Release me from this feeling of yearning you have created."

"I'd be delighted," he stated, seizing claim of her lips.

Not as before. Not tentative and searching. Firmly. Thoroughly.

All the while, working his finger. Stroking. In. Out. His palm creating the most delicious sensations as it rubbed steadily against the firm, peaked flesh at her entrance. Then more pressure, filling her, stretching her. Through the fog of desire came the realization he was using more than one finger.

"Open yourself," he whispered. "Let me in."

So single-mindedly intent was she on what his hand was doing that it took Julia several moments to grasp what Brandon was saying. Since everything he did thus far only added to her bliss, she was more than willing to oblige. Wondering at the pleasures to be had when Brandon finally took her the way a woman was meant to be taken, she willed her inner muscles to relax.

Unconsciously, a vision of the stableboy thrusting enthusiastically into the parlor maid came to mind. Gracious. No wonder the girl had been so shameless and vocal in urging her partner on.

Brandon knew she was close to climaxing. He could feel it in the way her body yielded, began tensing, her thighs tightening around his hand. As if she were preparing to jump off a great precipice. In a way she was. Her first leap into sexual gratification. One he'd brought her to.

She went rigid for a shadow of a second . . . and screamed, the sound lost a moment later against his shoulder as her arms clutched his neck and her womanhood clutched his fingers. Her breathing came out in short little puffs against his bare skin and her heart beat rapidly against his chest.

Allowing her to enjoy the full effects of her first climax, Brandon didn't move, only held her tightly, letting the lapping water gently rock them.

Julia felt dazed, adrift on the very water she was standing in. Never had she experienced anything so wonderful and yet so frightening. If his fingers could wreak such delightful mayhem, what undreamed-of ecstasy might his manhood cause when thrust up inside her? She shivered at the thought.

Why on earth would any woman refer to making love as a duty? Unless . . . perhaps all men were not as experienced in pleasuring as Brandon. The thought intrigued her.

"I never realized. . . . However could a young girl imagine. . . . What I mean to say. . . ." She sighed and looked up at him, eyes half closed, still in the thrall of pleasure. "Is it always so . . . ?"

"Delightful?" Brandon finished, smiling. "For some— not all." Without thought, he raised his hand to smooth back strands of damp, black hair from her flushed cheek. "There are men aplenty who are interested only in taking their own gratification, never realizing the rewards to be had from a fully sated woman. A well-bedded female is usually much more eager to linger and return the favor. Whereas those who

are not want nothing more than a quick end to what they consider a messy affair."

"Is that the reason a man seeks out a mistress, because she is more . . . amenable to his overtures than a wife?" The color of her cheeks heightened as she dipped her head.

Placing a finger beneath her chin, Brandon raised it back up. "The reason men seek out mistresses are many and varied. I do know that, although most men dream of a woman whose sexual appetites match his own, few are fortunate enough to find one."

For several moments, he stared deeply into her eyes. Cupping the back of her head, he tightened his arm around her waist, bringing her more fully against him.

Water ebbed from between them. Her knees bumped his thighs.

"I can mold you into that kind of woman, Julia. If that is your wish." Deliberately, he pushed his full-blown arousal against her pliant stomach, letting her feel his raging desire.

Her breath caught. Her small hands tried to find purchase on his wet, thickly muscled forearm.

"Under my tutelage you will learn every conceivable way to find pleasure and give it in return. But in doing so, I must warn you not to confuse lust with love. For no matter how adept you become in the art of seduction, I will not stray from my resolve to find a suitable wife."

Like smoke in a gentle wind, Julia's sense of fulfillment shifted and wavered. She should not feel hurt, but she did. Must he keep reminding her at every turn that she was no longer desirable as a wife? Or was it perhaps he who needed the constant reminding? Was it her imagination, or did the water seem a bit cooler?

"As I am of similar mind and wish no permanent attachments, you need have no worry, sir. I am under no illusions

as to the temporary status of my position. When the time comes, I shall move on with little regret."

"Splendid," he said, wondering why her indifference annoyed him when it was precisely what he wanted. "Since we are agreed on the matter, I see no reason to belabor the subject." Without warning, he scooped her up and began walking toward shore. "The air is turning cooler. It would be wise to allow our clothes to dry as much as possible before we begin our journey back."

Out of the water, he made his way to the blanket where he set her on her feet. The absence of his body heat produced a shiver.

"Cold?"

"No," she answered, trying hard to keep her voice even.

A quick assessment of her person had him shaking his head. "The tiny bumps covering your skin say otherwise." Placing his hands on her arms, he gave them a brisk rub. "Better?"

She nodded.

"Had I not been so pleasantly preoccupied, I would have noticed how cool it had gotten. Once we get you dry, I think it best to leave. I would not want you to take a chill."

"I have always enjoyed a healthy constitution. You need not treat me like a delicate flower. If you wish to stay longer—"

"What I wish is for a warm bed and us naked in it. But when the time comes, I would prefer you not be sniffling. So, let's get you out of these wet clothes. We'll use the blanket to dry you. Then you can put on your dress." Without so much as the smallest attempt to gain her permission, he turned her and began loosening the laces at the back of her stays.

The wet fabric made the task tedious, but through the entire process Julia remained silent. What was there to say?

He was right. If she remained in her damp clothes, the ride home would be most uncomfortable.

Still, the thought of once again being naked in his presence. . . . Her hands trembled as she slid them up to hold the front of her stays.

Oh, she knew she would need to get used to it, but she had hoped to be given more time. And the only thing to be accomplished by complaining would be giving him another reason to remind her of the choice she'd made.

When the final lace came undone and the sides fell open she clung tighter, half expecting him to rip it away.

"While you finish, I'll gather everything up," he said dismissively.

She glanced over her shoulder to see him crouched down and stuffing the remnants of their barely eaten meal back into the basket. "The longer you delay, the more likely it is that you will take a chill," he said without sparing her so much as a glance.

Wondering if he had eyes in the back of his head, Julia began removing the rest of her clothes.

By the time she was finished undressing, he was standing in front of her, holding up the blanket. But when she reached for it, he pulled it away. "Ahhh, but the day is not over, and neither is your lesson in touch. Come, my sweet, let me dry you."

Deciding it was better to step into the blanket than stand before him naked and shivering while his hot gaze seared her, Julia stepped forward. The moment she did, she was wrapped in both soft wool and his arms, enveloped in a cocoon of warmth.

He held her like that for a time, his cheek resting atop her head, her cheek against his shoulder.

Even as Julia's body warmed from the closeness of his,

she wondered how it was he seemed unaffected by the gentle breeze that had begun stirring the leaves on the trees.

"Your hair is wet, but there's nothing to be done about it now. If we attempt to take it down and dry it, I fear it would only make matters worse," he said softly.

Securing the ends of the blanket in one hand, he began moving the other. Slow . . . long . . . strokes. Down her back, over her hip, massaging the globes of her buttocks.

There, he lingered.

Exerting the gentlest of pressure, he brought her body more fully into his.

Julia mewed softly, her attention split between the large hand at her back and the large erection at her front. A tremble crawled through her body.

Brandon ceased all movement. "Does it scare you?" He pressed into her slightly.

"N . . . no. Well, perhaps a little. But. . . ."

The softly spoken denial surprised him. "What is it?"

"I'd like to know. . . ."

"Know what?" He leaned back the tiniest bit, creating a small space between them. "Look at me." When she obeyed, he continued. "Did I not say there would be nothing forbidden? You can *say* anything—*ask* me anything and I will answer." He could see indecision swirling in her expressive emerald eyes before she drew in a calming breath.

Catching her bottom lip between her teeth, she looked up. "Does it hurt?"

So that was it. Virginal misgivings. Her innocence brought a tender smile to his lips. "I fear it must the first time," he said. "But be assured, I will ease the way so that when the time comes, you will experience as little pain as possible. After that you will feel nothing but pleasure."

A shy smile touched her lips "No. Not that. I was fortu-

nate enough to have a mother who felt it prudent I be aware of the discomfort some women feel their first time with a man. What I wish to know is . . . do *you* hurt?"

His brow furrowed. "Do I—" Realization dawned. "It is not a *you*, Julia. If we are to deal well together you must call it what it is."

She blushed.

"In the eventuality you lack knowledge, I will supply you someoptions.Yard . . . shaft . . . rod . . . member . . . manhood."

Her blush deepened.

"If those are not to your liking, there are others. Although I always thought them to be rather silly. But if one must give a name, I suppose one could do worse. John Thomas . . . John Willie . . . *Little* Willie. An unflattering comparison you will be happy to know would not suit in my case," he said with a touch of arrogance. "Another—" he winced. "Hanging Johnny . . . a sad state to find oneself in, when in the company of a beautiful woman." He ran the back of his knuckles across her soft cheek and caressed her chin before continuing.

"Ah, and let us not forget Master John Thursday, though I have always wondered what one would call it the rest of the week. And then, there is the esteemed Julius Caesar. Or, the divine, Saint Peter."

Bowing her head, she pressed her face to his chest and began to quake.

It took Brandon a moment to realize it was not from embarrassment, but amusement. Damn the little chit if she weren't laughing. He could not help but feel a touch of admiration.

To bedevil her further, he went on. "For those wishing to wax poetic, there are these. Dart of Love, Lance of Love, Jack-in-the-Box, Torch of Cupid, and, one of my particular favor-

ites, though it will hold no meaning for you until we progress in your training . . . Sugar Stick."

His last statement had her looking up once more.

"Naturally, there are more crude versions, which I will refrain from telling you. Unless . . . " He arched a brow. "You desire to be so enlightened?"

She shook her head. "I believe the selection you have supplied shall be most sufficient," she said gamely, the beginnings of a grin on her lips.

Brandon found himself staring. She had the most amazing face. It held a demure innocence that made a man want to protect her from the world. At the same time, the mischievous sparkle in her eyes belied helplessness. Her skin was smooth, creamy, unblemished, depicting her youth. Her lips tempting as any courtesan's—full, ripe, and succulent as a summer plum.

Brandon lowered his head. A hairsbreadth from possessing her mouth he stopped.

Her eyes were closed, her head tilted back. If he kissed her now, he knew with certainty the training would come to an end. He forced himself to pull back.

"Now that I have given you a suitable list to choose from, would you like to pose your question once more?" he asked.

"Question?" Julia's lashes fluttered open, her eyes gradually filling with comprehension. She straightened. Gave him a challenging look. "I wish to inquire if your . . . rod hurts when it becomes rigid?"

A laugh sprung from his lips, filling the small clearing. "God, you are priceless." He gave her a quick squeeze, rubbing his stiffness more firmly against her. "Not in the sense I believe you to mean. Not the pain of a wound or injury. But with an ache for the want of you. An ache you too will soon become acquainted with."

Wrapping his arms around her waist, he lifted her off her feet, aligning his manhood with her cleft. Pressing deeply, he rotated his hips. "An ache to be between your widespread legs. An ache to have my *shaft* buried deep within you." Unable to resist, he locked his lips firmly against hers, catching her gasp. But no tongue. Not this time. It was too dangerous. He was too close to the brink.

He ended it. Placed her on the ground. Pushed her slightly away and resumed drying her.

Julia wanted to scream. He was driving her to distraction. Her emotions whirled like dandelion fluff in a mild breeze. Could he not end this torturous teaching and have done with it?

Then with a sense of heightened awareness, she became lost in the feel of his hands and the gentle rasp of the blanket over her naked body. A shiver passed through her. It was hard to believe something so mundane as drying one's body could elicit such sensations. But then, the hands moving over her were larger and much less subtle than any maid's had ever been.

Without removing the blanket entirely, he managed to shift it around and put the ends in her hands, leaving his free.

He began with her shoulders, his open palms smoothing over, around, and down. Moved to her breasts—pressing, lifting, causing her nipples to tingle, pebble, ache.

Julia's eyes drifted shut. Her body became languid, moving and swaying with the slightest pressure of his hands.

His fingers splayed across her ribs, slid to her stomach, captured her hips. His thumbs—kneading . . . circling . . . moving lower, tracing the outline of her pubic hair, grazing the creases at the tops of her thighs.

Awash in feeling, Julia tilted her hips forward.

"What is it you want?" Brandon whispered, brushing the side of his face against hers. "Are you wet between your legs? Shall I dry you there? You have merely to spread them." One of his hands slid down to encourage her.

With a whimper, she did as requested.

Julia was melting, she was sure of it. The friction his palm created as he moved it back and forth only added to the heat generated by a need she was barely beginning to recognize. A need for Brandon to pleasure her as he had in the lake.

And then it vanished. Not the need, not the heat, but his hand. Moved to her thigh, joined by his other. He bent to his knee, running a caressing stroke down to her ankle and back up. First one leg and then the other.

Raising her lashes, Julia clung more tightly to the blanket. She wanted his touch—his fingers inside her—but would not beg again. And he wanted her to. She could see it in the knowing gleam of his eyes.

By the time he finished and stood, she was warm and tingling all over. And disappointed, but she would die before admitting it.

"We need to get you dressed," Brandon said, trying his best to keep the lust from his voice—hoping that once her body was covered, he could staunch his burning need to take her. To spread the blanket on the ground, lay her on it, and slake his needs between the creamy thighs he had paid such diligent attention to moments before. It had taken all his will-power not to part the blanket, slip his hand between her legs, and push his fingers deep inside her body.

His member surged, became impossibly hard, the constriction of his wet buckskin breeches more pronounced, causing immense discomfort.

In need of immediate distraction, he bent to gather her gown and hasten her into it. When she moved to pick up

her stays, he blocked her with his body. "Leave it," he stated gruffly.

She jerked back in sudden surprise. "You . . . you cannot possibly mean for me to leave it here, out in the open," she sputtered.

"I see your point. Forgive me." He inclined his head.

Before she could reach again, he snatched it up and hurled it. The combination of wet fabric and the force of the throw sent it a good distance into the woods.

Numb with shock, Julia watched as it flew through the air, past the snagging fingers of several branches, smacked into a tree, and plopped to the ground.

"You beast!" she yelled, whirling to confront him. "That was my best stays." Intent on retrieving it, she turned.

Brandon grasped her arm, spinning her back. "I told you to never again wear one in my company. The next time I instruct you to do something, I expect to be obeyed."

The pleased grin on his face fanned the flames of Julia's indignation. "I took it to mean when we were *alone*."

He looked pointedly around the deserted area.

"You know perfectly well I am referring to the house."

"Then I suggest, the next time you are unsure as to my meaning, you ask for clarification."

"Perhaps," she began in a fit of pique, "you'd prefer me to dispense with all my clothing and merely walk around nak—" Realizing what she was saying, she bit off the remark. Too late.

"Naked? What a novel concept. I wonder why I hadn't thought of it," he murmured, appearing to seriously consider the idea. "Although, wandering around the entire house may not be quite proper, with the servants milling about. And there are the guests who will be arriving within the week to consider. However, inside the confines of our own rooms, I

can appreciate the advantages." The gaze he swept over her was licentious.

"Don't be absurd," Julia snapped. But at the hike of his brow and challenging glint in his eyes, she decided a less hostile approach would be better. "We shall simply forget the entire matter and I will endeavor to make sure there are no future misunderstandings." Her words were rushed, necessitating a deep breath when she finished. "Did you mention something about having guests?" She kept her tone painstakingly demure.

Brandon shook his head. "We shall get to that straight away. First we will finish the subject of your state of dress in the privacy of our bedchambers. Or, would lack of dress be more in keeping with what I have in mind?"

"Please, Brandon."

The tinge of panic in her voice immediately gained his attention.

"Surely even a mistress is allowed some modesty. Could we not come to an agreement on this? There are certain times when a woman. . . ."

She lowered her lashes and her cheeks turned a pretty shade of pink.

"Ahhh, I see. It is concern over your monthly courses that has you so flustered."

Her head snapped up, shocked that he could so casually discuss the intimate workings of a woman's body.

"Set your mind at ease, my dear. It is an inconvenience all men must endure, though I personally find no disgust in it."

Julia could not believe what she was hearing. *He* found no disgust in it. An inconvenience to men? He was not the one who had to lie abed for near half a day, his stomach cramping. Or, walk around with layers of rags stuffed between his legs. "Of all the unmitigated gall!"

"Hence," he went on, ignoring her agitation, oblivious to the vision she was having of drowning him in the lake with not the slightest bit of remorse. "You will be allowed every courtesy during that time. I will even volunteer my services to rub your stomach as I am given to understand some women find comfort in that."

Julia sucked in a quick breath. "You certainly will not. I am shocked that you would suggest such a thing. Have you not been schooled in at least the most trivial of decencies?" With an indignant toss of her head, she had every intention of walking away from him only to discover he was still holding onto her arm. "Release me." She shot a venomous look at where his large, tanned hand was wrapped around her much paler upper arm.

Brandon couldn't help but think her haughty display would have been considerably more effective had she not looked so adorably disheveled. It was hard to take a woman seriously when several tendrils of her wet hair were hanging down and dripping onto the bodice of her dress, rendering it nearly transparent. A woman whose feet were bare. A woman who, only a short while ago, had allowed him a most intimate knowledge of the same part of her body she was now refusing to discuss most vehemently.

"Have I overstepped your bounds of propriety, my dear? There is nothing shameful in the way a woman's body works. When you become intimate, it is not something you can hide. I should be more concerned if your courses *fail* to make an appearance—a matter we will address at a later time."

At his words, Julia felt a surge of panic. Oh, God. She was so confident she had considered all the consequences of her actions. But not that one. Not a baby. Of course, she didn't want one now, but she had always hoped that someday. . . .

Being a bastard himself, would Brandon allow her to

bring one into the world? Or would he deny her the one thing she had always wanted? A child of her own to lavish love upon. The love of a man she was resigned to forgo, but a child's love was a precious thing.

Unconsciously, she placed her hand on her stomach.

And swayed.

7

"JULIA?" BRANDON SHIFTED HIS grip to around her waist. He studied her face, which looked considerably paler than it had a moment ago. "Are you unwell?"

"No." Her voice was but a whisper. "I'm fine . . . really." She made an attempt to move away from him, but his grip tightened.

"You don't look fine."

"It. . . ." Searching for a plausible excuse, her gaze fell to the picnic basket. "A bit hungry is all. We ate so little."

His expression instantly turned contrite. "Forgive me. It was not my intention to starve you." He moved her toward the basket and stared down at the damp blanket lying crumpled next to it.

"Here, use this," he said snatching up his shirt, spreading it on the ground at her feet and solicitously helping her to sit down. She regarded him silently as he took the single plate he'd brought and heaped it with the choicest selection of food.

He was so incredibly handsome, with his dark good looks and sinfully delicious athletic form. And when he wasn't being an overbearing, demanding tyrant, he managed to be quite gallant as well. An occurrence that happened too infrequently for her liking. The man was vexing in the extreme.

Julia could admit now, if only to herself, she'd always been attracted to him.

As young girls often did, she'd imagined what her children might look like if sired by different men. Those she'd envisioned from Brandon had always been the most adorable of the lot.

It was easy to think his daughters the apple of their father's eye—precocious, spoiled, adventuresome. The boys handsome, polite, quite full of themselves—with a touch of the devil in them.

Once again, her stomach plummeted.

"Here, you must eat something."

Brandon's voice dispelled her thoughts. Unblinking, Julia stared at the mound of food he was offering and swallowed. How was she going to manage even the smallest bite?

"I'd be happy to feed you." He selected a cold piece of chicken and held it to her lips.

Julia tried concentrating on the meat and not the strong, lean fingers holding it. What those fingers were capable of. Where they'd been. How they'd made her feel.

Would they taste of her? Shocked to find herself leaning forward to find out, she quickly raised a hand between the food and her mouth.

"No. That's quite all right. I can manage." She took a calming breath. "Perhaps you should get the horse ready. I . . . I'm feeling a bit chilled," she improvised, supplying yet another false excuse.

She could see the objection in his eyes, but before he could speak, an ominous roll of thunder heralded from the distance.

Brandon glanced at the sky. "A storm is coming," he said, handing her the plate and getting to his feet. "While you eat, I'll prepare the horse. I think it best if we hurry. From the look of those dark clouds, I fear we'll not make the estate before the rain comes," he said over his shoulder as he left.

Julia stared after his broad, naked back. Her thoughts in turmoil. Her stomach in knots.

And for the first time since her father's death, she cursed him and the all-consuming love he had felt for her mother. A love that left him adrift and unable to cope without her. For if not for love, he would still be here and Julia would not find herself in the situation of being this man's mistress.

Determined not to give in to her melancholy, she drew a deep breath and managed to force down several pieces of food by the time Brandon returned with horse in tow.

"Ready?" he asked.

"Yes. What shall I do with the rest?"

Looking down at the near-empty plate, he smiled in approval. "Give it to me," he said, dropping Neptune's reins. Taking the plate, he flung its contents into some nearby bushes.

When he set the plate down and began helping her into her half-boots, Julia released the breath she'd been holding. And sent up a little prayer of thanks that he hadn't noticed the food she'd tossed earlier.

After assisting her to her feet and while she stood watching, Brandon repacked the basket with the careless efficiency only a man could manage. That task completed, he reached down, picked up the shirt she'd been sitting on, and slipped it over his head.

"Here," he said, taking his riding coat from across the saddle and handing it to her. "Slip this around your shoulders while I stash the basket somewhere for safe keeping. There won't be room enough for both you and it."

"A shame you did not take that into consideration *before* you turned my horse loose." She ended the statement with a short sniff.

"What makes you think I hadn't?" he said, unperturbed

by her surly demeanor. "I much prefer the feel of your sweet body to this scratchy, stiff hamper." He hoisted the object of discussion and with a smirk strode off a short way into the woods.

When he returned, Julia had his coat around her shoulders and her back to him.

Amused by her ill-humor, he was tempted to taunt her further. One look at the oncoming storm squelched that idea.

Wasting no more time, he threw himself into the saddle, helped her up, settled her across his thighs and set the horse in motion.

Knowing there was no avoiding the storm they were heading into, Brandon kept the stallion to a fast, steady pace. Julia, cuddled against his chest, seemed unusually quiet. And for the first time in his life, he found himself wishing for a chatty woman. Or, God forbid—one with the irritating penchant for complaint. Either would be preferable as it would help keep his mind off the soft feminine hip rubbing against the engorged flesh beneath his wet buckskins.

Never had a woman affected him so.

"We're nearly there," he said to divert his thoughts.

He felt her nod against his chest.

"Are you comfortable?"

Another nod.

Curse the woman! Did she intend to be silent the entire way? There must be something he could say. . . .

"I hope this storm is merely a passing one, for if not, travel from London will be most inconvenient." It was hard not to smile when she turned her face to look at him.

"I'd nearly forgotten. You did say something about guests." She shifted to straighten in his lap.

Brandon suppressed a groan. "I've extended an invitation to a few friends."

"Might I ask who?" Julia inquired, holding back her unease. Could he not have given her some time to adjust to her new status before announcing it to the world? For in essence that was what he was doing. One wagging tongue carrying word back to London and her circumstance would be bandied about like wagers at a horse race. Thankfully, she would not be there when the news became known. With a small amount of luck, some other scandal would have caught the *ton's* interest by the time they did make an appearance.

"My friend Malvern and his wife for one."

"Lord and Lady Malvern!" Though not intimately familiar with the pair, as one of the peerage Julia had attended their wedding. Lord Malvern, a second son, had attained the title upon the unexpected death of his elder brother. A year later, he'd met and reportedly fallen head-over-heels for his beautiful, somewhat unconventional American wife.

"The very same," Brandon stated, smiling into her surprised face. "Our other guests shall include my cousin Robert and your friend, Lady Isabella."

"Isabella?" She straightened farther. Unable to keep the excitement from her voice, she asked, "However did you manage to get her parents to agree?"

"I cannot take full credit. It seems Malvern's wife is quite the little diplomat and has vouched to play chaperone to your friend. A post she will not take lightly, given she has never taken a liking to Robert."

"Why is that?"

He shrugged. "She can give no other reason than he is *overly* nice and accommodating. I should think it a trait a woman would relish in a man. It seems the workings of the female mind shall forever be a mystery to me."

"Have you invited no one else?"

"No," he said. Possessed by a need to touch her, he gath-

ered the reins in one hand and brushed the backs of his fingers across her cheek. "I am not a cruel man, Julia, merely a determined one. I have no wish to set you up for ridicule. There would be little advantage in doing so. A man would find no joy in the arms of a mistress who harbors hate or resentment toward him. I would ease your way back into society by first surrounding you with people I believe will not judge you for your decision."

"Thank you. I—" The rest was lost in a roar of thunder as the sky opened above them.

Gathering her closer, Brandon leaned forward to offer what shelter he could from the ensuing downpour. He urged his mount to a faster pace. Though strong and fast, Neptune proved no match for the solid mass of black clouds that moved over them, swallowing the last traces of the late afternoon sun.

In seconds, they were drenched to the bone as lightning ripped across the heavens. When a quick bright flash lit the sky, enabling Brandon to see the dark shadowy outline of his home in the distance, he breathed a relieved sigh. "Not much farther, love," he shouted to the shivering woman clinging to his chest.

He felt Julia nod, opened his mouth to offer another reassurance when nature let loose its rendition of a naval bombardment.

Neptune shrieked. Reared.

Julia screamed.

Brandon, knowing it was a losing battle, fought for control. The horse lost his footing. Fell backward.

Hoping to avoid being crushed beneath the stallion, Brandon grabbed Julia around the waist, flinging them both sideways.

Opening her eyes, Julia shook off the wave of dizziness

that threatened to claim her. As her senses cleared, she found herself not on the wet, muddy ground, but sprawled across Brandon. Taking in a deep breath, she levered up on her arms to relieve him of her weight, only to realize his eyes were closed and he was not moving.

She put a trembling hand to his chest. "Thank God," she said, taking a relief-filled breath. Reassured by the strong, steady beat of his heart, she took a moment to collect herself. She gave his shoulder a gentle shake. "Brandon?" Getting no response, she slid to kneel by his side, uncaring of the muddy water seeping into her dress.

Neptune's snort momentarily drew her attention. The stallion stood a few feet away tossing its massive head and pawing the earth. He took two steps closer, then shied away. Taking comfort in his showing no sign of faltering, Julia returned her attention to her unconscious companion.

"Brandon, please. Wake up," she pleaded, futilely wiping rain from his face. Again, she shook him, softly at first and then harder. Her efforts were rewarded with a small moan. Weak with relief, she dropped her chin to her chest.

A moment later he stirred. His eyes opened. Blinked against the falling rain. Rising up to his elbows with great effort, he turned his head to look at her.

"Were you injured?" he asked in a pained whisper, tentatively exploring the back of his head.

"No. I am unharmed."

"Neptune?"

"Over there." She pointed, though he made no attempt to look. "And you?"

"Other than a lump the size of a small apple on the back of my head and some hellishly sore ribs, nothing seems broken."

"Can you stand?"

"I believe so."

When both his first and second attempt failed, Julia scrambled to her feet. "Here, let me help." Bending, she wrapped one of his arms around her neck, and placed an arm around his lower back. Even with her added strength, it took considerable effort to get him to his feet.

"Can you get me over to my horse?" At her hesitation, he added, "There is no reason to fear him. A more loyal brute you will never find. He's as gentle as a kitten."

Julia eyed the monstrous beast skeptically.

"I swear, in all the years I have owned him, he's never done anything like that before," he prompted.

Brandon's voice held such conviction, Julia found herself believing him. Securing her grip around his waist, and encouraging him to lean more heavily upon her, she moved toward the animal as quickly as Brandon's shaky legs would allow. She knew his strength was waning. His weight becoming heavier with each stumbling step. Julia also knew, had Brandon been thinking clearly, he would have suggested she bring the horse to him. Not wanting to waste time arguing and needing the reassurance of his warm, solid weight, she kept her silence. At the sight of him lying motionless she'd been gripped by an overwhelming fear. For him. For herself.

If something were to happen to him, where would she go—what would she do?

As they drew nearer to the horse, its sides quivered and it blew a loud breath through its nostrils, but remained where it was. Brandon stretched out his hand and ran it along Neptune's flanks. The stallion danced sideways.

"Closer," Brandon said to Julia, looking down onto her soft features.

They took two steps forward.

"Easy, boy." His tone low and soothing, Brandon reached

out to run a gentle hand along the animal's neck. This time the horse remained still, enabling Brandon to grasp the saddle and relieve Julia of his weight.

"Are you sure you are able to mount?" Julia asked. "I fear I will not be able to hold you should you fall." She placed one hand on the center of his back and leaned the opposite shoulder against the horse, steadying herself on the slick ground. She wanted to be prepared in the event Brandon's legs should buckle.

"Truth be told," he said, looking down at the top of her head, which barely met his shoulder, "I would have laid odds against your assisting me this far." A strained smile curved his lips. "You are much stronger than you appear."

Julia had received many compliments in her life, but none had ever given her as much pleasure as being called *strong* by this man. Especially at a time when she felt anything but.

"Allow me a moment," he said.

She gave him that and more as she stood in the rain, watching as he rested his head against the wet leather, his breathing labored.

He motioned her aside and, with what appeared to be his last bit of strength, pulled himself onto the horse. He wavered. Took several deep breaths. Straightened. Peering down from his lofty height, he extended his hand.

Instead of giving it, she turned to leave.

"What are you doing?"

"Your jacket," she said, looking toward the sodden heap not far from where they fell.

"Leave it."

"But—"

"Leave it," he repeated, offering his hand again.

She shook her head. "I think it best I lead the horse."

"Julia . . . I don't have time to debate the issue. This has nothing to do with my being gallant. My head hurts like the very devil. I need you seated in front of me so I have something to lean on in the eventuality I lose consciousness. Now, hike up your dress, give me your hand, and get your bottom in this saddle."

Julia would have taken issue with his demand if not for the pain etched across his chiseled features. Without further delay, she gathered up her sodden dress in one hand, gave him the other and placed her foot onto his boot. With an effort she knew cost him dearly, he yanked her up in front him. She made but one attempt to pull down the dress that had twisted high around her upper thighs. Relenting, she stuffed what fabric she could between her legs to retain her modesty.

She'd barely settled and taken up the reins when she felt Brandon's body press against her back and his arm slip around to clutch her waist tightly. The barest pressure of his thighs squeezing hers set the horse in motion.

It felt an eternity before Julia pulled the horse up in front of the manor. Her back ached from bearing Brandon's full weight, as he'd indeed lost consciousness before the horse had taken a dozen steps. It was evident by the immediate flooding of servants and lantern light into the yard their return had been diligently awaited.

"What happened?" Henry asked anxiously, coming to Julia's side, while two groomsmen gently eased Brandon off the horse. Showing no indication that he was shocked by the indecent exposure of her limbs, Henry courteously helped her to the ground.

"We were thrown from the horse," Julia replied, grateful when he temporarily diverted his gaze, giving her time to set her clothes to rights. "In an attempt to protect me, I fear Mr.

Barringer took the brunt of the fall and hit his head exceedingly hard. I would suggest you dispatch someone for a surgeon posthaste."

"I will do so immediately." He turned to the two men cradling Brandon between them. "Take him up to his room."

With the greatest of care not to jostle their master, the men left, leaving Henry to accompany Julia into the house after instructing a third man to fetch the surgeon.

The dozens of candles burning cheerily in the foyer contrasted starkly with the black, threatening night that loomed on the other side of the threshold. Safe, Julia thought, not delving too deeply to discover if the feeling stemmed from the house or the man who owned it.

At the foot of the stairs stood a maid, her smile welcoming and a blanket spread between outstretched hands. Julia's mind flashed the memory of Brandon in that exact position a short time ago. Exhausted beyond reason, she moaned. The maid's welcoming expression turned into a concerned frown.

"Henry, look," the maid said, clutching the blanket to her chest with one hand while pointing at Julia with the other.

"Good Lord, Miss Freemont," Henry declared, materializing at her side and gently grasping her arm. "Are you injured?"

"What? Injured? No. Somewhat sore and shaken, but—" Her gaze followed his to her shoulder. Where once the fabric was periwinkle blue, it now had a suspicious purple hue. But watered down or not, there was no mistaking it for what it was. Blood.

"Brandon!" Never realizing she'd called him by his Christian name, Julia's worried gaze flew between Henry and the sweeping staircase. "He must have been more seriously injured than I thought. He said it was only a bump."

"Are you sure you are uninjured, miss?" Henry persisted, refusing to relinquish his gentle but firm hold on her arm as she strained to be released.

"No . . . I mean, yes. I am sure. I must—" Her gaze flicked once more toward the stairs.

"Please, Miss Freemont. Your concern for Mr. Barringer is admirable," Henry said in his usual sensible, modulated tone. "I wish no disrespect, but under the circumstances, I doubt he will be in any condition to receive *visitors.*"

Julia ceased her struggles. She was exhausted and worried, not stupid. Brandon was probably being stripped of his clothes at this precise moment. Being neither wife, nor relative, if she ran up to his room, it would be a good as advertising her status in the *London Post*.

"Be assured he is receiving the best of care," Henry stated kindly. "It is you I am concerned with. You need to get out of your wet apparel, or we will soon have two patients to attend."

Demurring to his sensible reasoning, Julia made no further objections when he turned her over to the maid with instructions for a hot bath, warm meal, cup of tea liberally laced with brandy, and a promise to send word as soon as the surgeon had examined Brandon.

Two hours later, finished with her bath and sadly neglected supper, Julia sat curled up in the window seat, nursing a second cup of tea. Dressed in a ruffled linen nightgown, bundled under two covers with a pillow at her back, she split her attention between the steady splattering of rain against her windows and the drone of masculine voices coming from the adjoining room.

Julia found little consolation in the information brought to her earlier by a shy young maid who stated Mr. Barringer had suffered no serious injuries. The surgeon had arrived to

find his patient fully alert and refusing to be examined. The man was sent on his way with apologies for dragging him out on such a dastardly night and a goodly sum for his troubles.

Even tired and weak, it seemed Brandon was very much a man in command.

A clear, resounding *bloody hell* from the other room drew her gaze away from the night-shrouded landscape. Unable to discern anything more through the solid oak barrier between their rooms, she sighed and turned back to the window. It took immense effort to resist listening at the door as she had when she'd first come here.

In the next room, sitting up against the headboard, chest bare and lower half covered by a sheet, Brandon cursed several more times before regaining control of his anger.

"When neither you nor Miss Freemont proved the source of blood—"

"Blast!" Brandon cut short Henry's explanation. "I should have suspected a mere storm would not have caused Neptune to rear. How bad is the wound?" he asked his companion, who was seated next to his bed on a small wooden dressing chair.

"A graze to his flank. The stable master cleaned him off and treated the wound with salve. Said he'd be fit to ride again in no time."

"I guess that puts an end to any doubts. A random attack in London, on the docks, even a highwayman's bullet might be explained away. Being shot at on my own estates is another matter entirely. What bothers me most is that Miss Freemont was present on the last two occasions. Whoever is trying to kill me is becoming more desperate. Hence, more dangerous."

"What of your guests? Should I send word to them, retracting your invitation?"

Pinching the bridge of his nose, Brandon thought for

several moments. "I would like nothing better. But I know Malvern and that adorably meddlesome wife of his too well. If they discovered the reason behind the cancellation, he and Amelia would hound me to eternity. As for my cousin. . . . Robert would most likely feel slighted if Malvern were to come and not him." Brandon shot Henry a pained look. "There is nothing for it but to allow them all to visit. I shall apprise the men of the problem when they arrive and we will make arrangements to keep a close eye on the women."

Henry nodded. "If that is your wish."

Brandon barked a short, bitter laugh. "What I wish seems to matter little of late." He glanced at the closed door separating his room from Julia's, missing the fleeting smile that touched Henry's lips.

"When weather permits, send some men out to search the grounds." Closing his eyes, he leaned his head back against the headboard. "That will be all for tonight, Henry."

"Very good, sir," he said, and, rising, placed the chair he'd been sitting on in its proper place and closed the door soundlessly as he left.

Alone, Brandon stared once again at the door separating him from Julia. Feeling the need to see her, he whipped back the sheet and carefully eased himself from the bed.

8

BRANDON GAVE NO CONSIDERATION to knocking as he quietly turned the knob and let himself into Julia's room. Nor had he felt it necessary to don any clothing, since his intention was to crawl right back under the covers. He moved toward the bed, a smaller version of his own. Discovering it empty, he frowned.

A quick perusal of the room revealed his quarry to be curled up asleep on the window seat. He took his time making his way to her, partly because he was still sore from his tumble off the horse and partly because he wanted to enjoy this opportunity of being able to observe her at his leisure.

She must have dozed off gazing out the window, as her face was turned that way. It had finally stopped raining, and the light of a full moon drifted through the wet panes of glass, bathing her in a soft light.

In repose, her features looked as soft and innocent as a babe's. Her long, inky lashes were fanned across her porcelain cheeks and, for the first time, Brandon noticed a faint smattering of freckles across her slightly pointed, upturned nose. Her bottom lip was a tad larger than her upper, giving her a pouty, willful look. A look that had men falling over each other to do her bidding at many of the balls they'd both frequented. But he would see an end to that, now that those lips belonged to him. Those lips and the rest of her.

"Come, my sweet," he whispered. "I have a much more comfortable place for you to spend the night." Sliding supportive arms beneath her, he gathered her up, covers and all.

Her head lolled against his shoulder, her brow scrunched, and she expelled a delicate little grunt. Brandon smiled when he detected the faint smell of brandy on her breath.

He had thought to take her to his room, but after several steps, realized he was weaker from the fall than he'd been willing to admit. With a jaundiced eye, he looked toward her bed with its frilly, white, feminine covers. With reluctant resolve, he moved toward it. After a bit of inventive maneuvering, he was able to relieve her of the blankets, get her under the covers, and join her. Adjusting her back to his front, until her sweet bottom was nestled snugly into his pelvis, he settled in behind her.

For a very long time, Brandon lay awake, listening to each soft breath she took and inhaling her fragrance—a subtle wisp of gardenia and the special essence he'd come to recognize as Julia.

The soft underside of her generous breasts moved across the top of his arm, the delicate lace of her fine linen nightgown tickling his flesh. His thoughts turned to the many nights she would share his bed and her reaction when she awoke to find herself in his arms.

A smile touched his lips.

THE FIRST THOUGHT JULIA had on awaking the next morning was that either the chamber maid had come in earlier and placed one too many logs upon the fire, or there were one too many blankets on the bed. Unwilling to open

her eyes, it took a few moments to notice both her feet were under the covers, an odd occurrence given she usually slept with at least one foot hanging off the side of the bed. Seeking the coolness of the morning air, she extended her leg toward the edge.

Her eyes flew wide at the realization something solid and heavy was pinning her down.

Brandon.

Heart pounding, she became very much aware of the weight of his arm across her ribs and the warm, large hand cupping her left breast.

Everywhere there was contact . . . there was a delicious heat and her delicate, slightly damp nightgown was a negligible barrier between his flesh and hers. There was no need to imagine the contour of every muscle, every sinew, every curve or plane of his body—she could feel it. Where her flesh yielded, his did not.

She closed her eyes, wanting to experience every nuance of a man sharing her bed for the first time. The even cadence of his breathing across the back of her neck. The steady rise and fall of his chest against her spine. The heat of his loins, warming her backside. The weight of his thigh atop hers. The feel of his fingers, gently massaging her breast.

Julia's breath caught. What should she do? Perhaps if she kept her eyes closed and feigned sleep. . . .

Before the thought was complete, she felt the slightest shake of Brandon's chest at her back. The brute was laughing.

"It's no use pretending, sweet." His breath blew warm on her neck. "The moment your breathing changed, I knew you were awake."

A soft squeeze to her breast brought her eyes open. Never having been a man's mistress or having spent the night with a man in her bed, Julia didn't know quite what to say.

When he leaned away, creating a cool space of air between them, Julia thought he meant to release her. Instead, he rolled her to face him, his hand still firm on her breast.

"I must say you've managed to surprise me," he said, studying her features, nonchalantly stroking his thumb across the soft mound he held, making it peak.

"In what way?" Julia asked, trying to suppress a delicious shudder.

"I half expected you to scream down the house at finding me in your bed."

"Had I thought for an instant it would gain your extrication, I would have done so," she replied, haughtily. Or as haughtily as one could, when looking up into the face of a man whose thumb and finger were currently rolling the tip of one's nipple.

The warming sensation it produced flowed down to settle between her legs. Hoping to hide her reaction, Julia slid the hand that wasn't trapped between their bodies under the side of her nightgown and clutched the sheet. "In any event, did you not inform me yesterday I would not be *allowed* to demur? I am merely following your dictate. Was this not what you wanted?"

Brandon's smile turned into a full-blown grin. "Did I believe in sprites, I would think one stole the fiery, responsive woman I fell asleep with and left me this indifferent, biddable one in her place. But I wonder. . . ."

He bent his head to nuzzle aside her hair, enabling him to nibble the lobe of her ear, while his hand continued to torment her breast. Shifting for better balance, he began a rubbing motion with the leg he had thrown over hers. To taunt her further, he added his foot into the fray, caressing the length of her shin with his instep. It wasn't until it moved

almost up to her knee that she realized he'd hooked her hem with his toe and had brought it along.

Julia compressed her lips and tightened her fist, but was unable to conceal the small squeak that broke in the back of her throat.

Brandon lifted his head. "You are such a delight." His words rang with a faint chuckle. "But the glint in those beautiful green eyes of yours and the reactions of your body do little to support your words."

Uncaring of hiding her displeasure, Julia frowned up at him. "Now that you have been sufficiently amused and are done proving your point, would you kindly remove yourself from my person?" Yanking her arm out from between them and the other from her side, she shoved at his chest.

Unperturbed, Brandon grasped her wrists and shifted to his back, bringing her across his chest.

Stunned by his action, it took Julia a moment to gather her senses and react. Her struggles to get off him merely ended with him hooking his heels around her ankles, leaving her legs slightly spread and her lower half pressed intimately to him by the heavy arms he locked around her hips.

Hands braced against his wide, solid chest, Julia glared down at him.

"I should like for you to release me and return to your room before the maid comes."

The sharp staccato tone of her voice put Brandon in mind of an elderly etiquette instructor he once had. So he reacted the same way he had when scolded by her—he gave Julia a roguish smile. "I hate to be the bearer of bad tidings, my dear, but your maid has come and gone." He turned his head, directing her attention to a silver tea service and two china cups on the small round cherry table by the hearth, where a newly refurbished fire burned.

"You cad. How could you? Only yesterday you said you would allow some discretion."

He shrugged. "I changed my mind. I find I much prefer you in my bed. Or . . . me in yours. At any rate, it matters not. It was never my intention we sleep apart."

Julia struggled, his strength making a mockery of her efforts. The only thing gained: her body higher on his chest, her legs more widely spread by his, and the tip of his fully erect shaft wedged snugly between her thighs, not to mention the blanket somewhere down around her hips. She froze and looked at Brandon, who appeared quite pleased with the new position.

"Did I not know better, I would say you are determined to make a muddle of my teaching schedule," he said, and with a subtle flex of his hips, pressed into her the barest bit.

Julia was fairly sure he would go no farther, since the thin barrier of her nightgown was still between them, but it did little to prevent her from feeling the thickness—the heat.

More intrigued than frightened, she wondered how it might feel once inside her. It seemed physically impossible. But she had merely to close her eyes and remember the satisfaction on the stableboy's face and the pleased expression on the parlor maid's to know it would be. Without realizing it, her body relaxed more fully and the head of Brandon's erection slid in the slightest bit more. She gasped.

Brandon's hands flew up to grasp her shoulders. "Julia." He gave her a small shake. "Open your eyes," he gritted out softly.

Screwing them tighter, she shook her head.

In agonized amusement, Brandon watched her cheeks flare a most becoming red. After taking several deep breaths, he reversed their positions.

Her eyes remained shut.

In a mood to indulge and needing time to contain his own raging desires, he allowed her this short respite.

His gaze moved leisurely down the length of her linen-clad body—the prim, white nightgown, buttoned tightly at the neck, doing little to disguise her luscious womanly figure. Even it if had, he was all too aware of what lay beneath. It would be forever imprinted on his palms and in his mind after drying her at the lake.

Her breasts were full and firm, and at the moment showing a bare minimum of movement from her efforts to contain her breathing. Her waist small. Her stomach slightly rounded. Hips wide and inviting, melting into plump, fleshy thighs. The perfect cushion to cradle a man as he pushed deeply into her.

He paused his perusal at the small wet spot on the front of her nightgown. A reminder of his body's reaction to the warm portal he had yet to fully penetrate. Still, it was not all from him. Her body was extremely responsive for a virgin. And he was determined to see it more so. By the time he was ready to take her, her young, tight passage would be dripping and slick in response to his slightest touch.

It was time to commence with her lessons.

Reaching down, he laid his hand atop her mound. As he knew they would, her eyes sprang open.

"*Touch*, Julia." He worked his finger against her nightrail until it was wedged into the slit created by the folds of her womanhood. Pressing, rocking. "We will continue the lesson of touch."

With a soft moan, she arched up.

He removed his hand. "No, my sweet," he said, seeing confusion in her eyes and a disappointment that pleased him. "It is your turn to touch me. Anywhere. You must learn my body as I will learn yours." Leaning over her, he captured her

hand in his. Placing a gentle kiss in her palm, he pressed it to the center of his chest.

Watching, with an unsettling intensity, he began drawing it over his warm skin.

Slower.

Lower.

Julia knew what he intended, knew where he was taking her hand, but she was too lost in wonderment to care.

9

BRANDON'S SKIN SCORCHED HER fingers. Hot and smooth—not soft. Like taut strings on a harp, his flesh stretched over muscles and tendons, forming fascinating ridges and valleys.

She wanted to linger, discover all that was different between a man and a woman. The texture of his skin, the light covering of brown hair across the top of his chest, the tiny nuggets of flesh protruding from his flat nipples, his firm stomach. To journey her finger leisurely along the faint line of hair that extended from the middle of his chest and follow it down, down, down to the one place, he would be shocked to know, she wanted most to explore.

But he gave her no time, moving her hand as he wished, where he wished, until it reached the base of his stomach, where he released his hold.

For a long moment neither spoke.

Her splayed fingers resting lightly on his stomach, Julia remained motionless, unsure what to do . . . what he expected of her.

He reached up, framed her face with his hands, and kissed her. Not an urgent kiss, but passionate, a brewing storm that had yet to reach its full capacity.

He drew back. "The rest is up to you," he murmured. "My body is yours as yours is mine. But I warn you, a man's body is no less sensitive than a woman's. If I tell you to stop,

you must do so immediately, or risk pushing me beyond the bounds of restraint."

"How so?" She tilted her head, intrigued with the idea that she might possess that kind of ability. To make Brandon lose control as he did to her. . . .

Instead of answering, he reached down, careful not to dislodge her hand from him, and touched her between her legs.

Julia flinched, but did not move away.

"This small wet spot on the front of your gown . . . " he began a light, circular motion over the area with his fingertips, "is merely a prelude to what a man's shaft expels when brought to pleasure. Should I not be buried deep inside you when that occurs, I fear not only your gown will be wet, but the bedding as well."

"Oh." The word was soft, strained. Julia tried to concentrate on what he was saying and not the wicked sensations thrumming through her body. How was it possible that only after having his fingers inside her once, his slightest touch could make her long to have them there again?

With a playful growl, he retracted his hand, and nipped the tip of her chin. "You are too tempting by half, sweet vixen. We had best commence with your lesson before my hunger for both you and sustenance prevents it." At the conclusion of his warning, he sprawled out comfortably on his back and, with a swing of his leg, kicked back the covers.

Not as ready as she'd thought to see a man in a complete state of undress, Julia focused her gaze on the ceiling. Beside her, Brandon was silent, except for the sound of his heavy breathing. Inhaling deeply, she turned her head to encounter his smiling face.

Drat the man. If it were the last thing she did, she vowed to overcome every ounce of her maidenly reservations.

Mentally squaring her shoulders, she looked him straight in the eye, leaned up, and looked down.

Oh, my! It was not quite what she expected. Nothing at all like the young stableboy's shaft she'd caught a glimpse of. His had been considerably shorter and thinner, where Brandon's was long and thick, the tip reaching nearly to his navel. It was rather intimidating, lying extended and firm against his stomach, but in an odd sort of way soft and vulnerable as well. Which didn't make the least bit of sense, especially when she thought of it penetrating her body.

She found herself fascinated, thinking herself most fortunate to be allowed this opportunity to become acquainted with a man's body. Perhaps if more men were as accommodating, there would be less speculation and trepidation about the entire bedding process.

"Julia."

Brandon's quiet entreaty brought her head up.

"I would much prefer the heat of your hand to the heat of your gaze. Although I find your assiduous attention most arousing."

"Are you saying I can arouse you by merely looking?"

Brandon could see she was enticed by the thought, but he did not want to encourage her in that particular vein at the moment. "It is not the mere fact that you are looking, but the *way* you are looking. Another stage of your instruction I had planned for later this evening. Though a particular lesson I think you will need little instruction on."

His words brought a small, satisfied smile to her lips.

"I can see that pleases you. But *sight* is a multifaceted lesson."

"I don't understand." Her head tilted, the ends of her hair brushing his chest.

Momentarily distracted, he slowly shook his head. "That

is something you must wait to see. The sooner we get back to this lesson, the sooner you will gain the answers you seek."

As he had before, he took hold of her wrist and placed it on his chest, drawing it down.

This time, she resisted. "No . . . please. You said—I wish to do it on my own."

She pleaded so prettily, Brandon was compelled to relinquish his hold and fold his hands behind his head, giving her unobstructed access to his body.

"Do your worst," he said with good grace. "Only heed my warning."

"I will. I promise to stop if you say I must."

After one penetrating, searching look, he closed his eyes.

For some time, Julia could do nothing but stare, disbelieving her good fortune. She had expected him to watch her, scrutinize her every move. Since the day of their bargain, not once had he abandoned his control over even the smallest situation. And yet, for some reason, he was doing it now.

Where before she was feeling a good deal of unease, she now felt giddy. She shimmied around to her knees and sat back on her heels, deliberately pressing her hip against his thigh. The first step in her vow to overcome her maidenly qualms.

Brandon's leg tensed and then relaxed. Through the thin barrier of her nightgown, she could feel the heat emanating from him. It brought to mind his comment about their sharing a bed, how it had felt to wake up next to him, and how pleasant it might be to snuggle against his warmth in the winter months to come.

But now was not the time to mull over her sleeping arrangements. Not when she had a naked man lying complacently before her, willing to let her explore.

With a thrill of anticipation, she placed her hands lightly on his chest.

The large slab of muscle beneath her palms twitched. A quick look revealed Brandon's eyes still closed and his hands secured behind his head. Although there seemed to be a slight tenseness to his jaw Julia hadn't noticed previously. Confining her touch to her fingertips, she feathered them up to the tops of his shoulders, bringing them together again at the base of his neck.

He swallowed, drawing her attention to his Adam's apple.

Fascinated, Julia lightly covered it with the fingers of one hand.

Brandon swallowed again, appeasing her curiosity. She smiled as it slid up and down beneath her touch, eliciting a slight tingling sensation. Like a blind person, she continued down to his flat male paps and their tiny hardened nipples, the sparse whorl of hair surrounding them, down to where the hair became thicker in the middle of his chest. It was soft, springy, tickling her fingertips as she dragged them down farther. Her fingers rolled over each rib, into each indentation, like a small boat riding waves to end in a tiny whirlpool around his navel. His stomach clenched.

Julia pulled away. "Does my touch not please you?" she asked softly, glancing at his face.

He gave a clipped, closed-mouth chuckle, but his eyes remained closed. "Please me? You cannot imagine the pleasure your touch brings. I bid you, continue."

The words sounded strained and Julia found herself wishing his eyes were open, so she might better gauge his reactions. But unobserved, she felt freer to do as she pleased.

Before continuing, she scooted down on the bed, her hip to his knee, and allowed herself her first blatant look at a man's privates. Tentatively, she reached out to run her fingers lightly along its length. It twitched, causing her to snatch her hand back.

"A natural reaction, I assure you," Brandon murmured, once again bringing her gaze to his face. As before, his eyes were closed, but there was now a strained smile curving his lips.

Encouraged, she took his member in hand, applying a gentle squeeze. It wasn't at all what she expected.

Steel covered in satin was her immediate thought.

She heard a soft moan, and held her breath, afraid to look up. Afraid to find him watching, or that he would stop her when she'd only begun. Fingers wrapped lightly around him, she extended her thumb, running the pad across the tip of his member. Immersed in its velvety feel, she was startled when Brandon's hand came down, encompassing hers. Thinking he meant to stop her, she felt a stab of disappointment.

"Like this," he whispered, and began guiding her hand with a firm pressure, moving up and down . . . slowly . . . rhythmically, eventually aiding the motion with a light thrust of his hips.

Enthralled, Julia watched as the pliable skin covered and revealed the round, smooth head in succession. The warm flesh beneath her fingers pulsed, strained, surged. Thick from the start, it grew impossibly thicker, more rigid. Filling her palm. She expanded her grip beneath his. A tiny translucent pearl appeared at the tip, glistening, beckoning. Without thought, her thumb slipped from beneath his, to lightly graze the tip of his shaft.

The hand over hers tightened. "Enough."

The one-word command held a wealth of desperation. Julia looked up, to meet eyes burning with an intensity that should have frightened her. Instead, it thrilled her to her feminine core. She watched as his chest rapidly rose and fell as if each breath were an effort.

If the little she had done caused such a reaction, how

would he respond should she do more? Again her thumb moved.

"Julia—" Her name was forced through clenched teeth, his neck arching back. Inhaling a deep breath, he looked at her. "Unless you wish for this lesson to go far beyond what I intended, you had best release me."

"But—"

Sliding his grip to her wrist, he took her hand away. The simple motion caused him to suck a quick breath.

A tug on her arm brought her down alongside him. Careful not to brush his lower half against hers, Brandon leaned over her. Staring down into her lovely face, he found it hard to believe a worldly man such as himself had been ready to explode at a few brief strokes from the faltering hand of a virgin. The only conceivable explanation was that he'd been so absorbed in acquiring a wife, he'd been too busy to acquire another mistress to satisfy his mounting needs.

Wanting nothing more than to possess her pouty lips, but knowing therein lay folly, he brushed a light kiss to her forehead and said, "As much as I would like to lie abed all day with you in my arms, I feel it prudent I take my leave. There are things I must attend to. And I would venture to guess your maid will be arriving shortly, along with the bathwater I requested. When Marie does arrive, I would suggest you order another pot of chocolate as I am quite sure the one she brought earlier is cold."

"Chocolate? Not tea?" Surprised, Julia wondered if he'd delved so deeply into her life in the past few days that he'd learned her preference for the sweet drink.

"If you prefer tea, you need only ask and it will be brought to you. I'm afraid due to my mother's preference for chocolate, tea was rarely served when I was growing up

so I've never acquired a taste for it. Though I will drink it on occasion, if the social proprieties dictate I must."

She was mildly disappointed that he hadn't done it to cater to any liking of her own, although she couldn't quite say why it bothered her. But she did not dwell on it overlong, more intrigued by the tiny tidbit he had revealed regarding his childhood. "Your mother—"

"No time for questions, love. I will return in precisely one hour to escort you down to breakfast." Giving her one last languorous kiss, he rose from the bed. Looking down at her, he sighed heavily and shook his head. "I fear you shall prove to be a most distracting mistress." Turning, he moved across the room without a care for his nakedness to disappear behind the adjoining door.

Staring after him, Julia rose to a sitting position, tossed a thick length of her black hair behind her shoulder, and gathered her legs in front of her.

He had left her much to ponder upon. Not the least of which the way the muscles in his bare backside flexed as he strode into his room.

He had such a remarkably fascinating body, she doubted she would ever tire of it. So different from her own. Corded muscles, hard angles and ridges, a light dusting of dark hair in the most deliciously appealing places.

Julia smiled, thinking what fun it was going to be to discover every tantalizing masculine inch that was Brandon.

BRANDON HAD BEEN IN his room barely two minutes when there came a light tap on his door.

Smiling, he slipped into a thick blue velvet dressing gown. "Come in, Henry."

"Good morning, sir," the elderly man said, maneuvering carefully through the doorway, a tray between his hands. Making his way over to where Brandon was seated in an overstuffed green chair near the fireplace, he set the tray down on a table. "Your bath will be here momentarily." He poured a cup of chocolate and handed it to Brandon. "Shall I lay out the gray jacket and black breeches today?"

"As always, I leave myself in your capable hands."

"Very good, sir."

Brandon watched fondly as Henry went about his business. The man was nothing if not efficient—and loyal. They had been together since the day his grandfather had brought him home and delivered him into Henry's care. Most of what he knew about being a gentleman he'd learned from Henry. His one failure, held over from Brandon's rebellious first weeks, was to get his ward to stop addressing him by his given name. But the old fellow was getting on in years, although one would hardly notice. His appearance had not changed much over time. He still held himself erect and moved with quiet dignity, but Brandon had noticed his movements to be a bit slower of late.

"Henry?"

"Yes, sir?" he asked, turning his attention from the clothes he was meticulously placing on the bed.

"I was thinking I might hire a few extra people to help around the house. Especially now that Miss Freemont is here. After all, you are a gentleman's gentleman, yet you act as butler, errand boy, and have stitched a wound or two on occasion. Even acted the lady's maid when the need arose. Perhaps it is time you slowed down a bit."

Henry straightened. "Might I inquire if you find fault in the performance of my duties, sir? Perhaps you would prefer a younger man to attend you?"

The cup halfway to Brandon's mouth, it landed back into its saucer with a clink. "Good God . . . No!" He was quick to refute the notion, shocked that Henry would think such a thing. "You know deuced well I could never get along without you."

Henry visibly relaxed.

"I had thought only to reward you for your loyalty and make things easier for you in some small way. After all, you are not as youn—" Brandon broke off with a quick clearing of his throat at the slight rise of Henry's brow. "I was merely wondering if you felt it demeaning that you perform so many different duties for me."

"Not in the least, sir." He inclined his head slightly. "I would be quite disappointed should I discover you could get along without my services."

"On that score, you can set your mind at ease. I doubt that day will ever come." Brandon breathed easier at the faint upturning of Henry's mouth.

While Henry finished fussing over the clothes, Brandon allowed his thoughts to wander. Not until hearing a small noise from Henry's direction did he realize he'd been staring at the door between his room and Julia's. Would she be lounging in her own bath . . . her body covered by nothing but the silken caress of the water?

The rasp of velvet against his awakening phallus caused him to clear his throat and sit up straighter. Glancing out the window to the gray, cloud-covered day, he picked up the cup once more. "I assume since it has ceased raining, you have sent men out to search the grounds for any evidence of last night's assassin."

"Yes. But none have returned as yet."

"You will inform me as soon as they do."

"Of course."

Their conversation was interrupted by another knock on the door and, while Henry let in the young boys bringing hot water to fill the tub, Brandon contemplated the measures necessary to keep Julia and his guests safe.

Yet once alone and soaking in the tub, Brandon's thoughts inevitably turned to the woman in the next room and her delicious, tempting body.

Closing his eyes, Brandon could easily imagine the warm caressing heat of his bathwater to be her small hand.

Exploring . . . caressing . . . gently brushing the entire length of his body. Delicate slender fingers, spiraling over his rigid flesh. Preparing it to penetrate her sweet, hot mound.

His body tensed, his testicles tightened, and his shaft strained.

With a moaned curse, Brandon hastily reached for the washcloth.

10

TRUE TO HIS WORD, precisely sixty minutes later, Brandon strode through the connecting door, startling both Julia and Marie, who was in the process of pinning up her charge's hair at the dressing table.

"One would wonder why a door exists between these rooms at all since you never avail yourself of knocking upon it," Julia stated with exaggerated sweetness, meeting Brandon's gaze in the dressing table mirror.

"Marie." He addressed the maid, though his gaze never wavered from Julia's as he came to stand behind her chair.

"Yes, Mr. Barringer?" The girl's voice was pleasant and passive, as was her expression.

"You may leave us."

"Shall I come back later to finish Miss Freemont's hair?"

"There will be no need. Miss Freemont shall be wearing her hair loose, unless we are entertaining or going out," he said, ignoring the slight thinning of Julia's lips.

"Very good, sir. Will there be anything else?"

"Yes, one more thing," he said, his gaze fixed on Julia's face. "Please tell Henry to send someone up to remove the door between these two rooms."

A small gasp escaped before Julia could catch it, but she would not allow the mocking challenge in Brandon's eyes to reduce her to arguing in front of a servant.

"Yes, Mr. Barringer." Marie dipped a curtsy and left the

room without so much as a flicker of surprise at the outrageous order.

The minute the door was closed, Julia started to rise. "How dare—"

With firm hands on her shoulders, he pushed her back down, his gaze grabbing hers in the reflection. "You're becoming redundant, my dear. You should know by now that where you are concerned I dare anything. You have only yourself to blame in regard to the door. You should stop giving me such delightful suggestions if you do not wish me to act upon them."

She glared in stony silence until the unconscious clenching of her fist abruptly reminded her of the hairpin she'd been about to hand to the maid. With a small intake of breath, she looked down and placed the pin on the dressing table.

When she looked up again, it was to find Brandon's attention no longer on her face, but lower, absorbed in the quick rhythmic heaving of her breasts. His hands slipped from her shoulders, came together at the base of her throat, and slid lower to flatten against her exposed flesh. His fingers reached down to idly fiddle with the lace edging of her plunging neckline.

Presented with a new worry, Julia forgot all about her hair, the door, Brandon's total disregard for propriety. It was impossible to concentrate on anything but the warmth of his touch and the fact that by merely extending his fingers a bit farther, he could reach her nipples.

To her utter dismay, she found herself leaning back, tempting him to do exactly that—wanting him to take the peaked flesh between his fingers. But although his fingertips disappeared beneath the material, he merely traced a lazy curve along the outer circles of her nipples. Once, twice, a

third time, before removing his hands and once again placing them on her shoulders.

Lost in a daze of anticipation and yearning, Julia barely felt the playful tug on the section of her hair still hanging down.

"You have no idea how that look of regret on your face pleases me, my dear."

Julia jerked upright and picked up her brush. "You mistake me, sir. I am not disappointed, merely impatient to finish here and go down to breakfast. I find I am suddenly famished."

Brandon was famished also, but what his appetite craved was not down in the dining room. He had a brief image of Julia lying in front of him on the rosewood table. Naked. Her knees hooked over his shoulders. His tongue lapping up the delicious cream between her legs. The strain of his erection beneath his breeches brought him back to his senses.

"Then I shall not detain you further," he said, removing the ivory hairpins from her hair. "Like you, I much prefer to . . . titillate my palate with something *hot*."

There it was again, Julia thought. That tone. The one he always used when saying one thing and meaning another. And having a good laugh at her naïveté no doubt. But it would not always be so. It was not necessarily the words themselves, but the way they were used, or so he had said. And she was ever a fast learner. Doubly so when determination plagued her as it did now.

When he'd removed the last pin, he held out his hand for the brush.

Julia handed it over.

At his slight nod of approval, she clenched her teeth. She was beginning to feel like an obedient puppy. Please the master—get a pat on the head. Well, he would soon discover

he could not bring her to heel. But she would not show her retaliation like an angry mastiff, taking one large chunk out of his hide. Oh, no. She was more subtle than that, more inventive. She would watch and learn and bide her time, and like a small, tenacious terrier, annoyingly nip at his ankles from time to time. And perhaps a few other parts while she was at it. She pictured him naked and her nipping her way down his body.

Good gracious. Julia jerked as realization struck, causing the brush to snag on a tangle.

"Sorry," Brandon said from behind her.

"Quite all right. My fault." She gave him a smile in the mirror that had nothing to do with reassurance and everything to do with the fact that she'd just figured out how Brandon Barringer's word game worked.

Later, in the dining room, after getting over the shock of Brandon's seating her next to him rather than at the opposite end of the table, Julia found her first opportunity to test her theory.

She cut a sliver of cow's tongue from the piece on her plate and held it in front of her, as if to study it. Taking a deep breath, she asked innocently, "I do so love a good *tongue*, don't you?" When Brandon's gaze snapped up, she slid the piece past her lips, following up with a lazy lick. "Mmmm . . . it must have something to do with the feel when placed in one's mouth. Don't you agree?"

Brandon coughed around a mouthful of eggs, which he quickly covered with his napkin as he commenced choking.

Exuberant on the inside, all solemn concern on the outside, Julia shoved a glass of water into his hand.

Once he could catch his breath, he settled a searching gaze on her, to which she responded with her most innocent child-like expression. "Better?" she inquired.

"Yes, thank you."

Tempted to try for another reaction, but not wanting to make him too suspicious, she eased back to finish the rest of her meal.

After they shared a second cup of chocolate sprinkled with cinnamon, courtesy of Brandon's French chef, Henry entered the room.

"Pardon my interrupting, sir. I thought you might like to know a delivery has arrived from Madame LaFleur's."

"Excellent."

"Shall I have the packages taken up to Miss Freemont's room?"

"No, mine," Brandon corrected, offhandedly. "We'll be looking through them together."

Shock clogged Julia's throat at the outlandish reply, but neither man seemed to be paying her the slightest attention.

"Very good, sir," the older gentleman answered. "Shall I see to the driver?"

"Is it one we're familiar with?"

"One-eyed Jerry, and I hear his wife, Leona, is expecting their sixth."

Chuckling, Brandon shook his head. "Apparently the loss of his eye has not affected the aim of his *pistol.*"

The men shared a knowing smile, making Julia wonder what the man's shooting a gun had to do with his wife having a baby.

"Two guineas then?" Henry asked.

Julia's eyes widened at the outrageously high amount.

Brandon nodded. "Along with a note for Mau . . . Madame LaFleur expressing my gratitude for her expediency."

"I will see to it, sir." With a slight bend of the waist, he left the room.

"Now," Brandon said, turning his attention to Julia. "I

think it time I apprise you of the decision I came to after taking my leave of you this morning."

Julia regarded Brandon suspiciously. "Oh, and what decision was that?"

"I fear I sadly overestimated the time it would take to prepare you for your role as my mistress. A miscalculation that disrupts my schedule considerably, but one I can see a distinct advantage to."

Julia stared in dumbfounded amazement. He actually sounded put out that things were progressing so quickly. Her receptiveness was *disrupting his schedule?*

His indulgent smile caused her to grind her teeth.

"I had assumed being a sheltered young lady unaccustomed to a man's touch and unfamiliar with a man's body, you would find the entire ordeal rather unnerving. I can only offer you the excuse that I had never endeavored to be in the company of virgins before my decision to marry. They are such an annoyingly insipid and giggly lot. I suppose if you had been of their ilk, I would have never found myself attracted to you in the first place."

A backhanded compliment if ever Julia heard one, and quickly replaced by resentment about his looking for a wife. Still, she knew if she were to carve herself a niche in his life, she had best bury those types of feelings deep down inside where even she could not remember where they dwelled.

"What is it you have in mind?" she asked, wanting to feel in control of something, even if it were a mere conversation. "Or, will this be a lesson in *anticipation*?" She deliberately pitched her voice low, hoping to sound sultry. The gleam in Brandon's eyes attested to her success.

He leaned forward, slid his hand beneath her hair to cup her neck, and drew her closer. "I believe it shall," he whispered before his lips seared hers.

At first Julia resisted. Then, to her utter disgust, found herself not only giving in, but participating. His tongue slipped inside her mouth, washing her taste buds with cinnamon and chocolate. She returned the favor.

Brandon's low groan passed from his mouth into hers, a slow moving vibration that floated to the back of Julia's throat, tickling, beckoning, prompting, until she answered with a moan of her own.

Through hazy recollection, she found herself in his lap, her arms around his neck, his hand warm against her outer thigh, his mouth still devouring.

The clearing of a throat wrenched them back to reality.

Mortified, Julia froze.

Brandon sighed.

"What is it, Henry?" he asked imperturbably, moving his head to look past her.

Julia quickly took the opportunity to hide her face against his shoulder.

"Beg pardon, again, sir. Several of the men have returned, and you did say you wished to be informed upon their arrival."

"Have them wait in the library. I'll be there directly."

The roar of shame loud in her ears, Julia was unaware if Henry answered or not. All she knew for certain was that he had left the room, and the reason she knew was because of Brandon's whispered, "You can come out now, love. He's gone."

It took a steady pull of his fingers beneath her chin to make her do so.

"You need not worry about Henry; he is the soul of discretion."

"How shall I ever look him in the face?" she bemoaned, closing her eyes.

Brandon grasped her chin between thumb and fore-finger. "Look at me, Julia."

He waited patiently, until she did. "Believe me when I tell you, if I can look Henry in the face after some of the monumental indiscretions I've committed in my youth, I see no reason why you can't. However, should you insist you will be unable to, I guess there's nothing for it but to pack him off to London."

"No! I would not have you do that," she exclaimed, grabbing onto the lapels of his jacket.

"Taken a liking to the old fellow, have you?" he asked with a boyish grin that told Julia he hadn't meant it at all.

"It is mean of you to make fun of someone who is distressed, you beast," she said trying to sound disgruntled, but not quite accomplishing it. He could be so infuriatingly charming at times.

Treating her to a quick, hard kiss, Brandon stood, setting her on her feet. His hands on her hips kept her close. "I'm afraid I must leave. I shouldn't like to keep the men waiting overlong. As I will be fairly busy most of the day, I shall not see you at luncheon, but will be joining you for a late supper. Feel free to wander and make yourself acquainted with your new home. If you require anything, you have merely to ask a servant. My only request is that you do not venture outside."

"Am I to be restricted to the house?" A surge of apprehension filled her at the thought of being so confined.

"Certainly not. You are free to come and go as you please. It is only that we seem to have a poacher problem of late, and until the matter is dealt with I should not forgive myself if anything were to happen to you," he lied easily. "I shall be happy to take you out riding when weather permits. But you must promise to never go alone."

"I promise," she said, not completely satisfied, but

relieved he did not intend to keep her sequestered inside the house.

"Excellent." He removed one hand from her hip long enough to verify the time from his pocket watch. "I really must go. But I would have a kiss to take with me." Tightening his hold, he brought her more fully to him and bent as she rose to meet him. After a few moments, he reluctantly broke away. "The next time I kiss you . . . will be tonight . . . in my room . . . where no one will interrupt us."

The seductive promise hung in the air long after Brandon was gone.

11

"SORRY TO KEEP YOU waiting," Brandon said, striding into the library. His footsteps silent on the jewel-toned Oriental rug, he made his way past the two men standing in front of his desk and took the seat behind it. "Were you able to find anything, Matthew?" He leaned forward, placing his forearms on the gleaming mahogany, his gaze fixed intently on the larger of the two men.

"Yes, sir." A smile spread across the man's weary, rugged features as he stepped forward. "This," he said, holding out a crumpled handful of dirty fabric in his meaty hand.

Stretching to accept it, Brandon smoothed out the long, thin piece of filthy, tattered cloth in front of him. It lay stark against the dark wood, giving the appearance of dirty snow on a muddy road.

Henry, who'd been standing quietly by his side, tested the fabric between thumb and forefinger. "Silk," he stated quietly with a frown, meeting Brandon's gaze. "A gentleman's cravat." The clarification was unnecessary. Only the very wealthy could indulge in the quality of silk used to make this fabric.

"Where was it found?" Brandon asked the men.

"Less than a mile east of here, sir," the second man contributed, confirming it was in the proximity of the place where Neptune had been shot. "Wrapped well and tight on a branch, it were. Might of missed it, if not for a small piece flapping like the wing of a riled chicken."

Brandon's grip tightened on the end of the fabric he'd unconsciously been toying with. "You've done well. Both of you. Expect a little something extra in your wages this month," he said, eliciting a grateful nod from each man. "Matthew."

"Yes, sir?" His tone matched the seriousness in his master's.

"You were raised near here, were you not?"

"Yes, Mr. Barringer." The large man nodded and gave him a quizzical look.

"Would you have knowledge of five or six trustworthy men in the area who would like to enhance their yearly income by working for me for the next few months?"

"I surely would, sir."

"Any more like you at home?" Brandon asked as he sized up Matthew's towering, hulking length.

"Two brothers and three sisters, sir." His grin was full of pride.

"The brothers will do nicely," Brandon said.

Matthew heaved a great sigh and shook his head in mock regret. "The girls will be none too happy, I'm bettin'. They're a raucous bunch."

"I can well imagine," Brandon returned, interrupting his serious demeanor with a partial uplift of his lips. "But for this job, I seek only young, strong men who are familiar with handling a pistol. And I want them fully aware of the risk involved."

"Understood, sir."

"One more thing. The safety of the women on the estate is to be our first priority." Brandon speared Matthew's gaze and then the other man's. "Especially Miss Freemont." When both men nodded their understanding, Brandon continued. "However, I should not like to see them unduly distressed

over this matter; therefore, discretion is of the utmost importance."

"You can count on us, sir." Matthew answered for both of them.

"I never doubted it. Now, I know you are both cold and tired, so I suggest you seek the warmth of the kitchen where Etienne will make sure you get a hot meal. After that, a few hours' rest before resuming your duties. The same for the others who went out this morning."

"Very good, sir."

Both men bowed and exited the room, hauling the door shut behind them.

Brandon looked to Henry. "Thoughts?"

"You've no doubt acquired enemies from your business dealings."

Brandon gave a negligent wave of his hand and sat back in his chair. "Yes, but I had no business dealings when James and I were attacked on the docks after selling our commissions. And, although that was years ago, I cannot help but think all these attempts related. What puzzles me is . . . " he once again fingered the fabric in front of him "if a man could afford this kind of quality, why risk doing the deed himself? Why not hire some underling to do his dirty work?"

"Perhaps he is getting more desperate," Henry offered.

"Yes, but desperate for what? Who has anything to gain from my death?"

"Your cousin Robert?" Henry suggested quietly.

"Rubbish," Brandon scoffed. "Robert, God love him, has about as much backbone as a bowl of Etienne's holiday plum pudding. He's barely begun to stand up to his harridan of a mother that society forces me to claim as my aunt. I don't think I shall ever forget the fear on Robert's face the day we were to leave for Oxford and his mother refused to let loose

of him. I had to tear him out of the old witch's grip, while Uncle William held onto her." The memory made Brandon scowl.

"Add to that the number of times I rescued him from scrapes during our school years, and you cannot possibly expect me to believe Robert capable of plotting my demise. The man worships me like a besotted puppy."

"Even a puppy will turn on its master, given the right provocation."

"What provocation? It was Robert who received the title, not me." Brandon knew the tinge of bitterness he could never manage to suppress was there for Henry to hear.

"Yes, but not the greatest part of the old Duke's fortune. That went to you," Henry persisted.

"Enough." Brandon bent his head to rub the tips of his fingers across his forehead. "We have had this discussion before. You will never convince me Robert is behind the attempts on my life. He is wealthy in his own right. Uncle William, rest his tolerant soul, married for wealth, if nothing else."

"You would think the gentry would have learned better by now," Henry mumbled, regaining Brandon's attention.

"My parents risked everything for love, and where did it get them?" Brandon retorted, with ill-disguised resentment.

"At least they were happy for the short time they were together."

"Henry, this also is a much-belabored subject I do not wish to discuss."

"I merely wish to see you settled with a woman who will give you love and comfort. As well as children and the status you seek."

"Ahhh, then you need worry no more. For that is precisely what I *will* be getting. A wife for status and children,

and Miss Freemont for love and *comfort*. The kind of comfort every man seeks, but rarely finds in the bed of his wife."

"Yes, Miss Freemont," Henry repeated, without offering further comment.

Surprised by the older man's sudden silence, Brandon offered him a speculative look. "Henry?"

"Is there anything else you wish me to do to ensure the estate's security, sir?" he asked smoothly, as though they had never strayed from the subject.

All thoughts of women and his future vanished as Brandon focused on the more immediate matter. "Yes, I wish every man acquainted with a firearm to be given one. If there are not enough here, send Matthew to purchase more. Later, you and I will go through the house and conceal one in each of the rooms. Again, discretion is the key, but on the off chance one of the women makes mention of the increase in weapons, the men are to say we are planning a sporting event for our guests."

"Excellent idea, sir. Will you be remaining in the study?" Henry asked as he was leaving.

"Yes. It seems I have some much-neglected correspondence to see to." Brandon scrunched his nose at the pile of invitations lying on a large silver tray at the corner of his desk. It hadn't taken long for the local gentry to learn he was in residence.

But two hours later found him leaning back in his chair, the heels of his black Hessians resting upon the desktop and not one invitation answered. The center of his attention: a rare edition of the *Kama Sutra* he'd fingered from the many books on the shelf behind him. Not that he'd spent much time actually reading. Nor would he have, even had he been able to translate the words. What had him so enthralled were the beautifully detailed, hand-painted pictures of couples

entwined in every position imaginable. For one purpose and one purpose only. To enjoy the many delights the human flesh had to offer.

And he'd pictured himself with Julia in every contorted and not-so-contorted pose.

Straightening the book from its sideways position, an angle he'd often found necessary to understand the achievability of a goodly number of the positions, he made a mental reminder to ask that more pillows be placed on his bed.

Closing the book, Brandon carefully slid it back into its resting place, smiling when the small letters on the spine were rendered indistinguishable from the hundreds of other books on the shelves.

"Well, my good fellow," he said, glancing down at his straining rod and then at the pile of still-unanswered invitations. "Since it seems we can do nothing but think about *her*, I suppose there's nothing for it but to bring her here and make her assist in the distasteful task of answering these." He flicked an end of a vellum sheet with a flowery script across its surface. "What better way for Julia to become acquainted with our neighbors."

Knowing no adjustment would aid in his discomfort, Brandon merely stood and slipped back into the brown morning coat he'd slung over the back of a chair earlier.

AFTER WANDERING THE GLEAMING paneled halls and meandering through dozens of well-appointed and impeccably decorated rooms, Julia was returning to her own room when a commotion stilled her steps. Peeking around the wall, she was just in time to see a man carrying the door that had separated her room from Brandon's disappear down the

servant's stairs. This is the most disgustingly fastidious staff Julia had ever had the misfortune to encounter, she thought with annoyance.

Why, the entire house reeked of efficiency. She had not found so much as a dust mote on a single shiny surface. All she needed do was mention something casually and it was carried out.

Clear her throat—a glass of water appeared in the next room she would explore. Hungry—tasty butter scones in the next. Thirsty—a tea service in the one after that. She had made the mistake of sneezing once and a maid had magically appeared, and, smiling, had offered a white linen, lace-edged handkerchief with a delicately embroidered "B."

And the smiles. They were everywhere. Given freely, not forced. Bows and curtsies, but never a cower. Polite answers without a glimmer of disrespect, though she had to assume most of the staff had guessed what role she was to play in Brandon's life.

What kind of man would instill such respect? More importantly, what kind of man would give it? For Brandon surely did, evidenced by the staff's healthy appearance and flawless attire.

She had to wonder what Brandon's wife would do to fill her time, since the staff ran like a full-sailed clipper in a high wind.

As a thought took hold, she gave voice to the words. "Why, she'd more than likely have nothing to do, but—" Julia clamped her lips together, unwilling to complete the sentence, but her mind finished for her—*while away the hours in the bed of her husband.*

"Not bloody likely. At least not while I'm his mistress," she hissed into the empty corridor and headed for her room.

Once there, she sat in front of her dressing table and

picked up a brush. After raking the bristles through her hair for five minutes, she tossed it aside. Where usually she found solace in the mundane chore, this time she found nothing but a tender scalp. And every time she glanced into the mirror, she imagined meeting Brandon's mocking blue gaze or that of his yet-to-be wife's.

Not for the first time, she looked toward the beckoning, gaping hole between their rooms.

Standing, she checked her image in the mirror and adjusted the lace edge of her low-cut square bodice. She pinched the puffed sleeves at her shoulders, and smoothed a hand down her sides, following the peach stripes running the length of the cream dress.

"He did say I should make myself acquainted with my new home and there is one room I have yet to explore," she said to her smiling reflection.

12

MASCULINE. WARM. AND INCREDIBLY cozy, were Julia's first impressions as she peered into Brandon's room from the threshold:

An orchestrated blend of Sardinian blues, dark earthy greens, and rich golds.

Inhaling deeply, Julia moved inside and instantly became surrounded by Brandon's presence.

He was in the room, *everywhere*. Bold, darkly handsome, anchored in masculinity. And like him, the room seemed to offer a safe haven.

The atmosphere was so totally, utterly male. With one exception. A large number of floral boxes with colorful ribbons and big floppy bows lay piled next to a massive mahogany clothespress in the far corner. So out of place she had to smile, even as her curiosity swelled.

Deliberately avoiding that section of the room, she began on her left. Past the black marble fireplace, flanked by two overstuffed, green brocade chairs, between which stood a small round table suitable for intimate dining. If one were so inclined.

Moving on to the shaving stand, which held Brandon's personal grooming paraphernalia, she stopped. Titillated by the strong odor of musk fused with the faint smell of beeswax from the furniture, she inhaled deeply.

The bed was next. Unable to resist the urge, Julia placed

her face to his pillow, knowing it would hold his scent as her own pillow had after he'd left her that morning. As she raised her head, a metallic glimmer caught her eye.

In the middle of the headboard hung a large gold ring. Shadowed by the dark blue velvet canopy and side curtains, Julia was unable to make out the carving around it. Curious, she hiked her dress up past her knees and knelt on the bed for a closer look.

Intrigued by what she found, she reached out to run her fingertips over the intricately carved smiling faces of the two mischievous elfin creatures tugging over possession of the ring.

"How delightful to find you in one of my favorite positions," a deep baritone voice said.

Shrieking in surprise, Julia lost her balance and landed face first on the bed.

Before she could gather her senses or her dignity, two big masculine hands encircled her waist and drew her to an upright position on her knees. With her back pressed to Brandon's warm chest, and his thighs wedged between her legs, she was well and truly caught.

"Must you continuously sneak up on me?" she demanded waspishly, her heart thundering against her ribcage. Not entirely the result of her scare, given that she could feel the length of his hard, long shaft snugged up tightly into the crease of her backside. "Your lack of manners is appalling."

"*My* lack of manners?" His voice was tinged with humor. "I suppose it is mannerly to snoop through a man's room."

She stiffened slightly—a most pleasant feeling from where Brandon was standing.

"I was not snooping." She strained to look at him over her shoulder.

He held back a groan.

"Was it not you who told me I should become familiar with my new home?" she quipped, defiantly.

"Am I to understand that you feel my private quarters a part of your domain?"

"Why should you be afforded any privacy when I am not?" Her gaze was triumphant, gloating.

He nodded. "Point well taken."

A self-satisfied smile spread across her lips and he gave her a few moments to savor her victory.

"While we dine this evening, I will have the majority of your things moved into my rooms, and some of mine moved into yours. From this day forward, no area of this house will be either yours, or mine—but ours. Even my library, which you may feel free to enter and distract me any time you wish. The only exception being a pressing business meeting. At which time I will place one of the servants outside the door to avoid misunderstanding."

"Damn you, Brandon Barringer," she spewed, not caring a fig that she'd cursed, and began struggling in earnest. "Must you twist and turn my every meaning to suit your own purpose? You know deuced well that was not what I meant."

"Then perhaps you should guard your tongue more carefully, or put it to better purpose."

Her next words were lost against his warm lips and his seeking tongue. He traversed the warm recesses of her mouth, grazed her teeth, searched out every hidden, moist crevice. He enticed her tongue to dance with his, until Julia's legs wobbled and the only thing holding her up was his hard body and strong steadying hands.

"You are a jackanapes of the first water, sir," Julia stated as firmly as her sluggish mind would allow after his lips left hers.

He chuckled softly. "Why thank you, my dear. If I must

be labeled impertinent and a rascal, I am honored that you think me one of the highest quality."

She made a half-hearted effort to twist from his hold. Brandon merely shifted his grip, cupping her breast with one hand and her sweet womanly mound with the other. She stilled instantly.

He bent his head and nuzzled the curve of her neck. "I see a distraction is in order," he murmured against her sweet, floral-scented skin before gracing it with a light kiss.

He tightened his arm across her chest, still gripping her breast in one hand, while burrowing the other deeply between her legs. Satisfied with the position, he lifted her from the bed.

With a squeal, Julia threw one arm up and around the back of his neck, the other clasping tightly to his forearm, her thighs clutching his hand.

Brandon flexed the middle finger of the hand between her legs and smiled when Julia moaned.

Holding her suspended against him, he walked to the cheval glass standing next to the clothespress. Once their images were centered in the full-length mirror, he relaxed his arms enough to let her slide very, very slowly down the front of his body until her feet touched the floor. His hands remained where they were, gently massaging. Pressing his cheek next to hers, he whispered, "A brief introduction into tonight's lesson of *sight*. Feast your eyes, Julia."

"Dear Lord," she exclaimed breathily. Confronted with the sight of herself in Brandon's arms, of where his hands were, was so shocking, so—compelling, Julia found herself speechless.

She looked . . . wanton. Her arm thrown back behind his neck, her breasts thrust forward, inviting the hand that was slipping beneath the neckline of her dress to tease a hard-

ened nipple. So mesmerized was she by the sight, she hadn't noticed the fingers of his other hand busily inching up her dress until she felt a slight coolness around her legs.

"Brandon, no. You must stop." She clenched her thighs, only to discover it intensified the pressure of his palm against her mons.

"I will, my sweet. Only give me a small taste to take away with me. But know this," he said, his voice dropping a notch. "Tonight there will be no stopping."

She gave a barely perceptible nod.

It was all the encouragement Brandon needed.

He slipped his hand from her bodice to assist the other in raising her gown. Inch by inch, he revealed more of her pantalets until he was able to gather the entire skirt of the gown into his fist and hold it at her waist. He splayed the fingers of his free hand across her stomach. At her soft little mewl, Brandon smiled into the curve of her neck.

Holding her gaze, he slid his finger through the slit of her undergarments and then into her.

Her eyes closed, she arched back against him. His arms tensed.

"God, you feel so good." He rubbed his cheek softly against hers.

Heeding his promise to her, he gave one sweet, short, but thorough swirl in her wet depths before pulling his hand away.

Julia's knees almost gave out. Her eyes opened.

"Later, my love, we'll do much, much more, but the lesson in sight cannot be accomplished with your eyes closed." With a tender smile, he released her dress. It fell to the floor and swayed around his black Hessians.

Giving her a look filled with promise and a fleeting kiss, he led her from the room.

THE NEXT FEW HOURS together in his study were nerve-racking for Julia. How he could sit so calmly answering invitations was beyond her. Since they'd left his room, Brandon had made not one reference to what had occurred between them. Neither by word, nor look, nor deed. If she hadn't known better, she would have thought she'd been alone in front of that blasted mirror.

He hadn't thought she'd been watching. She had. From beneath lowered lashes. She'd felt so small surrounded by his much larger body. Small and wickedly feminine.

Her peach-striped dress framed by his brown jacket. His strong, sun-darkened hands against the white of her delicate linen undergarments. His manicured finger with bluntly cut nail slipping past the fabric and then into her. She was getting wet merely imagining it. A *wet* she had not understood until him. A wet she now thrilled in.

Frustrated beyond endurance, she felt like screaming. There must be some way to get him to react. Deep in thought, she ran her tongue across her dry lips and removed the seal from the wax on the letter she'd been sealing.

On a soft sigh, she looked up to catch his blue gaze on her mouth. Intense. Hungry.

Peering at the mantel clock over her shoulder, Brandon realized he'd been watching her for several minutes from across the expanse of his wide desk. He'd purposely placed her there, knowing if she was within easy reach the correspondence would have still sat in a pile, unanswered. But the distance had been a poor barrier. Her very presence was a distraction. Her soft feminine sighs, her light gardenia scent, her sweet innocent excitement at some of the invitations he'd accepted. He'd been extremely selective, picking only those from people he knew to be more tolerant in their judgment of others.

Christ, she had even convinced him to issue invitations to a small impromptu gathering of his own. Something he never did unless there was some business advantage to be gained. But that was two months away, and he had more preferable things to occupy his mind.

"Come here," he stated, holding out his hand.

He waited patiently, wondering if he would have to repeat the request. Setting aside the response to an invitation she was holding, she laid her fingers lightly on his palm and stood. With a light grip, he guided her around the desk.

When she was standing in front of him, Brandon spread his legs and patted his knee.

Julia caught her bottom lip between her teeth and gazed at the broad, muscular thigh that was to be her seat. Where once she would have flushed at the impropriety of the demand, the heat she felt now came from her desire to be held by him, to snuggle into his lap, to feel his hardness against her softness.

An unexpected yearning for him to do more than hold her shook her to the soles of her feet. Was it possible to become so addicted in so short a time? Would it be worse after they made love? Would she crave him like an opiate?

God help her, she couldn't seem to make herself care. She slipped onto his thigh, thrilled at the pleased smile that shaped his lips. But the smile quickly disappeared.

"I fear I have come to regret my decision to ask you to join me here in the library," he stated seriously.

Julia's spirits plummeted. She had so enjoyed sharing the afternoon with him, the light banter, the laughter, even the long periods of companionable silence. She had thought him of similar mind.

She bowed her head. "I apologize if I have caused you unease. If you wish me to leave. . . ." But when she made to

rise, he tightened the hand that had been resting lightly around her waist.

"You are correct in your assessment. You have indeed caused me a great deal of *unease*." Placing his free hand alongside her neck, he caressed her cheek with his thumb. "And, I have little doubt I am to suffer a great deal more in future. But I'm terribly afraid the unease that plagues me will not lessen by your being in another area of the house." For emphasis, he pressed his stiff member against her thigh.

"Oh. . . ."

"Yes, oh!" he repeated, leaning in to place a brief kiss at the corner of her mouth. "And the *regret* I make reference to is that I did not strip you naked and take you to my bed when the opportunity presented itself earlier. But tonight I have something special planned, and I do not wish to spoil it by whisking you upstairs now. Or laying your naked luscious body upon my desk and pummeling your wet depths with my recalcitrant rod."

"Your desk?" Julia trembled, finding herself tantalized by the shocking notion.

"Yes, among other places. Places you never imagined. We shall experiment in every room and on every piece of furniture in the house . . . when you are ready. For now, I will content myself by showing you with words." He bent to her ear and whispered, "Close your eyes."

Intrigued, Julia did as requested.

Brandon continued in a low, husky tone. "I will begin by kissing you beyond reason, devouring your sweet lips as I back you against the desk. My need to be inside you is so fierce, one sweep of my arm clears the surface. One obstacle out of the way, I move to the other—your garments. Eager to have you naked. . . ."

Julia whimpered.

A smile touched Brandon's lips. "I start on the buttons at the back of your gown, nearly ripping them off in the process. The dress dispensed with, I move on. The delicate fabric of your chemise proves an inadequate barrier to my hands and mouth as I alternately squeeze and suckle. But alas, that too must go. Along with your pantalets, for I am anxious for the sight and feel of your tender flesh. In only stockings and garters, you are a vision, firing a need in me I can no longer control."

"Brandon, I—"

"Shhh." The sound caressed her earlobe. "Listen. See yourself as I will see you. You will make such a beautiful offering."

He waited for her nod. "I slowly lay you onto the desk. The cool wood at your back. My warm hands caressing your front, moving slowly across every inch of your exposed flesh."

Julia shifted against him.

"I spread your legs . . . " his voice dropped, ". . . wide. I stand between them. Your heels are balanced at the edge of the desk, giving me total access to your luscious body."

She shivered.

"I release my manhood. Wrap my fingers around your waist and draw you toward me. Watching. Watching your sweet, dripping cleft move closer."

Julia gasped. Squirmed.

"But I don't drive into you, though both our bodies demand I do so. I need to hear you beg. Will you beg, sweet?"

"Yes. Yes. Brandon, pleeease." Julia arched in anticipation. Her head fell back, her thighs fell open. She was afraid to open her eyes, afraid if she did he would stop talking.

"With my fingers, I spread you wider . . . impale you inch by inch, filling you, stretching you."

Her body jerked, tensed, her pelvis thrust forward—seeking release.

"I want to keep toying with you, but my swelling shaft will no longer be denied. I lunge—

She clutched his forearm. Screamed his name . . . and shattered.

13

EYES CLOSED, BRANDON RESTED his head against the back of the chair and gathered Julia closer. One arm around her waist, the hand of the other making slow, soothing motions on the back of her thigh. Her dress once again in place, he chafed at the fabric between them, but dared not venture beneath it lest he be tempted beyond his limits. For now, he must take satisfaction in the little erratic puffs of breath she blew against his neck.

Although he himself had not climaxed, he was content in sharing the aftermath of her orgasm as he held her clinging body—absorbing the small tremors still radiating through it.

Never had he encountered a woman so responsive, so willing to learn. No man could be blessed with a more perfect mistress.

"Brandon?"

He felt her head shift to look up at him. "Hmmm?" He responded without opening his eyes, the stroking motions of his hand lengthening to include her hip.

"I don't understand how. . . . You didn't even touch me."

The wonder and uncertainty in her voice brought a smile to his lips. Devil take it, he was feeling a bit of wonder himself. "Believe me when I tell you it is not a common occurrence. You are unusually responsive to suggestion. That you are . . . pleases me beyond saying."

"Is that not my job . . . to please you?" she murmured.

"Yet in these past few days, I have been pleasured and you have not." The last was offered shyly, barely above a whisper.

He opened his eyes, pressed a feather-soft kiss to her brow. "It is best for one to know what pleasure is before one can give it. A great deal of pleasure can be gained from giving as well as receiving. To have it given unselfishly makes it all the sweeter. *Sex* is for self-satisfaction. A man can obtain sex anywhere. What he looks for in a relationship with his mistress is a shared passion. I shall teach you what pleases you and you in turn will gain insight into what pleases me. Ofttimes they are one and the same."

She remained silent for a moment, her forehead wrinkled in thought. "Are you saying I can do the same thing to you that you did to me?"

"With considerably less effort, to be totally honest." There was a slight chuckle in his voice as he drew her closer, letting her feel his state of arousal. "Sometimes the mere sight of something sexually arousing can send a man over the edge."

"Can you supply an example?" she asked, snuggling deeper, a definite calculating edge to her voice.

This time he laughed outright. "For that, minx, you will have to wait for this evening's lesson."

He stood abruptly and placed her on her feet. He loved the way she pouted. Not a childish pout, but a sultry one. Her cherry lips plump and full, tempting him to capture them beneath his own. For half a heartbeat he thought to deny himself. He grabbed her up against him, uncaring if he startled her.

The kiss was fraught with his building frustration. Hot, possessive, a man fully aroused. He slid his hands down her back, pausing at her waist, venturing down to cup the sweet firm cheeks of her ass. With a steady pressure, he ground his hard shaft against her soft stomach.

The low whimper that filled his mouth was one of need, driving him one step closer to the precipice of no return. He broke all contact. Holding her at arm's length, staring at her mouth, he gently pushed her back a step.

"You must leave, Julia. Now," he stated abruptly, passion making his tone seem harsher than he'd intended. But she seemed not to take exception to his brusque words. On the contrary, he thought he read a hint of smugness in her expressive green eyes.

He had wondered how long it would take the *real* Julia to shed her temporary cloak of insecurity. Not as long as he had contemplated. It seemed he was forever underestimating her.

No longer.

"Take yourself off and tell Henry I would like dinner served an hour earlier than originally planned."

"What shall I do after that?"

Brandon responded to the feigned meekness in her voice with a devilishly sexy smile. "I suggest you take a long nap. I want you well-rested for this evening."

Her lips curved upward, she nodded and then walked away.

He watched with appreciation as she swayed to the door, all grace and self-confidence.

Once she had the handle firmly in her grasp, she turned back. "Your every wish is my command, master," she tossed over her shoulder as she slid from the room.

"One night soon, I will put those words to the test," he said, staring at the solid door that stood between them. Turning, he reached down to open the bottom drawer of his desk and retrieved several sheets of paper.

He looked at his strong, bold script neatly penned across the pages. It had taken him hours to accomplish the final product. With a small sigh, but less remorse than he would

have imagined, he walked to the fireplace and consigned the lot of them to the low burning fire.

It seems there would be no further need for the lesson schedule he had planned for Julia.

AFTER RELAYING BRANDON'S orders to Henry, Julia found herself left to her own devices for the next few hours with little to do. She had never been adept at needlework, and thankfully her mother had realized early on no amount of effort on either of their parts would change that. She felt a little twinge of guilt, knowing more times than not the knotted mess of threads had been of her own making. Her mother would take one look at the hopeless snarl and uneven stitches, sigh loudly, and shoo her daughter off to go riding with her father.

Looking back now, Julia was sure her mother had known the threads were tangled on purpose. The fond memory made her smile.

There had also been many days like this one. Days when the rain beat a steady rhythm against the windowpanes. While her mother's nimble fingers plied a skilled needle to tautly stretched linen, creating elaborate garden scenes, Julia would curl up with a good book and lose herself for hours. She regretted not having the foresight to snatch a few volumes before leaving the library earlier, but she dare not tempt fate by going back.

With a sigh, she turned from the window. A knock sounded at her door. Moving to answer it, she was surprised to find a young male servant with an armful of books.

"Afternoon, Miss Freemont. Mr. Barringer thought you might like something to read."

"Mr. Barringer must have a bit of the gypsy in him, for I was thinking that very thing," she answered, resisting the urge to snatch them out of his hand. Instead, she pointed to a small round table flanked by two chairs. "You may place them over there."

"Yes, miss." Gauging his steps carefully over the top of the books, he moved across the room and set them down.

"Thank you," Julia said as he made to leave. "Please relay my gratitude to Mr. Barringer for his thoughtfulness and ask one of the maids to send up a pot of tea."

"I surely will, miss."

Hastily shutting the door behind him, she hurried over to the table. Sitting in one of the floral-cushioned chairs, she began leafing through the titles. Halfway through the pile she paused. Stuffed between a work by Samuel Johnson and a volume of *Gulliver's Travels* was a book she was totally unfamiliar with.

"*The Escapades of Lady Weathersby*," she whispered aloud. "A romantic tale? What an odd reading choice for a man's library." She ran her fingertip gently over the intricate, raised, gold overlay border on the black leather face of the book. Deciding it might make a good afternoon read, she picked up the tome and carried it to the window seat. Propping her back against several green brocade pillows and tossing a woolen throw over her legs, she settled in comfortably before turning back the cover.

Lady Weathersby and the Highwayman . . .

Twenty minutes later, Julia barely heard the knock at the door. "Come in," she said without looking up.

"Your tea, Miss Freemont," a young maid's voice rang out.

"Place it on the table, please. I shall serve myself, thank you," she said giving a distracted wave. Absorbed in the erotic tale, she never heard the servant leave.

"I tell you I have given you all my jewels," stated Lady Weathersby with hands on hips, heaving bosom thrust forward.

"I say you are lying, wench," the highwayman growled, his dark eyes glimmering through the slits in his mask.

"I will not stand here and allow you to blacken my character, sir. You leave me no recourse but to prove I am telling the truth." With an upward tilt of her chin, she raised her arms out to her sides. "I insist you search me."

The wicked smile that crossed his lips caused her heart to flutter.

"With pleasure." Safe from the bound and gagged driver in a nearby ditch, the highwayman tucked his pistol into the leather pouch attached to his saddle and peeled off his gloves. Shoving them in with the gun, he turned to face her.

"Now, if you would be so kind as to remove your clothes," he requested silkily.

"All my clothes?"

"If I am to do this properly, I fear you must. You will find I am a most thorough gentleman."

"If you were a gentleman, sir, you would know it would be quite impossible for me to manage such a feat without a lady's maid. But I suppose a lowly thief such as yourself would have little knowledge of these things."

"On the contrary," he said, his burning gaze riveted on the fleshy mounds of her bountiful bosom. "I am well aware of the assistance a lady's maid provides. I intend to lend myself to your service." With deliberate slowness, he reached down and casually plucked a knife from the top of his calf-high black leather boots. "If you would oblige

me by turning." He made a twirling motion with the tip of the blade.

Meeting his lecherous perusal, Lady Weathersby suppressed a delicious shiver and hastily obeyed.

He moved up behind her. A few quick swipes of the blade found her clothes in a billowy heap around her booted ankles. In nothing but silk stockings and pink satin garters, she whirled to confront him. "Are you quite satisfied? I told you I was hiding no other jewels."

"And once again, I say you lie, my pretty. For there are no more precious jewels than those of a woman's body."

He stepped closer, crowding her until her back was up against the coach.

"The diamond sparkle in a woman's eyes." The heated promise in his gaze seared through her. "The opal shimmer of her creamy skin," he murmured, drifting the backs of his fingers lightly across her collarbone, over her shoulder, down her arm.

She sucked in a gasp.

"The ruby of her lips." He yanked her to him, crushing her mouth beneath his.

The rasp of his clothes against her naked flesh caused her to moan into his mouth and squirm against him.

Moving a hand up to firmly squeeze her breast, he broke the contact. "The garnet of the luscious tips of her bubbies." He bent his head to suck and lick one hardened nipple and then the other.

"You go too far, sir," Lady Weathersby complained, her voice breathy, her body arching toward him.

He ignored her feigned protest. "Then there is the most precious gem. . . ." His voice was low, throaty. "The hidden pearl." He reached down, grazing his thumb

across her clit. "Which guards the greatest treasure of all." He slid two fingers so far inside her he filled his palm with her sweet hot honey pot."

At the rap on her door, Julia emitted a breathy squeal and slammed the book shut. Shocked to find her own legs slightly spread, the flesh between them damp, and her breathing heavy, she tossed the novel into the corner of the window seat and quickly gained her feet.

"Come in," she said, hastily smoothing the sides of her dress.

The maid who had brought the tea earlier entered. "Mr. Barringer thought you might like more hot tea and to freshen up a bit before joining him for supper," she said, scooting into the room with another silver pot. Following close behind was a male servant with a steaming bucket of water.

Julia watched silently as the boy poured water into the porcelain basin on a stand in the corner and then, bowing, left the room.

"How odd," the maid stated, drawing Julia's attention back to her.

"What?" she asked, seeing the maid heft the silver teapot as if weighing the contents.

"The pot is still full."

"Oh, yes. Well, I'm afraid I became so captivated by the book I was reading, the fact that it was here slipped my mind entirely."

"Mr. Barringer stated as much himself when he requested another be brought to you. How did he know, do you suppose?"

"I have no idea." Feeling her face heat, Julia glanced away. "But I will be sure to thank him when next I see him."

"Very good, miss. Will there be anything else you require?"

"Please send Marie up in fifteen minutes; I should like to change."

Once the maid was gone, Julia glanced toward the window seat where the book she'd been reading lay closed, its outward appearance revealing nothing of the explicit material inside. If Brandon thought to embarrass her by his certainty that she would find the material intriguing, he was in for a surprise.

With a secretive smile, she walked over, picked up the novel, and slipped it beneath several pillows. For the first time in a long time, she hoped it would rain on the morrow.

14

SEATED AT THE LONG dining room table, Brandon stood and watched Julia move toward him. She was grace personified, her bearing regal but not stiff. Her approach was more a glide than a walk, her sheer blue gown stirring slightly around her legs.

"Good evening, sweet," he said, pulling out the chair next to him. Once she was seated he rested a hand on her bare shoulder and placed his cheek next to hers. "I don't know what I'm more hungry for—Etienne's roast duck, or *you*. I suppose it matters little . . . since I plan to appease one appetite fully, the other just enough until I can possess you completely." He smiled at her delicate shiver.

After a discreet clearing of her throat, she said, "I wish to thank you for the books you sent up this afternoon."

Returning to his chair, he allowed the temporary change in subject. "As I am not yet familiar with your literary preferences, I hope you were able to find something suitable among the selections I made." Although his voice was nonchalant, his gaze was searching.

"Oh, yes. I do so love Shakespeare. *Macbeth* has always been one of my favorites."

"Were there no others you found interesting?" A mild frown marred his brow.

Julia reached for the glass of wine in front of her, drowning a giggle at his obvious disappointment. Enjoying

his frustration, she took her time in returning her drink to the table. "To be perfectly honest, I became so absorbed in reading the first book, I barely thought of the others. But I am quite sure I will find more to my liking," she stated, picking her words carefully to infuse as much truth as possible. She was determined not to give him the satisfaction of an admission. She'd learned at a very young age it was never to a woman's advantage for her man to think he knew her too well.

Her man. The significance of the words sent warm tingles through her body.

"Are you all right, my dear? You seem a trifle flushed." He leaned in solicitously, his nearness muddling her senses even more.

"Fine, thank you. Wine on an empty stomach has always had a rather odd effect on me."

"I shall keep that in mind." Giving her a devilish grin, he rang for supper.

When it was served and they were once again alone, Brandon reached over to take Julia's hand. "I must confess to missing you after you left the library this afternoon. Do I dare hope you missed me also?"

Julia felt the onset of another flush, but this time had no wine to blame it on. She had missed him. Proven by the many times she had mentally substituted herself for Lady Weathersby and Brandon for the Highwayman. "Yes," she said, deciding to tell the truth. "A little." The hasty addition brought a smile to Brandon's face and, before she could glean his intentions, he leaned closer, capturing her lips.

For the first time, Julia had no inkling of resisting, but shifted nearer for better contact. His lips were firm, warm, and all consuming. It amazed her how quickly she'd come to relish his kisses. Enraptured, she opened her mouth wider, aiding the sweet invasion of his seeking tongue.

Brandon deepened the kiss. Needing to feel her body against his, he placed his hands on her shoulders and began to rise, taking her with him.

Before they could gain their feet, the sound of heavy footsteps and the clink of delicate china broke them apart.

Julia fell heavily back into her chair, picked up her fork, and made an intense study of the food on her plate. Keenly disappointed by the servant's ill-time arrival, she sought solace in the warm afterglow of Brandon's nearness.

Brandon, no less disappointed, took his seat more leisurely.

During the remainder of the meal, he did his best to be charming, keeping the conversation casual and entertaining, trying to prevent his mind from wandering to what he had planned for her later. It was frustratingly hard. Every time she moved, sighed, laughed . . . her breasts rose and fell in the low bodice of her dress, tempting him to reach out, slip one from its confines, and suck a peaked nipple into his mouth. Every time she spoke, drank, or ate something . . . the spread of her plump, rosy lips beckoned him to claim them. One look at her delicate fingers wrapped around her wine glass . . . and he yearned to have them wrapped around his stiff shaft—caressing, squeezing.

"Perhaps we should skip dessert," he stated abruptly. "After the turtle soup and roast duck, I could hardly appreciate it."

"Must we?" Her lips formed into pout. "I was so looking forward to the cherry pie. It is one of my favorites, and Marie told me Etienne's is beyond delicious."

Brandon clamped down on his mounting passions. If he did not get her to his room soon. . . . "Marie is right, of course. I would not think to deprive you of such a delectable treat."

"Thank you," she said sweetly, reaching for the second glass of wine he had poured her, now half empty.

Brandon watched closely, wanting to see if she would subtly lick the edge, as she had done earlier in an effort to tease him. When she did, he nearly rose from the chair and seized her. Let her play her games now. He would play his later.

Barely had she set her spoon down after the last bite of flaky pie when Brandon stood and offered his hand. Placing hers in his, she rose to her feet.

Instead of leading her immediately from the room as he knew she expected, Brandon drew her closer. Inhaling the sweet, clean scent of her perfume, he said, "Tonight, you will see yourself through my eyes. View yourself as you never have before. Once we enter my room, you will not leave until morning." Wanting to judge her reaction, he pulled back, placed his hand beneath her chin, and tilted her head up. "Are you sure you are ready for this?"

Julia licked suddenly dry lips. "Yes," she said, holding his searching gaze.

"Then let us proceed." He brushed her lips briefly with his.

She extended her hand, expecting him to offer his arm. Instead, he whisked her up into his arms. The air in her lungs escaped on a gasp. "If you drop me down the stairs, I shall never forgive you," she said, striving to sound unconcerned by what was to come. Heart pounding, she sighed dreamily and placed her head on his shoulder.

Delighted by her cheeky reply, Brandon stared down at the top of her head and said, "You will never find yourself in a safer place than my arms."

Detecting an unexpected seriousness in his voice, Julia glanced up. But the only thing his face revealed was a rakish grin.

He took the stairs two at a time, giving no indication her extra weight mattered in the least. In what seemed seconds, she was standing in the middle of his room, staring at a large red beribboned box in the middle of his bed.

"I took the liberty of selecting your attire for the evening." When she said nothing, he prompted, "Go ahead, open it."

She recognized the package as one of the many from Madame LaFleur's, and, on any other occasion, she would have been bubbling over with excitement at the thought of a new outfit. But this was different. This time, it wasn't she who had made the selection, it was Brandon. What was it he'd said? *There are things you will wear for my pleasure alone.* She felt a wave of nervous excitement.

"I can assure you, it will not bite." With a challenging smile he placed a hand at her back, giving her a small nudge.

Not wanting to appear unsophisticated in his eyes, Julia stepped forward and began untying the bow. Lifting the lid, she peeked inside. The box held several ruby-colored garments the exact color of the bow. She pulled one out, intrigued when the light from the numerous candles around the room shined through the delicate, shimmery silk fabric.

"What do you think?"

Unaware he'd stepped up behind her, she sucked in a quick breath. "I would venture to say the weavers were woefully short on thread."

He gave a deep throaty chuckle, reaching around her to test the sheer material between thumb and forefinger. "It feels like liquid ice." He brought his lips to her ear. "Imagine how it will feel against your skin."

A ghost of a tingle skittered along Julia's flesh. "I—"

"Look at the rest," he insisted, tugging the over-gown from her fingers and tossing it onto the bed.

She pulled out the next item, eyeing it skeptically. "I thought you said I was to wear no stays?" she asked, slanting a look over her shoulder.

"Ahhh, but this is a special corset . . . from France. Meant to display a woman's assets to best advantage, not confine them." It too was consigned to the bed.

Wide-eyed, Julia stared at what remained in the bottom of the box. Two lacy garters, sporting tiny ribbon rosettes, and a pair of sheer long stockings, all in the same crimson color. Her gaze swung to the pile of unopened boxes against the wall, each with a different color bow, and wondered if their contents would also match.

With a light hand at her waist, Brandon turned her into his arms. "It would be my greatest pleasure to see you dressed in this outfit." Picking everything up, he placed them in her arms. "Should you require assistance in changing, I am only too happy to oblige."

"No, I believe I can manage well enough on my own." She half turned, intending to go to her own room.

A hand on her shoulder prevented her. "There is no need to leave; you can change here."

Her eyes widened slightly. "You expect me to change here? In front of you?" she asked, barely succeeding in keeping her voice steady.

Brandon grinned. "Not today, but eventually. Tonight, you may change behind there," he said, and with a slant of his head, indicated an elaborately carved oriental screen in the far corner.

Julia wondered if it had slipped her notice earlier, or had he requested it be placed there for her convenience? Taking a quick glance around, she realized that some of her own things were also in the room. Brandon was without doubt a man whose word could be depended on.

"Allow me a few minutes," she stated with a level gaze as she walked toward the screen and disappeared behind it.

No longer able to see her, Brandon made his way over to the table by the fireplace. Picking up a crystal decanter, he poured himself a glass of brandy with the intention of taking the edge off his anticipation. He was doubtful it would help, but it was worth a try. Removing his jacket and cravat, he tossed them across the back of a chair. Sitting in another chair, he unfastened the buttons at the top of his white shirt, picked up the drink, and made himself comfortable.

Behind the screen, Julia found a small chair onto which she placed the clothes she was holding. She immediately began removing her gown, knowing the longer she delayed the more nervous she would become. It was a difficult endeavor, but she managed to open enough fastenings to enable her to tug it over her head without ripping it. Hanging it on a brass hook on the wall she continued until she stood totally naked. The thought of nothing between her and Brandon but a three-paneled piece of wood caused a shiver to race up her spine. Not wholly due to apprehension.

She started with the stockings. Never had she seen any of such fine quality. Carefully gathering one up between thumb and finger, she slipped it over her foot and smoothed it to mid-thigh. Securing it with a garter, she repeated the process on the other leg. Next, the corset—if you could call it that. Made of delicate lace, it was shockingly scant. Her fingers shook as she carefully tightened the front laces and tied it off at the top with a bow. Last came the sheer over-dress.

Unwilling to think of the picture she presented, Julia took a deep breath, captured her bottom lip between her teeth, and stepped from behind the partition, enveloped in little else but a *frisson* of forbidden excitement.

The glass Brandon was in the process of bringing to his

lips never reached its destination. Distractedly consigning it to the table beside him, his gaze locked on the vision standing across the room. Breathtaking.

Backlit by dancing candlelight, the sheer gown became virtually transparent. She was a portrait in shades of red. Cherries, roses, rubies, and rich red wines. A feast for the eyes.

He could see the dark outline of her nipples above the specially made low-cut cups of the corset. And where the corset ended, he could make out the dark, shimmery triangle at the juncture of her thighs.

His body reacted instantly. His shaft pressed insistently against his black evening breeches. He extended a hand, willing Julia to him.

Silent, she walked toward him, her steps so hesitant and carefully placed, one might think she were walking on eggshells. Brandon was not inclined to complain. The longer she took, the longer he could appreciate the alluring picture she presented. The front opening of the gown, held closed by only three satin frogs, revealed enticing glimpses of creamy flesh and red silk as she made her way toward him.

An arm's reach away, she placed her hand tentatively into his.

He spread his thighs and, with a steady pull, drew her between his legs. Sitting forward, Brandon brought his lips to within inches of her breasts. "You have no idea how beautiful you look at this moment."

The heat of his whispered words cascaded over her scantily covered breasts, triggering her nipples to form into hard little pearls. Aware there was no way of hiding her reaction from him, Julia didn't try. Taking a deep breath, she met his steady gaze with her own.

The glint in his blue eyes should have given her warning,

but she still gasped when he grazed his lips lightly across one distended peak and suckled it. His warm, wet mouth against the cool silk caused the fabric to rasp across her sensitive flesh. A small moan escaped from between her trembling lips. With one last strong suck, he released her. Encircling her hips with his hands, he moved her back a step, deliberately brushing against her as he stood.

"Come, I want to show you something." Taking her hand, he took her over to the cheval glass. He positioned himself behind her, his hands on her shoulders. "Look."

Reluctant to view herself in the scandalous attire, Julia kept her head down, gaze averted. When she felt his fingers beneath her chin, lifting, she lowered her lashes.

"Open your eyes. See yourself for the desirable woman you are. A woman capable of bringing a man to his knees."

His husky whisper enticed her to obey. Mesmerized by the image that greeted her, she could do little but stare. The small flicker of shame she felt disappeared when she caught Brandon's gaze in the mirror. The blatant desire flaming back at her scorched her to her very soul.

This time when she took in the reflection, she tried to see herself as he would. She had never considered herself small, but there was nowhere she looked that she didn't see Brandon as well. She appeared soft and petite next to his strong, sturdy body. His broad shoulders, hips, and thighs framing her own. His large hands encompassing her slender shoulders. His chin resting on the top of her head. She had never felt so . . . so feminine, so much a woman.

"Watch," he instructed, as he slid his hands slowly down her upper arms, over her elbows to her wrists. Clasping both in a gentle grip, he guided them up and positioned them behind his neck.

The position emphasized the thrust of her breasts,

making her look like a shameless wanton. She tried tugging from his light grip.

"No. Leave them there . . . please."

Well aware that her current position left her vulnerable to his touch, she nodded.

With the back of his fingers, he skimmed down the insides of her arms until his knuckles brushed the tender plump curves of her breasts. "No courtesan in the world could look more desirable than you do at this moment."

The sound of his hoarse, deep voice set her nerve endings thrumming with anticipation and, dare she admit it—a burning need to feel his hands on her. "I need for you to touch me, Brandon," she admitted, softly.

"Oh, I will, love. Until you beg me to stop. But tonight's lesson is sight, and you must allow me to savor the way you look, drink in your loveliness. Shall I tell you what I see?"

"Yes, tell me." She knew her own voice sounded breathless, needy, but Julia seemed unable to muster a single ounce of concern.

"You are a study in shadow and light beneath a shimmering layer of red." He widened his stance to allow more light to pass between their legs, accentuating the outline of her thighs, the juncture at the top of her legs. "Your nipples give the appearance of ripe cherries, begging to be plucked." He tweaked them between thumb and forefinger.

She muffled a whimper.

"The lightness of your skin, the crevice between your breasts." Taking advantage of a small gape in the sheer gown caused by her arched back, he slid a finger deep within the valley of her breasts, ran it slowly up and down. Their eyes locked, and Julia knew he was thinking of what he'd done to her in the lake, just as she was.

He withdrew his hand, wrapped an arm around her

waist, and rotated his pelvis against her, showing her what she did to him.

"I want to see more." His hand went to the first fastening at her collarbone. It came undone with practiced ease. He moved to the next.

The feel of his palms against her sensitized nipples as he worked it open forced a moan from her constricted throat.

With the second frog undone, the material parted slightly, but, held at her sides by Brandon's arms, did not part fully.

"I feel like a young boy opening his first present," he murmured into the curve of her neck and, placing a warm kiss there, slid his hands down to the final closing. The one at the juncture of her legs.

Julia held her breath in anticipation. But instead of undoing it, he merely rested his fingertips lightly over the area and began making a skimming circular motion. The heat of his skin penetrated through the material and thatch of springy hair to make her throb with need.

He opened the clasp. The material cascaded from her body, to hang trapped between them in a shimmering froth of red.

Julia felt the air leave her lungs at the sinfully sensual image. Was this really her?

A woman whose full breasts and dark nipples jutted proudly above the cups of the corset. The corset itself, a ruby confection that hugged a trim waist making it look even smaller, accentuating slightly flared hips, ended mere inches above a nest of thick black hair. The white creaminess of her thighs disappeared beneath red garters and stockings. Slowly her gaze rose until it once again met Brandon's.

"Stay as you are," Brandon commanded, his voice gruff with restrained desire.

Receiving a small nod, and with her still clinging to him, Brandon created a minimum of space between them in order to rid himself of his shirt.

The red overdress that had been trapped between them floated to the floor.

15

OVERWHELMED BY HIS NEED to have Julia's delectable body pressed against him, Brandon grabbed the neck of his shirt in both hands and ripped it right down the center.

The heat of her back seared through his chest like a hot poker. Her red corset rasped over his chest hair, sending lust racing straight to his groin. It wasn't close enough. He needed to be inside her—making her a part of him.

Two more days, he promised himself. After tomorrow night's lesson in taste, he would make her his. In every way.

"You could tempt a sailor to forsake the sea," he said in a gruff voice.

The reflecting candlelight dancing in her expressive green eyes, she asked, "And what could I tempt you to forsake?" Closing her eyes, she leaned her head back against his shoulder.

When the hands tenderly caressing her hips abruptly stilled, Julia realized what her words seemed to imply. She braced for another *mistress lecture*. It never came. Her gaze sought his. The face she saw in the mirror was not set in hard lines of disapproval, but pensive consternation.

She pulled away. "I did not mean—"

Catching her hips and drawing her back against him, Brandon said, "I know." His hands drifted up, caressing her stomach, spanning her midriff, lifting her breasts. His thumbs slowly circled her nipples, occasionally flicking the tips.

Any thoughts Julia had of explaining herself vanished.

The contrast of his big hands and thick fingers against the dainty red lace corset was both mesmerizing and arousing. Without conscious thought, her arms slid from around his neck, her hands covering his.

He stilled. "You are breaking the rules, love. This is not how the game is played." He placed his lips next to her ear and whispered, "Must I tie your hands to keep them there? If you wish it, I have merely to retrieve my cravat. . . ."

"Surely you jest," she said, eyes rounding, but underlying her shock, a tiny seed of fascination had been planted.

He smiled and shook his head. "I assure you, I do not." He rubbed his cheek against hers, depositing a feathery kiss on her temple.

"How can one find pleasure in being rendered helpless?"

"Someday it will be my infinite delight to show you that particular diversion." His gaze searched her face. "When you are ready. Now, place your arms back around my neck, so I may continue with this evening's lesson."

She did without comment.

Brandon gave her ribs a slight press before venturing down to her stomach. He began by kneading, then making small circles, ever widening, until his fingertips were grazing the top of her pubic hair. Bypassing the spot Julia most wanted him to touch, his large, tan hands slid down until he could slip his fingers beneath her garters and the tops of her stockings, his thumbs resting in the crease where hip met thigh.

"Do you know what I see, Julia?"

There was a deep rumble to Brandon's voice. Julia felt his arousal pressed firmly against the small of her back, her backside enveloped in the heat of his pelvis. "Tell me," she said, her own voice gone husky, her eyes locked on their image as if hypnotized.

His hands standing out starkly against her pale thighs, his thumbs toying lightly at the edge of the hair between her legs, he whispered, "I see a raven's wings on newly fallen snow. And like a raven's wings, they must be spread in order to fly." He moved his fingers to the insides of her thighs, rubbing the tops of his index fingers against her wet outer lips. Applying steady pressure with his palms, he encouraged her into a wider stance.

Her senses heightened, along with her desire. Against her back, Julia felt the strong rapid thud of his heart and every hard-muscled plane of his chest.

Using the tips of his fingers, he parted her hair, revealing the moist, glistening lips of her sex.

Hit with a sudden wave of maidenly modesty, Julia turned her face away.

"There is nothing to be ashamed of, my little innocent," Brandon coaxed in a low, soothing tone. "Every part of a woman's body is beautiful. Have you not heard of a woman's beauty causing men to wage wars?"

"They are speaking of her facial beauty," she said in a small, uncertain voice.

"So poets and romantics would have you believe. They dare not write the truth. It is this. . . ." He ran a finger tenderly over her opening, through her wet folds. "This is what men go to battle over. Kill for. Wager fortunes on. Make fools of themselves to attain. For there is nothing more beautiful than that which is nestled between a woman's legs." He paused to place a gentle kiss upon her cheek. "The only *true* source of a man's immortality. A place to plant his seed for future generations. Believe me when I tell you there is no other place on earth he can feel more a man than buried deep with n a woman's womb."

He waited until her gaze once again met his in the

mirror. "This is what you were born for, love. Look." A deeper penetration of his finger drew her attention down. "See what I see."

Julia could feel heat rush to her cheeks, but did not look away. She had touched herself under the covers, but never had she dared to look at herself. She stared at her reflection.

Naked except for a red corset, garters, and stockings with a half-naked man's hand between her legs, she should have felt like a whore. One look at the open admiration on Brandon's face made her feel like a revered queen.

How would he look at me if he loved me? The errant thought caused her world to tilt. She immediately pushed it to the far recesses of her mind. You're his mistress. Will never be anything more, she reminded herself.

Brandon raised a hand to unclasp her arms from around his neck, stepped to her side, and bent to one knee.

Julia watched as his dark head lowered to softly kiss her thigh where the corset ended, his lips warm on her flesh.

This must be every woman's fantasy. To have a man such as Brandon kneeling at her feet.

Shirtless, he was a delicacy for the eyes. Broad shouldered, a wide well-defined chest cleaved by a small patch of brown curls. Even bending, the only ripples to be seen were those of taut skin over bunched muscles. His narrow waist disappeared into snug black breeches. The thigh of the leg he braced himself on, thick and firm. The thought of those thighs between her own made her heart skip.

His finger, slipping deep inside her, brought her attention back with a snap.

"You are so wet. Shall I make you wetter? Or . . . leave you to ache as I am aching?"

"Please, Brandon." She reached out to stroke the soft,

wavy brown curls on his head. "Do not tease me. Not tonight. I could not bear it."

He took in her serious expression. Nodded. "On one condition." He rotated his finger to remind her of its presence. "You must promise not to look away," he requested quietly, retracting his hand slowly, allowing her to see the glistening wetness on his finger.

"Oh, God." She took a shaky breath. "I would have a promise from you also."

"What promise?"

The sight of two thick fingers disappearing beyond the thatch of black hair and between her sensitive lips, and the sensation of being stretched, caused her to momentarily lose her train of thought.

"What promise?" came his gentle reminder.

"I . . . " She licked trembling lips. "I want you to experience pleasure too."

His face registered surprise. "I will not take you. Not tonight. There is one more lesson to be learned before I do." He leaned forward to stroke his tongue through her pubic hair.

Julia gasped. From the act and the shock of his warm breath. On a shudder, she gathered her courage. "Then show me another way."

He raised his gaze to hers. "I promise. Before this night is through, we shall both experience pleasure." The sweep of his thumb across her clitoris put a delicious end to the conversation.

Determined not go back on her word, Julia fought to keep her eyes open. She watched his fingers slide in and out of her body, each stroke adding to the coiling tension building deep inside her until she could withstand no more.

He proved her wrong by adding a third finger. Would his

rod feel like this? Somehow, she knew with certainty it would fill her more.

The vivid thought sent her over the edge.

She moaned his name. One hand clenched. The nails of the other found purchase in the thick muscle of his shoulder.

She sagged heavily against him.

Carefully pushing her away, Brandon stood and kissed her hard. Scooping her into his arms, he strode to the bed. Giving thanks for the turned-down covers, he deposited her on the white sheets with the utmost care. Smiling down at her languid form, he brushed back the damp black curls from her face and stepped back.

She whimpered. Stretched out her hand.

"The last thing I would do is leave. Allow me a moment to discard the rest of my clothes and I will be only too happy to join you." He sat on the edge of the bed, made short work of his shoes and stockings and, regaining his feet, peeled down his breeches. Knowing she watched, he stood brazenly before her. The numerous candles in the room allowed her a detailed view of the thick, heavy shaft that sprung up proudly from the dense thatch of dark hair between his thighs.

"Does it frighten you?" he asked, noting a small trace of apprehension on her face as she stared fixedly at his manhood.

As if awakening from a spell, she looked up at him. "No. It's merely that yours looks so much bigger than—" She broke off.

Brandon's countenance turned stormy. "Than whose?"

The underlying menace in the question would have been evident to a deaf man. Julia took a deep breath, knowing there was no way out other than the truth. She sighed heavily. "The stableboy's. But it's not what you think," she hastened to say when his expression turned blacker still. "Hearing strange

sounds in the stables on numerous occasions, I was curious as to their source. So one day, I hid in the stables and—"

"And . . ." he prompted.

"And that's when I saw him . . ." she dropped her gaze, ". . . swiving a young parlor maid."

It took a moment for her words to penetrate the haze of anger surrounding Brandon. When they did, a cleansing mirth took its place. He barked a laugh, summarily consigning the surge of overwhelming jealousy he'd felt to simple male possession.

"So tell me, sweetling. Was it only the one time, or did you watch often?"

Her long silence was all the confession Brandon needed.

"Why you little Peeping Tom," he said, kneeling on the bed, and grasping her chin in his hand, urged her to look at him.

"I was young and curious, is all," she said, defensively. "I'm quite sure you would have done the same."

He grinned. "What? Watch, or *swive* the maid?"

"Oh! You are deplorable." She jerked her chin from his hold and rolled toward the opposite side of the bed.

Throwing his arm around her waist, he tugged her back, stretching out on his side next to her. "I thought you wanted to pleasure me?" He traced his fingers lightly over her stomach, making it quiver. "Have you changed your mind?"

"No," she said quietly, her pique over his teasing forgotten. "I want to very much."

Rolling to his back, he pulled her until she was resting on her side.

"Give me your hand."

She gave it.

Brandon couldn't fail to notice how small it was in comparison to his. The skin virtually translucent with tiny

roadways of blue veins, the bones delicate, fingers long and thin. He placed a kiss on the tip of each finger before firmly wrapping all of them around his jutting shaft.

With his hand over hers, he showed her the rhythm that would please him most. A long down stroke, with a slight squeeze before coming back up.

"This time, I won't ask you to stop," he murmured. Releasing her hand, he closed his eyes.

16

THE SUN HAD YET to rise when Henry's discreet knock on the door had disturbed Brandon's sleep with an urgent message that necessitated he leave for London immediately. Now, dressed and ready to leave, he stood looking down at Julia. She was curled onto her side at the edge of his bed with one slender leg sticking out from beneath the covers. By the time they had settled in for the night, she had been so exhausted, they'd barely gotten her out of the corset before she'd fallen into a deep sleep. The red stocking that had encased her shapely limb so sensually the night before lay in droopy ripples halfway down her leg. The crimson garter still hugged her creamy thighs. He smiled.

Leaning over her, he picked up a section of her long hair. It would probably take her maid a good hour to untangle the mess he'd made of it. Recalling the pleasure he'd gained from sifting his fingers through the silken tresses, he felt not the least remorse. He bent closer to inhale its clean scent. Laying the hair carefully back over her shoulder, he took in her beauty one last time.

He had never shared this particular bed with any other woman before. Julia looked so peaceful and natural lying there. So . . . *so at home.*

Staggered by the concept, Brandon took a step back, almost tripping over the discarded French corset. He toed it with the tip of his boot. Picking it up, he looked once more at

the woman asleep in his bed. Realizing he was crushing the delicate fabric in a tight fist, he draped it over the back of a chair and left.

"ARE YOU SURE IT was cut," Brandon asked Matthew, who stood next to him in the pre-dawn chill.

"Positive. See for yourself."

Brandon tried to get a grip on his seething anger as he followed the larger man into the stables to where the saddle hung over a side rail of one of the stalls. He inspected the girth, noting the short, clean slice. If not for Matthew's diligence, he most likely would have ended up in a ditch with a broken neck halfway to London. "No one heard or saw anything?"

"One of the younger boys said he heard the horses stirring in the middle of the night, but when he got up to check, everything seemed fine."

"I want someone on watch in here at all times to make sure something like this never happens again. Use only the older boys. They are apt to be more alert than the younger ones and better able to handle a situation should it arise. If necessary, borrow some men from elsewhere on the estate. No one is to be on guard any longer than four hours. I don't want to chance anyone's falling asleep."

"How long will you be gone?"

"Three days, four at most. You are to watch over things while I'm away. If you need me, send word round to the townhouse."

"I would rest easier if you would take someone with you."

"I appreciate your concern." Brandon clapped a hand on

the other man's shoulder. "But if I'm to make it back before my guests arrive, I will need to ride hard. There is no other horse in the stable that can keep up with Neptune."

"There's truth in that," Matthew acknowledged with a smile, which Brandon returned.

Brandon's countenance turned serious. "In regards to Miss Freemont. . . ."

"You need not worry. I promise to keep her as close as a mother cat with a newborn kitten."

Brandon made a short snuffling sound. "Even if you could, I doubt she would let you. All I ask is that you not allow her to venture far when outside and not to ride while I'm away. Henry shall keep watch over her in the house. She's a stubborn, independent little puss, so do not allow her to coerce you into doing what she wants," Brandon said with more admiration than annoyance.

"I'll be sure to heed your warning."

"Excellent. Now, if you'll get me another saddle, I'll be off."

BARELY AWAKE, JULIA SCOOTED her rump back, seeking Brandon's heat. What she encountered was cold, empty space. With a sleepy moan, she rolled onto her back to find the other side of the bed unoccupied. Where was Brandon? Why had he not awakened her?

After a good stretch, she trapped the covers securely over her breasts with one arm and sat up. Pushing the heavy, tangled mass of her hair from her face, she yawned.

How odd, she thought, looking around the room. She did not feel the slightest unease in the masculine surroundings where the only things feminine were a few of her own

personal belongings. She smiled at the pile of boxes in the corner and the red silk corset, which currently resided over the back of a chair. Had Brandon picked it up from the floor? She felt a warm glow at how he had taken it off her and then kissed every inch of the skin it had covered.

Her gaze continued to roam the room, lighting on her brush and a bottle of her perfume next to Brandon's cologne.

It was then she saw the folded note with her name scrawled boldly across it.

Slipping to the edge of bed, she dragged the sheet off as she stood and wrapped in around herself. Padding over to the chest of drawers, she picked up the missive. Flipping it open, she read.

Julia,

An urgent message from my solicitor requires my presence in London. Due to the early hour and knowing how little sleep I allowed you the night prior, I felt it best not to awaken you.

She paused, her cheeks flushing.

If you require anything, you have merely to ask Henry. You may entertain yourself in whatever manner pleases you. I should return no later than four days hence.

Regards
B

Not sure why, Julia felt a twinge of disappointment at the impersonal, hastily scrawled note. For some unexplainable reason, she had expected more.

Deciding a brisk morning ride would be just the thing

to clear her mind, she left the note where she'd found it, and went to her room.

"DRAT THE MAN!" JULIA cursed a short time later, storming back into her room. Must he attempt to control her even when he was nowhere near? Yanking the green bonnet from her head, she flung it on the overstuffed brocade chair off in one corner. The matching jacket to the outfit she wore soon followed.

She had gone down to the stables, only to be told *Mr. Barringer* had left instructions that she was to do no riding until his return. And no amount of smiling, pouting prettily, or insisting that she was a very skilled rider had persuaded the big oaf of a man blocking her way to allow her to go riding.

"Well, *Mr. Barringer*, you may well own my body, but you will soon be made to see you do not own every minute of my life," she vowed.

With a sigh of disgust, she threw herself upon the window seat. Seeking to ease her irritation, she leaned her forehead against a cool pane of glass and stared sightlessly across the well-tended garden to the distant woods beyond.

Entertain herself in whatever manner pleased her, indeed! He had failed to state: as long as it met with his approval.

She kicked the pillows at her feet and connected with something hard. Glaring down, she spotted the book she had tossed there yesterday.

Her foul mood instantly dwindled. Reaching for the novel, she scooched back comfortably and flipped it open to Chapter Two.

Lady Weathersby's Wager

"So kind of you to take me in, my lord," Lady Weathersby stated, smiling across the card table. "I was woefully ill-prepared to be caught in an early snowstorm. I had not expected the weather to turn treacherous so rapidly." Nor had she expected to end up at the estate of one of the most handsome and notorious rakes in all of England, she thought, not at all disappointed with the delay in getting to London.

"I assure you, the pleasure is all mine," Lord Dunley replied, tearing his gaze from her chest for a quick glance at the cards in his hand. "I can think of no one better to be snowbound with than a beautiful woman." His gaze caressed her face. "But since I know you to be a lady of action and opposed to inane conversation, I can only think your intention is to distract me. You have yet to counter my wager." He raised a brow.

Forming her lips into a little moue, Lady Weathersby drew in a very, very deep breath. "It seems you have me at a distinct disadvantage, my lord," she said, running a long, polished nail over the edge of her cards as she inspected them again.

"How so?" asked the Viscount, lounging back in his chair.

She looked up, giving him a sultry look from beneath heavy black lashes. "Although I believe myself to be holding a winning hand, I seem to be short of ready funds. Could I possibly entice you to accept a small personal wager?"

His eyes lit with interest. "It would depend on how personal . . ." His gaze noticeably dropped from her lips to the abundant display of bosom provided by her low-cut gown. ". . . and how small."

She presented a contemplative, yet suggestive look. "I can see where size might be a sensitive issue." Stretching out her satin slippered foot beneath the table, she slid it up his leg until it was wedged between his thighs. Wiggling her toes, she tickled the heavy sac at the base of his manhood through his breeches.

With a devilish arch of one thick black brow, he said, "State the terms of your wager."

Gracing him with a teasing smile, she removed her foot. "You can hardly expect me to venture into a gentleman's agreement, when I am hardly a gentleman," she purred, running her tongue over her lips. "If you would be so kind as to supply me with paper and quill, I will pen my wager. Thus eliminating any misunderstandings."

A snap of Lord Dunley's fingers brought a nearby servant who was immediately dispatched to fulfill the request. After returning with the items, he was dismissed for the evening.

When Lady Weathersby was finished penning the wager, she read it over. Satisfied with what she wrote, she formed her lips into a soft pucker and blew gently to dry the ink.

The Viscount moaned and shifted in his chair.

"Here is the wager, my lord," she stated, carefully folding the vellum sheet and sliding it to the middle of the table.

Before she could withdraw her hand, he covered it with his. "There is a considerable amount of money in the pot. Will I find the wager worthy of it, do you think?"

"Oh, I am quite sure you will be most satisfied. If not—you may collect a forfeit of your own choosing."

"Anything?"

The husky anticipation in his voice sent a ripple of

lust through her entire body. "Anything," *she replied, her eyes full of promise.*

Tracing the back of her hand with his fingertips, he worked one finger down between hers and slid the paper out from beneath her hand. Drawing it across the table, he picked it up. He perused the contents. Fixing her with a burning gaze, he refolded the wager and tapped it against his chin. "A most generous offer. Still, the pot is substantial and I would exercise my right to claim a forfeit."

"You are a greedy man, my lord." *She was surprised, but not in the least disappointed.*

"I am known for my voracious appetite."

"Yes, I have heard such."

"Then you are acquainted with my preferences?"

"I believe I have a fairly good idea," *she said as a ripple of heady excitement surged through her.*

"Very good. If you are agreeable, my forfeit is that I be allowed to perform the same service for you."

Smiling, she nodded.

The smile he returned was the Devil's own. He flipped the wager onto the stack of money. Holding her gaze, he reached for the cards in front of him and began turning them over. One by one. The last card was flipped with a great flourish.

"Oh, my. It appears you have bested me," *Lady Weathersby said, folding the cards she'd picked up and placing them face down on the table.*

"Are you not going to reveal your hand?" *Dunley asked with a tilt of his head.*

"What purpose would it serve, but to reveal my ineptness of the game?" *she countered saucily.*

"You are many things, my lovely Lady Weath-

ersby, but I doubt if inept would ever be a word used to describe your skills."

"Have we ceased talking about cards, Lord Dunley?"

"Truth be known, I wish to cease talking entirely," he said, rising and walking over to the door. Locking it, he turned back. "I believe it is time for you to make good on your wager."

"Here? In the library?" she mocked, a wave of her hand indicating the book-lined walls.

Coming to stand in front of her, his look was hot, unyielding. "Here." He jerked her into his arms and kissed her hard. "Now." His nimble fingers sought, found, and discarded the pins in her elaborate coiffure, freeing the long tresses to stream down her back. "Naked."

With an expertise that excited her, her clothes soon lay in a puddle around her feet.

"On the table," he continued. Lifting her, he set her bare bottom onto the table and spread her legs until the losing cards she'd held peeked out from beneath her nest of springy dark curls. "And. . . ."

Lady Weathersby moaned and shuddered when he raked the back of one finger between the moist folds of her womanhood.

"Me," he drew one card out from beneath her, rubbing it against her damp flesh and flipping it over, "between," the second card came into view, using the same technique, "your," the third, "luscious . . . tender . . . thighs," he finished in succession, brushing over her clitoris as he turned the remaining cards face up.

Lady Weathersby's squirmed, causing both money and cards to shift on the table.

"It appears, Madame, you have lied."

"How so?" The question was short . . . breathy.

"You have not lost, but won."

"My darling Lord Dunley, you are so very, very right," she purred. *Grabbing his cravat, she eased herself back onto the table, pulling him with her until the wager they'd placed was pressed beneath her back and his broad shoulders between her thighs, forcing them farther apart.*

"How fare you at chess, my lady? For I would dearly love to challenge your skills again on the morrow." Lord Dunley's voice rumbled as he positioned her legs over his shoulders and sealed his mouth to her hot cleft to lap up every drop of her sweet, heady nectar.*

"Holy mother of God," Julia intoned aloud, not daring to read more. Pressing her legs tightly together, she dropped the book to her lap.

That could not possibly be what Brandon meant by *taste*.

17

BRANDON MADE LONDON IN record time. Exhausted and rumpled from the breakneck ride, he dropped from Neptune's back as he relinquished the reins to the young groom who had run from the dimly lit carriage house at the sound of his arrival. A second boy sprinted toward the house.

"Sorry, old boy," he said to the horse, which stood lathered and blowing with sides heaving. Feeling in no better shape, Brandon gave the animal a gentle slap on the rump to send it off to the stables.

Knowing his horse would be well taken care of, Brandon made his way toward the back door, trudging up the steps where his housekeeper stood waiting.

"Good evening, Mrs. Goodman. If you would be so kind as to have a bath drawn for me."

"Already ordered, sir."

Brandon gave her a tired smile. "Would you have a man sent with a note to my solicitor saying I am in residence and wish to see him." Due to the lateness of the hour, Brandon was not surprised to see a flash of mild astonishment cross her face. Then with a nod, she left to do his bidding.

"WILLIAM, GOOD OF YOU to come," Brandon greeted his solicitor with a firm handshake as he entered the library.

"Forgive me for dragging you from your home at such an hour, but I was most anxious to see this letter you spoke of."

"Actually, I anticipated your arriving quickly, so was prepared for your summons, no matter the time."

"Thank you. You have the letter?"

"Right here." Reaching into his coat, William retrieved a sheaf of paper and immediately handed it over.

"Help yourself to a brandy and have a seat. The evenings have gotten damnably cold," Brandon said, but his attention was already on the missive.

Pouring himself a drink, William settled into a chair adjacent to the one Brandon had taken and stretched his feet toward the welcoming heat of the fireplace.

Done reading, Brandon looked up, a troubled look crossing his features. "What do you suppose it means?"

"I'm not sure," William admitted honestly. "Since your parents' deaths, rumors abounded that they were truly wed. But even the old Duke, with all his money and resources, could find nothing to validate the claims."

"Knowing who I am and my reputation of dealing ruthlessly with those who cross me, do you really think someone would ask five hundred pounds for worthless information?" Brandon stated without conceit.

"No one in their right mind."

"I assume you did some checking on the woman?"

"Yes. With the utmost discretion, of course. I did not want to chance scaring her off before you had an opportunity to speak with her."

"What did you find?"

"She did indeed live in the area around the same time as your parents, and visited your mother on occasion. Though I cannot say if an actual friendship existed."

"If she can offer proof, you know what that would mean, William?"

"Yes, *Your Grace*," the other man lifted his glass in salute before finishing off the contents.

Brandon barked a self-mocking laugh. "Rather premature, I would imagine. This could merely be another wild goose chase as so many others were." For several long seconds, Brandon remained quiet. "There is Robert to consider."

His solicitor wasn't quite fast enough to hide the hint of distaste that crossed his features.

Brandon chose not to comment.

"What is there to consider?" William asked. "If your parents' marriage can be validated, it would mean that you have been the one wronged."

"I know, but you have no idea what Robert has been made to endure. He deserves some happiness. Perhaps I was the lucky one after all. Better to have no mother, than one of my aunt's ilk."

"Forgive me for speaking ill of my betters, sir, but from what I know of your late uncle's wife, I would venture your mother was a saint in comparison and I am sure she loved you very much."

Brandon smiled as if remembering a cherished memory. "Yes, you are right, William. Thank you for reminding me. And," he added with firm warning as he got to his feet and walked around his desk. "I would not hear you refer to yourself in those terms again. You are a far better man than most I know. Regardless of social standing."

Seeing the ready denial on his solicitor's face, Brandon held up a forestalling hand and, opening a drawer, dropped the letter inside. Taking out a piece of clean linen paper, he sat down and promptly scratched out a note. When he was done, he walked back over to where William was sitting and

handed it to him. "As soon as the bank opens tomorrow, have a draft drawn against my account and meet me here. We shall see if this . . . Mrs. Henning has something worth five hundred pounds."

IT HAD BEEN SEVEN years since Brandon had visited the place where he spent his childhood. It seemed like yesterday. Stepping from the coach onto the uneven cobblestone, he could almost see his parents walking, talking, and laughing with those they met, Brandon's small hand tugging at his father's much larger one to hurry them along. Had the streets always been this dirty, the houses this shabby? It hadn't seemed so then. Wrapped in his parents' love, everything around seemed to shine. God, how he missed them.

Even after he'd left to live with his grandfather, his sharp young mind had made it possible for him to remember things most youngsters would have long forgotten. Mostly the people. And once he was able, he'd sought out and offered employment to those who had been kind to him and his parents.

But his kindness had not gone unrewarded. It had opened a network of channels to the docks, where important information was funneled from sailors to workers and eventually passed on to other relatives, some of whom worked in Brandon's various households. The information he garnered proved invaluable to his shipping investments.

While waiting for William to join him, he looked around and noticed a young woman stepping from between two buildings. Her black hair and green eyes instantly reminded Brandon of Julia. The woman looked him over, giving him a come-hither smile. Brandon knew the bolt of desire that

streaked to his loins had nothing to do with her, but her likeness to the woman he'd left sleeping in his bed only yesterday. He felt a sudden urge to have done with this business and return to her.

"Lookin' fer a good time, gov?" she said through a wide red-lipped smile, revealing the absence of two front teeth.

"Not today, love," he said to the prostitute, extracting a coin from his purse and tossing it to her.

Catching it, she eyed both him and the coin skeptically, placed the shilling between her teeth, and bit down. Confirming its authenticity, she smiled. "If ye happen by this way again, duckie, ask for Bouncing Betty." She hefted her sizable breasts in the palms of her hands. "I be more 'n happy to take care of ye."

"I'll be sure to do that. Now run along and let me tend to my business."

Watching the exaggerated sway of her hips as she walked away, both Brandon and William shared a smile before turning toward the building and more serious matters.

Brandon entered the tenement first, traversing the long deserted hallway, skirting a pile of something he neither knew, nor wanted to know, the composition of. Cautious of any movement from the shadowed doorways along the way, he kept his attention forward, secure in the knowledge that William was behind him, watching as diligently. At the fifth door on the right he stopped.

"Is this it?" he asked William, keeping his voice low.

William nodded.

Motioning for his companion to step away from the door, Brandon stepped to the opposite side. He gave several hard raps to the battered, well-worn oak.

The door unexpectedly squeaked open.

Both men took another hasty step back, Brandon

reaching inside his coat for his pistol. When no one appeared, he slid his foot beyond the frame, nudging the door wider.

"Hello."

Silence.

"Mrs. Henning? I've come regarding the note you sent to my solicitor, Mr. Farnsworth."

Still no answer.

"I think I should go have a look," Brandon said.

William, whose hand had also disappeared beneath his coat, withdrew his own pistol. In response to Brandon's quirked brow, he said, "I thought it best to be prepared."

With a nod, Brandon cautiously made his way through the open doorway.

Looking around nervously, William drew out his kerchief and dabbed at his forehead.

A few minutes later, Brandon reappeared. The look on his face revealed something was terribly wrong.

"It appears we were not the only ones interested in what Mrs. Henning had to say."

The solicitor's brow furrowed. "She sold the information to another?"

"No. But someone has made it quite impossible for her to pass whatever information she had on to me."

"Good Lord!" William exclaimed, glancing at the door and taking a step back as the import of the words took root. "Is there nothing we can do?" With an economy of movement, he slipped his pistol back into the inside pocket of his coat.

"Nothing." Brandon's fists clenched at his sides. "Except to see that she has a decent burial." Brandon swallowed, trying hard to block out the vision of the woman's bloody, gaping mouth where her tongue had once been. No atrocity he'd ever witnessed during his years as a commissioned officer

had ever affected him so. Needing to cleanse his mind of the gruesome scene and his lungs of the stench, he strode past William and headed for the front door.

William's feet hit the cobblestones one step behind Brandon's.

For several moments neither man spoke, each deep in their own thoughts.

Exhaling from a deep breath, Brandon said, "I should like to retain the services of the Runners to investigate this heinous crime, William."

"Very good, sir."

"You are to use whatever funds necessary. If anything should be discovered, send word immediately."

"Rest assured I will do as you ask."

Brandon clapped a hand on William's shoulder and then turned to step into the waiting coach.

"Bow Street," he instructed the coachman after William was seated.

THE FIRST THING BRANDON did upon his arrival back to his townhouse was bathe and change. A light meal and several brandies came next.

What he really wanted was to return to Julia and lose himself in her rebellious sweetness. Riding through the night was infinitely preferable to the many sleepless hours that undoubtedly lay ahead of him later. His attempt at closing his eyes in the tub earlier had told him that much. It seemed the image of the dead woman would not be dismissed so easily.

Unfortunately, he could not leave. If it were only himself to consider he would, but it would not be fair to Neptune. The horse needed another day's rest and Brandon could not

justify risking injury to the loyal animal for the mere sake of finding succor in a woman's arms.

He didn't stop to think why the thought of Julia seemed sufficient to hold the macabre memory at bay; he only knew it did.

Thinking another distraction in order, he requested his coach brought around.

"Madame LaFleur's," he instructed, climbing in and settling back into the plush tufted seat. He was sure a quick trip to see Maude would be just the thing.

"*Bonjour*, madame," Brandon said, his mood lightening considerably at the sight of his old friend. He took her hand.

Barely giving his lips enough time to make contact, she snatched it back.

Brandon smiled.

"Monsieur Barringer, what a delightfully unexpected surprise. What brings you to my humble establishment again so soon?"

"I merely stopped in on the off chance you might have completed anything more from the order I placed with you last week."

"*Oui*, you are in luck. Only this morning my girls have finished two more garments. If you would be so kind as to follow me, *s'il vous plaît*, I will be only too happy to show you."

As soon as they were out of hearing from any customers, Maude hissed in a soft voice. "Touch me bum and I swear on me dear mum's grave ye'll be missin' yer fingers and pickin' snot with yer knuckles from here on out."

When Brandon didn't immediately respond with his usual banter, she looked back over her shoulder. Stopped. "What be ailin' ye, luv?"

"Not here," Brandon said quietly, placing a hand at the small of her back and prompting her to move forward.

With a concerned narrowing of her eyes, she nodded and resumed walking. Once ensconced behind the closed door, Maude went straight for the whiskey bottle. Pouring them both a drink, she waited until Brandon was settled in a chair and handed one over. Without saying a word, she took the seat adjacent to his.

That was one of the things Brandon admired about Maude. She knew when to talk and when not to.

Thirty minutes later, Mrs. Henning's gruesome story told and a second whiskey consumed, Brandon felt more himself.

"I'll set some of my boys to askin' questions. See if they can find out anythin'," Maude said when he was done talking.

Boys? Brandon smirked at the reference, doubting he'd ever seen a more brawny, dangerous lot of sailors than the ones she was speaking of. "I appreciate the offer, but I would prefer you not get involved, sweetheart. Whoever is behind this has either gone stark raving mad, or has hired someone who has. I couldn't live with myself if you ended up like Mrs. Henning." He took a deep gulp from the third glass of liquor he was currently nursing.

"Don't ye be frettin' none. No dicked-in-the-nob woman-killer will be getting his filthy hands on me. I been takin' care of meself since I were five and doin' a right fine job of it. 'Sides, the boys ain't about to be lettin' anythin' happen to me. I take good care of them and they take good care of me."

"Maude." Brandon's voice was filled with warning.

"I'll be hearin' no more on the matter, so ye might as well start flappin' yer jaw about somethin' else."

Knowing any attempt at changing her mind would be futile, Brandon prayed she was right about the *boys* and decided it wouldn't hurt to have one of his men keep an eye on her too. "Is anything being said regarding Miss Freemont?" he asked, taking her advice.

Maude gave him a sly, knowing grin. "*Oui, monsieur*," she said, applying her fake French to perfection. "But of course. That the Duke and Duchess of Malvern have invited her to accompany them to their country estate."

Brandon smiled at both the accent and the information. "Thank you, Maude. You're a gem."

"Weren't nothin'. These uppity, trussed-up old magpies be waitin' to pounce on any juicy tidbit of information. They're like starvin' cats what's found the last mouse in London." She gave him a level look. "Her being yer mistress ain't gonna stay a secret forever."

"I know. I had merely thought to give her time to adjust to the situation before having to face the ridicule of people she's associated with her entire life."

"Yer a good man, Brandon." She shook her head. "But sometimes yer as blind as a sailor wearin' patches over both his peepers. I made my livin' being a good judge of character. That's why I never got meself beat up or cut up, like some of the other girls workin' the docks. And I'm here to tell ye, your Miss Freemont ain't like those other whey-faced misses that comes in here. Ye ought to marry the uppity wench, have yerself a house full of annoyin' little Barringers, and have done with it. She's got spirit, that one does. I'm bettin' she won't be runnin' at the first sight of a man's shaft."

Knowing that for a fact, Brandon smiled to himself. "God, I adore you. No one but you would take a man's life-long plans and slap them in his face, in the hopes that he might start doubting himself."

"Glad you're finally seein' the right of it. There may be hope for ye yet," she said, completely missing his sarcasm. "Now. . . ." She stood up. "Take these packages and yer bloody arse out of here. There be some of us has to work for a livin'," she said, patting the side of her elaborately curled blond hair

and running her hands down the front of her stylish pink gown.

18

LEAVING WELL BEFORE DAWN the next morning, Brandon was less than two hours from London when he felt the hairs on the back of his neck rise.

Someone was following him.

He'd sensed it the moment he'd left the townhouse. Deliberately keeping Neptune to an even pace, he allowed whoever it was to track him. He was biding his time until he was well away from the city and at a place where he could spring a little surprise of his own.

Around the next bend up ahead the road narrowed, but there was a small cut-off to the right—if one knew where to look. That's where he would wait.

With the bend in sight, he gave Neptune a light kick to quicken his pace and took the turn. Quickly finding the break in the trees, he guided the horse as far back as he dared before the noise would alert the follower. He slid from the saddle. With a pat and a one-hand command, the horse dropped to its belly. This neat little trick had come in handy a time or two when Brandon was being chased by an irate husband or father, during his young and reckless years. Now thirty, he was less inclined to do anything so foolish, although he cherished the memories fondly.

Still, the foliage wasn't as thick as Brandon would've liked, but unless someone was seriously looking, he felt fairly sure the huge animal would go unnoticed. Walking back

closer to the road, he crouched down to conceal himself, pulled out his pistol from the inside pocket of his riding coat, and waited.

Brandon had to give the man credit, he was no bumbling lackey. He came around the bend cautiously, pistol drawn, his head moving from side to side. But by the time he realized something was wrong, it was too late.

Brandon stepped out from his hiding place as the rider passed him. "If you wish to live," Brandon said in a low, menacing voice, "get down and keep your hands where I can see them."

The man stopped his horse, but didn't immediately dismount.

Bloody hell, Brandon thought as he noticed the stiffening of the man's back and the tensing of his shoulders. He wasn't going to comply.

Swiveling in the saddle, the man swung his gun in Brandon's direction. With a sharp stab of regret, Brandon squeezed the trigger.

The assassin dropped to the ground with a sickly thud, one boot heel still hooked on the stirrup. The horse shied, dragging the man several feet before Brandon could make his way around the frightened animal and grab the bridle.

Disengaging the man's foot from the stirrup, Brandon dropped it to the ground.

The man groaned weakly.

Kneeling down beside him, Brandon wrapped his fists around the lapels of the man's black coat. "Who sent you?" The man's mouth moved, but no words came out. His eyes glazed over. There would be no answer.

Releasing his grip, Brandon let the body sink to the ground. For several seconds he remained where he was and then jumped to his feet.

"Stupid . . . bloody . . . bastard!" The curse came from between clenched teeth and Brandon wasn't sure if he meant himself for administering the fatal wound, or the man for dying before he could relinquish any information.

Cocking back his arm, Brandon swung hard with the intention of hurling his gun down the road. At the last moment he regained his senses and never released it. Wiping a hand across his face, he bent his head back and swore at the sky before collecting his composure.

With little hope of finding anything, Brandon crouched once again by the body and went through the man's pockets. What he discovered was a substantial purse.

Apparently whoever wanted him dead had the means to pay well to get the job done.

After rolling the body off the road into the underbrush, Brandon whistled for his horse. Gathering up the reins of the other horse, he mounted Neptune and set off once again, knowing his trip would be delayed by a quick stop at the nearest town.

There, he would tell the local constable where to find the body. And leave instructions to give the horse and money to a local orphanage.

THE TRIP HAD BEEN long and tedious, the interview with the constable more so, but Brandon was finally home. Grateful to Henry for his steadfast efficiency, Brandon rose from the tub next to the fireplace in his room. Even roused from his bed in the wee hours of the morning, his loyal man had taken a firm control over the small chaos caused by Brandon's unexpected arrival. Without Brandon's uttering a single order, he was whisked upstairs, stripped of his road clothes, and a

bath drawn. Shortly after that, immersed in a tranquil liquid oblivion, the only thought in his head . . . to crawl into bed beside Julia and curve his weary body around hers.

He had hoped to find her in his bed, but did not. And if he weren't so damn tired, he would have carried her there. Eyes half-closed, he dried himself off and trudged naked into the room next to his. Lifting the covers, he gently settled his front to Julia's back and lightly laid one arm over her middle. "I cannot believe how much I missed you," he whispered against the soft hair covering the back of her neck. Soon he dropped into a deep sleep.

Julia's eyes shot open, her heart pounding. Still unused to having anyone else in her bed, her sleep-shrouded mind was slow to realize it was Brandon.

Too dark to see the German clock on the mantel, she had no idea what time it was, but was fairly sure it was well before dawn. Had he really said he'd missed her? Or had it been part of a dream? Deciding it to be the latter, she closed her eyes and allowed sleep to reclaim her.

When next she awoke, it was to the feel of teasing fingers sifting lazily through the thatch of hair between her legs and warm lips nibbling the curve of her neck.

"One would think, considering the hour you arrived, you would still be sleeping," she said, trying to ignore the warm, thrumming sensation building in the lower recesses of her stomach.

"Ah, so I did wake you. I hadn't meant to." His finger dipped lower, circling her sensitive clitoris.

"Only briefly," she admitted off-handedly, wishing to appear as nonchalant as he, even as her hips moved slightly to encourage his touch.

"What did you do to occupy yourself while I was gone?" he asked casually.

One minute she was there, complacent beneath his touch, despite her attempt at appearing unaffected. The next, she was off the bed and glaring down at him.

"You forbade me to ride!" she accused, maintaining a distance well out of arm's reach, clutching the neck of her white cotton nightgown.

"It was for your own good," came the swift, curt explanation as if he were speaking to a wayward child. "Now come back to bed. I have need of your closeness."

"I will not allow you to rule every aspect of my life. I am a grown woman, able to make my own decisions, and will be treated as such."

Sighing heavily, Brandon flopped to his back, throwing an arm over his eyes. "Must we discuss this now?"

She noticed a note of glumness in his voice that almost caused her to relent. Almost. "Now or later," she insisted. "But you will not lay a hand on me until this matter is resolved."

He peeked at her from beneath his forearm before removing it and sitting up.

Julia became distracted by the sight of his wide, naked shoulders, hard-muscled chest and the faint trail of brown hair disappearing beneath the covers that had settled into his lap. Oh, how she had enjoyed playing with what she knew lay beneath the white rumpled fabric the night before he had left her. How she wanted to do it again. To take him beyond his control until his thick, white cream once again pumped into her hand.

"Very well, later."

His dismissive reply jolted her back to what they'd been discussing.

"Later?"

He smiled at the bewilderment in her voice. "You gave me a choice. I chose later," he said calmly, tossing the covers off

and rising from the bed. "I do so detest starting the morning off with an argument. I find it tends to affect the rest of the day most unfavorably." With a wink, he disappeared through the gaping hole between their rooms.

If there were a door Julia could have stormed through and slammed behind her, she would have. But short of ending up in the hall, where any passing servant could view her in her nightclothes, the only thing she could do was stand there and fume.

When next she encountered Brandon, he was seated at the dining room table, sipping chocolate and reading the newspaper. She had purposely dallied at her toilet, hoping to find him gone by the time she came down, but it seemed he was in no particular hurry to be about his daily business.

"Come, join me," he said congenially, setting the paper aside—something most men would never have done. Even her father had rarely done so for her mother. "Sit. I will serve you."

She arched a brow and he smiled.

Still upset, she remained silent as he seated her and went to the sideboard to fill a plate and pour a cup of chocolate. She felt a small spurt of pleasure at his having paid such close attention to her eating habits, as he not only picked the things she most preferred, but the correct portions as well.

"Thank you," she said begrudgingly.

"You are quite welcome, my dear." Still smiling, he took his seat. "I would be most happy to discuss the issue of your not riding in my absence if you wish."

She gave him a scalding look and in her sweetest voice said, "Not now, if you don't mind. I find an argument before a meal tends to ruin the appetite."

He laughed. "As you wish, sweet. I will be happy to return to my paper and allow you to finish your meal in silence. If that is your desire."

"What a capital idea. You are extraordinarily astute for a man—in some areas."

He grinned, shrugged his shoulders, and went back to reading the two-day-old news from London.

The satisfaction Julia expected to feel was short-lived when faced with his inattention and the distraction of the occasional movement of Brandon's strong hand as he sipped his chocolate.

"I should like to discuss the matter of your overbearing attitude," she stated after hastily finishing her meal.

"A moment, please," he said, not bothering to lift his gaze. "I wish to finish this article."

Julia had the feeling he was laughing at her from behind the printed barrier, but there was little she could do, as she was unwilling to give him the satisfaction of revealing her annoyance.

"I assure you, I do not mind in the least. I shall simply help myself to another cup of chocolate," she answered in an airy tone.

Her cup empty and her patience nearing its end, Julia wanted nothing more than to rip the blasted paper from his well-manicured fingers, wad it up in a tight ball, and shove it—

He lowered the newspaper and, meticulously refolding it, set it aside.

By the time she had Brandon's undivided attention, Julia was in a high dungeon. She wasn't sure if she wanted to discuss her inability to ride while he was away, or merely rip his arrogant head from his too-broad shoulders and feed it to the bloody horse. With great effort, she schooled her features into what she knew appeared to be bored unconcern.

Brandon was hard-pressed not to laugh. How many times had he seen that look on a woman's face when she was

attempting to be uninterested in a gentleman's attentions? Did females really believe men were not privy to their over-practiced schoolroom expressions? A perceptive man had only to read the other signals her body was projecting to know the truth. Like the tight grip she had on the handle of the delicate china cup in front of her, which he would guess she'd like nothing more than to toss at his head.

After a slight clearing of his throat, he said, "I know you are upset at being restricted in your riding, but I feel it unsafe for you to venture out without me. You are unfamiliar with the grounds around the estate and, should you be unlucky enough to be tossed on your stubborn little backside, no one would know where to find you."

"That is the most ridiculous thing I have ever heard," she stated doggedly, flinging back a lock of hair that had fallen over her shoulder. "I have never been thrown from a horse in my entire life."

He raised a brow.

"With the exception of the other night," she quickly amended. "But even you must admit to the extenuating circumstance of that particular instance. I had the best riding instructor money can buy. My father never forbade—"

"I am not your father. I take my responsibilities very seriously."

She gasped at the implication that her father had not.

"While you are under my protection, you *will* comply with my dictates. I am a man accustomed to giving orders and having them obeyed without question."

She jumped to her feet, fists clenched at her sides. "Then I fear we shall forever be at odds, *Mr. Barringer*, since I am a woman accustomed to obeying no one and *always* questioning."

Brandon watched her stalk away, unconcerned with the

challenge she'd issued. The angry swish of her hips brought a smile to his lips.

God, he loved her fiery spirit. But she *would* learn to listen to him, if for no other reason than her own safety.

"You will join me for supper this evening," he called after her. "If you do not, I shall seek you out, bring you down myself, and tie you to the chair if necessary."

What she groused back at him in a low unintelligible voice sounded suspiciously like a foul curse more commonly heard around the East-End docks.

WITH A STRANGLING GRIP on the door handle to her room, Julia shoved the thick panel open, slamming it shut behind her.

Drat the self-important, high-handed fiend. How dare he think he could dictate to her and she would yield like some pudding-hearted, little ninny?

Thinking to dispel some of her anger by immersing herself in another episode of Lady Weathersby, Julia retrieved the book.

She soon found her current state of mind would not allow her to give the tale the complete attention it deserved.

Better to save it for a day she could more appreciate it.

Going over to the stack of books on the table, she picked up a volume from Byron.

SUPPER WAS A SUBDUED affair, Julia initiating no conversation, only offering polite replies to Brandon's inquiries. He was content to allow her to wallow in her anger for the time

being, but they had only two evenings left before his guests arrived and he would not permit her to waste them. After tonight's lesson in taste, he had every intention of claiming her fully on the following eve.

"If you are quite finished with your meal, I would like you to join me for dessert," Brandon said. Standing, he held out his hand.

"Join you?" She gave him a quizzical look. "Are we not to have dessert here?"

"No," he said, catching her under the elbow and bringing her to her feet. Placing her hand on his arm, he secured it beneath his and began leading her from the room.

"If not here, where?" Julia slowed her steps, forcing Brandon to take a smaller stride or risk pulling her along behind him.

"I've requested it be served in *our room*."

Julia came to an abrupt standstill, pulling him to a stop. Her gaze flew to his. "Why would you do such a thing?"

"Have you forgotten I had promised your next lesson in taste?"

Julia's heart stuttered in her chest. "Yes. I mean, no. I had not forgotten. Only I have been feeling a tad poorly of late. Perhaps we should postpone—"

"Julia." Brandon's voice was rife with warning. "I know you are upset with me over the riding issue, and a man would expect a rebuff and to even be barred from his wife's bed until she had gotten over her miff. That is precisely the reason why most men procure a *mistress*. So that when he goes to *her* he knows she will never refuse him her body or her bed." He allowed her time to think on his words.

"Of course, you are right. I had forgotten my place. It shall be as you say." Trying to keep the bitterness from her voice, she pasted a smile on her face and took a step forward.

Her hand, still trapped beneath his, held her back when Brandon refused to budge.

"You sound and look more like a woman meeting a dire fate than one about to partake of one of life's greatest pleasures. Making love is not an act to be endured, but savored." Angling his head, he positioned his lips so they brushed the shell of her ear. "As I intend to savor every inch of you this night."

His lusty promise sent a stream of rippling shivers through her body so forceful, she could barely remember her own name let alone the reason she was so angry with him. Or, was it because she really did not wish to remember? What he said was true. She was his mistress. It was her duty to keep him happy in bed. At any rate, there was always tomorrow to make him pay for his arrogance.

This time, the smile on her face was genuine as she permitted him to move her from the room.

The first thing Julia noticed as Brandon closed and locked the bedroom door behind them was the extra table next to the bed. It was filled with the most glorious display of confections. Cherries, honey, melting chocolate in a chafing dish, and what looked like strawberry preserves. A plate of sugared fruit, a bowl of whipped cream, and a bowl of vanilla ice cream, both sitting in silver containers filled with ice.

"It looks scrumptious," she exclaimed with delight, giving the appearance of a child set free in a confectioner's shop. After another quick perusal of the table, she turned to him with a frown. "I fear someone has forgotten the plates."

"No, I believe everything is as I requested."

"Are the plates elsewhere then?" She turned in a circle, looking around the room, her frown deepening when she could not locate any.

He stepped closer, placing his hands on her shoulders, his thumbs rubbing softly at her collarbone. "Julia."

At his soft entreaty, she gave him her undivided attention.

His handsome face split into a devilish grin. "Darling . . . you are the plate."

19

JULIA'S EYES WIDENED, HER gaze traveling back to the assortment of sweets on the table. A picture flashed across her mind—Lord Dunley's head between Lady Weathersby's widespread thighs.

Heaven help her . . . that was *exactly* what Brandon meant by taste.

She looked at the man standing next to her. Like a living flame, the hot sensuality in Brandon's eyes leaped into Julia. A scalding heat starting deep within her womb, spreading outward until she feared ending up a pile of cinders at the toes of his shined-to-a-mirror boots.

Every objection her mind formed was quickly rejected. How could she voice them without revealing where she'd learned about such an intimate act?

No, that was a lie. She wanted to share this with Brandon—his lips, his mouth, his tongue.

"I find myself with a sudden insatiable craving for something sweet, love," Brandon said.

His voice poured over her like thick molasses. His hands clutched her shoulders, drawing her closer until she was pressed securely into the heat of his body.

"I believe I shall start with your lips," he whispered, dipping his head to place little teasing nibbles and licks over and around her pliant mouth. Purposely evading any attempt on her part to deepen the kiss.

The hands Julia had brought up to his chest now clawed heedlessly at the material of his coat. She opened her mouth in invitation, moaning softly around the thrusting entry of his tongue. Vaguely aware of Brandon's fingers working the buttons down the back of her dress, Julia felt an overwhelming need to have him closer. Rising on tiptoes, she crushed her lips against his.

This time it was Brandon who moaned. Impatient to have her naked, he gripped the sides of the dress and pulled, sending the last few buttons flying.

"If you keep this up, we will both be in need of a new wardrobe," she murmured with a smile.

"I will gladly buy you a hundred dresses if the disposal of each garners me access to your luscious body," he said and, unwilling to be separated from her, managed to remove the rest of her clothes, along with his, while backing her up to the bed. Falling down with her, he framed her face with his hands and continued to devour her mouth until the need for air forced them apart.

"If your lips are that sweet, I can only imagine how delicious the rest of you will taste," he murmured.

The statement was followed by a slow glide of his tongue up the side of her neck before he caught the lobe of her ear between his teeth. Julia squirmed beneath him, the movement pressing her pelvis into his loins.

Growling a mild expletive, Brandon released her ear. He leaned back marginally. "There is an element to this lesson that would greatly enhance the experience, if you are agreeable."

When he made no attempt to explain further, she asked, "How can I agree unless you tell me what it is?"

"It involves a measure of trust." He gave her a searching look.

She raised her hand to stroke his cheek. "Trusting you was never an issue. If I had not, I never would have come to you with my offer. In all the years I have known you, I have never heard a single person question your integrity."

Her soft admission filled him with a sense of over-whelming pleasure. He slipped a hand up her arm, captured her wrist, and turned his head to place a kiss in her palm. "Then you have no objection to my tying your arms above your head?"

"Wh . . . what?" She attempted to snatch her arm back, but his light grasp held.

Seeing the shock on her face, he released a soft chuckle. "I promise you will not regret it. Once you see the pleasure to be had, someday you may even let me tie your legs."

"My legs?" she squeaked.

"You said you trusted me, did you not?"

She nodded.

"Well?" His look was sensually challenging.

She took a quick little breath. "Very well, I agree. But only my hands," she clarified quickly, hoping she was not making a terrible mistake. But she *had* told him the truth. She did trust him. And while she was being honest with herself, she might as well admit that her hesitation was not due to any worry that Brandon would abuse her in her helplessness, but that she might grow to enjoy this particular game a bit too much. The mere thought of being at the mercy of Brandon's every sexual whim caused her entire body to ignite.

"Do not move," he commanded, slipping from the bed and going to his wardrobe, only to return a moment later with a silk cravat. "Your arm, please."

She laid it in the hand he extended and watched with interest as he tied a loose knot around her wrist with one end and looped the other through the gold ring in the center

of his headboard. Was it her imagination . . . or were the two elfin creatures holding the gold circlet laughing down at her?

Walking around to the other side, Brandon secured the opposite arm in a similar fashion. Making his way to the foot of the bed, he paused to stare down at her. The unbridled lust in his gaze and his immensely rigid rod let her know how pleased he was with the picture she presented.

Brandon reached out to run a light finger across her ankle. "Are you quite sure your legs must remain free?"

"Quite," she replied, clamping her thighs together and drawing her knees up. Not taken in by the crestfallen, little boy look that appeared on his face, she was tempted to giggle.

"Very well. I suppose I shall have to make do."

"I suppose you shall," she quipped back.

With a look that vowed retribution, he walked to the table. Picking up a spoon, he filled it with ice cream and put it into his mouth. Without swallowing, he slid onto the bed next to her. Giving her a closed-lipped smile, he bent to her chest, touched his lips to her nipple and quickly sucked as much of her breast into his mouth as he could.

The shock of icy cold and moist heat caused Julia's entire body to clench and her nipple to contract. A curious blend of exhilarating discomfort, it had Julia writhing and her neglected breast aching for a similar experience.

Swallowing, Brandon painstakingly lapped the melted ice cream that had seeped between his lips from her breast and trailed his tongue over to the other firm, fleshy mound. He blew a frosty breath across the tip. It peaked instantly.

"Again," Julia implored, arching up. Forgetting her hands were bound, she tried to bring them down to clasp his neck. She frowned.

Brandon's lips quirked at her frustration. "Oh, but there

are so many other delicacies to sample. I believe I shall leave this breast," he licked the nipple, "for later."

This time, when Brandon got up, it was to drag the table within arm's reach of the bed. Sitting back down beside her, he picked up the bowl of chocolate and tested it with his finger. Deeming it adequate for his purpose, he drizzled it slowly over her entire ribcage and abdomen.

Julia sucked in a breath, drawing in her stomach at the warm, spidery sensation.

Next, a dollop of whipped cream filled her navel and, after pulling the stem off a cherry with his teeth, Brandon placed the glistening red fruit atop the fluffy white mound. Detaching another stem, he placed that cherry into his mouth and brought it to her lips.

Knowing instinctively what he wanted, Julia lifted her head and gently sucked the fruit into her mouth, only to be surprised a moment later when Brandon's tongue followed to scoop it back into his.

"Hmmm," he murmured as he chewed and swallowed.

"Am I to be allowed no dessert?"

Her tone was both sulky and sensual, sending a shooting star of desire straight through Brandon. "Would you like one?"

She nodded.

"You will have to work for it," he bantered as he placed a cherry into his mouth and bent over her once more. Opening his lips slightly, he allowed her tongue to dip in, only to initiate a playful searching dance with his own. When he finally relented, giving up the fruit, they were both breathless and smiling.

"I think I shall venture to other unexplored territories," he said, with a lift of one dark brow. Lowering his head, he began licking and sucking the syrup from her body.

By the time he reached her navel Julia had run the gamut of sensations, from flushing warmth to chilling shivers, deep moans to tinkling giggles. And when she thought she could withstand no more, he smeared the strawberry preserves over her arms, chest, and thighs, and started over again.

"Brandon," she gasped.

Reluctantly removing his lips from the inside of her right thigh, he looked up.

Julia felt consumed by his unflinching, piercing gaze. "I . . . I cannot . . . I need. . . ." Her breathing was labored.

"I know what you need, love." His eyes glowing in the candlelight with pure male satisfaction, he reached for the honey.

"Do you know what a honey pot is?" Brandon asked. Spreading her legs wider with one hand, he held the bowl suspended above the juncture of her legs.

Although she'd read it in Lady Weathersby's escapades, she wasn't about to admit it. Capturing her bottom lip between her teeth, she shook her head.

"No? Well, allow me to tell you. A honey pot is something filled with the most delectable nectar in the world." He tilted the bowl, watching as the liquid amber dripped into her pubic hair. "A place where a man can quench his thirst for the heavenly sweetness he craves." The sweet thick river moved slowly, oozing over her clitoris, flowing downward, coating the plump fleshy lips between her legs.

With his free hand, he reached in to spread those lips, allowing the honey to coat both inside and out.

The sensation was so sinfully erotic, Julia might have leaped from the bed if not for the sweltering heat radiating from Brandon's gaze. A look that made her feel wicked . . . wanton . . . desirable. As if she were the last drop of water in a burning desert and he a thirsting nomad.

"God, you are beautiful. Everywhere," he clarified, running the tip of his finger around the opening of her cleft. His words were breathy, labored, as if his lungs were under great strain. Righting the bowl, he set it aside. Returned to trail his fingers through the thick nectar—over, around, and dipping slightly into her pink opening.

Overwhelmed by the intense intimate attention, Julia attempted to close her legs. The position of Brandon's arm prevented her from attaining her goal.

"You have never been more beautiful to me than you are at this moment, Julia. *Every* part of you. You are perfection . . . an artist's dream come true. Do not hide yourself." He placed a tender kiss on each thigh and, when he moved her legs farther apart with the lightest pressure of his hand, she allowed it.

Keeping his gazed fixed on hers, he raised up and settled between her legs. His broad shoulders warm and solid against the tender flesh of her thighs, he placed a hand above her knee, caressed it, then sent his hand journeying. Over shapely sleek calf, circling a trim ankle, cupping a slender foot, pausing . . . fingers rubbing . . . learning the high arch, the curve of her instep.

In slow degrees, he brought her leg up until her foot rested next to his shoulder. Did the same to the opposite leg. The whole time, placing tiny nips and licks over her stomach, sucking gently at the tendon where leg joined pelvis. He stopped briefly when her head arched back and she whimpered, the sound coming from somewhere deep in her throat. Making a mental note of each and every sensitive spot on her body with the intention of revisiting, Brandon continued his sensual torment.

But, compelled to draw out the pleasure, he purposely avoided the place he most wanted to taste. The honey within.

Julia gripped her bonds tighter, her arms straining, over-whelmed by sensation both unbearable and excruciatingly wonderful. Brandon's expert lips and hands finding and exploiting every highly sensitized part of her body. But still she yearned—her body knowing, seeking. "Brandon. I can bear no more. You must release me."

His answer was a muffled, "Mmmm."

His tongue flitting in and out of the soft curly hair between her legs, both smearing and lapping at the sticky sweetness, made Julia forget what she was trying to say.

Wet and warm, dipping down, a slow glide up between swollen silky folds. He shifted, resting on his forearms, using his fingers to spread the lips to which he had been paying such luscious attention. His fingertips at her opening, his breath hot on her pulsing flesh.

"Paradise," he whispered, before slipping his tongue inside.

Slowly, achingly slowly. A tantalizing gentle roughness against her oversensitive, overheated inner canal. Easing in . . . slipping out. . . . Again and again until she thought she'd go mad.

He stopped.

"Nooo," she groaned, thrusting her hips toward his mouth, thinking he meant to leave her in this hellish antici-pation.

"Shhh, I'm here, love. I'll take care of you."

She felt his fingers stroking in a steady rhythm while he placed the heated cavern of his mouth on her clitoris—flicking, sucking.

Fingers thrusting.

"Brandon!" Julia screamed as intense white flashing lights burst behind her eyelids.

But he allowed her no respite, no mercy as he continued to feast.

She climaxed thrice more before he allowed her to rest, and as she lay boneless with satiation, he untied her and washed her with diligent, tender care.

BRACED ON ONE ELBOW, lost in thought, Brandon stared down at Julia's sleeping visage. Turned on her side, facing away from the banked fire and snuggled against him, her features were in shadowy relief. But he needed no light to recall every detail of her beauty. It was captured in his memory for all time.

Not being able to get enough of her, he had appeased his appetite throughout the night. The ice cream and whipped cream had long since melted, but his insatiable need to taste every inch of her had not waned. Still had not.

He'd offered her sugared fruit from his fingers and then from his teeth. Her reward . . . long, languorous kisses as they fed upon each other's lips. Brandon was hard-pressed to say which had been sweeter.

There was a subtle change in her now, as if she no longer feared her own sexuality, but reveled in it. Yet still, she kept something back. Brandon was not quite sure what; he only knew he wanted it. She had callously rejected the respectable life he'd been prepared to offer her, and much more, had she only known. He would see to it she never denied him again.

A wife would give him an heir and respectability—Julia would give him *everything* else.

Damn her aristocratic pride . . . damn her father to hell for committing suicide . . . and damn himself. Because with Julia's sumptuous body lying fully sated next to him, the mere thought of another woman left him cold.

Clearing his conscience of the disagreeable matter, he

snuggled down next to her. With a surge of intense anticipation that on the morrow he would claim her fully, he buried his head in the crook of her neck, placed his lips on her warm and slightly salty skin, and slid a hand between her unresisting thighs.

20

JULIA SAT ON THE small couch in the library, the book of poetry she'd selected forgotten in her lap. Toying with the small diamond heart on a gold chain around her neck, she stared out the window. She was oblivious to the sun playing peek-a-boo in the clouds, the gardener tending the grounds, a young groom riding down the tree-lined lane as he exercised one of the horses. But she was not oblivious to Brandon. Even without his physical being, he lingered in her mind. A formidable presence. What he'd done to her the night before—what he made her feel—what he planned for her this evening.

He'd awakened her with whispered promises and heated kisses. Told her in explicit detail how he intended to claim her that night as his touch showed her what he intended to do right then. One scalded her inner being, the other her flesh.

She had no time to dwell on either, her brain turning to mush at the first rasp of his tongue between her legs . . . the first touch of his lips where she'd never before dreamt a man would want to kiss. But he'd shown her the folly of her thinking over and over and over again until insanity beckoned.

Afterwards he'd held her, stroking his hand over her sensitized skin ever so lightly.

Three hours had passed since then. Both an eternity and a matter of moments as her body heated and burned with the memory.

Realizing that the pendant she'd been fiddling with had ended up between her teeth, she allowed it to drop to her chest.

The necklace had belonged to her mother. Easily not the most expensive piece of jewelry, it was her mother's favorite— a gift from Julia's father on the day she'd been born.

Her mother was forever the romantic, Julia remembered with a spasm of sadness. Love did that to a person. An emotion Julia was determined to avoid at all costs, for the price of not loving or being loved seemed an infinitely easier fee to pay than having and losing it.

Deep in thought, she was startled to her feet by a light tap on the door, nearly dumping the forgotten book from her lap in the process. A quick grab saved it. "Yes?" Closing the volume, she set it aside.

Henry entered with a respectful nod. "Mr. Barringer requests your presence in the front parlor, Miss Freemont. Shall I tell him you will be there directly?"

"No. I shall come now."

"Very good, miss." Keeping his position by the doorway, he allowed her to precede him. They walked in silence to the parlor where he discreetly closed the door behind her.

Brandon rose from the dark red leather chair he'd been sitting in.

"I have received word from Malvern."

From the expression on his face, Julia could tell he was not particularly pleased. Her gaze fell to the missive he was holding.

"It would appear they are arriving a day early." He looked over his shoulder, out the tall, paned-glass windows. "It seems the rider bringing the message was delayed when his horse threw a shoe. I would venture to say they should be arriving any time." He returned his attention to her.

"You sound disgruntled. I should think you would be happy. After all, you did invite them."

He tossed the letter on the mahogany table next to the chair and closed the distance between them. "The problem . . . sweet," he said, placing his hands on her bare upper arms and drawing her closer, "Is that the plans I had for you this evening just went to hell."

Her eyes lit with comprehension. "You mean. . . ."

"Precisely." He closed his eyes as if staving off pain and, when he opened them, kissed her.

The kiss was greedy, passionate, and fraught with frustration. Regrettably, albeit honestly, she could not say where the majority of the tumultuous emotion stemmed from. Him . . . or her. From the day she had gone to Brandon with her proposal, she both dreaded and anticipated her deflowering in equal measures. Each day since, the scales had become tipped more favorably toward anticipation. He had stirred feelings in her no respectable woman would admit to. And it seemed her respectability was fast losing ground.

With a soft moan, she kissed him back.

Realizing his control was slipping like a ship from its mooring, Brandon broke the contact. Murmuring an incoherent expletive, he buried his face against Julia's neck. "Dare I hope their carriage breaks a wheel and they not arrive for at least one more day?"

Julia smiled. It instantly faded. "Brandon?" She pushed out of his arms.

He tilted his head.

"The door."

"The door?" His mind tried to digest the quick change in subject. *Kiss . . . lips . . . warm body . . . hard shaft—door?*

"The door between our rooms. You must have it replaced."

Oh, that *door.* "Whatever for?" he asked as the fog of desire slowly dissipated.

"Isabella," she insisted as if that explained everything.

"What does Lady Isabella have to do with the door?"

"From the time we were young, Isabella and I have always shared a room."

Brandon's lips eased into a sympathetic smile. "Would it be terribly rude of me to point out that you are no longer a young girl, but a woman grown." The slow, thorough gaze he subjected her to was immensely suggestive. He reached for her again.

She took a step back. "Please. Won't you at least consider. . . ."

Brandon smiled when her face turned nearly the same shade of pink as her gown and she tucked her chin. "Perhaps you could persuade me," he suggested. Lifting her chin on the tips of his fingers, he skimmed his thumb in a leisurely stroll across her lips, resting it at the corner of her mouth.

Julia's eyes momentarily lit with the notion and then narrowed. "How?"

"I would not be adverse to . . . shall we say, a compensatory forfeit. Something to hold me over until I can arrange for some privacy."

She took a tentative step closer. "A kiss?" She lowered her lashes and offered her mouth. At his chuckle, her eyes sprang open.

"Come now, Julia. What you offer hardly seems fair, considering what I will be forced to give up."

"What then?"

"Your willingness."

"My willingness? You already have that." Her brows drew together. "Have I not submitted to your desires?"

"Ahh, but that is the crux. You submit." His thumb once

again strolled across her lips, this time pausing in the middle. Brandon applied the slightest pressure until she opened enough to take the tip inside. "I want you to begin offering yourself to me."

Her eyes rounded and she made a small sound in the back of her throat. He felt the vibration against his thumb, but she neither released his thumb nor backed up.

Encouraged, he continued. "For the duration of our guests' stay . . . " he grazed the top ridge of her teeth ". . . you will wear no undergarments except for stockings and garter." His tone was deep, mellow.

The sound floated over Julia like a warm summer's breeze. When had she become so enamored by his deep baritone voice? Unconsciously, her lips clamped down on his thumb. Giving her a smile, he pulled it out.

"Whenever we are fortunate enough to gain a moment of uninterrupted privacy, you will either bare your lovely breasts to me so that I may suckle and play with them. . . ."

He conformed his hands to the shape of her breasts. "Or . . . " he said, sliding both hands down her sides, following the indent of her small waist over the gentle flare of her hips. Resting his hands against her thighs, he began gathering the material of her dress. "You will raise your skirts, baring yourself to my explorations so I may whet my appetite on the sweet wetness between your legs." He angled his forearms so the material he'd gathered rested on his wrists. Sliding one hand around to encompass the cheeks of her bottom, he pulled her closer, while the fingers of the other hand ventured between her legs.

At the first touch of his warm fingers drifting through her curls, Julia's traitorous body swayed. To anchor herself, she placed both hands on his thick upper arms. She might have closed her eyes if not for Brandon's hypnotically captive

gaze. Unerringly, he found the rigid nub hidden within her velvety folds. His finger whispered over it.

Although his face revealed satisfaction at the breathy, needy whimper that escaped Julia's parted lips, he removed his hands.

Like the fall of a castle gate, the gown dropped to her ankles.

Determined to maintain control, Brandon centered his thoughts on regulating his breathing and away from the warm, honeyed moistness on his finger. Time and again, this woman seemed to bring him to the brink of losing all control. Control he was determined not to relinquish. Control meant power. He'd spent most of his lifetime attaining it and would be damned if he'd surrender so much as a single scrap. Not since coming to live with his grandfather had he done so.

He met the question in Julia's eyes with a shake of his head.

She studied his face, her hands braced heavily on his arms.

Brandon knew the exact moment she realized what he wanted by the spark of comprehension in her fathomless emerald eyes. Demonstrating a confidence that took him off guard, she slowly moved her palms up. Her hands seemed small, delicate, but sure as she slid them up the outside of his arms, over the breadth of his shoulders, cupping the curve of his neck. Her fingers were lightly caressing as they stole their way through the hair at his nape before she twined them together. Eyes shining like precious jewels, she levered onto her toes and determinedly pressed her lips to his.

At the onset, Brandon kept his hands hanging loose at his sides, but eventually found them drifting to her hips. The moment he tightened his grip, she slid her hands to his shoulders and steadily pushed him away.

"Wait." At the confusion in his eyes, she placed a hand against his cheek. "You did say uninterrupted. Did you not?" At the slight incline of his head, she turned, went to the door, and locked it. The click of the latch seemed to echo in the sexually charged silence. Strolling past him, she made her way to the windows and drew the heavy cream brocade drapes. The couple was immediately cocooned in a cozy, diffuse light.

Returning, she placed a hand against his chest and backed him into the seat from which he'd arisen when she'd arrived. Once he was seated, she boldly stepped between his legs.

Julia could only hope she appeared confident, for inside she was shaking. The tiniest bit due to insecurity, the majority due to excitement. She had this inexplicable feeling of power. For once she was the one in charge. She'd felt the rapid pounding of Brandon's heart when she'd pressed her palm against his chest. Realized the strung tension of his body, the tautness of his lower jaw. As if a torch flared, understanding dawned. Blinded by her own insecurities and maidenly modesty, she'd not recognized how hard it was for him to maintain the iron control he seemed to have over his body. She wasn't naïve enough to think she was capable of doing it yet, but she vowed silently to one day shatter that control. Reaching inside the neckline of her dress, she took the first step in doing so.

"Is this what you want?" The breast she held out to Brandon was plump, the nipple peaked, and unerringly in line with his mouth.

"That and more," he murmured.

Drawing her closer, he laid urgent claim to the rigid, rosy kernel with his hot, wet lips. In a daring move, Julia angled slightly to press her thigh into his crotch. Mere days ago,

she would have been shocked at the bulging, hard rod she encountered. Today, she gloried in it.

Brandon groaned, the sound humming against her tender flesh. His hands slid up her back, his fingers spanning the width of it, his thumbs slipping around to settle at the undersides of her breasts.

"Brandon," Julia pleaded.

"Ummm."

"Brandon!" She placed her hands on either side of his head, trying to draw him away.

Through the haze of desire, Brandon was slow to realize the urgency in her voice. Releasing her, he pressed his cheek to her cushiony softness. It took him a moment to realize it was not the rumbling of her stomach he was hearing, but the rumbling of coach wheels.

"MALVERN!" BRANDON CALLED AS he stepped into the foyer, his heels snapping smartly on the black marble floor. The men met in three long strides, exchanged a fierce hug and hearty slaps on the back.

"Damn your soul, I've missed your stiff hide," James said with a grin, sliding his fingers through his wind-tossed black locks. A sure sign he'd been riding instead of being confined inside his coach. "How have you been faring?"

"Well. For the most part," Brandon added belatedly.

James caught the subtle change in his friend's voice, and the men exchanged a we'll-talk-later look.

"Married less than three months and already ignored in favor of a male companion," said the playfully exasperated voice of Malvern's wife over his shoulder.

"Never, my love." With a lopsided grin, he spread his

arm and Amelia stepped into it to be cuddled against her husband's side. Like the Duke, her hair was less than perfect and the pert little dark green riding cap upon her head listed a bit to one side.

"Amelia." Brandon gathered the woman's hand, touching his lips to the back.

"Oh, Brandon. You know how I abhor formality in the company of friends. Is it not enough I have to tolerate it when in public?" So saying, she scooted from her husband's embrace, threw her arms around Brandon's shoulder, and gave him a hearty squeeze.

James laughed.

Brandon rolled his eyes.

"I see she has yet to learn the intricacies of deportment among the nobility," Brandon droned out teasingly, returning the enthusiastic hug.

"Why shucks, Mr. Barringer. I guess us little ol' Americans are a bit slow when it comes to all the fuss and pomp."

Julia, who had stayed well back, tried unsuccessfully to stifle a soft giggle.

At the sound, all gazes turned in her direction.

"Ah, the lovely Miss Freemont. So good to see you again," Malvern said, going over and bestowing the same treatment to her hand as Brandon had to Amelia's.

"Your Grace." Retracting her hand, Julia dipped a curtsy.

"I'm afraid I have to agree with my wife. Please call me James, or Malvern. Either will do. One gets rather used to it with Amelia around."

"If that is your wish, Your Gr . . . James."

Smiling, James turned and extended his hand. His wife immediately took it. "Darling, you remember Miss Fr—."

"Of course I remember Julia," Amelia cut in boldly. "She was the prettiest girl at my wedding. Next to me, of course."

Her smile was impish. "Had my husband's gaze not been on me the entire evening, I might have found myself terribly jealous."

"Not true," Julia was quick to correct. "You were radiant. I so envy your petite stature and beautiful flaxen hair. You outshined every woman there."

"James, dear." Amelia turned to her husband. "The House of Lords could use such a diplomat. It's a shame you English are so backwards where women are concerned. Back home—"

"I know you do not think me gullible enough to believe there are women holding government positions in America."

"That is not at all what I was going to say," Amelia said on an exasperated sigh.

"Excellent. Then whatever it was might best be debated later. Over some brandy."

"I shall have Henry bring up five or six bottles from the cellar," Brandon seconded with an agonized murmur, making both women smile. "For now, I am quite sure you would like to get settled in. Henry will show you to your rooms."

"Room," James quickly amended, stepping to his wife's side and looking down into her shining blue eyes. "We're working on the next Malvern heir."

Her husband's outspoken statement brought a beautiful blush to not only his wife's cheeks but also Julia's.

Misinterpreting the odd look on Julia's face for one of surprise, Brandon chuckled lowly and bent to whisper, "Do not fret, sweet. I assure you, by the time their visit has ended, you will have gotten quite used to their outlandish behavior. One of the disagreeable effects of being in love, I would suppose. Are we not fortunate we'll never have to make such muttonheads of ourselves?"

"Yes, very fortunate, indeed." Julia's answer was quick

and precise. But the loving, intimate smile the married couple was currently sharing at the thought of producing a child left her feeling more than a little envious and . . . empty. Unconsciously, her hand went to her stomach.

"Henry," Brandon called to the unobtrusive man who had been standing off in one corner by the door. "I think it best we give the Duke and Duchess the entire west wing. That way they can cavort to their hearts' content and leave the rest of us undisturbed."

"How thoughtful of you, old chap." Malvern grinned, totally ignoring the light sarcasm in his friend's tone. "Might it be too much to hope that dinner will be late this evening?" He wiggled his eyebrows in Brandon's direction.

Shaking his head, Brandon instructed Henry, "Please inform Etienne dinner will be an hour later this evening." He shot another glance toward James, easily reading the look in his friend's eyes. "Make that two hours later this evening."

"A man could not ask for a dearer friend," James expounded, giving Brandon a wink and a solid slap on the shoulder. "Henry, lead the way."

"Yes, Your Grace," the older man said with immense dignity, seemingly oblivious to the ribald exchange that had taken place.

"We shall talk later," Amelia said over her shoulder to Julia as she was being hustled toward the stairs by her husband. "I am so looking forward to getting to know you and becoming friends."

Julia was given little opportunity to do anything but smile in reply as Malvern seemed in a great hurry to whisk his wife away. It was easy to see the couple was very much in love. Julia had lived with the gloomy side of that emotion for so long, she'd forgotten what the sunny side was. The days before her mother's death, when her parents were happy, their

love filling the house, spilling over onto her. But that was before her father's slide into what seemed a living purgatory after the loss of his beloved wife.

"Julia?"

Startled from her thoughts, she realized Brandon was moving her aside and out of harm's way as several sturdy male servants began hefting in a steady stream of large trunks.

"Woolgathering?" Brandon inquired next to her ear. "Or ... perhaps, like I, you were thinking of what we were doing in the parlor before our guests arrived? If I know James, I feel fairly sure that we can enjoy at least a couple of hours of uninterrupted solitude." He slid an arm around her waist, but she stepped away.

"Brandon, please. I couldn't possibly. Not now." She was careful to keep her voice low as more servants traipsed by on their way up the steps.

"I'm sorry," he said, misconstruing her mood. "I should have realized. If their behavior has upset you, I will have a talk with Malvern."

"No. I wasn't offended in the least. I will admit to being a little shocked, but only a little. I think their affection for each other is charming. It's only ... I'm feeling a bit tired is all. I thought to rest a bit before this evening."

Immensely disappointed, Brandon studied her face. There was fatigue ... but something else. Her head dipped before he could discern what it was.

"Of course, my dear. After all, your lack of sleep was totally of my doing. Not that I can regret it. Would you like me to escort you to your room?"

"Thank you, no." She reached beneath his coat and, taking out his pocket watch, placed it into his hand. "Surely there are things you must attend to in light of your guests'

early arrival. I'll see you at the evening meal." Offering a small smile, she left him.

Brandon wrapped his fingers tightly around the timepiece. His gaze pensive, he stared after her as she ascended the curved staircase, reached a bend, and slipped from sight. He was left with the distinct feeling that it was more than tiredness that took her from his side.

ENTERING HER ROOM, JULIA closed the door softly behind her. With a sigh, she leaned her back against the sturdy wood and closed her eyes. Once again, she felt her hand drifting toward her stomach and staunchly thrust it away. Opening her eyes, she pushed to a standing position.

Her gaze immediately took in the door between her room and Brandon's. She frowned, her fingers curling into fists.

Damn his manipulating hide. He'd coerced the promise from her, knowing he'd already ordered the door put back in place.

But her annoyance at his duplicity took an unexpected turn when she remembered the blossoming feeling of power she'd experienced earlier. She smiled. Oh, she'd expose herself to him all right. Until he was crazed with wanting her. But not on his terms. On hers.

Her spirits lifted at the silent resolution, only to plummet as another thought occurred.

Admittedly she'd learned much in her short time with Brandon, but not enough to have him groveling at her feet with unrepressed desire. She'd have to gain more experience before that would happen. If only there was someone she could turn to for help. . . .

Her gaze swung toward the window seat. Her spirits
bloomed once again.

Lady Weathersby!

21

Lady Weathersby and the Russian Count

She could barely contain her excitement. Count Nicholi Torsukov was the handsomest man she'd ever seen. And the biggest. Why he could probably cup her entire arse in one large hand, leaving the other free to explore.

The mere thought of those thick, long fingers slipping inside her made her womanhood tingle and juices flow.

She had to have him.

Their eyes met across the long, crowded banquet table.

"So tell me, Count. What does one entertain oneself with on those long, cold, Russian nights?" She exaggerated a little shiver, pressing her forearms against her sides. The movement inevitably caused her breasts to come dangerously close to spilling from her bodice.

The count's gaze immediately riveted on her ample cleavage, his eyes lighting with unmistakable interest. "It vould depend on the company one is in. The distractions are many and varied. Never boring. Russians pride themselves in living life to fullest. Ve court adventure like beautiful voman. Such as you," he added with a rakish smile.

"Hmmm." As if pondering his answer, Lady Weath-

ersby leaned forward, filled her spoon with turtle soup, and slipped it into her mouth with slow deliberation. Assured the Count's gaze fell and rose with the movement of her bosom, she drew the utensil out, careful to leave a few drops so it dribbled onto her breasts.

"Oh, my. How careless of me," she cooed, watching heat flare in the Count's eyes as he followed the progress of the liquid until it disappeared into the deep valley between the bountiful twin mounds. She wondered if, like her, he was imagining his tongue traversing the same path.

She was rewarded with an answer when his tongue came out to lick his full, firm lips.

Stretching across the table, he offered her his serviette. "Thank you," she said, adding a hint of sultriness to the smile she gave him as she accepted the square of fabric. With fastidious care she dabbed . . . rubbed . . . dabbed a little more until satisfied every drop was sopped up.

Throughout the remainder of the dinner, Lady Weathersby continued her silent little game. Making sure her breasts jiggled with each breathy laugh at the most inane jokes from her dinner companions. Slowly licking a drop of pudding off her finger. Reaching farther than necessary to obtain something being handed to her. Or . . . licking lips left wet with ruby wine.

The look the Count gave her was in no way blasé when he rose to follow the men for port and cigars.

Secure in her conquest, she excused herself, feigning a headache, and called for her coach. All the way home, she wondered if she should receive the Count tomorrow when he would surely call, or make him wait another day.

Anticipation was such a potent aphrodisiac.

Later, in her bedroom as she combed her waist-length brown curls in front of the mirror, she was still pondering that exact thing when she was startled by a dark shape looming outside her balcony.

"Who's there?" she gasped, standing so quickly the chair she'd been sitting in toppled to the floor.

The French doors parted on a blast of frigid air. The large figure of a man remained in shadow, outside the reach of the light from the low-burning fire in the hearth.

Filling her lungs with air, Lady Weathersby was about to scream when the man stepped farther into the room, revealing his handsome, set features.

"Ven you tease a Russian, my little darling, you must be prepared to pay the price. I am no milksop Englishman to be toyed vit. There is Cossack blood running through my veins."

"I have no idea what you mean, Count Torsukov."

"Nicholi," he corrected. "Since ve are about to become lovers, there is no need for formality."

"You presume too much," she protested impudently. "How dare you come here uninvited—"

"Uninvited?" He tossed back his head for a deep-throated laugh. "Do you vish to explain to my hard shaft how uninvited it is? Even now, it strains to slip between your creamy thighs and lose itself in your deep honey pool. You are an expert, madame. Vith each look, flick of your tongue, and deliberate exposure of your lovely, large breasts, my rod grew harder and harder until I nearly embarrassed myself. Imagine how humiliated I vould have been vitout even tiny serviette to cover my shame, since I so generously gave it to you."

She couldn't help the tiny smile that caressed the

corners of her mouth. "I find it hard to believe you could ever be shamed—Nicholi. And I thank you for the compliment on my skills of seduction, but I fear you are terribly mistaken."

Within a heartbeat he was before her—his hands gripping her shoulders, his large body blocking the cold wind still streaming into the room.

She should be freezing, standing there in only a flimsy pink silk nightrail, while he stood covered in a heavy, lush, white fur coat. She wasn't.

"Shall I see for myself how mistaken I am?" He gripped the neckline of her sheer gown in both hands, his cold knuckles coming into contact with her breasts. Her nipples puckered.

He yanked.

The first contact of his chilled hands cupping her bosom caused her to gasp. "Cold. . . ."

"Not for long," he countered, squeezing and kneading and then surrounding her long, pointy nipples with the warm moist heat of his mouth.

She groaned. The luxurious fur of his coat brushed against her naked flesh, causing her entire body to tingle. She went limp.

Relinquishing her breast, he caught her in the circle of his arms. "Do you vish to tell me now how uninvited I am? Or do you vish to spread legs in invitation and make me velcome?"

"Yes, and more," she whispered, giving up any pretense of not wanting him.

"Allow me to make sure you get it," he growled, taking the lobe of her ear between his teeth and biting down until she yelped. "I must vorn you, men are taught stamina from a young age in my country. Is necessary for

riding long and hard over vast plains of Russia. I do not tire easily."

"Although I thank you for the consideration, I think you will find me an excellent rider with a stamina to match your own."

"Then let us delay no more," he said and, with a flourish, removed his floor-length coat and tossed it down before the fireplace.

When she tried to step around him, he grabbed her wrist. "Vhere are you going?"

"To close the doors."

"No need. I intend to make you so hot, you vill be only too glad to feel cold air rush across your fevered skin."

The promise in his voice made her tremble with lust. Never had she met a man so sure of himself, so domineering. The experience was daunting and thrilling. Had she finally met her match? A man who could deliver what he promised? She couldn't wait to find out.

Together they made short work of his clothes. When he was gloriously naked, she allowed herself the opportunity to relish the fact that his meaty member was proportionate to his large physique. Never had she seen a more delectable phallus. Her mound throbbed for wanting. Her mouth watered, anxious to taste.

She halted him when he made to lay her before the hearth. "A brief taste first," she stated and fell to her knees. Unresisting, he buried his hands in her hair as she wrapped both hands around his massive member. She ran her tongue lightly across the head. Sucked the tip into her mouth. Unable to consume the whole of it, she contented herself with half, the tiny veins and ridges of his velvety stiff rod tantalizing her lips. She traced

*each nuance with her tongue, learning the intricate
terrain.*

*"Enough." His soft roar was subdued by his passion.
Fisting his hands in her hair, he applied light force to
bring her to her feet where he proceeded to kiss her senseless.*

*Long, kiss-drugged minutes later, they plummeted
together to the opulent fur at their feet.*

*On his knees, between her legs,˙ he placed his large
hands at the back of her thighs and spread her wide. He
turned his head to either side, gracing each of her ankles
with a slow, licking tribute.*

*"I have come calling, my hot, juicy vixen. Invite your
Cossack in." His demand was accompanied ʋy an inces-
sant pushing against the soft, wet petals of her femininity.*

*"Oh yes, Nicholi. Please enter my humble domain."
His eyes sparkled, giving the appearance of black
diamonds in the firelight, and she buried her hands in
the thick animal fur beneath her.*

He crossed her threshold in one powerful lunge.

The air whooshed through Julia's lungs like a bellows.
The beating of her heart was so rapid, she feared fainting.
My God! She never dreamt a woman would do such a thing.
It had been shocking when Brandon had placed his mouth
on her, but to place hers on him? To take his shaft into her
mouth? She remembered the sensations that had enveloped her body when he'd pleasured her in that way. She'd felt
helpless and at his complete mercy. Would he feel the same?
Could that be the way to make him lose his staunch control?

But the main obstacle remained fixed in her mind. Could
she find the courage to do it?

* * * * *

DINNER WAS A FUN, informal affair. It could be nothing less with the animated Amelia present. Julia liked the other woman from the start. James and Amelia surely knew what Julia's unchaperoned presence meant in Brandon's house, but not once did the couple make her feel self-conscious or awkward. On the contrary, they seemed to go out of their way to make her feel anything but.

"I do hope Mandy likes England," Amelia said excitedly. "I'm so looking forward to her visit next season."

"Please tell me your cousin is nothing like you? I fear London may not be ready for another," Brandon said with droll agony, reaching for his glass of wine.

"Oh, Brandon, you are such a tease. But you need not worry. Mandy is nothing like me."

"My faith in divine intervention has miraculously been restored." Lifting his crystal goblet in toast, he took a drink.

Amelia smiled innocently. "Actually, she's much more outspoken and adventuresome."

Brandon choked on the liquid barely halfway down his throat.

Laughing, James immediately went to his friend's aid, applying several solid whacks between his shoulder blades.

Amelia giggled outright, while Julia stifled hers behind a napkin.

The remainder of the meal was relatively uneventful and, at its end, the men excused themselves to the library and the women retired to the parlor.

"Sherry?" Amelia offered, walking over to the crystal decanter on a side table. She'd barely begun to pour, when she stopped. "Oh, I'm so sorry. I hope I didn't offend you. As the lady of the household, I believe it's your right to serve." Placing the decanter back down, she heaved a little sigh. "I wonder if I'll ever become accustomed to all the little rules

you English live by." She smiled. "You know, if it were Mandy, she'd probably chug the stuff straight from the bottle." A challenging twinkle lit her eyes.

Julia looked at her a bit skeptically.

"Well?"

"It would be most improper," Julia warned, with dwindling conviction.

"Yes . . . it would," the other woman tempted, knowing her companion was wavering.

Years of staunch discipline and breeding warred inside Julia. She shouldn't. Oh, botheration. After all, what harm could it do to a reputation already torn to shreds by becoming Brandon's mistress? "As your hostess, I feel it my duty to instruct you in the proper way to see to a guest's comforts," she said in her most formal voice, trying to keep her lips from twitching as a small frown turned down the corners of Amelia's mouth. "Therefore, as is *proper* . . . I must insist you go first."

A radiant smile lit Amelia's face. "I knew we would get along *smashingly*," she said, mimicking Julia's British accent to perfection. She raised the bottle in salute. Tilting it forward and her head back, she took a deep, manly drink. "Your turn."

Taking in a large breath, Julia reached for the vessel.

At her hesitation, Amelia offered an encouraging smile. "Go on."

Closing her eyes, Julia placed her lips to the opening and allowed the liquid to fill her mouth. She swallowed. Her eyes shot open. She gasped. Coughed. Gasped again.

"Not bad. However, I do believe a bit more practice is in order." Grasping Julia's hand, Amelia pulled her over to the fireplace and plopping down on the dense, soft Oriental rug, encouraged her new friend to do likewise.

Tossing decorum to the wind, Julia copied the other woman's cross-legged position.

Amelia grinned in approval.

Several healthy swigs later, Julia stated in a subdued voice. "Thank you, Amelia."

"For what?"

"You must be aware of my status in this house, yet you have been gracious enough not to call attention to it. As a Duchess, you would be in your full right to give me the cut direct."

"Oh, p . . . Oh, pi . . . pish-posh as you English would say." Amelia beamed at having finally gotten the term past her numb lips.

"I will understand fully if you do not wish to acknowledge me should we ever meet in London. I suppose I shall have to get used to being shunned by society now that everyone knows."

Amelia gave an indelicate snort. "Julia. You are such a ninny." Ignoring the woman's startled expression, she continued, "No one in London knows of your *arrangement*. Brandon has seen to that. Why do you think we are here?"

"What are you thay . . . saying?" Julia asked, having a bit of difficulty with her own speech.

"He hasn't told you?"

"Told me what?"

"Why, that everyone thinks you have been spending the last week in the company of the exalted . . . " she gave a willy-nilly wave of her hand, ". . . Duke and Duchess of Malvern."

"What!"

"Even your friend, Lady Isabella. Who should be arriving tomorrow, by the way. Has no idea." She narrowed her eyes. "Unless, you told her."

"No, I have not. I could not bring myself to tell her. I—"

"Well, that cinches it. Your secret is safe."

"Why would he go to such le . . . engths?" Julia ended on a hiccup. Her hand flew to her mouth.

Amelia giggled and held up a finger. After taking another sip from the near-empty decanter, she passed it to Julia. Face frozen into a wide grin, she waited until the other woman drained the last drops before answering. "Who knows? Men in love do the strangest things."

The crystal left Julia's fingers, landing with a heavy thunk. "No. You are mistaken. Brandon has made it quite clear he wants nothing from me but my—my body," she finished, squaring her shoulders. No small effort, considering the mellowing effects of the alcohol she'd consumed.

"Oh, I am quite sure he has. Most likely because he doesn't even realize it himself yet. But I've seen the way he follows your every movement, devouring you with his eyes when he thinks no one is watching. Then, there is the way you watch him. . . ." Amelia's grin was a tad lopsided.

"Pre . . . prep . . . Preposterous," Julia sputtered. "Either the sherry has dulled your wits, or you yourself are so enamored of your husband you envision love where none exists."

"Perhaps," Amelia conceded. But the woman's secretive smile left Julia with the impression she did not agree in the least.

Brandon in love with her and she with him—what utterly ridiculous drivel!

But the niggling notion lingered. Right up until the time Julia eased down to lay her head on the floor and closed her eyes.

BYPASSING THE PORT SET out on a silver server, Brandon strode to the far side of the library to a tall cupboard and

extracted a bottle of his best cognac. Bringing the bottle and two glasses over to where James had made himself comfortable in a chair before the fireplace, he poured them both a drink.

Taking a sip of the dark golden liquid, James closed his eyes in appreciation before resting his gaze on Brandon. "Tell me what's happened," he stated without preamble. "Has there been another attempt on your life?"

"Four actually," Brandon returned, intently studying the liquor he was twirling in his glass before raising it to his lips.

"Curse the bloody bastard," James spat, springing from the chair to pace.

"And one murder," Brandon added before downing the rest of the drink.

James came to an abrupt stop. "Murder! Who, for God's sake?"

"Sit, and I will tell you everything. Pacing will accomplish nothing. Lord knows I have done enough of it to know."

When James did as bade, Brandon relayed the details of each circumstance. Before the litany was over, several more glasses of cognac were consumed with little thought to savoring the expensive liquor's flavor.

"If you wish to leave and take your wife to London, I completely understand," Brandon said.

"What of Miss Freemont? If she remains here, surely all your efforts to protect her reputation will have been in vain."

"Julia stays."

The speed with which the reply was delivered took James off guard. He smiled. "So that's the way of it, is it?"

Brandon gave him a warning look. "There is no *way of it*. I merely sought to allow her an adjustment period. Oftentimes things do not turn out as we wish." He frowned down into the glass dangling between his fingers.

James sat up straighter in his chair. "These words from the all powerful and mighty Brandon Barringer, who lets nothing stand in his way. I am humbly amazed," he chortled.

Brandon glared. "If you need assistance in packing, I shall be more than happy to aid you."

"That won't be necessary," James said, his tone serious. "Between the two of us, I'm sure we can provide enough safety for the women."

"And Robert," Brandon put in helpfully.

"Yes, of course. How could I have forgotten Robert ... the brave hearted," he finished on a note of disgust.

"Why is it I seem to be the only one to see the good in my cousin? As far as I know, he has done little—"

"The point, exactly. He has done little except live off the largess of his father and now your grandfather. He and that wretched mother of his."

"Please, James, enough. I fear we shall never be in accord where Robert is concerned. All I ask is that you afford him a bit of respect while he is here." He held up his hand at the deep frown on his companion's face. "If not for his sake, for the sake of our friendship."

"You know I would do anything for you. I consider you as a brother." The statement was followed by a heavy sigh. "I shall endeavor to try."

Brandon smiled, some of his humor restored at both his friend's declaration and his pained expression. Extracting his watch, he gave it a quick check. "Enough serious talk for one night," he said, tucking it back into his pocket. "I suggest we go and see what the women are up to."

22

THE MEN ENTERED THE parlor expecting to find a couple of chattering women. What they found was two sleeping and apparently soused ones—if the empty bottle of sherry was any indication. The fact that no glasses could be found among the yards of pink and yellow silk surrounding the women made Brandon shake his head and James grin.

"I see I shall have to limit Julia's exposure to your wife. Your Duchess is already teaching her inappropriate habits," Brandon whispered.

"In light of my wife's inability to take exception to that remark, I protest on her behalf. Who is to say it was not *your Julia* who instigated such behavior?"

Brandon leveled a playfully scathing look on his friend. "*Miss Freemont* is a well-bred English lady."

"Uh . . . uh . . . careful, old chap. I would hate to have to second my wife when she called you out for impugning her good character."

Both men chuckled softly, each bending to pick up their respective women.

James looked at Brandon. "Would you think it rather presumptuous for me to deduce the Malvern heir will have no chance of being conceived this night?" His smile faded only slightly as he placed a gentle kiss upon his wife's forehead.

"I would think it a safe bet to place in the book at White's,"

Brandon murmured, looking down at the limp woman in his arms. His voice was devoid of sympathy, knowing he would be experiencing a similar fate.

ARMS LINKED IN COMPANIONABLE agony, both Julia and Amelia slowly entered the breakfast room the next morning.

"Good morning, ladies," the men said together, hastily gaining their feet with a loud scrape of their chairs.

Both women winced, repeating the gesture when the men solicitously seated them amidst another grating of chair legs on the oak floor.

"Allow me to serve you," Brandon said, moving off before Julia could tell him she had no taste for anything but an entire bucket of coffee, something Amelia had assured her would have her feeling as feisty as a polecat in no time. She had no idea what a polecat was, but anything was bound to be better than how she currently felt.

"And I shall serve my lovely wife," James offered cheerfully, eliciting a low moan from Amelia.

Within moments, both women were served.

Through bleary eyes, Julia stared down at the heaping plate, easily three times more than her usual portion. Her stomach rolled uneasily as the aromas of fish and eggs wafted up to greet her. Glancing across the table, she saw that Amelia was faring no better.

As if in mutual agreement, the two women stood abruptly and, excusing themselves, fled the room, the men's laughter floating behind them.

"I would imagine," Brandon said, once able to catch his breath, "the heir you plan on conceiving will no doubt be delayed another week or so, after this bit of mischief."

"A day, perhaps. No more. Amelia has never been able to hold out very long against my masterful persuasion," James bragged with a grin. "That is one of the advantages of sharing a bed, my friend. It gives a woman little space to run."

Yes, Brandon was well aware of the concept. The only problem was there was currently a door between his bed and the woman he most wanted in it. And the situation was bound to get worse once Robert and Isabella arrived.

HAVING HAD THEIR FUN, the men were on their best behavior the next time the women appeared. The foursome was enjoying a light snack in the parlor. The women settled on green tea and biscuits; the men gorged themselves on plum cake, fruit tarts, and wine.

Amelia derived great pleasure from subjecting the men to a well-deserved lecture on the advantages American women enjoyed over those of their English sisters.

Brandon rolled his eyes on several occasions.

James grinned.

Julia listened intently.

Their conversation came to an abrupt end at the sound of a coach.

Henry swung the outer door open at the exact moment the two couples spilled into the foyer.

The first visitor to be handed from the coach was an immaculately coiffured blonde woman.

"Isabella!" Julia gasped out, rushing to greet her friend.

"Julia! I have missed you terribly." A long hug ensued. Isabella braced her hands on Julia's arms and stepped back to run an assessing gaze over her childhood friend. "How are you faring?"

Having seen Isabella but once after her father's suicide, Julia knew there was more to the question than casual courtesy. "Well. Very well," she added. "The Duke and Duchess have been most entertaining. I cannot thank them enough for their generosity and *discretion* . . . " Julia shot a meaningful glance toward Brandon. ". . . in dealing with the matter of my father's death," she finished for Isabella's sake.

Reading the silent gratitude in Julia's eyes, Brandon acknowledged it with a barely perceptible nod.

A low grunt from the direction of the coach caught everyone's attention as a generously proportioned, elderly woman began to descend with the aid of two stout servants.

"Oh, goodness. I forgot all about Winnefred," Isabella said, rushing over to the woman's side. "I'm terribly sorry, Winny. Are you in a great deal of discomfort?"

"Don't you be worrying about your old nanny, my little chick." She patted her ward on the cheek as if she were still a small child. "A little stiff is all. These old bones are not accustomed to so many hours in a carriage—fine as it is. If Mr. Barringer would be kind enough to allow me a few hours' rest and some food, I'll be continuing on."

"I would be happy to supply anything you need, madame. You need only to ask Henry."

Henry immediately stepped forward to offer his arm to the elderly woman.

"Most kind of you. I won't be imposing long, as I am on my way to visit my daughter. I was happy to escort Lady Isabella, and it will give me time to see my new grandson. I shall return in ten days' time to accompany her home." Leaning heavily on Henry's arm she ascended the steps. Before stepping through the front door, she paused to eye the men skeptically and run a shrewd glance over Amelia.

"Thank you for bringing Lady Isabella to us," Amelia stated sweetly.

The woman bobbed a quick curtsy. "No disrespect intended, Your Grace, but I still cannot fathom how you talked Lady Isabella's mother into allowing her to come. You're a trifle young to be a chaperone—married or not."

The new Duchess gave her a conciliatory smile. "Young perhaps, but with the eyes of a hawk. I will watch over her with the same devotion as you would. I give you my word."

"I believe you," the nanny said, taking the unheard-of liberty of patting the Duchess of Malvern's cheek. With a smile that only added more creases to a face already heavily crinkled with age, she allowed Henry to lead her away.

No sooner had Isabella's coach headed for the stables than another one pulled up.

Robert, the last of Brandon's houseguests, had arrived.

HAD AMELIA BEEN ANYONE other than Malvern's wife, Brandon would have taken the billiard stick he was holding and swatted her pesky backside.

Now here he was, because of Amelia's plea to be taught the game, watching Julia stretched low across the slate table, the long stick sliding rhythmically between her slender fingers as she attempted to make her shot.

It had been hard enough to concentrate on dinner and the lively conversation flowing around him with Julia constantly bending over her meal, her creamy breasts threatening to spill out. Not to mention the time she'd dabbed away a dribble of wine from her cleavage. And the incident with the pudding . . . when she'd slid her finger into her mouth and delicately sucked it clean.

He tightened his grip on the cue stick, in an attempt to clear his mind of the vivid memory. It took only one look at her to realize the attempt would be futile.

Had her necklines always been that low?

Perhaps if he concentrated on riding?

He got an instant image of her seated facing him in the saddle, his manhood slipping in and out of her hot welcoming canal to the cadence of the horse's stride.

Perhaps a cock fight? No, definitely not.

Ahh, pugilism. It worked for a short while until the thought of pummeling flesh took on a whole new connotation.

His jaw was so clenched Brandon could feel his back teeth grinding together. If he made it through the next hour without spending himself in his breeches, it would be a damned miracle. With Isabella now inconveniently ensconced in Julia's room, he would have relatively little access to his mistress other than in the company of others. One would think she was teasing him on purpose. But she was too new at this game of seduction to have learned such a blatant skill.

It took his overheated mind a moment to comprehend that the heavy sigh filling the room was not from him, but from Julia as she straightened.

"I fear I shall never get the hang of this game." She sighed, her mouth pursing into a pretty pout.

To Brandon the sound seemed more one of pleasure than frustration. And that mouth. . . .

"Might you show me again how to align the balls with the hole and stroke the stick, *Mr. Barringer*?"

A groan clogged Brandon's throat. Was she daring him to kiss her for addressing him formally?

"Perhaps Robert would consent to instruct you since he is on your side of the table," he suggested, as casually as his raging lust would allow.

"I shall be happy to assist you, Miss Freemont," Robert offered, coming to stand next to her.

Her attention slow in leaving Brandon, she smiled at the man whose light brown, curly hair lent him an air of innocent boyish appeal. "Please, call me Julia."

"Only if you return the favor by calling me Robert. It seems informality is the order of the day among everyone here. I would wish the same courtesy."

"Very well, Robert. Is this how it is done?" She bent over the table once again, so low the very tip of her breast brushed the stick as she repositioned it between her fingers.

The stick in Brandon's hand fell to the black walnut parquet floor with a clatter. "I beg pardon," he said, picking it up as all gazes centered on him. "A tad too much chalk on the hands." The roll of James's eyes told him at least one person in the room hadn't bought the lame excuse.

To hide the satisfied smile that threatened to break, Julia lowered her head, giving the appearance of aligning her shot.

Thank you, Lady Weathersby.

With a clean, even stroke, she knocked the winning ball into the pocket.

While the others gathered around Julia to extend their congratulations, Brandon pulled out his watch and flipped open the case. "I hadn't realized how late it was. I rather think Lady Isabella would benefit from a good night's sleep after her arduous journey," he stated before anyone could collect the balls for another game. He was relatively sure he'd be unable to control his mounting sexual urges. It had been one of the reasons he was careful to remain on the opposite side of the table whenever Julia bent over to make a shot. Knowing she wore no undergarments, all he could think of was walking up behind her, lifting her dress, spreading the sweet cheeks of her arse, and plunging deep inside her.

"How accommodating of you."

"Excuse me?" Brandon's gaze flew to Julia, only to realize it was Isabella who'd spoken.

"You are the most thoughtful of hosts," Isabella went on to clarify. "I *am* rather tired, and relish the thought of sleeping in a fresh, comfortable bed tonight. The one at the inn we stopped at last evening was as lumpy as oatmeal, and I decline to venture a guess as to the cleanliness. I would like to request something else of you if you would not mind?"

"Anything," Brandon said.

"Might I not be afforded the same courtesy as the others? Please call me Isabella."

"As you wish."

"Thank you. Now I believe I shall retire." She turned to her fiancé. "Good night, *Robert*," she said, addressing him by his given name for the first time.

"Isabella," he returned with his usual respectful nod, giving no indication if he took any pleasure from the informality.

"If everyone will excuse me, I believe I shall join Isabella," Julia stated and, hooking an arm through her friend's, began exiting the room. "Good night everyone."

"Julia?"

The two women paused, turning at the sound of Brandon's voice.

"Yes?" Julia asked.

"I had hoped for a *private* moment with you to discuss a matter of some importance that has recently *arisen*."

She belatedly covered a small yawn. "Could it not wait until morning? I slept most fitfully last night and find myself extremely exhausted," she demurred. "I am quite sure I would be unable to give the matter the attention it deserves."

"I suppose there is no choice but to wait. I would not be

so rude as to insist. Although I am *achingly* disappointed," he said.

"I promise to *present* myself to you at the first opportunity in the morning," she said, wisely softening the rejection. "Sleep well." Tugging Isabella from the room, she dared not look over her shoulder.

Amelia walked up to her husband. "If you don't mind, dear, I think I shall join them," she said, rising on tiptoes to kiss his cheek.

"Not at all. The additional rest would do you good." Bending closer to her ear, James whispered, "Since I plan on keeping you up for the better part of the night once I join you."

Giving him an inviting smile, she bid the other two gentlemen goodnight and quit the room.

When she was gone, James folded his arms across his chest and confronted Brandon with a disgruntled look. "Since you've managed to deprive us of the lovely female company we were enjoying, perhaps we should move to the library for some port. Unless, of course, you were thinking of sending Robert and me off to bed?"

Turning on his heel, Brandon placed his stick back in the wooden rack on the wall with a snap and stomped from the room.

Sharing a rare smile, Robert and James followed.

23

BREAKFAST HAD BARELY ENDED the next morning when Henry approached Julia with a discreet summons to meet Brandon in the library.

Entering the room, she found herself yanked into Brandon's arms for a demanding kiss, which, to her mild annoyance, she reciprocated wholeheartedly.

The door was latched. The bare cheeks of her backside were pressed against the rigid wood panels and her stomach locked against the swelling member inside Brandon's straining breeches. But she had no one to blame—*or credit*, said the wanton little devil's voice inside her—but herself. For, determined to continue her daring game of the prior evening, she had brazenly hiked up the skirt of her dress in bold offering, revealing her red-laced garters. And nothing more but that which she'd been born with.

Brandon had wasted no time in taking advantage.

"I love the way you get wet for me—your juices hot and creamy." His words were a warm gust of breath against the sensitized skin of Julia's neck. He flexed his wrist, deepening the caress of the fingers he had wedged inside her. "You're close. I can feel it," he whispered when she squirmed against his palm; he felt the walls of her womanhood flicker. He rotated his fingers, gliding easily back and forth.

Julia moaned, the sensation driving her to the brink.

He slid in a third finger—it went in easily, stretching

her wider. "Soon, it will be my shaft thrusting its way past this thin barrier at the tip of my fingers, bringing you into womanhood." Using his long middle finger, he made a tentative foray the slightest bit deeper and then retreated.

When he withdrew his fingers completely to suck them clean, Julia nearly screamed. To prevent it, she bit down on her bottom lip.

"God, you have no idea how much I want you right now. But the first time I take you will not be up against a door. The gift of your maidenhead deserves more respect than that."

"You're leaving me like this?" Julia inquired, hating the pleading tone in her voice. "Damn you and your control, Brandon Barringer."

Surprise flashed in his eyes. "My control? I hadn't realized my control had become such an issue with you." He chuckled lightly. "Sweetheart, men aplenty have attempted to batter down my control. I would not pin your hope on doing so. Although I will admit you have managed to put several rather large holes in it."

His tone was light and teasing, and she wanted nothing more than to slap him. "Release me," she demanded, trying to squirm out from between him and the door.

He pressed his body more fully into hers. Flattening his palms against the door on either side of her head, he boxed her in. "And leave you wanting? I wouldn't dream of it. I have been accused of many things, but never of being a selfish lover."

"I wish to—"

The kiss he silenced her with was hot and wet and consuming, melting her anger and her inclination to leave, like sun-warmed ice cream.

"And I . . . " He began kissing his way down her front, his hot, heavy breath and moist mouth searing her through the

delicate fabric of her dress as he lowered himself to his knees.
". . . wish to finish what I began." The last of the husky whisper
was muffled in the downy, black hair between her legs.

CHATTING HAPPILY WITH ISABELLA later that day, Amelia
paused as they entered the upper hall. "Do you hear that?"

Isabella listened. "It sounds like weeping."

"Precisely. And if I'm not mistaken, I believe it to be
coming from Julia's room." Frowning, Amelia hurried over
to the door and, disregarding all propriety, pressed her ear
against it. She knocked softly. Receiving no answer, her frown
deepened. Placing her hand on the door handle, she looked
at Isabella. At the other woman's nod, she pressed down the
lever and very slowly opened the door.

The sight of Julia huddled in the middle of her bed,
trying to stifle her sobs into a pillow, prompted both women
to rush forward.

"Julia, darling. What is it?" Scooting on the bed, Isabella
placed a comforting hand on her friend's back.

"Yes, do tell us. Perhaps we can help." Amelia's softly
spoken entreaty brought Julia to a sitting position.

"I'm afraid no one can help," she managed to get out on a
hiccup sob. "I am beyond redemption." She sucked in several
rapid, shaky breaths. Her attempt to wipe at her tear-swollen
eyes only managed to smear the dampness across her blotchy,
reddened cheeks.

"Was it Mr. Barringer?" Isabella demanded. "If the brute
has harmed you in any way—" Her words were cut short
when Julia placed her fingers lightly over her friend's lips.

Taking her hand away, Julia dropped it into her lap with
the other. Head bent, she said, "He has done nothing I haven't

allowed. That is the whole of the problem. But I beg you, do not press me to tell more, for you surely will scorn me once you have heard. I have lost so much, I could not bear to lose your friendship as well." Her gaze moved from Isabella to Amelia. "Either of you."

"Oh, Julia," Amelia sighed, joining the other two women on the bed. "Don't be such a lettucehead."

Even in her misery, the statement brought a watery smile to Julia's lips.

"I think you mean *cabbagehead*," Isabella corrected.

"Oh, sorry," Amelia said with a sheepish smile. "At any rate, my point is that a true friend would never scorn you. And although I cannot claim the pleasure of your acquaintance as long as Isabella, I would hope to be counted a true friend. You see, it is not easy for an *upstart American* to make friends here among the female aristocracy. Many regard me as something of a heathen." She shrugged, but there was no dismissing the pain beneath her words.

"She is right, you know," Isabella stated firmly. "There is nothing you can tell me that would make me denounce our friendship."

Offering a weak smile, Julia drew in two shuddering breaths.

For several moments, no on spoke.

Gathering her courage, Julia looked at Isabella and said, "I've become Brandon's mistress." Encouraged when her friend didn't immediately leap from the bed and run screaming from the room, she continued. "And . . ." her voice lowered in misery, ". . . I fear I have done the worse thing a woman could do in this situation—I have fallen in love with my benefactor."

Julia felt her eyes filling again, but refused to divert her gaze. "He is not at all the man I believed him to be. He is not

in the least pretentious or grasping. He puts on no airs. He is kind to everyone—his own servants, those in need. It is true he is exacting and stubborn. Determined to have his way in all things. But even with me he has shown great restraint and consideration. Especially for my . . . inexperience." One tear overflowed, followed by another and another, each drop falling on the clenched hands in her lap.

"You poor dear," Isabella said, throwing her arms around her friend.

Once released, Julia looked toward Amelia, who had remained suspiciously silent. "Have you nothing to say?"

"I'm waiting," Amelia said.

"Waiting? Waiting for what?"

"The really horrible thing you've done that will turn us away. Have you kicked a dog?"

Julia sat up straighter. "Of course not. I would never do such a thing?"

"No dog, huh? Slap a servant perhaps?"

"Absolutely not. How could you think such a thing?"

"Hmmm . . . no dog and no servant. I know, you've killed someone and buried them in the rose garden on some dark and stormy night."

Before Julia's ire could peak into a full-blown eruption, she heard Isabella's soft giggle. It was then she realized what the Duchess was doing.

"Perhaps I shall invite *you* to join me for a stroll in the *rose garden* the next time I go," Julia suggested, allowing a cleansing laugh to escape.

This time, all three women threw themselves together for a prolonged hug.

"Come on," Amelia said, taking charge after they broke apart. "Let's get you out of this bed and cleaned up so we can decide what to do." Pulling Julia to her feet, she tugged her

over to the window seat and settled her there, while Isabella
went to dampen a cloth.

Refreshed, relieved, and with her back propped up
by several pillows, Julia looked at the two women who had
settled in next to her. "So, you don't think ill of me?" Julia
asked, still in a euphoric state of disbelief that they hadn't
shunned her.

"Whatever for?" asked Amelia, frowning slightly. "So far,
all you have told us is that like many women before you, you
have given yourself to a man you love out of wedlock."

Julia had not been acquainted with her new friend long
enough to question the secretive glint that lit Amelia's eyes.

"I agree," Isabella chimed in. "Not so long ago I would
have questioned why you would do such a thing. Demanded
why you had not turned to me for help. I now realize there
are worse fates than being a rich, handsome, passionate man's
mistress. It is markedly preferable to being a rich, dispas-
sionate man's wife."

Julia's eyes narrowed at the dry tone in which the statement was delivered. "Isabella?"

"Well, it's true," she said, with a staunch gaze. "If you can
find the courage to bare your soul, I should think it only fair
I do the same."

"What could you possibly have to confess?" The question
was posed with a lift of one finely arched brow. "You have
ever been a model of decorum and virtue."

"Only because I was never brave like you," Isabella stated,
shocking her friend. "I have always envied you your bravery
and adventuresome nature. While you swept through life, I
merely picked up one foot and fastidiously placed it in front
of the other. Because it was expected of me."

"You never said."

"I know." Isabella lowered her lashes and sighed. "You

see . . . I was not even brave enough to tell you. Perhaps it is the reason Robert shows so little interest in me. Perhaps he abhors cowards."

"Why, that's utterly ridiculous," Amelia piped up. "If that were the case, why would he have asked for your hand? He must hold you in some affection."

Isabella turned a bland eye toward Amelia. "Now who is being naïve? We both know there are any number of reasons for a man to take a wife—the least of which having anything to do with love. Especially a wife with a large dowry and impeccable lineage."

Julia gave a notable wince.

"Oh, dear." Isabella cut her recitation short. "Forgive me, Julia, I didn't mean. . . ."

"No need to apologize. After all, it is the truth. I have no dowry, and my *impeccable lineage* ended with father's suicide." She could say the word now without the devastating pain that usually followed.

"At least the man you care for desires you, whereas I have yet to be kissed," Isabella divulged in a rush.

"Are you saying Robert has never—not even once—kissed you in the entire year you have been betrothed?" Julia's face registered her surprise.

"Not once."

"Maybe he needs a little encouragement," Amelia suggested.

A becoming pink tinged Isabella's cheeks. "I tried. Once."

"What happened?" her companions asked simultaneously.

"He told me there would be plenty of time for such foolish intimacies after we married. Therefore, no need to risk being caught in such an unsuitable public display."

Amelia's countenance turned sour. "It's times like

these that I miss my cousin, Amanda. And . . . that damned pepperbox she's so fond of carrying."

"Pepperbox?" Julia tilted her head.

"Pistol."

"Pistol!" Isabella squeaked. "Your cousin carries a weapon?"

"Yes. And I will be happy to tell you all about her and . . . her little eccentricities another time. But we are straying from the main problem—Julia's predicament with Brandon."

"I am afraid there is little to be done," Julia offered, her tone melancholy.

"Why do you think that?" Amelia shot back.

"Brandon has made it quite clear that although he is desirous of my body, I am no longer suitable to become his wife. A position, I shamefully admit, I found objectionable myself until only today when I realized my feelings toward him."

"Well, Brandon's wanting you is a *good* thing. Mandy always says a way to a man's heart is through his pecker."

"Through his chin?" Isabella looked askance.

"Oh, dear. I forgot some American words don't hold the same meaning here in England. Through his. . . ." Amelia fumbled for an appropriate word. "Oh, fiddlesticks. His *manhood*."

Julia laughed and Isabella blushed to the roots of her hair.

"Anyway," Amelia went on with an impish grin. "Now that he's taken your virtue, it will be easy to use his lust against him."

"Actually he hasn't," Julia stated softly.

"What do you mean he hasn't? You've been together almost an entire week, and you did say you were his mistress," Amelia said.

"I'm rather confused," Isabella inserted. "I thought Julia was in Bath with you?"

"We'll explain later." Amelia waved off her interruption. "Julia, tell us what you mean."

"Well . . . we haven't quite gotten around to *that*. It was to be the night you arrived. Your early arrival completely interrupted Brandon's plans. With Isabella currently sleeping in my room. . . ."

Amelia clapped her hands together. "This is perfect. The man is obviously in love with you by the way he's acting. And—"

"No, I told you he was quite clear on that particular matter."

"Don't interrupt. Besides, you're being a ninnyhummer."

"Hammer," both British women said in unison.

"Whatever. At any rate, why do you think he went to such pains to protect your reputation? Not that I'm an expert on mistresses, mind you, but I do think it rather odd. It seems to me most men would be only too happy to expound upon their prowess. Unless, of course, he cares deeply for the woman."

"You really think so?" For the first time, Julia felt a tiny hope for her future with Brandon.

"Oh, yes. I *really* think so," Amelia stated. "What we need is a plan. First, you need to continue what you were doing last night at billiards."

Julia's eyes widened, her posture becoming more rigid. The crimson blush that filled her cheeks rivaled the one Isabella had suffered earlier. "Was I so obvious?"

"What was she doing?" Isabella asked with furrowed brow.

"Apparently not so obvious to everyone," Amelia said, spearing Isabella with a sympathetic look. "We shall have

to sit down and have a long talk on the subject of men, my dear."

"I should like to know what makes you such an authority on men," Isabella grouched.

"I must agree," Julia said. "After all, we are of the same age."

At Julia's added skepticism Amelia blew a puff of breath out of the side of her mouth, stirring her bangs. "I see I must acquaint the two of you with a very unique and experienced lady by the name of Maude. And *the betting book*. But first, you both must swear, on your honor as women, never to divulge its existence to a single member of the opposite sex. Not even on the threat of death," Amelia ended dramatically.

Intrigued, the other women leaned in closer.

"I swear," Julia stated without hesitation.

"As do I," Isabella added.

"Very well, I shall tell you. But first, I suggest we ring for tea and sandwiches. Once they arrive, I will astonish you with a most entertaining battle tale."

"Battle?" Julia looked doubtful. "What does a war have to do with a betting book?"

"With this particular one, everything. You are about to hear the tale of the capture and downfall of none other than my husband, the Duke of Malvern."

24

"I NEVER DREAMED SUCH a book existed," stated Julia some time later, astounded at the tale Amelia had relayed.

"Well it does," the Duchess assured her with an assertive nod, reaching for her teacup.

"So if I am to understand correctly, one places the name of the man she intends to marry into the book and writes a wager next to it. Much like the men do at White's."

Before answering, Amelia swallowed a sip of tepid tea. "Precisely."

"And any of the previous entrants can take up the wager if they so desire, and if you do not leg-shackle the man you have chosen, you make good on the bet," Isabella clarified further, after taking a dainty bite of a small sandwich.

"Yes." Amelia smiled. "But to my knowledge, no one has ever been required to pay."

"Why is that?" Julia asked.

"Because no one has ever lost," Amelia said impudently.

"No one?" Julia's shock was mirrored by the expression on Isabella's face.

"Not a single one," Amelia confirmed. "You see, once your name is in the book, you become a part of a sisterhood of sorts. Able to draw upon the help of anyone whose name appears within the pages."

"Will I be allowed to enter my name, do you think?" The tone of Julia's voice was both hopeful and wary.

"Of course." Amelia nodded. "As your new friend, I will personally see to it."

"But how?"

"Yes, how?" Isabella placed her own china cup down to lean closer.

"We will simply take a trip to London. Two days should be sufficient to prepare for the journey, I would think. And of course, we cannot tell the men."

"Not tell them!" Isabella gasped. "You mean leave without their knowledge? Won't the Duke be angry?" she asked, sharing a worried look with Julia.

"Without a doubt," Amelia answered flippantly. "But I shall have ever so much fun making him forgive me."

The three women grinned, and an unbreakable bond was set.

"WHY HAVE YOU WAITED so long to tell me someone has been trying to kill you?" Robert had stopped his pacing in front of the book-lined shelves to face Brandon. "Was it because you suspected I had a hand in it?" Robert shot a searching glance toward James, whose face remained suspiciously impassive.

"Certainly not," Brandon said fervently. "If that were the case, I would hardly be telling you now. At first, the incidents were random and far enough apart to be believed mere coincidence. No longer. Now, I am quite certain they are of malicious intent. I did not wish to burden you with my problems, as you have had enough of your own to deal with of late."

"You mean Mother," Robert stated with jaw clenched. "I am no longer a young boy in need of your protection, cousin. I am quite capable of dealing with her." He paused to brush

at unseen lint on the sleeve of his immaculate brown jacket. "Though why I am surprised you chose James as your confidant I cannot say. The two of you have always been close."

Brandon was not in the least fooled by the air of nonchalance Robert was currently displaying. For some reason beyond comprehension, his cousin had always been tediously resentful of Brandon's close friendship with James.

Heaving a heavy sigh, Brandon rose from his chair and went to Robert. Planting a hand on the other man's shoulder, he gave a quick squeeze. "I am sorry if I have offended you. It was not my intent. We are cousins. I have always had great affection for you."

Robert glanced down at the hand resting upon him. A small smile creased his lips. "And I, more for you," he said, catching Brandon in a quick embrace.

Over his cousin's shoulder, Brandon caught Malvern's grimace. Shooting his friend a stern frown, he cleared his throat and extricated himself. "What needs to be decided is what's to be done," he stated, walking over to pour himself a brandy from the decanter on his desk. After downing it in one gulp, he turned back to the others. "Naturally, the three women upstairs are to be our first priority. They must go nowhere unattended. If we go riding, it would be preferable for the six of us to go together. At the very least two men with the women. My man Matthew is loyal and an excellent horseman, should either of you require his services. I have also retained his brothers, both excellent shots. Every precaution must be taken."

"Might it not be better to inform the women of the danger?" Robert inquired.

"Absolutely not," James said, coming up from his lounging position to sit on the edge of his chair. "Amelia has a damnable liking for intrigue. She would be more likely to go

out in search of the villain." His statement was a mixture of worry, humor, and pride.

"I must agree with James," Brandon said. "I think in this particular situation, the women are better left unaware. Until recently, I had not realized how deuced complicated a woman can make things."

When Brandon returned to the decanter to pour another drink, a frown formed on Robert's face, while James merely settled back once again in his chair with his own drink and grinned.

THE WOMEN'S PLAN WAS working beautifully.

Over the next day and a half, with the help of her friends, Julia made herself appealing on every level. From the lowest-cut gowns in the sheerest fabrics, to the soft, feminine, upswept coiffures Marie fashioned, their long loose tendrils brushing the delicate curve of her cheek and neck. The kind of tendrils a man liked to toy with while whispering intimacies into a woman's ear, her maid had proclaimed with a sly look.

Julia had practiced her deep, sultry voice and heated looks on her two companions until all three women had tumbled to the bed in a fit of laughter.

But Brandon hadn't laughed once.

His gaze followed her like a flame running a trail of gunpowder.

And, as requested, she offered herself to him whenever the occasion arose.

With one exception.

On each of those occasions, either Isabella or Amelia was close by for a timely interruption.

So when James suggested an early ride on the second morning, Brandon was more than ready to relieve some of his pent-up frustration with a pell-mell run over the length of his property. Even if it were a sad substitute for the kind of ride he would have preferred.

Watching from an upstairs window until the men were out of sight, Julia let the curtain she was peering through drop back into place. "They're gone," she announced, turning toward Isabella and Amelia, who were busy packing a few necessities into a small bag.

"And Robert?" asked Amelia, brushing at several strands of blonde hair that had fallen into her eyes.

"He must still be in the house," Julia supplied.

"No. I saw him ride out earlier." This from Isabella.

Amelia smiled. "That leaves only one more obstacle—Matthew."

"No need to worry, Marie is taking care of him. It seems he's taken quite a liking to her, and she's decided now would be a most convenient time to let him know his interest is shared. She has arranged for him to meet her in the buttery."

"You are sure we are doing the right thing, Amelia?" Julia, experiencing a last-minute case of the jitters, walked to her dressing table and began toying with her brush.

"Yes. Quite sure." She held out her hand.

Julia placed both brush and a matching silver mirror into it and watched as they too disappeared into the bag.

"What if he does not come after me? Perhaps he has already tired of me. There are so many more beautiful and experienced women he could have."

"Stop being such a rooster-hearted goosehat."

"*Hen-hearted*! *Goosecap*!" a duet of female voices rang out.

"Ooh, where do you English come up with such ridiculous words anyway? I shall never grasp all these odd sayings.

Well, in American terms . . . stop being such a silly coward." At Julia's wince, she hurriedly inserted, "Sorry. But the situation seemed to call for some bluntness. Of course Brandon will come after you. If there were ever a man who was besotted, it is he. I am more concerned that he shall catch up with us before we even reach London. Our only advantage is that the men will be gone for the better part of the morning and their horses fairly exhausted upon their return."

"How can you be so sure?" Isabella stopped stuffing another gown into the bag long enough to ask.

"Let's just say I have seen the Duke in a similar state a time or two before we wed," Amelia said. Her lips twitched at holding back a grin. "Now," her face smoothed out into more serious lines, "stop delaying before someone comes looking for us—most particularly, Henry. I swear the old gentleman is part hound the way he seems to track us down no matter where we are in this old, rambling house."

Making their way quietly through the *old, rambling house* a scant ten minutes later, Isabella went first. At each hall and turn, she made sure no one was about before waving her friends on. At the door she gave them both a quick hug, wished them Godspeed, and closed the door behind them.

"Was that the door, miss?" Henry inquired solicitously from behind her.

Still clutching the knob in her hand Isabella gasped and nearly reopened the door. Snatching her hand away, she turned.

"Why, yes, Henry, it was. I was feeling the need for a bit of cool air," she lied quickly, hoping the blush she felt rising in her face would not alert him to the bald lie. As he stood there, searching her face, Isabella fought the urge to squirm.

"You do look a bit flushed, miss. Perhaps I should call for the physician?"

"No!" At his startled expression, she tempered her tone. "I mean . . . thank you, Henry, but I am quite sure I will be fine in no time." She waved off the suggestion and headed for the stairs before he could question her further.

Julia and Amelia made it to the stables without mishap. Once there, it was easy to intimidate the young stableboy set to watch the horses. The youth was no match for an imperious, irate Duchess who demanded he saddle two horses.

By the time he gathered enough courage to ask where they were going, the women were situated in their saddles and ready to leave.

"Should anyone inquire, you can tell them we are taking some clothes to the church down the lane to ease the suffering of those less fortunate," Amelia stated calmly, without a blink at the blatant lie.

Turning the horses, the women shared a look of mild regret at the noticeable unease on the boy's face.

Their attention centered on an expedient escape, neither saw Robert standing at the corner of the building.

WALKING THE HORSES THROUGH a small copse of trees after an invigorating headlong ride across an open meadow, Brandon and James were enjoying a companionable silence when the shots rang out.

Brandon jolted at the excruciating burning sensation at his left temple.

Reared back from the impact to his torso.

Heard James shouting.

Felt himself falling.

Made contact with the hard ground.

25

"BRANDON! DAMN YOU, MAN! You had better not be dead," James gritted out, after dragging his friend several feet to take cover behind the first adequate tree he could find.

Setting his pistol down beside him, he began a tentative inspection of a deep gash on Brandon's head. Satisfied that it was more bloody than fatal, James began frantically ripping open his friend's jacket, waistcoat, and shirt. Finding only a large red mark on his lower left side, he rolled him gently to check his back. Nothing.

Easing Brandon to the ground, James leaned back against the tree that was shielding them and released the air trapped in his lungs. Sparing another second to thank the good Lord for his benevolence, he picked up his pistol and listened. A short time later, he heard the sounds of a rapidly retreating horse.

Still, he waited.

When enough time passed to ensure it was not a ploy to entice them out into the open, he carefully uncocked his gun. Setting it down within easy reach, he came to kneel over Brandon and flattened his hand against his friend's bare chest. Relief washed through him at the strong, steady heartbeat that greeted him. Closing his eyes, he sat back down on his heels. The feel of a heavy hand trapping his own brought them back open.

"Julia?" Brandon murmured drowsily.

"No," James exclaimed, snatching his hand back. "And before you try to kiss me, old chap, I suggest you open your eyes."

It took Brandon several seconds before he could focus on the man bending over him. "James?" An attempt to sit up found him again flat on his back. He groaned.

"Lie still. That looks to be a fairly good-sized chunk missing from your head."

"What—" The sound came out as a croak. Taking a deep swallow and licking his lips, Brandon tried again. "What happened?"

"You were shot. Twice," was the clipped reply as James began untying the cravat still around Brandon's neck to use as a bandage for his head.

"Twice?" Brandon's hand immediately went to where he felt a numbing pain below his ribs, frowning when it came away clean.

"Damned if I know," James said, in answer to the bewilderment on his friend's face as he finished securing the makeshift bandage.

Closing his eyes, Brandon let several moments pass before saying, "Get my watch."

"Watch?" James shook his head as if to clear his hearing. "Watch! Are you mad? You cannot possibly mean to check that infernal timepiece of yours!"

Opening his eyes, Brandon smiled. "I have no intention of checking the time. I merely wish to see it."

"Whatever for?" James's look was suspect.

"Indulge me. After all, I'm the one who's lying here half dead."

James gave a snort, but the look on his face was one of intense relief when he reached inside the pocket of Brandon's waistcoat. "I cannot believe you wish to check— Damn

me," he said, staring at the watch dangling from its chain in front of him. Shaking his head, he cupped it in his hand and showed it to Brandon.

Smack dab in the middle was a lead pistol-ball.

Turning it back for another look, James shook his head again. "If I had known how good it was at stopping bullets, I would have used it for target practice long ago." The humorous statement was laden with gruff emotion.

"Very amusing." Brandon's look of mild disgust turned into a grimace as he levered up to his elbows.

Scrambling to help, James assisted him to his feet.

"Did you perchance see who it was?" Brandon asked, once he was fairly steady.

"No. I was too busy dragging your sorry arse behind a tree before he could have another go at you."

"I am eternally in your debt, my friend."

"I will remind you of having said so," James replied with a smile, brushing off Brandon's attempt at being serious.

"I would expect no less," Brandon said, emitting a soft snort. "Now, perhaps we should see about finding the horses."

Brandon gave a short, sharp whistle. The sound shot ruthlessly through his head, but it wasn't long before Neptune appeared with James's horse following close behind.

Climbing onto Neptune's back proved slow and agonizing, but with James's help, Brandon was eventually seated. What should have been a one-hour trip turned into three. And even with Neptune's smooth, easy gait, Brandon's head felt like a well-used blacksmith's anvil by the time they arrived.

Leaping from his horse before it even stopped, James rushed to Brandon's aid. "Here, lean on me," he said lending his assistance to what proved to be a sluggish and ungainly dismount. Wedging his shoulder beneath Brandon's arm,

he helped him to the house. Mindful of maintaining his supportive position, he shoved open the door. "Henry! Amelia! Julia! Come quickly."

Brandon winced. "Bloody hell, man. Are you trying to kill me?" he groused, placing a hand to his head. "Perhaps you'd like to yell all the servants' names as well?"

"My apologies," James said. "I—" Before he could say anything more, Henry and Isabella rushed into the foyer.

"What happened?" Henry asked, seeing the blood on the bandage.

"A mere flesh wound. Nothing to fret over," Brandon replied readily.

Raising a brow, Henry looked to James for confirmation, while Isabella stood quietly wringing her hands.

James nodded. "He should be fine after a few hours' rest," he said, adjusting his hold on Brandon. "Unless a rib is broken."

"Ribs?" Henry looked at Brandon's torso through the torn opening of his shirt.

"I'll explain all after we get him to bed," James supplied.

"Not bed. My study," Brandon insisted, waving Henry away. "A short sit and a couple of brandies is what I need."

"Perhaps you should do as they say, Brandon," Isabella said, not quite meeting his eyes.

He gave her a gentle smile. "Don't looked so troubled, my dear. I assure you it is nothing serious. Although, it is nice to know at least one woman in the household is concerned with my welfare. Where are the other two?"

"Could this wait until we get you settled?" James interrupted, saving Isabella from answering. "You're deuced heavy, old fellow."

Before following the men, Henry gave Isabella a compassionate look.

Waiting until they were halfway down the hall, she began to follow. The men's progress was slow and measured, Isabella's more so. Cold fear surged through her.

Matthew's anger at having discovered the women's deception had been tempered due to his station. James and Brandon would have no such compunction.

"BLEEDING BLOODY DAMN!" BRANDON shouted, ignoring the pain in his head and, if not for James's heavy hand on his shoulder, he would have shot from the chair.

"Calm yourself, Brandon. You will accomplish nothing by frightening the poor girl." The Duke's voice was steady and tight, much like the grip of his hand.

"What do you mean . . . gone?" Brandon forced himself to ask more calmly.

"They . . . Julia . . . Amelia." Try as she might, Isabella could not force the words past her constricted throat.

Wanting nothing more than to shake the words from her, Brandon clutched the sides of the chair until his muscles quivered.

It was Henry who answered. "From what Matthew told me before leaving to find them, Miss Freemont and the Duchess commandeered two horses and left shortly after you did."

"Where were they going?" James split his gaze between Henry and Isabella.

"To London," came the subdued female answer.

"London?" Brandon roared. "What would possess them to leave for London? We must go after them immediately."

"Is it your intention to scare the girl into apoplexy?" James asked sternly, hooking Brandon's glare with a half-

warning, half-worried one of his own, while exerting more pressure to keep him sitting.

At James's nod, Isabella continued. "Amelia wanted to take Julia to meet a woman by the name of Maude."

"Maude?" James repeated dumbly, raking fingers through his hair. "Why in heaven's name would she do that?" he asked, looking down at Brandon.

"You're asking me?" Brandon snarled, narrowing his eyes.

James gave him a disgusted look. Replacing the expression with a calmer one, he turned his gaze to Isabella. "Thank you, my dear." Noting her trembling lips, he gave her a small, encouraging smile. "Don't fret. We shall find them. I think it best you go to your room now."

With head hung and eyes suspiciously glassy, she took her leave.

James turned to Henry. "Have a fresh horse readied for me. I will be leaving immediately to find my wife."

"Yes, Your Grace."

"Two horses," Brandon corrected. "I shall be going also."

"You, my friend, are going nowhere until you are able to sit a horse without falling off. Your stubbornness will accomplish nothing but to hold me back."

Brandon wanted to argue, fear for Julia clouding his mind, but recognized the truth in the other man's words.

"Do as he says, Henry," Brandon ordered, resigned to staying behind, but his dry tone indicated it was not in the least to his liking. "Wait."

Henry stopped before reaching the door. "Yes, Mr. Barringer?"

"In all the commotion, I only now realized Robert also is missing. Have you any idea where he might be?"

"Forgive the oversight, sir. After receiving an urgent note from his mother, he too has gone to London."

"Thank you, Henry. Have Prince saddled for Malvern. Next to Neptune, he's the fastest."

"I believe he's gone, sir."

"Hellfire, then."

"Gone also, sir."

"Storm. Unless the women have wiped out my entire stables," Brandon said in exasperation.

"No, sir. Storm it is."

Once he was gone, Brandon turned a frown on James.

"At least they had the foresight, or luck, to take two of the fastest horses in your stables," James said on a deep sigh and began pacing. "If Julia has half the equestrian skill of Amelia, they are probably halfway to London."

"Amelia." Brandon, expelled the name with a puff of annoyance. "Have you no control over your wife, James?"

James stopped in his tracks, struggling with the urge to come to Amelia's defense, but knowing in all probability much of the blame could be laid at her feet. Deciding it was best not to address the issue at all, he said wearily, "There is much you must learn about love, my friend. In particular, the emotion has nothing to do with *control* and everything to do with allowing the person you love to be themselves."

Brandon frowned.

"I can see by the stubborn set of your jaw you do not believe me, so inevitably you must learn that particular lesson the hard way. As did I," came the belated admission. "So I can offer you no sympathy on that score. The best I can do is wish you luck. I fear you are sorely going to need it, if you wish to reclaim your lady."

"And reclaim her I shall. She belongs to me." Disdaining the Duke's smug look, Brandon went on, "We made a bargain, she and I. And I intend to see she keeps her end of it. A man has every right to expect recompense from his *mistress*."

James's response was to shake his head and offer Brandon a sympathetic smile before saying a final goodbye.

AT THE SOUND OF the door opening, the innkeeper's wife looked up. "What can I do for you, sirs?" she inquired of the three large, travel-worn men who entered. She wiped her hands on her apron, adding to the wrinkles already there.

"We're looking for two noblewomen who might have passed this way. Have you seen them?" the largest of the three asked, glancing around the room. His gaze lingered on the two young dandies at a corner table, heads bent in conversation.

"Why would you be wantin' to know?" she asked with brow raised, regaining the man's attention.

"One of them is a duchess and we've been sent by her husband to fetch her."

"A Duke what lost his duchess! Well, don't that beat all?" Placing her hands on her ample hips, the woman guffawed, joined by several male patrons in the room. "That be the best clanker I heard in a long time. And the other?" She paused to wipe her eyes with the corner of her apron. "I suppose she be a runaway wife, too?"

"Yes," the man answered stiffly.

He wasn't close enough to hear the soft gasp from one of the dandies, but the innkeeper's wife did.

"As you can see, there be no noblewomen here," she said, swiping her hand to indicate the room. "These men be the only ones stayin' at present. You're free to check the rooms if you don't believe me. Then ye best be on your way. Me and my Samuel run a respectable inn and don't want no trouble."

"She be tellin' the truth," piped up a man enjoying a

pint of ale at a table near the door. "I been here all day." He leaned toward the men, lowering his voice. "The closest thing to a woman I seen is those two namby-pamby fellers in the corner."

"Thank you," the man said and tossed a coin to the unkempt old fellow. Before leaving, he took another look around the room, his gaze lingering for a moment on the two gents in the corner. It took all kinds to make up the world, but the way the men leaned toward each other caused the big man to shudder. Quickly looking away, he turned once more to the lady. "Good day, ma'am. We won't be botherin' you further."

"Where to, Matthew?" one of the other three men was heard to ask on the way out.

"London," was the brusque reply.

"WELCOME BACK, YOUR GRACE," the footman at the Malvern London residence said, without so much as batting an eye at the scandalous male attire Amelia was wearing. With a short-waisted bow, he accepted the man's hat she handed him.

"Thank you, Jeeves. This is Miss Freemont. She will be staying with us. If anyone should inquire, she has been in Bath with the Duke and me the entire time."

"Yes, Your Grace." The impeccably dressed servant turned to Julia. "A pleasure, Miss Freemont."

"Oh, and Jeeves," Amelia said. "If perchance a very tall, frustrated looking young man named Matthew comes calling—please inform him that yes, I am in residence, but am predisposed with a terrible megrim."

"Excuse me, Your Grace. But you never—"

"Yes, yes. I know. I never get them, but that will be our little secret."

His lips twitched at the corners. "Very good, Your Grace."

"Whatever would I do without you?" Amelia asked, smiling. Shocking both Julia and the footman, she gave the man a quick squeeze.

"Come along, Julia. Don't dally. We are both in need of a long soak and nap." Once out of the footman's hearing, she added, "But first, I must pen a quick note to Maude to inform her we have need of her services. I am quite sure she will have no objection to a private after-hours fitting." Giving Julia a sly look, she took her hand and began leading her up the wide, curving staircase.

"SO, THE DUCHESS HERE tells me yer wantin' to learn how to leg-shackle and please yer man. Be that so?" Maude asked from behind her desk in her private rooms.

Stupefied at the swift change from refined French modiste to earthy, no nonsense Englishwoman, Julia could only nod.

"Why?" Maude pinned a narrow gaze on the young woman sitting in a chair across from her. "The way I hear tell it, ye were wantin' nothin' to do with him when he wanted ye for a *wife*. Is this some evil plan ye have of gettin' even with him for makin' ye his mistress?"

"No! Not at all," Julia yelped, shocked not only by the woman's accusations, but her knowledge of the situation.

"Why then?" Maude demanded with a fierce look.

"Because...." Julia began meekly and then, refusing to be intimidated, raised her chin. Staring directly into Maude's eyes, she said, "Because I love him. And if you are not willing

to help me, I am quite certain I can find some other East End. . . ." She grappled for a less-insulting term than the one that came to mind.

"*Prostitute* be the word yer lookin' for, missy," Maude supplied without resentment, the beginnings of a grin stretching her lips. Settling back into her chair, she turned to Amelia. "You done right bringin' her here."

"So, you'll help her?"

"How much time do we have?"

"Not much. A couple of days, perhaps."

"Don't leave no time for sugar coatin'. Be ye sure she won't go runnin' outta here like a cat what got its tail stomped on?"

"Quite sure. She barely blinked an eye when I suggested we dress in men's clothes to escape detection on the way to London."

"I'll do it then."

"Do what?" Julia paused, dizzy from swiveling her head between the two women. "What are you two talking about?"

"Brandon be needin' a strong, determined female." Maude was the one to answer. "Been havin' his way too long, I'm thinkin'. Now, tell me what ye know."

"Know?"

The older woman heaved an inpatient sigh. "About pleasin' a man. And I don't mean cookin' him no apple tart."

"Only what Brandon has taught me."

Maude gave her an exasperated look when she didn't continue. "I be good at a lot of things. Mind-readin' ain't one of them."

"I apologize. This is all so new to me and more than a little embarrassing." She slanted Amelia an anxious glance.

"Would you like me to leave?" her friend offered.

"No." Julia's spine grew straighter and she consciously

released the clump of dress she'd been twisting since sitting down. "How can I ever hope to gain and hold a man's attention by acting like a silly schoolroom miss?" Drawing in a deep breath, she stated, "He told me love was an emotion of the senses. Seeing, hearing, smelling, touching, tasting. He said I must learn each nuance to become a good mistress. On the first day—"

Maude held up a silencing hand. "That be right fine. But we ain't got the time to hear all that. Tell us what ye know of making love. What he did to ye. What ye did to him."

"To be truthful, although he showed me several ways to attain sexual gratification, we had not quite gotten around to complete copulation."

"Are ye tellin' me ye been with that boy over a week and the only thing he got around to was friggin' ye and ye friggin' him?" Maude snorted a laugh. "Damn me if the boy's not in love." She looked toward Amelia, and the two women shared a conspiratorial grin.

"No. He definitely is not," Julia corrected in a hurry.

"That's where yer wrong, lovie. It were me business to know men. I weren't known to be the best whore on the docks fer nothin'," she stated with pride.

Julia looked at the woman in front of her and felt deep admiration, despite Maude's chosen profession. After all, what did Julia have to be proud of? Her innate sense of style? Her ability to sit through a boring dinner conversation and appear enraptured?

All her life, she'd merely allowed herself to be taken care of. Even after the death of her father, she'd sought out the one person she knew could take care of her in the style she'd come to expect as her due. At the expense of her pride. For the first time in her life, she felt an ineptness that was enlightening. Suddenly she realized there was something she wanted far

more than clothes, money, and a grand house to live in. And she was willing to sacrifice anything and everything to get it.

Barely allowing herself a moment to take a breath, she told Maude the bare necessities. "He showed how a man could bring a woman to fulfillment by painting a picture with words, by his fingers deep inside her or merely playing with the hard little nub between her legs. And with his tongue." Here she paused, her womb throbbing with the memory. With a small shake of her head, she continued. "And he showed me how to please him by using my hand."

Maude turned to Amelia and a mysterious look passed between the two. "Nothin' else?" Maude inquired with a raise of one artistically paint-darkened brow.

"Nothing. Although. . . ."

"Go on."

"I read something in a book recently that led me to believe a woman might pleasure a man with her—her mouth," she said, surprising the other women with her knowledge.

"Ye sure can," Maude confirmed. "And it don't surprise me in the least that boy didn't teach ye, since it be one of a man's favorite ways of bein' pleasured."

"If so, why wouldn't he show me?"

"Control," Maude stated. "He be a man who likes his control, and he knew once he taught ye that particular way to please him, he'd have to give it up."

"I would love nothing more than to see him lose that iron-clad *control* of his, but I suppose I shall have to find another way."

"Don't ye be worrying none, deary. Ye came to the right place. All ye be needin' is some practice."

"Practice? But without being with Brandon, how could I possibly. . . ." Julia shot a nervous look toward Amelia, who shrugged. What had her friend gotten her into?

Smiling, Maude reached down and pulled something from the bottom drawer of her desk and plunked it in front of her. "Amazing what a sailor can do with some spare time and a nice long piece of whalebone. Ain't it?" Her eyes twinkled.

Stunned into silence, Julia and Amelia could do little but stare open-mouthed at what appeared to be an amazingly detailed, large, shiny, white, male shaft.

"Course," Maude continued with a small shrug of her shoulders, "might be a bit bigger than what yer use to seein'."

Speechless, Julia shook her head. "Truthfully, I was thinking it was a bit on the small side." Her mouth snapped shut, her face heating into a ruby blush. "I . . . I mean—"

"Pfth . . . some women has all the damn luck," Maude grumbled.

There was a moment of silence. A quirk of lips. Then all three women erupted into a spurt of laughter.

"Can't say I'm surprised none," Maude said, drying her teary eyes. "I had me a pretty good idea that rascally rake wouldn't be light in the breeches."

"Maude, you wouldn't by any chance have more of those?" Julia asked with a mischievous glint in her eyes.

"All shapes and sizes. Bone or ivory."

"A small ivory one I think. And, do you think perhaps you might get one of your sailor friends to make a slight alteration for me?"

"Julia, whatever do you have in mind?" asked Amelia, her own adventuresome interest piqued.

"I have always been fond of gifts, giving them as much as receiving, and I do believe I have come up with the most perfect one for Mr. Barringer."

26

IT WAS DARK BY the time Julia and Amelia left Maude. Waving goodbye to the proprietress, both women grasped the neck of their pelisses to ward off the evening chill.

Stepping down onto the cobblestone walk, a light fog swirling around her ankles, Amelia spotted their coach a short distance down the street and waved to her driver. He too was snuggled deep inside his coat, his hat pulled low as he gave the reins a quick snap. The deserted street allowed the sound to carry over the crisp air to where the women stood waiting.

"I do believe Maude is the most colorful character I have ever had the pleasure of meeting," Julia said with a smile, each word producing a small mist of steam before her lips.

"Yes, she is delightful. I will be forever grateful that I met her. Without her advice, I doubt very much if I would be the Duchess of Malvern. And now that your name is in the betting book, there are any number of women you may call upon to aid you in your endeavor to capture Brandon's heart. Although I have a feeling he has already relinquished it. Your absence from his life should speed the process along quite nicely."

Praying her friend was right, Julia decided not to comment. "I am still in awe over the names entered in the book. I would have never believed . . . the Marchioness of Wilmington," she said, bringing her hand up to muffle a giggle. "And—"

"Shhh. Not now," Amelia cautioned as the driver, who had pulled to a stop in front of them, came around to hand the women into the coach.

"Forgive me. I should have known better."

"Do not concern yourself. I remember feeling the same astonishment when I viewed them." Her concentration on Julia, she distractedly gave the driver her hand to aid her up and into the conveyance.

Julia waited quietly for her turn, shifting her feet to deflect the cold seeping into her green leather slippers. Noting one felt looser than the other, she looked down and found the ribbon had come undone. She bent to fix it and straightened in time to see the driver viciously shove the Duchess into the coach. The screech Amelia expelled was cut short when she fell against the squabs.

The driver turned to Julia.

She opened her mouth to scream. But the sound was trapped in her lungs when a filthy hand reached from behind, covering both her mouth and nose.

Unable to breathe, Julia began struggling.

"Damn ye, bitch," the man holding her cursed when the heel of her foot connected with his shin.

"Hold her, you fool," came the gruff, muted demand through the muffler the driver was wearing around his face.

The hand cutting off her air tightened. Spots began to form before Julia's eyes. She heard the distant sound of a shrill, sharp whistle and a coach pulling up, then experienced the vague sensation of being lifted.

IT TOOK THE BETTER part of an hour for Amelia to rouse Maude from the rooms above her shop and for the two of

them to revive the real coachman. He'd apparently been coshed on the head while attempting to give helpful directions to a newly appointed driver.

Maude immediately sent word to some of her sailor friends, two of whom escorted Amelia home, while several others were placed on the trail of the kidnappers.

By the time Amelia reached her residence, not only was Jeeves there to greet her, but James, Matthew, and his brothers as well.

Immediately going to the coach and opening the door, James was surprised to catch a sobbing, blubbering Amelia in his arms.

"Oh, James. It's all my fault," she wailed, clutching tightly to her husband's neck and burying her face against his chest.

"What the devil happened?" he demanded, looking over her head at the men who were with her.

One burly seaman quickly stepped forward, his choice of profession easily identifiable by the lingering smell of salt and fish. "Yer Duchess be unharmed, yer Grace," he said, doffing the sea cap off his head. "Maude sent us."

"They took her. They took Julia." Amelia's words and tears seeped through James's shirt, warming his flesh.

"What are you saying?" James's gaze flew to the coach. Seeing no one other than the driver, who was currently being helped out by Matthew, he looked down at the top of his wife's head. "Amelia, where is Julia?"

"They took her," she repeated.

He moved her away from his chest and lifted her chin. "Who took her?"

"I don't know. Oh, James," she sobbed. "I'm to blame. I should have never brought her here."

Torn between agreeing with her and comforting his wife, James merely clutched her to him, glad for her safety. "It will

be fine. I promise. We shall find her." He gave her a squeeze. "Come, everyone into the house," he commanded. "Where we can sort this out without all of London being privy to our business."

With Amelia tucked beneath his arm and pressed tightly to his side, he led the way through the foyer, down the hall, and into his study. Once everyone had filed in behind him and both the coachman and Amelia made comfortable in the chairs closest to the fireplace, James took the seat behind his desk and began asking questions.

For several seconds after hearing each person's version of the story, the Duke said nothing. The only sound in the room was the light tapping of the small dagger he was toying with. "Matthew?" he said, tossing the sharp object down several inches from his hand.

"Yes, Your Grace."

"The first thing to be done is to send for Mr. Barringer. Can one of your brothers leave immediately?"

"It should be me to go." The big man's fists clenched at his side. "Had I been attending to my duties or found the women before they reached London—"

"The time is past to waste our energy on blame. It matters not what *should have* been done, only what *should* be done now. Have your brothers ever been to London before?"

"No, sir."

"Whereas you have. Your knowledge of the city will be needed if we are to find Miss Freemont." At Matthew's nod, he turned to his wife. "Amelia?"

"Yes, husband?" Her eyes were partially downcast, the flesh beneath them red and puffy.

At any other time he would have smiled at her uncharacteristic meekness. "Did you see the man's face, note his size? Anything else that might help?"

She scrunched her brow in concentration. "He was a short man, only a few inches taller than me." Standing, she leveled her hand above her head.

"Anything else?"

She searched her memory. "Slighter of form than our driver." She bowed her head. "I suppose I was too busy conversing with Julia to realize it then."

"Did you perchance notice what he was wearing, the color of his clothes?" James asked quickly to keep her mind off her guilt and focused on what she remembered.

"They were dark. Even in the dim light. I would think either black or blue."

"Smart bloke," one of the sailors interrupted. "Easier to blend with the darkness. Harder to make out details."

"Let us hope not too smart," James responded and then nodded for his wife to continue.

"His hat was like a hundred others and he wore his collar turned up and muffler around his face." Amelia shook her head in misery. "I can recall nothing else. I am sorry." She sank back down into the chair. "I suppose I have not helped a great deal."

James got up, walked over, and placed a consoling hand on her shoulder. "Calm yourself, my dear. I shall have a small army searching for her before the night is through. With the help of Maude's friends, we shall fetch her home in no time," he said resolutely, hoping his words proved true.

"Right ye are, gov," the shorter of the two sailors chimed in. "So if ye won't be needin' us longer, we best get to it."

"Send word if you learn anything. No matter the hour," James said, shaking each man's hand as they prepared to take their leave. "And, thank you for bringing my wife home. I shall see to it you're well rewarded."

"No need. Maudie'll be taking good care of us," the sailor

said with a near-toothless grin that turned into a frown when he received an elbow in the ribs from his mate.

"Wait," Matthew said. "If you'd not be mindin', my brother Davey would like to join you. Josh will be the one goin' for Mr. Barringer."

The two sailors gave Davey a scrutinizing look. They nodded to each other, and this time the tall sailor spoke. "He looks to have enough brawn to carry his own. Come on, then. We've wasted enough time."

When they'd gone, Matthew turned to James. "If you've no further need of us here, I'll be sending Josh on his way."

The Duke clapped the other man on the shoulder. "Allow me some time to take my wife upstairs and settle her in. Then meet me back here. Between the two of us, we should be able to devise a suitable plan and place it in motion before too much time passes. If God is with us, we'll have Julia safe with us before Brandon arrives. If not. . . ."

From where Amelia was sitting, the look the two men shared was not encouraging in the least.

AS IT TURNED OUT, there was no need for Josh to ride all the way to Brandon's country estate, for he encountered him barely a three-hour ride from London.

Brandon had waited but a half day after James took his leave to send Isabella home and drag himself onto Neptune's back to begin his trek to collect his mistress. He had been unable to think of anything save her, the large house seeming empty without her presence. How it was Julia could so quickly change the atmosphere of a place he once escaped to for solitude, Brandon was at a loss to say. The peace he'd always gained from being there now seemed a lonely, solitary

existence. All for the mere coming and going of one small, troublesome female.

And with every upturned clump of mud from the hooves of the mighty brown horse beneath him, Brandon told himself it wasn't the emptiness in his heart that demanded he risk falling to the ground in his weakened state, but the emptiness of his bed.

27

"WOULD YOU PLEASE STOP pacing?" James said, for what seemed like the hundredth time, as Brandon once again passed in front of him.

"Why the devil have we not heard anything?" Brandon asked, momentarily standing still. Automatically reaching for his watch, he cursed as he remembered it was no longer there. He resumed pacing.

Consigned to having a rut carved into the library carpet in front of his desk, James said, "We have seventy men out searching. Seventy-one if I am forced to count Robert."

During a pass, Brandon gave his friend a cautioning look.

James shrugged and said, "You never did tell me how he came to learn of Julia's disappearance so quickly. One would wonder—"

An abrupt knock on the door brought Brandon to a halt and James to his feet.

"Enter," James barked.

"Mr. Farnsworth to see Mr. Barringer, Your Grace," Jeeves said, opening the door wider to admit the man standing behind him.

"William," Brandon said, going over to meet his solicitor. "Thank you for answering my summons."

"No need to thank me. Any word regarding Miss Freemont?"

"Not yet," Brandon answered warily. "I believe I shall go out again—"

"Absolutely not," James said, coming to stand beside Brandon. "You barely made it back the last time without falling off your horse. I thought we agreed it would be best to save your strength until we had a good solid lead. And that infernal pacing you are doing is not helping."

The men glared at each other.

"Your Grace, Mr. Barringer, please. I think perhaps a drink is in order," William said, stepping between the two. "Nothing will be accomplished by losing your tempers."

Brandon's shoulders slumped and his head lowered on a deep sigh. "He's right," he said tiredly, scrubbing his hand across his face and then pinching the bridge of nose. "Perhaps a drink would help."

"Go. Sit," James instructed Brandon. "I will get them. You also, William."

"Thank you, Your Grace," William said, deciding to wait to impart his information until things had settled a bit.

Once they were all seated with drinks in hand, William looked over at his employer, who had yet to sample his. With his dark head bent, Brandon was staring into the amber liquid as if it were a gypsy's crystal ball.

"Although I am surprised to find you in London, sir, it is fortuitous," William said. "I have only this morning received word from the Bow Street Runner you had me hire."

"What did he discover?"

"That the day Mrs. Henning was murdered, she had been visited by a man. It may have gone unnoticed if not for the fact that the gentleman was so well turned out."

Brandon's head jerked up, giving William his full attention. "Are you sure it was not merely us someone saw?" he asked, generously including William in the description.

The solicitor smiled. "No, sir. It was much earlier in the day."

"Are you saying someone from the upper classes?" James asked, placing his drink on a side table and sitting forward in his chair.

"It would appear so, Your Grace. There is something else." He paused, looking first at the Duke before settling his gaze on Brandon. "It was said a black coach also was seen that day, although a good distance from Mrs. Henning's. And. . . ."

"Go on," Brandon encouraged, placing his drink alongside James's.

"It sported a ducal crest."

"Whose?" Brandon's voice was low and lethal.

"Durnwald. Your grandfather's, I would guess," James supplied angrily, gaining a nod from William. At the confirmation, the Duke surged to his feet, grabbed the glass he'd set down earlier, and heaved it into the fireplace. It exploded with a whoosh. "I knew it! The bloody, twiddlepoop bastard," James cursed, calling into question Robert's gender along with his parentage.

William shifted his gaze once again to Brandon, who remained suspiciously quiet.

"Impossible," Brandon insisted, shaking his head. "I cannot believe Robert would ever set out to willfully harm me."

"Open your eyes, man," James spat in frustration. "Who else but Robert has as much to gain?"

Before Brandon could answer, another sharp rap took their attention to the door. It was opened before anyone could grant admission.

"Mr. Barringer—ooph."

A large, burly sailor pushed his way past Jeeves and paused to gasp in several breaths. "Matthew sent me. With this." The man held his hand out to Brandon.

When Brandon reached out, the man dropped a small diamond heart pendant into his palm.

Brandon immediately recognized it to be Julia's. She had once told him it was the one thing she could not bring herself to sell after the death of her father. "Where?"

"Down at the docks. In a tavern. Some bloke in 'is cups was braggin' 'bout how 'e took it for payment for helpin' some gent snatch up a pretty piece-o-fluff." The sailor smiled, revealing several missing teeth, the remaining ones severely blackened. "After a little friendly persuasion," he brought his fingers up to dab at the swelling flesh beneath his eye, "'e were right 'appy to give it up." His grin widened. "Along with a bit of information on where the lady could be found." The entire recitation was delivered through a spate of labored breathing.

"Jeeves, have three horses saddled immediately," James ordered.

"Four," William added, causing the footman to pause.

A quick nod from the Duke sent the servant on his way.

With long strides, James walked behind his desk and removed several books from a shelf. Springing a hidden latch, a portion of the shelves swung open, revealing an impressive display of weapons. Snatching two pistols off their wooden pegs, he handed them both to Brandon. The next set went to the sailor. Taking two more, he held them out to William. "Can you shoot?"

"Yes," the solicitor answered, accepting the guns.

After arming himself, James and the three others spilled into the foyer, only to encounter Amelia on the bottom step of the staircase.

"James? What has happened? Have you found her? If so, I insist on going with you."

As the other men rushed out through the front door, the Duke stepped up to where his wife was standing. He

thumbed the puffiness beneath her tired eyes. "I can waste no time arguing with you, love. I have asked little of you since we wed. But I ask now that you stay here. It will not benefit Julia if we must concern ourselves with your safety as well."

He could see she wanted to object. "I promise to send word as soon as we know something."

"Be careful, James. I love you," she said, bracing a light hand against his chest.

"And I love you," he said, giving her a quick, passionate kiss before leaving.

JULIA SPIRALED UP FROM the black abyss of unconsciousness. Her dazed senses were slow to take in the musty smell and feel of the cool, hard-packed earth beneath her cheek. Something tickled her leg. She jerked. A sharp squeal and scurrying feet had her jumping to her own.

Heart pounding, unable to discern her surroundings through the darkness that cloaked the room, she took a step back. Her progress was instantly halted by a hard, solid object. Julia's heart stopped. Lurched back into rhythm.

Not daring to move, she concentrated on taking deep, even breaths, while she waited for her eyes to adjust.

Crates. She was surrounded by crates. Her eyes, now focused, sought out a small sliver of light shining from beneath a door. Another round of scurrying feet had her lunging into the small space left open to accommodate the door's opening and closing.

Fighting down a surge of panic, she reached deep within herself for the courage to face whatever fate awaited her.

It came to her. In an image of Brandon.

At the sudden calm she felt, Julia was able to concentrate

on her surroundings. It was then she heard the voices. Moving closer to the door, she pressed her ear to the rough planks. Though able to catch an occasional word, she could not discern the conversation or recognize the voices speaking.

But there was no mistaking the sound of flesh meeting flesh. Then the indistinct conversation on the other side of the door continued.

"I won't let you do it. I won't let you kill her," Robert insisted, bringing his head back around slowly from the impact of the slap. He had taken up a position between the person he was confronting and the door he knew Julia to be behind.

"How dare you think to oppose me?" the figure sneered, in a voice gaining in both volume and octave. "Get out of my way, you sniveling coward. If you think I will not kill you to attain what I want, you are mistaken. You have outlived your usefulness. I have come too far—killed too many—to allow you to stop me."

"Who else have you killed?"

The laugh that filled the ramshackle room was shrill and sinister. A person gone mad.

"Dare I tell you? Perhaps I shall if for no other reason than to see the shock on your face."

"What others?" Robert persisted, staring at the pistol being pointed at his chest, holding his own gun steadily aligned with the speaker's heart.

"Where shall I start? There have been so many. Brandon's parents for one. Or does that count as two? And that bitch, Mrs. Henning. She got greedy, you see. Wanted more money for slipping the poison into his parents' food every time she would visit her *new friend*."

It took great effort for Robert to appear unaffected by the villainy being revealed, but he knew any sign of weakness

would be his undoing. "Go on," he said in a calm, controlled voice.

"With pleasure. Your grandfather."

Robert felt the narrowing gaze upon him like a physical caress. Waiting. Hungry. He steeled himself against showing any reaction.

"And my most coveted accomplishment—your father."

Not only the deed, but the silky pleasure in which the statement was delivered, rocked Robert back on his feet.

Another shrill, hysterical laugh filled the air. This one longer and louder. Only this time, Robert took some comfort in it, because it concealed the presence of Brandon and the other men sneaking up from behind.

Robert swallowed deeply, hoping to ward off the bile he felt rising in his throat. There were other questions yet unanswered. "Why Miss Freemont? What does she have to do with this?"

"Nothing, really," came the off-hand reply. "Other than that Brandon wanted her. Before your grandfather brought him back, it was *I* who controlled you. It was Brandon who turned you against me, took you away to Oxford. When you came back, a grown man, you resented my control, rather than deferring to it as you had before leaving. It was only fitting that he be made to pay by losing someone he wanted."

The hand holding the pistol on Robert tightened in an unwavering grip, and the voice grew more resentful. "I was hoping her father's suicide would save me the trouble of disposing of her. But even after I spent a small fortune to attain her father's gambling markers and her home, the stupid girl ran straight to Brandon."

"Anyone else?" Robert asked, not really wanting to hear, but needing to have the words spoken for the benefit of the others.

"No. Not yet anyway. But I fear, now that you know, you must join your father and grandfather. Then it shall be Brandon's turn. After that, everything shall be mine. The money. The power. Everything."

Robert was about to state how impossible that was, when Brandon stepped from the shadows and said, "I'm afraid that will never happen. Put down the pistol and turn around."

The figure spun, aiming the weapon in Brandon's direction.

"Mother! No!" Robert yelled, pulling the trigger on his own gun.

The figure turned back. Smiled tenderly. The maniacal face of moments ago smoothed into one of a mother's deep affection for her child. "No one shall ever separate us again, my son." Before anyone could stop her, she brought up the gun that had been dangling loosely from her fingers and fired.

Both mother and son slumped to the ground.

A shrill female scream drew everyone's attention to a door at the far side of the room.

Leaping over the body of his aunt, Brandon took off running. "Julia!"

"Brandon. Brandon. In here," she yelled.

"Stand back," he ordered and, allowing her enough time to remove herself from harm's way, delivered a bone-jarring kick that sent the door crashing inward. Brandon had a quick glimpse of the room before the door bounced off some crates and came rushing back. His forearm received the brunt of the blow. Giving the door a less forceful shove, he moved into the room.

The force of the woman flying into his arms almost knocked him back out.

For long minutes, neither spoke, each clinging to the other. Not even when the arms clutching around his neck

threatened to deny him air did he think to relinquish his hold on her.

It took the request of a dying man to break them apart.

"I COULD NOT ALLOW her to kill you, don't you see?" Robert gave a negligent glance at the dead woman, dressed in men's clothing, barely five feet away.

He coughed several times, blood dribbling from the corner of his mouth.

"She was my mother, but you . . . you were my hero. Forever coming to my rescue. I shall never forget that day at Oxford. Do you remember? Do you know the day I'm speaking of?"

"Yes," Brandon replied softly. "I remember."

Robert glanced at Julia, who stood to the side of Brandon, her hand lightly resting on his shoulder. "We were freshmen. He took on three upperclassmen who were determined to beat me senseless for some minor infraction. While I cowered in a corner, he engaged in a bout of fist-to-cuffs, taking on each one in turn. In the end, Brandon stood the victor. Though I often wondered how he managed to see or speak for several days afterward with his eyes so swollen and face so bruised and cut."

He turned his gaze back to Brandon. "For the remaining years at school, I devised and discarded at least a hundred plans of retribution on your behalf. Only to find in the end, I was too cowardly to carry out a single—"

A bout of coughing ensued. Weaker and with much greater effort as his strength waned. The blood from his mouth was flowing more freely, spilling over, saturating what was once a pristine white cravat.

"You shouldn't talk. Save your strength," Brandon insisted.

Ignoring the plea, Robert continued, his breathing more labored. "You were ever the brave one. Never backing down. Regardless of consequence. That was one of the reasons she hated you so. Mother," he clarified needlessly. "You were never afraid of her. She despised you for that. You never guessed that when you stood up to her on my behalf, she would thrash me later. She said it was my fault you were so insolent."

"God, Robert. I'm sorry. I never knew." Brandon's words were pained.

"How could you? I never told you. I knew she was lying. It was merely an excuse to beat me. Not that she needed one."

In the face of what Robert had endured, some of the hurt and anger Brandon was feeling at his cousin's earlier confession melted away. Robert had seen Julia leaving that day and, thinking her unworthy of Brandon after spurning his suit and labeling him a bastard, had allowed her and Amelia to go. But if not for Robert's uncovering his mother's perfidy . . . following her here . . . Julia might well be—

Refusing to finish the thought, Brandon looked down at Robert and said, "I had always thought of you as more a brother than a cousin." He was careful to keep his voice low and modulated, but even to his own ears, his words sounded inept, hollow.

Robert's attempt to smile ended in a gurgling cough, producing more blood. "I should like to hear you say it." Robert's words were barely discernible.

"Say what?" Brandon asked, his brows lowering.

"Address me as the Duke of Durnwald. You have never done so, you know. Not once."

He started to deny it, but Robert was right. Brandon

knew, deep down in his heart, he had always harbored a deeply buried resentment that he could never inherit the title, and Robert could. A title that now seemed of little significance when compared to a man's life. Looking up at Julia, he took her hand.

She gave him a reassuring smile and tightened her fingers around his.

Knowing she understood and grateful for her understanding, he turned back to Robert and said with the greatest solemnity, "Miss Freemont, may I present to you, His Grace, the Duke of Durnwald."

"A pleasure to meet you, Your Grace," she said in an amazingly steady voice, given the circumstances. Releasing Brandon's hand, she executed a deep curtsy.

"Thank you. Both of you," Robert said, his voice a mere whisper. "Forgive me, Julia. I was consumed with jealousy. I love him, you know. I know you understand, because you love him also."

"I do understand, Your Grace," she said quietly, neither denying nor confirming the words.

Robert could see in her eyes that she understood him fully. For a moment, their gazes met in silent communication.

Taking a painful breath, Robert knew that she would hold her silence, never tell Brandon that he didn't love him as a brother, a cousin, or even a friend—he was *in love* with him. A love he would never have acted upon, but there nonetheless. Robert could die in peace, knowing he had the pleasure of declaring his love openly, but his secret was safe—it would die with him this night.

When the next spasm of coughing came, Robert's whole body shook as he tried to suppress it. It was no use. In the end all he managed to do was spray the front of Brandon's shirt with his blood.

"Look what . . . I've done," he murmured, raising a weak hand to wipe at the fabric.

Brandon caught the hand in his. "It's not important."

"Forever . . . my gallant . . . Brandon. Even at the last . . . you would not have me . . . feel bad. But there is something . . . something I can finally do . . . to repay you." Robert paused to draw breath. "Mother's wardrobe . . . " His voice began dwindling and, with a limp pull of his hand, he beckoned Brandon closer.

". . . false bottom . . . box." His eyes closed. "Fare—"

Brandon bent closer, barely able to hear.

"Fare . . . well . . . Y . . . Your . . . Grace."

Drawing a last rattling breath, he ceased breathing. His lips curved in a peaceful smile.

Brandon passed his hand over Robert's eyes, closing them. Sliding out from under his cousin's body, he lowered it carefully to the dirt floor. Standing, he held out his hand to Julia. "Come," he said. "Let us leave this place. James is waiting to take us home."

Placing her hand into his, Julia silently followed Brandon out of the building.

28

JAMES WALKED INTO THE house to find his wife sleeping in a chair in the sitting room. Quietly making his way into the room, he hunkered down next to her and touched his knuckles to her soft cheek. "Wake up, love."

"Hmmm." Amelia instinctively turned toward the touch. "James?" Her eyes flew wide. "Have you found her? Is she safe?"

"Yes, to both." He smiled. "She's in the foyer, waiting for you."

In a flash, Amelia was out of the chair, nearly knocking James to the floor. "Sorry, darling," she said with a sheepish grin over her shoulder as she fled the room.

Chuckling softly, James rose to follow.

"Julia. Thank God," Amelia cried, capturing her friend in a desperate hug.

"Thank Robert, Brandon, James, and all the rest of the men who came searching," Julia corrected.

"You are truly all right?" Amelia stepped back to survey her.

"Truly."

"You must be shaken and exhausted. Come along, you will feel better after a bath, and then I shall personally see you tucked into bed."

"She won't be staying," Brandon said, stepping up to place his arm around Julia's waist. "She will be coming home with me."

"She cannot possibly. Her reputation—"

"Amelia." The note of command in James's voice drew his wife's gaze. "It is not for you to say. It is Julia's decision to make."

Amelia turned to her friend. "And is it? Your choice, I mean."

Julia stepped from Brandon's light embrace and gave him an imploring look. When he nodded, she went to Amelia and drew her a few feet away for privacy. She hugged her friend, whispering, "Please understand, Amelia. I need this one night. We came so close to losing one another. I promise I shall be careful and return before first light."

"I understand totally, my dear," the other woman whispered back. "You've no need to explain yourself."

"Thank you."

Another fierce hug was exchanged.

As they broke apart, Brandon walked up behind them and placed a possessive arm around Julia's shoulders. "Ready?"

"Yes," she said, allowing him to guide her to the door.

"I shall have the coachman return as soon as he delivers us to my townhouse," Brandon told James.

"No need," Amelia hurriedly answered before her husband could. "The hour is late. He can return at *first light*." The women exchanged a knowing glance.

"Amelia is right," James said as he followed Brandon outside and to the coach. "After what everyone has been through, we could all use a good night's sleep, including the driver."

When Brandon and Julia were seated in the coach and the door closed, James latched onto the frame and looked up at his friend.

"Thank you," Brandon said, extending his hand through the open window.

James grasped it and squeezed.

"You are a true friend." The smile on Brandon's face was beholden.

"Think nothing of it. I'm sure there will come a time when I will call on you to return the favor." He looked back at his wife, who stood in the open doorway.

A soft male chuckle was shared between the men as the coach pulled away and James walked to his wife and led her inside.

WITH THE SAME QUIET efficiency Julia had come to expect from Henry, Mrs. Goodman had seen to their needs the instant the couple had set foot inside the green marbled foyer of Brandon's London residence.

Clean, fed, and ensconced in Brandon's large canopied bed with his warm body curled down the length of her back, Julia should have felt content, safe. She did not.

Eyes wide, she stared at the low-burning fire in the hearth. At the pop of a bursting ember, she jerked and started to tremble.

"What is it, sweet?" Brandon asked, turning her on her back as he braced up on his elbow to look down at her.

Even in the dim light, Julia had no trouble discerning the deep concern on his face. A tear slid down her cheek.

"I was so frightened." She blinked as her eyes filled, sending a stream of tears following the path of the first. A sob ripped free of her chest. One look into Brandon's compassionate face and she threw her arms around him, pressed her faced into his bare shoulder, and began sobbing in earnest.

Holding her tightly, uncaring of the discomfort it caused his sore body, Brandon rolled to his back, taking her with

him. He wasn't sure how long they stayed in that position; he only knew that each tear that made its way onto his shoulder and rolled down his neck into the pillow tore into his heart like a falcon's talons.

Eventually, the tears stopped and her breathing became even. Thinking her asleep, he closed his eyes, though he knew his own sleep would be long in coming.

"Make love to me." The feminine plea came to him on a whisper.

Sure he was in the midst of some erotic dream, he did not answer.

"Brandon?" Her soft voice flowed over him. This time he opened his eyes, to find hers wide open and staring at him.

"Make love to me. Please."

Brandon groaned. The sound deep, but subdued. "I can think of nothing I want more at this moment. But I would be the lowest form of man to take advantage of you at a time like this." Although it was killing him to deny her . . . and himself, he forced the words out. "It is not what you really want, Julia. Only the circumstance makes you ask. After your near brush with death, you yearn to experience something that will make you feel alive. I do not—"

She placed her fingers over his lips. "I am well aware of what I am asking. And it has nothing to do with what happened tonight." At the feel of his frown beneath her fingers her lips turned into a soft smile. "Well, perhaps it does . . . a little. But please, love, do not deny me this. I need you."

Her upper body rode the swell of his deep sigh. "Are you sure?" he asked, the movement of his lips tickling the tips of her fingers, making her realize she had yet to remove them.

"Absolutely sure." Taking her hand away, she pressed her lips softly to his.

This time the moan that welled up from his chest was

more a growl. Bringing his hand up to cup the back of her head, he deepened the kiss. Not wishing to overwhelm her with his lust, he immediately changed the intensity of both his hand and lips to a softer pressure.

Julia was having none of it. This was her night. And she was not going to waste it on virginal tentativeness. They had done too much, gone too far over the past week to start back at the beginning.

Sliding her hands into the valley where his broad shoulders met the back of his thick neck, she curved her fingers and drew them up. With a slow, upward drag, her nails made deep furrows in his thick hair. Cupping his head, she compressed her lips to his.

It was like striking a match.

Brandon's reaction was instantaneous, hot, and all-consuming.

The reversal of position was so fast and smooth it took Julia's dazed mind several seconds to realize she was now on the bottom, entirely covered by Brandon's much larger body. But she was given no time to dwell on the matter, her concentration now centered on the slow, sensual concerto of tongues currently being orchestrated inside the hot recesses of her mouth.

Refusing to allow Brandon to be the sole conductor, she sent her fingers on a venture down across the thick muscles of his back to settle on his firm buttocks. She was rewarded with a deep grind of his pelvis into hers, leaving no doubt of the reaction his body was having to her more than willing participation.

On a breath-taking gasp, Brandon broke the contact, planted his palms on either side of her shoulders, and levered up.

"This is going too fast. We must slow down."

Presented with the accessibility of his wide, lightly furred chest, Julia slid her hands up, skimming along slim hips and the taut muscles along his sides until her palms were planted firmly over his flat nipples. "I don't want to go slow."

"Julia. You are still a virgin," he reminded gently. "I would not have you remember this night as one of pain. Only pleasure." He lowered himself to sip at her lips, causing her elbows to fold. When he pushed up again, her hands came with him as if attached.

"You have never caused me pain," she confessed softly, her fingers searching out and finding his nipples, rolling them as he often did hers. Lifting her head, she sucked one hardened little nub into her mouth and bit down gently.

Again.

And again, increasing the pressure of her teeth each time.

Harder, yet.

Closing his eyes, Brandon moaned.

Julia nipped him.

The bolt of sexual sensation it sent through Brandon's body was so strong, it caused his back to arch and his elbows to collapse. It was only at the last possible instant he recalled enough presence of mind not to crush her beneath his weight.

"You have made your point, my dear. I hope you are prepared for what is to come. I fear it impossible for me to wait longer."

"Then don't," she purred, sliding her feet up the back of his hair-roughened legs, rotating her pelvis, spreading herself open to him.

He reached down between their sweat-dampened bodies, raked his fingers through her curly thatch of hair over her clitoris, smiling when her hips jerked, and slid a finger deep

inside. He wasted little time in adding a second, and third, until she was writhing and his fingers moved inside her with slippery ease.

He removed his fingers to encircle his shaft. Placing the hot, throbbing tip to her moist opening, he applied the slightest pressure, until the head slipped inside.

"If I hurt you, you must tell me. Though God knows I may be unable to stop even then." His words were low, strained.

Reaching up, Julia laid her hand alongside his face. Feeling the rigidity in his jaw, she smiled. Even now, he was exerting his formidable control. "It seems loss and pain are inseparable companions. But I am told once the pain is breached, only pleasure awaits. I had not believed that until now. I wish to get past the pain and on to the pleasure. It is you who can take me there." She knew her double meaning was lost on him, but she needed to say the words. She was now ready to let go of her hurt and fears, and open herself to love.

"Then prepare yourself to be pleasured, my sweet."

In mutual accord, they thrust their hips.

Hers up. His down.

Julia's small gasp of pain was lost on the tide of a fast-following moan of pleasure. She felt stretched and filled and oh, so wonderful. She could feel every luscious, soft glide of Brandon's shaft as he pulled it almost all the way out. Buried it to the hilt once again. It became a long, slow ritual.

Wrapping her hands around his bulging upper arms, she could feel the tension in his straining muscles. They were thick and hard, and under great restraint. Not unlike his rod pumping in and out of her, giving her undreamed-of pleasure. But this time, she exalted in his control.

"You're there, love. I can feel it in the way your body is opening to me. All you need do is reach out and take it."

And she did. Shuddering in her pleasure. Screaming his name as if calling for him to join her.

It was the only thing he was waiting for. The mental and physical control he was holding himself under broke free like a wild stallion being released from his tether. He held nothing back. His eruption rippled through his entire body, his seed flooding the welcoming womb into which it flowed. It seemed endless, or time stood still. Brandon was not sure which.

The only thing he was sure of was Julia's being his mistress was no longer an option. In his unbridled lust, he had failed to take precautions. No child of his would be born a bastard. Nor would the woman bearing his child have to suffer as his own mother had. Both would have every ounce of respect they deserved.

But as they both drifted into an exhausted, deep, satiated sleep, Brandon could not seem to muster so much as a farthing's worth of regret that the woman to be his wife would be the woman he had thought to make his mistress.

THE MOMENT BRANDON OPENED his eyes the next morning, he knew she was gone. He felt the lack of her presence even before he felt the cold bed beneath his hand. But instead of a frown a smile broke onto his lips.

Drat the slippery wench. He was going to have to break her of the appalling habit she had of leaving him without so much as a by-your-leave.

29

"WHAT THE DEUCE DO you mean, she will not receive me?" Brandon glared down at Amelia and then over the top of her head at James. The couple was currently playing the role of formidable sentinel to perfection by filling the entire entrance of their home.

Presenting himself at the residence shortly after discovering Julia gone, he was shocked speechless when instead of allowing him entrance, Jeeves had requested he wait and summarily closed the door in his face.

A moment later Amelia had appeared with her husband guarding her flank.

"I demand to see her. I have come to collect her. Immediately," Brandon stated, sounding more like a little boy denied his after-dinner treat than one of the most powerful men in England.

"Why, Brandon? So you can continue with this ludicrous idea of yours to make her your mistress?" Amelia demanded. "Has she not been through enough? She has asked me to inform you she no longer desires that position. Please leave. You are making a scene."

"*I* am making a scene? I come here with a simple request to see Julia, have a door slammed in my face, am left standing in the cold, and you are blaming me for this public spectacle?" His arm swung back, indicating the street in general.

"He has a point, dear," James said reasonably from

behind his wife. "Perhaps it would be best if you went inside and allowed me a moment to speak with Brandon. Alone."

"I do not—"

"Go, on," he said, gently shoving her beneath the arm he had braced high on the doorframe. "Go upstairs. You will accomplish nothing by arguing with him but to make him angrier."

Amelia hesitated only long enough to spear Brandon with a threatening look and disappeared into the house without further protest. No one saw the grin on her face as she went up the stairs and made her way to Julia's room.

"If you give me your word you will confine yourself to the library, I will allow you to come in." When several seconds ticked by, James gave Brandon a sympathetic look and tilted his head.

"My word," Brandon relented, crossing his arms and tucking his chilled hands into his armpits. "Now, may I come in and get warmed?"

James smiled and moved away from the door. Trusting in Brandon's word, he walked straight to his study. While Brandon walked over and took a seat near the fireplace, James went to where the brandy sat and poured them both a drink.

After passing one to Brandon, he leaned back against the front of his desk and crossed his ankles.

For several moments, neither man spoke.

"You need to give her time," James stated, breaking the silence. "She'll come around. Women do not see things as clearly as we men do. Especially when their emotions are involved. I should think she will need at least a week before she will be able to make any clear, sensible decisions."

"When did you become such an expert on women?" Brandon scoffed, tossing back the drink and placing the empty glass on the table beside him.

"Expert? Hardly." James's chuckle was laced with self-ridicule. "But I suppose being married to one gives me a slight advantage. You cannot imagine how complex is the working of the female mind."

"Damn it all, James. Julia belongs with me. I can protect her. Give her the things she wants."

"And are you so sure you know what she wants? If so, I am totally in awe, as I have yet to figure out Amelia's needs. Women seem to change their minds as quickly as a dragonfly changes direction."

The men shared a laugh and Brandon felt some of the tension leave his body. "So, you think I should give her time?"

"Yes."

"A week?"

"At the very least."

Brandon leaned his head back against the chair. "I will do as you suggest," he said, sounding none too happy about it. "I will give her one week. But not one second more." Bringing his head up, he shot to his feet. "At any rate, there are matters I need to see to. Robert's and *his mother's* burial arrangements for one." Even in death, Brandon could not give her the respect of calling her his aunt. "And then there is the mysterious puzzle Robert left me with. His last words were most disturbing."

"What did he say?"

"There was no time to tell you last evening, but upon his death, Robert said, 'Farewell, Your Grace.'"

James immediately pushed from his leaning position and placed his glass on the desk.

"Are you certain?"

"Fairly. And something about a box in the bottom of his mother's wardrobe. I had intended to go there immediately upon collecting Julia." He frowned.

"I should like to go with you if you wouldn't mind."

"I could use a friend's company," Brandon admitted. "There is no telling what will be found."

"Allow me a moment to get my coat. And to tell Amelia I shall be going out," he called back as he rushed from the room.

Brandon was left smiling at the thought of his once staunchly independent friend having to inform his wife of leaving. Shaking his head, he hoped he would never allow himself to become so enamored with a woman that he would be accountable to her for his comings and goings.

"ARE YOU QUITE SURE this will work, Amelia?" Julia asked anxiously, as she sat on her bed cross-legged opposite the Duchess. "I shan't like it at all were I to lose him. Even should I spend the rest of my days as his mistress."

"You love him that much?"

"Yes. I have no illusions on that score. I had thought to avoid the emotion entirely, seeing what the loss of it had done to my father. I now realize the weakness was not in the emotion, but within the man. Mother should not have liked for him to end his days pining away for her. Growing up, I had always believed Father to be the strong one, when all along it was Mother."

Amelia placed a hand on Julia's shoulder. "Women are much stronger than men give us credit for—stronger than we give ourselves credit for. That is why I know you will be able to do this. You *are* a strong woman, Julia. I fear you will need to be if you—*when* you find yourself married to Brandon. He does so love to control everything around him. That is his strength. You, my dear, will turn it into his weakness."

"How?"

"By not giving him the one thing he wants most at this particular moment." Amelia smiled. "You."

"Continue," Julia prompted her, leaning forward, intrigued.

"You shall refuse to see him should he call. Avoid him whenever you should meet at a social engagement. You shall make yourself as elusive as a butterfly, no matter the size of the net he attempts to use. Or, the *temptation*."

Julia blushed and felt a need to clear her throat before saying, "I cannot give him the cut direct."

"No, never that," Amelia was quick to agree. "Brandon is James's best friend and now one of mine. I would never suggest you hurt him or embarrass him in any way." She brought her hand up in front of her and began moving her fingers as if she were tinkling the keys of a harpsichord. "You shall merely flutter your pretty wings at him and flit away out of reach." She floated the hand high above her head. Giggling, she brought it back down. "And for that, we need to enlist the aid of some of the other women in the *Book*. Now that you are officially one of the *sisterhood*, you will be astonished at the lengths your new friends will go to aid you in your quest."

"But what if it fails?" Julia insisted, unable to suppress a niggling of doubt.

"I have it on the best authority that it will *succeed*."

"Whose authority?"

Amelia grinned widely and began her recitation. "The Marchioness DeVille, the Dowager Duchess Burkley, the current Duchess of Burkley, Contessa DeMonet, Baroness. . . ."

As the list grew, so too did Julia's confidence.

* * * * *

HEARING A DISTURBING COMMOTION outside his office, William Farnsworth looked up from the papers he was studying as the door swung wide to admit Brandon Barringer with the Duke of Malvern close on his heels. Quickly whipping off his glasses and setting them down on his desk, William came to his feet and reached for his jacket. "Mr. Barringer, forgive me if I have forgotten an appointment—"

"You know deuced well you have never forgotten anything, William," Brandon said, in clipped dismissive tones.

Ensuring their privacy, James firmly closed the heavy oak door on the curious faces of the clerks in the outer room, who were currently vying for a more advantageous view.

"How soon can you authenticate a document?" Brandon asked, as William shrugged into his jacket.

"It would depend on what it was."

"This," Brandon said, tossing down what looked suspiciously like a marriage certificate.

William reached for the vellum and sank heavily back into his chair at the names that leapt off the page. "Dear God in Heaven." He looked up. A slow, wide grin divided his lips. "Your Grace," he added.

"You persist in jumping to conclusions, William. A most annoying habit," Brandon said, but there was no heat to his words.

"I will personally look into the matter right away," the solicitor stated, once again coming rapidly to his feet.

Brandon waved him back down.

"Where did you find it?"

Plopping himself down in one of the chairs in front of William's desk, James answered. "In the bottom of his aun . . . that is to say, Esther's wardrobe," he finished at Brandon's sharp glare. "Right where Robert told him to look. With his dying breath."

William looked between the two men. "I don't understand. If Robert told you last night, we could have seen to it then."

"There were other, more important matters to see to last night," Brandon stated firmly, thoughts of Julia and the night they had shared seeming forever at the forefront of his mind.

"More important than the Dukedom?" William sounded scandalized, while James merely snorted and casually stretched out his legs as if all that were being discussed was a matter of minor import. Shaking his head, the solicitor wondered if he would ever understand the eccentricities of the nobility.

"There was more," Brandon stated, setting the small wooden box he was holding in the center of the desk. "It seems my cousin's mother was quite fastidious in keeping track of every shilling paid out for the nefarious deeds she orchestrated. She kept a ledger. Names. The amounts paid. And the deed for which they were paid. Mrs. Henning's name was among them. As was a servant's at my grandfather's house, who conveniently disappeared shortly after the elder Duke's death."

"Dead, I would imagine," James cut in. "Esther was sinisterly diligent in not leaving loose ends. The only chink in her armor being she believed she would never be discovered. Hence, feeling it unnecessary to destroy any evidence."

"So it would seem," William interjected. "But how did she get this?" He waved the certificate.

"It would appear that the estrangement between my father and grandsire was not wholly of their choosing. Letters were sent on both ends, requesting reconciliation. Mrs. Henning, a valued *friend*," Brandon spat the word, "was entrusted with the missives from my parents—one telling of their marriage and one of my birth. As was apparently the last

letter from my dying mother along with the marriage certificate. It was her hope that the proof of my legitimacy would
induce grandfather to seek me out and claim me."

"And the letters from your grandfather?" William asked
softly.

"Here also. They never left the house. Delivered straight
into Esther's hand by the servant in her employ."

"Sit down, Brandon," James said, reading the desolation
and exhaustion in his friend's face. "William, a drink if you
please."

Both men did as James suggested.

"I CAN HARDLY BELIEVE it," Amelia said, three days later.
"Brandon the true Duke of Durnwald."

"Yes. All that remains now is for him to be officially
recognized," James said, picking up the cup of coffee he was
enjoying after sharing a large breakfast with his wife and
Julia. "I should imagine that with his wealth, good looks, *and*
a Dukedom, the mamas that were so anxious to drag their
thoroughbred daughters from his path will be throwing them
into it."

Only too aware of Julia's hesitancy to move forward
with their plan in light of Brandon's lofty elevation in status,
Amelia gave her husband a quick kick to the shin.

"Ow. What was that for?" he asked, slipping his hand
beneath the table to rub his leg.

"For being such a bore, inconsiderate of Julia's feelings,
and for referring to women as if they were nothing more than
good breeding stock," Amelia stated bluntly, bringing a blush
to Julia's face and a sheepish grin to her husband's.

"I do beg pardon, Julia," James said.

"No need," she assured, raising her chin slightly. "Brandon will finally be able to attain that which he has always coveted."

"So it would appear," James said softly, reaching for the delicate china cup at his hand and taking a drink.

"At any rate, I should like to send him a gift," Julia went on, trying to sound nonchalant and ignore the dull ache in her heart. "Something fitting for a new Duke. Perhaps you might guide me in the matter, James."

"I had thought to also send one around. However, the one thing I know he needs is the one thing I cannot bring myself to give him."

"What might that be?" Amelia asked.

"A pocket watch," James said with a wrinkling of his nose. The two women smiled, well aware of Brandon's annoying habit of continually checking to see if he was on schedule.

"Thank you for the idea, love," Amelia said, placing a chaste kiss on her husband's cheek. Reaching for Julia's hand, she dragged her from her seat. "I believe Julia and I have some shopping to do."

Bringing his hand up to rub the exact spot his wife's lips had landed, James indulged himself in a moment of appreciation as he focused on the appealing sway of Amelia's backside as she made her way down the length of the table and left the room.

Still seated at the table a scant fifteen minutes later, James heard the hushed tones of female voices, a rustle of fabric, and the low murmur of his footman's voice as the two women took their leave. At the sound of the door being closed, he smiled and was struck with the oddest sensation that his friend's days as a bachelor were strictly numbered.

* * * * *

"WHATCHA MEAN, YER GIVIN' up because ye ain't good enough for him?" Maude stared hard at Julia, who was seated across from her in the modiste's private quarters. "As far as I'm concerned nothing's changed. Yer still in love with him. And he's still the same man he was before he got that fancy title."

"You wouldn't understand. Brandon is a *Duke*. He deserves a wife of unquestionable reputation. A wife whose father didn't commit suicide," she finished meekly, lowering her head.

Amelia, who'd been standing quietly behind the chair that Julia was sitting in, gave Maude a helpless shrug when the woman looked her way.

"You know, you might be right," Maude said, drumming her fingers on the arm of the blue damask chair.

At the comment Julia's head came up.

"Perhaps that boy does deserve to be leg-shackled to some bracket-faced chit who wouldn't know a man's erection from the dull end of a spoon. One what would faint dead away the first time Brandon even hinted she might pleasure him by taking his thick, hard shaft into her mouth and sucking it until his juices came squirtin' out. One what—" Maude waved a hand in the air. "Well, I'm sure ye take my meanin'."

Giving Julia time to ponder her words, Maude got up to pour herself a whiskey, winking at Amelia in the process. "Want one?"

"No, thank you," Amelia answered.

She held it out to Julia, who shook her head.

Coming back, Maude settled herself in the chair and continued as if the conversation had never been interrupted. "I'm supposin' he can always train her like he did you. Course she won't be havin' my expertise to refine her talents."

At Julia's deep frown, Maude hid a smile behind the rim of her glass. She took a sizable drink. "But I think it only fair he get to enjoy one night of being loved the way a man should be. Don't ye agree? No sense lettin' all that practice go to waste. I swear that old whalebone phallus you practiced on quivers every time your name is mentioned."

Julia couldn't hold back the small chirp of laughter at what her mind pictured. "Yes," she said, squaring her shoulders. "Brandon does deserve a night like that. And so do I. Will you help me, Maude?"

"Ye bet I will," said the older woman as Amelia grinned, clutched the back of Julia's chair, and did a little bounce.

"First things first," Maude said, rising to her feet. "I think that watch ye mentioned getting for the new Duke should be something special. One that will make him think of ye every time he looks at it. And I know just the person to see."

Amelia and Julia exchanged an excited smile.

"Come on, I ain't got all day to be taking tea and crumpets with the likes of ye two. Let's get going."

Hustling the two younger women out in front of her, Maude stopped only long enough to inform one of her helpers that she'd be steppin' out for the afternoon.

"A PACKAGE FOR YOU, Your Grace," Henry said, coming into Brandon's bedroom,

Brandon smiled at his man. Having arrived several days ago, Henry had taken over the townhouse like a general takes over his troops, making sure Brandon was accorded every privilege and courtesy of his new title. They had not moved into the ducal London residence as yet, but, seeing the tension mount between Mrs. Goodman and Henry, Brandon

had hastily sent the woman over to see to the initial organization. Eventually, he would have to mesh the two strong-willed people into one household, but there would be time enough to worry about that later. At the moment, he had more important matters on his mind. Like convincing the woman he had come to realize he loved to become the new Duchess of Durnwald. Which would be a damn sight easier if he were allowed to see her.

"Who is the package from?" Brandon asked.

"The messenger said it was from Miss Freemont, Your Grace." With a slight turning up of the corner of his mouth, Henry handed Brandon the small box and the note that came along with it.

Brandon wasted no time in tearing the missive open. "It seems she has sent a present in honor of attaining my rightful birthright." For several moments he said nothing as he stroked his thumb across the words she had written.

The light clearing of Henry's throat caught his attention. "If you would like me to leave, Your Grace."

"No need." He tossed the note onto the bed and began ripping into the package. "This way, you will not waste time sneaking back to see what it is," Brandon stated, with a light air.

Henry harrumphed.

Brandon smiled. A smile that grew wider when he discovered what the box contained. "A new watch," he proclaimed pulling it out and holding it up for Henry's viewing.

"Quite lovely, Your Grace."

"Yes, it is," Brandon said, angling the watch to catch the morning light coming through the window. The new position allowed him to appreciate the masterfully carved hunt scene depicted on the front. He turned it over in his hand. The back revealed a man sitting atop an impressive-looking stallion. I

instantly reminded Brandon of Neptune, and he wondered if perhaps Julia had thought the same.

Smiling, he flipped the watch open. There was an inscription on the inside front cover. *May every hidden pleasure in time be yours.* He repeated the words out loud.

"I do not believe I have ever heard that particular saying, Your Grace."

"Hmmm, nor I." Brandon distractedly ran his thumb over the edge of the timepiece. Feeling a small bump, he looked closer. "There appears to be some sort of latch. . . ." At the slightest pressure, a hidden compartment sprung open.

Brandon took one look at what was inside and roared with delight. "Henry, call the carriage around," Brandon requested once he was able to stop laughing. "I'm off to the Malvern residence."

"Very good, Your Grace," Henry said, hurrying from the room.

30

IN HIGH SPIRITS, BRANDON walked up to his carriage and started giving instructions when he realized it was not his usual driver.

"Jerry, what are you doing here? What happened to George?"

"His wife be ill," Jerry said, making an unnecessary adjustment to his eye patch, "Mr. Barrin—Yer Grace. I be called to take ye where yer needin' to go."

"Very well. To the Duke of Malvern's residence, and hurry," Brandon said, hopping into the carriage.

When they arrived, he barely gave Jerry enough time to pull the horses to a stop before he pushed open the door and jumped out. His long, hurried strides, the furthest thing from a dignified ducal stroll as one could get, took him to the front of the house in seconds. Giving the large brass ring on the door several sharp raps, he waited.

"Good day, Jeeves," Brandon said cheerfully when the footman appeared. "Would you please inform Miss Freemont I have come to call."

"I am sorry, Your Grace. Neither Miss Freemont nor the Duchess are in residence at the moment."

Brandon's cheerful demeanor slipped marginally. "Would you happen to be privy to where they went?"

"I believe shopping, Your Grace. The Duchess made mention of Madame LaFleur's."

"Thank you, Jeeves. You are a font of knowledge. I shall inform Malvern you deserve a generous raise in wages." Striding swiftly back the way he'd come, Brandon stopped in front of Jerry, who stood holding the door open. "Madame LaFleur's, please. And give the horses a light taste of the ribbons." Grabbing both sides of the frame, Brandon hoisted himself into the carriage.

They arrived at the modiste's in record time, Brandon rewarding Jerry with a wide smile and the toss of a guinea. The lead horse received an affectionate pat.

He couldn't wait to set eyes on Julia. It had been days since he'd seen her. Touched her. Smelled her. Made love to her. God, how he missed having her near, in his bed at night. Or, during the day for that matter. As if sensing she was within reach, his wayward shaft stiffened like a divining rod.

He burst through the door of the establishment, startling several women. One shrieked, two older women gave him a mildly reproachful look, and one quickly dashed behind the curtain of a dressing room. The last occupant of the room gave him a threatening glare.

"Your Grace," Maude said, her flawless French accent holding a slight note of annoyance. "Is there something you are in such need of that you would so readily forget your manners? It was quite rude of you to scare my customers. I am sure that in England as in France a gentleman is taught to enter an establishment with a measure of finesse. *Oui*?"

"*Oui, madame*. Please accept my most humble apology. As I hope you will, ladies," he said, turning to present each of the women with a courtly bow.

A chorus of *Certainly, Your Grace* rang out, although Brandon paid little attention as his eyes moved around the room. Seeing no sign of the woman he sought, he said to Maude, "Might I impose upon you to grant me a private

moment, madame? I have a matter of great urgency to discuss."

"Oui, Your Grace. This way, *s'il vous plaît*."

Once behind closed doors, Maude turned on him in a flash. "If ye think gettin' that bloody title entitles you to come stormin' in me place like some three-sheets-in-the-wind sailor, I'll be settin' ye straight right quick."

With her hands crammed on her hips and giving him a lofty glare, she looked nothing like the refined lady she was dressed as and more like the Maude of old. Brandon grinned.

"Instead of standing there grinnin' like a fool, ye best start explaining, or I'll be tossin' ye head-over-arse out the back door," Maude warned.

"I'm sorry, love. Truly. I was rather in a rush to find Julia and was told she might be here." His grin faded. "I must have missed her. Did she or Amelia mention where they were going next?"

"Seems yer having a bit o' problem keeping track of yer mistress of late. Appears to me she might have changed her mind. Maybe she ain't wantin' to be no mistress to some lofty *Duke*."

Brandon gave her a soft glare.

"I hear tell she's currently residing with James and that new wife of his."

At that comment Brandon's frown deepened, until his jaw felt ready to snap. "I have every intention of seeing that situation changed."

"If you say so," Maude said, turning to conceal the glee on her face. Though he hadn't said so in words, Maude had no doubt Brandon was smitten with Julia. In all the time she'd known him, she'd never seen him reveal that much emotion over a woman before. "Here," she said, handing him a drink. "Sit yerself down. You look like you could use this."

Relenting, Brandon took the offering and sat in one chair while Maude made herself comfortable in another.

"Go on, drink up," Maude encouraged. "Ye know how I hate drinkin' alone."

Giving her a weak smile, Brandon downed the contents of his glass in one swallow. Toasting her with the empty glass, he set it aside. As it occurred to him that she had yet to answer his question concerning Julia's whereabouts, he opened his mouth to ask. Only to find himself unable to form a single word.

Maude's triumphant smile was the last thing Brandon saw as his eyes shuttered closed.

BRANDON MOANED. OPENED HIS eyes. God, he was so tired. Thinking to bring his hand up to rub his face, he found he could not.

"Bloody hell!"

It was the least offensive of the expletives that left his mouth when he found himself tied to a chair.

Naked.

His first instinct was to strain against the bonds, but availed him little. Whoever had done the deed was no bungling amateur. But who would want him in this position? Not merely tied to a chair, but vulnerably naked? His blood chilled at the options that flew through his mind. He swallowed. What perverted son-of-a-sea-cook would do such a thing?

A small noise behind him alerted him to another's presence.

"Who's there? Show yourself, you cowardly whoreson."

His demand brought forth a soft, feminine laugh. "For

someone newly relieved of his illegitimacy, it seems you have little compunction tossing it at another."

"Julia?"

"Yes," she answered. "Were you expecting another?"

"I knew not what to expect, awakening to find myself tied to a chair—without so much as a single thread to cover me." His words were heavy with relief and exasperation. "What is the meaning of this? Release me at once." He craned his neck in an effort to see her.

"You should save your strength and your commands. The one you will need in the coming hours, the other will gain you nothing. I am the one in control here."

"What—"

She stepped out from behind him.

Brandon knew he'd been about to say something. But had a cutthroat been holding a knife to his heart, he'd be unable to say what it was. "Devil take me," he finally managed to utter.

Julia smiled. "Not the devil. Only one of his lady minions."

From heaven or hell, Brandon would have willingly followed her to either. Followed? More likely dragged her there himself if he knew she would belong to him upon arrival. He was dazed, bedazzled, his mind struggling to comprehend the situation. His member was having no such problem. It was hard, throbbing, straining, caring little for the why, only for the when and how.

She was dressed similarly to the night he'd held her in front of the mirror. The difference being this time the corset, garters, and stockings were black. There were two other changes. The first: she was wearing a pair of black kid gloves. The second: her attitude was far removed from the woman she'd been that night. This Julia was calm, sophisticated, and

boiling over with self-confidence. The sexual effect it was having on Brandon was awe-inspiring and immediate.

"Remember the day you took me to the lake for a picnic?"

Struck dumb with lust, unable to take his eyes from her luscious body, he managed a slight nod.

"You removed my gloves, saying the taste of leather had never appealed to you. But I wonder if perhaps it is only what it is served *with* that is not to your liking." As she spoke, she brought one gloved hand up, resting it at the top of her breast.

Brandon's gaze followed.

Assured of his total attention, she moved her hand round to cup her breast, lifting, squeezing. Taking the nipple between her fingers, she lightly pinched and rolled.

Brandon's whole body clenched, his muscles straining in the soft glow of the multitude of candles placed to best advantage around the room. Julia wanted to miss nothing. To remember vividly every strain of his beautiful muscles, every clench of his strong jaw, every caress of his eyes as they followed her slightest movement.

Glorying in her power, she slid her hand from her breast, smoothing it over her ribcage, massaging her slightly rounded stomach, and rested it above the hair at the juncture of her legs.

"Untie me, Julia. If it was your intent to torture me, you have succeeded beyond your wildest imaginings."

"Oh, love. Your torture has merely begun. And you are about to find out how *wild* are my imaginings . . . but if you persist in making demands, I shall have no other choice but to gag you. The only demands to be heard this night will be mine."

Her hand dropped. She stepped up to him and reached

behind him. A light tickling sensation on his shoulder took his attention there. She was slipping a white cravat from the back of the chair. He hadn't noticed it earlier.

With a daring-him-to-say-anything look, she slid it around his neck and arranged the loose ends down his chest. The silk was cool against his burning flesh. He barely noticed—his attention was fixed on the two firm, lovely globes within a hairsbreadth of his lips.

Julia stepped back.

"Jul—"

She brought a leather-clad finger up to her lips in warning. Made him watch as she slowly, playfully slid it down her body until it lay in the same spot where she had stopped before.

"Taste, Brandon. I wish to show you how well I have learned my lesson in *taste*." She spread her legs. "Watch."

Bound as he was, Brandon could do little else. But every fiber in his being screamed for his release. To be able to touch her. Throw her to the bed standing off to one side. He knew not whose house he was in, nor did he care. He knew only one thing. When she released him from this chair, she would pay. The price—her body. Her soul. Her love. She would give him all those things and he would exult in the taking.

Further thought was impossible. He was capable of only two things, watching and feeling.

She spread her legs wider still, moving her index finger slowly through the dark wavy hair at her pubis, and lower only to disappear from view. The sight of her leathered hand cupping herself as she rotated the finger deep up inside her caused the tension in Brandon's body to intensify. His heart thundered in his chest, his muscles swelled.

The ropes binding his wrists behind the back of the chair and his legs to the chair legs became almost painful. But eve

that could not distract him from the sensual drama being played out in front of him. Eyes closed, head thrown back, Julia was a study in erotic perfection.

Taking deep, measured breaths, Brandon forced himself to relax.

Julia's head came up, her eyes opened. She slid her finger from the depths of her body. Even in the low light, Brandon could see the leather was darker, glistening with her essence.

Taking the steps that would bring her to him, she slid onto his lap. Rubbing against him provocatively, she held the finger to his lips. "Taste," she reminded him needlessly. Without hesitation, he opened his mouth.

Heaven, he thought. Not hell.

He bit down gently, holding it there, sucked. It tasted like leather and her. Julia. His Julia.

Brandon groaned, thrusting his hips into her.

She laughed, the low mellow throaty laugh of a woman in control. Of the moment. Of the man.

Withdrawing her finger from his mouth, she stroked his cheek, touched her mouth to his, laved his lips with her tongue, devoured him with an open-mouthed kiss. And moved off him.

"Damn it all, Julia," Brandon said through clenched teeth, his breathing harsh. "Are you attempting to kill me?"

"Only with ecstasy, my love. Nothing more," she said, stripping the gloves from her hands. Letting them drop to the plush carpet beneath her feet, she lowered herself to her knees between his widespread thighs.

31

JULIA LOOKED UP INTO the face of the man she loved. The man she could never have. She slid her hands up to cup his high cheekbones, running them down each side of his thick, corded neck. Across his broad shoulders. Lower.

Palms flat, she splayed her fingers across the bulging muscles of his chest, hoping his strength would somehow seep into her. Allow her to walk away with no regrets—with only a wish for Brandon to find his heart's desire. A woman who would come to him with no disgrace attached to her name.

"I don't believe I ever told you how beautiful you are," she whispered.

"Men are not beautiful, Julia." He studied her face. "But you are." His tone was low, serious. "More beautiful to me than you can fathom. I—"

"Shhh." She cupped her hand lightly over his mouth. A gentle reminder. One he heeded without protest.

Taking her hand away she sent it, along with the other on a journey to feel, enjoy, memorize. She lingered over every individual muscle and tendon, following each until it connected with another. She stopped at his thighs.

"Taste," she whispered again, glancing back up into his face. Bringing her hands together to capture his shaft, she bent her head and touched her lips to the smooth, satiny cap.

Brandon groaned, threw back his head. His hips arched, his shaft probing softly, seeking more.

She gave it.

Her mouth took him in. In slow degrees. Sliding down . . . down. Her tongue lapping. When she felt the tip touch the back of her throat, she reversed her journey, with the same degree of slow attentive skill.

She felt Brandon move. Knew he was watching. She could feel his erratic breathing stir the hair on the top of her head. Coming to the top, she released him. Dipped her head and, starting at the bottom of his taut, lightly haired sacks, she rode her tongue up the length of him.

He jerked. Had he not been tied to the chair, he might have bucked her free.

"Julia." Her name was a soft croak.

Showing no mercy, she sucked him in again, this time adding her hand. Encircling the rigid, pleasure-giving flesh with her fingers, she stroked. Up. Down. Up. Her mouth sucking. Her hand stroking.

Brandon's breathing became more erratic.

"You . . . must . . . Stop. . . ."

She obeyed. Long enough to murmur, "Never." Nipping the head of his member lightly with her teeth, she sucked it back into her mouth.

When her free hand reached down to toy with the tight sack between his legs, Brandon could hold back no more. His thighs clenched, his hips shot forward.

His seed spurted out in an erupting flood, coating her tongue, her mouth, the back of her throat.

Surprised at the force, titillated by the salty taste, enthralled with what she had done, it took her a moment to wallow.

"Lord help me," Brandon murmured weakly as his head

dropped forward to rest against the top of hers. "If I live to be a hundred, I vow I shall never forget this moment." He felt the smile of Julia's lips on flesh sated but still rigid.

With one last lick, Julia sat back on her heels and looked up at him. A sultry desire in her eyes.

"Now, if you will untie me, I should like to return the favor."

She shook her head.

"Julia. . . ." The command was back in his voice.

With a sigh, she stood, grasped his chin in her small hand, and kissed him. Brandon closed his eyes to savor her taste. She mouthed something against his lips. Something Brandon knew was important, but before his sluggish mind could grasp the words, she slid the cravat from his neck, placed it in his mouth, and tied it off with efficient haste.

His eyes sprang open.

She stepped back.

At the sight of such a large, powerful man tied, gagged, and at her complete mercy, a surge of feminine power rocked Julia to the center of her being.

"One last thing before I go," she purred, ignoring the narrowing of his eyes and muffled sounds from behind the white silk fabric.

"I have one more gift for you." She momentarily left his sight, returning seconds later. "I had this specially made for you. A cane fit for a *Duke*. Something that will always remind you of me." She held out the elegant walking stick for his inspection:

A handsome piece with an ebony shaft tipped with brass. The handle white ivory, intricately carved, with ripples and lines in no particular pattern, capped with a large, round brass knob.

As she spoke, Julia began unscrewing the top.

A hidden rapier, Brandon thought. A handy weapon to have, although a latch would have been more practical than having to unscrew it. Although he had no intention of hurting her feelings by saying so.

He would be more than happy to show his appreciation for it and the pocket watch, if the wench would only untie him.

But when the top was removed, he blinked twice at what he saw. Not a rapier at all, but a very cleverly carved version of a man's phallus.

Shocked, heart pounding, he watched Julia do something that would have knocked him from the chair, had he not been bound.

She spread her legs, inserted the fake shaft up into her unresisting flesh, gave it a slow rotation, and pulled it back out.

"In case you should ever feel the need to *taste* me," she said, setting the cap back on and screwing it in place. "If you dare."

Picking up the gloves she had set aside earlier, she placed both them and the cane across his bare thighs, well away from his jutting shaft.

Their gazes locked.

His confused, shocked, angry.

Hers triumphant, loving, sad.

"Goodbye, my love." She placed a sweet kiss on his forehead and, turning her back on the muffled curses and thumping chair legs, she left.

What felt to Brandon an eternity later, he heard the opening of the door. Drained from his exertions to attain escape, his wrists and ankles burning, he glared at the man who walked in.

"I been sent to release ye, Yer Grace. But from the look

yer givin' me, I ain't sure it be such a good idea," Jerry stated, remaining a good distance away.

Brandon made an attempt to gain control over his anger and relax the locked muscles of his jaw.

"That be some better. But I'll be havin' yer promise not to kill me afore I be a-lettin' ye loose."

"Umf."

"I be takin' that for a yes," Jerry said, walking behind Brandon and, taking out a small knife, sliced the rope at his wrists.

Brandon brought his aching arms forward and winced at the painful tingling sensation that raced up their length. Regaining some feeling, he reached up to untie the cravat. Once removed, he held out his hand as Jerry came back around.

Keeping well out of reach, Jerry stretched to drop the knife in Brandon's open palm and stepped back.

Once his legs were free, Brandon grabbed both cane and gloves from his lap and surged to his feet, receiving some satisfaction when the coachman jumped back another step.

Too angry to talk, Brandon looked around the room and, spotting his clothes neatly laid out on the bed, went over to get dressed. Once properly attired, he felt more in control.

"Ain't ye gonna say nothin'?" Jerry's one good blue eye peered out of a face wreathed in wary contrition.

"Where is she?"

"I weren't told much. Only that Maude needed a favor. I be owin' her a few. She been good to me and mine when things be rough. She said ye wouldn't be holdin' me accountable," he finished, giving Brandon a hopeful look.

"This has nothing to do with you, Jerry. But never lie to me again."

"Didn't. It be a fact yer driver's wife be sick and all I

said was I be called to take ye where yer needin' to go," Jerry repeated the words he'd said.

Faced with that convoluted truth, Brandon could do little but smile and say, "Right now, the only thing I *be needin'* is to go home, take a very *cold* bath, and get some rest. After which, I believe I shall go on a little hunting trip."

"Whatcha be huntin'?"

"Vixen," Brandon answered as he strode from the room. "A devilishly annoying one."

BUT OVER THE NEXT weeks, the vixen Brandon was hunting proved to be a very elusive one. By the end of the third week, he was ready to strangle something. Or someone. Preferable a lot of someones. Females, every last one.

Time and again, when he got close to cornering Julia, either at the Malvern residence, or a social function, some meddlesome female would find a reason to whisk her away. If they hadn't been from the highest peerages in England, Brandon might have thought there was a conspiracy against him. Had Julia always had so many female friends?

Even the Dowager Duchess of Burkley seemed to be taking an extraordinarily high interest in Julia's welfare. And damned if the old harridan wasn't proving to be a most diligent chaperone.

But tonight would be different. Brandon had seen to that. He was not without friends of his own.

Tonight, every single female that had come between him and the woman he wanted would be otherwise occupied. Including the most meddlesome. The Duchess of Malvern.

With a grin, Brandon allowed his feet to slide off the top of his desk with a thump. Picking up the open pocket watch

he'd been entertaining himself with, he came to his feet and picked up the cane Julia had given him.

Leaving his library, Brandon entered the foyer. He stood still long enough for a last inspection by Henry, who made a slight adjustment to his cravat, smoothed the shoulders of his black evening jacket, and helped him slip into his black wool overcoat. With a nod of thanks, Brandon placed his hat atop his head and went out to his carriage.

JULIA HADN'T THE HEART to tell all her new friends to desist in their machinations. There was no possibility of her marrying Brandon. She would not, could not, allow it to happen. Yet, in all fairness, she could not put the entire blame on them. She had enjoyed being allowed the fantasy, if only for a short while longer.

"I do so wish Isabella were here," Julia said, turning away from the swirling couples on the dance floor to Amelia, who was the current chaperone of the hour.

"As do I, dear. But who can blame her for seeking seclusion after what happened. To find out one's betrothed is a fake, his mother a murderer."

"But she must know no one would expect her to mourn, under the circumstances," Julia said. "After all, it was she who was wronged most grievously."

"True, but she took the news badly, and she will need some time to forget. Six months, I should think," Amelia said on a more cheerful note. "Then we shall see to it she returns to London in time for the Season. Amanda shall be here then and can help to make sure Isabella does not wallow in her doldrums. Mandy is ever so good at livening things up a bit."

"I cannot wait to meet her. She sounds such fun."

"Excuse me, my dear," James said, walking up to his wife and interrupting the conversation. "I believe you owe me a dance."

Amelia quickly glanced around. "Could it not wait a bit? Julia—"

"Will be fine," he said, sending a smile Julia's way.

"Your husband is right. You have yet to dance with him. Go. I will be fine," Julia said, shooing the other woman off.

"If you are sure."

"Go."

James gave Amelia no time to answer as he whisked her onto the dance floor, his smooth, beautifully executed steps quickly taking her to the other side of the room.

Julia had barely enough time to appreciate her momentary solitude before she found herself the center of attention by a growing number of attentive, fawning gentlemen.

Shielded from a view of the entire room, Julia was totally unaware that Brandon had arrived.

He stood at the entrance of the ballroom, uncaring of everything and everyone except the one woman he was searching for. Unlike prior times when he had to work his way through the crush, a path was immediately opened in deference to his newly acknowledged title. He looked neither right nor left as he began walking, somehow knowing she would be at the end of the path he had set upon.

Had his mission been less purposeful, he might have lingered to relish the disappointment on the faces of those who tried unsuccessfully to gain his attention. Mothers who had previously snatched their daughters from his path, men who had shunned him for other than business dealings. But he had no interest in either them or their insipid, childish daughters—he had a much more voluptuous, desirable quarry on his mind.

One he had spent the past nights dreaming of, when his overheated body and painfully rigid shaft would allow him to sleep. A woman he was determined to reclaim. Whether the headstrong little termagant was agreeable or not. After all, as a Duke, he should be entitled to pretty much what he damn well wanted.

Breaking through the crush, he saw her, standing in sophisticated comfort, holding her fan loosely in one hand, the tip resting in the other. She was surrounded by a toadying group of gentlemen, both young and old. Some he was well acquainted with, some he was not. All, obviously enraptured by her beauty.

When one of the bolder bucks bent over her shoulder in the guise of hearing better and stared avidly down the valley of her plump, creamy white breasts, Brandon had to physically contain himself from rushing over and blackening the man's eyes. Or worse.

Holding on tenuously to his raging jealousy, he broke through the milling crowd and stepped up behind her. The wary look on the face of the man in front of her must have alerted her to his presence. Studying Julia closely, Brandon was privy to the small start her body gave.

Julia turned casually, struggling to appear unconcerned by the presence behind her. Within, her heart was beating so fast she wondered that it did not fly from her chest. "Your Grace," she said, acknowledging him with a deep curtsy.

"Miss Freemont." He bent over her hand, pressing his lips to the back, lingering.

Distracted by the familiar feel of his mouth and fighting her body's yearning to have it pressed intimately between her thighs to lap at the moisture she knew was already gathering, she realized too late that he'd drawn her several steps away from the others.

"Are you enjoying the evening?" she asked, pulling her hand from his.

"Not as much as I intend to." The words were low, meant for her ears alone. Straightening, he said more loudly, "It is too early to tell, but one has merely to place oneself in the right company, focus his efforts on the object that will gain him the greatest pleasure, and enjoyment will inevitably follow."

Not as adept at the game of seductive innuendo as he, she allowed Brandon to detect a gleam of startled interest in her eyes before she affected a look of mild indifference.

"I wish you luck in finding that pleasure, Your Grace."

When she turned, he placed a detaining hand on her arm. "What would give me great pleasure, Miss Freemont, is for you to honor me with a dance."

"I do not think—"

"I insist." His eyes took on a challenging glint.

Unwilling to make a scene and risk ruining the tenuous beginning of her acceptance back in society, she knew he left her little choice but to comply.

He offered his arm.

Julia glanced around nervously.

"Come, Julia. You will find no one to intervene. This time. have taken measures to make sure of it."

Her startled gaze flew to his. Seeing the determined look there, she allowed him to lead her onto the dance floor.

Once there, he pulled her into his arms.

He held her too tight and too close. Julia could not find the will to insist otherwise as every fiber in her being responded to his familiarity. The sight of his chiseled, clean-shaven face. The woodsy scent of his soap, mingling with the musk of his cologne. The feel of his broad shoulders beneath the soft black wool of his tailored jacket. The solid touch of his hand as he guided her through the dance. The dark heat

of his gaze, burning a slow trail from her lips to the generously displayed tops of her breasts.

In reaction, her nipples puckered into hard little peaks. The rasp of the delicate blue fabric covering them almost caused her to moan.

"Dare I hope I am the reason for that look on your face and the firm little nubs currently straining against your bodice? Or perhaps it is merely a chill in the room?"

Upset with herself and the wolfish smile on his face, Julia tried to pull away.

His arms tightened, drawing her closer still.

"I demand you release me, before you cause a scene."

"It is not I who will cause the scene, but you, with your struggling. Not that I am averse to your wiggling against me. I have always found it quite pleasurable."

Shocked at his audacity, she immediately halted her efforts to escape.

"Is it your intention to embarrass me in front of the entire *ton*?"

"If that is what it will take for you to hear me out."

"What are you saying?"

"I am saying I no longer care what anyone thinks of me. Of us. I want you to become my wife. I love you."

His bald declaration so shocked her, for several seconds she could not think what to say. Her heart soared. He loved her. He wanted her. Then reason intruded.

"I see. If your concern stems from the night we spent together, you need concern yourself no further. You may continue your pursuit of a proper wife without guilt. My courses appeared last week. If that is all, Your Grace, I would like for you to release me."

It had not been the reaction Brandon had expected. Tears, laughter, her own declaration of undying love perhaps.

Not this. Stunned by her erroneous reasoning, Brandon nearly allowed her to get away.

"Julia, I do not want another woman for my duchess, I want you." He tried once again to reason with her. "What will it take to prove what I say is true? To prove I want no other woman but you?"

"Nothing. There is nothing you can do. You have been honest with me from the outset of our arrangement." She was careful to keep her voice low. "Now you have that which you desired most. The respect you so craved. A title. You need do nothing but find a respectable wife to enjoy it with." Julia knew she needed to get away soon, before her resolve broke. She could feel the burning in the back of her eyes. The thought of Brandon with another woman churned her insides. "Good bye, my love."

This time, he made no effort to retain her, but allowed her to whirl from his embrace. She got as far as his hand, still clutching the tips of her fingers, would allow.

"Miss Freemont?" Brandon called in a loud voice.

Shocked, Julia looked around to find many of the couples around them had stopped dancing and were now staring at them with interest.

Hurrying back to him, she placed a hand over his mouth. "Brandon, please."

She felt the grin of his mouth against her fingers before he grasped her wrist lightly and drew her arm down.

"You say there is nothing I can do to prove I love you? That you mean more to me than any scandal that might be attached to my name?" As his voice grew louder, more and more couples stopped dancing and stood watching in captivated silence.

"Brandon, hush."

"Well, I say you are wrong."

Before she could breath, before she could blink, Brandon used the wrist he was still holding to yank her against him. And in front of the entire *ton*, he kissed her. Hard, demanding, announcing his ownership to one and all.

He released her and, giving her one of his devilishly intriguing smiles that instantly put her senses on alert, hauled her up over his shoulder.

With a shriek, Julia found herself bottom up in front of half of London society.

"Everyone, your attention please." Brandon's voice boomed to be heard in the far corners of the silent ballroom. "I would like to present to you the new Duchess of Durnwald."

For a moment Julia could have sworn she could hear every candle in the ballroom flicker. And then little else but her own heartbeat as male laughter and congratulations began rippling through the crowd. Gradually it became mixed with the tinkling of feminine giggling and ended in a crescendo of resounding applause.

"Now, if you will please excuse us. I believe I still have a bit more persuading to do."

Julia buried her face deeper into Brandon's back as he carried her out. "I think I shall kill you," she said into his jacket, but the words were lost in an explosion of cheers and laughter.

Coming to the first room that would afford them some privacy, Brandon strode inside, breathing a sigh of relief to find the sitting room empty. Taking no chances that Julia would flee, he locked the door before setting her down.

"That is without doubt the most outrageous thing you could ever have done," Julia said, glaring up at him, fists clenched at her sides. "Have you lost what little sense God gave you?"

"I have come to the conclusion that where you are concerned, I have no sense," Brandon stated, calmly peeling off his gloves and tossing them onto a nearby chair. When he advanced a step forward, she took one back. He stopped.

"What of your precious reputation?" she asked, her heart thudding in anticipation of his answer.

"I suppose you shall just have to marry me to save me from the wagging tongues of society."

Encouraged by the slight easing of her stern expression, he continued. "I love you, Julia. I love the way you look, the way you smell, the way you taste. Especially the way you taste." At her raised brow, he smiled and pushed on. "I love everything about you. I was a fool to think I could ever marry another." His countenance turned more serious. "I suppose it took having you and then nearly losing you to make me realize it."

Julia looked into his beloved face. What she saw was nothing but love shining back at her. "Oh, Brandon." She stepped forward, slipping into his arms to be encompassed by his warm embrace. With her head tucked into his familiar strong warmth, she confessed, "I was such a fool to allow myself to be influenced by society's intolerance of one's birthright. It is not the title that makes the man, but the man that makes the title."

He hugged her tightly and kissed the top of her head.

She looked up at him. "You do not deserve the title of Duke."

He stiffened perceptibly.

Bringing her hand up, she caressed his cheek. "You deserve nothing less than to be named King. King of my heart." Her smile was dazzling. "I love you," she whispered and, wrapping her arms around his neck, pulled him to her for a tender, soul-melding kiss.

When they broke apart, Brandon eyed her lovingly and asked, "Does this mean you will marry me?"

Julia gave him a pitying look and heaved a deep sigh. "I suppose I must," she said, unable to keep a smile from creeping to her lips. "It seems the only way to save *your* reputation, after that scandalous display you put on."

Brandon's loud, barking laugh filled the room. Snatching her to him, he lifted her off the floor and swung her around to the tune of her lilting laughter.

Dizzy, from both love and spinning, Brandon placed her back on her feet.

"Are you ready to face the masses?" he asked.

"No."

The conviction in Julia's voice garnered Brandon's full attention. "Do you wish to leave then?"

"Yes. I would."

"If you will wait here, I shall make our excuses to our host and hostess," he said, his voice heavy with resolved disappointment. "Then I shall inform James and Amelia I will be returning you to their residence."

Julia peeked at him through lowered lashes. "You may tell the others any excuse you wish, but I prefer you not lie to James and Amelia. You should merely tell them I shall be returning at first light. Of a sudden I feel the greatest need for one of your expert *lessons*. After which, I plan on teaching you a little something I learned from a very dear friend of mine . . . Lady Weathersby."

JAMES LET LOOSE A deep, frustrated sigh. Unable to concentrate on *The Edinburgh Review* he was holding out in front of him, he folded the newspaper neatly and let it plop down next

to his chair. He looked over at Brandon, whom he'd dragged to one of their favorite clubs to keep him company.

Brandon consigned his own paper to the floor. "Hang in there, old fellow," he said. "It won't be much longer. It could be worse."

"How so?"

"I had chance to visit Exeter 'Change in the Strand only yesterday with Julia, and have picked up the bit of information that an elephant carries its young for nearly two years."

James shuddered at the thought. "It escapes me how such an amiable person as my wife," here James studiously ignored the skeptical look he received from Brandon, "can turn into such a shrew one moment only to burst into tears the next."

"Look on the bright side. You have merely one month to go."

"Which I am sure will seem an infernal eternity," James groaned out.

Giving his friend a sympathetic look, Brandon reached for his pocket watch and flipped it open.

"I see *your* wife has yet to break you of that annoying habit," James slurred in mild disgust. "If anything, you seem to be doing it more."

Without looking up, Brandon merely smiled.

"Well, what time is it?"

"I haven't the slightest," Brandon shot back cheerfully, unperturbed by his friend's dour mood.

"You are staring at your watch, yet have no idea what time it is?"

"Precisely. But it has served to remind me there are infinitely more pleasurable things I can be doing instead of keeping you company in your present ill-humored state."

"For instance?"

"For instance. . . ." Brandon surged to his feet. "Going

home to my wife, where Julia and I can work on attaining the next *Durnwald* heir. So, if you will excuse me," Brandon said, tugging down the sleeves of his grey worsted jacket and shifting slightly to accommodate the bulge forming in his breeches. "I believe I will take my leave." Before departing, he snapped his watch closed and flicked his wrist, tossing the watch to James. "Look for the hidden latch on the side," Brandon instructed with a wink. Grinning widely, he strode from the club.

The Duke of Malvern looked down at the timepiece he held and pressed the opening latch. He read the inscription. *May every hidden pleasure in time be yours.* As instructed, he ran a finger down the side, found the latch Brandon had spoken of, and pressed.

His immediate shout of laughter chased after Brandon like an outgoing tide, causing younger men to turn in his direction with curiosity and older men in disapproval.

Shaking his head at his friend's retreating back, James leashed in his humor and stared down at the watch.

There, in a secret compartment, was a graphically detailed rendition of a naked couple. The man's shaft, nearly half the size of his body, stroked down and sprang back in tandem with the opening and closing of the woman's legs to the chiming of the quarter hour.

c

most businesslike tone, while all the time her anxiety was rising and the questions were pounding through her head.

Did he know?

Had he found out?

A faint smile touched his mouth and the movement distracted her. There was an almost deadly beauty in the sensual curve of those lips. Everything about the man was dark and sexual, as if he'd been designed for the express purpose of drawing women to their doom. If rumor were correct, he did that with appalling frequency.

Fia wasn't fooled by his apparently relaxed pose or his deceptively mild tone.

Santo Ferrara was the most dangerous man she'd ever met.

Will Santo discover Fia's secret?

Find out in THE FORBIDDEN FERRARA
by USA TODAY bestselling author Sarah Morgan,
available this June from Harlequin Presents®!

The legacy of the powerful
Sicilian Ferrara dynasty continues in
THE FORBIDDEN FERRARA
by USA TODAY *bestselling author Sarah Morgan.*

Enjoy this sneak peek!

A Ferrara would never sit down at a Baracchi table for fear of being poisoned.

Fia had no idea why Santo was here. He didn't know.

He *couldn't* know.

"*Buona sera,* Fia."

A deep male voice came from the doorway, and she turned. The crazy thing was, she didn't know his voice. But she knew his eyes and they were looking at her now—two dark pools of dangerous black. They gleamed bright with intelligence and hard with ruthless purpose. They were the eyes of a man who thrived in a cutthroat business environment. A man who knew what he wanted and wasn't afraid to go after it. They were the same eyes that had glittered into hers in the darkness three years before as they'd ripped each other's clothes and slaked a fierce hunger.

He was exactly the same. Still the same "born to rule" Ferrara self-confidence; the same innate sophistication, polished until it shone bright as the paintwork of his Lamborghini.

She wanted him to go to hell and stay there.

He was her biggest mistake.

And judging from the cold, cynical glint in his eye, he considered her to be his.

"Well, this is a surprise. The Ferrara brothers don't usually step down from their ivory tower to mingle with us mortals. Checking out the competition?" She adopted her

Harlequin *Romance*

A touching new duet from fan-favorite author

SUSAN MEIER

First Time **DADS!**

When millionaire CEO Max Montgomery spots
Kate Hunter-Montgomery—the wife he's never forgotten—
back in town with a daughter who looks just like him, he's
determined to win her back. But can this savvy business tycoon
convince Kate to trust him a second time with her heart?

Find out this June in

THE TYCOON'S SECRET DAUGHTER

And look for book 2 coming this August!

NANNY FOR THE MILLIONAIRE'S TWINS

Saddle up with Harlequin® series books this summer
and find a cowboy for every mood!

REQUEST YOUR FREE BOOKS!
2 FREE NOVELS PLUS 2 FREE GIFTS!

Harlequin®

Romance

From the Heart, For the Heart

YES! Please send me 2 FREE Harlequin® Romance novels and my 2 FREE gifts (gifts are worth about $10). After receiving them, if I don't wish to receive any more books, I can return the shipping statement marked "cancel". If I don't cancel, I will receive 6 brand-new novels every month and be billed just $4.09 per book in the U.S. or $4.49 per book in Canada. That's a savings of at least 14% off the cover price! It's quite a bargain! Shipping and handling is just 50¢ per book in the U.S. and 75¢ per book in Canada.* I understand that accepting the 2 free books and gifts places me under no obligation to buy anything. I can always return a shipment and cancel at any time. Even if I never buy another book, the two free books and gifts are mine to keep forever.

116/316 HDN FESE

Name _____ (PLEASE PRINT)

Address _____ Apt. #

City _____ State/Prov. _____ Zip/Postal Code

Signature (if under 18, a parent or guardian must sign)

Mail to the **Reader Service:**
IN U.S.A.: P.O. Box 1867, Buffalo, NY 14240-1867
IN CANADA: P.O. Box 609, Fort Erie, Ontario L2A 5X3

Not valid for current subscribers to Harlequin Romance books.

**Are you a subscriber to Harlequin Romance books
and want to receive the larger-print edition?
Call 1-800-873-8635 or visit www.ReaderService.com.**

* Terms and prices subject to change without notice. Prices do not include applicable taxes. Sales tax applicable in N.Y. Canadian residents will be charged applicable taxes. Offer not valid in Quebec. This offer is limited to one order per household. All orders subject to credit approval. Credit or debit balances in a customer's account(s) may be offset by any other outstanding balance owed by or to the customer. Please allow 4 to 6 weeks for delivery. Offer available while quantities last.

Your Privacy—The Reader Service is committed to protecting your privacy. Our Privacy Policy is available online at www.ReaderService.com or upon request from the Reader Service.

We make a portion of our mailing list available to reputable third parties that offer products we believe may interest you. If you prefer that we not exchange your name with third parties, or if you wish to clarify or modify your communication preferences, please visit us at www.ReaderService.com/consumerchoice or write to us at Reader Service Preference Service, P.O. Box 9062, Buffalo, NY 14269. Include your complete name and address.

HRI1B

CLASSIC

Harlequin *Romance*

COMING NEXT MONTH
AVAILABLE JUNE 12, 2012

#4315 THE TYCOON'S SECRET DAUGHTER
First Time Dads!
Susan Meier

#4316 THE SHERIFF'S DOORSTEP BABY
Teresa Carpenter

#4317 THE REBEL RANCHER
Cadence Creek Cowboys
Donna Alward

#4318 PLAIN JANE IN THE SPOTLIGHT
The Falcon Dynasty
Lucy Gordon

#4319 SECRETS AND SPEED DATING
Leah Ashton

#4320 THE SHEIKH'S JEWEL
Melissa James

LESSONS OF THE SENSES

Brandon placed his mouth to the sensitive area below her ear and sucked gently. Moving lower, he laid a trail of tiny nips, soothing each with a caress of his tongue, working down to the tops of her soft, fragrant breasts. When he reached the edge of her gown she tensed. He foraged on, slipping his tongue beneath the fabric. When Julia expelled a soft whimper, Brandon raised his head and basked in the wonder evident in her eyes.

D1304490

I

Als Otto von Lambert von der Polizei benachrichtigt worden war, am Fuße der Al-Hakim-Ruine sei seine Frau Tina vergewaltigt und tot aufgefunden worden, ohne daß es gelungen sei, das Verbrechen aufzuklären, ließ der Psychiater, bekannt durch sein Buch über den Terrorismus, die Leiche mit einem Helikopter über das Mittelmeer transportieren, wobei der Sarg, worin sie lag, mit einem Tragseil unter der Flugmaschine befestigt, dieser nachschwebend, bald über sonnenbeschienene unermeßliche Flächen, bald durch Wolkenfetzen flog, dazu noch über den Alpen in einen Schneesturm, später in Regengüsse geriet, bis er sich sanft ins offene von der Trauerversammlung umstellte Grab hinunterspulen ließ, das alsobald zugeschaufelt wurde, worauf von Lambert, der bemerkt hatte, daß auch die F. den Vorgang filmte, seinen Schirm trotz des Regens schließend, sie kurz musterte und sie aufforderte, ihn noch diesen Abend mit ihrem Team zu besuchen, er habe einen Auftrag für sie, der keinen Aufschub dulde.

2

Die F., bekannt durch ihre Filmporträts, die sich vorgenommen hatte, neue Wege zu beschreiten und der noch vagen Idee nachhing, ein Gesamtporträt herzustellen, jenes unseres Planeten nämlich, indem sie dies durch ein Zusammenfügen zufälliger Szenen zu einem Ganzen zu erzielen hoffte, weshalb sie auch das seltsame Begräbnis gefilmt hatte, verblüfft dem massigen Mann nachschauend, von Lambert, der regennaß und unrasiert mit offenem schwarzem Mantel sie angeredet hatte und grußlos von ihr gegangen war, entschloß sich nur zögernd, die Aufforderung anzunehmen, weil ein ungutes Gefühl ihr sagte, etwas stimme nicht und außerdem laufe sie Gefahr, in den Sog einer Geschichte zu geraten, die sie von ihren Plänen ablenke, so daß sie eigentlich widerwillig mit ihrem Team in der Wohnung des Psychiaters erschien, allein von der Neugier getrieben, was dieser von ihr wolle und entschlossen, auf nichts einzugehen.

3

Von Lambert empfing sie in seinem Studierzimmer, verlangte unverzüglich gefilmt zu werden, ließ willig alle Vorbereitungen über sich ergehen, erklärte dann vor der laufenden Kamera, hinter seinem Schreibtisch sitzend, er sei am Tode seiner Frau schuldig, weil er die oft unter schweren Depressionen Leidende immer mehr als Fall statt als Frau behandelt hätte, bis sie, nachdem ihr seine Notizen über ihre Krankheit durch Zufall zu Gesicht gekommen, kurzerhand das Haus verlassen habe, nach der Meldung der Hausdame nur in ihrem roten Pelzmantel über einen Jeansanzug geworfen und mit einer Handtasche, seitdem habe er nichts mehr von ihr gehört, doch habe er auch nichts unternommen, von ihr etwas zu erfahren, um ihr einerseits jede Freiheit zu lassen, andererseits ihr, käme sie auf seine Nachforschungen, das Gefühl zu ersparen, sie würde von ihm weiterhin beobachtet, doch jetzt, da sie ein so entsetzliches Ende genommen und er nicht nur in seiner Methode ihr gegenüber, jener der kühlen Beobachtung, die der Psychiatrie vorgeschrieben sei, sondern auch in seinem Unterlassen jeder Nachforschung seine Schuld erkenne, erachte er es für seine Pflicht, die Wahrheit zu erfahren, mehr noch, sie der Wissenschaft zugänglich zu machen, herauszufinden, was sich ereignet habe, sei er doch an die Grenze seiner Wissenschaft gestoßen, die sich im Schicksal seiner Frau abzeichne, gesundheitlich sei er eine Ruine und nicht im Stande, selber hinzufahren und so gebe er denn ihr, der F., den Auftrag, mit ihrem Team das Verbrechen an seiner Frau, wovon er als Arzt der Urheber sei, der Täter jedoch nur einen zufälligen Faktor darstelle, an jenem Orte, wo es sich offensichtlich abgespielt habe, zu rekonstruieren, festzuhalten was festzuhalten sei, damit der so entstandene Film an Fachkongressen und der Staatsanwaltschaft vorgeführt werden könne, als Schuldiger habe er wie jeder Verbrecher das Recht auf das Geheimhalten seiner Verfehlung verloren und damit händigte er ihr einen Scheck in beträchtlicher Höhe, mehrere Fotos der Verstorbenen, sowie ihr Tagebuch und seine Notizen aus, worauf die F. den Auftrag zur Verwunderung ihres Teams annahm.

4

Nachdem die F. sich verabschiedet, auf die Frage ihres Kameramanns, was der Unsinn denn bedeute, keine Antwort gegeben und während der Nacht fast bis zur Morgendämmerung das Tagebuch und die Notizen durchgesehen hatte, organisierte sie nach kurzem Schlaf noch von ihrem Bett aus mit einem Reisebüro den Flug nach M., fuhr in die Stadt, kaufte die Boulevardpresse auf deren Titelseite Bilder der seltsamen Beerdigung und der Toten waren und setzte sich, bevor sie einer flüchtig hingeschriebenen Adresse nachging, die sie im Tagebuch gefunden hatte, im italienischen Restaurant, wo sie frühstückte, zum Logiker D., dessen Vorlesung auf der Universität von zwei, drei Studenten besucht wurde, zu einem scharfsinnigen Kauz, von dem niemand wußte, ob er dem Leben gegenüber hilflos war oder diese Hilflosigkeit nur spielte, der jedem, welcher sich in dem stets überfüllten Restaurant zu ihm setzte, seine logischen Probleme erklärte, derart wirr und gründlich, daß sie niemand zu begreifen vermochte, auch die F. nicht, die ihn jedoch amüsant fand, ihn mochte und ihm gegenüber oft ihre Pläne erläuterte, so jetzt, indem sie ihm vom merkwürdigen Auftrag des Psychiaters erzählte und auf das Tagebuch seiner Frau zu sprechen kam, ohne sich bewußt zu werden, daß sie davon berichtete, so sehr war sie noch mit dem engbeschriebenen Heft beschäftigt, sagte sie doch, sie habe noch nie eine ähnliche Schilderung eines Menschen gelesen, Tina von Lambert habe ihren Mann als ein Ungeheuer beschrieben, aber allmählich, nicht sofort, sondern indem sie eine Facette dieses Menschen um die andere von ihm gleichsam losgelöst, dann wie unter einem Mikroskop mit immer steigender Vergrößerung und in immer schärferem Licht betrachtet, seitenlang beschrieben habe, wie er esse, seitenlang wie er in den Zähnen stochere, seitenlang wie er sich und wo er sich kratze, seitenlang wie er schnalze oder sich räuspere, huste, niese oder andere unwillkürliche Bewegungen, Gesten, Zuckungen und Eigentümlichkeiten, die mehr und weniger bei jedem Menschen vorzufinden seien, aber dies alles sei in einer Art und Weise dargestellt, daß ihr, der F., nun das Essen an sich unerträglich vorkomme, und wenn sie jetzt noch nichts von ihrem Frühstück angerührt habe, so nur, weil sie sich vorstelle, sie esse ebenso abscheulich, man könne gar nicht ästhetisch essen, es sei, lese man dieses Tagebuch, als ob sich eine Wolke aus lauter Beobachtungen zu einem Klumpen von Haß und Abscheu verdichte, es komme ihr vor, als hätte sie ein Drehbuch gelesen zur Dokumentation jedes Menschen, als ob jeder Mensch, filme man ihn so, zu einem von Lambert werde, wie ihn dessen Frau beschrieben habe, indem er durch eine so unbarmherzige Beobachtung jede Individualität verliere, dagegen habe ihr der Psychiater einen ganz anderen Eindruck gemacht, er sei ein Fanatiker seines Berufs, der an seinem Beruf zu zweifeln beginne, er habe etwas ungemein Kindliches wie viele Wissenschaftler, und Hilfloses, er hätte geglaubt seine Frau zu lieben und glaube es immer noch, aber man bilde sich allzuleicht ein, jemanden zu lieben und liebe im Grunde nur sich selber, die spektakuläre Beerdigung habe sie mißtrauisch gemacht, die kaschiere nur seinen verletzten Stolz, warum nicht, und mit dem Auftrag, nach den Umständen zu forschen, die zum Tode seiner Frau geführt hätten, versuche er, wenn auch unbewußt, vor allem sich selber ein Denkmal zu setzen, sei die Schilderung Tinas über ihren Mann ins Übertriebene, ins allzu

Anschauliche geraten, so die Notizen von Lamberts ins allzu Abstrakte, nicht ein Beobachten, sondern ein Abstrahieren vom Menschen sei hinter diesen Notizen zu lesen, die Depression definiert als psychosomatisches Phänomen, ausgelöst durch die Einsicht in die Sinnlosigkeit des Seins, die dem Sein an sich anhafte, der Sinn des Seins sei das Sein selber und damit sei das Sein prinzipiell nicht auszuhalten, Tina sei dieser Einsicht einsichtig geworden und eben diese Einsicht in diese Einsicht sei die Depression und so seitenlang immer derselbe Quark, weshalb es ihr gänzlich unmöglich sei zu glauben, Tina sei geflüchtet, weil sie diese Notizen gefunden hätte, wie von Lambert anscheinend vermute, auch wenn ihr Tagebuch mit dem zweimal unterstrichenen Satz »ich werde beobachtet« geendet habe, sie deute diese Bemerkung anders, Tina sei dahintergekommen von Lambert hätte ihr Tagebuch gelesen, dieses sei ungeheuerlich, nicht von Lamberts Notizen, und für jemanden, der im Geheimen hasse und plötzlich wisse, der Gehaßte wisse es, gebe es keinen anderen Ausweg als die Flucht, worauf die F. ihre Ausführungen mit der Bemerkung schloß, etwas stimme an der Geschichte nicht, es bleibe rätselhaft, was Tina in die Wüste getrieben habe, sie, die

F., komme sich wie eine jener Sonden vor, die man ins All schieße, in der Hoffnung sie könnten Informationen zurück zur Erde senden, deren Beschaffenheit man noch nicht wisse.

5

D. hatte sich den Bericht der F. angehört und sich zerstreut ein Glas Wein bestellt, obwohl es erst elf Uhr war, und stürzte es ebenso zerstreut hinunter, bestellte sich ein zweites Glas und meinte, er sei zwar immer noch mit dem unnützen Problem beschäftigt, ob der Identitätssatz A = A stimme, da er zwei identische A setze, während es nur ein mit sich identisches A geben könne und wie es auch sei, auf die Wirklichkeit bezogen sei es unsinnig, kein Mensch sei mit sich identisch, weil er der Zeit unterworfen und genau genommen zu jedem Zeitpunkt ein anderer sei als vorher, manchmal scheine es ihm, er sei jeden Morgen ein anderer, als hätte ein anderes Ich sein vorheriges Ich verdrängt und machte nun von seinem Hirn Gebrauch und damit auch von seinem Gedächtnis, daher sei er froh sich mit der Logik abzugeben, die sich jenseits jeder Wirklichkeit befinde und jeder existentiellen Panne entrückt, darum könne er nur sehr allgemein Stellung zur Geschichte nehmen, die sie ihm aufgetischt habe, der gute von Lambert sei nicht als Ehemann erschüttert, sondern als Psychiater, vor dem Arzt sei die Patientin davongelaufen, aus seinem menschlichen Versagen mache er gleich ein Versagen der Psychiatrie, nun stehe der Psychiater da wie ein Wärter ohne Gefangene, was ihm fehle, sei sein Objekt, was er als seine Schuld bezeichne, sei nur dieses Fehlen und was er von der F. wolle, sei nur das ihm fehlende Dokument zu seinem Dokument; er wolle, indem er zu wissen versuche, was er nie begreifen könne, die Tote gleichsam wieder in sein Gefängnis zurückholen, das Ganze ein Stück für einen Komödienschreiber, verbärge sich nicht dahinter ein Problem, welches ihn, D., seit langem beunruhige, besitze er doch in seinem Haus in den Bergen ein Spiegelteleskop, ein ungefügiges Ding, das er bisweilen gegen einen Felsen richte, von wo aus er von Leuten mit Ferngläsern beobachtet werde, worauf jedesmal, kaum hätten die ihn mit ihren Ferngläsern Beobachtenden festgestellt, daß er sie mit seinem Spiegelteleskop beobachte, sich diese schleunigst zurückzögen, wobei sich nur die logische Feststellung bestätige, zu jedem Beobachteten gehöre ein Beobachtendes, das, werde es von jenem Beobachteten beobachtet, selber ein Beobachtetes werde, eine banale logische Wechselwirkung, die jedoch, werde sie in die Wirklichkeit transponiert, sich bedrohlich auswirke, die ihn Beobachtenden fühlten sich dadurch, daß er sie durch sein Spiegelteleskop beobachte, ertappt, ertappt zu werden erwecke Schmach, Schmach oft Aggression, mancher der sich verzogen habe, sei zurückgekehrt, wenn er, D., sein Instrument weggeräumt hätte, und habe Steine nach seinem Haus geworfen, überhaupt sei, was sich zwischen denen, die ihn beobachteten, und ihm abspiele, der seine Beobachter beobachte, für unsere Zeit symptomatisch, jeder fühle sich von jedem beobachtet und beobachte jeden, der Mensch heute sei ein beobachteter Mensch, der Staat beobachte ihn mit immer raffinierteren Methoden, der Mensch versuche sich immer verzweifelter dem Beobachtet-Werden zu entziehen, dem Staat sei der Mensch und dem Menschen der Staat immer verdächtiger, ebenso beobachte jeder Staat den anderen und fühle sich von jedem Staat beobachtet, auch beobachte wie noch nie der Mensch die Natur, indem er immer sinnreichere Instrumente erfinde, sie zu beobachten, wie Kameras, Teleskope, Stereoskope, Radioteleskope, Röntgenteleskope, Mikroskope, Elektronenmikroskope, Synchrotrone, Satelliten, Raumson-

den, Computer, immer neue Beobachtungen ent-
locke man der Natur, von Quasaren, Milliarden
Lichtjahre entfernt bis zu Billionstelmillimeter
kleinen Partikeln, bis zur Erkenntnis, die elektro-
magnetischen Strahlen seien verstrahlte Masse und
die Masse gefrorene elektromagnetische Strah-
lung, noch nie hätte der Mensch soviel von der
Natur beobachtet, sie stehe gleichsam nackt vor
ihm, jeder Geheimnisse bar, und werde ausge-
nutzt, mit ihren Ressourcen Schindluder getrieben, daher scheine es ihm, D., bisweilen, die
Natur beobachte nun ihrerseits den sie beobachtenden Menschen und werde aggressiv, bei der
verschmutzten Luft, dem verseuchten Boden,
dem verunreinigten Grundwasser, den sterbenden
Wäldern handle es sich um einen Streik, um eine
bewußte Weigerung, die Schadstoffe unschädlich
zu machen, die neuen Viren, die Erdbeben, Dür-
ren, Überschwemmungen, Hurrikane, Vulkan-
ausbrüche usw. dagegen seien gezielte Abwehr-
maßnahmen der beobachteten Natur gegen den,
der sie beobachte, so wie sein Spiegelteleskop und
die Steine, die gegen sein Haus geworfen würden,
Gegenmaßnahmen gegen das Beobachtet-Werden
seien, desgleichen was sich zwischen von Lambert
und dessen Frau abgespielt habe, um auf die

zurückzukommen, auch dort sei Beobachten ein Objektivieren und so habe denn jeder den anderen ins Unerträgliche objektiviert, er habe sie zu einem psychiatrischen Objekt, sie ihn zu einem Haßobjekt gemacht, worauf, aus dem plötzlichen Erkennen heraus, daß nämlich sie, die Beobachtende, vom Beobachteten beobachtet werde, sie sich spontan den roten Mantel über ihren Jeansanzug geworfen und den Teufelskreis von Beobachten und Beobachtet-Werden verlassen habe und in den Tod gelaufen sei, aber, fügte er hinzu, nachdem er plötzlich in ein Gelächter ausgebrochen war, wieder ernst geworden, was er da entwickelt habe, sei natürlich nur die eine Möglichkeit, die andere bestehe im puren Gegenteil dessen, was er ausgeführt habe, ein logischer Schluß hänge von der Ausgangssituation ab, wenn er in seinem Hause in den Bergen immer seltener beobachtet würde, so selten, daß, richte er sein Spiegelteleskop gegen solche, von denen er annehme, sie würden ihn vom Felsen aus beobachten, diese mit ihren Ferngläsern nicht ihn, sondern irgend etwas anderes beobachten würden, kletternde Gemsen oder kraxelnde Bergsteiger, dieses Unbeobachtet-Sein würde ihn mit der Zeit mehr quälen als das Beobachtet-Sein vorher, er würde die Steine gegen sein Haus geradezu herbeisehnen, nicht mehr beobachtet, käme er sich nicht beachtenswert, nicht beachtenswert nicht geachtet, nicht geachtet bedeutungslos, bedeutungslos sinnlos vor, er würde, stelle er sich vor, in eine hoffnungslose Depression geraten, ja, würde wohl seine ohnehin erfolglose akademische Laufbahn gar als etwas Sinnloses aufgeben, die Menschen, würde er dann zwangsläufig folgern, litten unter dem Unbeobachtet-Sein wie er, auch sie kämen sich unbeobachtet sinnlos vor, darum beobachteten alle einander, knipsten und filmten einander aus Angst vor der Sinnlosigkeit ihres Daseins angesichts eines auseinanderstiebenden Universums mit seinen Milliarden Milchstraßen, wie der unsrigen, besiedelt mit Abermilliarden durch die ungeheuren Distanzen hoffnungslos isolierten belebten Planeten, wie dem unsrigen, eines Alls unaufhörlich durchzuckt von explodierenden und dann in sich zusammensackenden Sonnen, wer anders sollte den Menschen da noch beobachten um ihm einen Sinn zu verleihen als dieser sich selber, sei doch gegenüber einem solchen Monstrum von Weltall ein persönlicher Gott nicht mehr möglich, ein Gott als Weltregent und als Vater, der einen jeden beobachte, der die Haare eines jeden zähle, Gott sei tot, weil er undenkbar geworden sei, ein im Verstande gänzlich wurzelloses Glaubensaxiom, nur noch ein unpersönlicher Gott sei als ein abstraktes Prinzip denkbar, als ein philosophisch-literarisches Gedankengebäude, um in das monströse Ganze doch noch einen Sinn hineinzuzaubern, vage und verblasen, Gefühl ist alles, Name ist Schall und Rauch, umnebelnd Himmelsglut, eingefangen in den Kachelofen des menschlichen Herzens, aber auch der Verstand sei unfähig, sich noch einen Sinn außerhalb des Menschen vorzuschwindeln, denn alles Denk- und Machbare, Logik, Metaphysik, Mathematik, Naturgesetze, Kunstwerke, Musik, Dichtung, bekomme nur Sinn durch den Menschen, ohne den Menschen sinke es ins Ungedachte und damit ins Sinnlose zurück, vieles was heute geschehe, folge er dieser logischen Spur weiter, sei dann begreifbar, die Menschheit taumle in der irren Hoffnung dahin, doch noch von irgendwem beobachtet zu werden, so etwa wenn sie wettrüste, natürlich zwinge es die Wettrüstenden, einander zu beobachten, weshalb sie im Grunde hofften, ewig wettrüsten zu können, um sich ewig beobachten zu müssen, ohne Wettrüsten versänken die Wettrüstenden in der Bedeutungslosigkeit, doch falls das Wettrü-

sten durch irgendeine Panne den atomaren Feuer-
brand auslöse, wozu es längst fähig sei, stelle
dieser nichts weiter als eine sinnlose Manifestation
dar, daß die Erde einmal bewohnt gewesen sei, ein
Feuerwerk, das niemand beobachte, es sei denn
irgendeine vielleicht vorhandene Menschheit oder
so etwas Ähnliches in der Nähe des Sirius oder
anderswo, ohne Möglichkeit dem, der so gern
beobachtet sein möchte, die Nachricht zu über-
mitteln, er sei beobachtet worden, weil dieser
dann nicht mehr existiere, auch der religiöse und
politische Fundamentalismus, der überall hervor-
breche oder immer noch herrsche, weise darauf
hin, daß viele und offenbar die meisten sich selber
unbeobachtet nicht aushielten, sie flüchteten in
die Vorstellung eines persönlichen Gottes oder
einer ebenso metaphysisch begründeten Partei
zurück, der oder die sie beobachte, wovon sie das
Recht ableiten, nun ihrerseits zu beobachten, ob
die Welt die Gebote des sie beobachtenden Gottes
oder der sie beobachtenden Partei beachte, bei den
Terroristen sei der Fall verzwickter, ihr Ziel sei
nicht ein beobachtetes, sondern ein unbeobachte-
tes Kinderland, aber weil sie die Welt, in der sie
lebten, als ein Gefängnis begriffen, in das sie nicht
nur rechtlos eingesperrt seien, sondern worin sie

auch unbeobachtet und unbeachtet in einem der Verliese lägen, versuchten sie verzweifelt, die Beobachtung der Wärter zu erzwingen und damit aus ihrer Nicht-Beobachtung ins Rampenlicht der Beachtung zu treten, was sie freilich nur vermöchten, wenn sie sich paradoxerweise immer wieder ins Unbeobachtete zurückzögen, aus dem Verlies ins Verlies, und nie kämen sie ins Freie, kurz, die Menschheit sei im Begriff, wieder zu den Windeln zurückzukehren, Fundamentalisten, Idealisten, Moralisten, Politchristen mühten sich ab, einer unbeobachteten Menschheit wieder eine Beobachtung und damit einen Sinn aufzuhalsen, weil der Mensch nun einmal ein Pedant sei und ohne Sinn nicht auskomme, weshalb er alles ertrage außer der Freiheit, auf den Sinn zu pfeifen, auch Tina von Lambert hätte davon geträumt, durch ihre Flucht von der Weltöffentlichkeit beobachtet zu werden, worauf der zweimal unterstrichene Satz, »ich werde beobachtet«, hinweisen könnte, als siegesbewußte Bekräftigung ihres geplanten Unterfangens, doch, akzeptiere man diese Möglichkeit, so beginne damit erst die eigentliche Tragödie, indem ihr Gatte ihre Flucht nicht als einen Versuch begriffen, beobachtet zu werden, sondern als eine Flucht vor dem Beobachtet-

Werden interpretiert und jede Nachforschung unterlassen habe, sei Tinas Ziel vorerst vereitelt worden, ihre Flucht sei unbeobachtet und damit unbeachtet geblieben, vielleicht habe sie sich dadurch in immer kühnere Abenteuer eingelassen, bis sie durch ihren Tod erreicht habe, was sie ersehnte, ihr Bild sei nun in allen Zeitungen, jetzt habe sie die Beobachtung und damit die Beachtung und ihren Sinn gefunden, den sie gesucht habe.

6

Die F., die dem Logiker aufmerksam zugehört und sich einen Campari bestellt hatte, meinte, D. werde sich wundern, warum sie den Auftrag von Lamberts angenommen habe, der Unterschied von beobachten und nicht-beobachtet sei zwar eine amüsante logische Spielerei, aber sie interessiere, was er über den Menschen gesagt habe, dem er jede Identität mit sich selber abgesprochen habe, da er immer ein anderer sei, hineingeworfen in die Zeit, wenn sie D. recht verstanden habe, was aber bedeuten würde, daß es kein Ich gebe, besser, nur eine zahllose Kette von aus der Zukunft auftauchenden, in der Gegenwart aufblitzenden und in der Vergangenheit versinkenden Ichs, so daß denn das, was man sein Ich nenne, nur ein Sammelname für sämtliche in der Vergangenheit angesammelten Ichs sei, ständig anwachsend und zugedeckt von den aus der Zukunft durch die Gegenwart herabfallenden Ichs, eine Ansammlung von Erlebnis- und Erinnerungsfetzen, vergleichbar mit einem Laubhaufen, bei dem die untersten Blätter längst zu Humus geworden und der durch das frisch fallende und heranwehende Laub immer höher steige, ein Vorgang, der zu einer Fiktion eines Ichs führe, indem jeder sein Ich zusammenfingiere, sich in eine Rolle dichten würde, die er mehr oder weniger gut zu spielen versuche, demnach komme es auf die schauspielerische Leistung an, ob einer als Charakter dastehe oder nicht, je unbewußter, unabsichtlicher er eine Rolle spiele, desto echter wirke er, sie begreife nun auch, warum Schauspieler so schwer zu porträtieren seien, diese spielten ihren Charakter zu offensichtlich, das bewußt Schauspielerische wirke unecht, überhaupt hätte sie, schaue sie auf ihre Laufbahn zurück, auf die Menschen, die sie porträtiert habe, das Gefühl, vor allem Schmierenschauspieler gefilmt zu haben, besonders unter den Politikern, wenige seien Schauspieler großen Formats ihres Ichs gewesen, sie habe sich vorgenommen, keine Porträts mehr zu filmen, aber wie sie diese Nacht das Tagebuch Tina von Lamberts gelesen, immer wieder, und wie sie sich vorgestellt habe, wie diese junge Frau in einem roten Pelzmantel in die Wüste hineinge-schritten sei, in dieses Meer aus Sand und Stein, sei es ihr, der F., klargeworden, daß sie mit ihrem Team dieser Frau nachspüren und wie diese in die

Wüste hinein zur Al-Hakim-Ruine gehen müsse, koste es, was es wolle, in der Wüste, ahne sie, liege eine Realität, der sie sich wie Tina stellen müsse, für diese sei es der Tod gewesen, was es für sie selber sein werde, wisse sie noch nicht und dann fragte sie D., den Campari austrinkend, ob sie nicht verrückt sei, diesen Auftrag anzunehmen, worauf D. antwortete, sie wolle in die Wüste gehen, weil sie eine neue Rolle suche, ihre alte Rolle sei die einer Beobachterin von Rollen gewesen, nun beabsichtige sie, das Gegenteil zu versuchen, nicht zu porträtieren, was ja einen Gegenstand voraussetze, sondern zu rekonstruieren, den Gegenstand ihres Porträts herzustellen, damit aus einzelnen herumliegenden Blättern einen Laubhaufen anzusammeln, wobei sie nicht wissen könne, ob die Blätter, die sie da zusammenschichte, auch zusammengehörten, ja, ob sie am Ende nicht sich selber porträtiere, ein Unterfangen, das zwar verrückt sei aber wiederum so verrückt, daß es nicht verrückt sei und er wünsche ihr alles Gute.

7

War es schon am Morgen schwül gewesen, als wäre es Sommer, so donnerte es, als sie zum Wagen trat und sie vermochte gerade noch das Schutzdach ihres Kabrioletts zu installieren, bevor ein Platzregen einsetzte, durch den sie an der Altstadt vorbei zum Altmarkt hinunterfuhr und trotz des Verbots am Trottoirrand parkte, hatte sie sich doch nicht geirrt, die an einer Seite des Tagebuchs flüchtig hingekritzelte Adresse war die des Ateliers eines seit einigen Wochen verstorbenen Malers, der seit vielen Jahren die Stadt verlassen, und das längst von jemand anderem benützt werden mußte, wenn es überhaupt noch existierte, denn es war in einem so lamentablen und baufälligen Zustand gewesen, daß sie überzeugt war, es nicht mehr vorzufinden, aber weil die Adresse in irgendeiner Beziehung zu Tina stehen mußte, ohne die sie nicht in ihr Tagebuch gekommen wäre, legte sie den kurzen Weg vom Wagen zur Haustüre trotz der niederstürzenden Regenmassen zurück und obwohl sich die Türe öffnen ließ, war sie schon durchnäßt als sie in den Korridor gelangte, der sich nicht verändert hatte, auch der Hof, von dessen Kopfsteinpflaster der Regen aufspritzte, war derselbe, ebenso die Scheune, worin sich das Atelier des Malers befunden hatte, auch die Türe hinauf erwies sich zu ihrem Erstaunen unverschlossen, die Treppe verlor sich oben im Dunkeln, sie suchte vergeblich nach einem Lichtschalter, stieg hinauf, die Hände tastend vor sich, spürte eine Türe und sie befand sich im Atelier, auch dieses zu ihrer Verblüffung unverändert im fahlen Silberlicht des Regens, der außen an den beiden Fenstern niederlief, der lange, schmale Raum war immer noch voller Bilder des Malers, der doch seit Jahren die Stadt verlassen hatte, großformatige Porträts, die abenteuerlichsten Gestalten der Altstadt standen herum, Pumpgenies, Quartalsäufer, Clochards, Straßenprediger, Zuhälter, Berufsarbeitslose, Schieber und andere Lebenskünstler, die meisten unter der Erde wie der Maler, nur nicht so feierlich wie dieser, bei dessen Begräbnis sie dabeigewesen war, höchstens daß bei jenen einige weinende Dirnen zugegen gewesen waren oder einige Zechbrüder, Bier ins Grab nachgießend, wenn es überhaupt zum Begräbnis kam und nicht zur Kremation, Porträts, wovon sie die meisten längst in Museen geglaubt, ja gesehen hatte, andere kleinformatigere Bilder stapelten sich zu Füßen der nur noch auf der Leinwand Gegenwärtigen, eine Straßenbahn darstellend, Klos, Pfannen, Autoruinen, Velos, Regenschirme, Verkehrspolizisten, Cinzanoflaschen, nichts gab es, das der Maler nicht dargestellt hätte, die Unordnung war ungeheuer, vor einem halb zerrissenen mächtigen Ledersessel war eine Kiste, auf der ein Tablar voller Bündnerfleisch, am Boden Chiantiflaschen und ein Wasserglas halb gefüllt mit Wein, Zeitungen, Eierschalen, überall Farbtuben, als wäre der Maler noch am Leben, Pinsel, Paletten, Terpentin- und Petroleumflaschen, nur eine Staffelei fehlte, der Regen klatschte gegen die zwei Fenster an der Längsseite, um besser zu sehen räumte die F. einen Stadtpräsidenten und einen Bankdirektor, der seit zwei Jahren im Zuchthaus ein etwas minder flottes Leben führte, vom Fenster an der Vorderwand weg und stand vor dem Porträt einer Frau im roten Pelzmantel, das die F. zuerst für das Bildnis Tina von Lamberts hielt, aber dann war es wieder nicht jenes der Tina, es konnte ebensogut das Porträt einer Frau sein, die Tina ähnlich war, doch zuckte sie plötzlich zusammen, es schien ihr, diese Frau,

die trotzig vor ihr stand mit weit aufgerissenen
Augen, sei sie selber, von diesem Gedanken
durchzuckt hörte sie Schritte hinter sich, sich
umwendend war es zu spät, die Türe war schon ins
Schloß gefallen, und als sie am späten Nachmittag
mit ihrem Team ins Atelier zurückkehrte, war das
Porträt verschwunden, dafür fand sie ein anderes
Team vor, welches das Atelier filmte, sie hätten es,
erklärte der Regisseur seltsam fahrig, vor der
Gesamtausstellung im Kunsthaus noch einmal so
rekonstruiert, wie es zur Zeit des Malers ausgesehen habe, seitdem sei es leer geblieben, sie blätter-
ten den Katalog durch, das Porträt war nicht zu
finden, auch sei es ganz unmöglich, daß das
Atelier nicht verschlossen gewesen sei.

8

Noch immer verwirrt durch dieses Erlebnis, das ihr wie ein Vorzeichen erschien, sie suche in der falschen Richtung, hätte sie beinah ihren Abflug annulliert, doch zögerte sie, die Vorbereitungen nahmen ihren Lauf, schon flogen sie über Spanien, unter ihnen der Guadalquivir, der Atlantik kam in Sicht und als sie in C. landeten, freute sie sich auf die Fahrt ins Landesinnere, es mußte noch grün sein und sie erinnerte sich, als sie vor Jahren diese Fahrt unternommen, an eine Dattelpalmenallee, durch die ihr Autos mit Skis auf den Dächern vom verschneiten Atlas her entgegengekommen waren; indessen wurden sie und ihr Team in C. gleich bei der Landung auf der Piste von einem Polizeiwagen abgeholt und ohne durch den Zoll zu müssen samt der Filmausrüstung in einen Militärtransporter gebracht und ins Landesinnere geflogen, in M. von vier Motorradpolizisten eskortiert in rasender Fahrt an Kolonnen von Touristen vorbei, von denen sie neugierig betrachtet wurden, in die Stadt gebracht, begleitet von zwei

Wagen, hinter und vor ihnen, eines Fernsehteams, das unaufhörlich filmte und, mit der Eskorte im Polizeiministerium angekommen, die F. und ihr Filmteam filmte, als dieses den Polizeichef filmte, der unglaublich dick, in weißer Uniform, an Göring erinnernd, an den Schreibtisch gelehnt erklärte, wie glücklich er sei, der F. und ihrem Team trotz der Bedenken seiner Regierung erlauben zu dürfen, auf seine Verantwortung freilich, die Schauplätze des scheußlichen Verbrechens zu besichtigen und zu filmen, aber am überglücklichsten sei er, weil die F. bei ihrem Versuch, die Untat zu rekonstruieren, auch die Gelegenheit ausnutzen wolle, die untadlige Arbeit seiner Polizei festzuhalten, die aufs modernste ausgerüstet jedem internationalen Maßstab nicht nur standhalte, sondern ihn auch übertreffe, ein derart schamloses Ansinnen, das den Verdacht verstärkte, den die F. seit ihrem Erlebnis im Atelier hegte, sie sei auf falscher Fährte, war doch ihr Unternehmen, kaum begonnen, sinnlos geworden, weil sie für den Fettwanst, der sich immer wieder den Schweiß mit seinem seidenen Taschentuch von der Stirne wischte, nur eine Gelegenheit darstellte, für ihn und die ihm unterstellte Polizei Propaganda zu machen, aber einmal in die Falle gegangen, sah sie vorerst keine Möglichkeit zu entkommen, denn nicht nur die Polizei nahm sie und ihr Team gefangen, indem sie zu einem Jeep geführt wurden, dessen Fahrer, ein Polizist mit Turban im Gegensatz zu den andern weißbehelmten Polizisten, die F. mit einer Handbewegung anwies, sich neben ihn zu setzen, während der Kameramann und der Tonmeister hinter ihr Platz nehmen und der Assistent mit den Geräten einen zweiten Jeep besteigen mußten, dessen Fahrer ein Schwarzer war, auch das Fernsehen folgte ihnen, als sie sich der Wüste näherten, zum Ärger der F., die es vorgezogen hätte, vorerst Erkundigungen einzuziehen, sich aber nicht zu verständigen vermochte, weil, sei es aus Absicht oder aus Nachlässigkeit, kein Dolmetscher zugegen war und die sie mehr herumkommandierenden als begleitenden Polizisten nicht Französisch verstanden, was man doch in diesem Lande hätte voraussetzen können, aber auch weil die Fernsehteams außer Rufweite in die Steinwüste hineinpreschten, seitwärts von F.s Jeep, wie denn auch die Wagenkolonne jede Ordnung verlor, so sehr, daß die anderen Wagen samt des Jeeps mit dem Assistenten und den Geräten sich in den Weiten, die in der Sonne kochten, zu zerstreuen schienen, so wie es jedem Fahrer ein-fiel, je nach Laune, sogar die vier Motorradpolizisten, die ihre Eskorte bildeten, lösten sich vom Jeep, in welchem sie saßen, brausten davon, hetzten einander, knatterten zurück, schlugen weite Bogen, indes die Fernsehteams dem Horizont zuschossen und plötzlich nicht mehr sichtbar waren; dafür aber begann ihr Jeepfahrer unverständliche Laute ausstoßend einem Schakal nachzujagen, kurvte ihm nach, der Schakal rannte und rannte, schlug Haken, rannte in anderer Richtung weiter, der Jeep ihm nach, einige Male drohte er umzustürzen, dann ratterten wieder die Motorradfahrer heran, schrien, machten Zeichen, die sie, an ihre Sitze geklammert, nicht begriffen, bis sie plötzlich in die Sandwüste gerieten, offenbar allein, ohne ein anderes Fahrzeug zu sichten, sogar die vier Motorradfahrer waren verschwunden, dermaßen fegten sie mit ihrem Jeep über eine asphaltierte Straße, wobei rätselhaft blieb, wie es ihrem Fahrer, der den Schakal nicht hatte überfahren können, möglich gewesen war, diese zu finden, war doch die Straße teilweise mit Sand bedeckt, wobei sich zu beiden Seiten die Sanddünen häuften, wodurch es der F. schien, sie pflügten durch ein von Sandwellen aufgepeitschtes Meer über das die Sonne immer längere Schatten warf, doch unvermittelt tauchte vor ihnen die Al-Hakim-Ruine auf, die in einer Mulde lag, in die sie unvermutet hinunterrasten, dem Monument entgegen, das, die Sonne verdunkelnd, schwarz vor ihr aus dem Gewimmel von Polizisten und Fernsehleuten aufwuchs, die sich schon vor ihm versammelt hatten, vor einem rätselhaften Zeugen einer unvorstellbar alten Zeit, den man um die Jahrhundertwende gefunden hatte, ein riesiges, durch den Sand spiegelglatt geschliffenes steinernes Quadrat, das sich als die Oberfläche eines Kubus herausstellte, der, als man weitergrub, immer gewaltigere Dimensionen annahm, doch als man ihn gänzlich freilegen wollte, hatten sich Heilige einer schiitischen Sekte, zerlumpte ausgemergelte Gestalten eingefunden, die sich an einer der Kubusseiten niederkauerten, in schwarze Mäntel gehüllt, auf den wahnsinnigen Kalifen Al-Hakim wartend, der nach ihrem Glauben im Innern des Kubus lauerte und jeden Monat, jeden Tag, jede Minute, jede Sekunde hervorbrechen konnte, seine Weltherrschaft zu übernehmen, schwarzen Riesenvögeln gleich hockten sie da, niemand wagte sie fortzutreiben, die Archäologen gruben die drei anderen Seiten des Kubus aus, gerieten immer tiefer, die schwarzen Sufi, wie sie genannt wurden, weit über ihnen, unbeweglich, auch wenn der Wind über sie strich, sie mit Sand überhäufend, rührten sie sich nicht, nur einmal jede Woche von einem riesigen Neger besucht, der auf einem Esel zu ihnen geritten kam, in ihre Mäuler einen Löffel voll Brei schlug und Wasser über sie goß und von dem es hieß, er sei noch ein Sklave, und als die F. sich ihnen näherte, weil ein junger Polizeioffizier, plötzlich des Französischen mächtig, ihr erklärt hatte, Tinas Leiche sei zwischen den »Heiligen« gefunden worden, wie er sich respektvoll ausdrückte, jemand müsse sie zwischen diese geworfen haben, es sei jedoch unmöglich, von ihnen Auskunft zu erhalten, da diese Schweigen bis zur Rückkehr ihres »Mahdi« gelobt hätten, die Unbeweglichen lange betrachtend, die vor ihr in langen Reihen kauerten, eins mit den schwarzen Quadern des Kubus, ein Gewächs an einer seiner Flanken, Mumien gleich, lange weiße strähnige sandverkrustete Bärte, die Augen unsichtbar in tiefen Höhlen, dicht mit Fliegen bedeckt, die überall auf ihnen herumkrochen, die Hände ineinandergekrallt mit langen Fingernägeln, die ihre Handteller durchbohrten, und nun einen von ihnen vorsichtig berührte, um vielleicht doch eine Auskunft zu erlangen, fiel dieser um, er war eine Leiche, auch der nächste, hinter ihr surrten die Kameras, erst beim dritten hatte sie den Eindruck, er sei noch am Leben, doch gab sie auf, nur ihr Kameramann schritt die Reihe ab, seinen Apparat an sein Auge gepreßt, und als sie den Vorfall dem Polizeioffizier meldete, der bei seinem Wagen geblieben war, meinte dieser, die Schakale würden den Rest besorgen, auch die Leiche Tinas sei zerrissen aufgefunden worden, und in diesem Augenblick setzte die Dämmerung ein, die Sonne mußte hinter der Mulde untergegangen sein, und der F. schien es, die Nacht falle sie an wie ein gnädiger Feind, der schnell tötet.

9

Auch am nächsten Tag war die Rückkehr nicht möglich, noch bevor die F. den Rückflug hatte buchen können, machte der Kameramann ihr Vorhaben mit der Meldung zunichte, ihm sei das abgedrehte Material abhanden gekommen, die Rollen seien vertauscht worden, die Fernsehleute beteuerten, es sei sein Material, der Kameramann verlangte wütend, dann sollten die Rollen entwikkelt werden, damit man es feststellen könne, was man ihm für den Abend versprach, zu einem Zeitpunkt also, der die Abreise unmöglich machte und schon waren sie wieder von der Polizei verschleppt und dies in einer Weise, die es klüger erscheinen ließ, so zu tun, als mache man mit, wurden ihnen doch in den unterirdischen Anlagen des Polizeiministeriums Menschen vorgeführt, mit denen die F. zwar sprechen und die sie filmen durfte, Männer, die, betraten sie den Raum, von ihren Handschellen befreit wurden, denen aber, hatten sie auf dem Schemel Platz genommen, ein Polizist seine Maschinenpistole in den Rücken drückte, wobei es sich um schlecht rasierte Individuen handelte, denen Zähne fehlten, die gierig mit zittrigen Händen nach der Zigarette griffen, die ihnen die F. anbot, und nach kurzem Blick auf Tinas Foto und auf die Frage, ob sie diese Frau gesehen hätten, nickten und auf die Frage wo, leise antworteten, im Ghetto, alle in schmutzigen weißen Leinenhosen und -kitteln, ohne Hemd, wie uniformiert und immer mit der gleichen Antwort: im Ghetto, im Ghetto, im Ghetto und dann erzählte jeder, man hätte versucht ihn anzuheuern, die Frau umzubringen, deren Foto ihm gezeigt wurde, es handle sich um die Gattin eines Mannes, der die arabische Widerstandsbewegung verteidigt und sie nicht als Terrororganisation bezeichnet habe oder so was Ähnliches, er sei nicht klug daraus geworden, warum die Frau dafür hätte sterben sollen, er habe das Angebot abgelehnt, die Summe sei zu schäbig gewesen, in seinen Kreisen seien die Tarife geregelt, Ehrensache, der Mann, der das Angebot gemacht habe, sei klein und dick gewesen, Amerikaner wahrscheinlich oder – er wisse nichts Näheres, die Frau habe er nur einmal gesehen, in dessen Begleitung, im Ghetto, er habe es schon gesagt, ähnliche Aussagen machten alle anderen, mechanisch, gierig die

Zigarette rauchend, nur einer grinste, als er das Foto sah, blies der F. Rauch ins Gesicht, er war fast zwerghaft, mit einem großen faltigen Gesicht, sprach Englisch wie etwa Skandinavier Englisch sprechen, sagte, er habe diese Frau nie gesehen, keiner habe diese Frau gesehen, worauf der Polizist ihn hochriß, ihn mit der Maschinenpistole in den Rücken schlug, doch schon war ein Offizier da, herrschte den Polizisten an, plötzlich waren andere Polizisten im Raum, der mit dem großen faltigen Gesicht wurde hinausgeführt, ein neuer Häftling wurde von außen hereingeschoben, saß da im Licht der Scheinwerfer, wieder Klappe, das Surren der Kamera, nahm mit zittrigen Händen eine Zigarette, schaute auf das Foto, erzählte die selbe Geschichte wie die anderen, mit unwesentlichen Varianten, manchmal undeutlich wie die andern, weil auch er wie die andern fast keine Zähne besaß, dann kam der nächste, dann der letzte, worauf sie vom kahlen Betonraum, wo sie die Männer vernommen hatten, worin sich nur ein wackliger Tisch, ein Scheinwerfer und einige Stühle befanden, durch die unterirdische Gefängniswelt, an Eisengittern vorbei, hinter denen in den Zellen etwas Weißliches lag oder kauerte, mit einem Lift zum Untersuchungsrichter gelangten, in ein modernes Büro, das behaglich eingerichtet war, mit einem Juristen, einem sanften Schönling mit randloser Brille, die nicht zu ihm paßte, der die F. und ihr Team, nachdem sie in bequemen Sesseln um einen runden Tisch mit Glasplatte Platz genommen, mit allen erdenklichen Delikatessen bewirtete, sogar Kaviar und Wodka waren vorhanden, wobei der Untersuchungsrichter, fleißig einem elsässischen Weißwein zugetan, den ihm ein französischer Kollege zugeschickt habe, dem Kameramann abwinkend, der aufnahmebereit lauerte, weitläufig beteuerte, er sei ein gläubiger Muslim, ja in vielem geradezu ein Fundamentalist, Khomeini hätte durchaus seine positiven, ja grandiosen Seiten, aber der Prozeß, der zu einer Synthese der Rechtsauffassung des Korans mit dem europäischen juristischen Denken führe, sei in diesem Lande nicht mehr aufzuhalten, zu vergleichen mit der Integration des Aristoteles in die mohammedanische Theologie im Mittelalter, schwafelte er weiter, doch endlich, mit einem ermüdenden Umweg über die Geschichte der spanischen Umayyaden kam er wie zufällig auf den Fall Tina von Lamberts zu sprechen, bedauerte, er verstehe durchaus die Emotionen, die der Fall in Europa ausgelöst habe, Europa neige dem Tragischen, die Kultur des Islam dem Fatalistischen zu, wies dann Fotos von der Leiche vor, sagte: na ja, die Schakale, meinte dann, die Leiche sei erst nach der Tat zu den schwarzen Sufi bei der Al-Hakim-Ruine gebracht worden, was, er entschuldigte sich, für einen christlichen oder – na ja – Täter spreche, kein Muslim hätte es gewagt, eine Leiche unter die Heiligen zu werfen, die Empörung darüber sei allgemein, legte den gerichtsmedizinischen Befund vor, Vergewaltigung, Tod durch Erwürgen, einen Kampf habe es offenbar keinen gegeben, die der F. vorgeführten Männer seien ausländische Agenten, welche Macht Interesse an der Ermordung gehabt habe, er brauche nicht deutlich zu werden, von Lamberts Weigerung am internationalen Antiterroristenkongreß, arabische Freiheitskämpfer als Terroristen zu bezeichnen, ein gewisser Geheimdienst habe ein Exempel statuiert, als Täter komme einer der Agenten in Frage, das Land sei voller Spione, natürlich auch sowjetische, tschechische, ostdeutsche vor allem, doch hauptsächlich amerikanische, französische, englische, westdeutsche, Italiener, warum alle aufzählen, kurz, Abenteurer aller Länder, der gewisse Geheimdienst, sie wisse ja welchen er meine, arbeite am gerissensten, er dinge andere

Agenten, dinge, das sei das Perfide, mit der Ermordung Tina von Lamberts habe er sich einerseits rächen, andererseits die guten Handelsbezie-
hungen seines Landes zur Europäischen Gemein-
schaft stören, insbesondere die Ausfuhr solcher
Waren erschweren wollen, Produkte, deren Ex-
port nach Europa der Hauptsache nach von – na
ja – getätigt worden sei, und dann, als der Untersuchungsrichter einen Anruf entgegengenommen,
starrte er die F. und ihr Team schweigend an,
öffnete die Türe, winkte ihnen ihm zu folgen,
schritt durch Korridore voran, dann eine Treppe
hinunter, wieder Korridore, öffnete mit einem
Schlüssel eine Eisentüre, wieder ein Korridor,
schmäler als die andern, worauf sie zu einer Wand
gelangten, in der sich eine Reihe kleiner Gucklö-
cher befand, von denen aus sie in einen kahlen Hof
hinunterzublicken vermochten, der offenbar vom
Gebäude des Polizeiministeriums umschlossen
wurde, doch sahen sie nur glatte, fensterlose
Mauern, was dem Hof ein schachtartiges Aus-
sehen gab, in den nun der zwerghafte Skandinavier an aufgereihten Polizisten mit geschulterten
Maschinenpistolen, weißen Helmen und weißen
Handschuhen vorbei hereingeführt wurde, in
Handschellen, hinter ihm ein Polizeihauptmann

mit gezücktem Säbel, der Skandinavier stellte sich an die Betonwand der Polizeireihe gegenüber, der Offizier schritt zu ihr zurück, stellte sich neben die Reihe, hielt den Säbel steil vor sein Gesicht, alles wirkte wie eine Operette, der fette Polizeichef wälzte sich herein, was den Eindruck des Operettenhaften erhöhte, wälzte sich mühsam und schwitzend zum Zwerghaften, Grinsenden, steckte ihm eine Zigarette in den Mund, zündete sie an, wälzte sich wieder aus dem Blickfeld derer, die oben hinter den Gucklöchern standen, die Kamera surrte, irgendwie hatte der Kameramann es fertiggebracht, den Vorgang doch noch zu filmen, unten rauchte der Zwerghafte, die Polizisten warteten, legten die Maschinenpistolen an, an deren Mündung etwas befestigt war, offenbar Schalldämpfer, warteten, der Offizier hatte seinen Säbel wieder gesenkt, der Zwerghafte rauchte, schien endlos zu rauchen, die Polizisten wurden unruhig, der Offizier riß seinen Säbel wieder hoch, die Polizisten zielten aufs neue, ein dumpfes Geräusch, der Zwerghafte griff mit den gefesselten Händen nach der Zigarette, ließ sie fallen, trat sie aus, stürzte dann in sich zusammen, während die Polizisten die Maschinenpistolen wieder gesenkt hielten, lag unbeweglich am Boden, während Blut aus ihm floß, überall, gegen die Mitte des Hofes zu, wo sich ein Abflußgitter befand und der Untersuchungsrichter sagte von seinem Guckloch zurücktretend, der Skandinavier habe gestanden, er sei der Mörder, leider sei der Polizeichef voreilig, es tue ihm leid, aber die Entrüstung im Lande – na ja –, und wieder ging es zurück, durch den schmalen Gang, durch die Eisentür, wieder durch die Korridore, doch jetzt durch andere, Treppen hinauf und hinab, dann ein Vorführraum, in ihm saß schon der Polizeichef, sesselfüllend, gnädig, animiert von der Hinrichtung, parfümdurchtränkte Bäche schwitzend, Zigaretten rauchend wie jene, die er dem Zwerghaften angeboten hatte, an dessen Geständnis weder die F. noch ihr Team, noch offenbar der Untersuchungsrichter glaubten, der sich nach einem erneuten »na ja« diskret zurückgezogen hatte, auf der Leinwand die Al-Hakim-Ruine, die Fahrzeuge, die Fernsehteams, die Polizisten, die vier Motorradfahrenden, die Ankunft der F. mit ihrem Team, der Kameramann den blöde lächelnden Assistenten unterweisend, der Tonmeister an seinen Geräten hantierend, dazwischen die Wüste, ein Polizist auf einem Kamel, der Jeep, der Fahrer im Turban am Steuer, die F. endlich irgendwohin starrend aber nicht wohin sie starrte, nach der Reihe der kauernden Gestalten am Fuß der Ruine, nach diesen fliegenbedeckten menschenähnlichen Wesen, halb im Sand versunken, über deren schwarze Mäntel der Sand strich, kein Bild von denen, bloß wieder Polizisten, dann ihre Ausbildung, in Schulzimmern, beim Sport, in den Schlafsälen, beim Zähneputzen unter der Massendusche, alles beklatscht vom weißen Göring, der Film sei großartig, gratuliere, um dann auf den Protest der F., es sei nicht ihr Film, erstaunt zu fragen, »wirklich?«, um gleich auch die Antwort zu geben, nun da werde das Material unbrauchbar gewesen sein, kein Wunder in der Wüstensonne, aber das Verbrechen sei jetzt ja aufgeklärt, der Täter exekutiert und er wünsche ihr eine angenehme Heimreise, worauf er sich erhob, huldvoll grüßte »lebe wohl, mein Kind« (was die F. besonders ärgerte) und den Raum verließ.

Wieder im Freien wurden sie vom Polizisten mit dem Turban erwartet, der am Steuer seines Jeeps ihnen spöttisch entgegenblickte, während hinter ihm die Touristen den weiten Platz zwischen dem Polizeiministerium und der großen Moschee füllten, von Kindern belagert, die ihnen die Hände aufrissen in der Hoffnung Geld zu finden, umkläfft von einer durch Lautsprecher übertragenen Predigt, die aus der Moschee drang, umtutet von Taxis und Reisebussen, die durch die Menge einen Weg suchten, durch ein Völkerdickicht von einander knipsenden und filmenden Ferienreisenden, das einen unwirklichen Kontrast zu den Vorgängen bildete, die sich im weißgetünchten Gebäudekomplex des Polizeiministeriums abgespielt hatten als ob sich zwei Wirklichkeiten durcheinanderschöben, eine unheimliche, grausame und eine touristisch banale, und als der Polizist mit dem Turban die F. noch auf französisch ansprach, was er doch vorher nicht gesprochen hatte, war es ihr zuviel: sie trennte sich von ihrem Team, sie wollte

allein sein, sie fühlte sich mitschuldig am Tod des
kleinen Skandinaviers, die Exekution war nur
unternommen worden, um sie an weiteren Nachforschungen zu hindern, sie sah immer wieder das
faltige Gesicht mit der Zigarette zwischen den
schmalen Lippen vor sich, dann die fliegenbedeckten Schädel der schwarzen Gestalten an der
Al-Hakim-Ruine, es war ihr als sei sie in einen
Alptraum geraten, der kein Ende nehmen wollte,
seit sie dieses Land betreten hatte, auch war sie
zum ersten Mal in ihrem Leben gescheitert, wollte
sie weitermachen gefährdete sie nicht nur ihr
Leben, sondern auch das ihres Teams, der Polizeichef war gefährlich, er würde vor nichts zurück-
schrecken, hinter dem Tod von Tina von Lambert
war ein Geheimnis verborgen, was der Untersuchungsrichter gesalbadert hatte, war allzu durchsichtig gewesen, ein plumper Versuch etwas ab-
zuschirmen, vor der Öffentlichkeit zu verbergen,
aber was, sie wußte es nicht und dann machte sie
sich wieder Vorwürfe, daß jemand das Atelier
hatte verlassen können, als sie das Porträt mit der
Frau im roten Mantel betrachtet hatte, die in ihrer
Erinnerung immer mehr ihre eigenen Züge annahm, hatte es sich um einen Mann oder um eine
Frau gehandelt, die im Atelier versteckt gewesen

war, hatte ihr der Regisseur etwas verschwiegen, wer hatte das Bett benutzt, das hinter dem Vorhang zum Vorschein gekommen war, auch darüber weiterzuforschen hatte sie unterlassen und so war sie noch wütend über ihre Schlamperei, geschoben von schwitzenden Touristen, in die Altstadt geraten, hatte sie doch auf einmal Mühe zu atmen, derart war der Geruch, der sie umgab, und zwar nicht ein spezieller Geruch, sondern der Geruch aller Gewürze auf einmal, durchzogen vom Geruch von Blut und Exkrementen, von Kaffee, Honig und Schweiß, sie bewegte sich durch dunkle schluchtartige Gassen, immer erhellt von Blitzlichtern, da jederzeit irgendwer der Menschenmenge fotografierte, an Stapeln von Kupferkesseln und Schalen, Töpfen, Teppichen, Schmuckgegenständen, Radios, Fernsehkisten, Koffern, Fleisch- und Fischständen, Gemüse- und Früchtebergen vorbei, eingehüllt in eine so penetrante Duft- und Gestankswolke, bis sie plötzlich etwas Pelzartiges streifte, sie blieb stehen, neben ihr zwängten sich Menschen vorbei, schoben sich ihr entgegen, Einheimische, nur keine Touristen mehr, wie sie verwirrt feststellte, über ihr hingen an Kleiderbügeln aus Draht billige knallige Frauenröcke in allen Farben um so grotesker, weil niemand solche Röcke trug, und was sie gestreift hatte, war ein roter Pelzmantel, von dem sie auf der Stelle wußte, daß es der Mantel Tina von Lamberts war, der sie wie ein magischer Gegenstand zu sich hergezogen haben mußte, wie ihr schien, weshalb sie geradezu zwanghaft ins Innere des Geschäfts lief, vor dem die Kleider hingen, es war eigentlich mehr eine Höhle, in die sie gelangte und es dauerte lange, bis sie im Dunkeln einen Greis erriet, den sie anredete, der aber nicht reagierte, worauf sie ihn ergriff und an der Hand gewaltsam ins Freie führte, unter seine Frauenröcke, ohngeachtet der sich inzwischen angesammelten Kinder, die F. mit großen Augen anstarrend, die den Pelzmantel vom Bügel, an welchem er hing, heruntergezerrt hatte und, entschlossen ihn zu erstehen, koste er was er wolle, erst jetzt bemerkte, daß sie einem Blinden gegenüberstand, dessen einzige Kleidung ein langes schmutziges einmal weißes Gewand war mit einem großen verkrusteten Blutfleck auf der Brust, halb verdeckt vom schütteren Bart, das Gesicht mit den weißgelben Augen ohne Pupillen unbeweglich, er schien auch nicht zu hören, sie nahm seine Hand, fuhr mit ihr über den Pelz, er antwortete nicht, die Kinder standen da, die Einheimischen blieben stehen, neugierig, was die Stockung bedeute, der Alte sagte immer noch nichts, die F. griff in ihre Tasche, die sie wie immer über ihren Jeansanzug umgehängt trug, in der sich, sorglos wie sie war, ihr Paß, ihr Schmuck, ihre Utensilien und ihr Geld befanden, drückte dem Blinden Geldscheine in die Hand, zog sich den Mantel an und ging durch die Menge davon, von einigen Kindern begleitet, die auf sie einredeten, ohne daß sie etwas verstand, dann aus der Altstadt gelangt, sie wußte nicht wie und auch nicht, wo sie war, fand sie ein Taxi, das sie in ihr Hotel führte, in dessen Halle sich ihr Team aufhielt, in den Sesseln herumlungernd, sie anstarrend, die im roten Pelzmantel vor ihnen stand, vom Tonmeister eine Zigarette verlangend und sagte, der rote Pelzmantel, den sie in der Altstadt gefunden habe, sei von Tina von Lambert getragen worden, als diese in die Wüste gegangen sei, so absurd es auch scheine, sie kehre nicht zurück, bis sie die Wahrheit über deren Tod erfahren habe.

Ob das vernünftig sei, fragte der Tonmeister, der
Assistent grinste verlegen und der Kameramann
erhob sich und sagte, er mache den Unsinn nicht
mehr mit, kaum hätte sie die F. verlassen, seien
Polizisten gekommen und hätten das im Ministerium gedrehte Material beschlagnahmt und als sie
hierher gekommen seien hätte der Portier schon
den Rückflug gebucht und auf morgen in aller
Herrgottsfrühe ein Taxi bestellt, er sei froh, dieses
verfluchte Land verlassen zu können, die Männer,
die sie verhört hätten, seien gefoltert gewesen und
deshalb ohne Zähne, und die Erschießung des
Zwergs, er habe in seinem Zimmer eine Stunde
lang gekotzt, sie seien alle Narren, sich in die
Politik des Landes zu mischen, seine Befürchtun-
gen hätten sich bestätigt, hier seien Recherchen,
welche diesen Namen verdienten, nicht nur unmöglich, sondern auch lebensgefährlich, was ihm
nichts ausmachen würde, wenn er die geringste
Chance für ihr Vorhaben sähe, und dann, sich
wieder in den Sessel werfend, fügte er bei, offen-

gestanden sei das ganze Projekt derart unklar, ja konfus, daß er auch der F. rate, das Projekt aufzugeben, gut, sie habe einen roten Pelzmantel aufgetrieben, aber ob sie auch sicher sei, daß dieser der Lambert gehört habe, worauf die F. gereizt antwortete, sie habe noch nie etwas aufgegeben, und als der Tonmeister, der nichts so sehr liebte wie den Frieden, noch meinte, es sei vielleicht doch besser, daß sie mit ihnen käme, gewisse Tatsachen hätten die Eigenschaft, nie ans Tageslicht zu kommen, ging sie grußlos auf ihr Zimmer, um dort freilich in der Türe stehenzubleiben, saß doch im Lehnstuhl unter der Stehlampe der sanfte Schönling mit der randlosen Brille, der Untersuchungsrichter, der die ihn stumm Betrachtende ebenfalls stumm betrachtete, darauf mit der Hand auf den zweiten Lehnstuhl wies, in den sich die F. mechanisch setzte, weil es ihr schien als ob beim Schönling hinter dem Weichen, Sentimentalen etwas Hartes, Entschlossenes, bis jetzt Verstecktes zum Vorschein komme, auch war seine Sprache, die vorher vage und ausschweifend gewesen war, wie er nun zu reden begann und ihr gratulierte, daß sie Tina von Lamberts Mantel aufgetrieben, nun hart, sachlich und oft spöttisch wie die eines Mannes, der sich freut, jemand hinters Licht geführt zu haben, weshalb sie nur stumm nicken konnte, als er ihr eröffnete, er sei gekommen, ihr für das Material zu danken, das sie gefilmt habe, es sei hervorragend, die schwarzen Heiligen und die Hinrichtung des Dänen großartig für seinen Zweck geeignet, und als sie fragte, was denn seine Absicht sei, antwortete er ruhig, im übrigen habe er sich erlaubt in den Kühlschrank neben die hier üblichen Fruchtsäfte, Limonaden und Mineralwasser eine Flasche Chablis stellen zu lassen, und neben dem Kühlschrank sei eine Flasche Whisky, und als sie sagte, sie ziehe Whisky vor, sagte er, das habe er gedacht, Nüsse seien auch vorhanden, stand auf, hantierte am Kühlschrank, kam mit zwei Gläsern mit Whisky zurück, Eis und Nüssen, stellte sich vor, er sei der Chef des Geheimdienstes und über ihre Gewohnheiten im Bilde, sie solle ihm sein Geschwätz im Ministerium verzeihen, der Polizeichef hätte seine Wanzen überall, er die seinen übrigens auch, jederzeit könne er abhören, was der Polizeichef abhöre, und dann berichtete er mit knappen Worten über die Absicht des Polizeichefs, die Macht im Lande zu übernehmen, außenpolitisch den Kurs zu ändern, die Ermordung Tinas einem fremden Geheimdienst zuzuschieben, darum die Erschießung des Skandinaviers, aber der Polizeichef wisse nicht, daß diese gefilmt worden sei, er wisse auch nicht, daß er von ihm, dem Chef des Geheimdienstes, beobachtet werde, ja der Polizeichef wisse nicht einmal, wer der Chef des Geheimdienstes sei, dem Polizeichef gehe es darum, als der starke Mann zu erscheinen, der über die Polizei wie über eine Privatarmee verfüge, damit, wenn er die Macht im Lande übernommen, diese als gesichert erscheine, ihm dagegen, dem Chef des Geheimdienstes, gehe es darum, den Polizeichef bloßzustellen, zu zeigen, wie dieser die Polizei korrumpiert habe und daß dessen Macht unsicher, labil und schon am zerfallen sei, doch vor allem gehe es darum, anhand des Verbrechens an Tina von Lambert dessen Unfähigkeit nachzuweisen, weshalb er denn alles unternommen habe, ihr weitere Nachforschungen zu ermöglichen, freilich mit einem neuen Team, das er ihr zur Verfügung stelle, der Polizeichef dürfe nicht mißtrauisch werden, ihr altes Team reise ab, er, der Chef des Geheimdienstes, habe jede Vorkehrung getroffen, die notwendigen Männer instruiert, das Hotelpersonal agiere in seinem Auftrag, eine ihm befreundete Person werde ihre Rolle übernehmen, bitte sehr, und damit öffnete er die Türe und eine junge Frau trat ein, gekleidet wie die F. in einen Jeansanzug, einen roten Pelzmantel über die Schulter gehängt, der genau so geschnitten war wie jener der Tina von Lambert, ein Umstand, der die F. mißtrauisch machte, weshalb sie fragte, ob die Bitte, sie solle dem Schicksal der unglücklichen Tina von Lambert weiter nachgehen, nicht vielmehr ein Befehl sei, eine Frage auf die sie die Antwort erhielt, daß sie es sei, die den Auftrag von Lamberts angenommen habe und er, der Chef des Geheimdienstes, es als seine Pflicht erachte, ihr dabei behilflich zu sein, dann fügte er noch bei, er lasse die F. anderswo unterbringen, sie habe nichts zu befürchten, sie sei von nun an unter seinem Schutz aber es wäre gut, wenn sie ihr Team informieren würde, in ihrem eigenen Interesse nur so weit als gerade noch nötig und damit verabschiedete er sich, die junge Frau hinausführend, die mit der F. nur insofern eine gewisse Ähnlichkeit aufwies, als, von weitem gesehen, eine Verwechslung nicht auszuschließen war.

12

Der Kameramann war schon im Bett, als die F. anrief, er kam im Schlafanzug in ihr Zimmer, wo sie ihren Koffer packte, und hörte sich ihren Bericht schweigend an, wobei sie nichts verschwieg, auch nicht den Rat des Chefs des Geheimdienstes, dem Team nur das Nötigste mitzuteilen, doch erst als sie geendet hatte, schenkte er sich einen Whisky ein, vergaß aber zu trinken, dachte nach und sagte endlich, die F. sei in eine Falle gegangen, Tina von Lamberts roter Pelzmantel sei nicht von ungefähr in die Altstadt zu einem blinden Verkäufer gekommen, der rote Pelzmantel sei der Köder gewesen, es gebe sehr wenige solcher Mäntel, vielleicht nur einen, daß jetzt eine Frau mit einem zweiten auftauchen könne, weise auf eine sorgfältige Planung hin, man hätte damit gerechnet, daß die F. in die Altstadt gehe, ein roter Pelzmantel zwischen billigen Röcken hängend falle auf und einen zweiten für eine Doppelgängerin herzustellen brauche Zeit, daß der Chef des Geheimdienstes den Polizeichef unschädlich machen wolle, leuchte ihm ein, aber wozu er dafür die F. brauche, begreife er nicht, wozu so viel Umstände, da sei noch etwas anderes im Spiele, Tina von Lambert sei nicht aus bloßer Laune in dieses Land gekommen, sondern aus einem bestimmten Grund, der auch mit ihrem Tod zu tun habe, das Buch von Lamberts über den Terrorismus habe er gelesen, den arabischen Widerstandskämpfern widme er zwei Seiten, er wehre sich dagegen, sie Terroristen zu nennen, wobei er freilich betone, daß auch Nichtterroristen zu Verbrechen fähig seien, Auschwitz zum Beispiel sei nicht das Werk von Terroristen, sondern von Beamten gewesen, es sei ausgeschlossen, daß deswegen von Lamberts Frau ermordet worden sei, auch der Chef des Geheimdienstes verschweige ihr das Wesentliche, sie sei ihm ins offene Messer gelaufen und könne nicht mehr zurück, aber es sei unvorsichtig von ihr gewesen, ihn, den Kameramann, einzuweihen, überhaupt würde es ihn wundern, wenn der Chef des Geheimdienstes ihr Team ziehen lasse, sie solle ihnen das Glück wünschen, das er ihr wünsche, damit umarmte er sie und ging, ohne den Whisky berührt zu haben, was er noch nie getan hatte, und der F. war es plötzlich, als ob sie ihn nie mehr sehen würde, wieder dachte sie an das Atelier zurück, sie war nun sicher, die Schritte hinter ihr seien Frauenschritte gewesen, trank wütend das Glas Whisky leer und packte weiter, schloß den Koffer und wurde, den roten Pelzmantel über ihrem Jeansanzug, durch den Hinterausgang des Hotels von einem Pagen, der so aussah, als sei er keiner und ihr den Koffer trug, zu einem Landrover gebracht, wo zwei Männer im Burnus sie erwarteten, sie aus der Stadt zuerst über die Staatsstraße, dann auf einem staubigen Weg über einen abenteuerlichen Paß, soviel sie in der mondlosen Nacht erkennen konnte, an Schneeflächen und Geröllhalden vorbei, Schluchten hinab und hinauf, in die Berge zu einem unbestimmbar durch die anbrechende Morgendämmerung schimmerndes Gemäuer brachten, das sich, als sie aus dem Landrover stiegen, als ein verwittertes zweistöckiges Gebäude erwies, mit der Inschrift GRAND-HÔTEL MARÉCHAL LYAUTEY über der Eingangstüre, die im eisigen Winde auf- und zuschlug, in welchem ihr von einem der Männer – da im Parterre, spärlich erleuchtet von einer Glühbirne, auf sein Rufen niemand erschien – im ersten Stock ein Zimmer zugewiesen wurde, indem er dort kurzerhand eine Türe geöffnet, sie hineingeschoben und den Koffer auf den hölzer-

nen Zimmerboden gestellt hatte, worauf sie, verblüfft über die rüde Behandlung, ihn die Treppe
hinunterpoltern und kurz darauf den Landrover
davonfahren hörte, offenbar nach M. zurück,
mißmutig schaute sie sich um, von der Decke hing
ebenfalls eine Glühbirne, im Bad funktionierte die
Dusche nicht, die Tapete hing in Fetzen von der
Mauer und das einzige Mobiliar bildeten ein
wackliger Stuhl und ein Feldbett, das freilich
frisch bezogen war, und immer wieder schlug
unten die Haustüre auf und zu und noch im Schlaf
hörte sie die Türe.

Es war schon Mittag als sie erwachte, vielleicht
weil die Türe jetzt nicht mehr auf und zu schlug,
vom Fenster aus, das so verschmutzt war, daß der
Tag kaum durchschimmerte, erblickte sie ein stei-
niges, von Buschgestrüpp überwuchertes und von
Schluchten durchzogenes Gelände, hinter dem
sich jäh ein steiler Bergrücken erhob, in dessen
Eishängen und Schründen sich eine Wolke verfan-
gen hatte, die den Gipfel verhüllte und im Sonnenlicht zu kochen schien, eine öde Gegend, die sie
fragen ließ, wozu das Hotel, wohin sie geführt
worden war und das offensichtlich keines mehr
war, einst gedient habe und jetzt diene, eine
Holztreppe hinuntergehend, in den roten Pelzmantel gehüllt, da es bitter kalt war, fand sie
niemanden, sie rief, in der Halle, mehr ein schäbi-
ges Zimmer, war niemand, auch in der Küche
niemand, bis plötzlich eine alte Frau aus einem
Nebenraum schlurfend in der Türe zur Halle
stehenblieb, die F. entgeistert anstarrte, um endlich auf französisch »ihr Mantel, ihr Mantel«

hervorzubringen, »ihr Mantel«, dabei zitternd auf den roten Pelzmantel zeigend, »ihr Mantel« plappernd, immer wieder, so offensichtlich durcheinander, daß sie, als die F. auf sie zuging, zurückwich in den Nebenraum, der offenbar einmal als Speisezimmer gedient hatte, und mit dem Rücken zur Wand, hinter dem Eßtisch und einigen alten Stühlen verschanzt, die F. angstvoll erwartete, die jedoch, um die alte Frau zu beruhigen, keine Anstalten mehr machte, auf sie zuzugehen, sondern in diesem trostlosen Zimmer stehenblieb, dessen einziger Schmuck ein großes gerahmtes Bild eines französischen Generals war, stark vergilbt, offenbar Marschall Lyautey, und auf französisch fragte, ob sie frühstücken könne, was die Alte mit einem heftigen Nicken bejahte, auf die F. zuging, sie bei der Hand nahm und auf eine Terrasse zog, wo sich an der Hausmauer unter einer einmal orangenen zerrissenen Markise ein gedeckter Holztisch befand, auch das Frühstück war schon vorbereitet, denn die Alte trug es herein, kaum hatte sich die F. gesetzt, war jedoch von ihrem Zimmer aus nur ein Schluchten-, Busch- und Steindurcheinander zu sehen gewesen mit dem kochenden Bergrücken dahinter, so blickte nun die F. einen sanften noch grünen

Hügel hinunter, an den weitere, immer niedrigere Hügel brandeten, sich aneinander brechend, bis weit unten es weißgelb hinaufschimmerte, die große Sandwüste, auch glaubte sie am Ende des Sichtbaren etwas Schwarzes zu ahnen, die Al-Hakim-Ruine, der Wind war frisch, die F. war froh sich in den roten Pelzmantel schmiegen zu können, den die Alte immer wieder beäugte, auch mit der Hand zaghaft über ihn fuhr, fast zärtlich, neben der frühstückenden F. verweilend, als müsse sie diese bewachen, aber zusammenzuckte, als die Frühstückende unvermittelt fragte, ob sie Tina von Lambert gekannt habe, eine Frage, welche die Alte aufs neue zu verwirren schien, indem sie immer wieder »Tina« stammelte, »Tina, Tina«, auf den Mantel wies, dann fragte, ob die F. eine Freundin sei und als diese bejahte, sich vor Aufregung in ihren Sätzen verhaspelnd berichtete, soweit es die F. zu verstehen vermochte, Tina sei mit einem gemieteten Auto allein hierhergekommen, wobei sie das »allein« mehrmals wiederholte, auch etwas Unverständliches über das gemietete Auto hervorstammelte, sie habe ein Zimmer für drei Monate gemietet und die Gegend durchstreift und sei bis zur großen Sandwüste vorgedrungen, ja bis zum schwarzen Stein, womit sie offenbar die

Ruine meinte, doch plötzlich nicht mehr zurückgekehrt, aber sie, die Alte, wisse, aber was die Alte wußte war unverständlich, sosehr die F. sich auch bemühte, hinter den Sinn der angefangenen, sich wiederholenden und abgebrochenen Sätze zu kommen, die Alte schwieg vielmehr plötzlich, wurde mißtrauisch, starrte wieder auf den roten Pelzmantel, wobei die F. spürte, die ihr Frühstück beendet hatte, daß die Alte etwas fragen wollte, aber nicht zu fragen wagte, weshalb die F. entschlossen aber nicht ohne Brutalität sagte, Tina werde nicht wiederkommen, sie sei tot, eine Nachricht, die von der Alten zuerst gleichgültig entgegengenommen wurde, so als hätte sie nicht begriffen, doch plötzlich fing sie an zu feixen, in sich hineinzukichern, aus Verzweiflung, wie es der F. allmählich aufging, und, indem sie die Alte bei der Schulter packte und schüttelte, verlangte sie, in das Zimmer geführt zu werden, das Tina gemietet hätte, worauf die Alte etwas murmelte, das, weil sie dabei wieder kicherte, wie »ganz oben« klang, um dann, wie die F. die Treppe hinaufging, in ein Schluchzen auszubrechen, um welches sich die F. freilich nicht mehr kümmerte, hatte sie doch im zweiten Stockwerk ein Zimmer gefunden, das vielleicht das Zimmer Tina von

68

Lamberts gewesen war, ein Zimmer besser als jenes, in welchem die F. geschlafen hatte, ausgestattet mit Anzeichen eines gewissen Komforts, der zu dem Hotel nicht paßte und die F. überraschte, als sie sich umschaute: ein breites Bett mit einer alten Steppdecke undefinierbarer Farbe, ein Kamin, offenbar noch nie gebraucht, auf ihm einige Bände Jules Verne, über ihm wieder das vergilbte Bild des Marschall Lyautey, eine alte Schreibkommode, ein Bad, die Kacheln nur noch teilweise intakt und in der Wanne Rostflecken, zerschlissene Sammetvorhänge, ein Balkon, gegen die ferne Sandwüste gelegen, und wie sie ihn betrat, sah sie hinter einem kleinen Gemäuer etwa hundert Meter wüstenabwärts etwas verschwinden, sie wartete und dann kam es wieder, es war der Kopf eines Mannes, der sie mit einem Fernglas beobachtete, so daß sie an den von Tina zweimal unterstrichenen Satz »ich werde beobachtet« denken mußte und als sie ins Zimmer zurücktrat, war in ihm schon die Alte mit dem Koffer, dem Bademantel und der Tasche der F., als sei es selbstverständlich, auch hatte sie Bettwäsche mitgebracht, worauf die F. gereizt fragte, ob sie telefonieren könne, nach unten gewiesen fand sie in einem dunklen Korridor neben der Küche das

Telefon, trotzig beschloß sie, den Logiker D. anzurufen, überzeugt, daß die Verbindung nicht zustande käme, aber entschlossen, das Unmögliche zu versuchen, hob sie den Hörer von der Gabel des alten Apparats, er war tot, es konnte sich um eine Vorsichtsmaßnahme des Chefs des Geheimdienstes handeln, er hatte sie hierher bringen lassen, wo auch Tina von Lambert gewesen war, aber plötzlich mißtraute sie dessen Begründungen, vor allem deshalb, weil sie sich nicht vorstellen konnte, was Tina bewogen haben sollte, mit einem Wagen, wie die Alte erzählt hatte, in der Wüste herumzufahren, vor der offenen Balkontüre auf dem Boden sitzend, dann wieder indem sie sich aufs Bett legte und zur Decke starrte, versuchte sie Tina von Lamberts Schicksal zu rekonstruieren, sie ging aufs neue vom einzig sicheren Ausgangspunkt aus, von Tinas Tagebüchern, und versuchte alle Möglichkeiten durchzuspielen, um zum sicheren Ende zu gelangen, zu Tinas von Schakalen zerfleischter Leiche bei der Al-Hakim-Ruine, doch nie kam sie zu einer schlüssigen Annahme, das Verlassen ihres Hauses, »kurzerhand« wie sich von Lambert ausgedrückt hatte, war eine Flucht gewesen, aber in dieses Land war sie nicht wie eine Flüchtende gekommen, sondern mit einem ganz bestimmten Ziel, so wie sie sich benommen hatte, hätte sich eine Journalistin benommen, die einem Geheimnis nachspürte, aber Tina war keine Journalistin, eine Liebesgeschichte war denkbar, aber nichts deutete auf eine Liebesgeschichte hin, ohne eine Lösung gefunden zu haben trat sie später vors Haus, die Wolke am Bergrücken hatte sich vergrößert, begann sich heranzuschieben, sie ging den Weg zurück, den sie gekommen war, geriet auf eine steinige Hochebene, der Weg verzweigte sich, sie wählte einen Weg, der sich nach einer halben Stunde wieder verzweigte, sie ging zurück, stand lange vor dem einsamen Haus, das sinnlos dastand, mit der Haustür, die wieder auf und zu schlug, und mit dem Schild darüber GRAND-HÔTEL MARÉCHAL LYAUTEY und über dem Schild das schwarze Rechteck eines Fensters, das einzige in der Hausmauer, die einmal weiß gewesen sein mußte und nun alle Schattierungen von Grau aufwies, das in alle Farben des Spektrums hineinspielte, derart als wäre es vor Urzeiten von Riesen angekotzt worden, und nicht nur während sie dastand und nach dem Haus schaute und nach dem Fenster, hinter dem sie geschlafen hatte, sondern auch Stunden vorher, eigentlich kaum

hatte sie das Haus verlassen, wußte sie und hatte
sie gewußt, daß sie beobachtet wurde, auch wenn
sie niemanden sah, der sie beobachtete und als der
Sonnenball hinter der fernen Sandwüste versank,
auf einmal so schnell, als ob er fiele, und die
Dämmerung hereinbrach, in der nur noch die
gewaltige Wolkenwand in ihren obersten Schich-
ten brennender Sand zu sein schien und sie ins
Haus hineinging, waren im Speisezimmer unter
dem Bild des Marschalls der Tisch schon gedeckt
und die Speisen aufgetragen, in einer Schüssel
Schaffleisch in einer roten Sauce und Weißbrot,
dazu Rotwein, die Alte war nicht zu sehen, sie aß
wenig, trank Wein, ging dann in das Zimmer, in
welchem auch Tina von Lambert gehaust hatte,
trat auf den Balkon, war es ihr doch gewesen, als
hätte sie, während sie aß, ein fernes Donnern
gehört, die Wolkenwand mußte wieder zurückge-
wichen sein, vor ihr und über ihr brannten noch
die Wintersterne, doch fern am Horizont sah sie
einen gleißenden Widerschein und ein Aufblitzen,
es war wie ein Gewitter und doch nicht und über
allem hing das ferne unbestimmbare Donnern und
wieder war es, als ob sie aus dem Dunkeln, das zu
ihr heraufdrang, beobachtet werde und wieder im
Zimmer, schon im Bademantel, in welchem sie

auch schlief, mit Grausen die rostige Badewanne
betrachtend, hörte sie ein Auto herankommen,
doch ohne anzuhalten vorbeifahren, kurz darauf
ein zweites, das hielt, dann ein Rufen, jemand
mußte das Haus betreten haben, rief weiter, ob
jemand da sei, kam in den ersten Stock hinauf, rief
»hallo, hallo« und als die F. hinunterging, den
roten Pelzmantel über den Bademantel geworfen,
fand sie einen jungen strohblonden Mann vor, der
im Begriff war, zu ihr hinaufzusteigen, der eine
blaue Cordhose, Joggingschuhe und eine wattierte
Jacke trug, sie mit weit aufgerissenen blauen Augen
anstarrte und stammelte »Gott sei Dank, Gott sei
Dank«, und als sie fragte, wofür denn Gott zu
danken sei, die Treppe hinaufstürzte, sie umarmte
und schrie, weil sie lebe, er habe es dem Chef gesagt und mit ihm gewettet, daß sie noch lebe und
nun lebe sie noch und damit sprang er die Treppe
wieder hinunter, dann die zweite und als die F. ihm
folgend die Halle erreicht hatte, sah sie den Strohblonden Koffer hereinschleppen, was sie auf den
Gedanken brachte, daß es sich um den ihr verspro-
chenen Kameramann handeln könne und sie fragte
ihn, worauf er antwortete, »erraten« und die
Kamera aus dem Wagen holte, aus einem vw-Bus
wie sie durch die offene Türe bemerkte, vor der das

Auto stand, dann sagte er an der Filmkamera
hantierend, die könne er auch in der Nacht brauchen, Spezialoptik, ihre Berichte seien phantastisch gewesen, eine Bemerkung, die sie stutzen
und fragen ließ, ob er sich denn nicht vorstellen
wolle, worauf er rot wurde und stammelte, er heiße
Björn Olsen und sie könne ruhig Dänisch mit ihm
reden, was sie an den zwerghaften, grinsenden
Mann denken ließ, der eine Zigarette rauchend an
der Wand gestanden, die Zigarette ausgetreten
hatte und in sich zusammengefallen war, und sie
antwortete, sie könne nicht Dänisch, er müsse sie
mit jemandem verwechseln, was ihn beinahe die
Kamera fallen ließ, und schreiend und auf den
Boden stampfend, nein, nein, das dürfe nicht wahr
sein, sie trage doch einen roten Pelzmantel, trug er
die Kamera und die Koffer wieder in den Bus,
kletterte in den Bus und fuhr los, doch nicht nach
M. zurück, sondern dem Gebirge zu, und als sie in
ihr Zimmer hinaufging, erschütterte auf einmal
eine Explosion das Haus, doch war alles wieder
ruhig, als sie den Balkon betrat, auch das Wetter-
leuchten und das gleißende Licht in der fernen
Sandwüste war erloschen, nur die Sterne brannten
so bedrohlich, daß sie ins Zimmer zurückkehrte
und die zerschlissenen Sammetvorhänge zuzog,

wobei ihr Blick auf die Schreibkommode fiel, sie war unverschlossen und leer, dann erst bemerkte sie den Papierkorb neben der Schreibkommode und in ihm ein zerknülltes Papier, das sie auseinanderfaltete und glättete, in einer Handschrift, die sie nicht kannte, war etwas geschrieben, offenbar ein Zitat, denn es stand in Anführungszeichen, aber da es eine nordische Sprache war, verstand sie es nicht, hartnäckig wie sie war, setzte sie sich an die Schreibkommode, die sie heruntergeklappt hatte und versuchte zu übersetzen, wobei ihr freilich Wörter wie »edderkop« oder »tomt rum« oder »fodfaeste« Mühe bereiteten, es war Mitternacht als sie glaubte, das Zitat enträtselt zu haben: ›Was soll da kommen, was sollen fremde Zeiten (fremtiden) bringen? Ich weiß das nicht, ich ahne nichts. Wenn eine Kreuzspinne (edderkop?) sich von einem festen Punkt in ihre Konsequenzen niederstürzt, da sieht sie beständig einen leeren Raum (tomt rum?) vor sich, worin sie keinen festen Fuß (fodfaeste?) finden kann, wie sehr sie auch zappelt. So wie dies geht es mir; vorn beständig ein leerer Raum (tomt rum?), was mich vorantreibt ist eine Konsequenz, die hinter (bag) mir liegt. Dieses Leben ist verkehrt (bagvendt) und rätselhaft (raedsomt?), nicht auszuhalten.‹

14

Als sie am nächsten Morgen früh hinunterging, in den roten Pelzmantel gehüllt, entschlossen nach dem Frühstück dem Gebirge zu zu gehen, weil die Explosion nach der Abfahrt des Dänen sie nicht in Ruhe ließ und das Zitat, das vielleicht eine verklausulierte Botschaft darstellte, ihre Unruhe steigerte, saß auf der Terrasse am Holztisch frühstükkend der Chef des Geheimdienstes, ganz in Weiß mit einem schwarzen Halstuch, an Stelle der randlosen Brille eine Sonnenbrille mit massiver Fassung, der sich erhob, die F. einlud, neben ihm Platz zu nehmen, ihr Kaffee einschenkte und Croissants anbot, die er für sie aus dem europäischen Teil von M. mitgebracht habe, bedauerte ihre notdürftige Unterkunft und legte ihr, nachdem sie gegessen hatte, eine Boulevardzeitung vor, in welcher auf dem Titelbild Tina von Lambert abgebildet war, strahlend, in den Armen ihres strahlenden Mannes, und darunter stand, sensationelle Rückkehr einer sensationell Beerdigten, die Gattin des bekannten Psychiaters habe sich infolge einer Depression im Atelier eines verstorbenen Malers versteckt gehalten, ihr Paß und ihr roter Pelzmantel seien gestohlen worden, was offenbar dazu geführt habe, daß sie mit jener Frau verwechselt worden sei, die bei der Al-Hakim-Ruine ermordet wurde, wobei man nun nicht nur vor dem Rätsel stehe, wer der Mörder, sondern auch wer die Ermordete sei, worauf die F. das Boulevardblatt bleich vor Entrüstung auf den Tisch warf, da stimme etwas nicht, das Ganze sei zu banal, dabei fühlte sie sich dermaßen blamiert und in ein unsinniges Abenteuer gelockt, daß sie in Tränen ausgebrochen wäre, aber die eiserne Ruhe des Chefs des Geheimdienstes neben ihr zwang sie zur Gelassenheit, um so mehr als dieser nun erläuterte, was an der Geschichte nicht stimme, sei der Diebstahl, Tina sei eine Freundin einer dänischen Journalistin, Jytte Sörensen, gewesen und habe dieser ihren Paß und ihren roten Pelzmantel gegeben, nur so habe die Dänin einreisen können, eine Auskunft, welche die F. nachdenklich machte, während er ihr eine weitere Tasse Kaffee anbot, fragte sie, woher er das wisse, und er antwortete, weil er die dänische Journalistin vernommen habe, sie hätte alles zugegeben und auf die Frage, warum diese ermordet worden sei, antwortete er, die Sonnenbrille anhauchend und reinigend, das wiederum wisse er nicht, Jytte Sörensen sei eine sehr energische Persönlichkeit gewesen und erinnere ihn in vielem an die F., er habe nicht herausbekommen, was sie mit ihrem Täuschungsmanöver bezwecke, da der Chef der Polizei sich habe täuschen lassen, habe er keinen Grund gesehen, seinerseits einzugreifen und sie samt dem falschen Paß und ihrem roten Pelzmantel ziehen lassen, weshalb auch, daß sie ein so schreckliches Ende genommen, tue ihm leid, hätte sie ihn eingeweiht, wäre es nicht dazu gekommen, das zerknüllte Zitat im Papierkorb habe sie, die F., sicher auch gelesen, es stamme von Kierkegaard, ›Entweder - Oder‹, er habe einen Spezialisten beigezogen, er habe zuerst an eine verschlüsselte Botschaft geglaubt, sei aber nun der Überzeugung, es handle sich um einen Hilferuf, er habe die tollkühne Dänin bis hierher überwachen können aber dann ihre Spur verloren, er hoffe, daß der junge Mann, der wie ein germanischer Recke ausgesehen habe, mehr Glück gehabt habe als seine Landsmännin – wenn das Wort richtig sei – offensichtlich seien beide im Auftrag einer dänischen privaten Fernsehanstalt eingereist, bekannt durch ihre Sensationsreportagen, und wenn sie jetzt, die F., in ihrem roten Pelzmantel in der Rolle einer anderen, als sie ursprünglich glaubte, ins Gebirge und vielleicht sogar in die Wüste gehe, so könne er ihr nicht mehr helfen, das Team, das er habe auftreiben wollen, habe sich geweigert mit ihr zusammenzuarbeiten, auch sei es für ihn leider nicht möglich gewesen, ihr Team ausreisen zu lassen, unglücklicherweise habe sie, die F., trotz seiner Warnung geplaudert, dieses schäbige Hotel sei der letzte noch irgendwie zu kontrollierende Punkt, von da an sei Niemandsland, völkerrechtlich noch nicht abgegrenzt, aber er sei gerne bereit, sie zurückzuführen, worauf die F. sagte, nachdem sie ihn um eine Zigarette gebeten und er ihr Feuer gegeben hatte, sie gehe trotzdem.

15

Als sie im roten Pelzmantel das Haus verließ, wies nichts mehr darauf hin, daß der Chef des Geheimdienstes sie besucht hatte und auch von der Alten fehlte jede Spur, das Haus schien leer gewesen zu sein, die Haustüre unter dem Schild GRAND-HÔTEL MARÉCHAL LYAUTEY schlug auf und zu und sie kam sich vor wie in einem alten unwirklichen Film, indem sie mit umgehängter Tasche, den Koffer in der Hand, in der menschenleeren Einöde den Weg wählte, den der junge Däne genommen haben mußte, ohne Wissen wohin die Straße führte, auf der sie nun sinnlos, stur, gegen jede Vernunft dem Berg zu wanderte, an dessen Flanken immer noch die Wolke hing, und an ihr Gespräch mit dem Logiker D. dachte, wie sie sich damals ein Bild von einer Tina von Lambert gemacht hatte, aus dem einzigen Grunde etwas zu unternehmen, nicht untätig zu sein, in Aktion zu treten, doch nun, wie sich dieses Bild als Phantasiegebilde herausgestellt hatte, wie hinter ihm eine banale Ehegeschichte zum Vorschein gekommen und sich das Schicksal einer ganz anderen Frau enthüllte, von der sie keine Ahnung gehabt hatte, aber deren roten Pelzmantel sie trug, der wiederum der gleiche war, den Tina getragen hatte, fühlte sie sich in diese andere, in diese dänische Journalistin Jytte Sörensen verwandelt, vielleicht vor allem durch das Zitat Kierkegaards, auch sie fühlte sich hilflos wie eine in den leeren Raum fallende Spinne, dieser Weg, den sie nun ging, staubig, steinig, der unbarmherzigen Sonne ausgesetzt, die längst durch die Wolkenwand gebrochen war, die unter ihr kochte, der sich Hängen entlang krümmte und sich zwischen seltsam geformten Felsen hindurch zwängte, war eine Konsequenz ihres ganzen Lebens, sie hatte immer spontan gehandelt, es war das erste Mal gewesen, daß sie gezögert hatte, als sie von Otto von Lambert aufgefordert worden war, ihn mit ihrem Team zu besuchen und dennoch war sie zu ihm gegangen und hatte seinen Auftrag angenommen, und nun schritt sie gegen ihren Willen diesen Weg entlang und konnte doch nicht anders, den Koffer in der Hand wie eine Autostopperin auf einer Straße, auf der keine Autos fuhren, bis sie plötzlich vor dem nackten Leichnam Björn Olsens stand, so unvermittelt, daß ihr Fuß an ihn stieß, er lag vor ihr, immer noch lachend, wie es schien, wie das erste Mal als sie ihn unten an der Treppe gesehen hatte, von weißem Staub bedeckt, so vollständig, daß er mehr einer Statue glich als einer Leiche, die Cordhose, die Joggingschuhe, die wattierte Jacke lagen im Material, das er mitgenommen hatte, in den runden Blechdosen, die meisten geborsten, aufgesprengt, aus denen die Filmbänder wie schwarze Gedärme quollen, und hinter diesem Wirrwarr der vw-Bus, von innen heraus zerrissen, ein groteskes Durcheinander von Blech und Stahl, ein verbogener und zerrissener Schrotthaufen von Maschinenteilen, Rädern, Glaskristallen, ein Anblick, der sie erstarren ließ, die Leiche, die Filmrollen, die herumgestreuten und geborstenen Koffer, die Kleidungsstücke, die Unterhose, die wie eine Fahne an einer geknickten Antenne flatterte – erst allmählich nahm sie Details wahr –, die Busruine, deren Lenkradüberreste noch von einer vom Arm abgetrennten Hand des Dänen umklammert waren, all das sah sie, vor der Leiche stehend, und doch schien ihr unwirklich, was sie sah, irgend etwas störte sie, machte die Wirklichkeit unwirklich, ein Geräusch, das sie auf einmal wahrnahm, das jedoch schon gewesen war, als sie auf den Toten gestoßen war, und als sie nach der Richtung schaute, aus der das Geräusch, dieses leise Surren kam, sah sie einen großen, hageren, schlaksigen Mann in einem weißen, schmutzigen Leinenanzug, der sie filmte, ihr zuwinkte und sie weiter filmte, dann zu ihr hinkte mit seiner Kamera, mit einem mühsamen Schritt über den Toten herüber, neben ihr diesen filmend, wie von ihr aus gesehen und dabei sagte, sie solle doch endlich ihren blöden Koffer abstellen, zur Seite hinkte, die Kamera wieder auf sie schwenkte, ihr nachhinkte, als sie zurückwich und ihn anherrschte, weil sie den Eindruck hatte, der Mann sei betrunken, was er wolle und wer er sei, worauf er die Kamera sinken ließ, man nenne ihn Polyphem, wie er sonst heiße, habe er längst vergessen, sei auch nicht wichtig, daß er sich nicht gemeldet habe, als der Geheimdienst für sie ein Kamerateam gesucht hätte, sei von der politischen Lage des Landes aus verständlich, für sie, die F., zu arbeiten, sei zu riskant, was die Polizei wisse, wisse der Geheimdienst und was der Geheimdienst wisse, wisse die Armee, etwas dicht zu halten, sei unmöglich, er sei ihr lieber heimlich gefolgt, er wisse ja, was sie suche, der Chef des Geheimdienstes habe es allen Kameramännern erzählt und es wimmle in diesem Land von Kameramännern, sie, die F., wolle den Mörder der Dänin finden und womöglich überführen, wozu sie auch deren roten Pelzmantel angezogen habe, er finde das phantastisch, er werde ihr später die Filme zeigen, die er von ihr, der F., gedreht habe, nicht nur seit sie im ›Grand-Hôtel Maréchal Lyautey‹ abgestiegen sei, wie sich der verlotterte Steinhaufen nenne, nein, schon vorher, als sie den roten Pelzmantel in der Altstadt beim Blinden gefunden und gekauft habe, auch diese Szene sei von ihm gefilmt worden und sicher auch von anderen, an ihrem Unternehmen sei nicht nur er interessiert, auch jetzt würde sie von überall her mit Teleobjektiven beobachtet, die selbst durch den Nebel drängen, wie ein Katarakt stürzten diese Erklärungen aus dem Munde des großen schlaksigen Mannes heraus, aus dieser Höhle mit schlechten Zähnen von weißen Stoppeln umgeben, aus einem hageren durchfurchten Gesicht mit kleinen brennenden Augen, aus einem Antlitz eines hinkenden Mannes in einem schmutzigen, verschmierten Leinenkleid, der mit gespreizten Beinen über der Leiche stehend, die F. immer wieder mit einer Videokamera filmte, und als sie fragte, was er nun eigentlich wolle, antwortete er, einen Tausch, und als sie fragte, was er darunter verstehe, erklärte er, er hätte ihre Filmporträts stets bewundert, es sei sein größter Wunsch, ein Porträt von ihr herzustellen, auch die Dänin, die Sörensen, hätte er gefilmt und weil sie am Schicksal dieser Journalistin interessiert sei, biete er für das Porträt, das er von ihr, der F., herzustellen gedenke, die Filme an, die er von der Dänin gemacht habe, er sei imstande, die Videokassetten in konventionelle Filme zu verwandeln, die Sörensen sei einem Geheimnis auf der Spur gewesen, für sie, die F., biete sich die Gelegenheit die Spur wiederaufzunehmen, er sei bereit mit ihr ein Gebiet der Wüste aufzusuchen, in welches die Sörensen verschlagen worden sei, von allen, von denen sie beobachtet werde, habe sich dorthin bis jetzt keiner vorgewagt, aber sie könne ihm vertrauen, er gelte in gewissen Kreisen als der wohl unerschrockenste Kameramann, wenn auch die Kreise, in denen er bekannt sei, nicht genannt und seine Filme nicht gezeigt werden könnten, aus wirtschaftlichen und politischen Gründen, die er angesichts der Leiche des jungen Dänen nicht erläutern möchte, aus Pietät, auch der sei diesen Gründen zum Opfer gefallen.

16

Er hinkte ohne eine Antwort abzuwarten zum Bus
zurück, wobei sich ihr Eindruck, er sei betrunken,
verstärkte, und als er hinter dem Bus verschwunden war, wußte sie, daß sie im Begriffe war,
nochmals einen Fehler zu begehen, doch wenn sie
das Schicksal der Dänin aufklären wollte, mußte
sie sich dem Manne anvertrauen, der sich Polyphem nannte, auch wenn ihm nicht zu trauen
war, den man offenbar ebenso beobachtete wie
man sie beobachtete, ja vielleicht wurde sie nur
beobachtet, weil man ihn beobachtete, sie kam
sich vor wie eine Schachfigur, die hin- und her-
geschoben wurde, eigentlich widerwillig stieg sie
über den Toten und gelangte um die Busruine
herum zu einem Geländefahrzeug, verstaute ihren
Koffer auf der Pritsche und nahm neben ihm
Platz, der nun deutlich nach Whisky stank und ihr
riet, sich anzuschnallen, nicht grundlos, denn die
Fahrt, die nun begann, war höllenmäßig, Staub-
wolken aufwirbelnd sausten sie dem Bergrücken
entlang tief in die kochende Wolkenwand hinab,

86

oft so nah am Straßenrand, daß Steine in die Abgründe unter ihnen prasselten, später ging es in Haarnadelkurven noch steiler hinunter, wobei der Betrunkene die Kurven manchmal übersah und mit dem massigen Fahrzeug geradewegs hinunterstob, während die F., durch den Gurt an die Rücklehne ihres Sitzes gepreßt, die Beine nach vorne gestemmt, den Bergrücken, den sie hinabfegten, kaum wahrnahm, auch das Grasland, dem sie entgegenfielen und über welches sie nun der Wüste entgegenrasten, Schakale und Kaninchen aufscheuchend, Schlangen, die wie Pfeile davonschossen, und anderes Getier, hinein in die Steinwüste, von einem schwarzen krächzenden Gewölk umhüllt, stundenlang wie es ihr schien, dann als die Vögel zurückblieben, in grelles Sonnenlicht getaucht, bis der Geländewagen eine Staubwolke aufwirbelnd, vor einem eher flachen Schutthaufen jäh stoppte, mitten in einer Ebene, die wie eine Marslandschaft schien, ein Eindruck, der vielleicht durch das Licht zustandekam, das sie ausstrahlte, war sie doch von einer seltsamen halb metallisch rostigen, halb felsigen Materie bedeckt, in der gigantische verbogene Metallformen, unförmige Stahlsplitter und Stacheln steckten, wie hineingewuchtet, was die F., als die Staubwolke,

die sich endlich gelegt hatte, gerade noch wahrzu-
nehmen vermochte, denn schon sank der Geländewagen nach unten, über ihm schloß sich eine
Decke, wonach sie sich in einer unterirdischen
Garage befanden und auf die Frage, wo sie sei,
antwortete er etwas Unverständliches, eine Eisentür glitt auf und er hinkte ihr durch weitere
aufgleitende Eisentüren halb keller-, halb atelier-
hafte Räume voraus, die Wände eng mit kleinen
Fotos bedeckt, als wären entwickelte Filmrollen
absurderweise in lauter Einzelbilder zerschnitten
worden, in einem wilden Durcheinander mit Stö-
ßen von Fotobüchern auf Tischen und Stühlen
lagen Großaufnahmen zerschossener Panzerwa-
gen herum, dazu Stöße vollgekritzelter Papiere,
Berge von Filmrollen, Gestelle, an denen Filmaus-
schnitte hingen, auch Körbe voll mit Filmresten,
dann ein Fotolabor, Kästen voller Dias, ein Vorführraum, ein Korridor, worauf er sie, mit dem
hinkenden Bein immer wieder einknickend und
schwankend, so betrunken war er, in einen fen-
sterlosen Raum führte, dessen Wände mit Fotos
bedeckt waren, mit einem Jugendstilbett und einem kleinen Tisch des gleichen Stils, ein grotesker
Raum, an den sich eine Toilette und ein Dusch-
raum anschlossen, das Gästeappartement, wie

er sich mühsam ausdrückte, gegen die Wand des Korridors taumelte und die F., die mißmutig das Innere der Zelle betrat, allein ließ, doch als sie sich wandte, hatte sich die Türe geschlossen.

17

Erst allmählich wurde sie sich der Furcht bewußt, die sich ihrer bemächtigt hatte, seit sie in dieser unterirdischen Anlage war, eine Erkenntnis, die sie bewog, statt das Unvernünftigste das Vernünftigste zu tun, von der Türe, die sich nicht öffnen ließ, zu lassen, ihre Furcht zu ignorieren, sich aufs Jugendstilbett zu legen und zu überlegen, wer Polyphem sein könnte, von einem Kameramann, der diesen Übernamen trug, hatte sie noch nie gehört, auch war rätselhaft wozu diese Anlage dienen könnte, sie mußte mit enormen Kosten erstellt worden sein, aber von wem, und was bedeuteten diese riesenhaften Trümmer um die Anlage herum, was ging hier vor und was sollte der seltsame Vorschlag, ihr Porträt gegen das der Jytte Sörensen zu tauschen, Fragen über denen sie einschlief und als sie jäh aufwachte, war es ihr als hätten die Wände gezittert und das Bett getanzt, was sie geträumt haben mußte, unwillkürlich begann sie die Fotos zu betrachten, mit steigendem Grauen, stellten sie doch dar, wie Björn Olsen in die Luft gesprengt wurde, die Fotos mußten mit einer Kamera von einer technischen Präzision aufgenommen worden sein, die für sie unvorstellbar war, erblickte man auf dem ersten Foto nur den vw-Bus in Umrissen, erschien auf dem nächsten, dort wo man die Kupplung vermuten konnte, eine kleine weiße Kugel, die sich auf den folgenden Fotos ausweitete, der Bus schien im Verlauf der Serie gleichzeitig durchsichtig und verformt zu werden und auseinanderzufallen, auch war zu sehen, wie Olsen von seinem Sitz gesprengt wurde, die verschiedenen Phasen wirkten um so gespensterhafter, als Olsen, von seinem Sitz in die Höhe gehoben, während seine rechte Hand, das Lenkrad umklammernd, sich von seinem Arm löste, vergnügt zu pfeifen schien, und, entsetzt über die fürchterlichen Fotos, sprang sie aus dem Bett und näherte sich instinktiv der Tür, die sich zu ihrer Verwunderung öffnete, doch froh aus dem Zimmer zu sein, das sie als Gefängniszelle empfand, trat sie in den Korridor, der war leer, sie witterte eine Falle, blieb stehen, irgendwo hämmerte jemand gegen eine Eisentüre, sie ging dem Geräusch nach, die Türen glitten auf, wenn sie sich ihnen näherte, sie ging durch die Räume, die sie schon gesehen hatte, sie ging zögernd, immer neue Korridore, Schlafstellen, technische Räume, deren Apparaturen sie nicht begriff, die Anlage mußte für viele Menschen gebaut sein, wo waren sie, mit jedem Schritt fühlte sie sich bedrohter, es mußte sich um eine List handeln, sie allein zu lassen, sie war sicher, sie werde von Polyphem beobachtet, sie kam dem Hämmern immer näher, einmal war es ganz nah, dann ferner, plötzlich stand sie am Ende eines Korridors vor einer Eisentüre, die ein normales Schloß hatte, in welchem ein Schlüssel steckte, gegen die gehämmert wurde, und manchmal war es, als ob sich jemand von innen mit den Schultern gegen die Türe werfe, schon wollte sie den Schlüssel drehen, als ihr der Gedanke kam, es sei Polyphem, der sich hinter der Eisentüre befinde, er war betrunken und sein Abschied war sonderbar gewesen, ihm mußte irgend etwas durch den Kopf geschossen sein, er hatte sie geradezu angestarrt und dann doch wieder nicht, als wäre sie nicht vorhanden, und dann konnte er sich selber aus Versehen eingesperrt haben indem sich das Schloß verklemmt hatte, auch konnte ihn ein Dritter eingeschlossen haben, die Anlage war riesig, vielleicht war sie nicht so unbewohnt wie es schien und warum öffneten sich plötzlich alle Türen automatisch, es polterte und hämmerte weiter, sie rief Polyphem, Polyphem, nur Hämmern und Poltern als Antwort, aber vielleicht war hinter einer Eisentüre nichts zu hören, vielleicht war alles keine List, vielleicht wurde sie nicht beobachtet, vielleicht war sie frei, sie lief in ihre Zelle, fand sie nicht, lief Irrwege, betrat eine Zelle, die sie zuerst für die ihre hielt, die jedoch nicht die ihre war, endlich fand sie die ihre doch, hängte sich die Tasche um, eilte wieder durch die unterirdischen Räume, immer noch war das Hämmern und Poltern zu hören, endlich fand sie die Garagentüre, sie glitt zur Seite, das Geländefahrzeug stand bereit, sie bestieg den Führersitz, betrachtete das Armaturenbrett, fand neben dem üblichen Instrumentarium zwei Knöpfe mit eingelassenen Zeigern, einer nach oben, einer nach unten, drückte auf den Knopf, dessen Zeiger nach oben wies, die Decke öffnete sich, das Geländefahrzeug wurde hinaufgeschoben, sie befand sich im Freien, über ihr der Himmel, in ihm Trümmer wie Speerspitzen, lange Schatten von einem grellen Funken geworfen, der erlosch, mit einem Ruck war die Erde rückwärts gekippt, der rote Streifen Lichts am Horizont begann sich zu schließen, sie war im Schlund eines Weltungeheuers, das seinen Rachen schloß, und wie sie den Ein-

bruch der Nacht erlebte, die Verwandlung von
Licht zu Schatten und von Schatten zu Finsternis,
in welcher die Sterne plötzlich da waren, ging ihr
die Gewißheit auf, daß die Freiheit die Falle war,
in die sie laufen sollte, sie ließ das Geländefahrzeug wieder nach unten gleiten, die Decke schloß
sich wieder über ihr, das Poltern und Hämmern
war nicht mehr zu hören, sie rannte in ihre Zelle
zurück und als sie sich auf das Bett warf, spürte sie
etwas heranheulen, ein Einschlag, ein Zerbersten,
fern und doch ganz nah, ein Erzittern, das Bett,
der Tisch tanzten, sie schloß die Augen, sie wußte
nicht wie lange, auch nicht ob sie ohnmächtig
gewesen war oder nicht, es war ihr gleichgültig
und als sie die Augen öffnete, stand Polyphem vor
ihr.

18

Er stellte ihren Koffer neben ihr Bett, er war
nüchtern und frisch rasiert, trug einen sauberen
weißen Anzug und ein schwarzes Hemd, es sei
halb elf, er habe sie lange suchen müssen, sie liege
nicht in ihrem Appartement, sie müsse es letzte
Nacht verwechselt haben, offenbar sei sie durch
das Erdbeben erschreckt worden, er erwarte sie
zum Frühstück, und hinkte hinaus, die Türe
schloß sich hinter ihm, sie erhob sich, das Bett war
eine Couch, die Fotos an den Wänden stellten in
verschiedenen Etappen die Explosion eines Pan-
zerwagens dar, ein im Turm eingeklemmter Mann
verbrannte, wurde zu Kohle, starrte verrenkt in
den Himmel, sie öffnete den Koffer, zog sich aus,
duschte, zog sich ein frisches Bluejeans-Kleid an,
öffnete die Türe, wieder das Hämmern und Poltern, dann Stille, sie verlief sich, dann Räume, an
die sie sich erinnerte, in einem Raum ein Tisch von
Fotos und Papieren leergefegt, Brot, auf einem
Brett in Scheiben geschnittenes Corned beef, Tee,
ein Krug mit Wasser, eine Büchse, Wassergläser,

Polyphem hinkte aus einem Korridor herbei, eine leere Blechschüssel in der Hand, als hätte er einem Tier zu fressen gegeben, befreite einen Stuhl von Fotobüchern, dann einen zweiten, sie setzte sich, er schnitt mit einem Taschenmesser das Brot in Scheiben, sie solle sich bedienen, sie schenkte sich Tee ein, nahm eine Scheibe Brot, Corned beef, sie spürte plötzlich, daß sie Hunger hatte, er schüttete ein weißes Pulver in ein Glas, füllte Wasser nach, am Morgen trinke er nur Milchpulver mit Wasser, er müsse sich entschuldigen, er sei gestern betrunken gewesen, er trinke in der letzten Zeit, scheußlich diese Milch, es sei kein Erdbeben gewesen, sagte sie, nein, es sei keines gewesen, antwortete er, goß sich Wasser nach, es sei angebracht, daß er sie aufkläre, in welche Geschichte sie unfreiwillig geraten sei, denn offenbar wisse sie nicht, was sich im Lande eigentlich abspiele, fuhr er fort und hatte etwas Spöttisches, Überlegenes, schien überhaupt ein anderer Mensch zu sein als der, den sie am explodierten vw-Bus kennengelernt hatte, natürlich, über den Machtkampf zwischen dem Polizeichef und dem Chef des Geheimdienstes sei sie im Bilde, selbstverständlich bereite der erste einen Staatsstreich vor, versuche der zweite diesen zu verhindern, doch seien dabei noch andere Interessen im Spiel, das Land in welches sie mehr als leichtsinnig gekommen sei, wie ihn dünke, lebe nicht nur vom Fremdenverkehr und von der Ausfuhr pflanzlicher Stoffe für Polsterzwekke, die Haupteinnahme sei ein Krieg, den das Land mit dem Nachbarstaat um ein Gebiet in der großen Sandwüste führe, wo außer einigen verlausten Beduinen und Wüstenflöhen niemand lebe, wohin sich nicht einmal der Tourismus vorgewagt habe, ein Krieg, der nun schon seit zehn Jahren dahinmotte und längst nur noch dazu diene, die Produkte aller waffenexportierenden Länder zu testen, nicht nur französische, deutsche, englische, italienische, schwedische, israelische, schweizerische Panzer kämpften gegen russische und tschechische, sondern auch russische gegen russische, amerikanische gegen amerikanische, deutsche gegen deutsche, schweizerische gegen schweizerische, überall in der Wüste fänden sich verlassene Panzerschlachtfelder, der Krieg suche sich immer neue Schauplätze, folgerichtig, weil nur durch den Waffenexport die Konjunktur einigermaßen stabil bleibe, gesetzt, die Waffen seien wettbewerbsfähig, fortwährend brächen wirkliche Kriege aus, wie der zwischen Iran und Irak zum Beispiel, er brauche weitere nicht aufzuzählen, da komme das Erproben von Waffen zu spät, daher kümmere sich die Waffenindustrie um so intensiver um den unbedeutenden Krieg hierzulande, der längst seinen politischen Sinn verloren habe, es handle sich um einen Scheinkrieg, die Instruktoren der waffenliefernden Industrienationen bildeten der Hauptsache nach Einheimische aus, Berber, Mauren, Araber, Juden, Neger, arme Teufel, die durch diesen Krieg privilegiert worden seien, kämen sie einigermaßen davon, doch nun sei das Land unruhig geworden, die Fundamentalisten sähen in diesem Krieg eine westliche Schweinerei, was ja stimme, zähle man den Warschauer Pakt auch dazu, der Chef des Geheimdienstes versuche aus dem Krieg einen internationalen Skandal zu machen, dazu sei ihm der Fall Sörensen willkommen, auch die Regierung möchte ihn einstellen, möchte, stehe dann aber vor einem wirtschaftlichen Desaster, der Generalstabchef schwanke noch und die Saudis seien unentschlossen, der Polizeichef wolle ihn weiterführen, er sei von den waffenproduzierenden Ländern bestochen, auch, wie man munkle, von den Israelis und vom Iran, und versuche die Regierung zu stürzen, unterstützt von den aus allen Windrichtungen herbeigeeilten sonst arbeitslosen Kameramännern und Fotografen, dieser Krieg sei ihr tägliches Brot, denn sein Sinn liege ja nur darin, daß er beobachtet werden könne, nur so seien die Waffen zu testen und ihre Schwächen und Fehlkonstruktionen zu erkennen und zu verbessern und was ihn betreffe – er lachte, nahm neues Milchpulver und Wasser, während sie ihr Frühstück längst beendet hatte –, nun, da müsse er wohl etwas weiter ausholen, jeder habe seine Geschichte, sie die ihre, er die seine, er wisse nicht wie ihre begonnen habe, wolle es auch nicht wissen, die seine habe an einem Montag abend in New York in der Bronx begonnen, sein Vater habe einen kleinen Fotoladen gehabt, Hochzeiten fotografiert und jeden, der sich fotografieren lassen wollte und einmal habe er das Foto eines Gentlemans ausgestellt, von dem er nicht gewußt habe, daß er es nicht hätte ausstellen dürfen, das habe ihm dann ein Mitglied der Bande beigebracht, mit einem Maschinengewehr, so daß sein Vater durchlöchert hinter dem Ladentisch über ihn gesunken sei, der am Boden sitzend seine Schulaufgaben gemacht habe, an jenem Montag abend eben, habe sich doch sein Vater in den Kopf gesetzt, ihm eine höhere Bildung zu geben, Väter wollten immer zu hoch hinaus mit ihren Söhnen, aber er, als er nach einer Weile, da niemand mehr geschossen habe, unter seinem Vater hervorgekraxelt sei, habe beim Anblick des zerschossenen Ladens begriffen, daß die wahre Bildung darin bestehe, zu kapieren wie man durch die Welt komme, indem man sich der Welt bediene, durch die man kommen möchte, er sei mit der einzigen Kamera, die nicht wie sein Vater durchlöchert gewesen sei, in die Unterwelt gestiegen, als Dreikäsehoch sozusagen, zuerst habe er sich auf Taschendiebe spezialisiert, die Polizei habe seine Schnappschüsse nur mäßig bezahlt und nur wenige verhaftet, so sei keiner auf ihn aufmerksam geworden, darauf sei er kühner geworden und habe sich an die Einbrecher herangemacht, die Ausrüstung habe er sich teils zusammengestohlen, teils zusammengebastelt, er habe mit der Intelligenz einer Ratte gelebt, um Einbrecher zu fotografieren, müsse man wie Einbrecher denken, die seien gewitzt und lichtscheu, einige Fassadenkletterer seien von seinem Blitzlicht geblendet abgestürzt, sie täten ihm noch jetzt leid, aber die Polizei habe immer noch schäbig bezahlt und mit den Fotos zur Presse zu laufen, hätte die Unterwelt alarmiert, so habe er denn Glück gehabt, niemand habe im schmächtigen Gassenjungen ei-

nen Fotografen vermutet, darum sei er größen-
wahnsinnig geworden und habe sich an die Killer
herangemacht, ohne eigentlich zu überlegen, auf
was er sich da einlasse, die Polizei sei zwar splen-
dide geworden, ein Killer nach dem anderen sei
nach Sing-Sing und auf den elektrischen Stuhl
gewandert oder aus Vorsicht von seinen Auftrag-
gebern abgeknallt worden, aber dann sei ihm aus
Zufall im Central Park ein Fangschuß unterlaufen,
der einem Senator die Karriere vermasselt und eine
Lawine von Skandalen ausgelöst habe, wodurch
die Polizei gezwungen worden sei, dem parlamen-
tarischen Untersuchungsausschuß seine Existenz
bekanntzugeben, von der sonst niemand wußte,
von dem FBI aufgestöbert, habe ihn der Ausschuß
auseinandergenommen, und mit seinem Bild in
der Zeitung habe er, in sein Atelier zurückgekehrt, dieses im gleichen Zustand vorgefunden
wie seinerzeit den Laden seines Vater, eine Zeit-
lang habe er sich noch über Wasser gehalten,
indem er der Polizei Fotos von Killern und den
Killern Fotos von Detektiven verkauft habe, aber
bald hätten ihn alle gejagt, Polizei und Killer, und
ihm sei nichts anderes übriggeblieben als sich bei
der Armee in Sicherheit zu bringen, auch die hätten
Fotografen gebraucht, legale und illegale, doch

wenn er sage, er habe sich in Sicherheit gebracht, fuhr er fort, auf dem Sessel nach rückwärts gelehnt und die Beine auf dem Tisch, so sei das reichlich übertrieben, Kriege, auch wenn sie nur administrative Maßnahmen genannt würden, seien unpopulär, Abgeordnete und Senatoren, Diplomaten und Journalisten müßten überzeugt, seien sie nicht überzeugt, bestochen, seien sie nicht zu bestechen, erpreßt werden, zu diesem Zwecke hätten ihm Luxusbordelle zur Verfügung gestanden, die Fotos, die er da geschossen habe, seien politisches Dynamit, er sei dazu gezwungen gewesen, die Armee hätte ihn jederzeit nach Hause schicken können und in Anbetracht dessen, was ihn dort erwartete, habe er nachgegeben, mit dem Erfolg, daß er, als wieder ein Untersuchungsausschuß anrückte, von der Armee zur Luftwaffe geflüchtet sei, dann, weil nichts hartnäckiger sei als rachsüchtige Politiker, von der Luftwaffe zur Waffenindustrie, in die alle Interessen zusammengelaufen seien, so daß er hoffen durfte, sich dort endlich in Sicherheit zu finden, so sei er denn hier gestrandet, arg zugerichtet, ein stets gejagter Jäger, eine legendäre Gestalt für die Insider seines Berufs, die ihn denn auch zu ihrem Boß gewählt hätten und es sei denn auch eine der größten

Schnapsideen seines Lebens gewesen, diese Wahl anzunehmen, denn damit sei er der Chef einer illegalen Organisation geworden, von der man jede Information über alle eingesetzten Waffen erhalten habe, deren Aufgabe auch definiert werden könne, daß sie die Spionage überflüssig mache, wer etwas über einen feindlichen Panzer oder über die Wirksamkeit einer Panzerabwehrkanone habe wissen wollen, habe sich nur an ihn zu wenden brauchen, dank seiner habe sich der Krieg weitergefrettet, durch seine allzu mächtige Position sei aber die Administration wiederum auf ihn aufmerksam geworden, um die Organisation zu zerschlagen, habe sie sich mit ihm in Verbindung gesetzt, er gelte auf seinem Spezialgebiet als der größte Experte, man wolle ihn nicht zwingen, aber einige Senatoren – nun gut, er habe ihren Auftrag angenommen und nun beginne die Organisation zu zerfallen, die Fortdauer des Kriegs sei fraglich, daß man ihm von Seiten seiner alten Kollegen nun nachstelle und ihn, tauche er auf, beobachte, sei nur allzu natürlich, um so mehr als er zugebe, einige allzu subtile Informationen zurückgehalten zu haben.

19

Er schwieg, er hatte geredet und geredet und sie
spürte, daß er reden mußte, daß er ihr erzählt
hatte, was er vielleicht noch niemandem erzählt
hatte, aber sie spürte auch, daß er ihr etwas
verschwieg und daß, was er verschwieg, mit dem
Grund zu tun hatte, weshalb er ihr sein Leben
erzählte, er saß da, zurückgelehnt, die Beine auf
dem Tisch, schaute vor sich hin, als ob er auf etwas
wartete, und dann heulte es erneut heran, erneut
ein Einschlag, ein Zerbersten, von der Decke
rieselte es, dann Stille, sie fragte, was das gewesen
sei, er antwortete, der Grund, weshalb sich niemand hierher wage, hinkte ins Labor, von oben
senkte sich eine Treppe, sie stiegen hinauf und
gelangten in einen kleinen flachkuppligen Raum,
der sich über eine geschlossene Reihe kleiner
Fenster wölbte, doch erst als sie neben ihm saß,
bemerkte sie, daß die Fenster Monitoren waren,
in deren einem sie die Sonne sinken sah und den
Boden der Wüste sich öffnen, den Geländewagen
auftauchen und sich selber auf dem Geländewagen

sitzen, dann sah sie den rotgelben Streifen sich schließen, sah den Einbruch der Nacht, das Versinken des Geländewagens, die hereinbrechenden Sterne, etwas schoß heran, grelles Licht, der Monitor erlosch, nun Spezialzeitlupe, sagte er, das Gleiche noch einmal, ruckweise wurde es Nacht, ruckweise erschien der versinkende Geländewagen, ruckweise brachen die Sterne herein, ruckweise vergrößerte sich einer, ruckweise wuchs er kometenhaft an, ruckweise bohrte sich schlankes, weißglühendes Gebilde in die Wüste, explodierte ruckweise, schleuderte ruckweise Steinbrocken auf, vulkanartig, dann nur noch Licht, Dunkel, das sei die erste gewesen, die zweite vorhin sei näher explodiert, meinte Polyphem, die Genauigkeit nehme zu, und auf die Frage der F., was sie gesehen habe, antwortete er, eine interkontinentale Rakete, und in einem Monitor erschien das Bild der Wüste, das Gebirge, auch die Stadt, die Wüste kam näher, ein Fadenkreuz legte sich über das Bild, hier sei die Anlage, worin sie sich befänden, die F. und er, die Aufnahme stamme von einem Satelliten, dessen Umlaufzeit derart jener der Erde angepaßt sei, daß er immer über ihnen schwebe, darauf setzte er einen weiteren Monitor ein, alles automatisiert, wie er sagte, wieder die Wüste, am linken Bildrand ein kleines schwarzes Viereck, die Al-Hakim-Ruine, rechts oben die Stadt, am rechten Bildrand das Gebirge, immer noch die Wolke, ein blendendweißer Wattebausch, in der Bildmitte eine kleine Kugel mit Antennen, der erste Satellit von einem zweiten Satelliten beobachtet, um zu beobachten was dieser beobachte, damit schaltete er die Monitoren aus, hinkte zur Treppe, stieg hinunter ohne sich um sie zu kümmern, ging wieder zum Raum zurück, zum Tisch, nahm mit bloßen Händen Corned beef, setzte sich, lehnte sich zurück, legte die Füße auf den Tisch, sagte, bald komme die nächste, aß, erklärte dabei, würden im Krieg in der Wüste die modernen konventionellen Waffen getestet, so sei es für die strategische Konzeption beider Seiten notwendig, die Zielgenauigkeit der interkontinentalen, kontinentalen und der von atomaren Unterseebooten abgefeuerten Raketen zu überprüfen, das Funktionieren jener Waffensysteme, die als Träger der Atom- und Wasserstoffbomben dienten, wodurch einerseits der Friede auf Erden erhalten werde, wenn auch auf die Gefahr hin, er und die Erde würden damit zu Tode gerüstet, indem entweder allzu sehr auf die Einschüchterung des andern oder auf den Computer oder auf eine Ideologie oder gar auf

Gott vertraut werde, der andere könnte den Kopf verlieren und handeln, der Computer sich irren, die Ideologie sich als falsch und Gott sich als desinteressiert erweisen, andererseits würden gerade jene Mächte, die nur konventionelle Waffen besäßen und sich doch eigentlich ducken müßten, dazu verführt, im Schatten des Weltfriedens der Abschreckung konventionelle Kriege zu führen, diese seien angesichts der Möglichkeit eines atomaren Krieges stubenrein geworden, was wiederum die Herstellung konventioneller Waffen ankurble und den Krieg in der Wüste rechtfertige, ein genialer Kreislauf, die Waffenindustrie und damit die Weltwirtschaft auf Touren zu halten, die Station, worin sie sich befänden, diene dazu, diesen Prozeß zu beschleunigen, sie sei durch ein Geheimabkommen ermöglicht und mit phantastischen Kosten errichtet worden, allein für die unterirdische Stromzufuhr seien im Gebirge ein Staudamm und ein Elektrizitätswerk gebaut worden, nicht zufällig habe man diesen Teil der Wüste als Zielfeld gewählt und zahle man jedes Jahr eine halbe Milliarde dafür, er sei nicht weit von jenen Ländern gelegen, die durch ihren Ölreichtum immer wieder der Versuchung nachgäben, die Industrienationen zu erpressen, die Beobachtungsstation sei mit über fünfzig Spezialisten belegt gewesen, alles Techniker, er als einziger Kameramann unter ihnen, der Hauptsache nach noch immer mit der alten Kodak aus dem Laden seines Vaters ausgerüstet, nur in der letzten Zeit hantiere er mit Video, er habe nie die Beobachtungsstation aufgesucht, sei ein noch so dicker Brocken angekündigt worden, ihm seien sensationelle Aufnahmen gelungen, zugegeben, ein Splitter habe sein linkes Bein zertrümmert, aber als er zurückgekommen sei, endlich wieder zusammengeflickt, habe er die Beobachtungsstation halb verlassen gefunden, man habe sie vollautomatisiert, die Techniker, die noch geblieben seien, hätten mit Computern gearbeitet, eigentlich habe man ihn nicht mehr gebraucht, er sei durch automatische Videokameras ersetzt worden, dann habe man einen Satelliten über die Beobachtungsstation lanciert, sie seien nicht einmal informiert worden, die Beobachtungsstation für den Satelliten befinde sich auf den Kanarischen Inseln, nur durch Zufall habe ein Fernsehspezialist den Satelliten über ihnen entdeckt, später den zweiten, dieser von den andern, wenig später sei der Befehl gekommen, die Station zu räumen, sie sei nun in der Lage vollautomatisch zu arbeiten, was eine

Lüge sei, wozu wäre dann der Satellit da, er allein, Polyphem, sei geblieben, er verstehe nichts von all diesen Installationen, er sei gerade noch fähig nachzuprüfen, ob die Videoanlagen noch funktionierten, sie funktionierten noch, aber wie lange, der Strom für die Beobachtungsstation stamme nur noch von den Batterien, der Strom vom Elektrizitätswerk sei seit heute morgen eingestellt, seien die Batterien erschöpft, sei die Beobachtungsstation nutzlos und nun habe man auch begonnen die Interkontinentalraketen zwar nicht gerade mit atomaren, aber doch mit hochbrisanten konventionellen Bomben zu bestücken, wenn er auch den Gedanken, man ziele von beiden Seiten nicht so sehr auf die Station, sondern mehr auf ihn, weil er im Besitz verschiedener Filme und Fotonegative sei, die für gewisse Diplomaten mehr als peinlich seien, nun doch für übertrieben halte, aber seitdem trinke er, er habe vorher nie getrunken, worauf die F. fragte, ob diese Dokumente, die er besitze, der Grund seien, warum er Björn Olsen umgebracht habe.

20

Er nahm die Füße vom Tisch, stand auf, holte zwischen den Filmrollen eine Flasche Whisky hervor, goß sich Whisky ins Glas, woraus er die Pulvermilch getrunken hatte, schwenkte es, trank es aus, fragte, ob sie an Gott glaube, schenkte sich neuen Whisky ein und setzte sich wieder ihr gegenüber, die von seiner Frage verwirrt wurde, die sie zuerst unwirsch beantworten wollte, aber dann im Gespür, daß sie von ihm mehr erfahre, wenn sie ernsthaft auf seine Frage einging, antwortete, sie könne nicht an einen Gott glauben, weil sie einerseits nicht wisse, was sie sich unter einem Gott vorzustellen habe, und daher nicht an etwas zu glauben vermöge, unter dem sie sich nichts vorstellen könne, andererseits keine Ahnung habe, was er, der sie nach ihrem Glauben frage, unter Gott verstehe, an den sie glauben solle oder nicht, worauf er entgegnete, wenn es einen Gott gebe, sei dieser als reiner Geist reines Beobachten, ohne Möglichkeit in den sich evolutionär abspulenden Prozeß der Materie einzugreifen, der im reinen Nichts münde, da selbst die Protonen einmal zerfielen und in dessen Verlauf die Erde, Pflanzen, Tiere und die Menschen entstanden seien und untergingen, nur wenn Gott reines Beobachten sei, bleibe er von seiner Schöpfung unbesudelt, was auch für ihn den Kameramann gelte, auch er habe nur zu beobachten, wäre es nicht so, hätte er sich längst eine Kugel durch den Kopf gejagt, jedes Gefühl wie Furcht, Liebe, Mitleid, Zorn, Verachtung, Rache, Schuld trübe nicht nur die reine Beobachtung, mehr noch, mache sie unmöglich, färbe ihr die Gefühle ein, so daß er der ekelhaften Welt beigemischt statt von ihr abgehoben wäre, die Wirklichkeit sei nur vermittels der Kamera objektiv erfaßbar, aseptisch, diese allein sei fähig, die Zeit und den Raum festzuhalten, worin sich das Erlebnis abspiele, während ohne Kamera das Erlebnis davongleite, sei es doch, kaum erlebt, schon Vergangenheit, damit nur noch Erinnerung und wie jede Erinnerung verfälscht, Fiktion, weshalb es ihm vorkomme, er sei kein Mensch mehr – da zum Mensch-Sein der Schein gehöre, die Einbildung eben, etwas direkt erleben zu können –, er sei vielmehr wie der Zyklop Polyphem, der die Welt durch ein einziges rundes Auge mitten auf der Stirne wie durch eine Kamera erlebt habe, er habe deshalb den vw-Bus nicht nur in die Luft gesprengt, um zu verhindern, daß Olsen dem Schicksal der dänischen Journalistin weiterhin nachspüre und in eine Lage gerate, in die sie, die F., jetzt geraten sei, sondern, fügte er hinzu, nach einem erneuten Heranheulen, Einschlagen, Zerbersten, Erzittern, doch ferner, sanfter, und einem nachlässigen »weit daneben«, es sei ihm vor allem darum gegangen, die Explosion zu filmen – sie solle ihn nicht falsch verstehen –, ein schreckliches Unglück, gewiß, aber dank der Kamera ein verewigtes Ereignis, ein Gleichnis der Weltkatastrophe, denn die Kamera sei dazu da, eine Zehntel-, eine Hundertstel-, ja Tausendstelsekunde festzuhalten, die Zeit aufzuhalten, indem sie die Zeit vernichte, auch der Film gebe ja die Wirklichkeit, lasse man ihn ablaufen, nur scheinbar wieder, er täusche einen Ablauf vor, der aus aneinandergereihten Einzelaufnahmen bestände, habe er einen Film gedreht, so zerschneide er den Film wieder, jede dieser Einzelaufnahmen stelle dann eine kristallisierte Wirklichkeit dar, eine unendliche Kostbarkeit, aber jetzt schwebten die zwei Satelliten über ihm, er habe sich mit seiner Kamera wie ein Gott gefühlt, aber nun werde beobachtet, was er beobachte und nicht nur was er beobachte, sondern auch er werde beobachtet, wie er beobachte, er kenne das Auflösungsvermögen der Satellitenaufnahmen, ein Gott, der beobachtet werde, sei kein Gott mehr, Gott werde nicht beobachtet, die Freiheit Gottes bestehe darin, daß er ein verborgener, versteckter Gott sei, und die Unfreiheit der Menschen, daß sie beobachtet würden, doch noch entsetzlicher sei, von wem er beobachtet und lächerlich gemacht werde, von einem System von Computern, denn was ihn beobachte seien zwei mit zwei Computern verbundene Kameras, beobachtet von zwei weiteren Computern, die ihrerseits von Computern beobachtet und in die mit ihnen verbundenen Computer eingespeist, abgetastet, umgesetzt, wieder zusammengesetzt und von Computern weiterverarbeitet in Laboratorien entwickelt, vergrößert, gesichtet und interpretiert würden, von wem und wo und ob überhaupt irgendwann von Menschen wisse er nicht, auch Computer verstünden Satellitenaufnahmen zu lesen und zu signalisieren, seien sie auf Einzelheiten und Abweichungen programmiert, er, Polyphem, sei ein gestürzter Gott, seine Stelle hätte nun ein Computer eingenommen, den ein zweiter Computer beobachte, ein Gott beobachte den andern, die Welt drehe sich ihrem Ursprung entgegen.

21

Er hatte ein Glas Whisky um das andere getrunken, kaum daß er ihn hin und wieder mit Wasser verdünnte, er hatte sich auch wieder in den Menschen verwandelt, den sie an der entstellten Leiche des Dänen kennengelernt hatte, in einen Säufer mit einem durchfurchten Gesicht mit kleinen brennenden Augen, die dennoch wie versteint wirkten, als hätten sie seit Ewigkeit in ein kaltes Grausen geblickt, und als sie fragte, aufs Geratewohl, wer den Einfall gehabt habe, ihn Polyphem zu nennen, stutzte sie –, kaum hatte sie die Frage gestellt, setzte er die Flasche Whisky an den Mund und dann antwortete er schwerfällig, sie sei zweimal in Todesgefahr gewesen, als sie ins Freie gegangen sei durch die Raketen und vorher vor der Eisentüre, hätte sie die geöffnet, wäre sie nicht mehr am Leben, denn der Name Polyphem sei ihm auf dem Flugzeugträger Kittyhawk gegeben worden, zu einem Zeitpunkt als der Rückzug aus Südvietnam schon beschlossen worden sei, in der Kajüte, die er mit einem rothaarigen Hünen geteilt habe, mit einem seltsamen Kauz, Professor für Griechisch an irgendeiner Hillbilly-Universität, der in seiner dienstfreien Zeit Homer gelesen habe, die ›Ilias‹, deren Verse laut rezitierend, dabei ein ausgekochter Bomberpilot, den man Achilles genannt habe, teils um den Sonderling zu veräppeln, teils aus einem Heidenrespekt vor dessen Tollkühnheit, ein Einzelgänger, den er immer wieder fotografiert und gefilmt habe, das Beste, was ihm je gelungen sei, denn Achilles habe nie darauf geachtet, habe auch nie mehr als gleichgültige Worte mit ihm gewechselt, bis er, wenige Stunden bevor sie mit einem Bomber eines neuen Typs einen nächtlichen Angriff auf Hanoi durchführen mußten, ein Auftrag, von dem sie beide geahnt hätten, er könne schiefgehen, von seinem Homer aufschauend ihn betrachtet hatte, als er gerade die Kamera auf ihn gerichtet hatte, du bist Polyphem, habe er gesagt, du bist Polyphem, und gelacht, das einzige Mal, daß er gelacht habe und dann nie mehr und darauf habe er zu reden begonnen, auch zum ersten Mal, und gesagt, die Griechen hätten Ares, den Gott des Kampfgetümmels, von Pallas Athene, der Göttin der Schlachtordnung, unterschieden, im Nahkampf sei jede Überlegung gefährlich, nur blitzschnelles Reagieren sei möglich, einem Speerstoß ausweichen, ein Abfangen eines Schwerthiebes mit dem Schild, ein Zustoßen, ein Zuschlagen, der Feind sei zugegen, Leib an Leib, dessen Wut, dessen Schnauben, dessen Schweiß, dessen Blut vermische sich mit der eigenen Wut, dem eigenen Schnauben, dem eigenen Schweiß, dem eigenen Blut zu einem wilden Knäuel von Angst und Haß, der Mensch verkralle sich im Menschen, verzahne sich in ihn, zerfleische, zerhacke, ersteche ihn, zum Tier geworden, zerreiße er Tiere, so habe vor Troja Achilles gekämpft, es sei ein haßerfülltes Morden gewesen, dazu habe er gebrüllt vor Wut und gejubelt nach dem Tod jedes Feindes, aber er, den man auch Achilles nenne, welche Schmach, je technischer der Krieg geworden sei desto abstrakter der Feind, für den Scharfschützen mit Zielfernrohr nur noch als ein in die Ferne entrücktes Objekt erkennbar, für die Geschütze nur noch vermutbar, und als Bomberpilot könne er zur Not noch angeben, wie viele Städte und Dörfer er bombardiert, aber nicht wie viele Menschen er getötet habe, auch nicht wie er sie getötet, zerfleischt, zerquetscht, verbrannt habe, er wisse nicht, er beobachte bloß seine Instrumente und folge den Angaben seines Funkers, um das Flugzeug dorthin zu bringen, an jenen abstrakten Punkt im stereometrischen Koordinatensystem von Längen-, Breitengrad und Höhe, abhängig von der eigenen Geschwindigkeit und der Windrichtung, dann das automatische Auslösen der Bomben und nach dem Angriff fühle er sich nicht als Held, sondern als Feigling, der finstere Verdacht tauche in ihm auf, ein ss-Schinderknecht in Auschwitz habe moralischer gehandelt als er, dieser sei mit seinen Opfern konfrontiert gewesen, auch wenn er sie als Untermenschen und Lumpengesindel betrachtet habe, zwischen ihm, Achilles, und seinen Opfern jedoch gebe es keine Konfrontation, die Opfer seien nicht einmal mehr Untermenschen, sondern irgend etwas Ungefähres als würde er Insekten vertilgen, wie der Flieger, der Gift versprühe, ja auch nicht die Mükken sehe, Ausbomben, Vernichten, Ausradieren, Ausschalten, gleichgültig welche Vokabel man brauche, sei abstrakt, rein technisch, nur noch summarisch zu erfassen, finanziell am besten, ein toter Vietnamese koste über hunderttausend Dollar, die Moral werde exstirpiert wie ein böser Tumor, der Haß injiziert wie ein Aufputschmittel gegen einen Feind, der ein Phantom sei, sehe er einen realen gefangenen Feind, könne er ihn nicht hassen, gewiß, er kämpfe gegen ein System, das seiner politischen Auffassung widerspreche, aber jedes System, auch das verbrecherischste, sei aus Schuldigen und Unschuldigen geflochten und in jedes System, auch in die Kriegsmaschinerie, der er zugeordnet sei, mische sich das Verbrechen ein, überwuchere und ersticke die Begründung, er komme sich wie eine Unperson vor, ein bloßer Beobachter von Zeigern und Uhren, und besonders im Angriff, den sie diese Nacht zu unternehmen hätten, ihr Flugzeug sei ein fliegender Computer, er starte, fliege ins Ziel, werfe die Bomben ab, alles automatisch, sie beide hätten nur Beobachterfunktion, er wünsche sich manchmal, ein echter Verbrecher zu sein, etwas Unmenschliches zu tun, ein Tier zu sein, eine Frau zu vergewaltigen und zu erwürgen, der Mensch sei eine Illusion, entweder werde er eine seelenlose Maschine, eine Kamera, ein Computer oder ein Tier, nach dieser Rede, der längsten, die Achilles je gehalten, sei dieser verstummt und sie seien Stunden später im Tiefflug mit doppelter Schallgeschwindigkeit Hanoi entgegengefegt, einem Feuerschlund der Flugabwehrgeschütze entgegen, die CIA hätte Hanoi gewarnt, zum Test gehörte auch die Abwehr, trotzdem habe er einige von seinen besten Aufnahmen gemacht, dann sei nach Abwurf der Bomben ihr Flugzeug getroffen worden, die Automatik sei ausgefallen, blutüberströmt, am Kopf verletzt, habe Achilles die schwerbeschädigte Maschine mit ihm zurückgeflogen, nicht mehr wie ein Mensch, sondern nun selber wie ein Computer, denn als sie auf der Kittyhawk gelandet seien und die Maschine zum Stillstand gekommen sei, habe ihn das blutige und leere Gesicht eines Idioten angeglotzt, er habe Achilles nie vergessen können, er stehe solange er lebe in dessen Schuld, er habe die ›Ilias‹ gelesen, um diesen Hillbilly-Professor zu verstehen, der ihm das Leben gerettet habe und seinetwegen ein Idiot geworden sei, er habe nach Achilles geforscht aber ihn erst nach Jahren aufgestöbert, in der psychiatrischen Abteilung des Militärspitals, wo man ihm, Polyphem, das Bein zusammenflickte, er habe einen idiotischen Gott vorgefunden, den man in eine Zelle gesperrt habe, weil er, einige Male aus der Anstalt entwichen, Frauen vergewaltigt und umgebracht habe, worauf er wieder vor sich hinschaute und auf ihre Frage, ob das Wesen hinter der Tür Achilles sei, antwortete er, sie müsse verstehen, daß er diesem den einzigen Wunsch, den es noch fühle, erfüllen müsse, wenn sich eine Gelegenheit biete, und im übrigen habe er ihr das Porträt der Jytte Sörensen versprochen.

22

Er hatte Mühe, den Projektor in Gang zu setzen, vorher hatte er lange nach der Filmrolle suchen müssen, endlich war es soweit, zurückgelehnt in einen Kinosessel, die Beine übereinandergeschlagen, sah sie zum erstenmal Jytte Sörensen, eine schlanke Frau im roten Pelzmantel, die in die große Sandwüste hineinging, wobei sie zuerst glaubte, sie sei es selber, die da gehe, an ihrem Gang bemerkte sie, daß die Frau getrieben wurde, wenn sie stehenblieb, schreckte etwas sie auf, das Gesicht der Frau sah sie nie, aber am Schatten, der von Zeit zu Zeit sichtbar wurde, ahnte sie, daß sie von Polyphems Geländewagen in die Wüste gezwungen wurde, Jytte Sörensen ging und ging, Steinwüste, Sandwüste, doch war es kein planloses Gehen, auch wenn sie getrieben wurde, hatte die F. das Gefühl, daß die Dänin auf ein Ziel zuging, das sie erreichen wollte, doch plötzlich lief sie einen steilen Hang hinunter, überschlug sich, die Al-Hakim-Ruine wurde sichtbar mit den schwarzen Vögeln der kauernden Heiligen, sie erhob sich, lief zu ihnen, umklammerte die Knie des ersten, wollte um Hilfe bitten, dieser fiel hin, wie er bei der F. hingefallen war, die Dänin kroch über den Leichnam, umklammerte die Knie des zweiten, auch dieser war eine Leiche, der Schatten des Fahrzeugs tauchte auf, pechschwarz, dann ein hünenhaftes Wesen, das sich auf sie warf, die, plötzlich willenlos, alles mit sich geschehen ließ, vergewaltigt und getötet wurde, alles überdeutlich, in Nahaufnahme ihr Gesicht, zum ersten Mal, dann jenes des Wesens, stöhnend, gierig, fleischig, leer, was dann folgte mußte mit einer Spezialkamera und in der Nacht aufgenommen worden sein, die Leiche lag zwischen den Heiligen, die zwei Toten wieder sitzend, Schakale kamen, schnupperten, begannen Jytte Sörensen zu zerfleischen, und erst jetzt bemerkte sie, daß sie sich allein im Vorführraum befand, sie erhob sich, verließ den Vorführraum, blieb stehen, entnahm der Tasche eine Zigarette, zündete sie an, rauchte, am Tisch saß Polyphem, schnitt an einem Filmband herum, neben ihm ein Gestell mit Filmresten, auf dem Tisch ein Revolver neben aus den Filmen geschnittenen Einzelbildern, am Tischende eine kahlköpfige Masse, Verse skandierend, griechische Hexameter, Homer, hin- und herwippend im Takt der Verse, die Augen geschlossen, und Polyphem sagte, er habe ihn mit Valium vollgestopft, dann, ein Bild ausschneidend, wie ihr sein Material gefallen habe, ein Video auf 16-mm-Film übertragen, eine Frage, auf die sie keine Antwort wußte, er schaute sie an, gleichgültig, kalt, was er Wirklichkeit nenne, sei inszeniert, sagte sie, worauf er, das Einzelbild betrachtend, das er aus dem Filmband geschnitten hatte, antwortete, ein Spiel werde inszeniert, die Wirklichkeit könne nicht inszeniert, sondern nur sichtbar gemacht werden, er habe die Sörensen sichtbar gemacht, wie eine Raumsonde die noch aktiven Vulkane eines Jupitermondes sichtbar gemacht habe, worauf sie sagte, Sophisterei, und er, die Wirklichkeit sei nicht sophistisch und dann, wie alles wieder erzitterte und es erneut von der Decke rieselte, wollte sie wissen, warum er Achilles einen idiotischen Gott genannt habe, eine Frage, die er damit beantwortete, er nenne ihn so, weil Achilles wie ein von seiner Schöpfung infizierter Gott handle, der seine Geschöpfe vernichte, die Dänin sei nicht ein Geschöpf des Idioten, warf sie zornig ein, um so schlimmer für Gott, entgegnete er ruhig und auf ihre Frage, ob es hier geschehen solle, sagte er, nein, auch nicht bei der

Al-Hakim-Ruine, die seien von den Satelliten zu beobachten, das Porträt über die Dänin weise Mängel auf, das Porträt über sie werde sein Meisterwerk, er habe den Ort schon ausgewählt, sie solle ihn und Achilles nun allein lassen, Achilles könnte wach werden und er habe zu packen, in der Nacht brächen sie auf, er nehme sie mit, und die Filme und Fotos um derentwegen man ihn jage, er verlasse diese Station für immer, darauf wandte er sich wieder seinem Filmband zu, während es ihr nicht bewußt wurde, daß sie ihm gehorchte, daß sie in ihre Zelle ging, sich aufs Jugendstilbett oder auf die Couch legte, so gleichgültig war es ihr, was sie tat, war es doch unmöglich zu fliehen, er war wieder nüchtern geworden und bewaffnet, Achilles konnte erwachen und immer wieder erzitterte die Station und wenn sie auch hätte fliehen wollen, wußte sie nicht, ob sie fliehen wollte, sie sah das Gesicht der Jytte Sörensen vor sich, lustverzerrt, und dann, wie die riesigen Hände ihre Kehle umschlossen, auf einen Moment, bevor es sich entstellte, stolz, triumphierend, willig, die Dänin hatte alles gewünscht, was ihr widerfuhr, die Vergewaltigung und den Tod, alles andere war nur ein Vorwand gewesen und sie, sie hatte den Weg zu Ende zu gehen, den sie gewählt hatte, ihrer Wahl zuliebe, ihrem Stolz, sich zuliebe, ein lächerlicher und dennoch unerbittlicher Zirkelschluß der Pflicht, aber war es die Wahrheit, die Wahrheit über sich selber, die sie suchte, sie dachte an ihre Begegnung mit von Lambert, sie hatten seinen Auftrag gegen ihren Instinkt angenommen, von einem vagen Plan hatte sie sich in einen noch vageren geflüchtet, nur um etwas zu unternehmen, weil sie sich in einer Krise befand, sie dachte an ihr Gespräch mit D., er war zu höflich gewesen ihr abzuraten und wohl auch zu neugierig, wie das alles enden solle, von Lambert könne ja noch einmal einen Helikopter schicken, er war noch einmal der Schuldige, dachte sie und mußte lachen, dann sah sie sich im Atelier, vor dem Porträt, es war wirklich jenes der Jytte Sörensen, aber sie hatte sich zu spät umgewandt, es mußte Tina gewesen sein, die den Raum verlassen hatte und sicher war der Regisseur ihr Geliebter, sie war nahe der Wahrheit gewesen, aber hatte ihr nicht nachgespürt, die Verlockung, nach M. zu fliegen, war zu groß, aber auch dieser Flug war vielleicht nur eine Flucht gewesen, aber eine Flucht vor wem, fragte sie sich, vor sich selber, möglich, vielleicht hielt sie sich selber nicht aus und die Flucht bestand darin, daß sie sich treiben ließ, sie sah sich als Mädchen, an einem Bergbach stehen, bevor er sich über eine Felswand in die Tiefe stürzte, sie hatte sich vom Lager entfernt und ein kleines Papierschiff in den Bach gesetzt, war ihm dann gefolgt, bald wurde es von diesem Stein aufgehalten, bald von jenem, doch immer wieder befreite es sich und nun trieb es unaufhaltsam dem Wasserfall entgegen, und sie schaute zu, das kleine Mädchen, unbändig vor Freude, denn sie hatte das Schiffchen mit all ihren Freundinnen besetzt, auch mit ihrer Schwester, mit ihrer Mutter und ihrem Vater und mit dem sommersprossigen Jungen in ihrer Klasse, der später an Kinderlähmung starb, mit allen, die sie liebte und die sie liebten, und wie die Fahrt des Schiffchens pfeilschnell wurde, wie es über die Klippe schnellte, hinab in die Tiefe, jubelte sie laut, und plötzlich wurde aus dem Schiffchen ein Schiff und aus dem Bach ein Strom, der einem Katarakt entgegenfloß, und sie saß in diesem Schiff, das immer schneller dahintrieb, dem Fall zu, und über diesem, auf zwei Klippen, hockten Polyphem, der sie mit einer Kamera fotografierte, die wie das Auge eines Riesen aussah, und Achilles, der lachte und mit dem nackten Oberkörper auf und ab wippte.

23

Sie brachen kurz nach einem Einschlag auf, der so
heftig war, daß sie glaubte, die Station stürze ein,
nichts funktionierte richtig, der Geländewagen
mußte nach oben gehebelt werden, endlich im
Freien wurde sie von Polyphem mit einer Hand-
schelle an eine Stange der Pritsche gefesselt, wo sie
zwischen Bergen von Filmrollen lag und dann
raste er davon, doch kam keine Rakete mehr, sie
fuhren ungestört die ganze Nacht immer tiefer
nach Süden, über ihr die Sterne, deren Namen sie
vergessen hatte, bis auf einen, Kanopus, den
würde sie auch sehen, hatte D. gesagt, aber nun
wußte sie nicht, ob sie ihn sah oder nicht, was sie
seltsam quälte, war es ihr doch, Kanopus würde
ihr helfen, wenn sie ihn erkennen könnte, dann
das Verblassen der Sterne, als letzter einer, der
vielleicht Kanopus war, das eisige Versilbern der
Nacht zum Tage, sie fror, das Heraufsteigen des
Sonnenballs, Polyphem ließ sie frei, trieb sie in
ihrem roten Pelzmantel in die große Wüste, in eine
zernarbte Mondlandschaft aus Sand und Stein,

Wadis entlang und zwischen Sanddünen und abenteuerlichen Felsformationen hindurch, in eine Hölle von Licht und Schatten, Staub und Trockenheit, so wie Jytte Sörensen hineingetrieben worden war, hinter ihr, bald sie fast berührend, bald entfernter, bald nicht mehr hörbar, bald heranbrausend, ein Untier, das mit seinem Opfer spielte, der Geländewagen, von Polyphem gesteuert, neben ihm Achilles, immer noch halb betäubt hin und her wippend aus der ›Ilias‹ zitierend, Verse, das einzige was der Stahlsplitter, der ihn getroffen hatte, nicht zerstören konnte, doch brauchte Polyphem sie nicht zu lenken, sie ging und ging, in ihren Pelzmantel gehüllt, lief der Sonne entgegen, die immer höher stieg, dann ein Lachen hinter ihr, der Geländewagen jagte sie wie der Polizist im weißen Turban den Schakal gejagt hatte, vielleicht war sie dieser Schakal, sie blieb stehen, der Geländewagen auch, sie war schweißüberströmt, sie zog sich aus, es war ihr gleichgültig, daß man ihr zusah, hüllte sich nur noch in den Pelzmantel, ging weiter, der Geländewagen hinter ihr, sie ging und ging, die Sonne brannte den Himmel weg, wenn der Geländewagen stand, zurückblieb, hörte sie das Geräusch einer Kamera, der Versuch eine Ermordete zu porträtieren wurde nun unternommen, nur daß sie selber die Ermordete sein würde, doch nicht sie porträtierte, sondern sie wurde porträtiert und sie dachte, was mit ihrem Porträt geschehen werde, ob Polyphem es weiteren Opfern vorführen werde, so wie er es ihr gegenüber mit dem Porträt der Dänin getan hatte, dann dachte sie an nichts mehr, weil es sinnlos war, an etwas zu denken, in der flirrenden Ferne tauchten bizarre niedere Felsen auf, sie dachte, vielleicht eine Fata Morgana, sie hatte immer geträumt, eine Fata Morgana zu sehen, doch als sie, schon taumelnd, näher kam, erwiesen sich die Felsen als ein Friedhof zerschossener Panzer, die sie wie schildkrötenhafte Riesentiere umstanden, während mächtige ausgebrannte Scheinwerfermasten in die gleißende Leere stachen, welche die Panzerschlacht beleuchtet hatten, doch kaum hatte sie den Ort erkannt, wohin sie getrieben worden war, warf sich der Schatten des heranrükkenden Geländewagens wie ein Mantel über sie, und wie Achilles vor ihr stand, halb nackt, staubbedeckt, als käme er von einem Schlachtgetümmel, die alten Militärhosen zerfetzt, die nackten Füße sandverkrustet, die Idiotenaugen weit geöffnet, wurde sie vom ungeheuren Anprall der Gegenwart erfaßt, von einer noch nie gekannten Lust zu leben, ewig zu leben, sich auf diesen Riesen, auf diesen idiotischen Gott zu werfen, die Zähne in seinen Hals zu schlagen, plötzlich ein Raubtier geworden, bar jeder Menschlichkeit, eins mit dem, der sie vergewaltigen und töten wollte, eins mit der fürchterlichen Stupidität der Welt, doch er schien ihr zu entweichen, drehte sich im Kreise, ohne daß sie begriff, warum er ihr entwich, sich im Kreise drehte, hinfiel, wieder aufstand, zu den amerikanischen, deutschen, französischen, russischen, tschechischen, israelischen, schweizerischen, italienischen Stahlleichen glotzte, aus denen es zu leben und aus den verrosteten Panzerkampfwagen und zerschossenen Panzerspähwagen herauszuklettern begann, Kameramänner tauchten gleich phantastischen Tieren auf, hoben sich ab vom kochenden Silber des Alls, der Chef des Geheimdienstes kroch aus den verbeulten Überresten eines russischen SU 100, während aus dem Kommandoturm eines ausgebrannten Centurions, als liefe Milch über, der Polizeichef in seiner weißen Uniform quoll, jeder hatte Polyphem beobachtet und jeder jeden und wie nun überall Kameramänner auf Panzertürmen, Panzerplatten, Panzerketten stehend filmten und die Tonmeister ihre Angeln hoch- und querreckten, griff Achilles, von einem zweiten Schuß getroffen, in ohnmächtiger Raserei einen Panzer um den anderen an, prallte von Fußtritten traktiert zurück, kam immer wieder auf den Rücken zu liegen, wälzte sich, rappelte sich hoch, keuchte zum Geländewagen, auf die Brust beide Hände gepreßt, zwischen deren Fingern Blut rann, fiel, von einem dritten Schuß getroffen, aufs neue auf den Rücken, dem ihn filmenden Polyphem zubrüllend, Verse aus der ›Ilias‹, kam dann noch einmal hoch, wurde von einer Salve einer Maschinenpistole zersiebt, fiel wieder zurück und verschied, worauf Polyphem, während alle ihn und einander filmten, den Geländewagen um die Panzerruinen herumkurvte und davonstob, denen, die ihn verfolgten, entschwindend, die nur der Spur zu folgen brauchten, auch das sinnlos, denn als sie sich gegen Mitternacht der Beobachtungsstation bis auf wenige Kilometer genähert hatten, erschütterte eine Explosion die Wüste wie ein Erdbeben und ein Feuerball stieg hoch.

24

Wochen später, mit ihrem Team heimgekehrt, nachdem die Fernsehanstalten ihren Film ohne Begründung abgewiesen, las im italienischen Restaurant der Logiker D. aus dem Morgenblatt der F. beim Frühstück vor, in M. habe der Generalstabchef den Chef des Geheimdienstes und den Polizeichef erschießen lassen, den einen, weil er sein Land verraten, den andern, weil er die Regierung habe stürzen wollen, nun selber Chef der Regierung geworden, sei der Generalstabchef zu den Truppen im Süden des Landes geflogen um den Grenzkrieg fortzusetzen, ferner habe er die Gerüchte dementiert, ein Teil der Wüste sei ein Zielplatz fremder Raketen, sein Land sei neutral, eine Nachricht, die D. um so mehr belustigte, als er auf der folgenden Seite die Nachricht las, Otto und Tina von Lambert sei ein langgehegter Wunsch in Erfüllung gegangen, indem die schon Totgeglaubte und Beerdigte einem gesunden Knaben das Leben geschenkt habe, so daß D., die Zeitung zusammenfaltend, zu der F. sagte: Donnerwetter, hast du aber Glück gehabt.

Friedrich Dürrenmatt
4. 6. 86

Friedrich Dürrenmatt
im Diogenes Verlag

Werk- und Studienausgaben in Diogenes Taschenbüchern

● **Woody Allen**
Werkausgabe in bisher
6 Einzelbänden
detebe

● **Also sprach der Erhabene**
Eine Auswahl aus den Reden Gotamo Budd-
hos. detebe 21443

● **Eric Ambler**
Werkausgabe in bisher
19 Einzelbänden
detebe

Über Eric Ambler
Aufsätze von Alfred Hitchcock bis Helmut
Heißenbüttel. Herausgegeben von Gerd Haff-
mans. detebe 20607

● **Alfred Andersch**
Studienausgabe in
18 Einzelbänden
detebe

Einige Zeichnungen
Essay. detebe 20399

Das Alfred Andersch Lesebuch
Herausgegeben von Gerd Haffmans
detebe 20695

Über Alfred Andersch
Herausgegeben von Gerd Haffmans
detebe 20819

● **Angelus Silesius**
Der cherubinische Wandersmann
detebe 20644

● **Honoré de Balzac**
Die großen Romane
in 10 Bänden. detebe 20901–20910

Erzählungen
in 3 Bänden. detebe 20896, 20897, 20899

Das ungekannte Meisterwerk
Erzählungen. detebe 20477

Das Mädchen mit den Goldaugen
Erzählung. Mit einem Nachwort von Stefan
Zweig. detebe 21447

Über Balzac
Herausgegeben von Claudia Schmölders
detebe 20309

André Maurois
Das Leben des Honoré Balzac
Eine Biographie. Aus dem Französischen von
Ernst Sander und Bruno Berger. detebe 21297

Charles Baudelaire
Die Tänzerin Fanfarlo
Prosadichtungen. detebe 20387

Die Blumen des Bösen
Gedichte. detebe 20999

● **Gottfried Benn**
Ausgewählte Gedichte
Herausgegeben und mit einem Nachwort
von Gerd Haffmans. detebe 20099

Das Gottfried Benn Lesebuch
Ein Querschnitt durch das Prosawerk,
herausgegeben von Max Niedermayer und
Marguerite Schlüter. detebe 20982

● **Giovanni Boccaccio**
Der Decamerone in 5 Bänden
Sämtliche 100 Novellen in der berühmten
Propyläen-Edition. Aus dem Italienischen
von Heinrich Conrad. Mit den Kupfern und
Vignetten von Gravelot, Boucher und Eisen
der Ausgabe von 1757. detebe 21060–21064

● **James Boswell**
Dr. Samuel Johnson
Leben und Meinungen. detebe 20786

● **Ray Bradbury**
Werkausgabe in bisher
11 Einzelbänden
detebe

● **Ulrich Bräker**
Werke in 2 Bänden
Herausgegeben von Samuel Voellmy und
Heinz Weder. detebe 20581 und 20582